D0620576

MIDWINTER OF
THE SPIRIT

&

A CROWN
OF LIGHTS

Phil Rickman was born in Lancashire. He has won awards for his TV and radio journalism, and his highly acclaimed ealier novels *Candlenight*, *Cybbe*, *The Man in the Moss*, *December*, *The Chalice*, and *The Wine of Angels* are also available from Pan Books in paperback, as is *Midwinter of the Spirit*, which charts Merrily Watkin's eventful debut as diocesan exorcist. He is married and lives on the Welsh Border.

Phil Rickman

MIDWINTER OF THE SPIRIT

&

A CROWN OF LIGHTS

PAN BOOKS

Midwinter of the Spirit first published 1999 by Macmillan.
First published by Pan Books 2000
A Crown of Lights first published 2001 by Macmillan.
First published by Pan Books 2001

This omnibus edition published 2005 by Pan Books
an imprint of Pan Macmillan Ltd
Pan Macmillan, 20 New Wharf Road, London N1 9RR
Basingstoke and Oxford
Associated companies throughout the world
www.panmacmillan.com

ISBN 0 330 44097 7

Copyright © Phil Rickman 1999, 2001

The right of Phil Rickman to be identified as the
author of this work has been asserted by him in accordance
with the Copyright, Designs and Patents Act 1988.

All rights reserved. No part of this publication may be
reproduced, stored in or introduced into a retrieval system, or
transmitted, in any form, or by any means (electronic, mechanical,
photocopying, recording or otherwise) without the prior written
permission of the publisher. Any person who does any unauthorized
act in relation to this publication may be liable to criminal
prosecution and civil claims for damages.

1 3 5 7 9 8 6 4 2

A CIP catalogue record for this book is available from
the British Library.

Printed and bound in Great Britain by
Mackays of Chatham plc, Chatham, Kent

This book is sold subject to the condition that it shall not,
by way of trade or otherwise, be lent, re-sold, hired out,
or otherwise circulated without the publisher's prior consent
in any form of binding or cover other than that in which
it is published and without a similar condition including this
condition being imposed on the subsequent purchaser.

MIDWINTER OF
THE SPIRIT

Part One

IMPRINT

ONE

It

This is where it walks . . .

Washing her hands, Merrily looked up and became very still, convinced in this grey, lingering moment that she was seeing the *imprint*.

What she saw, in the cracked and liver-spotted mirror, was a smudgy outline hovering beyond her left shoulder in the women's lavatory with its stone walls and flagged floor. Through the bubble-glass in the door, a bleary ochre glow seeped from the oil lamp in the passageway where, for some reason, there was no electricity.

This was where it walked, Huw had explained in his soft, mat-flat Yorkshire voice – David Hockney on downers.

It.

Rumoured, apparently, to be the shade of a preacher named Griffith who heaped sermons like hot coals on hapless hill-farming folk towards the end of the nineteenth century. But also known as the Grey Monk because this was what it most resembled, and this was where it walked.

Where it walked.

Merrily focused on her own drained face in the mirror.

Was this where madness began?

'Are they often caught short, then?' the ex-Army chaplain, Charlie Headland, had asked a few minutes earlier, while

3

Merrily was thinking: *Why do they always walk? Why don't they run like hell, in desperation, looking for a way out of this dismal routine?*

The course tutor, Huw Owen, had blinked, a crumpled old hippy in a discoloured dog-collar.

'No, I'm serious,' Charlie insisted. 'Do any of them still feel a need to pee, or do they leave all that behind?'

'Charles . . .' Huw being patient, not rising to it. 'There hasn't always been a lavatory at the end of that passage.'

Not smiling, either.

Huw would laugh, sometimes wildly, in the pub at night, but in the stone-walled lecture room he never lost his focus. It was about setting an example. Outside of all this, Huw said, you should always strive to live a full, free life but in 'Deliverance' remain watchful and analytical, and careful not to overreact to something as innocuous as an imprint.

This whole Grey Monk thing had arisen because of Huw needing an example of what he meant by '*imprints*'.

As distinct from '*visitors*', who usually were parents or close friends appearing at your bedside or in a favourite chair on the night of their deaths, often a once-only apparition to say: Everything is OK. Or '*volatiles*' – loose-cannon energy forms dislodging plates and table lamps, and commonly but sometimes inaccurately called poltergeists.

When this place was a Nonconformist chapel, Huw had told them, the present women's toilet had been some kind of vestry. Which was where Griffith the preacher – apparently helpless with lust for a married woman in Sennybridge – had been drinking hard into the night, was subsequently seen striding white and naked on the hill at dawn, and then had been found dead back here, his head cracked on a flagstone, the room stinking of brandy.

Sure – these things happened in lonely parishes. Merrily pulled down a paper towel and began to dry her hands, not hurrying – resisting the urge to whirl suddenly around and catch Griffith, crazed and naked, forming out of the dampness in the wall.

She would *not* be bloody-well scared. She would observe with detachment. *Imprints* were invariably harmless. They appeared, vanished, occasionally messed with the atmosphere, but they never accosted you. They were, in fact, unaware of you, having no feelings, no consciousness. Their actions rarely varied. They appeared like a wooden cuckoo from a clock, only silently. And, no, they did not appear to feel the need to pee.

If an *imprint* responded to you, then it was likely to be something else – a *visitor* or, worse, an *insomniac* – and you had to review your options.

'And how, basically, do we know which is which?' big, bald Charlie Headland had demanded then. Charlie was simple and belligerent – Onward, Christian Soldiers – and needed confrontation.

'We have tests,' Huw explained. 'After a while, you might start feeling maybe you no longer have to apply them. You'll feel you know what's required – been here before, already done that. You'll feel you've attained a sensitivity. Now you've got to watch that temptation, because—'

'Meaning psychic powers, Huw?' Clive Wells interrupted. Clive was old-money and High Church, and naturally suspicious of Huw with his ancient blue canvas jacket, his shaggy grey hair, his permanent stubble. 'Psychic powers – that's what you mean by sensitivity?'

'No-oo.' Huw stared down at the holes in his trainers. 'It's not necessarily the same thing. In fact I'm inclined to distrust people who go on about their powers. They start to rely on what they think of as their own ability, and they – and anybody else who relies on what they say – can be deceived. I was about to say I've found it dangerous to rely too heavily on

your perceived sensitivity. That feeling of heightened awareness, that can be an illusion too. We still need, all the time,
to stay close to an established procedure. We need that discipline, Clive; it's one of the Church's strengths.'

Charlie the chaplain nodded briskly, being all for discipline
and procedure.

'Make sure you put reason above intuition,' Huw said.
'Beware of inspiration.'

'That include divine inspiration?' Clive demanded.

Huw directed a bleak blue gaze at him. 'How do you
know when it's divine?'

Clive stiffened. 'Because I'm a priest. Because I have faith.'

'Listen, beware of being too simplistic, man,' said Huw
coldly.

They'd all gone quiet at this. Dusk clogging the grimy,
diamond-paned window behind Huw, melding with mountains and low cloud. Late October, long nights looming.
Merrily wishing she was home in front of the vicarage fire.

'I mean, don't get me wrong . . .' Huw was hunched up
on a corner of his desk by the bare-stone inglenook. 'All I'm
saying is' – he looked suddenly starved – 'that we must strive
to know the *true* God. Evil *lies* to you. Evil is plausible. Evil
butters you up, tells you what you want to hear. We need to
beware of what you might call disinformation.'

'Hell's bells.' Charlie chuckled, trying to diffuse the
atmosphere. 'Times like this you begin to wonder if you
haven't walked into the wrong course. More like MI5 –
imprints and *visitors, weepers, breathers, hitchhikers*, indeed.

'Important to keep them in their place, lad. If we overdramatize, if we wave our arms and rail against the Powers of
Darkness and all this heavy-metal crap, if we inflate it . . . then
we glorify it. We bloat what might simply be a nasty little
virus.'

'When all it requires is a mild antibiotic, I suppose,' said Barry Ambrose, a worried-looking vicar from Wiltshire.

'If you like. Take a break, shall we?' Huw slid from the desk.

Cue for Merrily to stand up and announce that she was going to brave the ladies' loo.

Deliverance?

It meant exorcism.

When, back in 1987, the Christian Exorcism Study Group had voted to change its name to the Christian Deliverance Study Group, it was presumably an attempt to de-sensationalize the job. 'Deliverance' sounded less medieval, less sinister. Less plain weird.

But it changed nothing. Your job was to protect people from the invasion of their lives by entities which even half the professed Christians in this country didn't believe in. You had the option these days to consider them psychological forces, but after a couple of days here you tended not to. The journey each morning, just before first light, from the hotel in Brecon to this stark chapel in the wild and lonely uplands, was itself coming to represent the idea of entering another dimension.

Merrily would be glad to leave.

Yesterday, they'd been addressed by their second psychiatrist, on the problem of confusing demonic possession with forms of schizophrenia. They'd have to work closely with psychiatrists – part of the local support-mechanism they would each need to assemble.

Best to choose your shrink with care, Huw had said after the doctor had gone, because you'd almost certainly, at some time, need to consult him or her on a personal level.

And then, noticing Clive Wells failing to smother his scorn, he'd spent just over an hour relating case histories of ministers who had gone mad or become alcoholic or disappeared for long periods, or battered their wives or mutilated themselves. When a Deliverance priest in Middlesborough was eventually taken into hospital, they'd found forty-seven crosses razored into his arms.

An extreme case, mind. Mostly the Deliverance ministry was consultative: local clergy with problems of a psychic nature on their patch would phone you for advice on how best to handle it. Only in severe or persistent cases were you obliged to go in personally. Also, genuine demonic possession was very rare. And although most of the work would involve hauntings, real ghosts – unquiet spirits or *insomniacs* – were also relatively infrequent. Ninety per cent were basic *volatiles* or *imprints*.

Like the monk.

Ah, yes . . . monks. What you needed to understand about these ubiquitous spectral clerics, Huw said, was that they were a very convenient shape. Robed and cowled and faceless, a monk lacked definition. In fact, anyone's aura – the electromagnetic haze around a lifeform – might look vaguely like a monk's cowl. So could an *imprint*, a residue. So that was why there were so many ghostly monks around, see?

'Oh, just bugger . . . *off*!' Merrily crumpled the paper towel, tossed it at the wall where the smudge had been and went over to investigate.

The smudge turned out to be not something in the air but in the wall itself: an imprint of an old doorway. The *ghost* of a doorway.

Three days of this and you were seeing them everywhere.

Merrily sighed, retrieved the towel, binned it. Picked up her cigarette from the edge of the washbasin. There you go . . . it was probably the combination of poor light and the smoke in the mirror which had made the outline appear to move.

It was rare, apparently, for Deliverance ministers or counsellors actually to experience the phenomena they were trying to *divert*. And anyway, as Huw had just pointed out, a perceived experience should not be trusted.

Trust nothing, least of all your own senses.

Merrily took a last look at herself in the mirror: a small dark-haired person in a sloppy sweater. The only woman among nine ministers on this course.

'Little dolly of a clergyperson . . . nice legs, dinky titties.'

Dermot, her church organist, had said that the day he exposed to her his own organ. She shuddered. Dermot had worn a monkish robe that morning, and no underpants. So naturally she no longer trusted monks. Or, for that matter, priests like Charlie Headland who looked as if they wouldn't mind spanking you. But she *was* inclined to trust the Reverend Huw Owen, faded and weary on the outside but tough and flexible as old leather. Something of the monk about Huw, also – the Celtic hermit-monk in his lonely cell.

She dropped her cigarette down the loo.

Oh well, back into the twilight zone.

The passage still had lockers and iron hooks on the wall, from when the chapel had been an Outward Bound centre owned by some Midland education authority. It had changed hands discreetly a couple of years ago, was now jointly owned by the Church of England and the Church in Wales, although it seemed few people, even inside the Church, knew it was currently used as a training centre for exorcists.

The door to the big stone room was open; she heard muted discussion from inside, a shrill, affected laugh. Charlie Headland was wedged against the jamb, crunching crisps. He shook the packet at Merrily.

'Prawn mayonnaise flavour.'

Merrily helped herself to a crisp. Charlie looked down at her with affection.

'You've got a lot of bottle, Mrs Watkins.'

'What? Just for going for a wee in a haunted loo?'

Charlie chuckled. On occasion, he would fling an arm around Merrily and squeeze her. Twice he'd patted her bottom.

'You wouldn't be laughing,' Merrily said, 'if that thing was in the gents' instead.'

Charlie grimaced and nodded, munched meditatively for a while, then patted her arm lightly. 'Got a little girl, I hear.'

'Not any more. A woman, she tells me. She's sixteen – just.'

'Oh, blimey. Where'd you leave her? Suitably caged, one hopes.'

'She's staying with friends in the village. Not this village – back home.'

Charlie balled his crisp packet, tossed it in the air and caught it. 'I reckon he made that up, you know.'

'Who?'

'Huw. That story about the hellfire preacher-man who died in the ladies' bogs. It's too pat.'

Merrily pulled the door to, cutting off the voices from the stone room. 'Why would he do that?'

'Giving us all little tests, isn't he? You particularly. You're the only woman amongst us, so there's one place you need to visit *alone*. If you'd suddenly started crossing your legs and holding it till you got back to the hotel, he'd know you were a little timid. Or if you came back rubbing your hands and saying you'd detected a cold patch, you'd be revealing how impressionable you were.'

'Be difficult to *spot* a cold patch in this place.'

'You're not wrong,' said Charlie. 'Talk about Spartan. Not what most of them were expecting. Neither's Huw. Awfully downmarket, isn't he? Clive's quite insulted – expected someone solemn and erudite like his old classics master at Eton.'

'What about you?'

'After fifteen years with the military? No problem at all for me. Funny chap, though, old Huw. Been through the mill, you can tell that. Wears the scar tissue like a badge.' Charlie dug his hands into his jacket pockets. 'I think Huw's here to show us where we stand as of now.'

'Which is?'

He nodded at the closed door. 'Out in the cold – lunatic fringe. Half the clergy quite openly don't believe in God as we knew Him any more, and here we all are, spooking each other with talk of *breathers* and *hitchhikers* and *insomniacs*.'

Not for the first time since her arrival, Merrily shivered. 'What exactly *is* a *hitchhiker*, Charlie?'

'What's it sound like to you?'

'Something that wants a free ride?'

'All the way to hell, presumably,' said Charlie.

'Mustn't overdramatize,' Merrily reminded him as the door opened and Huw stood there, unkempt, his dog-collar yellowing at the rim.

'Putting the telly on now,' Huw said hesitantly. 'If that's all right?'

Merrily said cheerfully, 'I didn't notice anything at all in the lavatory, Huw.'

Huw nodded.

There was a clear dent in the woman's forehead. Also a half-knitted V-shaped scab over her left eye, the bruised one.

Merrily had seen several women in this condition before, although not recently. And not under these circumstances, obviously. Mostly in the hostel in Liverpool, when she was a curate.

'This was what done it.' The woman was holding out a

green pottery ashtray. An old-fashioned pub ashtray like a dog bowl. 'See? Chipped all down the side. Not from when it hit me, like. When it fell on the floor afterwards.'

'I see.' The man's voice was calm and gentle and unsurprised. Not Huw – too deep, too posh. 'So it came flying—'

'I should've saved the other pieces, shouldn't I? I didn't think.'

'That's quite all right, Mrs . . . *bleep* . . . We're not the police. Now, the ashtray was where?'

'On the sideboard. Always kept on the sideboard.'

You could see the sideboard behind her. Looked like early Sixties. Teak, with big gilt knobs on the drawers. On the once-white wall above it was a half-scrubbed stain. As though she'd started to wipe it off and then thought: *What's the bloody point?*

'So you actually *saw* it rising up?'

'Yeah, I . . . It come . . . It just come through the air, straight at me. Like whizzing, you know?'

This was a very unhappy woman. Early thirties and losing it all fast. Eyes downcast, except once when she'd glanced up in desperation – *You've got to believe me!* – and Merrily could see a corona of blood around the pupil of the damaged eye.

'Couldn't you get out of the way? Couldn't you duck?'

'No, I never . . .' The woman backing off, as though the thing was flying straight at her again. 'Like, it was too quick. I couldn't move. I mean, you don't expect . . . you can't believe what's happening, can you?'

'Did you experience anything else?'

'What?'

'Was there any kind of change in the atmosphere of this room? The temperature, was it warmer . . . or colder?'

'It's always cold in here. Can't afford the gas, can I?' Her eyes filling up.

'No,' he said. 'I'm sorry. Tell me, where was your husband when this was happening?'

'What?'

'Your husband, did *he* see anything?'

'Nah, he . . . he wasn't here, was he?' Plucking at the sleeve of her purple blouse.

Merrily wrote down *husband* on her pad.

'He was out,' the woman said.

'Has he had any experiences himself? In this house?'

'He ain't seen nothing. Nothing come flying at *him*. I reckon he's heard, like, banging noises and stuff, though.'

'Stuff?'

'You better ask him.'

'Have you discussed it much between yourselves?'

Minimal shake of the head.

'Why not?'

'*I* dunno, do I?' A flicker of exasperation, then her body went slack again. 'What you supposed to say about it? It's the kids, innit? I don't want nothing to happen to the ki—'

The woman's face froze, one eye closed.

'All right.' Huw walked back to his desk pocketing the remote control, turning to face the students. 'We'll hold it there. Any thoughts?'

Merrily found she'd underlined *husband* twice.

They looked at one another, nobody wanting to speak first. Someone yawned: Nick Cowan, the former social worker from Coventry.

Huw said, 'Nick, not impressed?'

Nick Cowan slid down in his canvas-backed chair. 'Council house, is this, Huw? I don't think you told us.'

'Would that make a difference?'

'It's an old trick, that's all. It's a cliché. They want rehousing.'

'So she's faking it, is she?'

'Well, obviously I can't . . . I mean you asked for initial impressions, and that's mine, based on twenty-five years' experience and about a thousand reports from local authorities after that rubbishy film came out . . . *Amityville* whatever. It's an old scam, but they keep on trying it because they know you can't prove it one way or the other. And if you don't rehouse them they'll go to the press, and then the house'll get a reputation, and so . . .'

Nick felt for his dog-collar, as if to make sure it was still there. He was the only one of the group who wore his to these sessions every day. He seemed grateful for the dog-collar: it represented some kind of immunity. Perhaps he thought he no longer had to justify his opinions, submit reports, get his decisions rubber-stamped and ratified by the elected representatives; just the one big boss now.

'All right, then.' Huw went to sit on his desk, next to the TV, and leaned forward, hands clasped. 'Merrily?'

He was bound to ask her, the only female in the group. On the TV screen the woman with one closed eye looked blurred and stupid.

'Well,' Merrily said, 'she isn't faking that injury, is she?'

'How do you think she got the injury, Merrily?'

'Do we get to see the husband?'

'You think he beat her up?'

'I'd like to know what he has to say.'

Huw said nothing, looked down at his clasped hands.

'And see what kind of guy he is.'

Huw still didn't look at her. There was quiet in the stone room.

There'd been a lot of that. Quite often the course had the feeling of a retreat: prayer and contemplation. Merrily was starting to see the point: it was about being receptive. While you had to be pragmatic, these weren't decisions which in the end you could make alone.

Beyond the diamond panes, the horn of the moon rose over a foothill of Pen-y-fan.

'OK.'

Huw stepped down. His face was deeply, tightly lined, as though the lines had been burned in with hot wire, but his body was still supple and he moved with a wary grace, like an urban tomcat.

'We'll take another break.' He switched off the TV, ejected the tape. 'I'd like you to work out between you how you yourselves would proceed with this case. Who you'd involve. How much you'd keep confidential. Whether you'd move quickly, or give the situation a chance to resolve itself. Main question, is she lying? Is she deluded? Merrily, you look like you could do with another ciggy. Come for a walk.'

TWO

Fluctuation

The mountains hunched around the chapel, in its hollow, like some dark sisterhood over a cauldron. You had to go to the end of the drive before you could make out the meagre lights of the village.

It was awesomely lonely up here, but it was home to Huw, who sniffed appreciatively at Merrily's smoke, relaxing into his accent.

'I were born a bastard in a little *bwddyn* t'other side of that brow. Gone now, but you can find the foundations in the grass if you have a bit of a kick around.'

'I wondered about that: a Yorkshireman called Huw Owen. You're actually Welsh, then?'

'Me mam were waitressing up in Sheffield by the time I turned two, so I've no memories of it. She never wanted to come back; just me, forty-odd years on. Back to the land of my father, whoever the bugger was. Got five big, rugged parishes to run now, two of them strong Welsh-speaking. I'm learning, slowly – getting there.'

'Can't be easy.'

Huw waved a dismissive arm. 'Listen, it's a holiday, luv. Learning Welsh concentrates the mind. Cold, though, in't it?'

'Certainly colder than Hereford.' Merrily pulled her cheap waxed coat together. 'For all it's only forty-odd miles away.'

'Settled in there now, are you?'

'More or less.'

They followed a stony track in the last of the light. Walkers were advised to stick to the paths, even in the daytime, or they might get lost and wind up dying of hypothermia – or gunshot wounds. The regular soldiers from Brecon and the shadowy SAS from Hereford did most of their training up here in the Beacons.

No camouflaged soldiers around this evening, though. No helicopters, no flares. Even the buzzards had gone to roost. But to Merrily the silence was swollen. After they'd tramped a couple of hundred yards she said, 'Can we get this over with?'

Huw laughed.

'I'm not daft, Huw.'

'No, you're not that.'

He stopped. From the top of the rise, they could see the white eyes of headlights on the main road crossing the Beacons.

'All right.' Huw sat down on the bottom tier of what appeared to be a half-demolished cairn. 'I'll be frank. Have to say I were a bit surprised when I heard he'd offered the job to a young lass.'

Merrily stayed on her feet. 'Not *that* young.'

'You look frighteningly young to me. You must look like a little child after Canon T.H.B. Dobbs.' Huw pronounced the name in deliberate block capitals.

'Mr Dobbs,' Merrily said, 'yes. You know him, then?'

'Not well. Nobody knows the old bugger well.'

'I've never actually met him – with him being in and out of hospital for over a year.'

'There's a treat to look forward to,' Huw said.

'I've heard he's a . . . traditionalist.'

'Oh aye, he's that, all right. No bad thing, mind.'

'I can understand that.' Merrily finally sat down next to him.

'Aye,' Huw said. 'But does your new bishop?'

It was coming, the point of their expedition. The pale moon was limp above a black flank of Pen-y-fan.

'Bit of a new broom, Michael Henry Hunter,' Huw said, as a rabbit crossed the track, 'so I'm told. Bit of a trendy. Bit flash.'

'So he appoints a female diocesan exorcist,' Merrily said, 'because that's a cool, new-broom thing to do.'

'You said it.'

'Only, he hasn't appointed me. Not yet. Canon Dobbs is still officially in harness. I haven't been appointed to anything.'

'Oh, really?' Huw tossed a pebble into the darkness.

'So are you going to tell him?'

'Tell him?'

'That he shouldn't.'

'Not my job to tell a bishop what he can and can't do.'

'I suppose you want *me* to tell him: that I can't take it on.'

'Aye.' Huw gazed down at the road. 'I'd be happy with that.'

Shit, Merrily thought.

She'd met the Bishop just once before he'd become the Bishop. It was, fatefully, at a conference at her old college in Birmingham, to review the progress of women priests in the Midlands. He was young, not much older than Merrily, and she'd assumed he was chatting her up.

This was after her unplanned, controversial speech to the assembly, on the subject of women and ghosts.

'Shot my mouth off,' she told Huw, sitting now on the other side of the smashed cairn. 'I'd had a . . . all right, a psychic experience. One lasting several weeks. Not the kind I could avoid, because it was right there in the vicarage. Possibly a former incumbent, possibly just . . . a *volatile*. Plenty of sensations, sounds, possibly hallucinatory – I only ever actually *saw* it once. Anyway, it was just screwing me up. I didn't know how to deal with it, and Jane saying: "Didn't they teach you anything at theological college, Mum?" And I'm thinking, yeah, the kid's right. Here we are, licensed priests, and the one thing they haven't taught us is how to handle the supernatural. I didn't know about Mr Dobbs then. I didn't even know that every diocese needed to have one, or what exactly they did. I just wanted to know how many other women felt like me – or if I was being naive.'

'Touched a nerve?'

'Probably. It certainly didn't lead to a discussion, and nobody asked me anything about it afterwards. Except for Michael Hunter. He came over later in the restaurant, bought me lunch. I thought, he was just . . . Anyway, that was how it happened. Obviously, I'd no idea then that he was going to be my new bishop.'

'But he remembered you. Once he'd got his feet under the table and realized, as a radical sort of lad, that he could already have a bit of a problem on his hands: namely Canon T.H.B. Dobbs, his reactionary old diocesan exorcist. *Not* "Deliverance minister". *Decidedly* not.'

'I'm afraid "Deliverance consultant" is the Bishop's term.'

'Aye.' She felt his smile. 'You know why Dobbs doesn't like the word Deliverance? Because the first two syllables are an anagram of *devil*. That's what they say. Must've been relieved, Mick Hunter, when the old bugger got his little cardiac prod towards retirement.'

'But he hasn't gone yet, and I'm only here because the Bishop wants me to get some idea of how—'

'No, luv.' Huw looked up sharply. 'This *isn't* a course for people who just want to learn the basics of metaphysical trench warfare, as Hunter well knows. He wants you, badly.'

*

'It's a sensitive job. It's very political. It throws up a few hot potatoes like the satanic child-abuse panic – God, what was all that about, really? Well, I don't want any of this bell-book-and-candle, incense-burning, medieval rubbish. I want somebody bright and smart and on their toes. But also sympathetic and flexible and non-dogmatic and upfront. Does that describe you, Merrily?'

Mick Hunter in his study overlooking the River Wye. Thirty-nine years old and lean and fit, pulsing with energy and ambition. The heavy brown hair shading unruly blue eyes.

'So,' Huw Owen said now, mock-pathetic, slumped under the rising moon. 'Would you come over all feminist on me if I begged you not to do it?'

Merrily said nothing. She'd been expecting this, but that didn't mean she knew how to handle it. Quite a shock being offered the job, obviously. She'd still known very little about Deliverance ministry. But did the Bishop himself know much more? Huw appeared to think not.

'I do like women, you know,' he said ruefully. 'I've been *very* fond of women in me time.'

'You want to protect us, right?'

'I want to protect everybody. I'll be sixty next time but one, and I'm starting to feel a sense of responsibility. I don't want stuff letting in. A lot of bad energy's crowding the portals. I want to keep all the doors locked and the chains up.'

'Suddenly the big, strong, male chain's acquired all these weak links?'

'I've always been a supporter of women priests.'

'Sounds like it.'

'Just that it should've all been done years ago, that's the trouble. Give the women time to build up a weight of tradition, some ballast, before the Millennial surge.'

'And how long does it take to build up a weight of tradition? How long, in your estimation, before we'll be ready to take on the *weepers* and the *volatiles* and the *hitchhikers*?'

'Couple of centuries.'

'Terrific.'

'Look . . .' Silver-rimmed night clouds were moving behind Huw. 'You're not a fundamentalist, not a charismatic or a happy-clappy. You've no visible axe to grind and I can see why he was drawn to you. You're in many ways almost exactly the kind of person we need in the trenches.'

'And I would keep a *very* low profile.'

'With Mick Hunter wearing the pointy hat?' Huw hacked off a laugh. 'He'll have you right on the front page of the *Hereford Times* brandishing a big cross. All right – joke. But you'll inevitably draw attention. You're very pretty, am I allowed to say that? And *they'll* be right on to you, if they aren't already. Little rat-eyes in the dark.'

Merrily instantly thought about Dermot Child, the organist in the monk's robe. 'I don't know what you mean.'

'I think you do, Merrily.'

'Satanists?'

'Among other species of pond life.'

'Isn't all that a bit simplistic?'

'Let's pretend you never said that.'

A string of headlights floated down the valley a long way away. She thought of Jane back home in Ledwardine and felt isolated, cut off. How many of the other priests on the course would agree with Huw? All of them, probably. A night-breeze razored down from crags she could no longer see.

'Listen,' Huw said, 'the ordination of women is indisputably the most titillating development in the Church since the Reformation. They'll follow you home, they'll breathe into your phone at night, break into your vestry and tamper with your gear. Crouch in the back pews and masturbate through your sermons.'

'Yes.'

'But that's the tip of the iceberg.'

'Rather than just a phase?'

'Jesus,' Huw said, 'you know what I heard a woman say the other week? "We can handle it," she said. "It's no more hassle than nurses get, and women teachers." A priest, this was, totally failing to take account of the . . . the overwhelming glamour the priesthood itself confers. It's now a fact that ordained women are the prime target for every psychotic grinder of the dark satanic mills that ever sacrificed a chicken. And there are a lot of those buggers about.'

'I've read the figures.'

'Exaggerated – two million in Britain alone, that sort of level. I don't think so. I'd guess no more than a thousand hard-liners and another five or six thousand misfit hangers-on. But, by God, that's enough, in't it? It's a modern religion, see, masquerading as something ancient. I've not said much about it down there yet.' Jerking a thumb towards the chapel. 'I like to save it for the end of the course, on account of some priests find it harder to take seriously than spooks.'

A blur of white: an early barn owl sailing over on cue.

Merrily said, 'What do you mean by a modern religion?'

'Well, not in principle, though it got a hell of a boost in the Eighties. All that worship of money and sex and wordly success – Lucifer as patron saint of greedy, self-serving bastards, the Lord of this World. Goes back to some of the old Gnostic teachings: God's in His Heaven, while the other feller runs things down here.'

'You can't imagine people actually believing that.'

'Why not? If you want to get on in the world, you have to join the winning team. That's not evil, it's pragmatic. It's being level-headed, recognizing the set-up. A jungle, every man for himself, that's the manifesto. That's the spin. Got this amazing charge in the Eighties. Took off faster than mobile phones.'

'Which was when you—?'

He lifted a hand. 'I only talk about me when I'm drunk, and I don't like to get drunk any more.'

She stood up and walked, with determination, around to his side of the stones. 'Why are you here, really, Huw? I mean out here in the sticks. Are you in hiding?'

'Eh?'

'I just don't go for all that Land of my Fathers bullshit. Something happened to you in Sheffield and you felt you couldn't—'

'Cut it any more?'

'I'm sorry. It's none of my business.'

She *was* sorry. She wished she could see his eyes, but his face was in deep shadow.

'Aye, well, it wasn't Sheffield,' Huw said.

'You don't have to—'

'I won't. I'm just saying it wasn't Sheffield. I just . . . Look, don't try and turn this round, Merrily. You should consider your situation. You're on your own, your daughter won't be around much longer—'

'And I can't possibly hold myself together without a man.'

Huw stood up, the rising moon blooming on his left shoulder. 'This is not just wankers in the back pews, you know.'

She looked at him. 'I've encountered evil.'

'Face to face? Hearing it call your name? And your mother's name, and your daughter's name? Feeling it all over you like some viscous, stinking—'

He turned away, shaking his head, shambled back on to the track towards the chapel.

'Look, those blokes down there – solid, stoical, middle-aged priests: I can tell you four of them won't go through with it. Out of the rest, there'll be one broken marriage and a nervous breakdown. Are you listening, Merrily?'

'Yes!'

She stumbled after him, and he shouted back over his shoulder, 'Woman exorcist? Female guardian of the portals? You might as well just paint a great big bullseye between your tits.'

When they got back, the chapel was in near-darkness, only an unsteady line of light under the door of the stone room.

Inside, the oil lamp which normally hung in the passage now stood on Huw's desk, next to the TV.

'Power's gone,' someone said. They were all standing around in the lamplight looking guilty like small boys. There was a smell of burning.

'Ah, Huw, ah . . .' The Rev. Charles Headland flicked at the letter-box mouth of the VCR. 'Some of us wanted to have another look at that lady. Couldn't make up our minds. Dodgy items, poltergeists.'

'It was mainly me,' said Barry Ambrose, the worried vicar from Wiltshire. 'I half-believed her, but I think I'd have wanted to go back and talk to her again.'

'Yes.' Huw closed the door of the room. 'That was what they did. It was a rector in Northampton. He felt bad about them recording the first interview on tape for the likes of us, and just giving her a token prayer, so he went back to talk to her in private.'

Merrily felt a tension in the room.

'Sorry, Huw.' Charlie held up his hands, something ribboning and rustling there, and glistening in the lamplight. 'Don't know what happened here.'

Holding up the video cassette. About four yards of tape had become unravelled.

'Screen went blank. Ejected the tape, and the damn thing

was on fire. Had to rip it out and stamp on it. Extraordinary thing. Wasn't your only copy, was it?'

'Doesn't matter.' Huw accepted the remains of the video. 'Coming to the end of its shelf-life anyway, that particular case-history.'

'Need a new player, too, I'd guess.'

Merrily leaned in and saw that the lips of the machine were scorched and warped. She'd never known this happen to a VCR before.

'That's the fourth one in two years,' Huw said. 'It's a right difficult place, this.'

'Jesus.' Merrily's legs felt weak; she clutched at a chair. 'You're not saying . . .?'

'No, luv. I don't say anything, me.'

Silence in the stone room. One of those moments when spiderwebs of cracks appeared in the walls of reality, and Merrily thought: *Do I really want to be doing this? Should anyone be doing it?*

Huw looked over the lamplit assembly of bemused vicars and rectors and priests-in-charge. *God's elite commando unit*, Merrily thought, and wanted to give in to hysterical laughter, except one or two of them might then think she was possessed.

'So, lads,' Huw said, 'which of you would like to practise his cleansing routine?'

Charlie Headland's mouth tightened. Merrily guessed he was wondering if Huw had rigged this. And she even wondered that, too. *Tests – little tests. Lies. Disinformation.*

'And should we bless and cleanse the entire premises? Or perhaps each other?'

Merrily thought, horrified: *It's getting completely out of hand. How quickly we all rush to the edge.*

'This is insane,' Nick Cowan, the ex-social worker, said.

'It's nonsense. There was obviously some sort of electrical fluctuation. A power surge, that's all.'

Huw beamed at him. 'Good thought, Nicholas. You do get problems like that in the mountains. That's a very good thought. There you are . . .' He spread his hands. 'Lesson for us all. Always consider the rational nuts-and-bolts explanation before you get carried away. Why don't you go and check the fuse-box, Charles? In the cupboard over the front door. There's a torch in there.'

When Charlie had gone, Merrily sat down. She felt tired and heavy. To break the uncomfortable silence, she said, 'Was that a genuine case – the woman on the video?'

'Ah,' said Huw. In the wavery light, he looked much younger. Merrily could imagine him in some rock band in the Sixties.

'You said they went back to talk to her again.'

'Well.' He began to wrap the unravelled videotape in a coil around his hands until it was binding them together. 'Our man in Northampton knocks on the door and gets no answer, but he can hear a radio playing loudly inside the house, and the door's unlocked, so he goes in and calls out, like you do. And the radio just goes on playing, and our man's beginning to get a funny feeling.'

'Oh, dear God, no,' said Clive Wells. 'Don't say that.'

'Afraid so, Clive.' Huw held out his hands, pressed together as though in prayer but bound tight, somehow blasphemously, with black videotape. 'There she is on the settee with a bottle of whisky, nearly empty, and a bottle of pills, *very* empty, and Radio Two playing comforting Sixties hits.'

Merrily closed her eyes. Huw wouldn't be lying about this. He wouldn't be that cruel.

'And we still don't know if she was genuine or not,' Huw said sadly. 'The bottom line is that our man in Northampton should not have left before administering a proper blessing to leave her in a state of calm, feeling protected. Psychological benefits, if nothing else. The worst that could've happened then was he'd have looked a pillock if it came out she'd made the story up. But, then, looking like a pillock's part of the clergyperson's job, in't it, Merrily? Get used to it, don't we?'

Merrily was still staring into the scorched and grinning maw of the VCR when the lights came on again.

'First law of Deliverance,' Huw said. 'Always carry plenty of fuse wire.'

Part Two

VIRUS

THREE

Storm-trooper

They went to look at Hereford Cathedral – because it was raining, and because Jane had decided she liked churches.

As distinct, of course, from the Church, which was still the last refuge of tossers, no-hopers and sad gits who liked dressing up.

Jane wandered around in her precious Radiohead sweat-shirt, arms hanging loose, hands opened out. Despite the presence of all these vacuous, dog-collared losers, you could still sometimes pick up an essence of real spirituality in these old sacred buildings, the kid reckoned. This was because of where they'd been built, on ancient sacred sites. Plus the resonance of gothic architecture.

Merrily followed her discreetly, hands in pockets, head down, and didn't argue; a row was looming, but this was not the place and not the time. And anyway she had her own thoughts, her own decision to make. She wondered about consulting St Thomas, and was pleased to see Jane heading for the North Transept, where the old guy lay. Kind of.

They passed the central altar, with its suspended corona like a giant gold and silver cake-ruff. On Saturdays, even in October, there were usually parties of tourists around the Cathedral and its precincts, checking out the usual exhibits: the Mappa Mundi, the Chained Library, the John Piper tap-estries, the medieval shrine of . . .

31

'Oh.'

In the North Transept, Merrily came up against a barrier of new wooden partitioning, with chains and padlocks. It was screening off the end wall and the foot of the huge stained-glass window full of Christs and angels and reds and blues.

Jane said, 'So, like, what's wrong, Reverend Mum?' She put an eye to the crack in the padlocked partition door. 'Looks like a building site. They turning it into public lavatories or something?'

'I forgot. They're dismantling the shrine.'

'What for?' Jane looked interested.

'Renovation. Big job. Expensive. Twenty grand plus. Got to look after your saint.'

'Saint?' Jane said. 'Do me a favour. Guy was just a heavy-duty politician.'

'Well, he was, but—'

'Thomas Cantilupe, 1218 to 1282,' Jane recited. 'Former Chancellor of England. Came from a family of wealthy Norman barons. He really didn't have to try very hard, did he?'

Well, yes, he did, Merrily wanted to say. When he became Bishop of Hereford, he tried to put all that behind him. Wore a hair shirt. And, as a lover of rich food, once had a great pie made with his favourite lampreys from the Severn, took a single succulent bite, and gave the rest away.

'Must have had something going for him, flower. About three hundred miracles were credited to this shrine.'

'Look.' Jane pushed her dark brown hair behind her ears. 'It's the power of *place*. If you'd erected a burger-bar here, people would still have been cured. It's all about the confluence of energies. Nothing to do with the fancy tomb of some overprivileged, corrupt . . .'

She stopped. A willowy young guy in a Cathedral sweatshirt was strolling over.

'It's Mrs Watkins, right?'

'Hello,' Merrily said uncertainly. Was she supposed to recognize him? She was discovering that what you needed more than anything in this job was a massive database memory.

'Er, you don't know me, Mrs Watkins. I saw you with the archdeacon once. Neil Cooper – I'm kind of helping with the project. It's just . . . I've got a key if you want to have a look.'

While Merrily hesitated, Jane looked Neil Cooper over, from his blond hair to his dusty, tight jeans.

'Right,' Jane said. 'Cool. Let's do it.'

Under the window, a fourteenth-century bishop slept on, his marble mitre like a nightcap. But the tomb of his saintly predecessor, Thomas Cantilupe, was in pieces – stone sections laid out, Merrily thought, like a display of postmodern garden ornaments.

There were over thirty pieces, Neil told them, all carefully numbered by the stonemasons. Neil was an archaeology student who came in most weekends. It was, he said, a unique opportunity to examine a famous and fascinating medieval tomb.

Jane stood amongst the rubble and the workbenches, peering around and lifting dustcloths.

'So, like, where are the bones?'

An elderly woman glanced in through the door, then backed quickly away as if dust from the freshly exposed tomb might carry some ancient disease.

Jane was prepared to risk it. She knelt and stroked one of the oblong side-slabs, closing her eyes as though emanations were coming through to her, the faint echo of Gregorian chant. Jane liked to feel she was in touch with other spheres of existence. Nothing religious, you understand.

'Sorry,' said Neil. 'There aren't any.'

'No bones?'

Hands still moving sensuously over the stone, Jane opened her eyes and gazed up at Neil. He looked about twenty. An older man; Jane thought older men were cool, and *only* older men. It was beginning to perturb Merrily that the kid hadn't found any kind of steady boyfriend her own age, since they'd arrived in Herefordshire.

Neil glanced at Jane only briefly. 'What happened, Mrs Watkins, is some of the bones were probably taken away for safekeeping at the time of the Reformation. And some were apparently carried around the city during the plague in the hope they might bring some relief, and I expect a few of those didn't come back. So he's widely scattered, although part of the skull's supposed to be back in Hereford, with the monks over at Belmont Abbey.'

Jane stood up. 'So it was like completely empty when you opened it, yeah?'

'Lot of dust,' said Neil.

The side-slab was divided into six sections; on each a knight in armour had been carved, their swords and shields and helmets and even chain-mail fingers crisply discernible, but all the faces gone – flattened, pulped. It didn't look as if time was entirely responsible.

'So, in fact,' Jane said, 'this great historic, holy artefact is like an empty shell.'

'It's a shrine,' Merrily said.

'Of course, that's one of the continuing problems with the Anglican Church.' Jane smiled slyly, before sliding out the punchline. 'So *much* of it's just a hollow shell.'

Merrily was careful not to react. 'We're delaying you,' she said to Neil Cooper. 'It was good of you to let us in.'

'No problem, Mrs Watkins. Drop in any time.' He smiled at Merrily, ignoring Jane.

Jane scowled.

'I expect you'll be around quite often,' Neil said. 'I gather they're giving you an office in the cloisters.'

'Nothing's fixed yet,' Merrily said, too sharply. 'And, anyway, I'd only be here one-and-a-half days a week. I have a parish to run as well.' *God*, she thought, *does everybody know about this?* So much for low-profile, so much for discretion.

'Look in anytime,' Neil repeated. 'Always nice to see you.'

'The trouble with older men,' said Jane, as they left the Cathedral, 'is that the cretins seem to fancy even *older* women.'

As they walked into Broad Street, the rain dying off but the sky threatening more, Merrily noticed that Jane seemed taller. A little taller than Merrily in fact, which was not saying much but was momentarily alarming. As though this significant spurt had occurred during the few days they'd been apart: Merrily experiencing weirdness in Wales, Jane staying with trusty villagers Gomer and Minnie, but returning to the vicarage twice a day to feed Ethel the cat.

Merrily felt disoriented. So much had altered in the ten days since she'd last been to the Cathedral. Ten days which – because the past week had been such a strange period – seemed so much longer, even part of a different time-frame.

She felt a quiver of insecurity, glanced back at the ancient edifice of myriad browns and pinks. It seemed to have shrunk. From most parts of the city centre, the spires of All Saints and St Peter's were more dominant. The Cathedral had long since lost its own spire, and sat almost modestly in a secluded corner between the River Wye and the Castle Green and a nest of quiet streets with no shops in them.

'Tea?' Merrily said desperately.

'Whatever.'

The late-afternoon sky was a smoky kind of orange.

Merrily peered around for cafés, snackbars. She felt like a stranger, needing to ground herself.

'The Green Dragon? They must do afternoon tea.'

Jane shrugged. They crossed towards Hereford's biggest hotel, nineteenth-century and the longest façade on Broad Street.

'So you've learned about Thomas Cantilupe at school?'

'Only in passing. He didn't figure much nationally. Nothing that happened in Hereford seems to have made much of a difference to anything in the big world.'

Useless arguing with Jane in this mood. The kid had consented to come shopping, a big sacrifice on a Saturday; it was now Merrily's task to tease out of her what was wrong, and Jane wasn't going to assist. Tiresome, time-honoured ritual.

They found a window table in The Green Dragon, looking back out on to Broad Street, the Saturday crowds thinning now as the day closed down. Sometimes November could bring a last golden surge, but this one had seemed colourless and tensed for winter. Merrily was aware of a drab sense of transience and futility – nothing profound. Maybe just wishing she was Jane's age again.

'Cakes,' she said brightly.

'Just tea, thanks. Black.'

Merrily ordered two teas and a scone. 'Worried about our weight, are we, flower?'

'No.'

'What *are* we worried about then?'

'Did *we* say we were worried?'

The bored, half-closed eyes, the sardonic tuck at the corner of the mouth. It was pure Sean – as when Merrily was trying to quiz him about some dubious client. You don't see your daughter for a week, and in the interim she's readmitted her father's soiled spirit.

Merrily tried again. 'I, er . . . I missed you, flower.'

'Really?' Jane tilted her soft, pale face into a supportive hand, elbow on the table. 'I'd have thought you had far too much to think about, poncing about in your robes and practising your *Out, Demons, Out* routine with the soul police.'

'Ah.'

'What?'

'That's what this is about – the soul police? You think I'm . . .'

What? An anachronism? A joke? Though Jane was basically spiritual, she just didn't believe the Church of England was. Bad enough to have your own mother walking around in a dog-collar, never mind the holy water and the black bag now. Was that it?

That was probably too simple. Nothing about Jane was ever really simple.

A man striding up the street towards All Saints glanced through the window, blinked, paused, strode on. *Oh God, not him, not now.* Merrily turned away from the window, stared across the table at Jane.

The kid pushed back her tumbling hair. 'OK, look . . .'

Yes? Merrily leaned forward. A crack, an opening? *Yes . . .*

Jane said, 'I'm uncomfortable about what you're doing, Merrily.'

'I see.'

Jesus. *Merrily?* A major development. Now we are sixteen, time to dump this Mum nonsense. We are two grown women, equals.

This needed some thinking about.

'I don't think you do see,' Jane said.

'So tell me.'

'They're dragging you in, aren't they?'

'Who?'

'The Church. It's all political.'

37

'Of course it is.'

'All those fat, smug C-of-E gits, they're worried about losing their power and their influence, so they're appointing cool bishops: smooth, glossy people like Michael Hunter . . . *Mick* Hunter, for God's sake.'

'Bishops are still appointed by Downing Street.'

'Yeah, well, exactly. Old mate of Tony Blair's. I can just see them swapping chords for ancient Led Zeppelin riffs. Like, Mick's superficially cool and different, but he's really Establishment underneath.'

'Phew,' said Merrily theatrically. 'Thank God, my daughter has finally become a revolutionary. I thought it was never going to happen.'

Jane glared at her.

'You really don't understand, do you?'

'Sure. You think I'm a glossy, superficial bimbo who's—'

'More like a trainee storm-trooper, actually.'

'What?'

'Look . . .' Jane's eyes flashed. 'It seemed really interesting at first when you said you were going to do this Deliverance training. I'm thinking, yeah, this is what it's all about: the Church actually investigating the supernatural nitty-gritty instead of just spouting all this Bible crap. And this course and everything, it all seemed really mysterious. So, like . . . Wednesday night, I go back to the vicarage to feed Ethel. I think maybe I should check the answering machine, see if there's anything urgent. So I go into your office and I find . . . hang on . . .'

From a pocket of her jeans, Jane dragged a compacted square of printed paper which she opened out on the table-top.

'And suddenly I saw what it was all really about.'

Merrily pulled towards her a Deliverance Study Group

pamphlet heralding a forthcoming seminar entitled: NEW AGE . . . OLD ENEMY.

She'd forgotten about it. It had come in a package from the DSG the morning she left for the Brecon Beacons.

'I haven't read it, flower.'

'I bet.'

'But, sure, I can guess what it's about.'

She picked up the leaflet.

Meditation-groups, sweat-lodges, healing-circles . . . it may all seem innocuous, but so-called New Age pursuits are often the marihuana which leads to the heroin of hard-core Satanism. Introducing the discussion, Canon Stephen Rigbey will examine the allure of alternative spirituality and suggest ways of discouraging harmful experimentation.

Merrily said steadily, 'You happen to notice the key word in this?'

'Don't try and talk all around it.'

'It's "discussion" – meaning debate.'

'It's bloody spiritual fascism,' said Jane.

'Oh, Jane, listen—'

'*You* listen, for once. The New Age is about . . . it's about millions of people saying: I want to know more . . . I want an inner life . . . I want to commune with nature and the cosmos and things, find out about what we're really doing here and who's running the show, and like what part I can play in the Great Scheme of Things. Right?'

'Pretty much like Christianity, in fact.' Merrily lit a cigarette.

'No, that's bollocks.' Jane shook her head furiously. 'The Church is like: Oh, you don't have to *know* anything; you just come along every Sunday and sing some crappy Victorian hymns and stuff and you'll go to heaven.'

'Jane, we've had this argument before. You just want to reduce it to—'

'And anybody steps out of line, it's: Oh, you're evil, you're a heretic, you're an occultist and we're gonna like burn you or something! Which was how you got the old witch-hunts, because the Church has always been on this kind of paternalistic power trip and doesn't *want* people to search for the truth. Like it used to be science and Darwinism and stuff they were worried about, now it's the New Age because that's like *real practical spirituality.* And it's come at a time when the Church is really feeble and pathetic, and the bishops and everybody are shit scared of it all going down the pan, so now we get this big Deliverance initiative, which is really just about . . . about *suppression.*' Jane sat back in her chair with a bump.

'Wow,' Merrily said.

'Don't.'

'What?'

'You're gonna say something patronizing. *Don't.*' Jane snatched back the leaflet and folded it up again. Evidence obviously. 'I bet you were mega-flattered when *Mick* offered you the job, weren't you? I bet it never entered your head that they want people like you because you're quite young and attractive and everything, and like—'

'It did, actually.'

'Like you're not going to come over as some crucifix-waving loony, what?'

'It *did* occur to me.' Merrily cupped both hands around her cigarette; she wasn't sure if they allowed smoking in here. 'Of course it did. It's *still* occurring to me. Not your let's-stamp-out-the-New-Age stuff, because I can't quite believe that. But, yeah, I think he does want me for reasons other than that I'm obviously interested in . . . phenomena, whatever. Which is one reason I haven't yet said yes to the job.'

Jane blinked once and they sat and stared at one another. Merrily thought about all the other questions that were occurring to her. And what Huw Owen had said to them all as they gathered outside the chapel in the last minutes of the course.

'Maybe you should analyse your motives. Are you doing this out of a desire to help people cope with psychic distress? Or is it in a spirit of, shall we say, personal enquiry? Think how much deeper your faith would be if you had evidence of life after death. How much stronger your commitment to the calling if you had proof of the existence of supernatural evil. If that's the way you're thinking, you need to consider very carefully after you leave here. And then, for Christ's sake, forget this. Do something else.'

Merrily dragged raggedly on her cigarette.

'You really want it, though, don't you?' Jane said. 'You really, really want it.'

'I don't know,' Merrily lied.

Jane smiled.

'I have a lot of thinking to do,' Merrily said.

'You going to tell *Mick* you're in two minds?'

'I think I shall be avoiding the Bishop for a while.'

'Ha.' Jane was looking over her mother's left shoulder.

Merrily said wearily, 'He just came in, didn't he?'

'I think I'll leave you to it. I'll go and have a mooch around Waterstone's and Andy's. See you back at the car at six?'

The waitress arrived with the tea.

'The Bishop can have mine if he likes,' Jane said.

FOUR

Moon

It was what happened with the crow, after the rain on Dinedor Hill. This was when Lol Robinson actually began to be spooked by Moon.

As distinct from sorry for Moon. Puzzled by Moon. Fascinated by Moon.

And attracted to her, of course. But anything down that road was not an option. It was not supposed to be that kind of relationship.

Most people having their possessions carried into a new home would need to supervise the operation, make sure nothing got broken. Moon had shrugged, left them to get on with it, and melted away into the rain and her beloved hill.

There really wasn't very much stuff to move in. Moon didn't even have a proper bed. When the removal men had gone, Lol went up to the Iron Age ramparts to find her.

He walked up through the woods, not a steep slope because the barn was quite close to the flattened summit where the ancient camp had been, the Iron Age village of circular thatched huts. Nothing remained of it except dips and hollows, guarded now by huge old trees, and by the earthen ramparts at the highest point.

And this was where he found Moon, where the enormous

trees parted to reveal the city of Hereford laid out at your feet like an offering.

Lol was aware that some people called the hill a *holy* hill, though he wasn't sure why. He should ask Moon. The ancient mysteries of Dinedor swam in her soul.

She was standing with her back to him, next to a huge beech tree which still wore most of its leaves. Her hair hung almost to the waist of the long medieval sort of dress she wore under a woollen shawl.

Making Lol think of drawings of fairies by Arthur Rackham and the centrefolds of those quasi-mystical albums from the early Seventies – the ones which had first inspired him to write songs. The kind of songs which were already going out of fashion when Lol's band, Hazey Jane, won their first recording contract.

Moon would still have been at primary school then. She seemed to have skipped a whole generation, if not two. Hippy *nouvelle*. Down in the city, she sometimes looked pale and nervy, distanced from everything. Up here she was connected.

Dick Lyden, the psychotherapist, had noticed this and given his professional blessing to Moon's plan, despite the fears of her brother Denny, who was jittery as hell about it. '*She can't do this. You got to stop her. SHE CANNOT LIVE THERE! OUT OF THE FUCKING QUESTION!*'

But she was a grown woman. What were they supposed to do, short of getting her committed to a psychiatric hospital? Lol, who'd been through that particular horror himself, was now of the opinion that it should never happen to anyone who was not dangerously insane.

When he first saw Moon on the ramparts, even though her face was turned away, he thought she'd never seemed more serene.

She glanced over her shoulder and smiled at him.

'Hi.'

'OK?'

'Yes.' She turned back to the view over the city. 'Wonderful, isn't it? Look. Look at the Cathedral and All Saints. Isn't that amazing?'

From here, even though they were actually several hundred yards apart, the church steeple and the Cathedral tower overlapped. The sky around them was a strange, burned-out orange.

Moon said, 'Many of the ley-lines through other towns, you can't see them any more because of new high-rise buildings, but of course there aren't any of those in Hereford. The skyline remains substantially the same.'

Lol realized he'd seen an old photograph of this view, taken in the 1920s by Alfred Watkins, the Hereford gentleman who'd first noticed that prehistoric stones and mounds and the medieval churches on their sites often seemed to occur on imaginary straight lines running across the landscape. Most archaeologists thought this was a rubbish theory, but Katherine Moon was not like most archaeologists. *It's at least spiritually valid,*' she'd said once. He wasn't sure what she meant.

'Moon,' he said now, 'why do some people call it a holy hill?'

She didn't have to think about it. 'The line goes through four ancient places of worship, OK? Ending at a very old church in the country. But it starts here, and this is the highest point. So all these churches, including the Cathedral, remain in its shadow.'

'In the poetic sense.'

'In the spiritual sense. This hill is the mother of the city. The camp here was the earliest proper settlement, long before there was a town down there. Over a thousand Celtic people lived up here.' She paused. 'My ancestors.'

There was a touching tremor of pride in her voice.

'So it's kind of . . .' Lol hesitated, ' . . . holy in the pagan sense.'

'It's just holy.' Moon still had her back to him. 'This was before the time of Christ. Over a thousand people keeping sheep and storing grain, doing their spinning and weaving and dyeing. It would've been idyllic – for a time.'

'What happened to them? The Dinedor People.'

'Some of them never went away. And the spirit remains.'

Moon gazed down over the spread of the city towards the distant Black Mountains and Welsh border. Slowly she turned towards him.

'And some . . . some of us have returned.'

He saw tears shining in her eyes.

And then he saw the black thing clasped to her stomach.

Katherine Moon . . .

Dick Lyden, the therapist, had briefed Lol as best he could about three months ago.

Twenty-six. Bright girl, quite a good degree in archaeology, but an unfortunate history of instability. Runs in the family, evidently. Her brother Denny, he's the sanest of them; might look like a New Age traveller, but Denny's a businessman, has his head screwed on.

After university, Dick said, Katherine had spent a couple of years freelancing on various archaeological digs across Britain. This was how she became obsessed with dead Celtic civilizations. Began wearing primitive clothing and strange jewellery, smoking too much dope, tripping out on magic-mushroom tea. When she arrived back in Hereford, the Katherine bit had gone; she was just Moon, and more than a little weird.

The reason she'd come back to Hereford was the lure of the big Cathedral Close dig. Also, perhaps, the impending death of her mother – as if Moon had sensed this coming. Her mother had died after several years in and out of expensive psychiatric residential homes – one of the reasons Denny had kept working so hard. Now it looked like he had another one to provide for.

But Denny's wife, Maggie, had decreed that Katherine wasn't living with them, no way – this stemming from the Christmas before last, when Moon had come to stay and Maggie had found her stash under the baby's cot. What a dramatic Christmas *that* had been. Now it was: Let her take her inheritance, smoke it, snort it, inject it into her arm . . . Just keep the mad bitch well out of our lives.

No wonder Maggie was paranoid. Denny's mother seemed to have picked up psychiatric problems simply by marrying into the Moon family, like their instability was infectious.

Meanwhile, Katherine had flipped again. Bought some speed from a dealer in Hereford, disappeared into pubs and clubs for three days, and been pulled in by the police after nicking two skirts from Next. Denny had taken her to Dick Lyden, as part of the deal for a conditional discharge by Hereford magistrates.

He'd refurbished the flat over one of his shops for her, suggesting she ran the store for a while. Knowing this wasn't entirely satisfactory – right in the city centre, too convenient for pubs and clubs and dealers, it was not really where he'd wanted her. But where *did* he want her? Well, somewhere safe. Somewhere he wouldn't have to visit her too often and risk domestic strife.

But certainly not Dinedor Hill. Not in a million years. As for fucking Dyn Farm . . .

We got to stop her, man! Denny with his head in his hands, beating it on the shop counter when he heard about the barn. *She can't DO this!*

But Moon had the money from her mother's bequest.

She'd already signed the lease with the latest people to own the farmhouse and its Grade Two listed outbuildings.

'*Think about it this way, Denny,*' Dick Lyden had suggested. '*The hill might have terrible memories for you, but she was just a child at the time. She has no memories of it at all. To Moon it's simply the birthright of which she was robbed. So going back to the hill – to part of the actual family farm – could be a healing thing. Who knows? Might even be the making of her. If I were you, Denny, and I couldn't disguise my feelings, I'd keep my distance. Now she's done it, it would not be good for her to be exposed to any negativity.*'

And then Dick had said, '*Tell you what, why don't we get Lol here to keep an eye on her? Most inoffensive chap I know, this.*' Patting Lol on the arm. '*No threat, you see? She mustn't feel pressured in any way – that's the important thing.*'

So Lol Robinson, ex rock-star (almost), sometime songwriter, former mental patient, had become Moon's minder. Possibly because no one else really wanted to take that responsibility.

But that was OK. Lol needed some responsibility. It was fine.

Until this.

The rain had begun again. It misted Lol's glasses and made a glossy slick of Moon's waist-length hair, falling black and limp down her back.

As black and limp as the dead crow she held.

She was leaning back against the tree now, her right hand cupped under the bird.

'Moon?' Lol took a step backwards, stumbled to his knees in the mud, looking up at her. She was beautiful. Her big eyes were penetrating, like an owl's.

'Look,' she said.

There was a spreading patch of blood, already the size of a dinner plate, on her dress from the stomach to the groin.

'It fell dead at my feet,' Moon said, 'out of the sky. Isn't that incredible?'

'Is it?' Lol said faintly. Appalled to see that her left hand, bloodied to the wrist, was actually moving *inside* the body of the crow. Loose feathers were sticking to the blood on her dress.

'To the ancient Celts the crow or raven was a sacred and prophetic bird.' Moon spoke as though she was addressing not one person but a group of students in a lecture room. 'The hero Bran was possibly a personification of a raven god. There were also several crow or raven goddesses: Macha, Nemain, Badb and the Morrigan.'

Lol stood up but moved no closer to her.

'It fell dead at my feet,' she said again. 'It was a gift – from the ancestors. A greeting on this the day of my homecoming.'

'Like a housewarming present,' Lol said before he could think.

He expected her to flare up, but she smiled and her eyes glowed.

'Yes!' She looked at Lol for the first time, and began to cry. 'Oh, Lol, I can't tell you. I can't express . . .'

Her hand came out of the crow then, full of organs and intestines and bloody gunge.

Lol felt sick. 'Moon, if it's a gift—'

'The gift,' Moon said happily, 'is *prophecy*! And inner vision. The point is that the crow was endowed with super-natural powers. It was honoured and feared and revered, OK? When this one fell to the earth, it was still warm and there was a small wound in the abdomen and I put my little finger into the wound and it just . . .'

'Why did you do that?'

'Because it was *meant*, of course! By bathing my hands

48

in its blood, I'm acquiring its powers. There's a legend of Cuchulainn, where he does that. I . . .' She held out the bird to Lol. 'I don't know what to do next.'

'Bury it, I think,' Lol said hopefully.

And Moon nodded, smiling through her tears.

Lol let her put the mutilated bird into his hands, trying not to look at it, fixing his gaze out over the city, where the Cathedral tower still merged with the steeple of All Saints under an orange-brown cloudbank.

Down below the ramparts, in the bowl of the ancient camp, they covered the crow with damp, fallen leaves. Lol wondered if maybe he should say some kind of prayer, but couldn't think of one.

'You'll fly again,' he said lamely to the leafy mound. 'You will.'

He felt dazed and inadequate.

Poor crow. Poor bloody Moon.

She stood up, her long grey dress hemmed with mud. As he followed her out of the hollow, Lol thought of Merrily Watkins, whom he hadn't seen since leaving Ledwardine. Would a priest conduct a funeral service for a carrion crow? He thought Merrily would.

Moon gathered her dark woollen shawl around her. Numbed, he followed her along the slippery path. Ahead of them was a now-familiar oak tree with the single dead branch pointing out of the top like a finger from a fist. This was where another steep, secret path dropped towards Moon's new home in its dripping dell.

When the path curved to the left, and the barn's metal flue poked out of the trees, Moon's mood changed. Her face was a tremulous dawn.

'I still can't believe it.' She stopped where the path became a series of long, shallow earthen steps held up by stones and rotting boards. 'I'm back. I'm really back. And they *want* me back. They've given me their sign. Isn't that just . . .?' Moon shook her head, blown away.

Leaving Lol in a quandary – his hands sticky with crow bits and blood. Should he tell Denny about this? Or just Dick? Or not mention it at all?

'I'd like to sleep now, Lol,' Moon said.

'Good idea,' he said gratefully.

'I can't tell you how wonderful I feel.'

'Good,' Lol said. 'That's, er . . . good.'

Driving the old Astra back through the semi-industrial sprawl of Rotherwas and into the city, he couldn't even think about it. He thought instead about stupid things, like maybe buying a bike, too, and getting fit like Moon who insisted she'd be pedalling to the shop in Capuchin Lane six days a week all through the coming winter.

He parked in a private yard behind the shop, in a spot which would have been Moon's if she possessed a car, and he walked through an alley and into Capuchin Lane. It was also known these days as Church Street, but he and Moon both preferred its old name.

This was a wonderful street to live in: narrow, ancient, cobbled and closed to traffic, full of little shops and pubs, and ending at the Cathedral – presenting, in fact, the most medieval view of it, especially at dawn and in the evening when all the shops were closed and the hanging signs became black, romantic silhouettes.

The flat over the shop called John Barleycorn – one of Moon's brother's shops – had been semi-derelict when Moon had first lived here. This was when she was helping with the archaeological excavation in the Cathedral Close, before the digging site was released for a new building to house the Mappa Mundi and the Chained Library. More than a thousand skeletons had been unearthed, and Moon had spent her days among the dead and her nights on a camp bed in this same flat. Walking out each morning to the Cathedral – the dream developing.

She kept a photograph of herself holding two medieval skulls from the massive charnel pit they'd found – all three of them wearing damaged grins. When the excavation ended and the bones were removed, Moon wanted to stay on there and Denny wanted her to leave, so there was tension, and soon afterwards Moon stole the skirts from Next, and the police found her stoned on the Castle Green. And that was when Dick had finally agreed to renovate the flat over the shop as a proper home for her.

Moon had seemed fairly content here in Capuchin Lane. Only Dinedor Hill, in fact, could have lured her away – and it did.

Lol, in need of somewhere to live, had then himself taken over the flat. Denny was glad about that, as it meant Lol could keep an eye on Moon during her working hours, and watch out for any hovering dope-dealers.

He had his key to the side door, but went in through the shop to report to Denny.

Moon's much older, and very much bulkier, brother sat on a stool behind the counter, trying to tune a balalaika. Although there was only one customer in the store, a girl flicking through the CDs, it seemed quite full; for in a street of small shops this was the very smallest. And it was full of the busy sound of Gomez from big speakers – and Denny was here, a one-man crowd in himself.

'It go all right then, my old mate?'

'Fine.'

'Shit.'

As well as this shop, Denny ran a specialist hi-fi business, and his own recording studio in the cellar of his house up towards Breinton. Lol had produced a couple of albums for him there: local bands, limited editions. Denny was keen to get him back on to the studio floor, but Lol wasn't ready yet; the songs weren't quite there – something still missing.

Denny said, 'No fights, breakages, tears?'

'Would you count tears of joy?'

'Shit.'

Lol decided to keep quiet about the crow.

Denny twanged the balalaika and winced. 'Don't get yourself too comfy in that flat, mate. She changes like the wind, my little sister.' He shook his bald head, and his gold-plated novelty earring swung like a tiny censer.

'You hope.' Lol couldn't remember feeling exactly comfy anywhere.

'Yeah,' Denny said. 'Don't go back, that's my philosophy. *Never* in life do you fucking well go back.'

Lol shrugged, helpless. 'Whatever that place does to you, it has the opposite effect on her. You can't get around it: she's happy. She walks into the woods, up to the camp—'

'Yeah . . . and all the time passing the place where her fucking father topped himself! What does that say to you?'

Denny sniffed hard and plucked twice at the balalaika's strings, then laid it on the counter in disgust. 'What use is a three-string shoebox on a stick? Kathy bought it from this poor, homeless busker, probably got the BMW parked round the corner.'

'Soft-hearted,' Lol said.

'Soft in the head! I'll tell you one thing: first sign of unusual behaviour, any hint of dope up there – she's *out*. Kicking and screaming or . . .' The CD ended and Denny lowered his voice. 'Or however. Right?'

Lol nodded.

'Long as we agree on that, mate,' Denny said, as the girl

customer turned around from the CD racks clutching a copy of Beth Orton's *Trailer Park*, a slow delighted smile pushing her tongue into a corner of her mouth.

'Hey,' she said. 'Lol Robinson, wow.'

'Oh,' Lol said. It seemed like ages since he'd seen her. He smiled, realizing how much he'd missed her even though sometimes, like Moon, she could be trouble. Well, not *quite* like Moon.

'Hey, cool,' the girl said. 'And that same old Roswell sweat-shirt. *Is* that the same one, or did you buy a set?'

'Hello, Jane,' Lol said. He wondered how much she'd overheard.

'So, like who's Kathy?' Jane Watkins said. Dark mocking eyes under dark hair. A lot like her mother.

FIVE

The Last Exorcist

The Bishop smiled hard, talked fast, and wore purple as bishops do.

'The Church, OK?' His voice was public-school with the edges sanded off. 'The Church is . . . hierarchical, conservative, full of rivalry, feuding, back-stabbing. And inherently incapable of ever getting anything bloody well *done*.'

The Bishop wore purple all over: a tracksuit and jogging gear. The Bishop jogged all over the city and its outskirts, usually in the early mornings and the evenings, covering, according to the *Hereford Times*, a minimum of thirty miles a week.

'Now you'd think, wouldn't you, that organizing an office in the Cathedral cloisters would be the *easiest* thing? Scores of cells and crannies and cubicles, but . . . all of them the Dean's. And if the Dean says there isn't an office to spare, I'm not even permitted to argue. Within the precincts of the Cathedral, even God bows to the Dean. So we shall have to look elsewhere. I'm so sorry, Merrily.'

'It's probably meant, Bishop.'

'Mick,' corrected the Bishop. 'Meant? Oh it was meant, for sure. The bastard means to frustrate me. Who, after all, is the oldest member of his Chapter? Dobbs.' The Bishop tossed the name out like junk-mail. 'The old man's ubiquitous, hovering silently like some dark, malign spectre. I'd like to . . . I want to *exorcize* Dobbs.'

'Well, I feel very awkward about the whole thing.' Merrily poured tea for them both.

'Oh, why?' The Bishop quizzically tilted his head, as though he really didn't understand. He sugared his tea. 'You know the very worst thing about Dobbs? He actually *frightens* people – imagine. You have what you are convinced is an unwelcome presence in your house, your nerves are shot to hell, you finally gather the courage – or the sheer desperation – to go to the Church for help. And what should arrive at your door but this weird, shambling creature dressed like an undertaker and mumbling at you like Poe's doleful raven. Well, you'd rather hang on to the bloody ghost, wouldn't you?'

The Bishop, Merrily had noticed, said 'bloody' rather a lot, but nothing stronger, always conscious of the parameters of his image as a cool Christian. She was determined to be neither overawed nor underawed by Mick Hunter this afternoon, neither bulldozed nor seduced. She wished he was more like Huw Owen, but men like Huw never ever got to be bishops.

'Listen . . . Merrily . . .' His voice dropping an octave – late-night DJ. 'I realize how you must feel. If you were the kind of person who was utterly confident about it, I wouldn't want you in this job.'

' . . . *not a fundamentalist, not a charismatic or a happy-clappy, you've no visible axe to grind and I can see why he was drawn to you. You're in many ways almost exactly the kind of person we need in the trenches.*'

'Do you know Huw Owen?' she asked.

'Only by reputation. Quite a vocal campaigner for the ordination of women long before it became fa . . . feasible.'

Fashionable, he'd been about to say. Until it became

fashionable, Mick Hunter would have kept very quiet on the issue. Merrily was trying to see him as Jane saw him, but it wasn't easy; Mick's blue eyes were clear and blazing with a wild integrity. He had a – somehow unepiscopal – blue jaw. He smelled very lightly of clean, honest, jogger's sweat and of something smokily indistinct which made her think, rather shockingly, of what a very long time it had been since she'd last had sex.

'Your late husband was a lawyer, wasn't he?' he said, startling her upright, tea spilling.

'Yes.' She was blushing. 'I . . . me too. I mean, I was going to be one too. Until Jane came into the picture, and a few other things changed.'

'Shame,' the Bishop said. 'Road accident, wasn't it?'

'On the M5. He . . . he hit a bridge.'

They hit a bridge. Sean and Karen Adair, his clerk and girlfriend and accomplice in a number of delicate arrangements with iffy businessmen. Dying flung together in a ball of fire, at the time when Merrily was balancing an inevitable divorce against her chances of ordination, and Jane was just starting secondary school. How much of this did the Bishop know? All of it, probably.

'Look,' she had to say this, 'the thing is, Huw's position on the ordination of women doesn't extend to Deliverance ministry – did you know that? He doesn't think we're ready for all that yet.'

His eyes widening. She realized he'd probably sent her on this particular course precisely *because* he knew Huw was sympathetic to women priests.

'Not ready for all that?' The eyes narrowing again. 'All what?'

'He doesn't feel that we have the necessary weight of tradition behind us to take on . . . whatever's out there.'

'Which is a little bit preposterous' – Mick Hunter leaned back – 'don't you think?'

'It's not what *I* think that matters.'

'No, quite. At the end of the day, it's what *I* think. The Deliverance consultant's responsible to the Bishop, and only to the Bishop. And *I* think – without any positive discrimination – that, if anything, this is a job a woman can do better than a man. It demands delicacy, compassion . . . qualities not exactly manifested by Dobbs.'

'I've . . . I've been trying, you know, to work out exactly how you do see the job.'

Mick Hunter stirred his tea thoughtfully. Two tables away, a couple of well-dressed, not-quite-elderly women were openly watching him. Beefcake bishop – a new phenomenon.

'OK, right,' he said. 'While you were in Wales, we had some basic research carried out. Quick phone-call to all the parish clergy: a few facts and figures. Did you know for instance that in the past six months, in this diocese alone, there have been between twenty and thirty appeals to the Church for assistance with perceived psychic disturbance?'

'Really? My God.'

'And rising.' Mick smiled. 'If the Church was a business, we'd be calling this a major growth area.'

The Bishop then talked about apparent psychic blackspots revealed by the survey – the north of the diocese was worst – and Merrily thought about how fate pushed you around, all the unplanned directions your life took. Whether she would ever actually have become a lawyer had she not become pregnant while still at university. If she would ever have become a priest had Sean not died when he did and if she hadn't discovered he was a crook. If she would ever have been drawn into the strange shadow-world of Deliverance, had her own vicarage in Ledwardine not been tenanted by an essence of something which no one else had experienced.

She felt targeted, exposed. She wanted to leap up from the table and run to the car and smoke several cigarettes.

Instead she said, 'What exactly are we talking about here?'

The Bishop shrugged. 'Mostly, I suspect, about paranoia, psychiatric problems, loneliness, isolation, stress. Modern society, Merrily. Post-millennial angst. We're certainly *not* talking about the medieval world of Canon Dobbs. Nor, I think, should we be sending the local vicar along just to have a cup of coffee and intone a few prayers, which is what happens in most cases now.'

She began to understand about the office. He would want one that actually said DELIVERANCE CONSULTANT on its door. He wanted to bring the job out of the closet.

'I'm glad the awful word Exorcism's been ditched,' he said, 'though I'm not entirely happy with Deliverance either. A less portentous term would be "*rescue*", don't you think?'

Rescue Consultant? Spiritual Rescue Service? SRS? She raised her cup to mask a smile. He didn't notice.

'It would still be part of the parish priest's role to deal, in the initial stages, with people who think they're being haunted or little Darren's got the Devil in him or whatever. But the public also need to know there's an efficient machinery inside the Church for dealing with such problems, and that there's a particular person to whom they can turn. And I don't want that person to look like Dobbs. We need to be seen as sympathetic, non-judgemental, user-friendly. You've read Perry's book on Deliverance?'

'The set text, isn't it?'

'It's a start. I find Michael Perry rather too credulous, but I like his insistence on not overreacting. The job's about counselling. It's about being a spiritual Samaritan – about listening. You notice that Perry seldom seems to advocate exorcizing a place?'

'He suggests a Major Exorcism should primarily be focused on a demonically possessed person, and then only when a number of other procedures have proved ineffective.'

Mick Hunter put down his cup. 'I *never* want to hear of a so-called Major Exorcism. It's crude, primitive and almost certainly ineffective.'

Merrily blinked. 'You don't think that in the presence of extreme evil . . .?'

'Evil's a disease,' the Bishop said. 'In fact it's many diseases. If we're going to deal with it, we have to study the symptoms, consider the nature of the particular malady, and then apply the correct treatment with sensitivity, precision and care. The Major Exorcism, quite frankly, is the kind of medieval bludgeon which in my opinion the post-millennial Church can do without. Are you with me here?'

I don't know, Merrily thought wildly. *I don't know* . . .

'It's hard . . .' She took a breath to calm herself. Mick Hunter's enthusiasm picked you up and carried you along and then put you down suddenly, and you didn't know where you were. 'It's hard to express an opinion about something you've really had no experience of. I don't think anyone can possibly—'

'Merrily . . .' He put his hand over hers on the white tablecloth. 'One of my faults is expecting too much of people too soon, I realize that. But I know from my predecessor that you've proved yourself to be a resourceful, resilient person. The appalling Ledwardine business – I know you don't like your part in all that to be talked about . . .'

'No.'

'But you've shown you have nerve and wisdom and you can think on your feet. OK, I'm aware that we're breaking new ground here, but it's the direction I believe every diocese will be going in within five years.' He paused. 'I've had a word with Gareth, by the way.'

'The Archdeacon?'

'Under the reorganization, you were due to be awarded two extra parishes before the end of the year. I pointed out to Gareth that, under the circumstances, that would be far too much of a burden.'

'You mean it's either the Deliverance role or two more parishes to run?'

'The two parishes would be a lot easier, Merrily – a quieter life.'

'Yes.'

'If it's a quiet life you want?'

What she wanted was a cigarette, but she knew the Bishop hated them. What she wanted was for Huw Owen to have been proved wrong, but everything Huw had forecast had been dead right. She *would* wind up with her picture in the *Hereford Times*, although probably without the crucifix.

'I'm going to have to play this slowly and diplomatically,' Mick Hunter said. 'Dobbs won't go until he's too shaky to hold a cup of holy water, and as long as he's here he has the support of the Dean's cabal. Well, all right, he can still be an exorcist if he wants. That doesn't prevent me appointing a consultant to, say, prepare a detailed report on the demand for Deliverance services.'

Merrily said, 'I don't like this.'

'Merely politics. I'm afraid I'm quite good at politics.'

She sighed. 'You've given me a lot to think about, Bishop.'

'Mick.'

'Could I have some time?'

'To pray for guidance?'

'Yes,' Merrily said, 'I suppose that's what I'll do.'

'Call my office if you'd like another meeting.' Mick stood up, zipped his purple tracksuit top.

'Er . . . if you can't get an office in the cloisters, that means I'd be working from home then?'

At least she wouldn't have to see the rather scary Dobbs.

'Oh no.' Mick grinned. 'The Dean doesn't screw me so easily. I told you I'm quite good at this. I'm going to put you in the Palace.'

In the car going home, Merrily put on Tori Amos's *From the Choirgirl Hotel* because it was doomy and gothic and would keep Jane quiet. The kid would want to know what the Bishop had been so keen to talk about, but first Merrily needed to work it out for herself.

It certainly wasn't what Jane had imagined, a clandestine return to witch-hunting, sneaky rearguard action by a defensive Church. There was no sign of *New Age, Old Enemy* paranoia in Mick Hunter. He was simply enfolding the Deliverance ministry into his campaign to project the diocese further into the new millennium as a vibrant, caring, essential institution. Was that so wrong? But what did he see as the enemy?

' . . . *paranoia, psychiatric problems, loneliness, isolation, stress, post-millennial angst* . . .'

Clearly, the Bishop's liberalism did not extend to the supernatural. Merrily suspected he didn't believe in ghosts, and that for him the borderline between demonic possession and schizophrenia would not exist – which was worrying. To what extent was healthy scepticism compatible with Christian faith? And what did he mean: '*Put you in the Palace*'?

' . . . little record shop in Church Street?'

'Huh? Sorry, flower.'

Jane reached out and turned down the stereo. Merrily glanced across at her. Jane turning down music – this had never happened before.

'I said, who do you think I ran into in that poky little record shop in Church Street?'

It was almost dark, and they were leaving the city via the King's Acre roundabout, with a fourteenth-century cross on its island.

'Leonardo DiCaprio?' Merrily said. 'Richard Ashcroft of The Verve?'

'Close. Lol Robinson.'

'Oh,' Merrily said casually. There was a time when she could have become too fond of Lol Robinson. 'Right. How is he?'

Jane told her how Lol had just started renting this brilliant flat over the shop, with a view over the cobbles and two pubs about twenty yards away.

'Belongs to the guy who owns the shop. His sister used to live there but she's moved out. Her name's Katherine Moon, but she's just known as Moon, and I think she and Lol . . . Anyway, he looks exactly the same. Hasn't grown, same little round glasses, still wearing that black sweatshirt with the alien face on the front – possibly symbolic of the way he feels he relates to society and feels that certain people relate to him.'

'So, apart from the sartorial sameness, did he seem OK?'

'No, he was like waving his arms around and drooling at the mouth. Of course he seemed OK. We went for a coffee in the All Saints café. I've never been in there before. It's quite cool.'

'It's in a church.'

'Yeah, I noticed. Nice to see one fulfilling a useful service. Anyway, I got out of Lol what he's doing now. He didn't want to tell me, but I can be fairly persistent.'

'You nailed his guitar hand to the prayerbook shelf?'

'Look, do you want to know what he's doing or not?'

'All right.'

'You ready for this? He's training to be a shrink.'

'What? But he was—'

'Well, not a shrink exactly. He hates psychiatrists because they just give you drugs to keep you quiet. More a kind of psychotherapist. He was consulting one in Hereford, and the guy realized that, after years in and out of mental hospitals, Lol knew more -ologies and -isms than he himself did, so now he's employing him a couple of days a week for sort of on-the-job training, and Lol's doing these night classes. Isn't that so cool?'

'It . . .' Merrily thought about this. 'I suppose it is, really. Lol would be pretty good. He doesn't judge people. Yeah, that's cool.'

'Also, he's playing again. He's made some tapes, although he won't let anybody hear them.'

'Even you?'

'I'm working on it. I may go back there – I like that shop. Lots of stuff by indy folk bands. And I'm really glad I saw him. *I* didn't want to lose touch just because he moved out of Ledwardine.'

Merrily said cautiously, 'Lol needed time to get himself together.'

'Oh,' Jane said airily, 'I think he needed more than that, don't you?'

'Don't start.'

'Like maybe somebody who wasn't terrified of getting into a relationship because of what the parish might think.'

'Stop there,' Merrily said lightly, 'all right?'

'Fine.' Jane prodded the music up to disco level and turned to look out of the side window at the last of the grim amber sinking on to the shelf of the Black Mountains. A desultory rain filmed the windscreen.

'Still,' Merrily thought she heard the kid mumble, 'it's probably considered socially OK to fuck a bishop.'

*

That night, praying under her bedroom window in the vicarage, Merrily realized the Deliverance issue wasn't really a problem she needed to hang on God at this stage. Her usual advice to parishioners facing a decision was to gather all the information they could get from available sources on both sides of the argument, and only then apply for a solution.

Fair enough. She would seek independent advice within the Church.

She went to sit on the edge of the bed, looking out at the lights of Ledwardine speckling the trees. They made her think of what Huw Owen had said about the targeting of women priests.

Little rat-eyes in the dark.

She hadn't even raised that point with Mick Hunter. He would have taken it seriously, but not in the way it was meant by Huw.

Merrily shivered lightly and slid into bed, cuddling the hot water bottle, aware of Ethel the black cat curling on the duvet against her ankles, remembering the night Ethel had first appeared at the vicarage in the arms of Lol Robinson after she'd received a kicking from a drunk. She hoped Lol Robinson would be happy with his girlfriend. Lol and Merrily – that would never have worked.

Later, on the edge of sleep, she heard Huw Owen's flat, nasal voice as if it were actually in the room.

'*Little rat-eyes in the dark.*'

And jerked awake.

OK. She'd absorbed Huw's warning, listened to the Bishop's plans.

It was clear that what she had to do now, not least for the sake of her conscience, was go back to Hereford and talk to Canon Dobbs.

The Last Exorcist.

Merrily lay down again and slept.

SIX

Sweat and Mothballs

'Oh yes,' Moon said, 'he was outside the window, peering in – his face right up to the glass. His eyes were full of this awful, blank confusion. I don't think he knew who I was. That was the worst thing: he didn't *know* me.'

'He was in the . . . garden?' *How do I handle this?* Lol thought. *She's getting worse.*

'I ran out,' Moon said. 'Then I saw him again at the bottom of the steps leading up to the camp. And then he wasn't there any more.'

She was sitting on a cardboard box full of books. There were about two dozen boxes dumped all over the living area. Lol hadn't been into the kitchen or the bathroom but, except for the futon in the open loft, it looked exactly the way it had been the last time he was here. She'd refused offers of help from Denny and Lol, and from Dick Lyden's wife Ruth. You had to arrange your possessions yourself, she'd insisted, otherwise you'd never know where anything was.

But nothing at all seemed to have been put away, nothing even unpacked. It was as though she'd gone straight to bed when he left her on Saturday and had just got up again, four days later.

Sleeping Beauty situation, fairytale again.

The point about Moon was that she was utterly single-minded. Most of the time she had no small talk, and no interest in other people, although she could be very generous when some problem was put under her nose – like buying the busker's balalaika.

But now she'd found her father, and nothing else mattered.

'Oh,' she said, 'and he was wearing a flat cap which I recognized.'

Moon was wearing an ankle-length, white satin nightdress which had collected a lot of dust, a thick silver torc around her neck. She'd had on nothing over the nightdress when she'd opened the door to Lol. She didn't seem cold. It was wildly erotic. Lol wondered how doctors coped with this.

'It was this grey checked one with all the lining hanging out. Mummy always kept it – I mean for years, anyway. She talked about all the times she used to try and get him to throw it away. Denny threw it away in the end, I suppose. Now my father has it back.'

Delusional, Lol thought. *Because she doesn't seem scared. It has to be wishful thinking.* But what did it mean, that she'd wished up a father who didn't seem to recognize her?

The long nightdress rustled like leaves as Moon stood up, glided to the window.

'When I was little, I used to wonder if that was the cap he'd worn when he shot himself, so that was why it was all torn. Of course, the gun would have made much more of a mess than that, but you don't know these things when you're little, do you?'

It occurred to him that this was the first time she'd spoken about her father.

Her father had killed himself when she was about two years old. Denny said she had no memories of him, but there was probably some resentment because his folly was the reason they'd had to sell up and leave the hill.

'This fucking insane investment. Some mate of the old man's

had developed this sweet sparkling cider he reckoned was going to snatch at least half the Babycham market. Dad threw every-thing at it – sold off about fifty acres, left the farm non-viable.'

They'd lost the farm. Which was said to have been in the family since at least the Middle Ages. Or much longer, if you listened to Moon.

Denny had said, *'The day we left, the old man took his shotgun for a last, short walk. It's a thing farmers do when they feel they've let their ancestors down.'*

'How, um . . .?' Lol's mouth was dry. He sat down on another box of books. 'How do you feel about your dad now?'

Moon turned to Lol, her eyes shining. 'I have to reach out to him. The ancestors have enabled me to do that, OK?'

The crow. *'By bathing my hands in its blood, I'm acquiring its powers.'*

'They sent him back. He doesn't know why, but he will. He has to know who I am – that's the first stage. I have to let him know I'm all right about him.'

'You're not . . . just a bit scared?'

'He's my *father*. And I'm his only hope of finding peace. He knows he's got a lot of making up to do. To Mummy as well, but that's out of our hands now.'

She went silent, the fervour in her eyes slipping away.

'Your mum . . . do you feel *she's* at peace?' Lol didn't know why he'd asked that, except to get her talking again.

'I don't know. She was never the same afterwards. I mean, all my life she had problems with her nerves. It was lucky Denny was practically grown-up by then, and so he took charge. It was Denny who was always pushing me to do well at school, determined I should go to university because he hadn't. Taking the father's role, you know? He owes Denny too, I suppose.'

'How can he make it up to you?' Lol said softly. 'How can your father help?'

She blinked at him, as if that was obvious. 'With my book, of course – my book about the Dinedor People. He can help me with the book. He can make them talk to me. They sent him to me, so I must be able to reach them through him.'

'Who?'

'The ancestors.'

The barn was quite small: just four rooms. It had been converted initially as extra holiday accommodation by the present owners of the farmhouse, some people called Purefoy, who apparently ran a bed-and-breakfast business. But this had not been a very good summer for weather or tourism, and they'd presumably realized they could make more money with a long-term let. Not much ground, of course. No room for a garage, quite difficult access, but a beautiful rural situation.

Moon had come up here on the mountain-bike Denny had bought her in the aftermath of the shoplifting case. It was a hot day and she was pushing the bike up towards the camp when she suddenly, as she put it, felt her ancestors calling out to her.

It was the most incredible experience. Like the one Alfred Watkins must have had, when he first saw those lines in the landscape. Except I was aware of just one line, leading from me to the hill and back through the centuries. The hill was vibrating under me. I was shaking. I realized this was what I'd been training for, during all those years of digging people up. But that was only bones. I want to unearth real people. I want to communicate with them. I knew I had to discover the story of the hill and the Dinedor People. It was just an amazing moment. I felt as light as a butterfly.

Moon had been up here until the dusk came. She'd found herself almost frantically knocking on the doors of farmhouses and cottages all around the hill to find out who was living here and who had lived here for the most generations. Discovering, as she'd suspected she might, that the oldest Dinedor family was her own. Moon maintained that her family had come out of the original settlement on Dinedor Hill, all those years before the time of Christ.

But none lived here any more. Her father had snapped the line.

Close to sunset, Moon had arrived at Dyn Farm, at the old, mellowed farmhouse near to the camp, to find the Purefoys – Londoners, early-retired – in the garden.

'Usually, as you know, I'm so shy, unless I've taken something. But I was glowing. They didn't seem very friendly at first, a bit reserved like a lot of new people, but when I told them who I was, they became quite excited and invited me in. Of course, they were asking me all sorts of questions about the house that I couldn't really answer. I was just a toddler when we left.

'Then they showed me the barn. And I felt that my whole life had been leading up to that moment.'

Moon came over and stood in front of Lol, close enough for him to see her nipples through the nightdress. Oh God! He kept looking at her face.

'I wanted to tell him – my father – that it was OK, it was me, I was back. I was here. I wanted to tell him it was all right, that I'd help him to find peace.'

'You tried to talk to him?'

'No, not last night. I couldn't get close enough to him. This was the first night . . . last Saturday. Yeah, I had a sleep and then I went for a walk in the woods, where he shot himself. I went there when it was dark.'

'You saw him then?' *This is eerie. This is not good.*

'I didn't *see* him then. That was when I started to call out for him.'

'Literally?'

'Maybe. I remember standing in the woods and screaming, "Daddy!" It was funny . . . It was like I was a small child again.'

Lol said tentatively, 'You, um . . . you think that was safe, on your own?'

'Oh, nothing will ever happen to me on the hill. I intend to walk and walk, day and night, until I know every tree and bush of those woods, every fold of every field. I've got to make up for all those years away, you know? I have to absolutely immerse myself in the hill – until it goes everywhere with me. Until it fills my dreams.'

'So when you . . . when you saw him, *that* was a kind of dream, was it?'

She looked down at him. Her nightdress smelled of sweat and mothballs. Her hair hung down over each shoulder, like a stole.

She said, 'Are *you* supposed to be my therapist now, Lol?'

'I don't think so, not officially. I just help Dick.'

'Dick's hopeless, isn't he? Dick's a dead loss. He doesn't believe in anything outside of textbook psychology.'

'He's a nice bloke,' Lol said awkwardly. 'He wants to do his best for you.'

'He's an idiot. If you told Dick I'd seen my father, he'd come up with a beautiful theory involving hallucinations or drugs. But you see I don't *have* any drugs. I don't need anything up here; it's a constant, natural high. And it would be kind of an insult anyway. *And* I have never had hallucinations, ever.'

Her hair swung close to his face. It was the kind of hair medieval maidens dangled from high windows so that knights could climb up and rescue them.

'So it's not official,' she said. 'I mean us: we're not counsellor and patient or anything.'

Lol was confused. He felt himself blushing.

'We're a *bit* official,' he said.

'You have to report back to Dick?'

'I suppose so.'

'You'll tell him about this?'

'Not if . . .'

Moon turned away and dipped like a heron between two boxes, coming up with a dark green cardigan which she pulled on.

'Then it was a dream.' She bent and pouted at him, a petulant child. 'It was all a dream.'

SEVEN

Graveyard Angel

A mysterious summons to the Bishop's Palace.

Wednesday afternoon: market day, and the city still crowded. Merrily found a parking space near The Black Lion in Bridge Street. She might have been allowed to drive into the Palace courtyard, but this could be considered presumptuous; she didn't want that – almost didn't want to be noticed sliding through the shoppers in her black woollen two-piece, a grey silk scarf over her dog-collar.

Looking out, while she was in the area, for Canon Dobbs, the exorcist.

What she needed was a confidential chat with the old guy, nobody else involved. To clear the air, maybe even iron things out. If she took on this task, she wanted no hard feelings, no trail of resentment.

Contacting Dobbs was not so easy. In Deliverance, according to Huw Owen, low-profile was essential, to avoid being troubled by cranks and nutters or worse. But his guy was *well* below the parapet – not even, as she discovered, in the phone book. As a residential canon at the Cathedral he had no parishioners to be accessible to, but ex-directory?

Evensong at Ledwardine Church had recently been suspended by popular demand, or rather the absence of it, so on Sunday night – with Jane out at a friend's – Merrily had found time to ring Alan Crombie, the Rector of Madley. But he wasn't much help.

'Never had to consult him, Merrily – but I remember Colin Strong. When he was at Vowchurch, there was a persistent problem at a farmhouse and he ended up getting Dobbs in. I think he simply did it through the Bishop's office. You leave a message and he gets in touch with you.'

Well, that was no use. It would get right back to Mick Hunter.

'So ordinary members of the public have no real access to Dobbs?'

'Not initially,' Alan Crombie said. 'It's strictly clergy-consultation. That's normal practice. If you have a problem you go to your local priest and he decides if he can cope with it or if he needs specialist advice.'

'What happened at Vowchurch? Did Dobbs deal with it?'

'Lord knows. One of his rules is total secrecy. Anything gets in the papers, I gather his wrath is awesome to behold. Do you have another little problem in that department yourself, Merrily?'

'No, I . . .' *Oh, what the hell!* 'Off the record, Alan, the Bishop's asked me to succeed Dobbs when he . . . retires.'

'Oh, I see.' Silence, then a nervous laugh. 'Well . . . rather you than me.'

'I realize I may have to buy a black bag and a big hat.'

'God, you don't want to go in for that kind of thing,' Alan had said with another nervous laugh. 'Have all kinds of perverts following you home.'

Merrily walked along King Street, the Cathedral up ahead filling her vision. She had no idea what Dobbs looked like and saw no men in big hats with black bags.

Although it didn't look much from the front, the Bishop's Palace was perhaps the most desirable dwelling in Hereford:

next door to the Cathedral but closer to the River Wye, and dreamily visible from the public footpath on the opposite bank, with its big white windows on mellow red brick, tree-fringed lawns sloping to the water.

Inside, she'd never been further than the vastly refurbished twelfth-century Great Hall where receptions were held. Today she didn't even make it across the courtyard. Sophie Hill, the Bishop's elegant white-haired lay-secretary, met her at the entrance, steering her through a door under the gatehouse and up winding stone stairs, about twenty of them.

'It's not very big, but Michael thought you'd like it better that way.'

'I'm sorry?' Merrily pulled off her scarf.

'It could be quite charming' – Sophie reached beyond her to push open the door at the top of the steps – 'with a few pictures and things. To the left, please, Mrs Watkins.'

There were two offices in the gatehouse: a bigger one with a vista of Broad Street . . . and this.

Sloping ceiling, timbered and whitewashed walls, a desk with a phone. A scuffed repro captain's chair that swivelled, two filing cabinets, a small bookcase with a Bible and some local reference books, including Jane's one-time bible, *The Folklore of Herefordshire* by Ella Mary Leather.

Merrily walked uncertainly over to the window overlooking the courtyard and the former stables, a few parked cars and great stacks of split logs for the Bishop's fires.

'Welcome to Deliverance Tower,' said Sophie deadpan. 'The computer's on order.'

Walking dazed into the blustery sunshine on Broad Street, Merrily felt the hand of fate so heavily on her shoulder that she nearly threw up an arm to shake it off.

It had felt good up in the gatehouse, almost cosy. On top

of the city and yet remote from it – a refuge, an eyrie. It had felt right.

Careful. Don't be seduced on the first date.

Sophie had said the Bishop had planned to see her himself, but Mrs Hunter had an important appointment and her own car was being serviced. This appeared to be true; through the window, Merrily had watched Mick, in clerical shirt under what was almost certainly an Armani jacket, accompany his wife to a dusty BMW in British racing green. She saw that Val Hunter was very tall, nearly as tall as the Bishop. Angular, heronlike, tawny hair thrown back, a beauty with breeding. They had two sons at boarding school; although Mick had confessed, in an interview with the *Observer*, to having very mixed feelings about private education. Merrily suspected his wife didn't share them.

'He's still rather feeling his way,' Sophie had confided, 'but he does want change, and I'm afraid he'll be terribly disappointed if you walk away from this, Mrs Watkins. He regards it as a very meaningful step for the female ministry.'

At the top of Broad Street now, Merrily stared at the rings in a jeweller's window, and saw her reflection and all the people passing behind her – one man with a briefcase looking over his shoulder at her legs while her back was turned.

She began to tremble. She needed a cigarette.

Actually, even stronger than that, came the realization that she needed to pray.

Like now.

Abruptly, as though obeying some hypnotic command, she turned back towards the Cathedral, rapidly crossing the green and once again guiltily winding the scarf about her throat to cover the collar. She wanted no one to see her, no one to approach.

Within yards of the north door, she thought of going around the back to the cloisters, asking the first person she didn't recognize where Canon Dobbs lived, but by now the compulsion to pray was too strong, a racing in the blood.

She breathed out. *Jesus!*

It happened only rarely like this. Like the day she drove into the country with a blinding headache, and ended up following a track to a cell-like church dedicated to some forgotten Celtic saint where – when she'd most needed it; when she was just finding out the sordid truth about Sean's business – there'd been this sudden blissful sense of blue and gold, and a lamplit path opening in front of her.

A group was entering the Cathedral; it looked like a Women's Institute party. 'Isn't there a café?' someone said grumpily.

Merrily felt like pushing past, but waited at the end of the line as the women moved singly through the porch. When she was inside, she saw them fanning into the aisles, heard echoes of footsteps and birdlike voices spiralling through sacred stone caverns.

And she was just standing there on her own and tingling with need.

'Welcome to Hereford Cathedral.' An amplified voice from the distant pulpit, the duty chaplain. 'If you'd all please be seated, we'll begin the tour with a short prayer. Thank you.'

Sweating now, almost panicking, Merrily stumbled through the first available doorway and slithered to her knees in the merciful gloom of the fifteenth-century chantry chapel of Bishop John Stanbury, with its gilded triptych and its luxuriously carved and moulded walls and ceilings merging almost organically, it seemed, in a rush of rippling honeyed stone.

When she put her hands together she could feel the tiny hairs on the backs of them standing electrically on end.

'God,' she was whispering. 'What is it? What *is* it?'

That sensation of incredible potential: all the answers to all the questions no more than an instant away, an atom of time, a membrane of space.

'There's this picture of her,' Jane said, 'that she once threw away, only I rescued it from the bin for purposes of future leverage and blackmail and stuff. I think she knows I've got it, but she never says anything.'

They walked past the school tennis courts, their nets removed for the winter, and across to the sixth-form car park where Rowenna's Fiesta stood, six years old and lime-green but otherwise brilliant.

'She's wearing this frock like a heavy-duty binliner, right? And her hair's kind of bunched up with these like plastic spikes sticking out. She's got on this luminous white lipstick. And her eyes are like under about three economy packs of cheap mascara.'

Rowenna shook her head sadly.

'Her favourite band,' Jane said, 'was Siouxsie and the Banshees.'

'Don't,' said Rowenna, pained.

'Well, actually they weren't bad.'

Rowenna unlocked the Fiesta. 'You could always sell the picture to the tabloids.'

'Yeah, but she'd have to do something controversial first, to get them interested. Just another woman priest who used to be a punk, that isn't enough, is it? I suppose I could take it to the *Hereford Times*.'

'Who'd pay you about enough to buy a couple of CDs.'

'Yeah, mid-price ones.' Jane climbed into the passenger seat. 'No, the point I was trying to make: you look at that picture and you can somehow see the future priest there. You know what I mean, all dark and ritualistic?'

'What, she's some kind of vestment fetishist?'

'No! It's just . . . oh shit.'

Dean Wall and Danny Gittoes, famous sad Ledwardine louts, were leaning over the car, Dean's big face up against the passenger window. Jane wound it down. Dean fumbled out his ingratiating leer.

'All right for a lift home, ladies?'

'Not today, OK?' Rowenna said.

'In fact, not *ever.*' Jane cranked up the window. 'Like, no offence, but we'd rather *not* wind up raped and the car burned out, if that's OK with you.'

Dean was saying, 'You f—' as Jane wound the window the last inch.

'Foot down, Ro.'

Rowenna drove off, smiling.

'Nicely handled, kitten. Thanks.'

Rowenna was new at the school, but nearly two years older than Jane. On account of her family moving around a lot and a long spell of illness, she'd got way behind, so she'd needed to re-start her A-level course. She was a cool person – in a way a kind of older sister, a role she seemed to like.

'You don't mean,' said Jane, astounded, 'that you *have* actually given those two hairballs a lift? Like, how did you get the slime off the upholstery?'

Rowenna laughed. 'I see now it was a grave mistake, and I won't do it again. What were you saying about your mother? I didn't quite grasp the nature of the problem.'

'Oh, it's just . . .' Jane cupped her hands over her nose and mouth and sighed into them, ' . . . just she's worth more than this, that's all. Like, OK, maybe she was drawn into it by this spiritual need and the need to bring it out in other people, you know what I mean?'

'Maybe.' Rowenna drove with easy confidence. Within only a couple of hundred yards of the school, they were out into countryside with wooded hills and orchards.

'But I mean, the Church of England? Like, what can you really expect of an outfit that was only set up so Henry VIII could dump his wife? Spiritually they're just a bunch of no-hope tossers, and I can't see that the ordination of women will change a thing.'

'I suppose even the Catholics kind of look like they've got *something* together.' Rowenna's father was an Army officer, possibly SAS, and the family had spent some time in Northern Ireland.

'But you know what I mean?' Jane hunched forward, clasping her hands together. 'I imagine her in about forty years' time, sitting by the gas fire in some old clergyperson's home, full of arthritis from kneeling on cold stone floors, and thinking: What the hell was *that* all about?'

Rowenna laughed, a sound like ice in a cocktail glass. She looked innocent and kind of wispy, but she was pretty shrewd.

'And this Deliverance trip, right?' Jane knew she wasn't supposed to discuss this, but Rowenna's military background – high-security clearance, all that stuff – meant she could be trusted not to spread things around. 'It's obvious she thinks this is a kind of cutting-edge thing to do, and will maybe take her *closer*. You know what I mean?'

'To the spiritual world?'

'But it's actually quite the opposite. From what I can see, the job is actually to *stop* people getting close. She has to actively discourage all contact with the occult or anything mystical – anything *interesting*. I think that's kind of immoral, don't you?'

'It's kind of fascist,' Rowenna said.

'Let's face it, almost any kind of spiritual activity is more fun than going to church.'

'I wouldn't argue with that.'

*

And then, as usual, it was suddenly gone.

Sometimes you were left floating on a cushion of peace; occasionally there was an aching void. This time only silence coloured by the placid images of the Cathedral and the Wye Bridge in the small stained-glass window just above her head.

Merrily stood up shakily in the intimacy of Bishop Stanbury's exquisite chantry. She stood with her arms by her sides, breathing slowly. It was like sex: sublime at the time but what, if anything, had it altered? What progression was there?

Outside, in the main body of the Cathedral, the prayer was over and there was a communal rising and clattering. She stood quietly in the doorway of the chantry, her grey silk scarf dangling from her fingers.

'Go away. Go *away*.' A few yards away, a man's voice rose impatiently. 'I can't possibly discuss this here.'

'I don't understand . . .' A woman now, agitated. 'What have I been doing wrong?'

'Hush!'

A stuttering of footsteps. Merrily stepped out of the chantry, saw a woman, about sixty, who drew breath, stifled a cry, turned sharply and walked quickly away – across to the exit which led to the Cathedral giftshop. She wore a tweed coat and boots and a puffy velvet hat. She never looked back.

From the aisle to the left of the chantry, the man watched her go.

Merrily said, 'I'm so sorry, I didn't mean to—'

He wore a long overcoat. He glanced at her. 'I think your party is over in the Lady Chapel.'

Then he saw her collar and she saw his, and the skirt of the cassock below his overcoat. And although she'd never seen him before, as soon as she discerned cold recognition in the pale eyes in that stone face – the face of some ancient, eroded graveyard archangel – she knew who he was.

And before she was aware of them the words were out.

Possibly, under the circumstances, the stupidest words she could have uttered.

'Is there anything I can do, Canon Dobbs?'

He looked at her for a long time. She couldn't move.

Eventually, without any change of expression, he walked past her and left the Cathedral.

EIGHT

Beautiful Theory

For many years, Dick Lyden had been something stressful in the City of London. Now he and his wife were private psychotherapists in Hereford. Dick was about thirty pounds heavier, pink-cheeked, income decidedly reduced, a much happier man.

'And Moon – in her spiritual home at last?' He beamed, feet on his desk. 'How is Moon?'

'Moon is . . .' Lol hesitated. 'Moon is what I wanted to see you about.'

Dick and Ruth lived and practised in half of a steep Edwardian terrace on the western side, not far from the old watertower. Dick's attic office had a view across the city to Dinedor Hill, to which Lol's gaze was now inevitably being pulled. When Dick expansively opened up his hands, allowing him the floor, Lol turned his chair away from the window and told Dick about the crow which Moon claimed had mystically fallen dead at her feet.

Dick swivelled his feet from the desk, rubbed his forehead, pushing back slabs of battleship-grey hair. 'And do you think it really did?'

'I didn't see it happen.'

'So she may just have found it in the hedge and made the rest up.'

'It's possible,' Lol said.

'And the blood . . . she actually . . . That's extraordinary.' Dick rubbed his hands together, looking up at a plaster cornice above Lol's head. 'And yet, you know, while it might seem horrible to the likes of us, she's spent quite a few years scrabbling about in the earth, ferreting out old skulls with worms in their eyes.'

'This was a bit different, though.'

Yes, it was, Dick conceded. In fact, yes, what they were looking at here was really quite an elaborate fantasy structure, on the lines of one of those impossibly complicated computer games his son James used to play before he discovered rock music. Except this wasn't dragons and demons; this was built on layers of actual history.

'Let's examine it. Let's pull it apart.' Dick dragged a foolscap pad towards him, began to draw circles and link them with lines.

'What've we got? An extremely intelligent girl with a degree in archaeology, some years' experience in the field . . . and this absorbing, fanatical interest in the Iron Age civilization, which became an obsession – the Celtic jewellery, the strange woollens. She still wear that awful sheepskin waistcoat thing?'

'Not recently.'

'That's one good thing. Anyway . . . suddenly she's aware she can *explain* this obsession in the context of her own family history. She's been told the family roots in that particular spot go back to the Dark Ages and before – which is probably complete nonsense, but that's irrelevant. She forms the idea that this is what she was born to do, because of the *place* she was born – on the side of this Iron Age fort or whatever it is.'

Dick drew a crude hill with battlements.

'Perhaps believing . . . that there's some great *secret* here . . . that only she can recover. Some Holy Grail. But of course . . . what she *really* wants to find is a key . . . to her father's suicide.'

Dick smiled happily at Lol. He loved finding cross-references.

'Who knows, Laurence? Who knows what horrors lodged in the mind of a two-year-old child in circumstances like that? And Dinedor Hill never talked about, Denny going dark with anger if the subject of their father arises. So much *mystery*. Well, she doesn't want to believe her old man topped himself because he messed up his finances. It's got to be more profound than that.'

'It's profound enough,' Lol said. 'By losing the farm, he let down his family, and his ancestors. Scores of farmers have killed themselves in the past few years for similar reasons. And we're talking about a very historic family.'

'Absolutely. She's bunched all that together into an epic personal quest, with all the pseudo-mystical and supernatural overtones of James's trashy computer games.'

'Is that a good thing, though, Dick? Moon living at the centre of a fantasy?'

'I don't see that it's necessarily *bad*. And if it's all going to be providing material for her book . . . Do we know what kind of book she has in mind?'

'A history of Dinedor Hill seen through the eyes of the people who live there now—'

'Splendid,' Dick interrupted.

'—and the people who lived there over two thousand years ago.'

'Constructed from archaeological evidence and what she feels is her own instinctive knowledge of her ancestors? Well, that could be a very valid book, couldn't it? One can certainly imagine a publisher going for that. I could talk to some people myself.'

'I don't know.' Lol had been doubtful about this book

from the start. A book wasn't like a song; you couldn't knock it out in a couple of hours when the inspiration was there. 'She doesn't seem organized enough for anything like that. For instance, Denny's managing the shop for a few days while she gets the barn sorted – supposedly. But this morning virtually nothing had changed: everything still in boxes. Which was what Denny said it'd be like: chaos – and Moon living inside herself.'

Dick shrugged. 'So after the excitement of the move, there's a period of emotional exhaustion. Then she dusts herself off, starts to pick up the pieces. Then the rehab begins. I'll give her a couple of days and then I'll go and have a chat myself. Or we can both go, yes?'

'OK.'

'You don't seem too sure. Is there something else?'

'Dick's hopeless, isn't he? Dick's a dead loss. He doesn't believe in anything outside of textbook psychology.'

Moon had predicted that Dick would come up with a beautiful theory, and he had – without Lol even mentioning her story about seeing her father at the window.

'You have to report back to Dick? You'll tell him about this?'

Dick tore off the top sheet of the pad and crumpled it up. 'I think you'd better spit it out, Lol.'

Yes, he had to. There was a professional arrangement here. Dick had insisted Lol should be paid a retainer to keep an eye on Moon and report back once a week. It was complicated: at first Lol had been paying Dick for analysis; now Dick was paying Lol.

In his kindly way, Dick was devious. Lol was still not sure whether observing Moon was not supposed to be part of his own therapy.

Women had been Lol's problem. Women and religion.

He'd wound up first consulting Dick Lyden during the

summer, while still trying to sell his roses-round-the-door cottage on the edge of an orchard out at Ledwardine. To which he'd moved with a woman called Alison who he thought had rescued him from the past and the shadow of the psychiatric hospital. But Alison had her own reasons for coming to Ledwardine, and they didn't include Lol.

The people who actually *had* tried to rescue him had come from the village itself. They included a brusque old biddy called Lucy Devenish, now dead. And also the parish priest-in-charge.

At this stage in Lol's life, priests of any kind were to be avoided. His parents had been drawn into this awful evangelical-fundamentalist Christian church and had decided that Lol, with his strange songs and his dubious lifestyle, was no longer their son. At his mother's graveside, Lol's father had turned his back on him. Lol had henceforth been suspicious of everything in a dog-collar that was not a dog.

Until the Vicar of Ledwardine.

Who in the end had been the reason for him leaving the village. The Vicar was, after all, a very busy and respected person, and Lol was this pathetic little sometimes-songwriter living on hackwork and royalties from before the fall. He wasn't sure she realized how he felt. He *was* sure she didn't need this.

So he left her his black cat and moved to Hereford, putting his bits of furniture in store and lodging for a while in a pub just down the street from Dick Lyden. Dick's local, as it happened – also Denny Moon's. Which had led to several sessions in Denny's recording studio and a few consultation sessions with Dick, because Lol still couldn't rely on his own mental equilibrium.

'*Christ,*' Dick had said one afternoon, '*you know more about this bloody trade than I do.*' Fascinated by Lol's extensive knowledge of psychiatry – absorbed over hours, then weeks and months spent in the medical library at a lax and decaying loony-bin in Oxfordshire. *'Apart from a general self-esteem deficit, this is probably your principal problem – you're a kind of mental hypochondriac. Perhaps you need to help diagnose other people for a while, to take your mind off it.'*

Loonies taking over the practice. The idea had really appealed to Dick: the idea of Lol keeping an experienced eye on another of his clients – twenty-something, gorgeous, weird. Dick loved it when clients could help each other, his practice becoming a big family. It was still small, this city; he liked the way relationships and associations developed an organic life, spread like creeper on a wall, and therefore strengthened his own latent roots in Hereford.

Thus, Lol had been introduced to Katherine Moon – and perhaps also because Dick couldn't quite get a handle on Moon.

'Her father's ghost,' Dick said calmly.

'Twice.'

'Right.' Dick hunched intently forward. 'Now, think carefully about this, Lol. What effect did this alleged manifestation have on her? What kind of an experience was it? Soothing? Frightening? Cathartic?'

'Not frightening.'

'So, a man's face at the window at dead of night. A young woman all alone in a still-strange dwelling . . . and she's not frightened. What does that tell us?'

'She said she had the impression he was more scared than she was. Disturbed and confused. She thought he didn't recognize her. Didn't know who she was.'

'Interesting.'

'She said she wanted to tell him it was OK.'

Dick spread his hands. 'Moon as healer.'

'She wants him to find peace.'

'And when he does, she will too,' Dick said. 'I really don't see a problem there. Seems to be all bubbling away quite satisfactorily in Moon's subconscious. She finds a dead crow and inflicts upon the poor bird all of her not inconsiderable knowledge of Celtic crow-lore. The crow's been sent by the ancestors to give her *the sight*. So what's she going to see first?'

'That's very good, Dick.'

'It makes sense, my boy. It's about *belonging*, isn't it? Look at me. I do feel I've found my spiritual home here in this city – so tiny after London, and *knowable*. Ruth tells me I'm continually pulling this town to my bosom. But a hill . . . a hill's much more embraceable, isn't it?' Dick leaned over to the window to scan the horizon. 'You know, I'm not even sure I know which one it is.'

'The one with all the trees.'

In the afternoon sunshine, the woods were a golden crust on the long, shallow loaf.

'Hmm,' Dick turned away, 'not particularly imposing, is it? And this was where the first settled community was? This hill is what you might call the *mother* of Hereford, I suppose.'

'The holy hill.'

'Super,' Dick said with firm satisfaction. 'One must feel a weight of responsibility to one's ancestors if one was born on a holy hill. And her father's suicide . . . a ready-made open wound for her to heal?'

Lol felt unhappy. He didn't like the way Dick seemed to assume that once you'd made a neat psychological package out of something, that was it. Sorted. In Lol's experience, real life was endlessly messy.

Dick leaned back in his leather swivel-rocker, hands comfortably enfolded over his lightbulb gut. 'The way we create our destiny on an epic, computer-game scale – would that it was as simple for all of us. Do you know, I rather suspect there's a paper in this. Let's go and see her. What are you doing tomorrow morning?'

'So you think it was a dream?' Lol said.

'Hmm?'

'Her father – a dream? Or an invention?'

'Well, good God, man,' Dick threw up his arms, 'what the hell *else* could it have been?'

NINE

Clerical Chic

Driving home, Merrily hardly noticed the countryside: the shambling black-and-white farms and cottages, the emptied orchards. Over it all, as though bevelled in the windscreen glass, hovered the unchanging, weathered face of the archaic monument that was Canon T. H. B. Dobbs.

That silent confrontation in the Cathedral had erased time. She could no longer remember praying in Bishop Stanbury's beautiful chantry – only the stumbling in and the creeping out. The interim was like an alcoholic haze.

But she had her answer.

Didn't she just?

In the late afternoon the wind had died, leaving the sky lumpy and congealed like a cold, fried breakfast. Beneath it the historic village of Ledwardine looked sapped and brittle, the black-and-white buildings lifeless, as indeed several now were. Nothing remained, for instance, of Cassidy's Country Kitchen except a sign and some peeling apple-transfers on the dark glass; and five *For Sale* signs had sprouted between Church Street and Old Barn Lane.

The village looked like it needed care and love and a shot of something – an injection of spirit. Of God, perhaps? Introduced by a conscientious, caring priest without selfish ambitions she wasn't equipped to fulfil?

Confess: you were stimulated. You'd had a meaningful brush with the paranormal and you wanted to know more. In fact – admit it – it was you that Huw Owen was addressing when he said prospective Deliverance ministers should analyse their motives, consider if they needed evidence of life after death to sustain their faith, proof of the existence of supernatural evil to convince them of a power for good.

Huw had been full of foreboding. Jane had been dismissive. Only Mick Hunter was enthusiastic, and Mick Hunter was a politician.

And now God had arbitrated, signalling – in the silence of Canon T. H. B. Dobbs – His unequivocal negative.

Of course, that could have been pure coincidence – if we're being rational about this.

But the compulsion to rush into the Cathedral, the waiting chantry, Dobbs being right there when she emerged? She'd wanted a sign, she'd received a sign. End of story. Later this evening she would phone the Bishop and tell him what wasn't, after all, going to happen.

Mature trees seemed to push the old vicarage back from the village centre. Beneath them was parked a lurid luminous-green Fiesta.

Which had to be something to do with Jane. If it was a boyfriend, Merrily only hoped he was under twenty.

Because of the size of the house, Jane had taken over the entire top floor, formerly attics, as her private apartment, and had finally re-emulsioned her sitting-room/study as the Dutch painter Mondrian might have envisaged it – the squares and rectangles between the timbers in different primary colours. If the Inspector of Listed Buildings ever turned up, the kid was on her own.

She wasn't on her own up there now, though, was she? Merrily edged the Volvo around the little car and parked in the driveway. Although she talked a lot about 'totty', Jane's relations with boys had been curiously restrained. You waited with a certain trepidation for The Big One, because the kid didn't do things by halves, and the first stirring of real love would probably send her virginity spinning straight out of the window.

So Merrily was half-relieved when she opened the front door to find Jane in the hall with a girl in the same school uniform.

An older girl, though not as vividly sophisticated as Jane's last – ill-fated – friend, Colette Cassidy. This one was ethereal, with long, red, soft-spun hair which floated behind her as she gazed around.

'Oh, hi. I was just going to show Rowenna the apartment.' Jane gestured vaguely at Merrily. 'That's the Reverend Mum.'

The girl came over and actually shook hands.

Jane sat down on the stairs. 'Rowenna's dad's with the SAS.'

'With the Army,' Rowenna said discreetly. 'This is a really amazing house, Mrs Watkins. Wonderfully atmospheric. You can feel its memories kind of vibrating in the oak beams. I was just saying to Jane, if I lived here I think I'd just keep going round hugging beams and things. Our place is really new and boring, with fitted cupboards and wardrobes and things.'

'I bet it's a lot easier to heat and keep clean, though,' Merrily said ruefully. 'You live locally, Rowenna?'

'Well, you know, up towards Credenhill, where the base is.' Rowenna wrinkled her nose. 'I wish we *were* down here. It's on a completely different plane. The past is real here. You feel you could just slip into it.'

'Right,' Merrily said. 'If that's what you want.'

'Yes.' Rowenna didn't blink. 'Most of the time, yes.'

Merrily thought it was a sad indictment of society when young people wanted not so much to change the world as to change it *back* – to some golden age which almost certainly never was.

'Oh, hey, listen to this!' Jane sprang up. 'Rowenna's dad goes running – right? – with Mick Hunter.'

'Well, not exactly.' Rowenna looked a bit uncomfortable. 'The Bishop has this arrangement to go along with the guys on some of their routine cross-country runs. It's kind of irregular, apparently. I'm not really supposed to talk about it.'

God, thought Merrily, *he'd just have to go training with the SAS, wouldn't he?*

'Isn't that just so cool?' Jane drawled cynically, in her Rachel-from-*Friends* voice.

Merrily smiled.

'She's not what I expected at all.' Rowenna went to sit on Jane's old sofa, staring up at the Mondrian walls. 'Most of the women priests you see around look kind of bedraggled. But with that suit and the black stockings and everything, she makes the dog-collar seem like . . . I don't know, a fashion accessory.'

'Clerical chic,' Jane said. 'Don't tell her, for God's sake. She only stopped wearing that awful ankle-length cassock because this guy was turned on by all those buttons to undo.'

'Which guy?'

'Her former organist, creepy little git.'

'No special person in her life?'

'Only the Big Guy with the long beard – and the Bishop.'

Rowenna shot her a look.

'Hey, just professionally,' said Jane, 'I *hope*. Sure, the first time I saw him, I thought, wow, yeah, this is the goods. But then I couldn't believe I'd been that shallow. Besides, he's got a wife and kids.'

'Whatever that counts for these days.'

'Yeah, he'd probably quite like to get his leg over Mum. If

you can keep it inside the priesthood, it probably saves a lot of hassle. I just hope she's more sensible. You want a coffee?'

'No thanks, I have to be off in a minute.' Rowenna stood up and moved across to Jane's bookcase. 'You've got it all here, haven't you? Personal transformation, past-life regression, communicating with Nature spirits . . .'

'Yeah, I'm a sad New Age weirdo. Don't spread it around.'

'It's not weird to be interested in what's going to happen to us. Do you do anything like, you know, meditation or anything like that?'

'I've thought about it after . . . when I once had a couple of odd things happen to me.'

Rowenna sat down again. 'Go on.'

'It was probably just imagination. I mean, you can make something out of everything, can't you? Like, Mum, she reckons she sometimes gets these images of blue and gold when she's saying her prayers, and so she connects it with God because that's like the container she's in. But it could be anything, couldn't it?'

'So what happened to you?'

'I don't talk about it much. I reckon if you try to analyse this stuff it just evaporates.'

'Not around me, kitten.'

'OK, well, I just feel this intense connection to some places. Like you were talking about hugging beams, I feel I want to hug hills and fields and – Hey, this is really, really stupid. It's just hyper-imagination.'

'Oh, Jane! Don't stop *now.*'

'Sorry. OK, well, like time passes and you're not aware of it. It's like you're here but you're *not* here, and then you're here again – some kind of shift in reality. Maybe it happens to everybody but most people disregard it. There was an old woman in the village I used to be able to talk to about this stuff, but she's dead now.'

'I think there's another side to all of us we need to discover,' Rowenna said. 'Especially us . . . I mean our generation. We're growing up into this awesome millennial situation where all the old stuff's breaking down . . . like political divisions and organized religion. That's not knocking your mum or anything.'

'It's OK,' Jane said. 'She knows it's all coming to pieces. She got these quite sizeable congregations at first on account of being a woman, but the novelty's wearing off already. When the Church is just surviving on gimmicks you know it's the slippery slope. Go on.'

'All I was saying is that we shouldn't pass up on the opportunity to expand our consciousness wherever possible.'

'I'll go along with that. What sort of stuff have you done?'

'Oh, I've just kind of messed around the edges.' Rowenna flicked the pages of a paperback about interpreting dreams. 'Like, when we were in Salisbury I had this friend whose sister did tarot readings, and she showed me two layouts. I was doing it at school for a few weeks. It was really incredible how accurate it was. Then I did this reading for a girl who was getting to be quite a good friend, and it came out really horrible and she got meningitis soon afterwards and nearly died, and she never came back to school – which kind of spooked me.'

Jane shrugged. 'That doesn't mean it was the cards gave her meningitis. Can you still remember how? Would you be able to do a reading for me?'

'Mmm . . . don't think so. Rather not.'

'Wimp.'

'Maybe. Tell you what, though, I saw this poster down the health-food shop, right? There's a psychic fair on in Leominster next weekend.'

'Cool. What is it?'

'You've never been to one? There are loads about.'

'Rowenna, my mother's a vicar. I lead this dead sheltered life.'

Rowenna smiled. 'Well, actually I've just been to one and it was seriously tacky and full of freaky old dames in gypsy clobber, but good fun if you didn't take it too seriously. We could check it out.'

'OK,' Jane said. 'I suspect I'd better not tell Mum.'

'I suppose she wouldn't be cool about that stuff. Alternative spirituality – subversive.'

'Actually, she's pretty liberal. Well, to a point. Things could be just a tiny bit dicey at the moment, though. So I wouldn't want to, you know . . .'

Jane thought about the soul police. Then she looked at Rowenna and saw that this was someone intelligent and worldly and kind of unfettered. Someone she could actually share stuff with.

'I mean, I guess Mum feels that any kind of spirituality is better than none at all,' Jane grinned, 'which I suppose is how I feel about the Church of England.'

That night, Merrily and Jane made sandwiches and ate them in front of a repeat of an early episode of *King of the Hill*. And then Jane said she'd go to her apartment and have a read and an early night. So Merrily returned, as she usually did, to the kitchen.

She always felt more in control in the kitchen. It was a bit vast, but they'd had lots of cupboards put in, and installed a couple of squashy easychairs and some muted lighting. Recently, she'd converted the adjacent scullery into an office. She supposed this was *her* apartment.

Which meant that, with just the two of them, huge areas of the vicarage remained unused. Stupid and wasteful. No wonder the Church was selling off so many of its old properties, and installing vicars in modest estate-houses.

At least Merrily was no longer so intimidated by all those closed bedroom doors, which had played their own sinister role in the paranormal *fluctuations* that might – if she'd then heard of him – have sent her to consult Canon Dobbs. It had been quiet up there for several months now. A day or two ago she'd caught herself thinking she would almost welcome *its* return: a chance to study an *imprint* at close hand.

But, then, probably not. Not now.

It was ten fifteen. The Bishop had given her his private number, with instructions to call anytime, but she never had. This was probably too late.

Don't be a wimp.

Merrily went through to the scullery, switched on the desk lamp. The answering machine had an unblinking red light; for once, nobody had called. On the desk sat the Apple Mac she'd bought secondhand. God knows what was being installed in the Deliverance Office. If she didn't stop it now.

She pulled down the cordless phone and stabbed out the number very quickly. It rang only twice before Mick Hunter came on. The late-night DJ voice.

'Hi. Val and Mick are unavailable at the moment. Please leave a message after the tone. God bless.'

Merrily hesitated for a second before she cut the line. She'd do this properly tomorrow: call his office and make an appointment. She was aware that when you came face to face with Mick Hunter, your doubts and reservations tended to be tidal-waved by his personality, but that wasn't going to happen this time.

She thought of calling Huw Owen at his stark stone rectory in the Brecon Beacons. But to say what?

Realizing, then, that the only reason she would be calling Huw at this time of night was some tenuous hope that he'd changed his mind about the suitability of women priests for trench warfare.

Unhappy with herself, she switched out the lights, and went up to bed, Ethel the black cat padding softly behind her.

The bedside phone bleeped her awake.

'Reverend Watkins?'

'Yes.' Merrily struggled to sit up.

'Oh . . . I'm sorry to disturb you. It was your husband I wanted. Is he there?'

'I'm afraid he's dead.' Merrily squinted at the luminous clock, clawing for the light switch over the bed, but not finding it.

Nearly ten past two?

'I'm sorry,' the woman said. 'Have I got the right number? I'm trying to contact the Reverend Watkins.' Northern Irish accent.

'Yeah, that's me.'

'Oh. Well, I . . . This is Sister Cullen at Hereford General.'

'General? What . . . sorry?'

'The General Hospital.'

Jesus!

Merrily scrambled out of bed into a wedge of moonlight sandwiched between the curtains. 'Is somebody hurt? Has there been an accident?'

Jane!

She went cold. Jane had crept out again after Merrily had gone to bed? Jane and her friend in the car, clubbing in Hereford, too much to drink. *Oh no, please* . . .

'It's nothing like that,' the sister said, almost impatient. 'It was suggested we call you, that's all. We have a problem. One of our patients is asking for a priest, and the hospital chaplain's away for the night. We were given your number as somebody who should be the one to deal with this. There are some complications.'

'I don't understand. I'm ten miles away.' Scrabbling on the floor for her cigarettes. 'Who suggested . . .?'

'We were given your number. I'm sorry, they never told me you were a woman.'

'That make a difference?'

'I'm sorry, I didn't mean anything offensive. I don't know what to do now.'

'Look, give me half an hour, OK? I'll get dressed. What are the complications you mentioned?'

'I'm sorry, it's not the sort of thing we discuss over the phone.'

Give me strength!

'All right, the General, you said. It'll take me about twenty, twenty-five minutes, Sister . . .'

'Cullen. Ask for Watkins Ward.'

'What?'

It was starting to feel like a dream. The house had done this to her before.

'The Alfred Watkins Ward,' said Sister Cullen. 'Don't bother looking for your Bible. We've got one here.'

TEN

Denzil

Reversing the clanking Volvo out of the vicarage drive, she saw Dobbs's grim, stone face again, as though it was superimposed on the windscreen or the night itself. As if the old bastard had been in the car waiting for her. As if he was staying with her until she'd formally walked away from his job. As if—

This has got to bloody stop!

Merrily gripped the wheel, shaking it violently, but really shaking herself. She'd become oppressed by the dour image of Dobbs. When she'd had the chance to say a final *No, thank you* to Mick Hunter and to Deliverance, she was going to keep well away from the Cathedral precincts, because she – squeezing the wheel until her hands hurt – never ... wanted ... to ... see ... *him* ... again.

OK – steadying her breathing – this was no state in which to minister to a dying man.

On the cobbles of the marketplace she thought she could see a glaze of frost. The wrought-iron mock-gaslamps had gone out, leaving only a small, wintry security light by the steps to The Black Swan.

She drove slowly across the square, not wanting to wake anyone. She'd left a conspicuous note for Jane on the kitchen table in case she didn't get home by morning; you never knew with hospital vigils.

Virtually alone on the country roads, too tense to be tired, she found the kid's all-time favourite album, the complex *OK Computer*, on the stereo and tried to concentrate on the words. But her perception of the songs, full of haunted darkness, only reminded her of Dobbs.

She stopped the music. She would go over this thing once more.

The truth was, after the shock of seeing Dobbs in the Cathedral, when she'd been all charged up and unstable, her mind inevitably had contrived this divinely scripted scene: *he* was there because *she* was.

But what about the unknown woman Dobbs had been with?

'What have I been doing wrong?' the woman had cried. What was all that about?

Well, it made no obvious sense, so forget it. The simple, rational explanation was that Merrily had walked, unexpected, into *Dobbs's* scene. Perhaps *he* was just as shocked when who should suddenly emerge from the chantry but the notorious female pretender.

All right. Stop it, there. Stop looking for a way out. You made your decision, you stick to it.

The General Hospital was an eighteenth-century brick building with the usual unsightly additions. Messy at the front but, like the Bishop's Palace, with a beautiful situation on the Wye, a few hundred yards downstream from the Cathedral. No parking problems at pushing 3.00 a.m.; Merrily left the Volvo near a public garden where a path led down to the suspension footbridge over the river, all dark down there now.

Been here many times to visit parishioners, of course, but never at this hour. And never to the Alfred Watkins Ward, named presumably after the Herefordian pioneer photographer, brewer, magistrate and discoverer of ley-lines. No relation of hers, as far as she knew, but then she didn't know the Herefordshire side of the family very well.

'Bottom of the corridor,' a passing paramedic advised. 'Turn left and immediately left again, through the plastic doors, up the stairs, left at the top and through the double doors.'

These old buildings were wonderful, Merrily thought, for almost everything except hospitals. A plaque on the wall near the main entrance discreetly declared that this used to be a lunatic asylum and, as you walked the unevenly lit, twisting passages, you could imagine the first ever patients wandering here, groping vaguely for their senses, the air dense with disease and desperation.

Despite the directions received, she lost herself in the dim labyrinth, and it was over five minutes before she found a sign to Alfred Watkins Ward. At its entrance, two nurses were talking quietly but with a lot of gesturing. When they saw Merrily, they separated.

She smiled. 'Sister Cullen?'

'On the ward,' the younger nurse said. 'Who shall I say?'

'Merrily Watkins.'

The younger nurse pushed through the double doors into the gloom of the ward itself. Merrily unzipped her waxed jacket, feeling better now she was here. The presence of the dying used to scare her, but recently she'd become more comfortable with them, even slightly in awe – aware of this composure they often developed very close to the end, a calm anticipation of the big voyage – assisted passage. And she would sometimes come away with a tentative glow. Over her past three years as a cleric, several nurses had told her shyly that they'd actually *seen* spirits leaving bodies, like a light within a mist.

'Oh hell!' The older nurse spotted the dog-collar, took a step back in dismay. '*You're* the priest?'

'At 3.00 a.m.,' Merrily said, 'you don't get an archbishop.'

'Oh, look . . .' The nurse was plump, mid-fifties, agitated. 'This isn't right. Eileen Cullen shouldn't have done this. She's an atheist, fair enough, but she should've had more sense. Isn't there a male priest you know?'

Merrily stared in disbelief at the woman's face, pale and blotched under the hanging lights. And fearful too.

'Don't look at me like that. I'm sorry, Miss . . . Reverend. It's just that what we don't need is another woman. Look, would you mind waiting there while I go and talk to Sister Cullen?'

'Fine,' Merrily said tightly. 'Don't worry about me. I don't have to go to work until Sunday.'

'Look, I'm sorry, all right? I'm sorry.'

'Sure.' Merrily sat down on a leather-covered bench, pulled out her cigarettes.

'And I'm afraid you can't smoke in here.'

Sister Cullen was about Merrily's age, but tall, short-haired, sombre-faced. *More like a priest than I'll ever look.*

Behind her, the ward diminished into darkness like a Victorian railway tunnel.

'I may have misled you on the phone,' Cullen said. 'I was confused.'

'*You're* confused.' Merrily stood up. 'Forgive me, but sometimes, especially at three in the morning and without a cigarette, even the clergy can get a trifle pissed off, you know?'

'Keep your voice down, please.'

'I'm sorry. I would just like to know what this is about.'

'All right.' Cullen gestured at the bench and they both sat

down. 'It's Mr Denzil Joy . . . that's the patient. Mr Joy's dying. He's unlikely to see the morning.'

'I'm sorry.'

'With respect, Mrs Watkins, you'll be the only one.'

'Huh?'

'This is a difficult situation.'

'He's asked for a priest, hasn't he?'

'No, that . . . that's where I misled you. He hasn't.'

She jerked a thumb at the double doors. Behind the glass, Merrily saw the other two nurses peering out. They looked like they wanted to escape, or at least stand as close as possible to the lights outside.

'*They* did,' Sister Cullen said. '*They* asked me to call a priest.

Following Cullen through the darkened ward, she was reminded of those war-drawings by Henry Moore of people sleeping in air-raid shelters, swaddled and anonymous. The soundtrack of restive breathing, ruptured snores, shifting bodies was inflated by muted hissings and rumblings in the building's own decaying metabolism. And also, Merrily felt, by slivers of tension in the sour sickness-smelling air.

'He's in a side ward here,' Cullen whispered. 'We've always had him in a side ward.'

'What's his . . . his condition?'

'Chronic emphysema: lungs full of fluid. Been coming on for years – he's been in four times. This time he knows he's not going out.'

'And he isn't . . . . ready. Right?'

Cullen breathed scornfully down her nose. 'Earlier tonight he sent for his wife.'

Merrily looked for some significance in this. 'She's not here with him now?'

'No, we sent her home. Jesus!'

A metal-shaded lamp burned bleakly on a table at the entrance to the side ward, across which an extra plastic-covered screen had been erected.

'There's an evil in this man.' Sister Cullen began sliding the screen away. 'Brace yourself.'

Merrily said, 'I don't understand. What do you . . .?'

And then she did understand. It was Deliverance business.

Huw Owen had stressed: *'Compose, prepare, protect yourself – ALWAYS.'*

Directing them to the prayer known as *St Patrick's Breast-plate*, very old, very British, part of our legacy from the Celtic Church, Huw had said, and Merrily had seen the strength of the hermit in him, the hermit-priest in the cave on the island.

> *Christ be with me, Christ within me,*
> *Christ behind me, Christ before me,*
> *Christ beside me, Christ to win me,*
> *Christ to comfort and restore me,*
> *Christ beneath me, Christ above me,*
> *Christ in quiet, Christ in danger . . .*

Binding yourself with light Huw had said; this was what it was about. A sealing of the portals, old Christian magic, Huw had said. *'Use it.'*

But she hadn't even thought of that. She'd made no prep-arations at all, simply dashed out of the house like a junior doctor on call. Because that was all it was – a routine minis-tering to the dying, a stand-in job, no one else available. Nobody had mentioned . . .

'We were given your number as somebody who should be the one to deal with this. There are some complications.'

. . . it had simply never occurred to her that the hospital had been given her name as a trained Deliverance minister. It never occurred to her that this was what she now was. Who had directed them? The Bishop's office? The Bishop himself?

I've been set up, she thought, angry – and afraid that, whatever needed to be done, she wouldn't be up to it.

There were two iron beds in the side ward, one empty; in the other, Mr Denzil Joy.

His eyes were slits, unmoving under a sweat-sheened and sallow forehead. His hair was black, an unnatural black for a man in his sixties. A dying man dyeing, she thought absurdly.

Two pale green tubes came down his nostrils and looped away over his cheeks, like a cartoon smile.

'Oxygen,' Cullen explained in a whisper.

'Is he asleep?'

'In and out of it.'

'Can he speak?'

Trying to understand what she was doing here, looking hard at him, wondering what she was missing.

Like little horns or something? What do you expect to see?

'With difficulty,' Cullen said.

'Should I sit with him a while?'

'Fetch you a Bible, shall I?'

'Let's . . . let's just leave that a moment.' Knowing how ominous a black, leathered Bible could appear to the patient at such times, wishing she'd brought her blue-and-white paperback version. And still unclear about what they wanted from her here.

There was a vinyl-covered chair next to the bed, and she sat down. Denzil Joy wore a white surgical smock thing; one of his arms was out in view, fingers curved over the coverlet. She put her own hand over it, and almost recoiled. It was warm and damp, slimy somehow, reptilian. A small, nervous smile tweaked at Cullen's lips.

In the moment Merrily touched Denzil Joy, it seemed a

certain scent arose. The kind of odour you could almost see curling through the air, so that it entered your nostrils as if directed there. At first sweet and faintly oily.

Then Merrily gasped and took in a sickening mouthful and, to her shame, had to get up and leave the room, a hand over her mouth.

The other hand, not the one which had touched Denzil Joy.

One of the patients on the ward was calling out, 'Nurse!' as loudly as a farmer summoning a sheepdog over a six-acre field.

At the door Merrily gulped in the stale hospital air as if it was ozone.

'Dr Taylor found a good description for it.' Eileen Cullen was standing beside the metal lamp, smiling grimly. 'Although *he* never quite got the full benefit of it, being a man. He said it was like a mixture of gangrene and cat faeces. That seems pretty close, though I wouldn't know for sure. Never kept cats myself. Excuse me a minute.'

She padded down the ward towards the man calling out, one hand raised, forefinger of the other to her lips. As soon as she'd gone, the plump middle-aged nurse appeared from the shadows, put her mouth up to Merrily's ear.

'I'll tell you what that is, Reverend. It's the smell of evil.'

'Huh?'

'He can turn it on. Don't look at me like that. Maybe it's automatic, when his blood temperature rises. It comes to the same thing. Did you feel him enter you?'

'What?'

'We can't talk here.' She took Merrily's arm, pulled her away and into a small room lit by a strip light, with sinks and bags of waste. She shut the door. The disinfectant smell here, in comparison with that in the side ward, was like honeysuckle on a summer evening.

'I'm a strong woman,' the nurse said, 'thirty years in the job. Everything nasty a person can throw off, I've seen it and smelled it and touched it.'

'I can imagine.'

'No, you can't, my girl.' The nurse pushed up a sleeve. 'You have no idea. Look at that, now.' Livid bruising around the wrist, like she'd been handcuffed.

'What happened was: Mr Joy, he asked for a bottle – to urinate in, you know? And then he called me back and he said he was having . . . trouble getting it in. Well, some of them, they say that as a matter of course, and you have a laugh and you go away and come back brandishing the biggest pair of forceps you can find. But Denzil Joy was a very sick man and he seemed distressed, so I did try to help.' She pulled down her sleeve again. 'You see where that got me.'

'Oh.'

'Grip like a monkey-wrench, my dear. Thought I'd never get fooled again. You understand now why we wanted a male priest?'

Surely, what you wanted, Merrily thought, *was a male nurse*. 'Look, Nurse . . . I'm sorry?'

'Nurse Protheroe. Sandra.'

'Sandra, this is a dying man, OK? He knows he's dying. He's afraid. He's looking for . . . comfort, I suppose. That doesn't make him possessed by evil. I don't know what his background is. I mean . . .'

'Farm-labourer and slaughterman. Been in a few times before, he has. When he wasn't so bad – not so seriously ill, that is.'

'Farm-labourer? So his idea of comfort might be a bit . . . rough and ready?'

Sandra snorted. 'Oh, for heaven's sake, it's more than *that*, girl. You're not getting this, are you? I've dealt with that type more times than you've done weddings and funerals – rough as an old boar and ready for anything they can get. But Mr Joy, he's different. Mr Joy's an abuser, a destroyer – do you know what I mean? He likes causing pain and death to animals, and he likes doing it to women, too. Hurting them and humiliating them. Degrading them.'

'Yes. That might very well be true. But it doesn't—'

'That smell . . . that's not natural, not even in a hospital. That's *his* smell. That's the smell of all the things he's done and all the things he'd still like to do. We even put Nil-odour under his bed one night.'

'What's that?'

'Undertaker's fluid. They put it in coffins sometimes, so it's less offensive for the relatives.'

'You put undertaker's deodorant under a dying patient's bed?'

'It didn't work. You can't remove the smell of evil with chemicals. You spend a night in here with that man, you can't sleep when you goes home. You keep waking up with that . . .' Protheroe hugged herself. 'As for young Tessa – white, that girl was. This was after his wife come in this afternoon.'

'Sandra, look . . .' Merrily moved to the door. This wasn't how state-registered nurses were supposed to behave. She needed to talk to the duty doctor. 'You say I don't get this. You're dead right, I don't get this at all. All right, he might not be a very nice man, he may not smell very good, but that's no excuse to make his last hours a total misery. I mean, what does his wife say about all this?'

'Mrs Joy don't talk,' said Sandra. 'Being as how you're a priest, I'll tell you about Mrs Joy, shall I?'

'If you think it'll help.'

Sandra exhaled a sour laugh. 'About twenty years younger

than him, she is, but you wouldn't know it to look at her, state she's in, the poor miserable cow. No, not a cow, a rabbit . . . a poor frightened little wretch. We left them alone for about half an hour, as you do at times like this. Then Dr Taylor comes on his rounds and he has to see Mr Joy, obviously, and Tess goes in to ask Mrs Joy will she come out for a couple of minutes, and—'

Footsteps outside. Sandra stopped talking, looking at the door. The footsteps passed. Sandra lowered her voice.

'The chair's pushed right up next to the bed, see? That chair you were just sitting on?'

'Yes.' Merrily found her hands were clasped in front of her, rubbing together. She wanted to wash them, but not in front of Sandra Protheroe. 'Go on.'

'So Mrs Joy's standing on that chair, leaning over the bed. She's holding her dress right up above her waist. She's got her knickers round her ankles.'

Merrily closed her eyes for a moment.

'And Denzil's just lying there with his tubes up his nose and all the spittle down his chin, wheezing and rattling with glee, and his little eyes eating her up. But that's not the worst thing, see.'

She swallowed, backed up against a sink, looking down at her shoes and shaking her head.

'The worse thing is her face. What Tessa said was that woman's face was completely blank. No expression at all – like a zombie. She's just looking at the wall, and her face's absolutely blank. She knows Tessa's there, but she don't get down. Showing no embarrassment at all, though God knows she must have been as full up with shame and humiliation as it's possible to be. But she just stands there staring at the wall. Because *he* hadn't told her she could get down.'

Merrily's mouth was dry.

'This is a dying man,' Sandra said. 'And he knows it and

she knows it, and she's still terrified of him. In his younger days, see, he thought he was God's gift. A woman who knows the family, she told me about all the women and girls he'd had, and the way he abused them but they kept coming back. He charmed them back, he did. Not by his looks, not by his manners, he just *charmed* them. And then he got older and he got sick and he got married, and he controls the wife by fear. And he's lying there delighting in Tessa seeing the poor little woman giving him an eyeful of what he owns. If that's not evil then I don't know what evil is.'

'What is evil?' Huw Owen had said. *'It's the question you're never going to answer. But when you're in the same room with it, you'll know.'*

Merrily said, 'I'm sorry. I don't know what I can do.'

'Protection. She wants protection.'

The door had opened. Sister Cullen was standing there, the darkness behind her.

'She's right, he's a bad man with a black charm. But he's just a man, and that's where it ends as far as I'm concerned. I'm from Derry, so I've seen what religion does to people, and I want none of it. But this is one patient where I'm more concerned about his nurses.'

'It's getting stronger the nearer he comes to death,' Sandra said. 'Tell her.'

'Sandra's convinced the smell's getting worse.'

'And if *you* don't do something, when he dies this ward's going to be polluted for ever. And I'm not coming back tomorrow. I'm out.'

'Let me get this right.' Merrily looked from one to the other, the believer and the atheist, but both essentially of the same mind. 'You've called me out in the middle of the night, not because you want comfort for a distressed terminal patient but because . . . you want protection from *him*?'

Cullen said with resignation, 'If there's anything you think you can do about it, feel free, but I'd strongly advise you not to touch the evil bastard again.'

'Sister . . .' The young nurse Tessa in the doorway. She was crying. 'Can you come, please?'

ELEVEN

Scritch-scratch

Merrily thought of the almost-poetic abstraction of *imprints* and *visitors* and *weepers* and *breathers*.

She thought about the *hitchhiker* – the disembodied spirit which took over someone's body for a period, usually for some specific if illogical purpose, and then went away.

She considered probably the worst of them all – Huw had discussed this in detail over the last two days of the Deliverance course – the *squatter*.

And then thought about the pathetic, stinking, wheezing, nasal-cathe.red reality of Denzil Joy, who fitted into none of the slick categories which Charlie Headland had said reminded him of the fictionalized world of espionage. What was Denzil Joy other than an unpleasant man coming to the end of his run? Was he, indeed, any of her business?

There were several tests you had to implement before a subject could reasonably be considered possessed by an external, demonic evil – most importantly, the psychiatric assessment. Now, how could anyone assess a man apparently in the last hours of his life, a person unable to speak? It was an impossible situation.

'I'm sorry, Sister,' Tessa said. 'It was just that his breathing sort of altered and I thought he was starting to . . . go.'

All four of them stood watching Denzil from outside the door.

'Gone, has he?' An old man warbling from the ward. 'What's happening over there?'

'Everything's fine, Francis,' Eileen Cullen hissed. 'Go to sleep now, will you.'

Merrily took a closer look at Denzil Joy, his face half-lit by the lamp on a table just outside the door. Black hair over shallow forehead, small, sucking mouth. His frame thin and wiry, with bony arms. *'Grip like a monkey-wrench, my dear.'*

'Does he never say anything? Never ask for anything? Doesn't he talk to you?'

'Doesn't like talking to women,' Cullen said. 'Prefers to communicate with us in other ways.'

Sandra instinctively massaged her bruised wrist. 'I reckon he didn't do this on his own. That's what I think now.'

Merrily turned to her. 'You're a Christian, Sandra?'

'I attend St Peter's,' Sandra declared piously. 'Well, not every week – sometimes shifts don't allow, obviously. But one week in every three – at least that.'

'And you don't believe, Eileen.'

'I'm aware of evil,' she snapped. 'Of course I am. I just think there's quite enough of it on this earth to be going on with.'

'Tessa?'

'I'm scared.' In her uniform, no make-up, Tessa looked about Jane's age, although she surely must be several years older. She had quite a posh accent. 'I thought he was Cheyne-Stoking. I didn't want to be alone with him when he died.'

Merrily glanced at Cullen, who beckoned her away from the door.

'She means the kind of sporadic breathing that tells you they're on their way out.'

Merrily nodded, remembering other bedsides.

'The smell's gone, Eileen. At least it's not what it was.'

'I don't know, he seems to be able to turn it on and off at

will. That's what gets to Protheroe – him controlling his smell. Particularly when a woman gets close. There's a psychological solution, if you ask me.'

'He's kind of drawing energy through sexual arousal?'

'I can't imagine there's any physical arousal, and I don't feel inclined to check. I've about had it with this one.' Cullen wiped her brow with the side of a fist. 'See, earlier on, Sandra was threatening to walk out. That's when I called you. She knows if I took any disciplinary action over this there'd be unfavourable publicity of the kind nobody wants. I'm going through the motions, so I am, and I'd be happy if you could just do the same.'

'Primarily, we need to consider what's best for him.'

'I just think he's an evil bastard, you know? I wish he'd just die, then we could get him portered the hell out of here.'

Merrily sighed. No putting this off any longer. 'I'll go in and say a few prayers for him.'

'That's it? I thought you were an exorcist of some kind?'

'Some kind,' Merrily said.

> *I bind unto myself the Name,*
> *The strong Name of the Trinity.*
> *By invocation of the same,*
> *The Three in One and One in Three.'*

She was back in the sluice-room, alone this time, murmuring *St Patrick's Breastplate* to the pale grey walls. A window was open; she heard a siren coming closer – police, or an ambulance bringing someone into Casualty. The normal world out there – and here she was in a former lunatic asylum, getting into Dark Age armour. Relying on her God to pull her out of this, if it should turn out to be misguided.

'Don't ever fall into the trap of thinking it's you that's doing it,' Huw had stressed. *'You're never any more than the*

medium, the vessel. We don't want any of this Van Helsing crap, wielding the crucifix like it's a battle-axe. Always preferred a titchy little cross, meself. Lets you know where you stand in the great scheme of things.'

She wore her own cross under her jumper, and it too was pretty small.

What she could do was limited, anyway. She wasn't allowed to perform an exorcism – and quite right, too – without the permission of the Bishop. Knowing Mick Hunter, he'd call for a written report, spend at least two days considering the ethics of it and how he'd look if it leaked out.

Merrily stepped out on to the ward, where most of the patients slept noisily on, shuffling and muttering. Few people got a peaceful night in a hospital. The silent digital wall-clock said 4.25.

'I'd better come in with you,' the night sister said.

'Perhaps not, Eileen.'

'Whenever possible, have other Christians with you as back-up – or witnesses in case there's any shit flying round afterwards in the media. Or, put it this way, if you're having people with you, make sure you know where they've been.'

'Because I'm not a bloody Bible-basher? Jesus! All right . . . Nurse Protheroe, what about you? You started all this.'

Sandra shrank away. 'I can't.'

'Superstition,' Cullen said, with contempt. 'I can never accept that in a professional. Well, there has to be a staff nurse in there. This is a hospital, in case anybody's forgotten.'

'I'll do it,' Tessa said.

'Don't be stupid,' Sandra whispered harshly.

Merrily thought of Jane. She wouldn't want the kid within a mile of this. She thought: *My God, this is some kind of awful first. Four women gathering like a bunch of witches to plot against a dying man. This ever gets out, we'll look ridiculous or dangerously paranoid. Or cold conspirators – heartless, vindictive. Are we?*

'Look,' she said. 'I'll be all right on my own. I'm not going to be doing anything dramatic – no holy water. You can all watch through the window if you like.'

'No,' said Cullen.

'I teach Sunday school,' Tessa offered solemnly, and they all looked at her. 'I can handle it as long as I'm not alone in there.'

'All right, then.' Eileen Cullen shrugged, perhaps still wanting to shame Sandra Protheroe into it, but Sandra didn't react. 'Just as long as you realize it's not an instruction. And you make sure and stay well back from the Reverend, you hear? Any trouble, you come and get me. You know what I mean by trouble?'

'I think so.' Tessa nodded. She bit her upper lip, plucked a stray ash-blonde hair from her forehead.

Merrily put a hand on Tessa's shoulder, leaned in to look for her eyes. 'You sure about this?'

'It's best, isn't it?'

'All right. Do you want to come in here a minute.'

The sluice-room as temporary chapel. Merrily faced the girl over the rubbish sacks full of swabs and bandages soaked with bodily fluids and God-knows-what.

'Tessa, I . . . How old are you?'

'Nineteen.'

'OK, look . . . I just want to say I'm not too sure about any of this. Whatever Mr Joy's done in his time, it's not my job to judge him. We're just going in to pray with him and try to bring him some peace. To calm down whatever sick yearnings he's harbouring so that he can end his life in some kind of grace. I mean, probably none of this will be necessary, but when I've started, I've got rules to follow, so I'd like to . . . close our eyes a moment. *Our Father . . .*'

She said the Lord's Prayer softly, Tessa joining in, then placed her hands either side of the girl's bowed head.

'Jesus . . . surround her and hold her . . . safe from the forces of evil.'

It again entered her head that this was all a crazy, hysterical over-reaction; there were no forces of evil, no Je—

She kicked out mentally, sent the thought spinning away. She opened the door.

'Come on.'

Denzil Joy's terrible breathing was through the mouth: liquid, strangulated, the sound of an old-fashioned hot-water geyser filling up. In the side ward, with the door closed, it seemed all around them, underscored by that hum you couldn't seem to escape in hospital wards, and the throaty chortle of the overhead heating pipes.

The green oxygen tubes were clipped together behind his head, which was supported by three pillows. There were scabs of mucus where the tubes fitted into his nostrils.

'You want me to do anything?' Tessa asked.

'Just grab a chair from somewhere.'

'I'd rather stand. Is that OK?'

'However you feel comfortable.'

Merrily sat in the vinyl-covered chair on which the wretched Mrs Joy was said to have stood. Its seat was sunken in the middle.

OK. She pushed up a sleeve of her black jumper, reached over in the half-light and took Denzil's hand, instantly screwing up her eyes because it was undeniably vile, like picking up a cold turd.

Stop it!

Sliding her hand away from his fingers with their long yellow nails, and up to his bony wrist, holding it gently, calming her breathing.

'Denzil . . .' She cleared her throat. 'I don't know if you can hear me. My name's Merrily. I'm . . . er, the Vicar of Ledwardine. I'm just doing the rounds – as we vicars do.'

If he was even half awake, he wouldn't be aware of what time it was, how unlikely it was that a vicar would be doing the rounds. At all costs she mustn't alarm him.

'I wanted to say a few prayers with you, if that's OK.'

His breathing didn't alter. His eyes remained three-quarters closed. He seemed unaware of her. She looked down at his thin, furtive face, the spittle bubbling around his mouth. And she pleaded with God to send her some pity. Nobody should die an object of fear and hatred and revulsion.

'He's very, very weak,' Tessa murmured in her ear. 'I don't know how he's holding on.'

Merrily nodded. 'Almighty God, our Heavenly Father,' she said softly. 'We know, all of us, that we've done bad things and neglected to do good things we might've done.'

She felt Denzil's wrist turn under her hand: other than the breathing, the first sign of life. The wrist turned so that the palm was upwards, the position of supplication, as though he was responding, holding out his hand for forgiveness.

'For the sake of Jesus Christ, our Lord, Your Son, we beg You to forgive us, close the book on the past. Calm our souls.'

She squeezed the hand encouragingly. Outside, Nurse Sandra Protheroe passed the door without looking in.

'We know Your nature is to have mercy, to forgive. We beg You to free Denzil from whatever bonds are binding his spirit.'

One of Denzil's fingernails began to move slowly against her palm, like the claw of an injured bird. It felt, actually, quite unpleasant. Suggestive. She wished she'd never spoken to Sandra Protheroe.

Tessa was standing beside the door with her hands behind her back. She managed a rather wounded smile.

'We ask You this,' Merrily said, 'in the name of our saviour Jesus Christ.' She felt slightly sick and closed her eyes.

At once, the light scratching of Denzil's nail on her palm picked up momentum, acquired a rhythm. A small high-pitched wheeze was detectable under his rasping, snuffling breath, and the sweet sour stench was back – suddenly and rapidly unravelling from him like a soiled string, seeming to spiral through the thin, stale air directly into Merrily's nose and coil there.

'Cat faeces and gangrene.'

Oh God! She felt clammy and nauseous but also starved, like she had flu coming on.

'I'll tell you what that is, Reverend. It's the smell of evil.'

It's not evil. It's sickness. It's disgusting, but it's not evil.

Still, she tightened her lips against it, fighting the compulsion to snatch her hand away. She must *not*, she must let it lie there, mustn't react. *It's my job, it's my job, it's what I do, it's—*

She could almost hear it now. *Scritch-scratch* – the tiniest movement of a curling nail on the end of a yellow finger. Suspecting that in the mind of Denzil Joy this was not a mere finger.

He can enter you without moving an inch, that man.

Slide away, squirm away, get out of here.

Scritch-scratch, as though he was teasing away layers of skin in the centre of her palm to get his finger under the flesh. But that was imagination. His strength, his lifeforce, was so depleted this was the most he could manage: *scritch-scratch*. Poor guy – reach out to the humanity in him. *Poor guy, poor guy, poor guy, poor guy . . .*

She was aware of him taking in a long, long shuddering breath. Tessa moving towards the bed.

The breath was not released. There was an awesome cliff-edge of silence. The scratching stopped.

'This is it,' Tessa said quietly. So much composure in the kid. 'He's Cheyne-Stoking, no question this time.'

In the breathless silence, Merrily would swear she could feel the heat of him, slithering from his mind to her mind, while his finger lay still in her hand like a small cigar.

It seemed much darker and colder in here now – as though, in its hunger for life-energy, the shrivelled body in the bed was absorbing all the electricity, all the light, all the heat in the room.

'In fact I think he's gone,' Tessa said.

Darkness. Cold. Stillness. And the sinuous, putrid smell. Gently, Merrily attempted to slip her hand out of his.

And then it seized her.

'Grip like a monkey-wrench.'

Like a train from a tunnel, his breath came out and in the same moment his fingers pushed up between hers and tightened; a low, sniggering laugh seemed to singe the air between them.

And Merrily felt something slide between her legs.

Knowing in a second that she'd felt no such thing, that it was all imagination, conditioning. But it was too late: the cold wriggled fiercely into her groin, jetted into her stomach like an iced enema. She'd already torn her hand away, throwing herself back with so much force that she slipped from the chair to the shiny grey floor and slid back against the second bed, hearing herself squealing,

'*I bind unto myself the Name,*

'*The strong Name of the Trin—*'

And, hearing Tessa screaming shrilly, she cried out help-lessly.

'Begone!'

Not knowing who or what she meant.

There was a wrenching, snapping sound; she saw the green

tubes writhing in the air like electric snakes, torn from Denzil's nostrils as suddenly, in a single, violent ratchet movement, he sat up in his bed.

Tessa shrieking, 'Noooooooooooo!' and falling back against the door, stumbling out when it was flung open by Eileen Cullen – who just stood there with Denzil Joy's upright, stiffened, shadowed shape between her and Merrily.

TWELVE

Soiled

She discovered she was in the corridor outside. And that she was half sobbing and half laughing, but it wasn't *real* laughing. On the other side of a film of tears, a small flame was approaching.

'It's not allowed, is it?' Was that *her* voice, that mad cackle?

'The hell it isn't,' said Cullen, lighting Merrily's cigarette and then one for herself.

They sat on the bench outside the ward. It was no longer quiet in there.

'We told them Tessa had seen a mouse, but patients, especially old fellers – it's like spooking the horses in a stable, you know? We'll give them half an hour to get themselves back to sleep before we get somebody up here to take him out.'

'I'm sorry, Eileen.' Merrily blew her nose. 'This is ridiculous.'

'It's that, all right. How the devil he found the strength to sit up like that is beyond me. He was a husk, so he was. Nothing left. What the hell did you *do*?'

'Do?' She crushed the wet tissue into her palm – the palm of the *scritch-scratch*. 'God knows.'

'You reckon?'

'How would I know? I was completely out of my depth.

No real idea what I was supposed to be doing. This is a bloody mug's game, Eileen. A charade, maybe. Play-acting?'

My bit was play-acting; his was real.

'Hey, I didn't hear that. This is your profession.' Cullen put a hand on her knee. 'We'll go into my office for a cuppa, soon as I get Protheroe to do the necessary.'

'The necessary?'

'Lay the poor bastard out. We're none of us scared of dead bodies, are we? Not even this one, although . . . you didn't see his face, did you?'

Merrily shook her head. 'I was on the floor by then. Could only see the back of his head and those tubes flying out of his nose when he . . . rose up.'

She shuddered. The snapping of the tubes; she could still hear it.

'That's lucky. You'll maybe get some sleep tonight.' Eileen Cullen dragged on her cigarette. 'Jesus, he was frightened. I thought at first it was me he was looking at. But he's staring over my shoulder, out of the door into thin air. Nobody there. Nobody *I* could see. And the look on his face: like somebody was coming for him, you know? Like the person he feared most in all the world was standing in that doorway, waiting to . . . Oh, Jesus, the things you see in this job, you could go out of your mind if you hadn't so much to bloody do.'

'Waiting to take him away,' Merrily said drably. 'Whatever it was was waiting to take him away.'

'It's the chemicals is all it is. The chemicals in the brain. Some people that close to the end, the chemicals ease the way, you know?'

'The angels on the threshold.' Merrily blew her nose again into the sodden tissue.

'Or the Devil. Whatever cocktail of volatile chemicals was

sloshing round in that man's head, they must've shown him the Devil and all his works.'

'Which means I failed.'

'Natural justice, Merrily.'

'That's not the way it's supposed to work.' There was a question she needed to ask, a really obvious question. What was it? She couldn't think.

'Come and have that cuppa.'

'Thanks, but I need to get home. I've got my daughter.'

'You want someone to drive you? I think you're in shock, you know.'

'God no, I'll be fine. Maybe I should come back later and . . . cleanse the place?'

'What, with all the patients awake?' Cullen stood up. 'You in there flashing the big cross and doing the mumbo-jumbo? Forget it. Mop and bucket'll see it right. It's over.'

'Is it?'

'What do you want me to say? I'm a non-believer. Was all chemicals, Merrily, maybe a few of yours as well, don't you think? You go sleep it off. We'll tell the Bishop or who you like that you did a terrific job.'

The Bishop?

'I'd rather you said I'd never even been.'

'You don't mean that.'

'Tell them I didn't answer the phone when you rang.'

'Get yourself some rest. Call me at home sometime. I've written the number on your ciggy packet.' Sister Cullen squeezed her shoulder. 'Thank you, Merrily. You did OK, I reckon.'

'For a Bible-basher?'

The Bishop?

Had the Bishop set her up for it?

This was the question she'd meant to ask. She remembered

that as she was leaving the building, pulling on her coat. Who exactly had told them to contact her? Who had advised them that Merrily Watkins was Deliverance-trained and available for work?

Had to be him. He was dangerous. Michael Hunter – Bishop Cool – was a dangerous man to have organizing your career.

There was light in the sky and a cold wind. What the hell time was it? Where had she left the car all those hours ago when all she'd had to think about was Dobbs? She hurried down the drive and into the deserted street full of fresh cold air from the hills.

It was the cold *inside* that scared her. She stood and shivered by the entrance to the shambling jumble of a hospital where the body of Denzil Joy lay cooling.

I was raped. Like icy letters in the sky. *He raped me.*

She felt greasy, slimy, soiled, used. He'd made his smell go into her, had scratched himself an entrance hole. And then he'd died, he'd gone away, but he'd left his filthy essence inside her. She needed a long shower, needed to pray. Needed to think. Because this would not, *could* not have happened to a male priest, a male exorcist.

I need exorcizing.

Violently she zipped up her fading waxed coat and strode away into the pre-dawn murk. She would find a church that was open or, failing that, would go to her own church in Ledwardine. She couldn't take the pitiful, disgusting dregs of Denzil home to Jane. She would have to go into a church and pray for his soul. Pray for it to be taken away somewhere and stripped and cleaned.

She saw that the old blue Volvo had been very badly parked, even for three in the morning: standing half on the grass near the little gardens where the footpath went up and then down to the Wye. Another six inches and she'd have backed into a sign saying: NO PARKING. KEEP ENTRANCE CLEAR. She fumbled out her keys.

'Excuse me, madam.'

He'd blundered out of the bushes, a big heavy guy in some kind of rally anorak, luminous stripe down one arm. 'Is this your car?'

'Who are you?'

'Police. How long has the car been here, please?'

All she needed.

'Look, I'm sorry, I was in a hurry and I thought it'd be OK.'

'When did you park it?'

'About three, I suppose.'

'To go to the hospital?'

'Yes.'

'Can I ask why?'

'Look,' Merrily said, exasperated, 'it could've been parked a whole lot better, I agree. I'm very sorry. Give me a ticket or whatever. I'm a bit knackered, OK?'

'It isn't about parking, miss. Would you mind telling me your name, please?'

'After I see your ID.' Merrily unlocked the Volvo. If he took any time producing his warrant card, she was out of here. You didn't trust big guys in the semi-dark – not these days.

'It's all right, Peter. It's her.' A woman in a long white raincoat emerged from the river path. 'Ms Watkins, Person of the Cloth. I'll deal with this.'

The big man nodded, trudged back up the footpath.

Merrily sighed. 'DI Howe.'

'Acting DCI, actually.'

'The old fast track's moved up a gear, has it?' Weariness loosening Merrily's reserve. 'Let me guess, I've walked into some kind of stake-out. Colombian drugs barons are bringing a consignment up the Wye?'

Annie Howe didn't laugh. It occurred to Merrily that she had yet ever to hear Annie Howe laugh. Her short, ashen hair gleamed dully like a helmet in the early light.

'You priests work long hours. Sick parishioner?'

'Dead,' Merrily said. 'Just now.'

'Obviously a night for it, Ms Watkins.'

'For what?'

Annie Howe came to stand next to her, glancing into the Volvo. She was maybe five years younger than Merrily – a smooth, efficient, over-educated CID person, both feet on the escalator. During the police hunt in Ledwardine earlier this year, Jane had remarked that Howe reminded her of a Nazi dentist. You could tell where the kid was coming from.

'We've pulled a body out of the Wye, Ms Watkins. Just down there, not far from Victoria Bridge.'

'Oh God. Just?'

'Couple of hours ago.'

She remembered hearing the siren from the sluice-room window. 'What happened?'

'We're not sure yet. But it didn't appear to have been in the water an awfully long time, so we're rather keen to talk to anyone who might have seen something' – Howe smiled thinly – 'or heard a solitary splash, perhaps.'

'Not me.'

'You arrived about three, I hear that right?'

'Something like that.'

'Nobody about at all?'

'Not that I can recall.'

'You ever been down to the river this way?'

'Not really.'

'It's quite pretty,' Howe said. 'Come and see.'

Merrily sighed and followed her past some flowerless beds and a bench to a little parapet. Below them was a narrow suspension bridge, grey girders across the dark, misty river. A glimmering of pale plastic tape, and two policemen.

Howe said, 'It's just that if there's a particular parking place most convenient for the river, then your car's in it. We thought it might be the dead man's at first. Quite a disappointment really, when your name came up as the owner.'

'And when the body wasn't a woman about my age in a dog-collar.'

'Not quite what I meant. It just made it less easy to put a name to him. But we will.'

'How old was he?'

'Quite young. Thirties.'

'Suicide?'

'It's a possibility, given the time of day. So's accidental death.' Annie Howe looked at Merrily. 'So's murder.'

'He didn't drown?'

'We should know quite soon.'

'But he came off the bridge?'

Howe shrugged.

'If you knew it was my car, why didn't you come into the hospital and ask for me?'

'We did. Nobody seemed to know you were there.'

'The Alfred Watkins Ward, if you want to check. Ask for Sister Cullen. I've been with her for the last three hours or so.'

Howe nodded. 'So it's unlikely you would've seen anything. Ah, well, nothing's ever simple, is it, Ms Watkins? Thanks for your help. I don't suppose we'll be in touch, but if you remember anything that might be useful . . .' the wind whipped the skirt of Howe's raincoat against her calves, 'you know where to find me.'

Merrily looked down into the swirling mist and dark water. It looked somehow warmer than she felt – and almost inviting.

THIRTEEN

Show Barn

It was rare to see genial Dick Lyden in a bad mood.

When Lol arrived just after 8.00 a.m., Dick was pacing the kitchen, slamming his right fist into his left palm.

'The little shit,' he fumed. 'The fucking little shit!'

'He's just trying it on,' Mrs Ruth Lyden, fellow therapist, said calmly. 'He knows you too well. He's got you psyched out. He knows your particular weak spot and he goes for it.'

There was plenty of room for Dick to pace; the Lydens' kitchen was as big as a restaurant kitchen, more than half as big as Lol's new flat over the shop. It was all white and metallic like a dairy.

'His psychological know-how goes out of the window when he's dealing with his own son,' Ruth told Lol. She was a large, placid, frizzy-haired woman who'd once been Dick's personal secretary in London.

'Well, you can't, can you?' Dick sat down at the banquet-sized table. 'You simply can't distance yourself sufficiently from your own family – be wrong even to try. I think we're probably even worse than ordinary people at dealing with our own problems.'

Lol didn't like to ask what the present personal problem was; Ruth told him anyway.

'James has been chosen as Boy Bishop.' She searched Lol's face, eyebrows raised. 'You know about that?'

130

'Sorry,' Lol said. 'I'm not that well up on the Church.'

'Medieval Christmas tradition. Used to happen all over the place, but it's almost unique to Hereford now. A boy is chosen from the Cathedral choristers, or the retired choristers, to replace the Bishop on his throne on St Nicholas's Day. Gets to wear the mitre and wield the staff and whatnot. Terribly solemn and everything, though quite fun as well.'

'It's actually a great honour,' Dick said. 'Especially for newcomers like us. Little shit!'

'And of course James now says he's going to refuse to do it.' Ruth poured coffee for Lol. 'When they offered it to him, he was very flattered in a cynical sort of way. But now he's announced it would be morally wrong of him to do it – having decided he's an atheist—'

'What the fuck difference does that make?' Dick snarled. 'At least twenty-five per cent of the bloody clergy are atheists!'

'—and that it isn't in line with his personal image or his musical direction. He's sixteen now, and at sixteen one's image is awfully well defined. How quickly they change! One year an angelic little choirboy, and then—'

'A bloody yob,' said Dick. 'Where's his guitar? I'm going to lock it in the shed.'

'He's taken it to school with him.' Ruth hid a smile behind her coffee cup. 'Told you he had you psyched.'

'Devious little bastard.' Dick drained his cup, coughed at the strength of the coffee. 'Right, I'll get my coat, Lol. Be good to go out and deal with something straightforward.'

'Moon is straightforward?'

'Well, you know what I mean. Straightforwardly convoluted.'

'Poor Dick,' Ruth said when he'd left the kitchen. 'It's an honour for *him* rather than James. A sign that he's really been accepted into the city. He needs that – needs to be at the hub of things. He's a terrible control-freak, really, in his oh-so-amiable way.'

Lol said, 'Do you guys psychoanalyse one another *all* the time?'

Ruth laughed.

Outside, it began to rain, a sudden cold splattering.

'Wow.' Jane was observing her mother from the stove. 'You really do look like shit.'

'Thank you. I think we've established that.'

Merrily had told her about being delayed by the police investigating a body in the Wye. But that evidently didn't explain why she looked like shit.

'You need a hot bath,' Jane said. 'And then off to bed.'

'The bath certainly.' No question about that. Merrily watched the rain on the window. It looked dirty. Everything looked dirty even after twenty minutes before the altar. *Scritch-scratch.*

'So.' Jane shovelled inch-thick toast on to a plate. 'You want to talk about the other stuff?'

'What makes you think there's other stuff?'

'Do me a favour,' Jane said.

The kid had realized, from quite soon after Sean's death, that her mother would need someone on whom she could lay heavy issues. There were times when she instinctively became a kind of sensible younger sister – with no sarcasm, point-scoring, storage of information for future blackmail.

'Hang on, though.' Merrily looked up. 'What time is it? The school bus'll be going without you.'

'I'm taking the day off. I have a migraine.'

'In which case, flower, you appear to be coping with the blinding agony which defines that condition with what I can only describe as a remarkable stoicism.'

'Yeah, it's a fairly mild attack. But it could get worse.

Besides, when you've really sussed out the way teachers operate, you can take the odd day off any time you like without missing a thing.'

'Except you never have – have you?'

'A vicar's daughter has to be flexible. If I went to school, you'd stay up and work all day, and by the time I got home you'd be *soooo* unbearable.'

'Jane—'

'Don't argue. Just have some breakfast and bugger off to bed. I'll stick around, make a brilliant log fire – and repel all the time-wasting gits.'

Merrily gave up. 'But this must never happen again.'

Jane shrugged.

'All right,' Merrily said. 'No egg for me, thanks. My digestive system can just about cope with Marmite.'

'Right.' Jane brought the teapot to the table and sat down. 'What's disturbed it exactly?'

Merrily sighed a couple of times and watched the rain blurring the window. And she then told Jane about Denzil Joy.

Some of it.

Rain sheeted down on Dinedor Hill, the twisty road narrowing as they climbed.

Dick was clearly disappointed when they ran out of track for the massive Mitsubishi Intercooler Super Turbo-Plus he'd borrowed from Denny for the weekend. Dick was contemplating a move into four-wheel drive.

Lol unbuckled his seatbelt. 'If you go any further, English Heritage'll be down on you. It'll be in the *Hereford Times* – "City Therapist Squashes Ancient Camp".'

'You may scoff. But I *do* feel it's important to be a good citizen. We *chose* to come here – which confers responsibility.' Dick braked and reversed into something satisfyingly deep and viscous. 'Even to something that just looks like any other hill.'

'You have no soul, Dick.'

Dick squinted through the mud-blotched windcreen. 'Buggered if I'm staggering up there in this weather. What am I missing?'

'Nice view over the city. For the rest, you need a soul.'

'Imagination.' Dick leaned back in the driving seat, allowing the glass to mist. 'I have very little, thank goodness. The ancestors . . . Jung would have found plenty to go at, but I've never been particularly drawn to the idea of the collective-unconscious, race memories, all that. It *sounds* good, but . . . what do you think?'

'I'm inclined to believe it. I've got a bit in common with Moon, I suppose.'

'And you fancy her. Well, of course you do. Awfully sexy creature.'

'Yes.' Lol had been half expecting this. 'She is.'

'So what's the problem?' Dick started ticking off plus-factors on his fingers. 'You're both on your own. *I'm* her actual therapist, not you, so no ethical barriers. Do find her attractive, don't you?'

'She's beautiful.'

'But you think she doesn't fancy you – that it? Oh, I think she does, old son. I think she does.'

Lol felt awkward. 'Maybe we wouldn't be too good for each other. You don't get to laugh much around Moon.'

'Not a terrific sense of humour, no,' Dick conceded.

'Like, you want to make her happy, but you don't somehow think she'd be happy being happy.'

And that was it really: you couldn't help feeling that life with Moon was destined to end in a suicide pact.

'Lol,' Dick said, 'I realize you're a sensitive soul, but you don't particularly need to think about psychology when you're shagging someone, do you?'

'Yuk,' Jane said. 'I mean . . . *yuk*!'

'Quite.'

'I mean, it's awful, it's tragic, and everything. But it's also . . . really inconsiderate. I really think you should've walked out. Like, how were you to know these nurses weren't lying? Nobody should have to make a decision like that, with the old guy's clock running down the whole time.'

'It wasn't an actual exorcism. It wasn't much at all, in the end.'

'Sounds like that's what the older nurse wanted, though. An exorcism.'

'Possibly.' The parts Merrily hadn't mentioned included the scratching finger and other sensations. The subjective aspects.

'Face it.' Jane poured the tea. 'It's a crap deal, Mum. They send you in armed with a handful of half-assed prayers and platitudes which are supposed to cover all eventualities. You're holding a duff hand from the start.'

'Well, not—'

'It's like with these evangelical maniacs, where you like go along and you're looking a bit off-colour and in about three minutes flat they've discovered you're possessed by seventeen different demons and the next thing you're rolling around on the floor throwing up. You could really *damage* people.'

'It's a bit more disciplined than that but, yeah, I know what you mean. It *is* a minefield.'

'And it's just useless *liturgy*. Like, with all respect, what real actual practical training have you had? It's not like you've even done any meditation or yoga or anything. I mean . . . theological college? Does that even equal, say, two weeks at a respectable ashram?'

'I think it possibly does,' Merrily said, but wondering.

'But you're not really spiritually developed, are you? Not like Buddhist monks and Indian gurus and guys like that. Like, you can't – I don't know – leave your body or anything. You've just read the books. And yet they want you to mess with people's souls.'

'It's supposed to be God who does the actual messing. That is, we don't believe we have any special powers. We kind of signpost the way for the Holy Spirit.'

'You ever ask yourself, if the Holy Spirit is so ubi . . . all-over-the-place and on the ball, why does it *need* a signpost?'

'We have to invite the Holy Spirit in, you know?'

'Why?'

'Because that's one of the rules. Deep theology, flower.'

'Bollocks,' Jane murmured. 'Anyway, I wouldn't let Hunter get away with this.'

Merrily paused with the mug at her mouth. 'He's the guv'nor.'

'He's a tosser.'

'But I *will* call him. I'll have a bath and a rest and then I'll call him.'

'Maybe Rowenna could get some of the SAS cross-country guys to elbow the flash git into a deep ditch,' Jane mused. 'Muddy his fetching purple tracksuit.'

The rain was battering the barn windows, and Lol was sure there was an element of sleet to it now. But Dick was all sunshine, like his row with the boy James had never happened.

'Well, this is super.' Clasping his herbal tea to his chest. 'This is quite magnificent.'

And it was. The little barn was transformed. All the boxes had disappeared, everything put away, everything tidy. A bright coal-fire on the simple, stone hearth. Fragments of black pottery arranged on a small shelf. On the wall alongside the steps to the bedroom loft was a detailed pen-and-ink plan of, presumably, the Dinedor Iron Age community – round huts with stone bases and conical thatched roofs. Moon had made mysterious marks on it: dots and symbols – archaeologist stuff.

Ideal Homes show barn?

'You were right and we were wrong,' Dick told Moon. But he was smiling at Lol and the smile said: *I was right and you were wrong.*

Above the fireplace was a gilt-framed photograph of a smiling man leaning against a Land Rover. The man's smile was Moon's smile.

'We thought you'd be a bit, ah, cut off up here,' Dick said. 'A bit lonely? But this is your place, Moon. What are you going to do?'

'Well, I'm going back to work in the shop.' Moon wore the long grey dress, freshly washed; without mud on the hem it looked like a hostess dress. Her very long hair was in a loose, lush plait. 'For a while, anyway.'

'Playing it day by day.'

'I'm not an alcoholic, Dick.'

She didn't smile. She hadn't looked at Lol. He felt he'd betrayed her.

'What I *meant*, Moon,' Dick said, 'is that you clearly no longer feel the need to hurry – rush from one experience to another. You've been away, you've been through all kinds of changes, and now you've returned to repossess your past. *Your* past, *your* place, firm ground – it must feel wonderful.'

Moon said nothing. Dick took this as agreement, and nodded enthusiastically. It was the conclusion he wanted, the neat outcome of a very singular case. He had her all packaged up in his head: at least an article for *Psychology Today* or whatever he subscribed to. Moon was getting better. Moon was taking responsibility for herself.

So why, to Lol, had she never seemed more of an enigma? What had caused her suddenly to launch into this place like a team of industrial cleaners? As if she'd known they were coming. Or someone else? Determined that the barn should project the image of a balanced, settled academic individual.

It was a façade; it had to be.

And the picture of her smiling father disturbed him. If Dick had noticed it, he didn't comment. Lol looked closely at the photograph. When it was taken, Moon's father would have been about Denny's age – early to mid forties. He looked more like Moon than Denny did, the same smile and the same deep-sunk, glittering eyes. Something black and gnarled lay on the mantelpiece below the picture. Lol bent to examine it.

'Don't touch that!' Moon almost ran across the room, eased herself between Lol and the fireplace.

Lol stepped back. 'I'm sorry . . .'

'It's very delicate.'

'What is it?'

'I found it. It was only about ten yards from the barn. Someone had started digging out a pond some time ago and never finished it, and there was a heap of soil where the ground was turned over, and it was actually projecting – sticking out.'

She moved aside to let them see, now they realized they mustn't touch. It was knobbled and corroded, about ten inches long.

'Anyone else, if they didn't know about these things, they'd think it was just an old tractor part or something. I mean, nothing much has ever been found up here. A trench was once cut from the ramparts to the centre of the camp, and nothing much was found there except lots of black pottery and an axe-head.'

'It's a dagger,' Lol decided.

'A sword. Confirmation for me that this farm – not so much the house, but the *farm* – has been here since the Iron Age. It was waiting for me to find it. You see, now?'

'Fate,' Lol said hollowly.

'Oh no,' Moon said. 'Far less random than fate.'

'What's that mean?'

Moon shook her head. He thought she smiled.

'You could take it to a museum, have it cleaned up by experts.'

Moon was horrified. 'Nobody's going to touch it but me. I don't want the flow blocked by anyone else's vibrations.'

'Good for you, Moon,' said Dick. 'Look, we must have a good long chat.'

'Yes, but not today,' Moon said. 'My landlords are coming over for lunch. Tim and Anna Purefoy? From the farm?'

'Ah.' Dick nodded. 'Excellent. Getting to know the neighbours.'

'I'm meeting all the people who live around the hill – for my book. If I'm going to trace how the community's changed over two millennia, I have to examine its components. Quite a few of the newcomers here are very interested too. They're going to help me.'

'Terrific.' Dick looked like he wanted to pat her on the head. 'Can't wait to read it.'

Later, when Dick went to have fun reversing the Mitsubishi out of the morass in front of the barn where someone had once started to dig a pond, Moon came to stand next to Lol in the doorway.

'Don't bring him here again.'

'He'll hear you.'

'I don't care if he does. I don't want him here. He's an idiot. Denny only employed him to get the court off our backs.'

'*Your* back, Moon.'

'He's an idiot.'

'He means well.'

'Lol, If you come here again as Dick's assistant, I won't tell you anything in future. I don't need people around me I can't trust.'

The slanting rain plucked at the mud.

'I'm sorry,' Lol said. 'Do you want me to come back?'

She looked at him, smiling almost coyly. 'Only as yourself.'

As Merrily rolled gratefully into bed, the phone rang.

'Unplug it!' Jane screeched from the landing. 'Unplug it *now*! I'll get it downstairs.'

'Hello,' Merrily said. 'Ledwardine Vicarage.'

'Merrily? It's Sophie at the Bishop's office. Michael asked me to ring. We wondered if you'd be popping into town today and, if so, could you call in?'

'Well, I wasn't planning . . .' On the one hand, she very much needed to talk to the Bishop; on the other, not in this state. 'Bit tied up this morning.'

'Oh. Well, this afternoon there'll be nobody here. Better make it tomorrow, I suppose. It's just a little job – in connection with the Deliverance side of things.'

'Oh?'

'I don't imagine it's terribly urgent.'

'Good. Sophie, do all the Deliverance cases come through your office?'

'Well, it's intended that they should. I'm afraid Canon Dobbs was less organized.'

'What about the problem last night at the General Hospital?'

140

'At the hospital? *Was* there a problem?'

'So it didn't come through the office?'

'It didn't come through *me*.'

'If you weren't there, would the Bishop have handled it himself?'

'They wouldn't normally get through to the Bishop. Anyway he wasn't here last night. He was at his parents' home in the Forest of Dean. They thought his father had suffered another heart attack but it was a false alarm, I'm glad to say.'

'Oh,' Merrily said, 'good.'

'Did you have to go to the hospital, then, Merrily?'

'Yes, I did.' She gripped the phone tightly. If Hunter had been away, then who had directed the hospital to approach her? Who set her up for Denzil Joy's grisly farewell party?

'Merrily, are you all right?'

'Yes, I . . . This other job – can you tell me what that is?'

'I'm not sure I should over the phone.'

'You don't need to mention names.'

'Well, it's . . . a haunting. At a home for the elderly. Near Dorstone, out towards the Welsh border.'

'And where did *that* come from? Who told you about it?'

'It came from the new vicar of Dorstone, I believe. Michael had asked me to keep him informed of any reports of this nature, and when I mentioned it to him he said he'd like you to . . . take a crack at it, as he put it. He . . .' She hesitated. 'What he went on to say, if I'm not speaking out of turn, is that it would be a test of how committed you were.'

'Committed?'

'Frankly, he feels you're rather stalling. He'd expected a firm answer by now. When we spoke on the phone, he asked if I'd heard from you.'

'I see. So if I sidestep this haunting, or suggest the Vicar of Dorstone handles it himself, he'll take that as a no.'

'I may be wrong about that.'

Sophie was never wrong. Merrily felt she could almost see the hand of fate, grey-gloved in the half-light of the bedroom.

From the landing, Jane called out, 'For Christ's sake, Mum!'

In Merrily's head, the demonic Denzil Joy sat up in bed for the last time, tubes flying out of his nose in twin puffs of snot. Huw Owen's voice echoed over the Brecon Beacons. *'Might as well just paint a great big bullseye between your tits.'*

And, she thought, *it was Dobbs, wasn't it? It was bloody Dobbs – it has to be. Dobbs set me up.*

She felt light-headed with fatigue. She knew that later, when she awoke again, she was going to be very angry, but now the rage was still misty and distant.

So were the words she spoke, so faintly that she wasn't sure she hadn't merely thought them. 'I'll come in tomorrow then, Sophie. Ten? Ten-thirty?'

She didn't hear the reply, wasn't even aware of hanging up the phone.

There were no dreams, thank God.

FOURTEEN

The First Exorcist

She stopped at the top of the gatehouse stairs, rubbing circulation back into her hands. It seemed to have become winter overnight. The waxed jacket felt as flimsy as a bin-liner. No good, she'd have to get herself a proper coat when she had time.

When she saw the office door, she didn't know whether to laugh or cry or turn around and creep quietly away.

The white panels were adorned by a single, black gothic letter. Above it, a simple, black cross.

𝕯

The Rev. Charlie Headland was chuckling softly in her head. *'More like MI5 . . .'*

Too late to turn around and creep out. Sophie – grey suit, pearls, neat white bun, half-glasses on a chain – stood in the adjacent doorway.

'Merrily, good morning. Did you see a few specks of snow? I'm convinced I saw snow. Heavens, come up.'

'Do I have to sign in? Maybe pass through a detector?'

Sophie smiled wryly. 'Michael's specific instructions. In one respect I suppose it's rather elegant.'

'Sophie, it looks like the entrance to a bloody chapel of rest.'

'Oh.' Sophie looked put out. She *was* the Bishop's person, whoever the current bishop happened to be.

The new arrival on the office desk was an Apple Mac and a printer, and something Merrily took to be a scanner.

'Jesus,' she said. 'All I know how to do on one of these is type.'

'Don't worry,' Sophie said, a little cool now. 'I'm your secretary as well, for a while. Michael wants me to open a Deliverance database: filing and categorizing the various cases, and giving area breakdowns. He also wants me to arrange a meeting with the Director of Social Services, the Chief Executive of the Health Authority, charities like MIND – and also the police.'

Merrily flopped down behind the desk. 'What?'

'And you're to have an e-mail address, possibly a website.'

She looked into the blank computer screen as though it were a crystal ball, conjuring up Huw Owen's tired, rugged face. *'I don't want stuff letting in. A lot of bad energy's crowding the portals. I want to keep all the doors locked and the chains up . . .'*

Her new secretary stood by the window, hands linked demurely at the waist of her tweed skirt.

'Look . . . Sophie,' Merrily moistened her wind-roughened lips, 'the thing about Deliverance, it needs to be low-profile. I wouldn't go as far as to use the word "clandestine", but there's a danger of attracting time-wasters and fanatics and loonies and . . . other undesirable elements. The Bishop doesn't seem to have grasped this basic point.'

'Deliverance is getting a high priority, Merrily.' Sophie slipped into the visitor's chair. 'Look . . . I really wouldn't worry about this. Michael's a very young man to be a bishop, and he perhaps feels he's been put in place to make an impression, help push the Church firmly into the twenty-first century. He's also a very clever man, with an impeccable pedigree which he tends to underplay. Father and an uncle were both bishops . . . father-in-law's the Dean of Gloucester. Michael feels that if people are aware of the amount of work undertaken by the Deliverance ministry, they may be more inclined towards what you might call spiritual preventative medicine.'

'You mean what we used to call "Going to Church"?'

Sophie smiled wryly.

'I know,' Merrily said wearily. 'It all makes a kind of sense. I just wish there was less . . . bollocks.'

'I don't doubt that you'll cope, Merrily. You'll find the details of the Dorstone haunting on your computer, if you click on the desktop file marked *Memo*. I shall be next door if you want me.'

'Thanks.' Merrily shed her coat and switched on the computer.

And then closed the door and picked up the phone and rang Eileen Cullen at home.

'Timed it well, Merrily. Come off shift, whizz round Tesco, home to bed.' Away from the ward, Cullen's voice sounded softer. 'How are you now?'

'Bit confused.'

'Ah-ha. Well . . . what can I tell you? There's a palpable sense of relief on the ward. We laid him out – he made the scariest corpse I ever handled – then we fumigated the side ward. Too much to expect that he'd take his smell down to the mortuary with him.'

Almost immediately, Denzil's reptilian odour was in her head. Merrily stifled a cough.

'Oh, and later in the morning,' Eileen Cullen said, 'I'm told that the old man came in and said a prayer or two.'

'Old man?' Merrily tingled.

'I don't even know his name, but his collar was the right way round so nobody questions it.'

'His name is Dobbs,' Merrily said.

'Aye, that's the feller, I suppose.'

'He already knew about Denzil. Didn't he?'

'He must've. Though how he'd have found out the man was dead, I don't know. We've hardly got the time to put out a general bulletin to the clergy.'

'OK, look, let's not keep walking around each other – I'll explain. Canon Dobbs is the Diocesan Exorcist. I'm the one being set up to take over from him. He doesn't want to go, and he certainly doesn't want to be replaced by a woman. I'm coming round to thinking he set me up with Denzil last night to give me a taste of just how nasty and squalid the job could be. *And* why it's not a suitable job for a woman.'

After a moment Cullen said, 'That wasn't very nice of him then, was it?'

'Not awfully. So I'd appreciate just . . . knowing. Like, anything you can remember. Entirely off the record, Eileen.'

'Aye,' said Cullen, 'you get surgeons like that. They love to leave you holding the shit end of the stick. All right, I'll tell you what I know. He *did* know Denzil Joy. Whether this was from Denzil's life outside of hospital I wouldn't know. Probably. But he came in once – I didn't see this, I wasn't there, but Protheroe was – and they had to ask him to leave. Denzil's spitting at him, coming out with all kinds of foul stuff you don't want to be hearing from a sickbed, and it carried on that way after the priest was well out of the building. It's why we put him in solitary the past two times. Though obviously his wife lived to regret that.'

'Did anyone ask Dobbs about the incident?'

'Oh, he wouldn't talk to the likes of us – except very briefly to Protheroe. He said to let him know if we had any further trouble with Mr Joy. So, naturally, the other night, after the business with the wife, Protheroe's screaming, "Call the priest, call the priest, the man's possessed with evil." '

'And you called him?'

'I called the number she gave me and a woman answered, and I told her what it was about and she said to hang on, and then she came back and said to call the Reverend Watkins. Does that solve your problem?'

'Do you remember the phone number you rang for Dobbs?'

'Oh, I probably wrote it down and threw it away. Protheroe probably keeps it in a gold locket around her neck.'

'Well, thanks. You've been very helpful.'

'Aye.' A pause. 'How're you feeling yourself, Merrily? Like, did he do anything to you?'

'I . . . maybe.'

'I don't want to worry you,' Cullen said, 'but they say it comes back sometimes. Like the ache you get with the shingles, you know?'

'I've never had shingles.'

'Pray you never do,' Cullen said. 'Seems daft saying this to a priest, but if you ever want a chat about anything, you've got the number.'

'Thanks,' Merrily said. 'Thanks.'

She clicked on *Memo*.

STRICTLY PRIVATE AND CONFIDENTIAL

Mrs Susan Thorpe, proprietor, The Glades Residential Home, Hardwicke (between Dorstone and Hay-on-Wye) requests a discreet meeting with regard to unexplained occurrences.

Sophie's head came round the door just then, as if she'd heard the click of the mouse. 'Would you like me to call her for you? Make an appointment?'

'Just leave the number on the desk. Sophie, could you give me another bit of information?'

'It's what I'm here for, Merrily.'

'Could you tell me exactly where in the Close Canon Dobbs lives?'

Sophie removed her half-glasses. 'Ho-hum,' she said.

'The Bishop's specific instructions are to keep Dobbs and me well apart, right?'

'Michael doesn't discuss Canon Dobbs. Perhaps you could try the telephone directory?'

'Of which you know he's ex-.'

Sophie sighed. 'He moved out of the canonry when his wife died. He lives in a little terraced house in Gwynne Street.'

'That's . . .?'

'Less than fifty yards from where I sit – just down from the Christian bookshop. And I didn't tell you that.'

'Thank you.'

'I suppose you had to get this over at some stage.' Sophie refixed her glasses. 'Don't forget your haunting, will you?'

Frost-blackened plants dripped down the sides of a hanging basket next to the door. The green door needed painting. Paint was peeling from the wooden window ledge; the wood was rotting. The house itself rather let Gwynne Street down.

The street was narrow, almost like an alley, following the perimeter wall of the Bishop's Palace, and sloping downhill towards the river. The house was one of the lower ones, before they gave way to warehouses and garages near the banks of the Wye.

There was no bell, no knocker. Merrily banged on the door with a fist, which hurt and brought more paint flying off.

There was no answer. She peered in at the window. The

curtains were drawn against her. She looked around in frustration. There was no sign of another way in. Above her, the sky was tight and dark-flecked like stretched goatskin.

'Hello, Merrily. All right, luv?'

'I don't really know.'

'Oh.' Silence on the line as Huw Owen mulled this over. 'That sounds like you took on the job. I *thought* you wouldn't back out.'

'I was actually about to turn it down.' Merrily lit a cigarette, looking out of the window into the Bishop's Palace yard. 'Then a case happened.'

'Just happened, eh?' Huw said. 'Just like that. Well, what's done's done, in't it? How can I help?'

'I don't suppose any of the others've called. Charlie? Clive?'

'Never off, lass. "Do excuse me bothering you again, Huw, but I have a teensy problem, and I'm not entirely sure if it's a *weeper* or a *breather*." '

Merrily blew an accidental smoke-ring. 'So I'm the first to come crying to the headmaster.'

'I always liked you the best, anyroad, luv. Charlie and Clive'll fall on their arses sooner or later, but they won't tell *me*.'

She started to laugh, picturing him sitting placidly in his isolated, Brontë-esque rectory, like some ungroomed old wolfhound.

'Let's hear it then, lass.'

She told him about Denzil Joy. She told it simply and concisely. She missed out nothing she thought might be important. *Scritch-scratch.* And then the Dobbs link. It took over fifteen minutes, and it brought everything back, and she felt unclean again.

'My,' Huw said, 'that's a foxy one, in't it?'

'What d'you think?'

'Could be a few things. Could be just a very nasty little man. Or it could be a *carrier.*'

'A carrier. Did you tell us about carriers?'

'Happen I forgot.'

'Meaning you deliberately forgot. Would *carriers* be the people who pick up *hitchhikers*?'

'You're not daft, Merrily. I said that, din't I? Provable carriers are . . . not that common. And not easy to diagnose. And they can lead to a lot of hysteria of the fundamentalist type. You know, if one bloke's got it, it must be contagious? And then you get these dubious mass-exorcisms, everybody rolling around and clutching their guts.'

'Just one man,' Merrily said, 'so far.'

'That's good to know. Well, a carrier is usually a nasty person who attracts more nastiness to him – like iron filings to a magnet. Usually there's a bit of a sexual kink. An overly powerful sex-drive and probably not bright. Not a lot up top, too much down below.'

'Anything I need to do now he's gone?'

'To make sure he don't come back? Sounds like Mr Dobbs has done it. Not going quietly into that good night, is he?'

'Clearly not.'

'Might not work, mind. That's the big irony with Deliverance – half the time it don't work. But in somewhere like a hospital it'll fade or get consumed by all the rest of the pervading anguish. You could happen do a protection on yourself periodically. Oh, and leave off sex for a week.'

'Gosh, Huw, that's going to be a tall order.'

'Oh dear,' Huw said. 'So you're still on your own, eh? What a bloody waste. God hates waste.'

Before lunch, Merrily made an appointment to meet Mrs Susan Thorpe at The Glades Residential Home at eleven

o'clock the following morning. There must have been somebody in the room who didn't know about this issue, because
Mrs Thorpe kept addressing her as if she were Rentokil
coming to deal with an infestation of woodworm.

Sophie was meeting a friend for lunch at The Green
Dragon. Merrily decided to see what was on offer at the café
inside All Saints Church: a fairly ingenious idea for getting
bums on pews or at least *close* to pews.

But first – *Sod it, I'm not walking away from this* – she
slipped round the wall and back into Gwynne Street.

There was a weak, cream-coloured sun now over Broad
Street, but Gwynne Street was still in shadow. The only point
of light was in the middle of Dobbs's flaking green door.

It turned out to be a slender white envelope trapped by a
corner in the letterbox flap. As she raised a fist to knock on
the door and wondered if she ought to push the envelope
through, she saw the name typed on the front:

                    Mrs M Watkins

She caught a movement at an upstairs window and glanced
up, saw a curtain quiver. He was there! The old bastard had
been in the whole time. He'd watched her standing here
knocking more paint from his door.

And now he'd left her a letter.

The street was deserted: no cars, no people, no voices. She
felt like smashing Dobbs's window. Instead she snatched the
envelope out of the box and walked away and didn't look
back.

She walked quickly out of Gwynne Street, past the
Christian bookshop and the Tourist Information Shop, and
round the corner into King Street, where she stood at the
kerb and tore open the envelope. She hoped it was a threat,
something abusive.

There was a single sheet of notepaper folded inside. In the centre, a single line of type:

The first exorcist was Jesus Christ.

This was all it said.

FIFTEEN

Male Thing

The woman behind the counter was, by any standards, drop-dead gorgeous. Worse still, kind of pale and mysterious and distant, with hair you could trip over.

A woollen scarf masking her lower face, Jane watched from outside the shop window. Saturday morning: bright enough to bring thousands of shoppers into Hereford from all over the county and from large areas of Wales; cold enough for there still to be condensation on the windows, even in sheltered Church Street.

Jane had come in on the early bus, the *only* bus out of Ledwardine on a Saturday. At half-twelve, Rowenna was picking her up outside the Library. It was Psychic Fair day.

Which left her a couple of hours to kill. It was inevitable she'd wind up here at some point.

She almost wished she hadn't; this was *so* awful. Lol had written songs about creatures like this. And now he lived above the same shop. Maybe during the lunch hour the woman would weave her languorous way up some archaic spiral staircase, and he'd be waiting for her up on the landing, where they'd start undressing each other before making their frenzied . . .

'Jane?'

Damn. He must have come out of a side entrance. She must remain cool, show no surprise.

'So that's her, is it, Lol?'

'Who?'

He was shivering in his thin, faded sweatshirt. His hair needed attention; it had never looked the same since he'd cut it off at the back and lost the ponytail. Made him look too grown-up, almost like a man of thirty-eight.

'Moon?' Jane lowered her scarf. Inside the shop, the woman saw them looking at her and smiled absently, arranging a display of CDs on the counter. 'She's quite ordinary-looking, isn't she?'

'Almost plain,' Lol said. 'Jane, how much would it cost to make you go away and stop embarrassing me?'

'More than you've got on you. Much more.'

'How about a cappuccino?'

'Yeah, that'll do,' Jane said.

It was set in deep countryside, a kind of manor house, rambling but not very old, maybe early nineteenth-century. Squat gateposts with plain stone balls on top, and a notice in the entrance – THE GLADES RESIDENTIAL HOME – stencilled over a painted purple hill with the sun above it. A bright yellow sun with no suggestion of it setting, which would have been the wrong image altogether.

There was a small car park in front, with a sweeping view of the Radnor hills, but a woman appeared around the side of the house and beckoned her to drive closer to her.

Merrily followed the drive around to a brick double-garage and parked in front of it, the woman hurrying after her.

'You're wearing your . . . uniform,' she said in a loud, dismayed whisper, when Merrily got out of the car. 'I'm sorry, I should have emphasized the need for discretion.'

Merrily smiled. 'Don't worry about that.' *Don't worry yet; we may not even paste your case on the Deliverance website.*

'It's all been very difficult,' the woman said. 'We didn't want to call in the local vicar – *far* too close – so the obvious person was Mr Dobbs, but then . . . such a bombshell – we won't talk about that. I'm Susan Thorpe. We'll go in this way.'

She was a big woman, dark blonde hair pushed under a wide, practical hairslide. She led Merrily through a small back door, down a short drab passage and into what was clearly her private sitting room: very untidy.

'Have a seat. Throw those magazines on the floor. I've sent for some coffee, is that all right? God, I didn't need this, I really didn't *need* this. Everything comes at once, don't you find that? Now I discover I have to find a room for my mother.'

'Must be a problem, if you run a home like this and your mother gets to the age—'

'Oh, it's not like that. Mother's fitter than me. She's lost her job, that's all, *and* her home – she was someone's house-keeper. I'm sorry, I'm afraid I've forgotten your name.'

'Merrily Watkins.'

'Merrily. And you're the new diocesan exorcist. I was in quite a quandary, Merrily, so I rang the Diocese. I said, "Could you send *anybody* but Dobbs." '

Dobbs? Merrily still had his one-liner in her bag: *The first exorcist was Jesus Christ*. Hence, Jesus must be our role model, and Jesus was not a woman. 'Why didn't you want Canon Dobbs?'

'This problem . . . I was very loath at first to think it *was* a problem – your kind of problem, anyway. Old people can be such *delinquents*. They'll break a teapot because they don't like the colour, wet the bed because they don't like the sheets.'

'This is a *volatile* . . . er, poltergeist phenomenon?'

'Oh no, the point I was making is that, when one of the

staff complains of strange things happening, I immediately suspect one or other of the residents. In this case, neither I nor – so far, thank God – any of the residents have seen or heard a thing.'

'So who has?' Merrily still hadn't received an answer to her question about Dobbs. Was this another of his set-ups, another attempt to show her why she, as a woman, was unfit to follow in the footsteps of Jesus?

'Chambermaids,' said Mrs Thorpe. 'Well, domestic care-workers, actually, but we do try to make it seem like a hotel for the sake of the residents, so we call them chambermaids. The other week, one simply gave in her notice – or rather sent it by post, having failed to return after a weekend away. Gave no explanation other than "personal reasons". It was only then that my assistant manager told me the woman had rushed downstairs one evening white as a sheet and said she wasn't going up *there* again.'

'Where?'

'To the third floor.'

Merrily tensed, thinking of her own third-floor problem, currently in remission, at the vicarage. 'Did she elaborate?'

'No, as I say, she simply left and we thought no more about it and took on a replacement, a local woman who didn't want to live in but was prepared to work nights. Well, at least *she* couldn't just bugger off without an explanation.'

'She's had the same experience?'

'We presume it was the same. Do you want to talk to her?'

'If that's possible.'

'She'll be coming in with the coffee in a minute.' Mrs Thorpe pulled a half-crushed cigarette packet from between the sofa cushions. 'Does smoke interfere with whatever it is you do?'

'I hope not. Have one of mine.'

'I'm terrible sorry – with all the persecution these days,

one assumes other people don't smoke. Have you met Canon Dobbs?'

'Kind of.'

'He's going out of his mind, you know.'

'Oh?'

'Always been a very, very strange man, but it's been down-hill all the way for the past year. The man ought to be in a . . . well, a place like this, I suppose. Not this one, though.'

'So you know him quite well then.'

Susan Thorpe lit up and coughed fiercely. 'Sorry, thought I told you: my mother was his housekeeper.'

'Dobbs's housekeeper? In Hereford?'

'For five years. When his wife died he moved out of his canonry with about twenty thousand books. Bought two houses in a nearby terrace, one for the housekeeper – and more books, of course.'

'This is in Gwynne Street?'

'That's it. Quite a nice place to live if you like cities. Mother rather wondered if he might do the decent thing and leave it to her when he shuffled off his mortal coil, but then, a couple of days ago, absolutely out of the blue, he just tells her to go, leave. Gives her five thousand quid and instruc-tions to be out by the weekend – that's today. "Why?" she says, utterly dumbfounded. "What have I *done* to you?" "Nothing," he says. "Don't ask questions, just leave, and thank you very much." What d'you make of that?'

'Weird,' Merrily said. 'I—'

'*I don't understand . . . What have I been doing wrong?*' She heard the words, with their long, cathedral echo, saw a woman of about sixty, distressed, walking away in her sensible boots, her tweed coat, her . . .

'Mrs Thorpe, does your mother ever wear a green velvet hat, sort of Tudor-looking?'

'*Go away. Go away*,' Canon Dobbs had hissed. '*I can't possibly discuss this here.*'

Oh my God, Jane thought. *They are. They really are. An item!*

In the corner café, she and Lol had a slab of chocolate fudge cake each, which they had to take turns in forking up because the table had one leg shorter than the other three.

'So, like, this is serious, right? You and Moon.'

'We're just . . .'

'Good friends?'

'Kind of.' He seemed uncomfortable discussing Moon. She must be a good ten years younger. Not that that mattered, of course. Jane was a good *twenty* years younger than Lol, and she quite . . .

Anyway.

'So you're kind of looking after her flat here, while she's doing up this barn?'

'Sort of. Her family came from Dinedor Hill and she's always been keen to move back. Er . . . how's your mum?'

'Oh, you remember her? How *sweet*. She's OK. In fact she's actually working a couple of days a week out of an office just a few hundred yards from here.'

'Really?' He looked up.

'In the Bishop's Palace gatehouse. I haven't been there yet, but I gather it's cool.'

'What's she doing there?'

'*Not* so cool. She's been appointed Deliverance minister. You know – like used to be called exorcist? Like in that film where the kid's head does a complete circle while she's throwing up green bile and masturbating with a crucifix? Mum now gets to deal with people like that. Only, of course, there aren't many people like that, not in these parts – which is why it's such a dodgy job.'

Lol put down his cake fork. He looked concerned. 'Why would she want to do it?'

'Because she thinks the Church should be in a position to give advice on the paranormal, and there was nobody around to give *her* advice when she needed it.'

'I remember.'

'The question you should be asking is why would *they* want her to do that? And *I* think it's to put a pretty face on a fairly nasty, reactionary business. Like, for instance, they'd say that the reason there isn't much about ghosts in the Bible is that God doesn't want us to mess with ghosts, or study our own inner consciousness, that kind of thing. God just wants us to toddle off to church on a Sunday, otherwise keep our noses out.'

'That wouldn't necessarily be bad advice for everybody,' Lol said, and she could sense he was thinking about something in particular.

'That's the wimp's attitude, Mr Robinson.'

'Absolutely. And somebody's who's been banged up with mad people, and even madder psychiatrists.'

'So does that mean you'll be avoiding Mum like the plague?'

'Oh that's . . . not a problem. I've had the plague.'

What was on his mind? Did he still have feelings for Mum, despite the exquisite Moon? Or maybe she wasn't such a trophy.

'Lol?'

'Mmm?'

'Something bothering you?'

'Er . . .' Lol ate the last bit of his fudge cake. 'In the film – with the kid's head spinning round and the green bile and the crucifix? All that doesn't happen simultaneously.'

'What are you on about?'

'Those're completely different scenes – in the film.'

'Thank you, Lol,' Jane said, annoyed with him now. 'I'll tell Mum. She'll be ever so reassured.'

The care assistant's name was Helen Matthews. She lived in Hay-on-Wye, about five miles away. She was about thirty, had two young children, seemed balanced, reliable. 'It's the kids I worry about,' she said, and Merrily was reminded of the poor woman in the Deliverance Study Group video, who'd said something similar. 'I wouldn't want to go taking anything back to them, see.'

Despite having dependants and an iffy husband, the woman in the video had still killed herself – clear evidence that paranormal events could drastically affect a person's mental equilibrium.

Not a problem here. Merrily felt on relatively firm ground with this one.

'From what you say, this is what we call an *imprint*, and it usually belongs to a place. It won't follow you. It can't get into you. You can't take it away. It's like a colour-slide projected on a wall.'

'Mrs Watkins . . .' Helen Matthews was at the edge of the sofa. She wore a white coat, her short black hair was tied back, and her voice shook. 'You can tell yourself how it won't harm you, how it isn't really there, but when you're on your own in an upstairs passage and it's late at night and all the doors are shut and the lights are turned down and you *know* that . . . that something is following you, and you finally make . . . make yourself turn round, to reassure yourself there's nothing there . . . and there is . . . *There is.*'

She shuddered so violently it was almost a convulsion. She held on to the sofa, near tears. Even Susan Thorpe looked unnerved.

'OK,' Merrily said gently. 'Let's just be sure about this.

You say all the doors were closed and the lights were dimmed. Is it possible one of the doors opened and —'

'No! Definitely not. And if it was . . . Well, they're all old ladies. There are only old ladies here at present. This was a *man*. Or at least a male . . . a male *thing*.'

'What did he look like?'

'He looked . . .' Helen lost it. 'He looked like a bloody *ghost*. He walked out of the wall.'

'Could you see his face?'

'I think he had a moustache. And I think he was wearing a suit. Like in the old black-and-white films: double-breasted, wide shoulders sort of thing.'

Merrily glanced at Susan Thorpe, who shook her head.

'Description like that, it could have been anyone who lived here over the past three-quarters of a century. We've only been here four years – moved from Hampshire to be near my mother. I mean, there were no old photo albums lying around the place, and it was a guesthouse before we came. It could be anybody.'

'Are there any stories about the house? You're fairly local, Helen. Are there any . . . I don't really know what I'm looking for.'

'Murders? Suicides? I don't know, but I could ask around in Hay.'

'Christ's sake, don't do that!' Susan Thorpe rose up. 'I know what it's like in Hay. It'll be all over the town in no time. This is a business we're running here. Seven jobs depend on us, so let's not get hysterical. So far, we've managed to conceal it from the residents, let's keep it that way. And anyway, *we* haven't seen anything, and no residents have reported anything in the past four years. Why should this . . . thing start to appear now?'

'We believe imprints and place-memories can be activated

after years and years,' Merrily said. 'Sometimes it's a result of an emotional crisis or a disturbance.'

'Absolutely not! Nothing like that here at all.'

'You said yourself that old people can behave like delinquents. Sometimes mental instability, senile dementia . . .'

'Any signs of dementia, they have to go, I'm afraid. We aren't a nursing home. And the only signs of hysteria have been . . . well, not you, Helen, but certainly your predecessor . . .'

'*You* didn't see it,' Helen said quietly. 'Have you ever seen one, Mrs Watkins?'

'Possibly. Put it this way, I know what it feels like. I know how frightening it is. But I don't want to overreact either. I don't plan to squirt holy water all over the place. What I'd like to do is go up there now, with both of you, and say a few prayers.'

Susan Thorpe sat up. 'Aloud?'

'Of course, aloud.'

'Oh no, we can't have that. Some of the residents will be in their rooms. They'll hear you.'

Merrily sighed.

'I think it's a good idea,' Helen Matthews said. '*I'll* come.'

'I'm sorry.' Susan Thorpe stood up, adjusted her hairslide. 'I can't have it. Can't you do it outside – out of earshot? God's everywhere, isn't He? Why can't you go outside?'

'I could, but I don't think that would have any effect.'

Helen said, 'If *I've* seen it, Mrs Thorpe, it's only a matter of time before one of the old ladies does. What if someone has a heart attack?'

Merrily thought of the video again, and what Huw had said. *Bottom line is that our man in Northampton should not have left before administering a proper blessing, leaving her in a state of calm, feeling protected.* Yes, suppose someone *did* have a heart attack?

'God,' Susan Thorpe breathed, 'this is getting beyond a joke.'

'It never is a joke,' Merrily said. 'I'm starting to realize that.'

'The problem is finding a time when that passage and all the rooms off it are empty. Look, all right . . . most of the residents totter off to Hardwicke Church on a Sunday morning, as people of that age tend to. What are you doing tomorrow morning?'

'I'm going to my church, Susan. I'm a vicar.'

'Oh.' Susan Thorpe was unembarrassed. 'You don't do this sort of thing full-time then?' Like this diminished Merrily – a part-timer. Susan became agitated. 'Well, look . . . look, there's going to be a party. One of the residents is a hundred years old; we're having a small *soirée* for her. I can tell you, old people *never* miss a party. Suppose, while it was on, we could smuggle you upstairs and you could do your little ceremony? You do work at night?'

'Your mother will be here then, I suppose.'

'I should think.'

'I'll see what I can do,' Merrily said.

It would be very interesting to talk to Mrs Thorpe's mother. Five thousand quid, and instructions to be out by the weekend? Either Dobbs really was going out of his mind, or there was something very odd here. She had to go carefully, though: mustn't appear to be checking on him. Casually running into the former housekeeper while processing an *imprint* . . . that would do fine.

As she left The Glades, Merrily saw that it was snowing lightly out of a sky like stone. Winter deftly gatecrashing autumn's mournful party.

SIXTEEN

Real Stuff

The stall which made Jane laugh the most was the one selling something called:

The Circlet of Selene

It looked like three strands of copper wire bound together into a bangle or a necklet and secured by small curtain rings. The wording was a bit careful. It didn't actually promise you more energy, a better night's sleep and a dynamic sex life; it claimed, however, that many people had *found* that all this had *come about* after *only three weeks* of wearing the Circlet of Selene. Which cost a mere £12.75 for the bangle or £17.75 for the necklet, neither of which must have cost more than 75p to produce.

Still, people were buying them – women mostly. Well, ninety per cent of the punters here were women, in fact. The totty-quotient was pretty bloody lamentable, especially in the marquee which had been erected in a field behind the pub. Most of the blokes had stayed in the bar, as blokes were wont to do, and even that wasn't exactly crowded with intriguing, dark-eyed, gipsy-looking guys.

The marquee housed most of the stalls – crystals, incense-burners, cosmic jewellery – though it was far too cold a day for a marquee. You'd think the weather situation might have been foreseen, given the number of self-styled psychics and seers on the premises. Most had clearly taken cover in the pub, where it was warmer, but Jane hadn't felt drawn to consult any of them; they were probably all a bit pricey, too.

'Taste-lapse.' She sipped muddy coffee from a plastic cup. 'Serious, serious taste-lapse, Rowenna.'

They were in a cold corner behind a trestle table displaying lurid healing crystals and supervised by a gross middle-aged couple in matching bobble-hats. Tape-loop relaxation music was trickling out of little speakers, and it got on your nerves.

'I'm sorry.' Rowenna looked around. 'The last one I went to wasn't this bad, really. Oh, there's Kirlian Photography over there. You could have your aura photographed.'

'You ever have yours done?'

'Once. I got a picture of my hand with what looked like little flames coming out of the fingertips.'

'What does it prove?'

'That you've got an aura.'

'If you didn't have an aura you'd be dead, wouldn't you?'

'I'm glad I can't see yours today,' Rowenna said. 'It'd be all dark and negative. You having problems on the domestic front or something?'

'Not to speak of.'

'You can speak to me of anything at all, kitten.' Rowenna touched the tip of Jane's nose with a gloved forefinger. Her floaty red hair was topped by a black velvet beret. The coat she wore just had to be cashmere. She looked far too cool and upmarket for this shoddy bazaar.

'Well, I was talking to this bloke,' Jane said.

'Bloke?'

'A bloke I was sure was seriously into Mum at one time, and—'

'Oh, your mum. How do you mean *into*?'

'Well, not *into* – like not in the fullest sense. I just had it in mind that they'd be good together. He's quite insecure and vulnerable, but also kind of cool. He was a musician and songwriter when he was young – *too* young maybe – and he got led astray and into drugs, and wound up in a mental hospital.'

'The way you do.'

'It's surprising how easily that can happen. Anyway, I don't like guys who are too secure and full of themselves, do you? Like, a certain degree of pathos can be kind of sexy.'

Rowenna looked unimpressed by this. The sound of slow waves breaking on rocks cascaded serenely out of the speakers – which sounded pretty naff in a damp tent in a field near Leominster.

'So I was telling Lol that Mum was now an exorcist, like in that film where the kid gets possessed and spews green bile everywhere, and how there was no call for dealing with stuff like that around here. But like . . . I mean there is, you know? When you think about it, it's really like that. And, whereas in that film you had these heavy-duty, case-hardened Jesuit priests and even *they* couldn't handle it . . .'

' "Come into me . . . come into me," ' Rowenna intoned. 'And then he crashes out of the window to his death. What do you mean, it's really like that?'

'She had this mega-nasty job,' Jane said soberly. 'Nightmare stuff – and, like, no warning, you know?'

'I don't actually believe you.'

'That's all right, I'm not supposed to talk about it anyway.'

'All right, if you tell me I'll buy you a Circlet of Selene.'

'Not good enough. You have to promise never ever to buy me a Circlet of Selene.' It was probably OK to talk about this one, with him being dead and everything. 'All right. Guy in the hospital – this really awful rapist kind of slimeball, gets off on degrading women, and he's dying, OK?'

'OK by me,' said Rowenna.

'But he can't let go of his abiding obsession. You can see it glistening on his skin, like grease.' Jane shivered with a warped sort of pleasure. 'Like, she didn't tell me *all* of this, but I put it together. Anyway, the nurses, they're all like really shit-scared of this pervert, because he's got this totally tainted aura.'

'What was his name?'

'Mr Joy. Isn't that excellent?'

'You're embroidering this.'

'I so am *not*! His name was Denzil Joy, he was in the Watkins Ward, right up at the top of the hospital where it's old and spooky, and the nurses were genuinely scared of him. Takes a lot to scare nurses, all the stuff they've seen.'

'What did he do?'

'She wouldn't say, but I could tell she was still, like, trembling with revulsion hours later. Heavy trauma scenario. What I think it was . . . was that this man could like make you feel like you'd been raped; he could invade your body just by thinking about what he wanted to do to you. And that got all boiled together with the sickness and the frustration inside him. The nurses are convinced he was possessed.'

'Creepy.'

'The hell with creepy – this was bloody dangerous, if you ask me. And the Bishop just sends her in to sort out this evil scumbag without a second thought, on account of she's like a priest and priests know what to do. But – seriously – is she equipped for this? Does she know what she's doing? Does she hell. Occult-wise, she's probably as naive as all these idiots cooing over the frigging Circlet of Selene. Like, I feel there's probably a lot I could tell her – to help, you know – but would she listen?'

'Jane,' Rowenna said, 'listen to me. You cannot change other people – only yourself. In the end, the winners in this life are the people who go in with their eyes open and say: I'm not going to let God or Nature or the Bishop of Hereford or whoever fuck about with me. *I'm* going to call the shots.'

'Right,' Jane said. 'I suppose that's right.'

'And it's great if you can actually see that while you're still young enough to do something about it – like us, you know?'

And, of course, Jane knew it *was* right. When someone like Rowenna, who was just that bit older and a cool person too, said *this* is right, it conferred a kind of responsibility. You felt you had to do something about it.

She tossed her paper cup into a litter bucket. 'Let's get out of this amusement arcade.'

'Good idea,' said Rowenna. 'Go find the real stuff.'

'Huh?'

'This is just a front, isn't it? The real heavy-duty clairvoyants are in little back rooms in the pub.'

'You want to consult a clairvoyant?'

'Check them out, anyway – see if they're genuine. If they're not, it'll just be a laugh.'

'Cost an arm and a leg,' Jane said doubtfully.

'They usually leave the amount up to you. Hey . . .' Tenderly, Rowenna bent and stroked back Jane's hair and peered into her eyes. 'You're not apprehensive, are you?'

'Christ, no,' said Jane. 'Let's go for it.'

Twice Lol had been down to the shop. Once to see if Moon wanted any help; but she explained that running a record shop wasn't as easy as he might think, and shooed him away. The second time to see what she was doing for lunch; Moon had brought along two apples and a banana.

Moon insisted she was fine. Dick Lyden also said Moon was fine. If Dick was in two minds about anyone it was probably Lol, who'd claimed that Moon was living in squalor in the barn – until Dick had seen the place looking like a suburban villa, and Moon poised like she was ready to serve the canapés.

Denny also seemed a little happier when he called in, appearing at the door of the flat wearing a plaid overcoat and a big hat with a red feather, halfway to a smile.

'She's looking almost healthy,' he conceded. 'Is there something I don't know?'

Lol shrugged. What could he say to him without reference to ghosts or disembowelled crows?

'Listen, I don't mind.' Denny spread himself in the arm-chair. 'I think it's good. I'm glad, all right?'

'She's working on her book.'

'Book? Oh.' Denny looked uninterested, a touch pained. 'That's not really gonna happen, is it?'

'*Does* your family go all the way back to the Iron Age?'

Denny's smile shut down altogether. 'Could be.'

'Is it a Celtic name, Moon?'

'I really don't know. We weren't always called Moon. A daughter inherited the farm back in the eighteenth century, married a bloke called Moon. Look . . .' Denny pulled on his earring. 'There's a little something you gotta help me with here, mate.'

'Unblocking drains is not my responsibility. You are the landlord, Dennis.'

'Nothing that simple, little friend. This is a *really* dis-tasteful job. Dick Lyden fill you in about his kid? This Bishop-for-a-day crap – the kid refusing to play along?'

Lol nodded warily. 'If they'd told me at sixteen I'd been picked for Boy Bishop, I'd've tried to get expelled first.'

'This kid attends the Cathedral School,' Denny said. 'So his father pays good money for him to be publicly humiliated in front of his peers.'

Lol brought two lagers from the fridge, as Denny spelled it

out. Dick, it seemed, had resorted to bribery: if the boy James swallowed his cool for just a day, Dick would finance a professionally produced CD by James and his rock band.

Lol winced. 'What are they called?'

'Tuneless Little Twats with Fender Strats. Fuck knows, does it matter? I told him you'd do it, Lol.'

'Me?'

'Produce them. You'll get paid, of course.'

'Sod off.'

'Laurence, we're talking EP-length, that's all. Four tracks – two days' work, max. A hundred copies, which is where I make *my* profit. It's common enough these days – how I keep the studio up and running. I said you'd do it. James *knows* your stuff. James even *likes* your stuff.'

'Suppose I hate *his* stuff?'

'Good boy,' said Denny, 'I appreciate this. I said we'd give their material a listen tomorrow afternoon, OK? Good. And I'm glad about Kathy and you. I am really *glad*. God knows, I would do anything, *give* anything to get her away from there. Meanwhile, if she's not alone, that's the best thing I could hope for under the circumstances.'

Lol went still. 'What has she said?'

'I'm her brother,' Denny said. 'She doesn't have to say anything to me.'

Later, after Denny had gone, it started to snow a little.

Lol stood by the window in the dark, looking down into lamplit Church Street/Capuchin Lane, the centuries seeping away along with the colours of the day. It was snowing briskly, all the shops had closed, most of the people had gone. If he leaned into the top corner of the window he could see the blackening tower of the Cathedral. Below him, a young guy guided a young woman gently into a shallow doorway and they embraced.

Lol thought of Moon in her dusty white nightdress.
'*If she's not alone . . .*'

'Fucking hell, I didn't expect that.' Rowenna had gone in first, and when she came out she raised her eyebrows, pulled Jane over to the door.

'She was good?'

'She *was*, actually.'

'How much?'

'Twenty. I paid for you as well.'

'There was no need for that. I'm not—'

'Forget it. Go on, don't keep her waiting. She might hang a curse on you.'

'Shit,' said Jane.

'That was a joke.'

'Sure.'

She didn't, to be honest, like fortune-tellers one bit, and for the very reasons Rowenna had put to her earlier. Suppose the woman told her she was going to die soon? Or that Mum was? Not that they ever did; they just looked at you sadly from under their headscarves and said: *Take your money back, dearie. All of a sudden I'm not feeling too well . . .* And that was when you knew they were genuine and your card was marked.

'Go on,' Rowenna hissed.

The booth was just an alcove in the public bar with a wicker screen set up to hide it.

Angela. Tarot Readings.

Rowenna had opted for her because, like she'd said, she herself knew a bit about the tarot, so would be able to tell if Angela was the real McCoy.

Oh, shit. Another thing Jane didn't like was the way you

were kind of putting yourself and your future in someone else's hands. Whatever they wanted to tell you, it would stay with you, colour your dreams, frame your nightmares. *Not* Jane's idea of New Age, which was about self-exploration – wasn't it?

'Jane . . .'

'Yeah, OK.'

No alternative, no way out. Jane squeezed behind the partition.

SEVENTEEN

Wise Women

Angela smiled.

'You look worried,' she said. 'Why is that?'

'I'm not worried.'

'There's no need to be. Have you consulted the tarot before?'

'Once or twice,' Jane lied.

Angela smiled. She was sitting at a long pub table of scratched mahogany with wrought-iron legs. Behind her was a narrow window of frosted glass; the light it shed was cold and grey. It was going rapidly dark out there.

Angela's hands were already in motion, spreading the cards and then gathering them together. Her hands were slender and supple; there were no rings. Suddenly she pushed the full pack in front of Jane.

'Pick them up.'

'Me?'

Angela nodded. She was not what Jane had been expecting: no headscarf, no big brass earrings. Jane saw a long oval face and mid-length ash-blonde hair. She wore a pale linen suit which seemed no more suited to this event than Rowenna's cashmere. Jane reached out for the cards.

'And shuffle them.'

They were quite big cards and Jane was clumsy. Cards kept sliding out as she tried to mix them up. 'Sorry.'

'It's all right, you're doing fine. Now cut the pack.'

Angela's voice was the most unexpected thing. It was warm and surprisingly cultured.

Jane cut the cards and left them in two piles.

'What I want you to understand,' Angela said, 'is that the cards are merely an aid. They form a psychic link between us.' She put the pack together and then lifted her hand sharply as though it had given her an electric shock.

'Oh!'

'What's wrong?'

'Oh, Jane . . .'

Christ, what's she seen?

Jane said nervously, 'How do you know my name?'

'I'm psychic.' Angela laughed lightly. 'No, your friend told me, of course.'

'What else did she tell you?'

'Well, she certainly didn't tell me how powerful you were. Has no one told you that before?' Angela began to lay out the cards, one on top of another.

'Not that I recall.' Ah. Right. She was beginning to get the picture now.

'They will,' Angela said with calm certainty.

Oh, sure. I wonder how many other people you said that to today. Jane nodded and said nothing. Now she knew it was a scam, she was no longer worried. Did Rowenna realize it was a scam? Of course she did. When she came out she'd just been taking the piss, picking up on Jane's manifest trepidation.

Angela had the cards laid out in a neat semicircle. They were beautifully coloured, and Jane started looking for the ones she'd seen pictures of on the covers of mystery novels: *Death, The Devil, The Hanged Man, The Last Judgement.* But none of these was obvious in the dim light; all the designs were unfamiliar.

Angela placed one card face-down below the others, con-

templated it for a moment and then turned it over to reveal a
faintly smiling woman in a long white robe, sitting on some
sort of throne with mystical symbols and artefacts all around
her. There were lights on in the pub, but somehow they
didn't penetrate into this alcove, or at least not as far as
Angela.

'Tell me something, Jane. What do you know of your
ancestors?'

'Sorry?'

'I mean, are you aware of – how can I put this? – wise
women, in your family?'

'I guess that depends on what you mean by wise.'

'I'm picking up a . . . I suppose you would say a tradition.
I feel . . . I believe you have much to inherit. Whether it's
immediate ancestry or something further back, it's hard to
say, but it's there. It came up immediately, no mistaking it at
all. So I double-checked and the cards are reinforcing it.
There's a very strong tradition here.'

Mum? Does she mean Mum? Jane found herself holding her
breath.

'Do you know what I'm talking about?'

'Well . . . maybe.' Mum had sometimes talked of experiences she'd had in churches, visions of a cosmic benevolence
in blue and gold, the feeling that she really had to—

Don't tell her what Mum is!

Astonishingly, Angela held up a hand. 'No, you don't have
to explain – as long as you understand.'

'Yeah.' Jane breathed out. *Jesus Christ.*

Angela was gazing intently at the cards, her attention
locked on the layout. She was absolutely still, as though she
and the cards were encased in glass. Eventually, without
looking up, she said, 'It's a big, big responsibility.'

'Oh.'

'It needs to be nurtured.' Angela turned over two more

cards which seemed to be in conjunction. 'Ah, now . . . there's been a gap in your life, I think. Someone missing. Would you . . .? Do you perhaps have just the one parent?'

'Yes,' Jane said awed. 'How did you . . .?'

'I don't think that's been such a big handicap for you as it might have been for others. You have reserves of emotional and psychic energy which have been sustaining you. But now that reservoir of psychic energy ought to be plumbed, or it may overflow. That can cause problems.'

'How do you mean?' Jane felt a slow excitement burning somewhere down in her abdomen. She looked at Angela's half-shadowed face and saw intelligence there. And beauty too – fine bones. Angela must be over fifty but Jane thought men would find her awfully sexy.

'Jane, I don't want to alarm you, but if one is given a talent and one fails to develop it, or allows powerful energy to go its own way, it can become misdirected and cause all sorts of problems, physical and mental – chronic ailments, nervous trouble. Quite a lot of people in hospitals and mental institutions are simply people who have failed to recognize and channel certain energies.'

Angela looked up suddenly. Jane saw her eyes clearly for the first time; they were like chips of flint. She was serious about this. She was dead serious.

She said faintly, 'What does that mean?'

Angela reached over and touched her fingers. 'Oh, I'm sorry. Please don't worry. Sometimes I'm concentrating so hard I say the first things that come into my head. It's just so rare that I get anything as clear and specific as this . . . I'm probably getting carried away.'

'No, please go on.'

'I don't think so.' Angela swept all the cards together. 'I've been overloading you with my own impressions, and that's not a good thing to do. Let's relax a moment and I'll tell you about some less far-reaching aspects of your life.'

She asked Jane to shuffle and cut the pack again, then did a couple of smaller layouts and told Jane a few things about herself and her future which were more in line with the stuff you expected to hear. Well, a bit more *intimate* perhaps . . . like that she was a virgin but wouldn't be for long. That she would have more than one serious lover before she was twenty.

Jane smiled. At one time she'd have been fairly excited about that, not to say relieved, but right now it didn't seem as vital.

Angela told her that she was extremely intelligent and could have her pick of careers, but she might feel herself drawn towards communications or even performance art.

Cool.

But her main choices – Angela sighed, like she'd tried to get away from this but couldn't – would be in the spiritual realm. Other levels of existence were already becoming accessible to her.

'Other planes,' Angela said, 'other spheres. Someone who has gone before has opened the way. Does that make any sense to you?'

Jane thought at once of her old friend, the late Miss Lucy Devenish, writer of children's stories and proprietor of the magical giftshop called Ledwardine Lore, who had introduced her to rural mysteries and the mystical poetry of Thomas Traherne. And showed her that spirituality was a shining crystal, of which Christianity was only one face.

'What . . .?' Jane found it hard to speak, her mouth was so dry. 'What do you think I should do?'

'Don't know. It's not for me to say. This is a very personal issue.'

'You can't just leave it like that. I mean, I could buy books and things, but I already do that.'

Angela gathered up the cards. 'Have you had any personal experiences which have mystified you?'

'Maybe. Like, there was this time I kind of fell asleep in a field, and when I awoke I felt as though I'd been someone else. It's like really hard to explain, but—'

'Don't tell me. These are messages for you alone. Look, Jane, what I'm going to do is give you a telephone number. Not mine, because I don't think you should be entirely influenced by one person or feel that you're being pressed from one direction.'

Angela reached down to a handbag on the floor and pulled out a notepad and a pen. Jane felt a welling excitement and also a small, fizzing trepidation as Angela wrote.

'This is the number of a young woman called Sorrel, not far from here. You'll like her. She's very down-to-earth.'

'Who . . . is she?'

'Just another person with a questing spirit. She runs a healthfood restaurant in Hereford and holds meetings there for people of a like mind: to share experiences and consider methods of developing their skills.'

'Sounds a bit . . . I mean, I'd feel a bit . . .'

'If you did decide to go, you could always take your friend . . . Rosemary, was it?'

'Rowenna.' Jane felt *much* better. 'Yeah, that'd be cool. Er . . . develop skills? What sort of skills do you think I might have?'

'Healing? Clairvoyance? It's not for me to say. Perhaps you can find out.' Angela tore the top page out of her notebook and placed it in front of Jane. 'It's entirely up to you now.'

'Right,' Jane said. 'Right.'

When she stood up, her legs felt cold and trembly.

*

Moon was pulling down the old-fashioned rollerblind over the CLOSED sign on the door.

All the lights were out except for a brown-shaded one on the counter, so that the air in the shop had a deep-shadowed sepia density. The unsaleable balalaika hung forlornly on the wall behind the till. The low-level music from the speakers each end of the single seventeenth-century beam was by Radiohead at their most suicidal: the one about escaping lest you choked.

Lol swallowed. Moon said to him, as though he'd been here for some time, 'I asked Denny to come over for supper. He said he'd really love to but he was too busy. I knew he'd say that.'

'Well, he probably is. Work's piling up in the studio.'

Moon shook her head. 'It's his wife. Maggie thinks I'm still doing dope – and I'm poison in all sorts of other ways. Plus, he just doesn't want to come to the barn.'

She came to stand next to him. She was wearing a long brown cardigan over a too-much-unbuttoned white cotton blouse and jeans. Something dull and metallic hung from a leather thong around her neck.

'Moon, you can't go home on your bike, in the dark, up that hill. It's snowing hard.'

'I've got good lights – and nothing will touch me on Dinedor.'

'I could try and get it in the back of the car. Or I could take you back in the car now, and pick you up again tomorrow.'

He felt tense – the missing element here, as usual, was lightness. In any situation, Moon was a solemn person: no humour, no banter. As if all the family's irony genes had been been used up on Denny sixteen years before she was born.

'Silly making two trips,' Moon argued.

'I don't mind, really.'

'Or you could stay,' Moon said. 'Why not stay over?'

She was very close to him. 'What exactly did Denny say to you?'

'He said . . . that he was glad you weren't on your own.'

Moon laughed lightly.

'What did you tell him, Moon?'

'It doesn't matter. Poor Denny.' Moon took Lol's left hand and held it between both of hers. They were slim hands but strong, hardened by delving in the earth. 'And stupid Dick. I can't believe how timid and stupid people can be. Dick and his feeble psychology; Denny hiding behind a wall against the past. And you?' She looked closely at his hand. 'Are you timid too?'

'Oh, I'm more timid than any of them,' Lol said.

'What of? What are you frightened of, Lol?'

She was standing close enough now for him to see that there was dust on her blouse. She seemed to attract dust. *Dust of ages*, Lol thought. The past had become attracted to her.

A long way away, Radiohead were playing *Karma Police*, about what you got if you messed with Us; he could hardly hear it for the drumming in his head.

'I think I'm frightened of you,' Lol whispered in shame, 'and I don't know why.'

The movements were so minimal that he'd hardly noticed her creeping into his arms, until they were kissing and his hands were in the long, long hair and something flared inside him like when you finally put a match to a long-prepared fire of brittle paper and dry kindling.

'So what are you going to do?' Rowenna asked, as they drove into Ledwardine marketplace, which had a lacing of snow.

'Stop just here for a while,' Jane said. 'You haven't even told me what she said to *you*.'

The cobbled square, with its little timbered market-hall, was lit by electric gaslamps on wrought-iron poles and brackets. Rowenna parked under one of these, and its light turned her hair into shivering spirals of rose-gold.

'She told me my spiritual progression would be very much bound up with a friend's.'

'Oh, gosh.'

There were only two cars on the square, both in front of The Black Swan. There was a light visible between the trees which screened the vicarage, and Jane thought she could see a cluster of early stars around the tip of the church steeple, but that might just have been snow. She just so much wanted this to be a magical night.

'So, are you going to phone this other woman, kitten?'

'It's a big step.'

'No, it isn't. You can check it out first, and if it sounds iffy you don't get involved.'

'*I* don't get involved?'

'All right, *we* don't.'

'What about Mum?'

'We don't have to invite her, do we?'

'You know what I mean. Right now, she would not be cool about this. She's insecure enough as it is.'

'Of course she's insecure. She's a Christian.'

'I don't think I can do it to her.'

'You're not doing anything to her!'

'I'd be lying.'

'They expect us to lie,' Rowenna said.

The snow made spangles in the fake gaslight.

'I need to think about this.'

'Well, don't think too long. Like Angela said, repressing it may seriously damage your health.'

Jane sighed. The village seemed deserted. Through the snowflakes, the light in the vicarage looked very far away.

EIGHTEEN

Overhead Cables Cut

'Where did you get to, flower?'

'Oh, Hereford and places. Shopping and stuff.'

'What did you buy?'

'Nothing much. Rowenna got . . . some things.'

'She seems to have a lot of money,' Merrily said, heating soup at the stove. 'I suppose she's indulged quite a bit, having to be dragged around the country with her father stationed at different bases.'

'Yeah,' Jane said noncommittally. She'd arrived home about seven – looking a bit pale, Merrily thought. Outside, it was snowing quite hard and sticking impressively to the ground and the trees. November snow; it couldn't last, surely.

'Where did Rowenna live before?'

'What's this about?' said Jane.

'Just interest. You seem to be spending a lot of time with her, that's all.'

'That,' said Jane, 'is because she's interesting. They were at Malmesbury in Wiltshire. Her dad was with the Army at Salisbury or somewhere. They don't like to talk about it, the SAS, so I don't ask. Satisfied?'

Later, she said, 'I'm sorry, Mum. I'm being a pig. Tired, that's all. I think I'll have an early night.'

Merrily didn't argue; she wanted to be up early herself. She suspected there'd be a bigger congregation tomorrow than usual; people always liked going to church in the snow.

She was in bed by eleven, with a hot-water bottle. Less than ten minutes later, the phone bleeped.

'Ledwardine Vic—'

'Merrily, it's Sophie at the Bishop's office. I'm terribly sorry to bother you, but we're having a problem – at the Cathedral. I wonder, could you perhaps come over?'

Big grey snowflakes tumbled against the window. Merrily sat up in bed. It had never felt so cold in here before.

'What's happened?'

'I . . . it involves Canon Dobbs. I don't like to say too much on the phone.'

Merrily switched on the bedside lamp. 'Give me half an hour. Maybe forty-five minutes if the roads are bad.'

'Oh God, yes, I didn't realize. Do be careful.'

'I'll see you soon.'

When she came out of the bedroom, buttoning her jeans, she found Jane on the landing. 'I heard the phone.' She was in her dressing-gown, and mustn't have been asleep.

'Some kind of problem at the Cathedral.'

'Why should that concern *you*?'

'I don't really know.'

'Shall I come? It looks a bit rough out there.'

'God, no. You get back to bed.'

'What if you get stuck? These roads can be really nasty and the council's mega-slow off the mark – like about three days, apparently.'

'It's a big car. I'll be fine.'

'This is like Deliverance business again, isn't it?'

'To be honest, I just don't know.'

'Talk about secrecy,' Jane said, strangely wide awake. 'You

Deliverance guys make the SAS seem like double-glazing salesmen.'

Why had she imagined the Cathedral would be all lit up? Maybe because that was how she'd been hoping to find it: a beacon of Old Christian warmth and strength.

But in the snow and the night, she was more than ever aware of how set-apart it had become. Once it had stood almost next to the medieval castle, two powerhouses together; now the city was growing away from the river, and the castle had vanished. The Cathedral crouched, black on white, like the Church at bay.

Merrily parked on Broad Street, near the central library. The dashboard clock, always five to ten minutes fast, indicated near-midnight. It had been a grindingly slow journey, with her window wound down to let the cigarette smoke out and the arctic air in, just to keep her awake. She'd taken the longer, wider route east of the Wye, where there was always some traffic, even the chance of snowploughing if anyone in the highways department had happened to notice a change in the weather. The road-surface was white and brown and treacherous, snow-lagged trees slumped over it like gross cauliflowers.

It all still seemed so unlikely – what would Hunter want with her at this time of night? Was he trying to turn Deliverance into the Fourth Emergency Service?

Merrily locked the Volvo, put on her gloves, pulled up her hood and set out across the snow-quilted silence of Broad Street.

No one about, not even a drunk in view. No traffic at all. The city centre as you rarely saw it: luminous and Christmas-card serene, snowflakes like big stars against the blue-black. Merrily's booted steps were muted on the padded pavement. Behind her only The Green Dragon had lights on. She felt conspicuous. There was no sign of the Bishop or the Bishop's men. Hadn't a woman once been raped in the Cathedral's shadow? Hadn't the last time she'd been called out at night . . .?

Christ be with me, Christ within me.

The Cathedral was towered and turreted, the paths and the green lawns submerged together in snow, a white moat around God's fortress. But no other night defences; its guardians – the canons and the vergers – were sleeping in the warren of cloisters behind. Nobody about except . . .

'Merrily!'

Sophie came hurrying around the building, towards the North Porch, following the bouncing beam of a torch attached to a large shadow beside her.

Merrily breathed normally again.

'Thank heavens you made it.' The Bishop's secretary lived not five minutes' walk away, in a quiet Victorian villa near the Castle Green. She wore a long sheepskin coat, her white hair coming apart under a woollen scarf. 'We were just wondering whether to call Michael, after all.'

'But I thought the Bishop—'

'He doesn't know anything about this,' Sophie said quickly. 'Do you know George Curtiss?'

'Good evening, Mrs Watkins. I, ah, think we have met.'

'Oh, yes. Hello.' He was one of the Cathedral canons: a big, overcoated man with a beard of Greek Orthodox proportions and a surprisingly hesitant reedy voice.

'George called me to ask if we should tell Michael about this,' Sophie said. 'But I suggested we consult you. This is all very difficult.'

'Look, I'm sorry . . . Am I supposed to know what's happening?'

'You tell her, George.'

'Yes, it's . . . Oh dear.' George Curtiss glanced behind him to make sure they were alone, bringing down his voice. 'It's about old, ah, Tom Dobbs, I'm afraid.'

'Merrily,' Sophie was hugging herself, 'he's virtually barricaded himself in. We think he's . . .'

'Drunk, I rather fear,' George said.

'What?'

'He's behind that partition,' Sophie said. 'You know, where they're repairing the Cantilupe tomb?'

'He's in there with—?'

'Chained and padlocked himself in. He won't talk to us. He's just rambling. To someone else? To himself? I don't know. Rambling on and on. Neither of us understands, but I just . . . well, I rather suspected you might. It's all . . . it's rather frightening, actually.'

'So there is a' – Merrily swallowed – 'a Deliverance context?'

What a stupid question.

'Oh, yes,' Sophie said, 'I think so. Don't you?'

George Curtiss shuffled impatiently. 'I trust we can, ah, rely on your discretion, Mrs Watkins. I know he's an odd character, but I do have a long-standing admiration for the man. As does . . . as does the Dean.'

'But I don't know him. I've never even spoken to him.'

'He's, ah, had his problems,' George said. 'Feels rather beleaguered – threatened by . . . by certain recent developments. In view of these, we'd rather avoid involving the Dean – or the Bishop – at this stage.'

'But I don't *know* him. And he—'

'But you know what he *does*, Merrily,' Sophie whispered urgently.

'Do I?'

'Mrs Watkins.' George Curtis coughed. 'We all know what he *does*, if not the, ah, technicalities of it. It's just we're a little nervous about what's . . . going on in there.'

'You want me to try and talk to him?'

'Just listen, I suppose.' Sophie tightened her scarf. 'Interpret for us.'

'My Latin isn't what it used to be,' George said.

'Latin?'

George dragged a long breath through the brambles of his beard, but his voice still came out weakly. 'My impression is he's talking to, ah . . . to, ah . . . to St Thomas.'

'I don't understand,' Merrily said.

Sophie almost snapped at her, 'You think *we* do?'

They followed George Curtiss and his torch around the building to St John's door, which was used mainly by the clergy and the vergers. Snow was already spattered up the nearby walls.

'We'll go in very quietly,' George said, as though addressing a party of schoolchildren – he was one of the regular tour-guides, Merrily recalled. 'I sometimes think the Dean has ultrasonic hearing.'

Merrily stepped warily inside – as if a mad-eyed Dobbs might come rampaging at them, swinging his crucifix.

Drunk? If Dobbs had a drink problem, it was the first she'd heard about it. But if the old exorcist had become a public embarrassment, the Dean could no longer be seen to support him. That way the Dean would himself lose face. And if the Bishop found out, he would make the most of it – in the most *discreet* way, of course – to strengthen his position as an engine of reform, get rid of Dobbs, and perhaps the Dean as well.

Can of worms!

Although it felt no warmer inside, Merrily unzipped her waxed coat and put a hand to the bump in her sweater, her pectoral cross.

This was because the atmosphere in the Cathedral was different.

Live?

Sophie touched her arm. 'Are you all right?'

'Yes.' Merrily remembered reading once that gothic churches somehow recharged themselves at night, like battery packs. She felt again the powerful inner call to prayer she'd experienced on the afternoon she'd emerged from the shell-like chantry to encounter Dobbs and the woman.

'I won't put on any lights,' George whispered. 'Don't want to draw undue, ah . . . attention.'

He snapped off his torch for a moment. The only illumination now was the little aumbry light over the cupboard holding the emergency sacrament: wine and wafers in a silver container. Merrily felt a desperate, vibrating desire to kneel before it.

There was no sound at all.

'All right.' George switched on his torch again, and they followed its bobbing beam through the Lady Chapel and into the North Transept, where the great stained-glass window reared over the temporary screening partition hiding the dismantled tomb of St Thomas Cantilupe. George shone his torch over the various posters drawing-pinned to it, telling the story of Cantilupe – a wise and caring bishop, according to the Cathedral guidebook, who stood firm against evil in all its guises.

George stopped and called out harshly, 'Thomas?' as though he hadn't intended to – as though the word had been wrenched out of him.

Merrily quivered for an instant.

Thomas? – as if he was summoning the spirit of Cantilupe. He might as well have been. There was no response.

Merrily looked at Sophie. 'You're sure he's still . . .?'

George moved across and shone his torch on the plywood

partition door. Merrily remembered a padlocked chain con-necting steel staples on the outside.

'All this will be taken down quite soon,' George said. 'They're putting the tomb back together next week.'

The chain appeared to have been dragged inside through a half-inch crack between the ill-fitting door and its frame. Dobbs – or someone else – had to be still behind it.

Merrily said, 'Do you feel anything?'

'I feel quite annoyed, actually,' Sophie muttered. 'Why isn't he doing . . . what he was doing earlier? You'll think we only dragged you here on a such a dreadful night on some sort of perverse whim.'

'No. The atmosphere, Sophie – the atmosphere's some-how . . . I don't know . . . disarranged.'

'How do you mean?'

'I don't know. I've never been in here at night before. Not like this, anyway.'

She had a feeling of overhead cables cut, slashed through. Of them hanging down now, still live and dangerous.

'Thomas?' George rapped on the plywood door. 'Thomas, it's George. Getting a bit anxious about you, old chap.'

'Something's happened,' Merrily said suddenly. 'Can you break it down?'

'Thomas!' George slapped the partition with a leather-gloved hand. 'Are you there?'

'Break it down!'

He swung round. 'This is a cathedral, Mrs Watkins.'

'Maybe you can snap the chain?'

'I can't even *reach* the chain.'

'Kick the door.'

'I . . . I can't.'

Merrily hurriedly unzipped her coat and slipped out of it. 'Stand back, then. I'll do it.'

'No, I . . . Thomas! For God's sake!' George put an ear to

the crack between the door and the frame. 'Stop . . . wait . . . I can hear . . .'

Merrily went still.

'I can hear him breathing,' George said. 'Can you hear that?'

She turned her back to the plywood screen, steadying her own breathing. She rubbed her eyes. *Think practically, think rationally.* When she turned back, both George and Sophie were staring at her. And the air in the high transept was still invisibly untidy with snipped wires.

'All right.' Big George began to unbutton his overcoat. 'I'll do it.'

He wore fat, black boots. Doc Martens probably, size eleven at least. With equipment like that, he could bring the whole damned partition crashing down.

He gave Merrily the rubber-covered torch, which felt moist. By its light, she saw that his brown eyes were wide and scared, and a froth of spittle glistened in his beard.

'Christ be with us,' Merrily heard herself saying.

NINETEEN

Costume Drama

Siren warbling, blue beacons strobing – violently beautiful over the snow – the ambulance broke the rules by cutting from Broad Street across the Cathedral Green.

Merrily stood outside St John's door with Sophie. Feeling useless.

Even in his condition, Dobbs had reared up from the stones at the sight of her, one arm hanging limp, and his face like a waxwork melting down one side. George Curtiss had then taken charge, suggesting she and Sophie should phone for help from the office in the gatehouse.

Merrily had glanced back once before they hurried away, and had seen George fumbling at the wall under the aumbry light.

'The sacrament.' Sophie had started to shake. 'Oh, dear God, he's asked for the sacrament.'

Merrily wasn't sure Dobbs had been in any condition, at the time, to voice a request; this was probably George's own decision. Probably a wise one.

She and Sophie stood back while the paramedics brought the old man out. Multiple headlights creaming the snow and more people gathering – one of the vergers, a couple of policemen.

And the Right Reverend Michael Hunter loping towards them. The Bishop in a purple tracksuit.

'Merrily, what on earth are you doing here?'

'Michael, I sent for her,' Sophie explained at once. 'I thought—'

'That's good,' the Bishop said. 'That's fine. Entirely appropriate.'

Summoned from his bed, no doubt, by the ambulance siren, he seemed neither cold nor tired. Merrily could almost see his athlete's glow as an actual halo as he raised a palm over the two women, like a blessing.

'Poor Canon Dobbs,' Sophie said.

The Bishop nodded. 'A good and distinguished servant of God.'

Huh? Merrily recalled their discussion in The Green Dragon. '*The old man's ubiquitous. Hovering silently, like some dark, malign spectre. I'd like to . . . I want to* exorcize *Dobbs.*'

Classic episcopal hypocrisy.

'But he worked himself too hard – and for too long,' the Bishop said. 'A stroke, I gather.'

'Yes,' Merrily said, 'that's what it looks like.'

'No!' Cool, efficient Sophie started to cry. '*Two* strokes. It must have been two, don't you see? We thought he must be . . . must have been drinking. When we heard his voice all slurred, in fact he was simply struggling to speak after a first stroke – probably only a minor one. And then . . . I remember my father . . . Oh God, how stupid we were, how utterly thoughtless.'

'Sophie,' Merrily said, 'if it wasn't for you, he might still be lying there.'

'Perhaps it was us shouting at him to come out . . . perhaps all the fuss threw him into some sort of confused panic and that was what brought on the second stroke.'

'Sophie, listen.' The Bishop took his secretary by both shoulders, then eased back her scarf so as to look into her eyes. 'We all knew that Thomas was long, long overdue for retirement. His particular ministry put him under enormous pressure. Several of us, as you know, tried very hard to persuade him to give it up. I think it was becoming explicitly clear to everyone that this good man's mind was breaking down. Hey, watch yourself . . .'

He guided Sophie out of the path of the ambulance as it started up, preparing to bear the stricken Dobbs to the General Hospital. George Curtiss appeared from behind it, breathing hard through his beard.

'Bishop . . .'

'Well done, George.'

'I'm afraid I didn't do enough.'

'I'm sure you did everything humanly possible,' Mick Hunter said – then, after a pause, 'except to inform your bishop.'

'Oh, yes. I, ah, thought . . . hoped . . . that it wouldn't be necessary to involve you – or the Dean.'

'I want to be appraised of *everything*, George. You won't forget that again, will you?'

'No.' The big canon, a good ten years older than the Bishop, looked like a chastized schoolboy. 'I'm sorry, Bishop.'

'Get some sleep. We'll talk about this tomorrow. Merrily—'

'Bishop?' She was annoyed at the way he'd spoken to George, who'd administered the sacrament to Dobbs, stayed with him, tried to make him comfortable, keep him calm.

The Bishop said, 'What was Canon Dobbs actually doing when you found him?'

'He was having a stroke, Bishop,' Merrily said wearily.

Mick Hunter was silent.

'I'm sorry,' Merrily said. 'It's been a difficult night.'

'Has it? I see. I'll talk to you on Monday, Merrily. This is obviously going to have a bearing on your situation.' He turned and walked towards the Cathedral.

'I thought for a moment he was going to say something about God moving in mysterious ways,' Merrily muttered, 'to clear the way for the new regime.'

'He's wearing trainers,' Sophie said absently. 'His poor feet must be absolutely soaked.'

'Wellies wouldn't fit the image.'

'He's more than image, Merrily,' Sophie said quietly. 'I think you know that. He's a very young man. One day he'll be a great man, I should think.'

One day he'll probably be an archbishop, Merrily thought. *But I doubt he'll be a great man.*

But she'd said enough.

'Thank you for coming,' Sophie said, 'though clearly it wasn't a terribly good idea.'

'Sophie . . .' Merrily glanced over her shoulder at the Cathedral, which – although someone, probably the Bishop, had put on lights – was still not the imagined beacon of old Christian warmth, not now. 'When George said Dobbs was talking to Thomas Cantilupe, what did he mean by that?'

Sophie appeared uncomfortable. 'Does that matter now?'

'Yeah, I think it does.'

'That was George's surmise. I thought he was talking to himself. Thomas, you see – both of them Thomases. It was as though he . . . perhaps he was already feeling ill and he was urging himself to hold on.'

'What were his words?'

'Well, like that. He did actually say that at least once: "Please God, hold on, Thomas." And then he'd lapse into mumbling Latin.'

'How did he get *in*? Does he have keys?'

'He must have.'

'Does he often come here alone at night?'

'It . . .' Sophie sighed. 'So they say.'

'What else do they say?'

'They say he has rather an obsession with St Thomas Cantilupe. I do know he studied the medieval Church, so perhaps he sought some sort of deeper communion with the saint, on a spiritual level. I don't like to—'

'You mean because the tomb was lying open, for the first time in over a century, he thought the saint would be more accessible? You have to help me here, Sophie. I don't understand.'

'I don't know what to say,' Sophie said. 'I don't feel it's right to talk about it now, with the poor man probably dying. I mean, George gave him the *sacrament*.'

'Sophie, just let me get this right. Are you saying you called me in because you and George thought Canon Dobbs was attempting to make contact with a dead saint?'

'I don't *know*, Merrily.' Sophie was wringing the ends of her scarf. 'Look, I just wanted to protect . . . Oh, I don't know *who* I wanted to protect. The Bishop? Canon Dobbs? Or just the Cathedral? In the end it all comes back to the Cathedral, doesn't it? I . . .' She stamped a booted foot on the snow as if to emphasize it to herself. 'I work for the Cathedral.'

'Is there something . . . is there a problem in the Cathedral? Is that what you're trying to say?'

Maybe she should talk to George, who was still with the two policemen beside their car at the roadside.

'Can we talk about this . . . again?' Sophie said.

'If I'm going to help, you've got to trust me.'

'I *do* trust you, Merrily. That's why I telephoned for you. And I feel guilty now – you look so awfully tired. Do you really have to drive back? The roads are going to be dreadful.'

'No worse than when I came. I think the snow's stopping anyway.'

'But it'll probably freeze on top. That's rather treacherous – and it's always a little warmer in the city. Look, why don't you stay with us tonight? We always keep a room prepared, and Andrew will have hot chocolate ready.'

'Well, thanks. But there's Jane at home. And tomorrow's services.'

'I do feel so guilty about bringing you here.'

'Don't worry, I won't fall asleep at the wheel. I'll smoke.'

'Hmm,' Sophie said disapprovingly.

'Good night, Sophie.'

Watching Sophie walk away towards warmth and hot chocolate, Merrily felt damp and chilled inside her thinning fake-Barbour. She saw the police car pulling away into Broad Street, and George Curtiss had already gone.

Fatigue had induced detachment. She didn't *want* to be detached. She remembered how, when she and Sophie and George had first entered the Cathedral tonight, the urge to pray had washed over her like surf, a tide of need. *Dobbs's need?*

That had gone now; her prayers weren't needed – or not so urgently. She ought to have obeyed that call, fallen to her knees, and the whole bit.

Bloody Anglican reserve. The Church of the Stiff Upper Lip.

Abruptly, Merrily went back into the Cathedral, to pray for Dobbs, before it was all locked up again. Knowing she would make for the place where George had kicked down a partition door: the Cantilupe fragments.

What did she know about Cantilupe? Bishop of Hereford in the late thirteenth century. Born into a wealthy Norman baronial family. Educated for the Church. A political career before he came to Hereford in middle age, in the reign of Edward I. A row with the Archbishop of Canterbury which got him excommunicated. Reinstatement, then death, then sainthood. Then the miracles, dozens of miracles around the shrine: the tomb that no longer had a body in it, and that was now in pieces.

The aumbry light still shone: a relic of the medieval Church, seldom needed now. Tonight another medieval relic had required the last rites.

Merrily realized she very much did not want Dobbs to die. She went down on her knees, on the hard coldness, before the aumbry light itself. *Let him live. Please God, let him survive. Build some kind of bridge between us. Throw down some quiet light. Let there be . . .*

Useless, incoherent – she was just too tired. She couldn't find the words to explain herself.

'Merrily.'

She opened her eyes.

'I'm sorry I was so abrupt, Merrily. It wasn't you – it was me, I'm sorry. I felt excluded.'

The late-night DJ voice, resonant, burnt-umber. She should have realized he'd still be here. Perhaps she had.

'Hello, Mick.'

The Bishop extended a hand. He was very strong, and suddenly she was on her feet again.

'You look very tired,' Mick said. 'I hear you've been working hard tonight.'

'*Finding* it hard, that's all.'

'As you're bound to.' His lean face was crinkled by a sympathetic, closed-mouth smile. He surveyed her in the mellow light. 'It's a very taxing role: social worker, psychotherapist and virtuoso stage-performer, all rolled into one.'

'Stage-performer?'

'We're all of us actors, Merrily. The Church is a faded but still fabulous costume drama.'

'Oh.'

'And, to survive, it has to be considerably more sophisticated these days. Poor Dobbs is strictly Hammer Films, I'm afraid. He should retire, if he recovers, to one of those nice rural nursing homes for ageing clerics. There to write his memoirs, don't you think?'

'I don't know what I think.'

'You're overtired,' Mick said. 'Poor baby, I'm not going to let you drive home, you realize that.'

'It's only twenty minutes.' He was offering to drive her?

'In these conditions? At least an hour – and requiring rather more attention than I suspect you'd be able to summon. Consider this an executive ruling. Come to the Palace. We've lots of spare rooms I always feel guilty about. Perhaps we should make some available to selected homeless people, what do you think?'

'I think it would be very much an unnecessary imposition on Mrs Hunter.'

'What, accommodating the homeless? Or accommodating you? Either way, not a problem. Valentina's away for a couple of days, visiting her ageing parents in the Cotswolds. Old Church, Val's father – yesterday's Church. We have endless and insoluble theological arguments, so these days I tend to plead pressure of work.'

Merrily smiled. 'Look, it's very kind of you, Mick. It's just—' She moved self-consciously towards St John's door.

'*You*' – he followed her – 'need all your strength. Just let others look after you sometimes. We can get you back in good time for tomorrow's services, if that's what you're worried about. We have a wonderful old Land Rover at our disposal.'

'There's Jane, you know?'

'Jane?'

'My daughter.'

She thought he blinked. 'She's not a child any more, is she? She must be getting quite used to your nocturnal comings and goings.'

'I suppose she is.'

'Well, then . . .'

He put his hands on her shoulders, as he had on Sophie's earlier. His hands were big and firm and warm.

'Merrily, you have to stop shouldering the problems of the world. Besides, it would be a good opportunity for us to talk about the future. It'll be impossible to keep this out of the papers, you know, especially if the old guy dies on us. We need to be ready, hmm?'

As Mick Hunter lowered his arms from her shoulders, his head bent quickly, and she was sure his lips touched her forehead just once, on the hairline.

'This means we can stop quietly phasing you in and officially announce the establishment of a Deliverance consultancy. We need to discuss how we're going to handle that.'

'But not tonight.'

'Oh no, not tonight. Tomorrow.' He paused. 'Over our breakfast, perhaps.'

The way he said *our* breakfast. The way he had his arms by his sides now, but had not stepped back. The way he seemed to be closer than when his hands had been on her. She felt an awful compulsion to fall forward, collapse into that strong, muscular episcopal chest.

'Up to you, of course,' he said. 'Coincidentally, we've just had a guest suite refurbished. Bathroom with shower, small sitting room – that sort of set-up. You may find you have to overnight in Hereford quite often as your role expands. Consider it available at any time. As you'll be reporting exclusively to me, it would seem like an arrangement with considerable . . . possibilities, you know.'

She stayed silent, giving him an opportunity to qualify that, but he didn't. He just stood there gazing at her, and after a moment he calmly folded his arms – sometimes a defensive gesture, but not this time.

No, this couldn't be? Couldn't possibly be how it sounded.

'Everything's changing, Merrily,' Mick said easily. 'This is a time of transition when traditional values, old restrictions, should be allowed to drift away. We should stop presuming to know what God wants of us.'

Merrily backed against the door, needing cold air, space.

'We should be prepared to experiment,' Mick continued calmly, 'until the waters settle and we know where we are again. For a while.'

He followed her out of the Cathedral, leaving the door for the verger to lock. Outside, an unreal mauvish mist was gathering around white roofs, over white pavements, the grey-white road. A Christmas-card Hereford, out of time. Mick Hunter, in his purple tracksuit, seemed part of the picture. Part of the illusion. Not real.

'See, no traffic at all,' he said. 'Earlier, I believe, the TV and radio stations were warning motorists not to venture out unless it was absolutely vital.'

Time of transition? In the tingling mist, Merrily felt as though she was being drawn into a developing, lucid dream and had to go with it – some of the way, at least – to see if its destination could possibly be what she was half-imagining.

Or make a wild dash across Broad Street for her car. Or . . .

She heard Jane saying, '*It's probably considered socially OK to fuck a bishop*,' and felt appalled.

'Mick, look, I actually think it's beginning to thaw. I can be home in half an hour.'

'Nonsense. Merrily, you know you don't really want to do that.'

'I have to.'

She began to walk away from him towards the road, and then stopped and turned as the Bishop spoke again with quiet insistence.

'You only *have* to do what you want to do.'

'That's not true . . .'

This was not the Bishop talking but the bulge in his tracksuit trousers. She closed her eyes briefly and wished him gone.

'Oh . . . Excuse me, miss.'

A man stepped out from behind one of the trees like some accosting beggar – one of those homeless that Mick and Val would *not* be accommodating at the Palace.

'Not now,' the Bishop told him irritably.

'Sorry, sir. Not you – the lady. Are you by any chance the lady whose daughter ordered a minicab?'

'Huh?'

'Mrs Watson?'

'Watkins.'

'Yeah, that's it.'

Mick Hunter didn't move. Merrily shrugged and gave him a bashful smile. 'I didn't know she'd done that. Kid does my thinking for me. Thanks anyway, Bishop. What time do you want to see me on Monday?'

'Eleven o'clock,' the Bishop said tonelessly, 'in the Great Hall.'

She nodded.

'Good night,' he said.

'It's this way,' said the cabbie.

Mick Hunter had vanished by the time she found out that the cabbie did not have a vehicle with him.

TWENTY

Not Good

They walked in silence a short way along Broad Street until Merrily was sure the Bishop had returned to the Palace. Then Lol Robinson hurried her discreetly across the whitened green and into Church Street.

'Little Jane called me, about half an hour ago. Said you were heading this way and you might be able to use a cup of coffee at some stage. I've just been . . . hanging around.'

'So intuitive, that kid.' God, she was pleased to see him. Although, under the circumstances, anybody at all would have been a serious blessing.

'I think she was worried about you,' he said.

Merrily smiled. 'I'm sure.' She felt light-headed – glad, for the first time she could remember, to be out of the Cathedral.

'Who was that guy in the tracksuit?' Lol unlocked a recessed door in the alleyway next to the little music shop.

'That, Laurence, was the Bishop of Hereford.'

'Oh, I see.' Lol wore nothing over the familiar black sweatshirt with the Roswell alien face printed on it in flaking grey. He must be freezing. 'I had him down as some late-night jogger, who . . . I don't really know.'

'Thought I was a prostitute.'

'Like you always find in the Cathedral Close.' Lol grinned. 'Who was the bloke they put in the ambulance?'

'Canon Dobbs. He's had a stroke. We found him collapsed in the Cathedral.'

'Oh.' Lol shouldered the door open and turned on the light. They entered a hallway with a flight of stairs and a mountain-bike.

'They called me in,' Merrily said, 'because he was . . . still *is* the last diocesan exorcist. You know about all that, I suppose.'

'Well, you know, I've talked to Jane.'

'Then you know everything.'

She looked around the shapeless, lamplit room with its beams and trusses and sash windows with lots of little square panes. Lol's old guitar rested on a metal stand by the bricked-up fireplace. A stained and sagging armchair she remembered from his old cottage in Ledwardine.

'Ethel used to sleep in this,' she said.

'How *is* Ethel?'

'Ethel is fine. You get extra points for being a vicarage cat.'

Lol moved around, opening up radiators. His brass-rimmed glasses had half-misted.

'This place is better for you?' Merrily flopped into the chair without taking off her coat. 'Do you feel better here?'

'Haven't been here long enough to think too much about it. It's OK, I suppose.' He went into what was presumably the kitchen, leaving the door open, a blue-white light flickering.

'Very central. Convenient for the Cathedral.'

'Right.'

She forced herself out of the chair, and went to join him in the kitchen. It had barely room for two people. The fluorescent strip-lighting hurt her eyes, reminding her of the sluice-room next to the Alfred Watkins Ward.

'That was your idea, the taxi?'

'All I could think of at the time.' He had his back to her, filling the kettle.

'Thank you,' she said solemnly. 'You . . . got me out of something heavy.'

'Really?' He turned round, looking happy. 'Like you did for me and Ethel that night?'

'Oh, more than that. The way this was going, I might not have had a career.'

'Well, you know, I didn't really hear anything.'

'Yes, you did.'

'OK, I did. How many points for sleeping with a lady vicar?'

'For a bishop? I honestly can't recall a precedent. But bishops are survivors – especially this one, I suspect. Lady vicars . . . they're expendable. Especially ones caught in sin.'

She was startled at how easy it was to discuss all this with Lol, though they hadn't spoken for months. It might have been just this morning she last saw him. She looked around the little kitchen: plywood cupboards, a small fridge, a microwave, three mugs with hedgehog motifs on a shelf. Nothing suggestive of permanence. She was looking for a sign that Lol was out of limbo now and not finding one.

'Erm . . .' He turned to pull two of the mugs from the shelf. 'When you said just now that you might not have had a career, does that mean that if I hadn't shown up . . .?'

'What it would have meant,' Merrily said slowly, 'is that, in order to get away from him, I would probably have had to stop pretending he was simply offering me a room for the night.'

'Right.' Lol set down the mugs. His glasses had misted again. 'Jane'll be glad to know that.'

They sat and drank their coffee, Merrily in Ethel's old chair, Lol on the floor, his back to the window. She'd have to be going soon if she was going to grab a couple of hours before Holy Communion.

'Jane said you were training to be a psychotherapist.'

'Wild exaggeration. I've been helping *my* therapist. *Former* therapist, hopefully. That means I help a bit with other clients – as a kind of therapy. Well, one other client mainly: the woman who used to live in this flat.'

'Oh,' Merrily said, 'that would be this, er . . . Moon? Just that Jane implied—'

'I've got a vague idea what Jane implied.'

'That kid could start wars.' Merrily stretched. 'I don't want to move.'

'So don't move.'

'I have to. Anyway, I think you'd make rather a good psychotherapist.'

'Being an ex-loony?'

'Not only that.'

'Thanks.'

'You know what I mean. You've been swallowed by the system once. You could be good at keeping other people *out* of the system.'

Lol said, 'Maybe there are too many therapists and counsellors around already, all talking different kinds of bollocks.'

'Is this Dick paying you?'

'Kind of. There's no big problem with money: the song royalties trickle in. And I might have another album – sometime.' Lol stood up. 'I, er . . . I was thinking of ringing you sometime, actually. What do you do if someone insists they've seen a ghost. I mean, not just any old ghost – a close relative. And so maybe they *want* to see it. To see *more* of it.'

'Well . . . I'd try and find out if it was a real ghost. Maybe I'd ask a psychiatrist – or a psychotherapist – for some advice.'

'And say this psychotherapist – or somebody else who

knew this person well – was fairly convinced that there *was* something . . . unusual happening here.'

'Well . . .' Merrily lit a cigarette. 'I'd probably try and explain to the person that this was not a very good idea. It's not uncommon, actually, seeing relatives who've just passed on.'

'Twenty-five years ago?'

'That's *more* uncommon. A *visitor* is the loose term we, er, we tend to use for this kind of . . . phenomenon.'

'And it's a bad thing, is it? Even if the person is not scared by it.'

'Any prolonged contact with a . . . spirit, or whatever, is unhealthy. It can lead to all kinds of problems. Mental problems obviously, and also . . . Well, you might think that what you're seeing is your old mum, but it might be something else. I take it we're talking about this Moon?'

'Possibly.'

'Lol, you only *have* one client . . .'

'OK, it's Moon.'

'Who's she been seeing?'

'Her father. He died when she was two.'

'Any complications?'

'Shot himself.'

'Oh.'

'That's not good, is it?'

'That's not good at all,' Merrily said. 'Would she see me, do you think?'

'I don't know. Maybe if you weren't wearing . . . you know?'

'A dog-collar.'

'And I introduced you as a friend.'

'Sounds like a good idea.'

'She's working in the shop down below all week.'

'Maybe I'll call in on Monday, then,' Merrily said. 'I don't know what time yet. I'll be in the gatehouse if you want me – except mid-morning when I'm having discussions with my friend the Bishop.'

'Pity you can't see her house, really – a barn she's leasing up on Dinedor Hill. She's quite obsessive about the hill. It's where she was born, where the family have lived since the Iron Age – or so she claims.'

'This sounds awfully complicated, Lol.' Merrily yawned and forced herself out of the chair. 'Where'd I put my coat?'

'All I can say is that she's different when she's up there. A different person – half . . . half somewhere else.' He unhooked her waxed jacket from behind the door. 'I don't suppose . . . No, never mind.'

'I hate it when anyone says that.'

'Just that she left her bike here and I drove her home last night, because of the snow. So I have to pick her up on Monday morning, fetch her in to work.'

'Early?'

'Ish.'

'If you could get me back to the gatehouse by eleven, I can come up with you. What's my excuse, then?'

'Your car wouldn't start, so I'm giving you a lift somewhere? She'll buy that. This is really good of you, Merrily.'

'It's my job. We're told to work with shrinks. The Bishop would approve.'

'The shrink doesn't know,' Lol said. 'The shrink must *never* know.'

'A non-believer, huh?'

'Of the most intractable kind,' Lol said. 'You want me to drive you back now?'

'No, Lol,' Merrily annunciated carefully, 'you're – not –

really – a – minicab – driver. That was for the benefit of the Bishop.'

She went smiling into the snow. She must be overtired.

At least the roads were no worse. Back in the vicarage just before five, she called the General Hospital. She gave them her name and they put her through to the ward. She just knew which one it was going to be – there was an ironic inevitability about it.

'Reverend Watkins? Not the biggest surprise of the morning, to have you ring.'

'What *was* the biggest?'

'The biggest, to tell you the simple truth,' Eileen Cullen said, 'is that the auld feller's still with us.'

'Would that be an indication he might be coming through this?'

'Ah, now, I wouldn't go taking bets on that. He knows when you're talking to him – his eyes'll follow you around the room. But he's not talking back yet.'

'Mr Dobbs is not a big conversationalist, in my experience. The room? You haven't got him—'

'Christ no. We have this other wee side ward at the far end of the main ward. If Denzil was still with us, Mr Dobbs wouldn't even be able to smell him.'

Merrily shuddered.

'So, collapsed in the Cathedral, they say?' Cullen said nonchalantly.

'Yes, that's what they say.'

'Well, I'm off home in a while, but I'm sure they'll keep you posted on any developments. I'll mention it.'

'Thanks.'

A pause, then Cullen said, 'Funny, isn't it, how things come around. Mr Dobbs arranging like that for you to have a mauling from Denzil in his death-throes, and now . . . You ever find out why he did that to you?'

'I never did,' Merrily said. 'Maybe never will now.'

'Well,' Cullen said, 'a patient'll talk about all kinds of things, so he will – in the night, sometimes. I'll keep my ears open.'

TWENTY-ONE

Chalk Circle

She knew the words, of course she did, *she knew the words*. But they wouldn't come. She bent close to him – his breath uneven, his eyes closed against her, like this was an act of will. She brought the chalice close to his stoney face on the hospital pillow, white as a linen altar-cloth, and tipped her hand very slightly so that the wine rolled slowly down the silver vessel and trickled between his parted lips, a drop remaining on his lower lip, like blood.

Blood. Yes. Yes, of course.

'The blood of our Lord, Jesus Christ, which was shed for you, preserve your body and soul into everlasting life. Drink this in remembrance that Christ's blood was shed for you . . .'

Thomas Dobbs began to suck greedily at the wine. She was so grateful at having remembered the words that she tilted the chalice again, at a steeper angle, and wine flooded between his lips and filled his cheeks, and she began to murmur the Lord's Prayer.

'Our Father, Who . . .'

There was a cracking sound, like splintering stone, and his eyes flicked open, shocking her. Dobbs's eyes were grey and white and, when he saw who hovered behind the sacrament, they blurred and foamed like a stream over rocks in winter.

'Hallowed be . . .'

Dobbs's shoulders began to quake.

'Thy kingdom . . .'

She watched him rising up in the metal bed, his cheeks expanding. She could not move; this was her job. She kept on murmuring the prayer. When, eyes bulging in fury, he coughed the consecrated wine in a great spout into her face, it was indeed as warm as fresh blood, and she felt its rivulets down her cheeks.

This was her job; she could not move.

His hand snaked from under the bedclothes, and when it gripped her wrist like a monkey-wrench, the green tubes were ejected from his nose with a soft popping.

She didn't scream. She was a priest. She just woke up with a whimper, sweating – after a little over an hour's sleep on the sofa, and half a minute before the alarm was due to go off.

'You look awful,' said Ted Clowes after morning service. As senior churchwarden and Merrily's uncle, he was entitled to be insulting. 'This damned Deliverance nonsense, I suppose. I've told you, I have an extreme aversion to *anything* evangelical.'

Uncle Ted, a retired solicitor, had read 'widely' (the *Daily Mail*) about the Toronto Blessing and certain churches in Greater London where parishioners with emotional problems were exorcized of their 'devils' in front of the entire congregation. He was monitoring all Merrily's services for 'danger signs'.

'In addition, there's all the time it seems to take up – time that should be spent in this parish, Merrily.'

'Ted, I wouldn't have been doing anything here in the parish in the early hours of this morning.'

'But look at the state of you! Look at the shadows under your eyes. You look as if you'd been beaten up. I tell you, these things don't go unnoticed in a village. Half of those old women are not listening to a word of your sermon; they're examining you inch by inch for signs of disrepair. Anyway, I should get some sleep for an hour or two after lunch. Put that child of yours on telephone duty.'

Jane was sitting in Mum's scullery-office, with Ethel on her knees and her one purchase from the psychic fair open on the desk: a secondhand copy of *A Treatise on Cosmic Fire* by Alice A. Bailey. So far, she couldn't understand how a book with such a cool title could be so impenetrable. It sometimes read like one of those stereotype fantasy sagas she devoured as a kid – well, until about last year, actually – with all these references to The Sevenfold Lords and stuff like that. Except this was for real. But wasn't there a *simpler* way to enlightenment?

In her pocket, she had the phone number Angela had given her.

Sorrel.

She took it out, then put it back. Instead she rang Lol. Mum had said very little about last night apart from Dobbs and his stroke – like, tough, but the old guy was plainly out of his tree, as well as being seriously outdated on the issue of women priests. If you had to have soul police – and no way *did* you – better someone decently liberal like Mum; Dobbs should have bowed out long ago and gone to tend his roses or something.

Jane scratched behind Ethel's left ear until the black cat twisted her neck, purred luxuriously and faked an orgasm.

Lol wasn't answering his phone. Mum said she'd had a cup of coffee with Lol, that was all. Not as good as getting completely soaked through, and having to take off all her clothes on Lol's hearthrug, but a start.

Jane hung up, closed Alice A. Bailey, put Ethel on the carpet.

She took a long, long breath and got out the piece of paper.

*

Denny had upgraded his studio to 24-track. 'This is it for me,' he said. '*Finito*. I think we've all been getting too techno-conscious. It's not what rock and roll's about. When I was a kid you had a two-track Grundig in somebody's garage and you were bloody grateful.'

'What on earth is a Grundig?' asked James Lyden's friend Eirion, unpacking his bass.

'Forget it,' Denny said.

The house was no more than half a mile from Dick's place, about the same age but detached and with a longish drive. Just as well, with a studio underneath. However, Denny had also allowed for major soundproofing; the creation of an anteroom and homemade acoustic walls had reduced the main cellar to about two-thirds of its original size. Four of them now stood in the glass-screened control room, with Denny's personalized mixing-board. It was a warm, secure little world.

'This was the wine cellar?' James enquired, presumably wondering what Denny had done with all his wine.

'Coal cellar,' Denny snapped.

James didn't have a Stratocaster. He had a Gibson Les Paul copy – a good one; you had to look hard to be sure. He gazed around. 'I've got a *rough* idea how this set-up operates, but perhaps you could stick around for an hour or two, before you let us get on with it.'

Lol blinked. They expected Denny to leave them here alone with his gear? But Denny wasn't listening. He was underneath the mainboard now, with a hand lamp, messing with something. Lol wondered if James actually had got the wrong idea about this, or whether he was just trying it on. He looked like the kind of kid who would always try for more.

With a fair chance of success, Lol figured. The boy looked austere and kind of patrician, and tall – a good six inches taller than Dick. A good bit slimmer than Dick, too – who would have ceased to be James's role model many years ago. Like when James was about six.

'I used to rather like those Hazey Jane albums,' he said to Lol. 'You were a pretty good songwriter. You had that melancholy feel of . . . what was his name? I can't remember . . . Mum had an album of his.'

'Nick Drake?' Through the glass, Lol could see the two non-songwriting band members erecting a drum kit down on the studio floor.

'Oh, I know . . . James Taylor.'

'*That's* interesting,' Lol said.

James nodded knowledgeably. His mother, as a therapist, would have told him about the young James Taylor's psychiatric problems. Which would be why he'd made the comparison. Letting Lol know he knew the history.

He smiled compassionately down at Lol. 'You did absolutely the right thing, in my view. I mean packing in when you did. If everybody stopped recording at their peak, we'd have a hell of a lot less dross to wade through, in my view. Like, someone should've shot Lennon ten years earlier.'

'That's what you think?'

'They should have shot McCartney first,' said Eirion. He was from Cardiff – one of those wealthy, Welsh-speaking families – but Eirion spoke English with an accent straight out of Hampstead or somewhere.

'Eirion reckons twenty-five,' James said. 'I say twenty-seven, giving them the benefit of the doubt.'

'Compulsory retirement age for rock musicians,' Eirion explained. 'We argue about it a lot.'

'Personally, I think semi-voluntary euthanasia's probably the best answer,' Lol said. 'When they stop playing, their health goes or they take too many drugs and become a burden on the state.'

Eirion considered this. 'They could surely afford BUPA or something, couldn't they?'

Lol heard rumbles from underneath the mixing-board. Detected sounds resembling *fucking*, *little* and *shits*. He was beginning to enjoy this. In fact, he felt much better today about . . . well, most of it. This morning the disparate pieces of a song which had been lying around for most of a month had fallen exquisitely into place.

'So how many songs you actually got, James?'

'How many, Eirion? Twenty, twenty-two?'

'Well, yes, but some of them are fairly embarrassing now, actually – things we did over a year ago.'

'That old, huh?' said Lol.

James looked sullen. 'Dad says he's only paying for four. But he can cock off. That would be a pure waste of time and manpower. Besides, we've worked seriously hard and we're pretty fucking efficient. It wouldn't take that much longer to lay down the other six.'

'An album in fact?'

'Anything less isn't worth the hassle,' said James, 'don't you think?'

'We'll see how it goes,' Lol said. 'It's this bloke's studio.'

Denny came up, red-faced, from underneath the board, his big earring swinging furiously. 'Sorted,' he announced.

'Oh, I get it.' James tucked his rugby shirt into his jeans, and strapped on his guitar. 'You're the engineer, too.'

'And the cleaner,' Denny said menacingly. 'And the teaboy.'

'No, I mean . . . to be tactful about this, we don't mind you guys hanging around. We do want to be produced, but we need space to experiment, yeah? We're only into being . . . guided, up to a point. I mean, you know, I don't want to sound arrogant or anything.'

'Perish the thought,' Lol said.

He kept wondering how he would be feeling now if, instead of meeting Merrily Watkins again, he'd spent last night in Moon's barn – in Moon's futon.

But it hadn't worked out like that, and he was so glad.

Merrily lay awake, tasting the formless dregs of a dream. With the feeling of something wrong – of loneliness. And the recurrent domestic agoraphobia of two small women sharing seven bedrooms.

'*You're never really alone, you know.*' How often had she said that to a bereaved parishioner? Whichever way you looked at Him, God was never another warm body in a cold bed on a winter's night.

The luminous clock indicated 5.40 p.m. Time to leave for Evensong – except they'd dropped it last September because so few people liked turning out in winter darkness.

She remembered the essence of her dream. Oh God, an image of the lithe and tawny Val Hunter astride Mick under some high, moulded ceiling, with all the lights on. Merrily standing in the doorway, shocked to find herself wearing a very short black nightie. Cold legs, cold feet. '*Come on, Merrily!*' the Bishop had shouted impatiently. '*Don't be nervous. This is a time of transition. We have to experiment!*' The king-size bed, a four-poster, had shiny purple sheets.

But that confrontation under the aumbry light now seemed no less unlikely than the dream of the purple sheets. Merrily slid out of bed.

Downstairs there was no sign of Jane. Ethel eyed her sleepily from the basket beside the Aga, as Merrily made herself some coffee. She thought of the night Lol had first arrived with Ethel, after the cat had been savagely kicked by a drunk. They'd examined her on the kitchen table, just there –

Where a note lay, neatly printed from the computer.

MUM: Rowenna turned up. Didn't want to wake you, so left machine on. Back by ten . . . swear to God.
Here's list of phone calls so far.

1. Emily Price, from Old Barn Lane, wanting to firm-up a date for wedding rehearsal.
2. Uncle Ted, in Churchwarden Mode. Didn't say what it was about – probably usual pep talk about not neglecting parish for glamour of Hereford.
3. Sister Cullen. Can you ring her at home?

That's it. Love J.

Eileen Cullen said, 'Don't worry, the auld feller's not gone yet.'

'I was thinking of visiting him. Is he allowed visitors?'

Cullen laughed. 'Well, it's funny you should say that, Merrily. Mr Dobbs *has* had a visitor. That's why I called you. I thought you'd maybe want to know. Just the one visitor.'

'Someone I know?'

'You'll be on your own if you do.'

'You're going to spin this one out, aren't you?'

'All right,' Cullen said, 'I'll tell you. First off, I wasn't there. Young Tessa was there – you remember Tessa? Sunday-school teacher – the plucky kid holding Denzil's other hand?'

'I remember.' Like you could forget anybody there that night.

'This afternoon, all right, a man in an overcoat carrying an attaché case. A minister, he says, come to pray with Mr Dobbs. But Mr Dobbs can't speak, Tessa tells him. Doesn't matter, the priest says. They would like some peace and quiet and nobody coming in.'

'What was his name?'

'He didn't give his name. I told you Dobbs was in another wee side ward, all on his own? Well, the priest's drawn the curtain across the glass in the door. Except it's not possible to block the window fully. If you're nosy enough, you can stand on a chair and look down through the top. Which Tessa did, after she caught the light from the candles.'

'Candles?'

'We're always a bit careful, the range of religious fellers show up these days – and all quite legit, you know? Only Sister Miller's on her break and Tessa's a wee bit unsure about this, so she takes a peep. He'd about finished by then, so he had. He was picking up his wee bottles of holy water, scrubbing out his chalk circle.'

'Chalk circle?' Merrily sat down hard at the scullery desk.

'Me telling you like this, it sounds like a joke, but the child was terrified. He'd drawn a circle round the bed, if you please! Yellow chalk. Making a bit of extra room by pushing the visitor's chair under the door handle, the cheeky sod, so anyone'd have a job getting in even if they wanted to. And some bottles of water, with stoppers, placed around the circle. He also had a black book – very eerie, very frightening.'

'What did she do?'

'Went to find Sister Miller. Time the two of them got back, your man had gone. She rang me here during her break.'

'Well . . .' Merrily drew erratic circles on a pad. 'I'm lost. I don't understand this.'

'All *I* can say is that I was raised a Catholic, and it isn't one of our . . . things . . . our rituals.'

'Doesn't even seem like proper religion, Eileen. More like . . . magic. You sure this was a real priest?'

'I didn't see him. Tessa says he was wearing a dog-collar. He had a hat and scarf, so she couldn't see much of his face.'

'Did they check Dobbs over after he'd gone?'

'No change. He lies there still as corpse, so he does. Sometimes his eyes'll be open, but you never see it happen. What'll we do? Call the police, you reckon?'

'I don't know what the police could do, to be honest. But if he shows up again . . . would you mind calling me?'

'Merrily,' Cullen said, 'if it's me that's on when he shows, I'll be on to you before the divil's got both feet on the blessed ward at all.'

TWENTY-TWO

Edict

Monday morning, and Jane felt good – which was rare. She lay and watched for the dawn.

She'd seen like hundreds of dawns from here now, her bed facing the east window. This was not brilliant *feng shui*-wise, but you did get to see the sun come up over the wooded hill, and that was seriously important today.

Jane replayed last night's encounter – still amazed at how *cool* Sorrel had been, inviting her and Rowenna over at once to talk about it all. Jane calling Rowenna, and Ro saying, 'Look, better not tell them we're still at school. These people worry about parents finding out and making a fuss.' That was cool – so they were office working girls. Sorrel, who looked about Mum's age, had with her an elderly woman called Patricia who was kind of the head of the group and was obviously a really heavy person and had quizzed them in this really soft, knowing voice. *'How important is it to you to find the Path within yourself? Are you ready for so much hard work at a time when most girls your age are out having fun?'*

That made you think. You could spend years in search of enlightenment, and still wind up disillusioned at forty or something. The answer was: give it six months and then, if it wasn't working for you, let it go.

No sign of dawn, and it was getting on for seven. Mum

was probably up already, because – *yes!* – Mum was meeting Lol later in Hereford.

She didn't know what the meeting was about, and why it was so early, but that didn't matter. Their meeting was still a major coup for Mystic Jane, who had set the whole thing up the other night. Classic, when you thought about it: Lol taking Merrily in from the cold, offering her sanctuary just like she'd done for him that time. Mum still very big on the sanctuary concept, like with all those hookers she tried to rescue when she was a curate in Liverpool.

It would be really good to have Lol around again, so cool in his vulnerable, nervous way. This Moon – she was entirely wrong for him. You could tell, just by watching her in the shop, that she was remote and self-obsessed. So, OK, she was beautiful and about ten years younger than Mum. But Mum was still sexy. Well, she *could* be sexy, if she wanted to. If the bloody Church . . .

Or if they'd met way back – Mum in her Goth frock and her Siouxie Sioux make-up, Lol unhappily on the road with his band, Hazey Jane. You seemed to go all tightened up and inhibited when you got older. Especially when you had your whole life hijacked by the Church. The dog-collar – it was like some sick masochism trip. The punks used to wear actual dog-collars. Had Mum once been into bondage gear, and was that a natural progression to clerical costume?

Jane was just picturing Mum in the pulpit in her Sunday surplice and half a potful of coal-black mascara, when she became aware of the frozen night sky at last beginning to brown with heat from the east. Patricia said you were supposed to wait for the big orb itself but, like, what if it didn't show until you were on the school bus or something?

She scrambled out of bed and walked slowly to the east-facing window and opened it as wide as it would go. It was absolutely bloody *freezing*.

Well, good! Jane steeled herself and flung her arms wide.

Now her first exercise. She had the words Patricia had given them written out on the back of an old birthday card, all ready, balanced on the window ledge. She pictured Rowenna standing at her own window in the big modern house in Credenhill Jane hadn't yet visited.

She pictured Patricia and Sorrel – sisters, kind of.

OK. She took a mouthful of cold air and coughed. Then she looked into the sandy sky and read aloud from the card.

> *'Hail to Thee, Eternal Spiritual Sun*
> *'Whose symbol now rises in the Heavens.*
> *'Hail to Thee from the Abodes of Morning.'*

Jane lowered her arms, and stayed silent. By tomorrow, she wouldn't need the card.

She was on the Path.

This time, she was going to do it right.

Merrily dumped her waxed jacket on a front pew and went to kneel in the chancel.

Before her, the altar was a hazy-grey block under a stained-glass window, its colours still sleeping. She hadn't switched on the lamps or even lit a candle.

Unlocking the church, she'd thought what a shame it was to have to restrict the house of God to not much more than normal working hours. Ted wanted to lock it up at five each evening, but Merrily was insisting on seven at least, even if she then had to go along with her own keys. A church should really be offering sanctuary around the clock. Perhaps you could employ a sympathetic security patrol to filter out the vandals – try getting *that* one past the parish council.

Enough! Merrily knelt in silence for maybe ten minutes, letting thoughts drift away, and then began.

Her voice was hesitant, but steady. She kept it low.

> *'Christ be with me, Christ within me.*
> *'Christ behind me . . .'*

Christ and who else? A story in the *Church Times* last week had revealed two more attacks – one of them sexual – on women priests in their own churches. But you couldn't wrap yourself in cotton-wool like some religious statuette.

Equally she'd seen with the Denzil Joy incident the potential dangers of not protecting yourself before you went out on a case. And there was a lot about this Moon business she didn't like. Obsession, for a start, was always dangerous. She'd called Lol last night, while Jane was out, to get some more background. She didn't like the idea of that newly displayed photograph of the dead father in a room full of Iron Age relics. There was the possibility that this woman was drawing down pagan Celtic elements she would not be able to deal with.

Lol was right: it was necessary to go to the location on this one. To try to see it through Moon's eyes. But if there was something there, some lurking presence from way way back, would Merrily be able to sense it? While, at the same time, keeping it out?

> *'I bind unto myself the Name,*
> *'The strong Name of the Trinity.*
> *'By invocation of the same,*
> *'The Three in One and One in Three . . .'*

Pip-pop! The green tubes ejecting from the nostrils of dying Denzil Joy. *Pip-pop!*

Merrily cringed.

Stop!

She opened and closed her eyes and pulled the folds of blue and gold around her.

Start again.

Christ be with me, Christ within me . . .'

But Merrily's visit with Lol to Moon's barn was not going to happen. Something appalling already had. Something she could not ignore.

Jane took the call while Merrily was making breakfast.

'It's some really nasty, officious-sounding bastard.'

'Not so *loud*!' Merrily took it on the cordless phone in the kitchen.

'Merrily Watkins speaking.'

'This is Major Weston, area organizer for the Redundant Churches Fund. I make no apologies for calling you before eight. I find it ridiculous that I should have to call you at all. I wanted the *local* man to deal with it. Bizarrely, the local man tells me all matters of this nature have to be referred directly to you.'

'What's the problem, Major?' She wasn't aware that the Redundant Churches Fund even had an area organizer.

'Desecration is the problem, Mrs Watkins. At the Church of St Cosmas and St Damien at Stretford. Do you know where that is?'

'Vaguely.'

'I expect you'll manage to find it. The police already have, for what *they're* worth.'

'What kind of desecration?'

'What *kind*? Satanic desecration, of course.'

Jane was furious.

'You can't do this to Lol! Whatever it was, you *promised* him.'

'I have to. It's—'

'Your job – yeah, yeah. You know what I think? I think you're empire-building.'

'Flower, it's not *me*! I didn't even know about this, but apparently every vicar or rector or priest-in-charge in the diocese has received an edict from the Bishop's office to say that anything arising in their parishes possibly related to Deliverance should be referred initially to me. Through the Deliverance office, naturally, but this Major Weston's obviously had an earful from a local vicar happy to wash his hands of it, and so the Major's made a special point of finding my home number and getting me up nice and early in the morning. What can I do?'

'You don't have to go *now*.'

'I *do* have to go now. They've got to get the place cleaned up. It's a disused church supported by this charity.'

But she *was* annoyed. Neither Mick nor Sophie had mentioned this memo going out to all the priests. Yes, it did look like empire-building, and whilst a few vicars would be secretly relieved, the majority would resent it. *She* would have resented it.

'I'll call Lol,' she said.

TWENTY-THREE

Strawberry Ice

The main road was a brown channel between banks of snow. The Cathedral – usually seen at its most imposing from Greyfriars Bridge – skulked uneasily in half-lit mist.

Beyond the bridge, the car slid alarmingly towards the kerb where there was a pub called The Treacle Mine. This was not promising. The hill might still be a problem – like the other night.

White hell, then. Not ten minutes out of the city, but the snow had lain undisturbed for longer. Denny's monster Mitsubishi would, for once, have been useful. Don't even try the steep bit, Moon had said. You'll just get stuck. I can walk down from here.

'Oh, it's hazardous out there, Moon. Snow-blindness. Hypothermia.'

'Lol, the hill's only five hundred and ninety-five feet above sea level.'

Sometimes her humour-vacuum was almost endearing. Ever since they'd left the shop – Moon, in her green padded ski-jacket, snuggling into his shoulder – Lol had been thinking: *I was wrong, I'm crazy. There's nothing weird going on. All she needs is love.*

Anyway, he couldn't stop now; there was nowhere to turn the car around.

This morning, with no further snow, things were better.

Someone must have been up the hill with a tractor, perhaps even a snowplough. He made it without too much revving and sliding, as far as the little car park for visitors to the ancient camp.

The desolation of the day was getting to him. He'd been looking forward to bringing Merrily up here. But Merrily couldn't make it. Second thoughts, maybe, about loopy Moon – and loopy Lol, too. He'd misunderstood her.

From the back of the car, he pulled his wellies and his old army combat jacket. The snow around here was untrodden, lying in big drifts. Even where it hadn't drifted, it was four, five inches deep.

Lol ploughed through. The earth steps had disappeared, becoming a deceptive white ski-run. Lol stopped. He'd imagined the barn below would be winter-picturesque, but it was like a short, blackened toadstool under its snow-swollen roof. Neglected and charmless, most of its windows shrunken by snow.

On Saturday night, a gauzy moon had been nesting in the snow-bent treetops, and Moon had walked across where the patch of garden would be and looked all around like she wanted to establish a memory of how the barn and the surrounding trees looked in their moonlit winter robes.

And Lol had then thought, this is it. Dick whispering in his ear, *'You do find her attractive, don't you? Think she doesn't fancy you? Oh, I think she does, old son. I think she does.'* And then Denny. *'I would do anything, give anything to get her away from there. Meanwhile, if she's not alone, that's the best thing I could hope for under the circumstances.'*

Lol crunched carefully down the long earthen steps. It was fully light now, or as light as it was going to get. He knocked on the front door, set into the glassed-over barn bay, long curtains drawn on either side.

There was no answer. After a minute, Lol stepped back on to the snow-shrouded garden and looked around.

A big man was striding out of a wall of conifers on the other side of the barn. He stopped. 'Hello. Can I help?'

'I'm looking for Kathy Moon.'

'Yes, this is where she lives.' He had a high, hearty voice – not local. He wore a shiny new green Barbour and a matching cap. 'I'm from the farm. Tim Purefoy.'

'Lol Robinson. I'm a . . . friend of hers.'

'Yes, I'm sure she's spoken of you.' Tim Purefoy looked down at Lol, recognition dawning. 'I know . . . you were here helping Katherine move in, yes?' He ambled across to the glassed-over barn bay, squinting through a hole in the condensation. 'Bit odd – she's usually up and about quite early. Cycles into town, you know.'

Lol explained about driving Moon home on Saturday, and the bike being still at the shop.

'Well, I don't know what to say,' said Mr Purefoy. 'Gone for a stroll maybe? Perhaps she wanted to see what the hill was like under snow, before it all vanished. Bit of a romantic about this hill, as you probably know. Anyway, can't be far away. Come and wait at the farmhouse if you like, and have a coffee.'

'Actually,' Lol said, 'I don't suppose I could use your phone? It's possible her brother got worried about her being up here in the blizzard. Maybe he's collected her.'

'No problem at all. Follow me.' Tim Purefoy beat his gloved hands together. 'Like midwinter already, isn't it?'

The Dyn farmhouse was unexpectedly close – no more than fifteen yards behind the tight row of Leylandii. It was these conifers that deprived the barn of its view, but when you passed between them . . .

Lol almost gasped.

They were standing on a wide white lawn sloping away to a line of low bushes which probably hid the road. But it might as well have been a cliff edge.

Below it, the city – a timeless vision in the mist.

'Startling, isn't it?' Tim Purefoy folded his arms in satisfaction. 'Best view of Hereford you'll get from anywhere – except from the ramparts of the hillfort itself.'

The snow had made Hereford an island and softened the outlines of its buildings, so that the new merged colourlessly with the old. And because the city had somehow been bypassed by the high-rise revolution of the Sixties and Seventies, it might *all* have been seventeenth-century, even medieval, underneath. It was both remote and intimate; it made Lol feel very strange.

'See how the steeple of All Saints is superimposed on the Cathedral tower?' Tim said knowledgeably. 'That's one of Alfred Watkins's ley-lines. An invisible, mystical cable joining sacred sites – a prehistoric path of power.'

'And we're standing on it?'

'Absolutely. It goes very close to the house. We had a chap over to dowse it – the earth-energy. They're energy lines, you know. And spirit paths, so we're told.'

No wonder this guy had taken to Moon. Standing in the thin rain on the snowy lawn, Lol suddenly felt he could jump off and slide down that mystical cable from the hill to the steeple to the tower in the mist.

'Probably all nonsense,' Tim Purefoy said, 'but at sunset you can feel you own the city. Come and have some coffee, my friend.'

Lol shook himself.

The farmhouse was three-storeyed, ruggedly rendered in white. With lots of haphazard, irregular mullioned windows, it looked as old as the hill itself. How could Moon live out in that sunken, tree-smothered barn, knowing her own family had lost this house, and this view?

'Anna!' Tim Purefoy shouldered open the door of a wooden lean-to porch on the side of the house. 'Coffee, darling!' He held open the door for Lol. 'Come in, come in. Don't worry about the boots. It's a flagged floor, and the place is a damn mess this morning, anyway.'

Globular hanging lights were switched on in the vast, farmhouse kitchen. It was golden with antique pine, and had an old cream-coloured double-oven Aga which seemed actually to be putting heat into the room. Like a furnace, in fact. Lol felt almost oppressed by the sudden warmth.

'One second . . .' The woman kneeling at the stove wore jeans and a sackcloth-coloured apron tied over a long rainbow sweater. Her fair hair was efficiently bound up in a yellow silk scarf.

'My wife, Anna.' Tim Purefoy pulled off his cap, freeing springy white-blond curls. 'Darling, this chap's a friend of Katherine – who seems to have gone walkabout in the woods again.'

'Oh gosh. Not untypical, though.' Anna Purefoy closed an oven door, sprang up, patting floury hands on her apron. 'I'm making bread. One can buy a marvellous loaf at any one of a half-dozen places in town, but one somehow feels *obliged*, living in a house this old. Do you know what I mean?'

Lol nodded. 'Responsibility to the ancestors.'

'My God,' said Tim. 'This chap *does* know Katherine.'

'It's good to think someone does.' Anna pulled out chairs from under a refectory table. Concern put lines into her face. She was perhaps fifteen years older than she'd first appeared.

'Don't *interfere*, darling!' said Tim with affection. 'You know what we said about interfering. My wife's lost unless she can find someone to worry about.'

'There's a loaf in here for Katherine,' said Anna. 'Left to herself, she'd go days without food.'

'Oh, nonsense, Anna!'

His wife glared at him. 'Tim, I have been in her kitchen and found the refrigerator absolutely *bare*, while the girl sits there with all her books and her maps and her notes. Fascinating, what she's doing, of course, and we've learned a lot by helping her, but she's so *obsessive*, isn't she? I feel enormously guilty.'

'She thinks we twisted her arm to take on the barn.' Tim pulled off his Barbour, revealing a thick and costly cowboy shirt and a silk cravat. 'In fact, she virtually twisted ours.' He focused narrowed eyes on Lol. 'You know the history, I suppose.'

Lol nodded warily. 'I, er, know about her father.'

'Oooh.' Anna hugged herself with a shiver.

'Speaking personally,' Tim said, 'I wouldn't want to live within a hundred miles of here under those particular circumstances – but there we are. Telephone's in the hall. I say, do take off your coat, so you won't feel it so cold when you go outside again.'

From the square oak-pillared hall, Lol called the shop and got no answer. Then he called Denny at home.

Denny said angrily, 'Gone? How can she be gone?'

'So you haven't seen her? I came to pick her up here—'

'What you mean, came to pick her up?'

Lol said awkwardly, 'Denny, there's . . . there's nothing happening between Moon and me. There never has been.'

Denny was quiet for a few seconds, then he said, 'I don't believe this. You gay, Laurence?'

'No.'

'Then what the fuck . . .? I can't . . . She sometimes goes in to see the idiots next door . . . at the farm.'

'That's where I'm calling from, and they haven't seen her,

either. They say she sometimes goes out for walks, but I can't see any footprints.'

'I'm coming over,' Denny said. 'Fucking stay there.'

Lol went back outside with both Purefoys.

'You, er . . . you still own the barn, presumably?'

'Oh yes,' Anna said. 'Katherine's indicated several times that she'd like to buy it, but we're not awfully happy about that idea. It is very near to the house, and suppose she . . . Well, suppose she had a change of heart or had to sell suddenly?'

Meaning, Lol guessed, suppose she was removed by men in white coats.

'*Anyone* could buy it then, couldn't they?' Tim said. 'And it's awfully close to our house.'

'So you still have keys, presumably.'

'Well, we do. But we'd never dream of going in without permission. As I keep telling Anna, it's not our place to interfere. Or to be . . . over curious. That is, we try not to notice what we're not supposed to notice.'

What had Moon been doing?

Lol wondered how long the Purefoys themselves would stay here, once they'd got used to that view, and over the novelty of homemade bread. Houses like this, previously occupied by the same family for centuries, might then change hands half a dozen times in the following twenty years. It was hard to settle under the weight of someone else's tradition.

And costly, too. You bought a country residence for what seemed like peanuts compared with London, and then you found out how much you had to spend just to keep it standing. Moon must have been a gift to them. They'd probably run out of money halfway through converting the barn, and bodged the rest very quickly once she came on the scene.

'Are you something to do with the little shop?' Anna

asked, a scarlet parka now setting off her yellow scarf. 'That place where Katherine works?'

'Me? Not exactly, I'm just a . . . friend of hers. And of Denny.'

'Must be a busy man, her brother,' Tim said. 'Never seems to have time to visit her here.'

Lol tried knocking one more time, harder in case she was still asleep.

'OK if I go round the back and bang on one of the windows?'

'My dear chap, whatever you want.'

Lol pushed through bushes at one corner. Behind the barn there was, under snow, what must be a small square of lawn up against a low bank. It looked quite pretty – like a cake with pink icing.

Also, like some exotic confection, its design became more complex as he stared. Pink – but pale brown in places where the thaw had already eroded the snow. Strawberry ice-cream in the middle, sorbet round the edges, up against the back wall made of rubble-stone.

All it needed was a cherry in the middle, Lol thought in the wild surrealism of the moment. The red woollen beret Merrily used to wear, that would do. If you threw her beret into the centre of this lawn, it would lodge lusciously in the soft, wet, pink snow like a cherry.

There was a jagged hole in the snow under the nozzle of a pipe poking out of the wall about eighteen inches above the ground.

They'd bodged the plumbing, he thought. That was the overflow from the bath, and it should empty down into a drain.

Oh God!

Lol stood there remembering how completely Moon had changed once they'd reached the door of the barn. Her voice becoming sharp like the night, her eyes glittering like ice under the moon, as she pulled out her keys. She had been talking about Dick Lyden again, and what a clown he was. While separating a long black key and unlocking the door in the glass bay.

Maybe not *such* a clown, Lol had thought at the time. Confidence had seemed to click into place the minute Moon arrived back here – the strength of the old settlement around her, the child of the Hill. In Dick's terms of reference, a fantasy structure: *'The way we create our destiny. The way we form fate.'*

He'd moved to follow her into the barn, but she'd turned in the doorway, somehow stiffening.

She'd said, *'No.'*

'Moon?'

'I've changed my mind. I don't want you to come in.'

He'd stepped back.

'Thank you,' Moon had said. Once she had opened the door, the darkness inside seemed to suck her in and thrust him away.

Now, when Lol walked back round to the front of the barn, he was shaking.

'No luck, old chap?'

'I think we're going to need those keys, Mr Purefoy,' Lol said.

TWENTY-FOUR

Last Long Prayer

The medieval church of St Cosmas and St Damien was almost part of a farmyard situated on the edge of a hamlet among windy-looking fields in the north of the county. Not that far from main roads but Merrily, who thought she knew this county fairly well, had been unaware of it.

The church was tiny, the size of a small barn, with a little timbered bell-turret at one end.

St Cosmas and St Damien?

'Fourth-century Mediterranean saints,' said Major Weston, 'connected with physicians and surgeons, for some reason. Local doctors hold the occasional service here. Otherwise it's disused. Absolute bloody tragedy.'

'One of all too many these days, Major.' Powdered snow blew at Merrily's legs.

'Call me Nigel,' suggested Major Weston, whose belligerence had dropped away the moment he saw her. He was about sixty, had a moist and petulant lower lip, and a costly camel coat.

Merrily followed him around the raised churchyard, pine trees rearing grimly on its edge.

'I think it was the Bishop of Lincoln,' the Major said, 'who warned that disused churches were now increasingly falling prey to Satanism. The message seems to be that if your people don't want them, the Devil's only too happy to take them on.'

'It's not that we don't *want* them.'

'I know, I know, but you don't, do you? Otherwise my Fund wouldn't exist. We maintain nearly three hundred churches at present, and the figure's going up at an alarming rate. Now, when you think what a comparatively tiny population England had when these lovely old buildings were erected . . .'

'Yeah,' Merrily said, 'tell me about it.'

They stopped outside the porch. She saw that the single long gothic window in the wall beside it had an iron bar up the middle. On one side lay the farm, and some houses on the other – a stone's throw away.

'If I was a Satanist, Major, I really don't think I'd feel too safe performing a black mass here. You wouldn't be able to chant very loudly, would you, before somebody came in with a torch and a shotgun?'

'That's what the police said. Must've been lunatics – but then that's what they are, aren't they? Not normal, these people. Beggars belief.'

'I've never met one. I'd rather like to.'

He peered at her. 'Would you, by God?'

'Just to try and find out *why*.'

'What they've done in here may just change your mind. Ready to go in?'

'Sure.'

'Not squeamish are you?'

'Let's hope not.' She followed him into the porch, and he lifted the latch. 'There's no lock!'

'There should be – and there will be. A new one's in the course of being made, I believe. Perhaps these scum knew that.'

'Meanwhile, the church is left without a lock?'

'You can't just put any old lock on a building dating back to the twelfth century. In you go, m'dear.'

Holding the door for her, letting her go in first. A gentleman, ha.

It was dim and intimate, no immediate echo. None of that sense of Higher Authority you had in most cathedrals, and big churches like her own at Ledwardine.

It was in fact fascinating, the Church of St Cosmas and St Damien. Quartered by an arcade of stone and a wooden screen with a pulpit in the middle. Two short naves and what seemed to be two chancels with two altars, although she could only see one from where she was standing – a plain wooden table without a cloth.

Against the far wall, and close to the floor, the stone effigies of a knight in armour and his lady shared that last long prayer.

Merrily didn't move. She was reminded of nowhere so much as the little stone Celtic cell where she'd had the vision of the blue and the gold and the lamplit path. Only the smell was different.

She knew the smells of old churches, and they didn't usually include urine.

Before Tim Purefoy was even back with his keys, a big vehicle was roaring up to the barn bay, sloshing through the wet snow. The dull gold, bull-barred Mitsubishi, spattered from wheels to windscreen with snow-slicks and mud, skidded to within a couple of feet of the glass wall.

Denny Moon slammed out, looking once – hard – at the barn, as though angry it was still there; not burned out, derelict, toppled into rubble. He wore an old leather jacket and a black baseball cap. Wraparound dark glasses, like he feared snow-blindness. He took in the encircling trees and the over-grown Leylandii hedge, sucking air through his teeth.

'Fucking place!'

Lol walked nervously towards the car. 'Mr Purefoy's gone for his keys.'

'Fuck that. I'll kick the door down.' Denny gave him a black stare. 'Lol, what is it? What is it you know, man?'

'We just need to get in.'

'Look at you! Something's scared you. What is it?'

Tim Purefoy appeared, holding up a long key on an extended wire ring holding also two smaller ones.

At the same time his wife came round from the back of the barn. She looked stricken. 'Call . . . call the police,' she stammered. 'Better call the police.'

Denny gasped and snatched the keys.

The big room was brightened by snowlight from the highest window, exposed trusses the colour of bone.

'Kathy!' Denny bawled. '*Kathy!*'

The smell of candlewax. Blobs of it on the floor.

Denny's head swivelled. 'She sleep up there?' He made for the stairs to the loft. He hadn't seen the lawn, so he wouldn't know that what they really needed was the bathroom. 'Kathy!'

Two doors behind the stairs: one ajar, through which Lol could see kitchen worktops and the edge of a cooker; the other door shut.

Lol opened it and went in.

Into the square, white, bitter-smelling, metal-smelling bathroom, quietly closing the door and snipping the catch, sealing himself in with her. Like he should have done on Saturday night – resisting the hostile thrust of the barn – when she'd said, *'I don't want you to come in.'*

*

His back against the door, he saw first, on the wall over the bath like an icon, the photograph of a smiling man standing before a Land Rover.

On the rim of the bath were pebble-smooth shards of black pottery, arranged in a line.

'No sign,' he heard Denny shout from upstairs, sounding relieved, almost optimistic, because he hadn't found her dead in her futon.

Lol saw the crusted brown tidemark on the porcelain around the overflow grille, like sloppy dinner deposits around a baby's mouth. Presumably a tap had been left running and the overflow had gulped it all down and regurgitated it on to the snowy lawn, stopping only when the primitive water tank ran dry.

'Lol?' Denny's feet descending the stairs. 'Where'd he go?'

It was dreamlike. Lol thought at first – from the position of her, the stillness of the tableau – of Ophelia in that sad, famous Pre-Raphaelite painting.

The thin pine door bulged against him as Denny tried to open it, and then battered it with his fists, making it vibrate against Lol's back until Lol almost tripped and fell forward towards the bath. And he cried out, 'Oh God!' seeing it now as it was: graceless, peaceless, sorrowless – nothing like Ophelia.

Who wouldn't have been naked or grinning like Moon was grinning, congealing in her stagnant pool of rich, scummy, pinky-brown, cold water. With eyes open, like frosted glass, and lips retracted over stiff, ridged gums and sharp white teeth.

Beautiful Moon, so defiantly disgusting now with her cunning, secret, bloodless grin and her blood-pickled fingers below her breasts – on the waterline, on the bloodline. And the wrists ripped open: not nice neat slits – the skin was torn and ruched.

'Lol!' Denny screamed, and the pressure on Lol's back eased, telling him Denny was about to hurl himself against the door.

She'd been here a long time, you could tell. This hadn't happened this morning or even last night; this had to be Saturday night, maybe only hours after he'd brought her home and meekly taken no for an answer . . . almost gratefully, because he'd already had the sense of something dark and soiled. He should have said: Moon, there are things we have to talk about. He should have said this long ago – after the crow. He should have gone long ago to Merrily Watkins.

Swallowing his nausea, he went closer and bent over the bath. On the bottom, between Moon's legs, lay the eroded file-like blade, ragged and blackened and scabby and old, very old.

He remembered those slender but unexpectedly hardened hands fouled by crow's blood, and turned away, and opened the door to Denny.

'I'd like to sleep now, Lol.'

TWENTY-FIVE

Sad Tosser

Sophie said, 'Was it *very* horrible?'

'It was, actually.'

'It's so utterly distressing.' Sophie's face creased into shadows. 'I once read a book by a reformed Satanist who said that when they break into a church and do appalling acts, it has an almost intoxicating effect. Afterwards they feel a terrible elation. Almost . . . sexual.'

'Well,' Merrily said, 'by the very nature of what they are, they're not going to walk out feeling disgusted and nauseous, are they?'

Sophie shuddered.

When she'd gone, Merrily rang Huw Owen.

No reply, no answering machine.

She thought about calling Lol to rearrange that chance encounter with his troubled friend, Moon, but then Sophie came through again.

'Merrily, it's Chief Inspector Howe on the line.'

'Oh. Right.'

'Ms Watkins?'

'Good morning.'

'Ms Watkins, I, er . . . I'd like to consult you – as an expert.'

'Me?'

'Indeed,' Howe said.

'Heavens.' What seemed likely was that the Super-intendent, after a lunch with the Bishop, had strongly suggested Annie Howe consult Merrily over something, anything. Howe would be disinclined, as *acting* DCI, to make waves.

'Ms Watkins?'

'Sorry, just swallowing one of the pills I've been prescribed for moments of overexcitement.'

Howe sighed. 'Perhaps we could meet. I gather you've been cleaning up after devil-worshippers.'

'Blanket term, Annie. I'm not convinced.'

'Good. That's what I wanted to discuss with you.'

'One o'clock? Pub?'

'No, I'll come to your office,' Annie Howe said, keeping it official, hanging up.

Sophie came back again. 'The Reverend Owen now. Take it on my phone if you like. I have to powder my nose.'

It seemed that Sophie didn't feel she was ready to hear about this incident in detail.

'Hard to get rid of the taste, in't it, lass?'

'Hard to lose the smell.'

'Number twos as well?'

'Not that I could detect, but I didn't go prying into too many dark corners.'

'Aye, well, your problem here,' Huw said, 'is deciding whether this is the real thing or just kids who think it'd be fun to play at being Satanists for an hour or so.'

'I thought you didn't get away with just playing at it.'

'In my experience you don't, but let's not worry about poor little dabblers at this stage. Tell me again about the bird.'

'Well, it was . . . had been a crow or a raven. Is there much difference? I don't know. It had been cut open, and its entrails spread over the altar. There are kind of twin chancels in this church, but this was the real altar, on the right.'

'Two chancels?'

'Side by side. Very unusual. Quite a special little place.'

'Let me have a think.'

Merrily looked down from Sophie's window at white roofs on cars and people hurrying. Hereford people were essentially country folk, and country folk had no great love for snow. Certainly not November snow. Never a good sign; winter was supposed to settle in slowly. What if this went on until March or April?

'Two chancels,' Huw said. 'They might see this as representing a dualism: left and right, darkness and light.'

'Actually, there was some blood on the other table, too, as if the sacrificed crow had been brought from one side to the other.'

'How do you know it was sacrificed?'

'I don't. It would be nice – nicer – to think it was already dead, and they just wanted to make a mess. Huw, the way you're talking suggests you think this was the real thing.'

'It's possible.'

'If it *was* the real thing, what would be the motive? What would they be after?'

'Kicks . . . a buzz . . . power. Or – biggest addiction of the lot – the pursuit of knowledge. Nowt you won't do to feed your craving. Ordinary mortals – expendable like cattle. Kindness and mercy – waste of energy. Love's a drain, faith's for feeble minds. Can you understand that? To *know* is all. Can you get a handle on that?'

'No. That's why I'm a Christian.' *Working towards it, anyway. Made it to the pious bitch stage.*

'Mind, a crow splattered over a country church, that still has the touch of low-grade headbangers. What are you going to do about it?'

'Major Weston was asking for reconsecration. I said that wasn't necessary, as a consecration's for all time.'

'Correct. What you proposing instead?'

'A lesser exorcism, do you think?'

'When?'

'I was thinking early evening, if we could get some people together then. I wouldn't like to think of the place getting snowed in before we could do it.'

'You want me to come over?'

'I couldn't ask you to do that.'

'Give me directions,' Huw said. 'I'll be there at five.'

'I can't keep leaning on you.'

'I like it,' Huw said. 'Keeps me off the drink.'

Merrily smiled. She saw Annie Howe, in her white belted mac, walking rapidly out of King Street carrying a briefcase. 'I . . . suppose you've heard about Dobbs.'

'Aye.'

'Any thoughts on that?'

'Poor bugger?'

'That's it?'

'Let's hope so,' Huw said.

Sophie pulled up an extra chair for Howe and left them in her office. The Acting DCI kept her mac on. She hated informality.

'My knowledge of police demarcation's fairly negligible,' Merrily said, 'but aren't you a bit *senior* to be investigating the minor desecration of a country church?'

'I'm not sure I am.' Annie Howe brought a tabloid newspaper from her case and placed it before Merrily, on Sophie's desk. 'You've seen this, I imagine.'

A copy of last night's *Evening News*. The anchor story:

| **WYE DEATH: MAN NAMED.** |

'Oh, this is the guy . . .' Merrily had scarcely given it another thought. All memories of that night were still dominated by Denzil Joy. She scanned the text.

> . . . identified as 32-year-old Paul Sayer, from Chepstow. Mr Sayer had not been reported missing for over a week because his family understood he was on holiday abroad.
>
> Acting Det. Chief Inspector Annie Howe, who is leading the investigation, said, 'We are very anxious to talk to anyone who may have seen Mr Sayer since November 19. We believe he may have arrived in Hereford by bus or train and . . .

'No need to read the lot. It's mainly waffle. His relatives aren't going to talk, and we ourselves have been rather economical with any information given out to the press.'

'Aren't you always.'

'Need to Know, Ms Watkins,' Howe said, 'Need to Know. Let me tell you what we do know about Sayer.'

She brought out a folder containing photographs. Sophie, fetching in coffee for them on a tray, spotted one of them and made a choking noise.

'Would you mind?' Howe stood up and shut the door on both Sophie and the coffee.

'I believe it's known as the Goat of Mendes,' Merrily said.

A colour photograph of what seemed to be a poster.

Luridly demonic: like the cover of a dinosaur heavy-metal album from the Eighties.

'We'll return to that,' Howe said. 'But this is a photograph of Paul Sayer. He may, for all we know, have been around the city for several days before he was killed.'

He had a fox-like face, the lower half almost a triangle. No smile. Hair lank, looked as if it would be greasy. Though his eyes were lifeless, he was not dead in this picture.

'Passport photo.' Annie Howe unbelted her raincoat. 'Does look like him, though. Recognize him?'

Merrily shook her head. Howe looked openly around the office. Merrily wished the ☧ on the door was removable for occasions like this. She felt self-conscious, felt like a fraud.

Howe smiled blandly, her contact-lensed eyes conveying an extremely subtle sneer. 'You're like a little watchdog at the gate up here, Ms Watkins.'

'Look, if you're not here specifically to arrest me, how about you call me Merrily?'

'Actually, the people I call by their first names tend to be the ones I've *already* arrested. Standard interview-room technique.'

'But the suspects don't get to call you Annie.'

You might wonder if anyone did, under the rank of superintendent, she had such glacial dignity. She was only thirty-two, Merrily estimated, the same age as the man pulled out of the Wye – Paul Sayer whose photo lay on the desk.

'I expect you'll get round to explaining what this poor guy has to do with the Goat and me.'

' "This poor guy"?' said Annie Howe. 'Why do I suspect your sympathy may be short-lived?'

'He had, er, form?'

'None at all. He was, according to his surviving family, a quiet, decent, clean-living man who worked as a bank clerk in Chepstow and lived in a terraced house on the edge of the town, which was immaculately maintained. He was unmarried, but once engaged for three years to a young woman from Stroud who's since emigrated to Australia. I'll be talking to her tonight, but one can guess why the relationship foundered.'

Merrily took out a cigarette. 'Do you mind?'

'It's your office.'

'I'll open the window. Why did the engagement fall through?'

'Don't bother with the window, Ms Watkins. I'm paid to take risks. Well I suppose she must have seen his cellar.'

Cellar?

'Oh, my God, not a Fred West situation?'

'Let's not get *too* carried away. This is it.'

Six more photographs, all eight by ten. All in colour, although there wasn't much colour in that cellar.

'Christ,' Merrily said.

'So now you understand why I'm here.' Howe turned one of the pictures around, a wide-angle taken from the top of the cellar steps. 'Is this your standard satanic temple, then, would you say?'

'I've never actually been in one, but it looks . . . well, it looks like something inspired by old Dracula films and Dennis Wheatley novels, to be honest.'

'The altar,' Howe said, 'appears to have been put together from components acquired at garden centres in the vicinity – reconstituted stone. The wall poster's of American origin, probably obtained by mail-order – we found some glossy magazines full of this stuff.'

'Sad.'

'Yes, I admit I have a problem understanding the millions of people who seem to worship your own God, but this . . . How real are these people? How genuine?'

'I don't know . . . I'd be inclined to think the guy who built this temple is – I may be wrong – what my daughter would call a sad tosser.'

'But a dead tosser,' Howe said. 'And we have to consider that his death could be linked to his . . . faith.'

Merrily examined a close-up of the altar. 'What's the stain?'

'We wondered that – but it's only wine.'

'So, no signs of . . .?'

'Blood sacrifice? We haven't finished there yet, but no.'

'How did you find this set-up?'

'We had to break through a very thick door with a very big lock. The local boys were quite intrigued. Not that he appears to have broken any laws. It's all perfectly acceptable in the eyes of the law, as you know.'

'Makes you wonder why there are any laws left,' Merrily said. 'I've always thought Christianity would become fashionable overnight if they started persecuting us again.'

'So,' Howe gathered up the photos, 'you aren't very impressed by Mr Sayer's evident commitment to His Satanic Majesty.'

'No more than I was by the sick bastards who spread a crow over a lovely little old church, but . . .'

'Yes, that's the point. In your opinion, if we were to devote more person-hours than we might normally do to catching the insects who dirtied this church – which amounts to no more than wilful damage and possible cruelty to a wild bird, which is unprovable – might they be able to throw some light on the religious activities of Mr Sayer?'

'You're asking if there's a network in this area?'

'Precisely.'

'I've no idea. It *is* our intention to build up a file or database, but I'm only just getting my feet under the table, and

nothing like that seems to exist at present. My . . . predecessor—'

'Is not going to be saying an awful lot to anyone for quite a
while, from what I hear. If ever.'

'I'm sorry about this.' Merrily was desperate for another
cigarette, but unwilling to display weakness in front of Howe
– who leaned back and looked pensive.

'Ms Watkins, what's your gut feeling?'

'My gut feeling . . . is that . . . although there's no obvious
pattern, there's something a bit odd going on. I mean, I was
on a course for Deliverance priests. All of us were vicars,
rectors . . . Nobody does this full-time, that's the point. We
were told a diocesan exorcist might receive four, five assign-
ments in a year.'

'While you . . .?'

'You want to see my appointments diary already – plus two
satanic links within a week. Yes, you might find it worth
following through on the Stretford case. I wonder if they ever
return to the scene of the crime.'

'Why do you ask?'

'I'm going back tonight to do what we call a minor
exorcism.'

'Interesting. If they're local, they might not be able to
resist turning up.'

'That's what I thought.'

'Thank you, Ms Watkins, we'll be represented.' Annie
Howe snapped her briefcase shut.

'Just one thing.'

'Hmm?'

'Could you make them Christians?'

'Who?'

'The coppers.'

'Are you serious?'

'Two reasons,' Merrily said. 'One is that, if they're not, I can't let them in. Two, a few extra devout bodies at an exorcism can only help – I understand.'

'You understand.'

'I've never done one before, have I?'

TWENTY-SIX

Family Heirloom

Lol sat in the flat above Church Street – Moon's 'Capuchin Lane'. He was waiting for Denny.

He'd been waiting for Denny for several hours. It was going dark again. The shop below, called John Barleycorn, had been closed all day. Denny had not yet said he was coming, but Lol knew that sooner or later he would have to.

It was Anna Purefoy who had found the photocopy, about the same time that Lol left the bathroom and Denny went in and they heard him roar, in his agony and outrage, like a maddened bull. It was Mrs Purefoy, Lol thought, who – in the choking aftermath of a tragedy that was all the more horrifying because it *wasn't* a surprise – was the calmest of them.

'Is Katherine dead?'

Lol had nodded, still carrying an image of the encrusted overflow grille. Like the mouth of a vortex, Moon's life sucked into it.

'Tim,' Mrs Purefoy had said then, 'I think you should telephone the police from our house. I don't think we should touch anything here.'

And when Tim had gone, she'd led Lol to the telephone table by the side of the stairs. 'I was about to phone for them myself, and then I saw this.' Her red parka creaked as she bent over the table. 'Did you know about this, Mr Robinson?'

It was a copy of a cutting from the *Hereford Times*, dated November 1974 – twenty-five years ago, almost exactly. It took Lol less than half a minute to make horrifying sense of it. He was stunned.

'Did *you* know about it?'

A mad question maybe. Would anybody knowing about this have bought the old house?

By then, Denny had emerged from the bathroom, and was standing, head bowed, on the other side of the stairs. After a moment he looked up, wiped the back of a hand across his lips and shook his head savagely, his earring jangling. He didn't look at Lol or Mrs Purefoy as he strode through the room and out of the barn, the door swinging behind him. You could hear his feet grinding snow to slush as he paced outside.

Mrs Purefoy said, 'Did you know her very well, Mr Robinson?'

'Not well enough, obviously,' Lol said. 'No . . . no I didn't know her well.'

And then the police had arrived – two constables. After his first brief interview, not much more than personal details, Lol had gone out on the hill while they were talking to Denny and the Purefoys. He ascended the soggy earth-steps to the car, freezing up with delayed horror, a clogging of sorrow and shame backed up against a hundred questions.

He'd waited by the barn with Denny until they brought the body out. Hearing the splash and slap and gurgle and other sounds from the bathroom. Watching the utility coffin borne away to the post-mortem. And then he and Denny had gone to Hereford police headquarters, where they were questioned separately by a uniformed sergeant and a detective constable. Statements were made and signed, Lol feeling numbed throughout.

He and Denny had had no opportunity to talk in any kind of privacy.

The police had shown Lol the twenty-five-year-old cutting from the *Hereford Times* and asked him if he'd seen it before, or if he was aware of the events decribed in the story.

Lol had told them he knew it had happened, but not like this. He'd always understood it had been a shotgun in the woods, but he didn't remember how he had come to know that.

Later, the police let him read the item again. In the absence of a suicide note, they were obviously glad to have it. It made their job so much easier.

ANCIENT SWORD USED BY SUICIDE FARMER

Hereford farmer Harry Moon killed himself with a two-thousand-year-old family heirloom, an inquest was told this week.

Mr Moon, who had been forced to sell Dyn Farm on Dinedor Hill because of a failed business venture, told his family he was going to take a last look around the farm before they moved out.

He was later found by his teenage son in a barn near the house, lying in a stone cattle trough with both wrists cut. Dennis Moon, 15, told Hereford Deputy Coroner Colin Hurley how he found a ten-inch long sword, an Iron Age relic, lying on his father's chest.

> 'The sword had hung in the hall for as long as I can remember,' he said. 'It was supposed to have been handed down from generation to generation.'
>
> A verdict of suicide while the balance of mind was disturbed was recorded on 43-year-old Mr Moon, who . . .

'And when you left her at the door on Saturday evening,' the sergeant said, 'how would you describe Miss Moon's state of mind?'

'Kind of . . . intense,' Lol had said honestly.

'Intense, how?'

'She was researching a book about her family. I had the impression she couldn't wait to get back to it.'

The sergeant had shaken his head – not quite what he'd expected to hear.

Lol sat now in Ethel's old chair, shadows gathering around him.

Sometime tonight he'd have to ring Dick Lyden – most famous quote: *I realize you're a sensitive soul. But you don't particularly need to think about psychology when you're shagging someone, do you?* He couldn't face it.

Just before 4.30 p.m., he heard a key in the lock, and then Denny's footsteps on the stairs.

It had been Merrily's plan to spend an hour meditating in Ledwardine Church before driving nearly twenty miles to meet Huw at the church of St Cosmas and St Damien, but she'd been waylaid in the porch by Uncle Ted in heavy churchwarden mode.

'Where on earth have you been? I tried to ring your so-called office – engaged, engaged, engaged. It's not good enough, Merrily.'

'Ted, I've just spent nearly two hours trying to put together a small congregation that absolutely nobody wants to join. I have one hour to get myself together and then I've got to go out again.'

'I'm sorry, Merrily, but if you haven't got time for your own church, then—'

'Ted,' she backed away from him, 'I really don't want to go into this now, whatever it is. OK? Can we talk in the morning?'

It was not too dark to see his plump, smooth, retired face changing colour. 'Were you here this morning? Someone thought they saw you.'

'Early, yes.' God, was that only today?

'What time?'

'I don't know . . . sevenish maybe. What—?'

'Did you notice anything amiss?'

'I just went up to the chancel to pray. Don't say—'

'Yes, someone broke in. Someone broke into your church last night.'

'Oh God.' She thought at once of a dead crow and a smell of piss. 'What did they do?'

'Smashed a window.'

'Oh no.'

'Come and look.'

She followed him into the church, where the lights were on and they turned left into the vestry, where she saw that the bulb had been smashed in its shade and a big piece of hardboard covered the window facing the orchard.

The vestry. Thank God for that. No stained glass there.

'Did they take anything?'

'No, but that's not the point, is it?'

No blood, no entrails, no urine. Merrily took the opportunity to fumble her way to the wardrobe and pull out her vestments on their hangers. She'd have to change at home now.

'Have you told the police?'

'Of course we did – not that they took much interest.'

'I suppose if nothing was taken . . . Look, I'm sorry, Ted. I'll have to take a proper look round tomorrow. I have to tell Jane where I'm going.'

'And where *are* you going?'

'I have to conduct a service over at Stretford. Near Dilwyn.'

'This damned Deliverance twaddle again, I suppose,' he said contemptuously. 'You're on a damned slippery slope, Merrily.'

Denny's speech, his whole manner, had slowed down – like somebody had unplugged him, Lol thought, or stopped his medication. Denny seemed ten years older. His oversized earring now looked absurd.

'You see, Dad – he'd bought this house for us to move to when he sold the farm. At Tupsley, right on the edge of the city.'

Denny had the chair, Lol was on the floor by the bricked-up fireplace. A parchment-shaded reading lamp was on.

'Far too bloody close, that house,' Denny said. 'Christ. I used to wonder, didn't he ever think about that? How Mum was gonna be able to handle living around here with his suicide hanging over us? The whole family tainted with it? Everybody talking about us? The selfish bastard!'

Lol thought of that smiling man with the Land Rover who threw a shadow twenty-five-years long. Denny lit up a Silk Cut from a full packet Merrily had left behind.

'So after he . . . died, we flogged the Tupsley house

sharpish, and moved over to the first place we could find in Gloucester. We had relatives there, see, and nobody there to blab to little Kathy about what had happened, like kids would've done if we'd still been in town – whispers in the schoolyard. Jesus, *we* never talked about it. It never got mentioned in our house – let alone how it happened. If some bloody old auntie ever let it slip, Ma would go loopy for days after. And me . . . she's watching me all the time in case I'm developing the symptoms.'

'Of what?'

'Schizophrenia.'

Lol sensed Denny Moon's personal fears of inheriting some fatal family flaw, some sick gene – Denny keeping the anxiety well flattened under years of bluster, laughter and general loudness.

'So we . . . when Kathy's five or six and starting to ask questions like how come she didn't have an old man, we told her it was an accident. His gun went off in the woods. No big deal – she never remembered him anyway. When she was older, twelve maybe, I broke it to her that he topped himself, and why. But I stuck with the gun. You know why? Cause I knew she'd make me tell her what it was like, finding him. What he looked like in that trough – like one of them stone coffins you find around old churches.'

'Yes.' Lol found himself nodding, remembering the photo of Moon in the Cathedral Close charnel pit, gleefully holding up two ruined medieval skulls like she'd been reunited with old friends. So happy, so *at home* with images of death – reaching out to the image of her dead father, feverish eyes under the flat cap she thought he might have been wearing when he shot himself.

Sick!

Denny threw him a grateful glance. 'I was fifteen. All you can do with a memory like that is burn it out of your mind –

like they used to do with the stump when you lost an arm in some battle. So she leaves school, goes off to university in Bristol. I get the first shop – inherited, Mum's side. I come back to Hereford. I meet Maggie. You know the rest.'

'It never occurred to you she'd find out one day?'

'Why?' Denny croaked. 'Why should she? Twenty-five years, how many people remember anyway? It was *over*. And how could I ever have imagined, in any kind of worst-case scenario, that she was gonna rent this place – the same fucking barn? What kind of impossible nightmare coincidence is that? I was amazed it's still here. Like who'd want to live at a house with that abattoir right next door?'

'Somebody obviously tried hard to keep the barn out of view.' Lol thought of the wall of fast-growing Leylandii. Planted there, presumably, by the people who'd bought Dyn Farm from Harry Moon, or by the owners after that. Out of sight, out of mind, out of nightmares. 'And the Purefoys were incomers. How would they know?'

'Stupid gits.'

'You . . .' Lol hesitated. 'You didn't think of telling her before she moved in?'

'And what do you think that would've achieved, Laurence? You think that would've put her off?' Denny produced wild, synthetic laughter. '*Her*?'

Poor bloody Denny, who wanted to burn away his own last image of Harry Moon like cauterizing a stump – terrified of what might happen if he came up here and it all crashed back on him.

So he'd simply stayed away, paying Dick to look out for his sister, and both of them laying it on Lol. Wanting Lol to get close, move in with her. Lol imagined what Merrily would say about this – a situation so unbelievably flawed and precarious that only men could have allowed it to develop.

And in a way that was right. But Lol could see Denny's

skewed logic: why he'd gone to Dick Lyden instead of a real psychiatrist, and to Dick rather than Ruth. A guy he knew from the pub – a mate, nothing formal. Someone he could talk to, without having to tell all. *'He's an idiot,'* Moon had said.

'That paper,' Denny said. 'That copy of the *Times* – it never even came into our house. *You* know anything about this – how she got hold of it?'

Lol shook his head. 'First time I've seen it. I don't know . . . Did somebody give it to her? Was she going back through the old newspaper files, part of her research, and came across it that way?'

'And just laid it out there on the table, where the Purefoy woman found it? Had it all worked out, didn't she? So bloody *happy* to join the father she couldn't even remember.' Denny began to cry. 'Happy? You think she was happy?'

Some psychologist, Lol thought . . . maybe even Dick in his paper for *Psychology Today* . . . might draw a flawed parallel with the Heaven's Gate mass-suicides, all those people in San Diego who came to believe they could hitch a ride on the Hale Bopp comet.

'I never understood her,' Lol said.

And always just a little repelled.

'All down to me,' Denny said, his voice flat and dry like cardboard. 'It's all going down to me. She suddenly learns I lied to her all those years ago; that's what they're gonna say. And that fucking sword – and the bath. You know where that bath is, don't you?' He sprang up, fists clenched at his sides. 'That was exactly where the mangers were. For winter feed and water.'

Exactly? Lol felt cold inside.

'That stone trough . . . it was where the bath is now, I'd swear to it. They probably used the same holes for the fucking pipes. And the sword – that fucking sword, man! I want to *scream*. It is *not* possible.'

'She said she dug it up.'

'Where?'

'Just outside. Somebody had been trying to dig a pond and given up and she saw this thing sticking out where the ground had been excavated. Unless she knew all the time about what your father really did, there's no way she would have just found this thing and made that connection.'

'Nooo!' Denny leapt up, threw his cigarette on to the hearth. 'You don't understand, do you? The police . . . after the inquest, they asked if we wanted it back: the fucking family heirloom. The thing he'd specially sharpened on the old scythe stone, so it'd go through f . . . flesh . . . and veins, without much sawing.'

Lol thought about the blackened relic. *She* must have sharpened that too. Must have honed the edge, testing it on her thumb maybe – rehearsing. You didn't slash your wrists sideways, you cut upwards into the vein – a fellow patient in the psychiatric hospital had told Lol that. And warm water to prevent muscle cramps and stop the blood clotting. Dreamy, otherworldly, unstable Moon hadn't done a thing wrong.

'Police said what did we wanna do with it – this valuable antique. So I took it. Ma was in no state at the time, never would be again, so *I* took it. Ma signs for it, never knew what she was signing for. I was sixteen by then – big man taking charge. I knew what to do with it. I wrapped it up in some newspaper, stuffed it in my bike bag – brought it up here, back to the old farm. Come up on the bike early one morning, and buried the fucker.'

'*You* buried it?'

'And then, twenty-five years later, my poor little mental

sister comes along and digs it up – the *same* blade.' Denny hissed, 'It defies fucking *belief*.'

'You don't know that.' Lol leapt up aghast. 'You can't possibly know that.'

'Don't *know* it? It was on our wall for . . . I dunno, for centuries. That's why I knew Kathy wasn't talking total crap about us being in this direct line to the old Celtic village. My grandad, when I was little, he told me that artefact'd been in the family for two thousand years. Sounds balls, don't it? What family's been two thousand years in the same spot?'

'Where did you bury it?'

'In the shit.' A short, bitter laugh. 'There was this kind of slurry pit in front of here in those days. I dug down to the bottom of it. I put the sword in the shit.'

It all fitted so well. Perhaps the Purefoys or their predecessors had found the old pit, thought it was the site of a pond, so dug down – and when no water came up, they abandoned it. It all fitted so horribly well.

'You tell the police it was the same sword?'

'They never asked. They knew she'd dug up all this stuff. Far as they're concerned she was just obsessed with Dad's suicide. They're not connecting it beyond an obsession. If you were the police, would you wanner know all this shit about the ancestors? Would you want a hint of anything . . .' Denny drew breath and bit his lower lip. 'Anything paranormal?'

'You think that?'

'Sometimes,' Denny said, 'it's the least complicated option.'

'She said it was telling her things,' Lol said. 'She wouldn't even let me touch it. She said she didn't want the flow blocked by anyone else's vibrations.'

'Madness,' Denny said. 'Let's just call it madness.'

Lol stood up and moved to the window, looked down into Capuchin Lane, snow now in rags against the house walls after a day of shoppers' shoes. 'She just wanted to think she was in . . . almost physical contact with her ancestors.'

'She's with the primitive fuckers now,' Denny said sourly.

Protect Her This Night

The day after tomorrow it would be December. Amidst frozen fields, the Church of St Cosmas and St Damien, a small candle-shimmer behind its leaded windows, looked peaceful in a humble-stable-at-Bethlehem way. Or so she told herself.

Another attempt to dispel the fear.

'Always make time to prepare,' Huw would say. All the time she'd made, she'd blown.

An hour fending off Ted Clowes, who saw himself as her lay-supervisor, who was always credited with getting Merrily the Ledwardine living – to ease the worries of her mother, his sister in Cheltenham who was convinced that it was only a matter of time before any female curate in Liverpool was found raped and battered in the churchyard.

Ted would also dump her without a qualm if anything began reflecting badly on himself.

'I think,' he'd told her before they finally parted tonight, 'that this parish is beginning to realize precisely where it stands with you, Merrily.'

And she knew that this time he'd cause trouble. Perhaps a discreet call to the Archdeacon, a question at the parish council which would be recorded in the minutes.

It had left her less than an hour to see to the blessing and bottling of the water and to explain to Jane where she was going and why Jane, who would be more than a bit interested, could not come. The truth was, if there was anything in there, she didn't want Jane exposed to it. Kids her age were easy prey. It might even have been kids Jane's age who were behind the desecration.

But Jane seemed unconcerned, said that was OK, as she was going out anyway, to see a movie in Hereford with Rowenna.

Hardly for the first time, as she parked the Volvo at the side of the track next to a Suzuki four-wheel drive and a muddied Mondeo, Merrily wondered why Jane did not have a boyfriend.

She went round the boot to fetch her case, containing the Bibles, the prayer books, the rites of blessing and lesser exorcism that she'd hand-copied on to cards, and the holy water. She was freezing. She'd changed into her vestments before leaving, so now she put on her cowled clerical cloak of heavyweight loden, but it did nothing for the cold inside.

Lights shone from the cottages. The church, however, was in darkness, no candlelight visible from this side.

She saw figures waiting for her at the edge of the churchyard.

'DS Bliss.' He shone a torch upwards to his own ginger-topped face. 'Franny Bliss.' Merseyside accent. 'I'm a Catholic. You all right with that, Vicar?'

'That's . . . fine. I'm Merrily.'

'I know. Seen your piccy in the local rag. This big yobbo's PC Dave Jones. Nonconformist, him. What was that bloody chapel of yours again, Dave?'

'Pisgah, sarge. Pisgah Chapel.' PC Jones was in plain clothes: dark anorak and a flat cap. 'Not been back in years, mind.'

'I just love to hear him say it,' Bliss said. 'Now, just so's you know, Merrily, we've gor another lad hanging out by the farm. We don't talk about him – many years lapsed. That's why he gets to stay in the cold. Anyway, we're the best the DCI could put together in the time. Where do you want us?'

'I don't know how you want to handle it.' Merrily stood on the parapet surrounding the churchyard, looking out at the bare fields gleaming silver under a sizable moon. The wind plucked at her cloak. 'This could be a wild-goose chase for you.'

'Like most of our nights, that is,' said bulky Dave.

Merrily gathered the cloak around her. She was scared – and had been since changing into her priestly things. Under her cloak, the cassock had begun to feel clammy, the surplice stiff.

'For a start, who else knows about this?' Franny Bliss asked.

'Well, I told Major Weston, and made a courtesy call to my colleague at Dilwyn. Left a message on his machine, anyway. I also rang the farm here and got the numbers of about half a dozen people living in the area, giving them the opportunity to come along if they felt strongly about it.'

'Or if they fancied watching an exorcism?'

Merrily sighed. 'Unfortunately, yes. But I said the number allowed inside the church would be limited. And definitely no children.'

'Would it be all right if we talked to a few of the locals? In areas like this, people hear things.'

'Afterwards, though.'

'We'll ask them to hang on. And we'll pay particular attention to anyone who doesn't want to. I do feel quite strongly about it meself. It's only wilful damage, but if they can do this, they're capable of a lot of other stuff carrying stiffer sentences, you know what I mean?'

'I had a chat with Inspector Howe.'

'And your Bishop's had a chat with our Divisional Super. It's about community relations at the highest level.'

'Ah, I'm sorry about that.' The Bishop had been hard to pin down, and tonight's ceremony had, in the end, been cleared with him on his mobile via Sophie.

'Not that we wouldn't be here anyway,' Franny Bliss said, 'but maybe not *three* of us. Still, get *these* lads, and even if we don't get a line on the body in the Wye, we might get something else.'

'Might get possessed, sarge,' PC Jones said heavily.

'Merrily'll protect us, Dave. Won't yer, Merrily?'

There was nothing essentially *wrong* with Christianity, Patricia said. It promoted a useful, if simplistic, moral code. But it was an import. When it was introduced, it was revolutionary and brash and sometimes brutal and crass. It trampled over ancient wisdom.

Jane saw Rowenna's glance. None of the rest of the group knew her mother was a vicar. They thought she was a teacher. And they thought Jane was eighteen and working as a secretary.

Blinds were down over the window. A small brass oil lamp burned on a high table. Seven of them sat in a vague semicircle around Patricia, on mats and dark-coloured pillows. There was a faint scent, musty-sweet, perhaps from the oil in the lamp. It was mysterious but also cosy.

'And Christianity has always been used as a prop for prejudices,' Patricia continued, 'creating the myth of the cloven-hoofed devil and demonizing black cats, which were tortured and slaughtered in their hundreds.'

Jane thought about Ethel and seethed.

'So many of these things are forgotten now,' Patricia said.

Patricia had the look of someone much older than she possibly could be, someone who'd been soaking up wisdom for like *centuries*. She was the elder of the circle and the others deferred to her. Jane wasn't sure how many others there were in the group. They came from a wide area on both sides of the Welsh border. All women: a couple of old-hippy types – long skirts and braided hair – but mainly the kind you thought of as school-teacherish. Thank heavens none of their own teachers were here.

She and Rowenna were the youngest. The women called themselves 'The Pod', after the café itself.

Patricia was saying: 'It's the basis of many of our exercises that human beings are the central nervous system of the Earth. Thus we can receive impulses and also send them out. We can effect changes with our minds, and this is a responsibility not to be taken lightly.'

That was the definition of magic, wasn't it? Effecting change with the mind – Mum's lot would say that only God could effect changes. Which, from where Jane was sitting, was bollocks basically – all this Serving the Will of God stuff. Like the wholesale slaughter of black cats? The Spanish Inquisition?

But was The Pod a *pagan* thing? Because, OK, she was entitled to find her own spiritual path, but it would be better if it was like *parallel* to Mum's. She wasn't particularly looking for confrontation and heavy-duty domestic strife.

She just wished someone would explain simple things like that.

'It's about consciousness.' Patricia looked suddenly at Jane, as if she'd picked up her thoughts, her uncertainty.

Jane shivered. She was a little scared of Patricia, with her smoky-grey dress and her tight, parchment-coloured hair. She wanted to ask exactly what Patricia meant by 'consciousness'. But this was only their second meeting, and she didn't want to seem stupid. The nature of consciousness was something on which she'd be expected to meditate – she was establishing a special corner for that in her sitting-room/study, next to a big yellow rectangle on one of the Mondrian walls. She'd bought a little incense-burner but hadn't used it yet.

It was all a little bit frightening – therefore, naturally, wonderful.

Jane glanced up. Patricia was looking directly at her. In the gloom, Patricia's eyes burned like tiny torchbulbs.

Jane gulped, suddenly panicked. Christ, she'd been rumbled. They'd found out that her mother was an Anglican priest. They thought she was some sort of Church spy. She looked across at Rowenna, but Rowenna was staring away into the darkness. The others were gazing placidly down into their laps. She didn't really know any of them; Angela, the tarot lady, had not been present at either of the meetings.

Jane had expected all kinds of questions before she was admitted to the circle, but it hadn't been like that. It was only when you got here and experienced the electric atmosphere – as if this little room was the entrance to an endless tunnel – that you instinctively wanted to keep quiet about yourself. At least, you did if your old lady was a vicar.

'Don't worry, Jane,' Patricia said suddenly. 'We're here to help you.' The woman smiled thinly.

The wind whined in the rafters and the flame of the oil lamp shrank back, as though it was cowering.

Cool!

The church was now lit by two oil lamps supported on brackets, three candles and a hurricane lantern on the central pulpit. It looked deceptively cosy. Huw Owen was there with a curly-haired, jutting-jawed, youngish minister, who backed away from Merrily in her cloak, as if she was a vampire, throwing up his hands in mock defence.

'Mrs Watkins, I *beg* forgiveness.'

'From me?'

'I'm Jeffrey Kimball, from Dilwyn. Major Weston approached me this morning, to perform the necessary, and I'm afraid I threw a tantrum and gave him your home number, which I looked up in the telephone book. It was pure pique on my part after that memorandum from the Bishop on the subject of Deliverance, and I'm sorry to have taken it out on you.'

'I can understand your—'

'To be quite honest, Mrs Watkins, I tend to object to more or less anything this particular bishop does. I do so *hate* blatantly political appointments of any kind. Absolutely *everyone* thought Hereford should have gone to Tom Armstrong – a canon at the Cathedral for five years before he went to Reading as Dean . . . *Immensely* able man . . . and they used a very minor heart problem as an excuse to give it to Hunter. I make no secret of my feelings, and I realize you—'

'Happen you can save that till after, lad,' Huw Owen said.

'Oh.' The Rev. Kimball let his arms fall to his sides. 'Yes, of course. I should have thought.'

'Merrily needs a bit of quiet,' Huw said.

'Yes, I shall leave you alone and go out to contemplate the moonlight on the snow.'

'Aye, give us quarter of an hour, there's a good lad.'

'I know his type,' Huw said as the latch dropped into place behind Kimball. 'Gets to the age when the bishops are looking younger. How are you, lass?'

She hugged Huw. It was the first time they'd been together since the Deliverance course. He wore what looked like an airforce greatcoat and a yellow bobble-hat.

'You all right for this, Merrily?'

'Sure.' She looked around, sniffed the air, could only smell disinfectant.

'Who cleared it up?' Huw asked.

'I did. Couldn't ask anybody else, could I? Buried the . . . remains . . . just over the wall. Little ceremony.'

'Hands and knees wi' a scrubbing brush, eh? What you got in mind for tonight?'

'We're looking at minor exorcism.'

'Never go over the top.'

'A cleansing. Holy water.'

'Go right round it, I would. Take one of them coppers with you. Never had a copper at one of mine. Right, make a start? You want to pray together first?'

'That would be good.'

They sat side by side on the pew nearest the pulpit. 'I'll keep it simple,' Huw said, 'then we'll have a bit of quiet. Lord, be with us in this tainted place tonight. Help this lass, Merrily, to repossess it, in Your name, from whatever dark shadows may still hang around it. Protect her this night, amen.'

'Amen,' Merrily added.

And, during the ensuing period of quiet, she felt nothing – at first.

When she closed her eyes, she saw neither the blue nor the gold, nor the lamplit path. She saw nothing but a swirling grey untinged by the lamps and the candles.

She was not comfortable on the strange, sloping pew. Found she was squirming a bit, her cassock feeling clammy again. She was actually sweating; she felt damp down her spine. *Come on, calm down.* She undid the cloak, let it slip from her shoulders. Opened her eyes, but lowered the lids, letting them relax. Shifted position again, and was aware of Huw's brief sideways glance.

Lamplight flushed the sandstone faces of the knight and his lady, raised only inches above the floor to her left. They were believed, she now knew, to be John and Agnes de la Bere. The de la Beres were lords of the manor for much of the

Middle Ages. John wore armour and carried a shield; his wife was gowned and wimpled, slim and girlishly pretty. Another knight, probably John's father, Robert, lay in the sub-chancel in front with his wife Margaret. Some effigies were terrifying, but these were courtly and benign and truthful. John de la Bere was stocky, had narrow eyes and a big nose.

In other words, she felt OK about them. And about the church. So why was she so uneasy?

She closed her eyes again, pressed her hands formally together, like the hands of John and Agnes de la Bere, and murmured *St Patrick's Breastplate* in her mind. She smelled the pine disinfectant she'd borrowed from the farm, and ignored the slow-burning itch which occurred in the palm of her left hand and then the right, as though transmitted from one to the other.

Huw was watching her openly now. She was absolutely desperate for a smoke. She shifted again. The itch in her hands was worse; she couldn't ignore it, had to concentrate hard to stop herself pulling her hands apart and rubbing her palms on the edge of the pew.

When she could bear it no longer and yearned for relief, she was at last given some help.

Scritch-scratch.

The tiny bird-claw, the curling nail on a yellow finger. The smell of disinfectant had grown sweet and rancid, and was pulled into her nostrils like thin string and down into her throat.

Cat faeces and gangrene.

A rough cough came up like vomit. Merrily began to cough and cough and couldn't stop. She folded up on the pew, arms flailing, eyes streaming. She felt Huw's arms around her, heard him praying frantically under his breath, clutching her to him, and still she couldn't stop coughing and slid down his legs to the stone floor, and he pulled away from her and she heard him scrabbling about.

'Drink,' he said urgently. Then a hard ring of glass pushing at her lips, chinking on her teeth.

She gripped it and sucked and Huw held it there.

Merrily fell back against the pew, holy water dribbling down her chin, the lamps and candles blurring into a blaze. Huw brought her gently to her feet and put her cloak around her shoulders.

'Out of here, lass,' he said mildly. 'Don't come back, eh?'

TWENTY-EIGHT

Crone with a Toad

Lol saw that Dick Lyden had become aware of deep waters and was now backing into the paddling area. Dick poured Glenmorangie for Lol and himself. He still looked shaken: not terribly upset exactly, more like unnerved. Almost certainly this was the first time a client of his had taken her own life.

An unexpected minefield then, psychotherapy.

Dick sat down behind his desk lamp, some art-deco thing with a cold blue shade. It created distance.

'And the police, Lol . . . the police are saying what?'

'Keeping the lid on it. No crime, no guilty parties. Probably doing their best to disregard the bizarre bits.'

Dick had finally got through on the phone, demanding Lol should come round at once. Needing to know, for his peace of mind and his professional security, everything that had happened and how it might rebound on him.

This was no longer jolly old Dick revelling in his newfound status as analyst, delightedly knitting strands of experience together into some stupid woolly jumper.

Lol said, 'As I understand it, they don't particularly want to *know* if it's the same sword, basically.'

'That's quite understandable. A suicide is not a murder. This . . . this wrist-cutting is still not uncommon, I gather, in an age of subtler methods. Not a difficult way to go. More distressing, perhaps, for whoever finds the body. And the weapon? An important symbol for Moon, no doubt, under the regrettable circumstances, but irrelevant as far as the police are concerned. But what the hell was Denny doing sitting on this information? Would I have supported her plan to move into that place if I'd known her father had done it in that actual same . . . When's the inquest?'

Meaning: *Will I be called? What am I going to say?*

'Going to be opened tomorrow, but that's just so Denny can give formal identification of the body and they can release her for burial. It'll then be adjourned for weeks – maybe months – while they put the medical evidence together.'

'They haven't been to see me yet.'

'Maybe you don't matter, Dick,' Lol said coldly.

He'd hate to think that Dick was counting on the inquest being economical with the facts, so there'd be more unpublicized material available for his own psychological paper on Moon's case. He'd really *hate* to think that.

But the inquest was going to get it all wrong, wasn't it?

Just that Lol couldn't see through to the truth either.

'Look . . . ahm . . .' Dick leaned back, well behind his blue lamp. 'Lol, I don't want you to blame yourself for this. You tried to get close to her and it didn't work out. Perhaps that was a mistake, but we'll never know. We must accept we'll never know, and . . . and . . . and let it go.'

A subtle restructuring of history here: like it had been Lol's sole decision to try to get close to Moon, with Dick's tentative, guarded approval.

'Well,' Dick stood up, 'thanks for coming over. Ahm . . . this won't affect the boy's recording, will it? Denny . . . well, obviously something creative to occupy his mind.'

Tuneless Little Twats with Fender Strats.

'I'm sure it's exactly what he needs,' said Lol.

'Good man,' Dick said. 'The boy, you see . . . the boy's been very difficult and uncommunicative, and when he does communicate, it's with an unpleasant teenage sneer. Goes out every night now, pushing it as far as he can get. When he's not with his band, he's with some girl. Some girl's got her hooks into him, so I would rather he was with the band in Denny's studio. At least until after Sunday.'

'Why Sunday?'

'His enthronement as Boy Bishop in the Cathedral, during evensong. By the actual Bishop, and before a packed Cathedral. Just let's get that over with.'

'You still think he might back out, right?'

'Not if the little shit knows what's good for him,' Dick said through his teeth. Then he laughed at his own venom. 'Look, Lol, Moon was ill – more ill than any of us knew. Delusional. Shouldn't have been on her own there. We're all to blame for that – Denny, you, ah . . . me, and the Health Service. All I'm saying . . . the police are right. Let's not overcomplicate things, or see things that might not be there. That's how myths are created.'

'Right,' Lol said. A small fury ignited inside him.

'Good man.' Dick clapped him on the shoulder.

It was thawing at last. Clouds crowded the moon as Lol crossed the main road towards the refashioned ruins of the city wall.

This CD would be his last work for Dick Lyden. He hadn't been to his psychology night-class for over a fortnight.

The city wall glistened in the moonlight.

So the version of Moon's death which the inquest would establish would be untrue. The verdict – unless the post-mortem threw up something unexpected – would be a straightforward Suicide While the Balance of Mind was

Disturbed. And no blindingly obvious warnings from the coroner afterwards; there was nothing anyone else would learn from this.

'*And when you left her at the door on Saturday evening, how would you describe Miss Moon's state of mind?*'

'*Kind of . . . intense. She was researching a book. About her family. I had the impression she couldn't wait to get back to it.*'

It was true. When he'd left her, there was no indication at all that she might—

'*If you were the police,*' Denny had said, '*would you want a hint of anything paranormal?*'

Why had Denny said that? It was the first time he'd ever mentioned the paranormal in connection with Moon, or indeed any connection at all. But how well did he really know Denny? Only well enough to know now that Denny had been putting up a front to conceal unvoiced fears. Perhaps if he'd told Denny, rather than Dick, about the crow and about Moon seeing her father . . .

Oh, hell!

Lol stood on the medieval bridge, gazing over the parapet into the Wye, numbed by a quiet panic. He didn't know what to do, which street to go down. Directionless. Working with Dick, while it hadn't felt exactly *right*, at least had been a new rope to hold on to.

Very soon he would reach the main road again, having walked in a complete circle. He felt like some aimless vagrant – or worse, closer to the truth, a mental patient returned to the care of the community. He turned abruptly, moved back up Bridge Street, past the off-licence and Peter Bell's Type-writer Shop, the snow on the pavement reduced to slivers of slush.

Two young women walked out of a darkened doorway

about five yards ahead of him and he saw, by an all-night-lighted shopfront, that one of them was Jane Watkins. Perhaps she noticed him; she turned sharply away and hurried on, slightly ahead of her companion.

The doorway belonged to Pod's, a healthfood café. He'd been in there just once: it was dark and primitive and woody, with secondhand tables and rickety chairs – people who opened healthfood restaurants were into recycling and no frills. On the whitewashed walls, in thin black frames, he remembered, were reproductions of drawings by Mervyn Peake: twisted figures, spindly figures, bulbous figures, in gloomy landscapes. Lol recalled eating a soya-sausage roll under one showing a crone with a toad. He hadn't stayed long.

When she got in, she put out some food for Ethel and went up to the bathroom, which was still like a 1950s public lavatory, with black and white tiles and a shower the size of an iron streetlamp. She sat on the lavatory, head in hands, her stomach churning. She heard Jane's key turn in the door, but it was quite a while before Merrily could go down.

'You're ill,' Jane said. Looking up from the omelette mix in the pan. The sight of the yellow slop made Merrily want to throw up.

She shivered damply inside her dressing-gown. 'I'm sorry, flower, I can't eat . . . anything. I'm really sorry.'

'I'd better stay off school tomorrow and look after you,' Jane said promptly, 'if you're no better by then.'

'No, thank you . . . I mean, certainly not.'

'How long have you been in?'

'Not long.' Merrily leaned against the Aga rail next to her daughter.

'How did it go?'

'All right, I think.'

'Did you feel ill *then*?'

'Yes. In fact, I . . . couldn't do it. But Huw was there. Huw did it.'

Jane sniffed, her eyes narrowing. 'You've been drinking.'

'Hey, what is this? I called into a pub for something to settle my stomach.'

Everybody trying not to stare at the cloaked figure with the bottom of her cassock showing: the first female whisky-priest in the diocese.

'Hmm,' Jane said, 'why don't you go to bed? I'll bring you a drink up.'

'Thanks, flower.' She thought she might be about to cry. Again.

She took up a hot-water bottle, dumped her cassock and surplice in the wash-bin, lay between the sheets and sweated.

She'd been here before: a panic-attack at her own installation service at Ledwardine Church. And hallucinations . . .

But what kind of sick, warped mind conjures up the filth of Denzil Joy?

Dear God.

Franny Bliss and his colleague had watched her hobble to the car, perhaps waiting to see her safely back to the church of St Cosmas and St Damien, but she hadn't returned. *'Out of here, lass.'*

It was all over. Finished.

Jane brought her hot chocolate.

'There's a drop of brandy in it.'

'You'll have me at the Betty Ford Clinic, flower.'

Jane smiled wanly.

'Where did *you* go tonight?'

'Just . . . you know . . . to see a couple of friends.'

'They could come here sometime. Lots of room.'

'Yeah,' Jane said. 'Maybe sometime.'

Merrily sank back into the sweat-damp pillow and slithered into a feverish sleep. At times she heard bleeps and voices – which might have been on the answering machine or in her hot, fogged head – like satanic static.

Just before midnight, the bedside phone bleeped.

'Huw?' she said feverishly.

'You were asleep, Merrily?'

'Yes. Hello, Eileen.'

'Your man's back,' Cullen said, 'with his candles and his bottles.'

'Oh.'

'I said I'd call you.'

She clawed for consciousness. 'It's not . . . visiting time, is it?'

'Jesus, you *must* have been sound asleep. Being as Mr Dobbs is in a side ward, *any* time is visiting time, within reason. This is not exactly within my idea of reason, but the visitor's a very plausible feller. Whatever the hell kind of weirdness he's getting up to in there, I have to say I quite took to him.'

'You . . . talked to him?'

'He was very apologetic. Said he'd have come earlier but he had some urgent business to see to . . . Are you still there, Merrily?'

'What did he look like?'

'Oh . . . late fifties. Longish, straggly grey hair. He had a bobble-hat and he was in this auld blue airman's coat. Talked like . . . who's that feller? Alan Bennett? But a real auld hippy, you know?'

'Yes.'

'He's still in there, doing his stuff around Mr Dobbs with

his candles. Probably be gone by the time you get here. I could try to keep him talking, if you like . . .'

'No,' Merrily said bleakly, 'it's all right now, Eileen. I don't think I want to see him.'

TWENTY-NINE

Fog

At first it felt like the start of a cold: that filthy, metallic tainting of the back of the throat. And then she was fully awake – knowing what it was, panting in terror.

He's here!

Rolling out of bed, breath coming in sobs, rolling over and scrambling on to her knees, she began to mutter the *Breastplate*, groping on the carpet for her pectoral cross.

> '. . . *by invocation of the same*
> '*The Three in One and One in Three.*
> '*Of whom all nature hath creation.*
> '*Eternal Father, Spirit, Word . . .*'

And she fell back against the bottom of the bed, gulping air.

Gone? Perhaps.

After a while she sat up, before reaching instinctively for the cigarettes and lighter, pulling herself to her feet, into the old woollen dressing-gown and out of the cold, uncosy bedroom.

She ached. The light from the landing window was the colour of damp concrete. The garden below looked like her head felt: choked with fog. She stood swaying at the top of the stairs, dizzy, thought she would fall, and hugged the newell post on the landing, the cigarette dangling from her mouth. Repeatedly scraping her thumb against the Zippo, but the light wouldn't come. Sweating and shaking with panic and betrayal.

'Mum?'

What?

'Mum!'

The kid stood at the bottom of the stairs, looking frightened.

Merrily heard a single letter dropping through the box. The postman.

Normality.

She began to cough. *No such thing.*

Because there was no light, as such, penetrating Capuchin Lane, Lol overslept and awoke to the leaden grind of a harmonium from the shop below, a deep and doomy female voice.

Nico. Mournful, sinister old Nico songs from the Seventies. Unshaven, Lol made it down to the shop, past Moon's lonely mountain-bike, and found Viv, the new manager: a sloppy-hippy granny, old friend of Denny's.

'Do you like Nico, Lol?'

'Sometimes,' Lol said.

'I love her,' Viv said. 'I know she's not to everybody's taste. But it's Moon's funeral on Friday: a mourning time.'

'That's three days away.' He didn't know whether Moon had ever even liked Nico; it was not unlikely.

'I thought I'd play it for an hour every morning, to show that we're in mourning,' Viv promised. 'There's a letter for you, from London.'

Lol opened it over his toast in the corner café. Ironically it promised money – money, as usual, for nothing. The revered Norma Waterson wanted to use one of his songs on her next solo album. It was 'The Baker's Lament', the one about the death of traditional village life.

He was depressed. By James Lyden's rules, he should have been dead now for at least ten years. On the other hand, unless folk singers were exempt, Norma Waterson should have been dead for over twenty-five. He stared through the café window into the fog. There was nothing in the day ahead for him. It had come to this.

Whereas Moon, so excited by her research, so driven . . . had just simply ended it.

He could not believe that what she'd discovered had led her to the conclusion that the only way of repairing the broken link with her ancestors was by joining them.

He'd heard nothing more from Merrily.

Lol finished his toast, walked back to the shop. A customer was coming out, and Lol heard that endless dirge again through the open door. It sounded – because Nico was also dead – like an accusation from beyond the grave, a bony finger pointing.

Sophie was saying into the phone, 'Have they double-checked? Yes, of course, I'm sorry. But it seems so . . .'

Merrily pulled off her coat, tossed it over the back of her chair, slumped down into it. She was going to miss Sophie, and even the office with ⅅ on the door – almost a second home now, with none of the complications of the first.

Sophie put down the phone, tucking a strand of white hair behind one ear. 'It's bizarre, Merrily, quite bizarre. That was George Curtiss. The Dean's absolutely furious. You know the Cantilupe tomb was due to be reassembled this week, in time for the Boy Bishop ceremony on Sunday? But, would you believe, there's a piece missing.'

'A piece?'

'One of the side panels. You know the side-panels with the figures of knights? Knights Templar, someone suggested.'

'I know.' She remembered the knights, blurred by age, their faces disfigured.

'Well, one had broken away from the panel. Maybe through age or stone-fatigue. It was due to be repaired, but now it's vanished!'

'Someone pinched a slab of stone?'

'So it seems. When the masons were sorting out all the segments it just wasn't there. It's not huge – about a foot wide, eighteen inches deep – though heavy obviously.'

'Not easily shoved in your shopping bag,' Merrily said. 'But safely locked up behind that partition, surely?'

'That's the point.' Sophie looked worried. 'About the only time its removal could have happened was when we were all fussing over Canon Dobbs, after his stroke.'

'They suspect one of us?' *Maybe*, she thought insanely, *I could resign under suspicion of stealing a chunk of Cantilupe.* It would be easier, less complicated.

'This Dean will suspect anyone connected with the Bishop,' Sophie said with rare malice. 'He's already calling for a full inquiry. No, I don't for a minute think they suspect one of us. They just think we might have been more . . . I don't know . . . observant.'

'Who'd want to nick a single medieval knight not in terrific condition? And what for – a bird-table?'

'Don't joke about it in front of the Dean, whatever you do.'

'I never seem to meet the Dean,' Merrily said.

'Personally I *never* joke in front of the Dean.' The Bishop had appeared in the doorway. The Bishop at his hunkiest, with the possibly-Armani jacket over a denim shirt and jeans. The only purple now was a handkerchief carelessly tucked into his breast pocket. 'Good morning, Sophie. Merrily, how did it go last night? Nothing over the top, one trusts. Restraint is our new watchword.'

She said, 'You haven't heard?'

'What should I have heard?'

'Mick, look . . .' She came slowly to her feet. 'I need to talk to you.'

'Oh yes,' Sophie said quickly, 'the blessing at Stretford. I gather you weren't very well, Merrily.'

'Who told—?'

'She really shouldn't have turned out, Michael,' Sophie said. 'You can see how terribly pale she is.'

'Merrily?' The Bishop moved into the office, turned his famous blue eyes on her. 'Lord, yes, you don't look well at all.'

'Fortunately,' Sophie said, 'Huw Owen was present and able to take over and conduct the service, so that was all right.'

Merrily stared at her. *What are you doing?*

'Owen?' The Bishop's face stiffened with outrage. 'Who the *hell* invited Owen?'

'I did,' Merrily said. 'I'm sorry, I should have told you, shouldn't I?'

'Yes, you should. The man's from outside the diocese. He's *Church in Wales.*'

'It's my fault,' Sophie said quickly. 'Merrily told me she'd asked the Reverend Owen to come in as . . .'

'Hand-holder,' Merrily said. 'It was my first serious exorcism. As it was to be in a church, I didn't want to make a mistake.'

'Well, I should have been told,' the Bishop said almost peevishly. 'I realize he was your course tutor, Merrily, but I've appointed *you*, not him. In fact, if I'd known more about Owen at the time, we might not have sent you on that particular course.'

'I'm sorry?'

'Let's just say' – the Bishop's eyes were hard – 'that his roots are planted in the same general area as Dobbs's.'

'Oh, Michael . . .' Any further discussion of the dangers of medievalism was forestalled by Sophie informing the Bishop about the missing Cantilupe knight, apparently smuggled out of the Cathedral.

'And that's all they took?' The Bishop slowly shook his head, half-smiling now. 'Admittedly, we don't want opportunist tomb-robbers cruising the Cathedral, but it's hardly cause for a major panic. Surely our guys can construct a temporary substitute if they need to put the shrine together in a hurry. Reconstituted stone or something. Who, after all, is going to know?'

'Reconstituted stone?' Sophie said faintly.

'Poor old boy's bones are already widely scattered,' the Bishop said reasonably. 'It's not as if those knights have anything to guard any more, is it? Sophie, Val and I shall be leaving earlier for London than planned.'

'I'm sorry,' Sophie spun towards her office, 'I thought the reception was tomorrow.'

'Well, there's going to be a dinner now, tonight – with Tony and Cherie. And other people, of course.' He laughed. 'One can hardly reschedule these things according to one's personal convenience. We'll need to get off before lunch. So . . . Merrily,' turning his attention on her like a loaded shotgun, 'I want you to think about something.'

He stepped back and surveyed her – critically, she thought – in her black jumper and woollen skirt, flaking fake-Barbour over the back of the chair.

Whatever it is now, she thought, *not today.*

'Ironic that the question of Dobbs and Owen should arise. Traditionalism – I want all this to be raised at the next General Synod, and I want you, Merrily, to give some thought to producing a paper on what, for want of a better term, I'm officially calling New Deliverance.'

She stared at him. 'Me?'

'Very definitely you. I think I may be looking at the very *face* of New Deliverance.'

'Bishop, I don't know what you mean about "New". Surely the whole point of—'

'You know very well what I mean, Merrily. Think back to our discussion in The Green Dragon. Anyway, I don't have time to expand on it now. We'll talk again before Christmas, yes?'

She couldn't reply.

'Excellent,' the Bishop said crisply. As he left, Merrily's phone rang.

'Merrily. Franny Bliss. Remember? How are you?'

'I'm . . . OK.'

'You don't sound all that OK to me. You should've said something – us keeping you talking outside in the cold all that time. Not that it was much warmer inside. Sorry you had to go off like that, but you probably did the best thing. He's a card, that Huw, isn't he? Turned out well for us, anyway.'

'It did?'

'I'm not gonna bore you with the run-up to this, but we finally had a chat with two very nice elderly ladies: sisters, churchgoers, and active members of the Royal Society for the Protection of Birds. They put us on to a lad called Craig Proctor, lives out near Monkland. Now young Craig, for reasons you really don't want to know about, especially if you're not feeling well, is an expert at trapping wild birds. These old ladies've been after him for months, but he's clever is Craig – or he thought he was. Anyway, after a long and meaningful exchange at Leominster nick this morning, Craig has told us he was approached by a chap he didn't know, and given a hundred and fifty pounds to procure one live carrion crow.'

'Christ.'

The fog outside was like a carpet against the window.

'Yeh,' Franny said. 'Now, what's that say to you, Merrily?'

'It says you're not just looking for a bunch of kids who've seen some nasty films.'

'The real thing, eh?'

'Yes, though I don't know what I mean when I say that. Did you get a description out of him?'

'Young guy – motorbike, moustache, hard-looking. That's not much help. Craig's never seen him before, he claims.'

'You arrest him?'

'No. He knew we'd no evidence and he wasn't gonna confess.'

'You made a deal.'

'We don't make deals, as you well know, Merrily. Just have a little think about why somebody would blow a hundred and fifty on setting up some grubby little sacrifice in a church nobody uses.'

'And taking a considerable risk too,' Merrily said. 'Stretford itself might be a bit lonely, but the church is hardly lonely *within* Stretford.'

'That too.'

'Have you asked Huw?'

'Well, yeh, I did call Huw, to be honest, but he wasn't there.'

'He's a busy man,' Merrily said quietly.

Sophie had gestured to her something about popping out for a while. Merrily considered waiting for her to return, needing to find out how she'd learned about last night's disaster, and why she'd been so quick to cover up in front of the Bishop.

But, by lunchtime, Sophie had not come back, so Merrily switched on the computer and typed out the letter.

It had already been composed in her head on the way here. It was formal and uncomplicated. That was always best; no need for details – not that she felt able to put that stuff on paper.

Dear Bishop,

After long consideration and a great deal of prayer and agonizing, I have decided to ask you to accept my resignation from the role of Diocesan Deliverance Consultant.

I do not doubt that this is – or will become – a valid job for a woman. However, events have proved to me that I am not yet sufficiently wise or experienced enough to take it on. Therefore I honestly think I should make a discreet exit before I become a liability to the Church.

I would like to thank you for your kindness and – albeit misplaced – confidence in me. I am sorry for wasting so much of your very valuable time.

Yours sincerely,
Merrily Watkins

It hung there on the screen and she sat in front of it, reading it over and over again until she saw it only as words with no coherent meaning.

She could print it out and post it, or send it through the internal mail. Either way, he would not see it before he and Val left for London. Or maybe e-mail it immediately to the Bishop's Palace? That would be the quickest and the best, and leave no room for hesitation.

She read it through again; there was nothing more to say. She looked up the Palace's e-mail address and prepared to send. It would be courteous, perhaps, to show it first to Sophie. Perhaps she'd wait until Sophie returned, perhaps she wouldn't. What she would *not* do was ring Huw Owen about it.

As often, the only certainty was a cigarette. Her packet was empty, so she felt in her bag for another, and came up with a creamy-white envelope, the one pushed through the letterbox while she was shivering on the landing. She'd stuffed it into her bag, while arguing with Jane that she was perfectly fit to go to work – no, she did not have flu. *It's mental, flower. I'm coming apart and torturing myself with sick, sexual, demonic fantasies. God's way of showing me I'm not equipped to take on other people's terrors.* But she hadn't said any of that either.

She opened the letter, postmarked Hereford and addressed to The Reverend Mrs Watkins. It came straight to the point.

Dear Reverend Watkins,

You should know that your Daughter has been seen brazenly endangering her Soul, and yours, by mixing with the Spiritually Unclean.

Ask her what she was doing last Saturday afternoon at the so-called PSYCHIC FAIR at Leominster. It is well known that such events attract members of Occult Groups in search of converts. Ask her how long she has been consorting with a Clairvoyant who uses the Devil's Picturebook.

Many people have always been disgusted that your Daughter does not attend Church as the Daughter of a Minister of God ought to. Now we know why.

If it is true that you have been appointed
Exorcist then perhaps you should start by
cleansing the Filthy Soul of Your Own Daughter.

It was unsigned. Quite expensively done, judged by the standards set by these creeps. Usually the paper was cheap and crumpled, and whereas most of them were pushed into a letterbox, either here or at the church, this one had come by post.

Surprising how many anonymous letters you got. Or perhaps male ministers didn't get so many – quite a few of these letters muttered that you should stop pretending to be a priest and go out and get yourself a husband like ordinary, decent women did. One or two of them also offered to give her what ordinary, decent women were getting, but she evidently wasn't. She picked these ones up by one corner and washed her hands afterwards.

Some of them she felt she ought to file, or give to the police in case other women were receiving similar messages and the sender ever got nicked. Some she really didn't want to take to the police, in case anyone at the station suspected there was no smoke without fire.

But most of them got burned in the grate or the nearest ashtray.

Merrily flicked the Zippo. It would be true, of course. Jane had laid it on the line that altogether fateful afternoon in the coffee lounge at The Green Dragon. *'The Church has always been on this kind of paternalistic power-trip, doesn't want people to search for the truth. Like it used to be science and Darwinism and stuff they were worried about. Now it's the New Age because that's like real practical spirituality.'*

Psychic fairs were where people went in search of 'Real Practical Spirituality'. Merrily didn't doubt that what the letter said was essentially true. It would explain a lot of things, not least the allure of Rowenna.

She knew the Devil's Picturebook was the tarot – a doorway.

Et tu, flower. She felt choked by acrid fog. Her head ached. No option now.

She sent the Bishop his e-mail, walked out of the office and down the stone stairs.

Part Three

PROJECTION

THIRTY

Self-pity

She felt cold, and dangerously light inside, as though a dead weight had rolled away, but releasing nothing. She stepped through a tide of pensioners, a coach party heading towards the Cathedral. The sky was overcast. Nobody seemed to be smiling any more. One of the old men looked a bit like Dobbs.

She should tell Dobbs that it was OK now. That he could go ahead and recover. She'd do that, yes. She'd go to the hospital at visiting time and tell him. *Jesus Christ was the first exorcist; the pattern is unbroken.* This would draw a final line under everything.

Unless Huw was there, the bastard, with his holy water and his candles.

Jesus!

The city swirled around her in the fog, undefined. She mustn't look back at the Cathedral. It was no part of her life now. She should go back to her own parish and deal with the church break-in. Head Ted Clowes off at the pass. At Ledwardine – her home.

Or not?

Sweat sprang out on her forehead. She felt insubstantial, worthless. She had no home, no lover, no spiritual adviser, no . . .

Daughter?

Failed her. Too bound up in your own conceits. Sending her into the arms of New Age occult freaks, a reaction to living with a . . .

Pious bitch?

Her dead husband Sean had been the first to call her that. After a day quite like this, a headachy day, the desperate day when she'd found out just how bent he was, and screamed at him for his duplicity and his greed, and he'd screamed back: *'I was doing it for you, you pious bitch.'*

She hated that word. Don't ever be *pious*. Smoke, curse, never be afraid to say *Jesus Christ!* in fury or astonishment – at least it keeps the name in circulation. Strive to be a good person, a good priest, never a *pious* priest.

Once, up in Liverpool, she'd conducted a youth service wearing a binliner instead of a cassock. It was half a generation too late; some of the kids were appalled, others sneered. Not so easy not being *pious*.

Merrily found herself back on the green, watching the Cathedral placidly swallowing the coach party. The fog was lifting, but the sky behind it was darkening. She had no idea which way to go next.

Suppose she'd backed away from the lamplit path and supported Sean, had said, *Let's fight this together*? Would he have made the effort for her, found some fresh, uncorrupted friends, a new but much older secretary? Would he, in the end, have *survived*? Might she have saved his life by not following the Path of the Pious Bitch into the arms of God?

She stood at the barrier preventing cars turning into Church Street. She was panting, thoughts racing again. Wasn't it true that having women in the priesthood was creating a new divide between the sexes – because men could love both God and their wives, but no truly heterosexual woman could love both God and a man with sufficient intensity to make both relationships potent? Was it all a sham? Was it true that all she was searching for in God were those qualities lacking in ordinary men? Or, at least, in Sean.

Oh *Christ*. Merrily flattened herself against a brick wall facing the side of the Cathedral. The headache had gone; she wished it was back, she wanted pain. Fumbling at her dog-collar, she took it off and put it in her bag. A cold breeze seemed to leap immediately to her throat, like a stab of admonishment.

She zipped up her coat, holding its collar together, turned her back on the Cathedral and walked quickly into Church Street.

Lol saw Merrily from his window, through the drifting fog: gliding almost drunkenly along the street, peering unseeingly into shopwindows newly edged with Christmas glitter.

He ran downstairs, past the bike, past Nico's sepulchral drone and the very interested gaze of Big Viv.

'Merrily?' Close up, she seemed limp, drained.

'Oh,' she said. 'Hi.' And he was shocked because she looked as vague as Moon had often been, but that was just him, wasn't it – his paranoia?

But paranoia hadn't created the shadows and creases, the dark hair all mussed, dark eyes moist, make-up escaping.

He looked around. Not the flat now – it had been too awkward there the other night, as if foreshadowed by the death of Moon.

She let him steer her into the corner café where he and Jane had eaten chocolate fudge cake.

There was no one else in the back room. A brown pot of tea between them. On the wall above them was a framed Cézanne poster – baked furrowed earth under a heat haze.

The letter lay folded on the table, held down by the sugar bowl, revealing only the words 'known that such events attract members of Occult Groups in search of converts'.

'But surely,' he said, 'they mainly just attract ordinary people who read their daily horoscopes. It doesn't mean she's sacrificing babies.'

But he thought of seeing Jane and the other girl coming out of Pod's last night, long after it was closed. And Jane pretending, for the first time ever, not to have seen him.

'If this was London,' she said, 'I could get away with it. Or if Jane was grown-up and living somewhere else. If she'd even been up-front about it, I could have—'

'Merrily, it means nothing. I can't believe you've just quit because of this. It's the Bishop, isn't it?'

'Sorry?'

'He made another move on you, right?'

'No.' She smiled. 'He's been . . . fine. And anyway I might have taken that the wrong way: late at night, very tired. No, I'm just . . . paranoid.' She held up her half-smoked cigarette as though using it as a measure of something. 'Also I have filthy habits and a deep reservoir of self-pity.'

He nodded at the cigarette. 'What are the others, then?'

Merrily tipped it into the ashtray. He saw she was blushing. She had no filthy habits.

'Just . . . tell me to pull myself together, OK?'

'I like you being untogether. It makes me feel responsible and kind of protective – sort of like a real bloke.'

She smiled.

'So what are you going to do now?'

'Go back to my flock and try to be a good little shepherd. The Deliverance ministry was a wrong move. I thought it was something you could pick up as you went along. I didn't realize . . . I'm a fraud, Lol. I don't know what I'm doing, let too many people down. I even let you down. I said I'd go and see your friend, Moon . . .' She looked vague. 'Was that yesterday?'

'Mmm.'

'I mean, I could still see her. I'm still a minister, of sorts.'

'She's not there now,' he said too quietly.

'Lol?' She looked directly at him for the first time since sitting down at the table.

'She died.'

Her face froze up behind the smoke.

'No!' He put up his hands. 'She was dead long before you could've got there. There was nothing you could have done.'

And he told her about it: about the Iron Age sword . . . about the newspaper report from twenty-five years ago . . . why Denny had concealed the truth – why Denny *said* he'd concealed the truth . . . why Dick thought they should let it lie.

She kept shaking her head, lips parted. He was relieved at the way outrage had lifted her again.

'Lol, I've never heard anything so . . . There is something deeply, deeply wrong here, don't you think?'

'But what can you do about it? We can't bring her back. And we can't find out what was in her mind.'

'What about this book she was supposed to be writing?'

'Supposed to be, but I don't think she'd written a word. But if there is anything lying around, Denny will find it. And if it says anything he doesn't like, he'll destroy it without telling anyone.'

'Will you be called as a witness at the inquest?'

'I expect so. I was the first to . . . the first to enter the bathroom.'

'And what will you say?'

'I'll just answer their questions. That should cover about *half* of the truth.'

'And the rest of it *can't* be the truth, because it has no rationality.' She looked down into her cup as if there might be a message for her in the tea-leaves. 'I'm so sorry, Lol.'

The point at which people say, *Ah well, one of those things.* Except this wasn't.

After a while, she said, 'What if all your working life is concerned with things that three-quarters of the civilized world now consider irrational?'

'That could be stressful,' he said. There were lights on in the café now, but they didn't seem to reach Merrily. *What* was she not telling him?

She said, 'You know why some vicars busy themselves constantly with youth work and stuff like that? It's so that if, at any point, they realize there's no God, they can think: *Well, at least I haven't been wasting my time.*'

'Cynical.'

'Rational. For the same reasons, some Deliverance ministers prefer to think of themselves as Christian psychologists.'

'Psychology is wonderful,' Lol said grimly. 'Look how much it helped Moon.'

'Perhaps she had the wrong therapist.'

'We must get her a better one next time. I think *you* could have helped Moon. I wish to God I'd told you about her earlier. And I think . . . I think there must be a lot of other people you could help.'

'Thanks, but you're being kind.' She dropped the cigarettes and lighter into her bag, then folded up the anonymous letter very tightly.

This was not good: nothing had been resolved. He sensed that when she returned to her flock she would be different: a sad shepherd exiled, unfulfilled, into a community that wasn't a community any more. None of them were; village life, like he'd said in his song, was no more than a sweet watercolour memory. She'd grow old and lined, and end up hating God.

'Listen.' Lol lowered his voice to an urgent whisper. 'My life is pathetic. I'm a failed performer, a mediocre songwriter, an ex-mental patient who can't keep a woman. My sole function on this earth at the present time appears to be producing an album for a semi-talented, obnoxious little git who's blackmailing his father. Three days ago, a woman I couldn't love but needed to help just . . . shut me out in the snow. And then slashed both her wrists. Now somebody who I care about is holding out on me in exactly the same way. What does this tell me?'

Mega self-pity, he thought as she sat down again. *Occasionally it works.*

Merrily said, looking down at the table, 'Sometimes I think you're the only friend I have left.'

'Friend,' he repeated sadly.

She met his eyes. 'It's a big word, Lol.'

He nodded, although he knew there were bigger ones.

Outside, it was already going dark, and the fog had never really lifted.

THIRTY-ONE

Old Tiger

Jane stood on the vicarage lawn, Ethel the cat watching her from inside the kitchen window. There was fog still around, but a paler patch almost directly overhead; the moon was probably just there, behind layer upon layer of steamy cloud.

Right, then.

She'd been told that it was OK to do this from the inside of the house, but she didn't feel quite right about that. Not with the moon, somehow. And it *was* a vicarage. Whereas the garden bordered the old and sinister orchard which, though it belonged to the Church, had been here, in essence, far longer. Pre-Christian almost certainly.

The night was young but silent around Jane. You could usually hear some sounds from the marketplace or The Black Swan, but not many people seemed to have ventured out tonight. Also, the fog itself created this lovely padded hush. It lined the hills and blocked in the spaces between the trees in the dense woods above Ledwardine, as if the whole valley had acquired these deep, resonant walls like a vast auditorium.

She wondered if Rowenna was outside in *her* garden, too. The problem was that there were doubtless other houses overlooking that one, and Rowenna had younger brothers who would just take the piss, so she was probably now in her room – searching for the same moon.

Jane looked up, cleared her throat almost nervously. Probably Mum felt like this in the pulpit. *Don't think about Mum. This is nothing to do with her.*

She drew in a long, chilled breath, imagining moonbeams – unfortunately there weren't any – also being drawn down, filling her with silken, silvery light. And then she called out – not *too* loud, as villages had ears.

> '*Hail to Thee, Lady Moon,*
> '*Whose light reflects our most secret hopes.*
> '*Hail to Thee from the abodes of darkness.*'

Something about that *abodes of darkness* making it more thrilling than the sun thing in the morning. Especially in this fog.

And it did work, this cycle of spiritual salutation. It put the whole day into a natural sequence. It deepened your awareness of the connectedness of everything, and your role as part of the great perceiving mechanism that was humanity.

Jane felt seriously calm by now and not at all cold – like she was generating her own inner heat. Or *something* was. She looked up into the sky again, just as this really miraculous thing began to happen.

The moon appeared.

First as just a grey imprint on the cloud-tapestry. Then as this kind of smoke-wreathed silver figurine: the goddess gathering the folds of her cloud-robes around her.

And finally . . . as a core of brilliant white fire at the heart of the fog.

Winter glory.

Oh, wow! She heard me.

Jane just stood there and shivered in amazement and delight, like totally transported.

Cool!

Like really, really, *really* cool.

'Visiting time's not for another hour,' Sister Miller said. 'It's teatime and the patients have to eat. You'll need to come back.'

Sister Miller was all nurse: tough and ageless. Merrily concentrated on her seasoned face, because the view along Watkins Ward was dizzying and oppressive. It would have been hard to come up here alone tonight, any night.

She told Sister Miller that Sister Cullen had said visiting hours were less strict if the patient was in a side ward.

'Which one?'

'Canon Dobbs.'

'That old man?' said Sister Miller. 'Are you relatives?'

'I'm a . . . colleague.'

'Because my view is that he doesn't need to be here now, no matter what Dr Bradley says. Why can't someone look after him at home? He's just taking up a bed.'

'You mean he's recovering?'

'Of course he's recovering. I've been in nursing for nearly forty years. Mr Dobbs was walking perfectly well this morning. He can also feed himself. I believe he could also talk, if he wanted to.' Sister Miller turned on Lol. 'Have *you* any idea why he's refusing to talk?'

Lol thought about it. 'Perhaps he's just impatient with routine questions like "How are we today?".'

'You have ten minutes and no longer,' said Sister Miller.

It was like praying over a tomb. He lay on his back, as still as an effigy. Eyes shut. You were not aware of him breathing. He looked dead.

Just a short prayer, then. Nothing clever. Someone else

having seen to all the smart stuff. Afterwards, Merrily brushed her knees and sat in the bedside chair.

'Hello, Mr Dobbs.'

He didn't move. He was like stone. Could he possibly be awake?

'We haven't spoken before, as such. I'm Merrily Watkins.' Keeping her voice low and even. 'I've come to say goodbye.'

On the other side of the door's glass square, Lol smiled. OK, that was not the most tactful thing to say in a hospital.

'By which I mean that I've now decided not to accept the Deliverance . . . role. I just wanted you to know that. We never met formally, and now there's no reason we ever should.'

The side ward enclosing Dobbs was like a drab chapel. A faintly mouldy smell came from him – not organic, more like the miasma of old books in a damp warehouse.

'I'm sorry that you're in here. I'm sorry we didn't get to you sooner in the Cathedral.' She half-rose to pull the bedside chair a little closer and lowered her voice to below prayer level. 'I'm even sorrier you didn't feel able to tell any of us what you were doing there.'

She leaned her face forward to within six inches of his. They'd kept him shaved, but stubble had sprouted under his chin like a patch of sparse grass on a rockface.

'It doesn't matter to me now – not professionally. I'm out of it, feeling a little humiliated, rather slighted. I *know* Jesus Christ was the first exorcist, but also that half the world's population is female, and rather more than half the people with problems of psychic disturbance – or so it seems to me – are female too. I believe that one day there *will* be a female exorcist in this diocese, without the fires of hell burning in High Town. I just wanted you to know that too.'

No reaction. Yet he could apparently walk and feed himself. She felt angry.

'I probably felt less insulted, but more puzzled, when I heard you'd been avoiding *all* women. Dumping your housekeeper – that wasn't a terribly kind thing to do. Why are you scared of women?'

Her hand went instinctively to her throat. She still wasn't wearing the dog-collar.

'I don't know what makes you tick, Canon Dobbs. I've been trying to forgive you for setting me up for that final session with Denzil Joy.'

She felt tainted just uttering the name, particularly here. Too much like an invocation?

'If you wanted to scare me off, show me how unpleasant it could be, you very nearly succeeded. But that wasn't, in the end, why I decided to quit.'

She stood up. On his bedside table she placed two pounds of seedless grapes and two bottles of Malvern water.

'Maybe you could share these with Huw Owen – next time he comes with his candles, and his holy water, and his magic chalk.'

She waited. Not a movement. She took a last look at him, but he remained like a fossil.

When she reached the door, she stopped, noticing that Lol's eyes had widened. She resisted the urge to spin around.

Once out of the door, she turned left towards the ward entrance, refusing even to glance back along Watkins to the top side ward where Denzil Joy's spirit had left his body.

And gone where?

The sudden shudder ripped up her spine like a razor-blade.

'OK, he opened his eyes,' Lol informed her, outside the hospital. 'As soon as you turned your back and walked away, his eyes snapped open. Then closed again when he saw me standing on the other side of the glass.'

Merrily's Volvo was parked in a small bay near a little park.

By the path to the Victoria footbridge over the Wye. They leaned against it.

'He heard it all, then?' she said.

'Every word. His eyes were very bright, fully aware – and mad as hell when he saw me.'

'Good. My God!'

'Mmm.' Those eyes had spooked Lol. They were burning with the hard, wary intelligence of an old tiger. But the effect of this news on Merrily he found exciting.

The cold had lost its bite and the fog had thinned. He could see the three-quarter moon as through a lace curtain.

Merrily said, 'Could we go for a short walk? I need to clear my head.'

It was *very* short. He followed her through the patch of parkland to a kind of viewing platform overlooking the still dark Wye and the suspension footbridge.

'Last time I stood here, Inspector Annie Howe was showing me where a body had been found.'

'What exciting times you have, Merrily. Such drama.'

'Too much drama.' She stood with her back to the river, beside an ornate lamp standard. 'Well, this suggests Dobbs was an active participant in Huw's ritual, doesn't it? Or maybe even directing it?'

'You're the expert.'

'Obviously not, or I'd know what this was about.'

'And this Huw going behind your back, that's the reason you resigned?'

She shrugged.

'I still don't see it.'

'Lol, he was my course tutor: the Deliverance man. He's the nearest I've had or wanted to have to a spiritual adviser. I rated the guy. I really *liked* him.'

'I see.'

'No, you don't. A father-figure, just about. But, more

important, the person you trust to guide you through the . . .
through the hinterland of Hell, if you like. But what if there's
something iffy about what they were both doing?'

'Iffy?'

'I don't know.'

'And you want to?'

'Yeah.' Her dark hair shone in the lamplight.

'More than a professional interest?'

'I don't *have* a professional interest any more. I am just so
angry. That *shit*.'

'Excellent.'

'Huh?'

'I'm happy you're mad. When I first saw you in Church
Street you were about as animated as Mr Dobbs back there. I
worry easily.'

She smiled, shaking her head. 'Lol . . .'

'Mmm?'

'I said some stupid things, all right? Things that weren't
necessarily true.'

'Which in particular?'

'You choose,' Merrily said. Her face seemed flushed.

He thought for a moment. 'OK, I've chosen.'

'Don't tell me.'

'Why not?'

'Because . . .'

'Because little Jane doesn't know where you are?'

'Little Jane doesn't bloody care.'

'I think she does, Merrily. And it's not my place to say so
to a professional good person, but if you take this out on her
before you've gone into it properly, you might regret it.'

'You mean I should take steps to find out what she's doing
– and who with?'

'I can . . . help maybe, if you want.'

'Why are you doing this, Lol?'

'A number of possible reasons.' Lol stood close to her but looked across the river to the haze of misted lights on the fringe of the city. 'You choose.'

Merrily sighed. 'I can't go to bed with you, you know.' And, naturally, she looked soft-focus beautiful under the lamp. 'Not the way things are.'

'God,' Lol said sadly. 'He has a lot to answer for.'

'It isn't God,' Merrily said.

'Oh.' He wanted to roll over the rail into the black river. 'That means somebody else.'

'Yes.'

She turned away from him and from the light. In the moment before she did, he saw her eyes and he thought he saw a flash of fear there, and he thought there was a shudder of revulsion.

But he *was* paranoid. Official!

'I'll take you back now,' Merrily said.

THIRTY-TWO

Fantasy World

Jane threw open the bedroom window, and the damned fog came in and she started to cough. It was like being with Mum in the scullery-office on a heavy Silk Cut night.

Down on the lawn the last rags of snow had gone. Snow was clean, bright, refreshing. Fog was misery. It was December today, so only three weeks to Midwinter, the great solstice when the year had the first gleam of spring in its eye.

Always darkest before the dawn. This, Jane thought, was like a midwinter of the spirit. She cleared her throat.

> *'Hail to Thee, Eternal Spiritual Sun.*
> *'Whose visible symbol now rises from the Heavens.'*

That was a bloody laugh.

> *'Hail unto Thee from the Abodes of Morning.'*

It had been so brilliant last night out in the garden. Maybe she was a night person. Maybe a moon person. And yet the bedtime exercise had not gone too well, the great rewinding of the day.

> *Before you go to sleep, make a journey back through the day. Starting with the very last thing you did or said or*

thought, then going back through every small event, every action, every perception, as though you were rewinding a sensory videotape of your day. Consider each occurrence impartially, as though it were happening to someone else, and notice how one thing led to another. Thus will you learn about cause and effect. This reverse procedure also de-conditions your mind from thinking sequentially – past, present and future – and demolishes the web of falsehood you habitually weave to excuse your wrong behaviour.

It was impossible to stay with it. You got sidetracked. You thought of something interesting and followed it through. Or something bad, like Mum being ill, which could plunge you without warning into some awful Stalinist scenario at Gran's in Cheltenham: *'As long as your mother is in hospital, Jane, you are under my roof, and a young lady does not go out looking like THAT.'* Or you remembered seeing some cool male person and, despite what Angela had foretold, you were into the old dying-a-virgin angst. Rowenna never seemed prey to these fears; had she *no* hormones?

Gratefully, Jane closed the window. Mum had not looked too bad last night. Quiet, though: pensive.

'You're not OK! You're not! You look like sh—'

'Don't say it, all right?'

'It's true.'

And, Jesus, it *was* true. That ratty old dressing-gown, the cig drooping from the corner of her mouth. A vicar? Standing on the stairs, she looked like some ageing hooker.

'It's the weather,' Mum said.

'It so is *not* the weather! Maybe you should see a doctor. I don't know about exorcist; you look like completely bloody *possessed.*'

For a moment, Mum looked quite horrible, face all red and scrunched up like some kind of blood-pressure situation. And then . . .

'STOP IT! Don't you ever *ever* make jokes about that, do you hear?'

'And, like whatever happened to the sense of humour?' Jane backed away into the kitchen, teetering on the rim of tears.

They ate breakfast in silence apart from the bleeping of the answering machine: unplayed messages from last night. 'Aren't you going to ever listen to that thing?' Jane said finally at the front door.

'I'll get around to it, flower,' Mum said drably, turning away because, for less than half a second, Jane had caught her eyes and seen in them the harsh glint of fear.

No, please.

Standing desolate on the dark-shrouded market square, as the headlights of the school bus bleared around the corner, Jane thought, suppose it's not flu, nor even some kind of virus; suppose she's found symptoms of something she's afraid to take to the doctor.

Oh God. Please, God.

The only time Jane ever reverted to the Old Guy was when it was about Mum.

Bleep.

'*Merrily, it's Sophie. I'm calling at seven o'clock. Please ring me at home.*'

Bleep.

'*Ms Watkins. Acting DCI Howe, 19.27, Tuesday. I need to talk to you. Can you call me between eight-thirty and ten tomorrow, Wednesday. Thanks.*'

Bleep.

'*This is Susan Thorpe, Mrs Watkins, at The Glades. Could you confirm our arrangement for tomorrow evening? Thank you.*'

Bleep.

'*Merrily, it's Sophie again. Please call me. You must realize what it's about.*'

Bleep.

'*Hello, lass. Time we had a chat, eh?*'

Merrily didn't think so.

Lol said, 'Viv, *you* know the Alternative Hereford – I mean, most of the people on that side of things.'

'My love,' Big Viv laughed throatily, 'I *am* the Alternative Hereford. Just don't ask me to point you to a dealer.'

'What happens over that healthfood café in Bridge Street?'

'Pod's?' Viv gave him a sharp look. He saw she had two tight lip-rings on this morning. 'Well, they used to do a good cashewburger, then they got a different cook and it wasn't so good. You won't meet anybody there.'

'Uh-huh.' Lol shook his head gently. 'I'm not looking to score anything chemical.'

He collected another hard look. 'What then?'

'I don't know. Mysticism?'

'You won't score that either. Not at Pod's.'

He didn't know whether to be relieved or disappointed.

'Wrong gender, Lol. It's a woman thing there. I can put you on to a few other people, if you like, depending what you're into. Wicca . . . theosophy . . . Gurdjieff . . .?'

'I'll tell you the truth,' Lol said. 'It involves a friend of mine. She thought her daughter might be involved in something possibly linked to Pod's, and she'd like to know a bit about it. It's a peace-of-mind thing.'

'What's her name?'

'Jane. Jane Watkins.'

'Don't know her.' Viv went to sit behind the till. 'All right, I went there a few times, but it got a bit intense, yeah?'

'What was it into?'

'Self-discovery, developing an inner life, meditation, astral-projection, occult-*lite* – you know?'

'You manage to leave your body, Viv?'

'No such luck, darling. The best teacher they had just dropped out, then they got very responsible. A bit elitist – no riff-raff, no dopeheads. Like an esoteric ladies' club, you know? That was when I kicked it into touch. Life's too short.'

'For what?'

'For taking seriously. Plus, it was inconvenient. They started meeting in an afternoon on account of the kind of women they were attracting didn't want their oh-so-respectable husbands to find out. Anyway, it was all a bit snooty and bit too sombre.'

Lol wondered how sombre was too sombre for a Nico-fan.

'This is a very intense, intellectual kid, Lol?'

'Not how I'd describe her. Well . . . not how I *would* have described her.'

'They change so fast, kids,' Viv said.

The only call Merrily returned was Susan Thorpe's. A care-attendant answered: Mrs Thorpe had left early for Hereford Market. Merrily said quickly, before she could let herself back out, 'Could you tell her the arrangement still stands.'

She felt really unsure about this, but she very much wanted to speak to Susan Thorpe's mother – wanted every bit of background she could get on Thomas Dobbs.

And it was only an *imprint*: a redirection of energies. She could handle that – couldn't she? – if she protected herself.

'That's fine,' the woman said. 'Thank you, Mrs Watkins.'

'OK.'

She lit a cigarette and pulled over the phone book. This was something she should have done days ago.

Napier. Surprisingly, there were three in Credenhill. Would it say Major Napier? Colonel Napier? She didn't even know Rowenna's father's rank. A serving officer in the SAS would, anyway, be unlikely to advertise his situation. Might even be ex-directory. She called the first Napier – no reply. At the second, a woman answered, and Merrily asked if this was where Rowenna lived.

The woman laughed, with no humour. 'This is where she sleeps' – London accent? – 'sometimes.'

There was the sound of a morning TV talk-show in the background, a studio audience programmed to gasp and hoot.

'Is that Mrs Napier?'

'No, it's Mrs Straker.'

'Would it be possible to speak to Mrs Napier?'

'I wouldn't know, dear. Depends if you can afford long-distance.'

Merrily said nothing.

'I'm Rowenna's aunt,' Mrs Straker continued heavily, like she'd had to explain this a thousand times too many. 'I look after the kids for Steve. He's my younger brother. He and Helen split up about four years ago. She's in Canada now. If you want to speak to Steve, you'll have to call back tonight.'

'I'm sorry. I didn't know any of this. My name's Merrily Watkins. From Ledwardine. My daughter, Jane . . . she seems to be Rowenna's best friend, at school.'

No reaction. This wasn't what she'd expected. She wanted a warm, concerned parent, delighted to hear from little Jane's mother.

'I don't know any Jane,' Mrs Straker said. 'See, Mrs . . .'

'Watkins. Merrily.'

'Yeah. See, since her dad bought her that car we never

know where she is. I wouldn't have got it her, personally. I don't think she should have a car till she's at college or got a job, but Steve's soft with her, and now she goes where she likes. And she don't bring her girl friends back here. Or the men either.'

Merrily sat down, her picture of Rowenna and her family background undergoing radical revision.

'Sometimes,' Mrs Straker was saying, 'I think I should be bothering more than I do, but when she was here all the time it was nothing but rows and sulks, and this is a very small house for the five of us. Where we were before, down in Salisbury, things was difficult, but it was a bigger place at least, you know what I mean?'

'I suppose your brother has to go away a lot.' In the SAS, Merrily had heard, you could never rely on not having to be in Bosnia or somewhere at a day's notice.

'No,' said Mrs Straker.

'He *is* a . . . an Army officer, isn't he, your brother?'

Mrs Straker laughed. 'That's what she told you, is it?'

'Not exactly,' Merrily said. It was Jane who'd told her.

'Steve's a corporal. He works in admin.'

'I see.'

'That's not good enough for Rowenna, obviously. She lives in what I would call a fantasy world. Steve can't see it, or he don't want to. I dunno what *your* daughter's like, Mrs Watson.'

'Impressionable.' Merrily's stomach felt like lead. 'She's been out a lot lately, at night, and she doesn't always say where. I'm getting worried – which is why I rang.'

'You want to watch her,' Mrs Straker said. 'Keep an eye on her, that's my advice.'

'Why would you . . . advise that?'

Mrs Straker made a pregnant humming noise. There was a

lot she could say, would enjoy relating, but she apparently wanted more encouragement.

Merrily said, 'It's a bit difficult for me to keep an eye on Jane all the time, being a single mum, you know? Having to work.'

'Divorced?'

'Widow.'

'Yes, I'm a widow too,' Mrs Straker said. 'It's not easy, is it? Never thought I'd end up looking after somebody else's kids, even if they are my own brother's. But I can't watch that girl as well – I told Steve that. Not now she's got a car. What do you do?'

'Yes, I can see the problem.'

'No, what do *you* do? What's your job?'

The front doorbell rang.

'I'm, er . . . I'm a minister in the Church. A vicar.'

The line went quiet.

'Oh dear,' Mrs Straker said, 'that's not what I expected at all. That's very funny that is.'

The doorbell rang again, twice, followed by a rapping of the knocker.

'Why is that so funny?'

'That's your front door, dear,' Mrs Straker said. 'You'd best go and get it. Ring me back, if you like.'

'Why is that so funny, Mrs Straker?'

'It's not funny at all, Mrs Watson. *You* won't find it funny, I'll guarantee that.'

THIRTY-THREE

Wrong Number, Dear

Annie Howe stood on the step, young and spruce and clean, fast-track fresh against the swirling murk.

'Ah, you *are* there, Ms Watkins. I was driving over from Leominster, so I thought I'd call.' Her ash-blonde head tilted, taking in the dressing-gown – and the blotches and the bags, no doubt. 'You really *aren't* well, are you?'

'Not wonderful.'

'Flu?'

'No, it's OK to come in,' Merrily said. 'You won't catch anything.'

'I seldom do. Is this nervous exhaustion, perhaps?'

'That might be closer.'

Howe stepped into the kitchen, with a slight wrinkling of the nose. Her own kitchen would be hardwood and stainless-steel, cool as a morgue. She sat down at the table, confidently pushing the ashtray away.

'Ms Watkins, it's the Paul Sayer thing again.'

Merrily filled the kettle. 'That seemed to have gone quiet?'

'That's because we're still choosing not to make too much noise about it. I'm wondering if we ought to.'

'You want me to discuss it in a sermon?'

Howe smiled thinly. 'Perhaps a sarcasm amnesty?'

'Sure. Sorry, go on.'

So what did she do about this? If Howe knew she was in

the process of shedding the Deliverance role, this conversation would never reach the coffee stage. Difficult, since she was unable to square it with the Bishop until his return from London. OK, say nothing.

'You heard from DS Bliss, I believe,' Howe said.

'He told me about the supplier of crows. Did you get any further?'

'Unfortunately not. They appeared to have paid their money, taken their crow, and melted back into their own netherworld. But, as you agreed with Bliss, the fee suggests that the people involved in this are not the usual . . . how shall I say—?'

'Toerags.'

'Quite.'

'So, let me get this right – have you actually said publicly that Sayer was murdered yet?'

Howe shook her head. 'We're staying with the phrase "suspicious circumstances". The situation is, as you must realize, that we could doubtless get widespread national publicity if we told the press about Sayer's hobby.'

'Especially if you gave them the pictures.'

'Of course. But apart from producing an unseemly double-page spread in the *Daily Star*, I can't see that it would help. I'm no longer sure the people we want to talk to would ever read a tabloid. Yes, it's possible, Sayer *may* simply be a wanker. We've found some videotapes under a floorboard which seem to show ritual activities, but we don't know if these are events that Sayer was personally involved in or sado-pornographic tapes he acquired for his own gratification. They're quite explicit.'

'Not commercial films?'

'Oh, no, the quality's not good enough. Lots of camera shake and the picture itself is so poor it seems to have been recorded with either old or very cheap equipment – which suggests it's not simulated.'

'What kind of ritual activities?'

'You can view them if you like.'

'I'd rather you just told me.'

'Well, one shows a man penetrating a woman on an altar. She's wearing a blindfold and a gag, and it looks like rape. The man's face is not hidden, but well covered by long hair and a beard. In the background are several people whose faces are even less distinguishable. What does that sound like to you?'

'Any suggestion of location?'

'Possibly a church. And then there's the inevitable passing-round-the-chalice sequence.'

'Black Mass?'

'Someone drinks from the chalice, and there's residue on the mouth suggestive of blood. But, as I say, the quality is appalling.'

'You see, on the one hand,' Merrily said, 'the Black Mass is the best-known of all satanic rituals, and probably the easiest to carry out if you're just idiots with a warped idea of fun. You just do everything in reverse – say the Lord's Prayer backwards, et cetera. And you pervert everything – urinate in the chalice or . . . use blood instead of wine. Blood is the aspect which could, on the other hand, mean serious business. Blood represents the life-force, and it's seen as the most potent of all magical substances. If you want to make something happen, you use real blood.'

'Of course, we have no way of knowing whether *this* is. It looks too thin for ketchup, but it could be soy sauce or something.'

'I'm not being much help. Am I?'

'It's more a question of what help you might be in the future,' Howe said. 'We've failed to identify a single person who's been involved in any . . . any activity with Sayer. Or, indeed, with serious satanic activity of any kind. That's not including the self-publicists, of course.'

'When did you ever see a serious, heavy-duty, *educated* Satanist stripped off in the *News of the World*?'

'You mean – as with organized crime – the big operators are the outwardly respectable types you'd never suspect?'

'I suppose that's a good parallel.'

'It's also largely a myth,' said Howe. 'The Mr Bigs of this world are very rare, and we *do* know who they are. But I'm still interested. Do you personally believe there are high-powered practitioners with big houses and executive posts?'

'How would I know? I'm only a village vicar. But if Sayer *was* just a wanker, perhaps he was playing out of his league.'

'You mean, if he was regarded by some serious and outwardly respectable practitioner as a potential embarrassment . . .'

'Or he was getting too ambitious. Or he angered some rival . . . group. I'm told there's a lot of jealousy and in-fighting and power-struggling among certain occult sects.'

'Who told you that?'

'It was discussed during a course I was sent on. Is this what you wanted to hear?'

'Go on.'

'We were told that there are basically two classes of Satanist – what Huw, our tutor, calls the headbangers who are just in it for the experience or whatever psychic charge they can get; and the intellectuals. These are people who came out of Gnosticism and believe that knowledge is all, and so anything is valid if it leads to more knowledge.'

'Including murder?'

'Probably. Although they'd be as reluctant as the rest of us to break the law. Satanists, basically, are the people who hate Christianity. And they hate us because they see us as irrational. They despise us for our pomp and our smugness. All these great cathedrals costing millions of pounds a year to maintain, all the wasted psychic energy . . . to promote what they see as the idiot myth that you can get there by *love*.'

'I see.'

'Why do I get the feeling you also think it's an idiot myth?'

'Because I'm a police-person,' Howe said. 'Love is something we seldom encounter.'

When Howe had left, Merrily phoned Mrs Straker back four times, and never got an answer. Her own phone rang three times; she didn't pick it up, but pressed 1471 each time. The calls were from Sophie, Uncle Ted and Sophie respectively.

She owed Sophie an explanation, but couldn't face that now. And anyway, when Mick returned tomorrow, she'd have to talk to *him* – at length, no doubt. Before then, she wanted to have lost this . . . virus.

In the afternoon, she filled a plastic bottle with tapwater and took it across to the church and into the chancel, where she stood it before the altar. In the choir stalls, she meditated for almost an hour. *Blue and gold. Lamplit path.*

She went into the vestry and changed into the cassock and surplice she'd worn at St Cosmas and St Damien, since washed and replaced in the vestry wardrobe. She walked, head bowed, along the central aisle, back to the chancel, and stood before the altar.

'Lord God Almighty, the Creator of Life, bless this water . . .'

Back in the vicarage, she went up to her bedroom and sprinkled holy water in all four corners. Then across the threshold and at the window, top and bottom.

She went down on her knees and prayed that the soul of *our brother Denzil* might be directed away from its suffering and its *earthly obsessions* and led into the Light.

Filtered through fog, the fading light lay like a dustsheet on the bedroom.

Jane felt uncomfortable on the school bus home. Increasingly so, as more and more students got off. The buses had arrived early at the school, on account of the fog which was getting worse; classes had been wound up twenty minutes ahead of time.

The bus was moving very slowly, in low gear. It must be like driving through frogspawn. Jane just hoped to God that Mum was feeling better – was not going to be *really* ill.

Ledwardine was near the end of the line. Dean Wall, legendary greaseball, knew that, so there was no need at all for him to dump his fat ass on the seat next to Jane. He was on his own tonight, his mate Danny Gittoes off sick, supposedly.

'Just wanted to make sure you didn't miss your stop in all this fog. Seein' as how you en't much used to buses these days.'

Very funny! Jane gathered her bag protectively on to her lap. 'Don't worry about me. I have a natural homing instinct.'

The bus was crawling now. She had no idea where the *hell* they were.

'Only tryin' t'be helpful, Watkins.' Dean Wall shoved his fat thigh against hers, leaned back and stretched. The fat bastard clearly wasn't going to move. 'Goin' out tonight?'

'Probably not.'

'Off with some bloke tonight, then, is she?'

'I wouldn't have thought so.'

Wall's big fat lips shambled into a loose smile.

'Look, just sod off, OK?' Jane said.

'I wouldn't worry, Watkins – you'll still get yours. Er's likely bisexual.'

'Will you piss *off*?'

'You don't know nothin', do you? You're dead naive, you are.'

Jane gazed out of the window at dense nothing. 'Stop trying to wind me up.'

'I'm tryin' to put you *right*, Jane. You wanner talk to Gittoes, you do. 'Cept he en't capable of speech right now – still recoverin', like. His ma's thinkin' of gettin' him plastic surgery to take the smile off his face.'

'I don't want to know!'

'I bet you do.' Dean Wall leaned a little closer and Jane shrank against the streaming window. Dean lowered his voice. ''Er give Danny a blow job, back o' the woodwork building.'

She spun and stared at him.

'Listen, I en't kiddin', Jane.' He threw up his hands like she was about to hit him. 'Gittoes was pretty bloody gob-smacked himself, as it were.'

'You totally disgusting slimeball.'

''Er needed a favour, see.'

'I want you to sit somewhere else, all right?' Jane said. 'I'm going to count to five. If you haven't gone by then, I'll start screaming. Then I'll tell the driver you put your hand up my skirt.'

'Mrs Straker?'

'Yes?'

'Who's this?'

'It's Merrily Watkins again. I've tried several times to call back, but I suppose you had to go out.'

'Who'd you say you were?'

'Merrily – it's Jane's mum. She's Rowenna's friend. We spoke earlier.'

'I think you've got the wrong number, dear.'

'We spoke about an hour and a half ago. You said there was something I should know about Rowenna.'

You won't find it funny. I'll guarantee that.

'You must be thinking of somebody else,' Mrs Straker said. 'I've never spoken to you before in my life.'

She couldn't talk, Merrily decided. Someone had come into the house who shouldn't hear this. Or someone she was afraid of.

'Is there somebody with you? Has Rowenna come back? Is Jane with her? Could you just answer yes or no?'

'Listen,' Mrs Straker hissed, 'I don't know who you are, but if you pester me again I'll call the police. That clear enough for you, dear? Now get off the fucking line.'

She lay awake that night for over an hour, a whole carillon of alarm bells ringing.

It was the first evening this week that she and Jane had eaten together. Afterwards, they made a log fire in the drawing room and watched TV, all very mellow and companionable. Later they put out the lamps and moved out of the draughts and close to the fire, sipped their tea and talked. And then she got around to telling Jane about Katherine Moon.

'Dead?'

So she hadn't known. It was hard to tell how Jane really felt about this; she seemed to have assumed Moon and Lol had been, at some stage, an item. When Merrily came to Moon's use of the Iron Age knife – this kind of stuff never seemed to upset Jane particularly, as long as no animals were involved – the kid nodded solemnly.

'Sure. The later Celtic period, coming up to the Dark Ages, that was like this really screwed-up time.'

'It was?' Merrily curling her legs on to the sofa.

'Bad magic. The Druids were getting into blood sacrifices

and stuff. If your family was rooted in all that, you're quite likely to get reverberations. Plus, who knows what *else* happened on the site of that barn? I mean way back. It could be really poisoned, giving off all kinds of mind-warping vibrations. If you don't know how to handle these things, it could go badly wrong for you.'

'That's very interesting,' Merrily had said mildly. 'Where did you learn all that, flower?'

'Everybody knows that,' Jane said inscrutably. She was sitting on a big cushion at the edge of the hearth. 'So this Moon was bonkers all along?'

'She had a history of psychiatric problems.'

Which led to a long and fairly sensible discussion about Lol and the kind of unsuitable women into whose ambience he seemed to have been drawn, beginning with his born-again Christian mother, then the problem over a fifteen-year-old schoolgirl, when he himself was about nineteen but no more mature than the girl, and then some older woman who was into drugs, and later Alison Kinnersley who'd first drawn him to Herefordshire for entirely her own ends.

'How's he taken it?' Jane set her mug down on the hearth and prodded at a log with the poker.

'He thinks he should have known the way things were going, which is what people always say after a suicide. But in this case people were *trying* to help her. It's very odd. It doesn't add up.'

'So, like, Lol . . . was he in love with her?'

'I really don't think so, flower.'

And at this point the phone had rung and she'd waited and dialled 1471, finding it had been Lol himself. She called him back from the scullery-office, still answering monosyllabically, because Jane was sometimes a stealthy mover. So she never did learn how he'd discovered the kid had become involved with something called The Pod, which met above a café in

Hereford. It could be worse, however, Lol said: women only, nothing sexual. Self-development through meditation and spiritual exercises. Progressing – possibly – to journeys out of the body.

Oh, was *that* all?

When she went back to the drawing room, Jane had put on the stereo and it was playing one of the warmest, breathiest, Nick Drake-iest songs on the second and final Hazey Jane album. The one which went, '*Waking in the misty dawn and finding you there.*'

Merrily lay on the sofa and listened to the music, her thoughts tumbling like water on to rocks.

During the remainder of the evening, the phone rang twice. Merrily said the machine would get it, although she knew it was still unplugged.

The last caller, she'd discovered from the bedside phone, was Huw Owen. She fell asleep trying to make sense of him and Dobbs.

She lay there, half awake for quite a while, dimly aware of both palms itching, before the jagged cold ripped up her, from vagina to throat, and then she was throwing herself out of bed and rolling away into a corner, where the carpet was still damp from holy water, and she curled up dripping with sweat and terror and saw from the neon-red digits of the illuminated clock that the time was 4.00 a.m., the hour of his death in Hereford General.

Across the room, with a waft of cat's faeces and gangrene, a shadow sat up in her bed.

THIRTY-FOUR

A Party

The bulkhead light came on and the back door was tugged open.

Somewhere deep in the stone and panelled heart of The Glades a piano was being plonked, a dozen cracked sopranos clawing for the notes of what might have been a hymn.

'Ah.' Susan Thorpe stepped out in her Aran sweater, heathery skirt, riding boots. 'Splendid. We were beginning to think you weren't going to venture out.'

No 'How good of you to turn out on a night like this'. Mrs Thorpe appeared to think Deliverance was the kind of local service you paid for in your council tax.

The singing voices shrilled and then shrank under a great clumping chord.

'I can never say no to a party,' Merrily said.

She shed her fake-Barbour in the hall. Underneath, she wore a shaggy black mohair jumper over another jumper, her largest pectoral cross snuggling between the two layers. Susan Thorpe looked relieved that she wasn't in a surplice. But her husband Chris obviously thought she ought to be.

'This is a *proper* exorcism, isn't it?' He was extremely tall, with a shelf of bushy eyebrow and a premature stoop.

His wife glared. 'They aren't *all* bloody deaf in there, you know.'

'Let's get this clear,' Merrily said. 'It isn't going to be

328

an exorcism at all. An exorcism is an extreme measure only normally used for the removal of an evil presence.'

'How d'you know it isn't that?'

'I don't know *what* it is yet, Mr Thorpe.' *Yet* – that was optimistic. 'If it does turn out to be, er, malevolent, we shall have to think again.'

Believe me, if you had real malevolence here, you would know . . .

'Always believed in belt and braces, myself,' Chris Thorpe said gruffly. 'Go in hard. If you've got rats, you put down poison, block all the holes.'

Merrily smiled demurely up at him. 'How fortunate we all are that you're not an exorcist.'

'Let it go, Chris.' Susan Thorpe pushed him into the passage leading to the private sitting room, held open the door for Merrily. 'The truth is, my husband's a sceptic. He teaches physics.'

'Oh, where?'

'Moorfield High,' Susan said quickly. Oh dear, a mere state school. The Thorpes were no more than late-thirties, yet had the style and attitudes of people at least a generation older. You couldn't imagine this was entirely down to living with old people. More a cultivated image over which they'd lost all control.

The sitting room was gloomily lit by a standard lamp with an underpowered bulb, but it was much tidier tonight – possibly the work of the plump woman who sat placidly sipping tea. On her knees was a plate with a knife on it, and cake crumbs.

'This is my mother, Edna Rees. This is Mrs Merrily Watkins, Mother. She's Dobbs's successor.'

The former housekeeper to the Canon had raw red farmer's cheeks and wore her hat indoors; how many women did that these days? She put down her cup, and studied Merrily at length, unembarrassed.

'You seem very young, Mrs Watkins.'

'I'm not sure which way to take that, Mrs Rees.'

'Oh, I think you are, my dear.' Mrs Rees's accent was far more local than her daughter's – Hereford-Welsh. 'I think you are.'

Merrily smiled. *How do I get to talk to her in private?*

Susan Thorpe frowned. 'I don't know how long this operation normally takes you, Merrily. But our venerable guest of honour is usually in bed by ten.'

'So there's going to be nobody on that floor until then?'

'Nobody living,' said Mrs Rees blandly.

Chris Thorpe glanced at Merrily's shoulder-bag. 'You have some equipment?'

'We don't have to be near any power points, if that's what you mean.'

'Chris, why don't you go and do something else?' Susan said through her teeth.

'It's my house. I've a right to be informed.'

'But I don't feel you really believe it's going to achieve anything,' Merrily said. 'It's just that normally we like to do this in the presence of people who are a bit sympathetic – a scattering of actual Christians. I mean, *are* there any practising Christians around? What about the woman who saw . . . him? Helen?'

'Supervising the party,' Susan said. 'Making sure it doesn't get too rowdy. Anyway, she doesn't want to be involved. Christians? No shortage of *them* but they're the ones we're trying not to alarm. You're on your own, I'm afraid, Merrily. Can I offer you a fortifying cigarette?'

'Thanks. Afterwards, I think. If you could just point me at the spot.'

'Don't fret.' Mrs Rees put down her cup and saucer. 'I'll go with you.'

Excellent.

'Did you ever go with Canon Dobbs, Mrs Rees?'

'Oh no.' Mrs Rees stood up, shaking cake crumbs from her pleated skirt. 'Wasn't *woman's* work, was it?'

Jane and Rowenna ordered coffee and doughnuts at the Little Chef between Hereford and Leominster. Jane nervously stirred an extra sugar into hers. 'I didn't even tell her I was going out tonight. It's come to this: separate lives.'

Rowenna was unsympathetic. 'You're a woman now. You live by your own rules.'

'Yeah, well . . .' Jane looked through the window at the car park and a petrol-station forecourt. She kind of liked Little Chefs because they sold maps and stuff as well, giving you a feeling of being on a *journey.* They weren't travelling far this time, however.

Only to the pub where the psychic fair had been held – there to meet with the gracious Angela. Jane felt like Macbeth going for his second session with the Weird Sisters. Like, face it, the first meeting had changed Jane's life.

She hadn't seen much of Rowenna over the past couple of days. Then, this morning, the lime-green Fiesta had slid into Ledwardine market square while she was waiting for the bus.

She'd immediately wondered whether to tell Rowenna what Dean Wall had said. If somebody was spreading that kind of filth about you, you had a right to know. But the minute she got in, Ro was like: 'Guess who called *me* last night?'

Jane abandoned half her doughnut, pushed the plate away.

'Don't look so worried.'

Rowenna wore a new belted coat of soft white leather;

Jane was wearing her school duffel coat. People must think she was like some hitchhiker this genteel lady had picked up.

'Is she going to give us a reading?'

'I don't know,' Rowenna said. 'You scared of that?'

'I was so pissed off when I got up, I forgot to do the sun thing.'

'So what's she going to do about that?' Rowenna said quite irritably. 'Give you detention? Lighten up, these people are not like . . .' With a napkin over her finger, she dabbed a crumb from the edge of Jane's mouth. 'Listen, you know what your problem is? Your mother's dreary Anglicanism is weighing down on you. So *gloomy*, kitten. You spend your whole life making sacrifices and practising self-denial in the hope of getting your reward in heaven. What kind of crappy deal is that?'

'Yeah, I know.'

'Going to waste her whole life on that shit – and they get paid peanuts, don't they? I mean, that great old house and no money to make the most of it? What's the point? She's still attractive, your old lady. It's understandable that it pisses you off.'

'I can't run her life.'

'No? If it was me, I'd feel it was my responsibility to kind of rescue her, you know? She's obviously got talent, psychic-sensitivity, all that stuff, but she's just pouring it down the drain.'

Jane laughed grimly. 'Oh sure, I walk in one night and I'm, like: "Look, Mum, I can get you out of this life of misery. Why don't you come along to my group one night and learn some cool spiritual exercises?" '

'You underrate yourself, Jane. You can be much more subtle than that,' Rowenna said. There was something new about her tonight: an aggression – and a less-than-subtle change of attitude. Remember '*Listen to me. You cannot change other people. Only yourself.*' How many days ago did she say *that*?

'Come on,' Rowenna said, 'let's go.'

A bulb blew.

Merrily's right hand slid under her top sweater to grip the pectoral cross. A bright anger flared inside her.

The lights were wall-mounted: low-powered, pearlized, pear-shaped bulbs, two on each dusty bracket, the brackets about eight feet apart along the narrow passage. This was the one furthest away, so that now the passage – not very bright to begin with – was dimmed by new shadows and no longer had a visible end. Easy, in this lightless tunnel, to conjure a moving shadow.

Edna Rees chuckled. She was sitting in a pink wicker chair pulled out from a bathroom. Merrily was kneeling on the topmost of three carpeted steps leading up to the haunted east wing.

This was the third floor, and once was attics.

This was a stake-out.

Because you didn't simply arrive and go straight into the spiel. '*Spend some time with it,*' Huw Owen said. '*Let it talk to you. No, of course they seldom actually* talk. *And yet they do.*'

Could she trust anything Huw Owen had told her?

They'd been here twenty minutes. Downstairs, Susan Thorpe would be glaring at her watch. '*Always take your time,*' Huw said. '*Never let any bugger rush you. Where some of these customers come from, there* is *no time. Don't rush, don't overreact, don't go drowning it in holy water.*'

Merrily's bag contained only one small bottle of holy water, for all the use that was. Her only other equipment was a Christian Deliverance Study Group booklet of suitable prayers, most of which she knew off by heart anyway.

She was just going through the motions, with no confidence that it would work.

'*It doesn't always work*' – Huw's truest phrase. It should be printed on the front of the Deliverance handbook.

It should be the *title* of the Deliverance handbook.

And where was she really? How far had she come since the 4.00 a.m. horror? Since the fleeing of her bedroom, the vomiting in the kitchen sink, the stove-hugging, the burning of lights till dawn and the *Oh Christ, why hast thou forsaken me*?

There was then the Putting On A Brave Face Until The Bus Takes Jane Away interlude. She'd had the time – hours – to wash and dress carefully, apply make-up. To stand back from the mirror and recoil at the sight of age and fear pushing through like a disease.

Then the staring-at-the-phone phase. The agitated For God's Sake Ring, Huw moments. *He keeps calling you. He wants to explain. So you should call him back. It doesn't matter that he and Dobbs conspired against you. It doesn't matter what he did. You need him. You need him to take it away. You need to call him now and say, Huw, I am possessed. I am possessed by the spirit of Denzil Joy.*

Yet it was not like that. She might look rough in the mirror, but her dull, tired eyes were not the sleazed-over eyes of Denzil Joy. She didn't feel his greasy desires. She didn't *know* him.

Was not possessed by him.

Haunted, though – certainly that. Useless to paper it over with psychology; she was haunted by him. He followed her, had become her spirit-stalker. Because she'd failed, that night in the General, to redirect his malignant energy, its residue had clung to her. She'd walked out of the hospital with Denzil Joy crawling and skulking behind her like some foul familiar. He was hers now. No one else had caught his disease.

And she'd been unaware of it until – once again insufficiently prepared – she had been collecting herself for the assault on the crow-killer of St Cosmas. Collecting her energy. Then into the cocktail had seeped his essence.

Was that what happened? Had yesterday's holy-water exercise been a failure because it had been directed only at the bedroom – making the *room* safe – rather than herself?

Because she was the magnet, right? She'd *invited* him – sitting by his bedside, holding his kippered hands. The female exorcist attracting the incubus, just as the priest-in-charge had invoked the lust of the organist who'd flashed at her from a tombstone.

Today, she'd concentrated on cleansing herself. Leaving the answering machine unplugged, she'd set out on a tour of churches, a pilgrimage on the perimeter of Hereford. A full day of prayer and meditation.

Finally, parking in a back street near the Cathedral School, and slipping discreetly into the Cathedral, sitting quietly at the back for over an hour while tourists and canons she didn't know flitted through.

She had not called Huw, or Sophie. Had resisted the impulse to enter Church Street and find Lol. She had left the answering machine unplugged. At 4.00 p.m., she'd returned to the vicarage and fed the cat and made a meal for Jane and herself. Then one more visit to the church before the drive – leaving plenty of time – to The Glades.

It was not about proving herself as an exorcist any more. That was over. This was about saving her ministry.

And her sanity?

Leave sanity out of this. Sanity is relative.

Edna Rees looked along the passage, without apparent apprehension, to where the bulb had just blown. 'Surely that's not the first time it's happened to you, my dear?'

Merrily said nothing.

Edna shifted comfortably in her wicker chair. 'Regular occurrence, it was, in Gwynne Street. Wherever he lived, it happened. So I learned.'

'Bulbs blowing?'

'Might've put me off if I'd known before I took the job, see. But you get used to it.'

Merrily glanced along the line of bulbs. The loss of one seemed to make all the others less bright, as though they were losing heart. There was probably a simple scientific explanation; she should ask Chris Thorpe.

'One week we lost five,' Edna said. 'I said, you want to charge them for all these bulbs, Canon. Well, expensive they are these days, bulbs. We tried those economy things – cost the earth, take an age to come on, but they're supposed to last ten years. Not in that house, they didn't.'

'What else happened?'

'Some nights . . .' Edna pulled her skirt down over her knees, ' . . . you just couldn't heat that place to save your life, even with all the radiators turned up, the living-room fire banked all day. Wasn't even *that* cold outside sometimes, see. And yet, come the night, just when you'd think it'd be getting nicely warmed up . . .'

Cold spots?

This passage had five doors, all closed. Closed doors were threatening. Doors ajar with darkness within were terrifying. Merrily guessed she just didn't like doors. Otherwise, there was no sense of disturbance, no cold spots – and certainly nothing like the acrid, soul-shrivelling stench which had gathered around . . .

Stop!

She turned briskly to Edna. 'Are you saying that he . . . brought his work home?'

Edna looked at Merrily from under her bottle-green velvet

hat. Her eyes were brown and shrewd, over cheeks that were small explosions of split veins.

'My dear, his work *followed* him home.'

She froze. 'He told you that?'

'He never talked about his work,' Edna said. 'Not to me; not to anyone, far as I know. But when he came back sometimes, it was like Jack Frost himself walking in.'

'What did he do about that?'

'Not for me to know, Mrs Watkins.'

'No,' Merrily said, 'obviously not. I . . . saw you with him the other week, in the Cathedral.'

'Yes,' Edna said calmly, 'I thought it was you.'

'He was telling you to go away. He said there was something he couldn't . . . couldn't discuss there.'

'Sharp ears you have.'

'Is it none of my business?'

'You must think it is.'

'Why "here"? Why did he want to get you out of the Cathedral?'

'For the same reason he wanted me out of his house, Mrs Watkins.'

'Which is?'

'Why are you asking me these questions?'

'Because I can't ask him. Because he's lying in hospital apparently incapable of speech. Or at least he doesn't speak to the female nurses.'

Edna smiled.

'Any more than he'd speak to me before his stroke. He froze me out, too, on the grounds that I wasn't fit to do his job. His sole communication with me was a cryptic note saying that Jesus Christ was the first exorcist. There. I've told you everything, Edna.'

It was what she wanted.

'Merrily . . . Can I call you Merrily?'

'Please do.'

'Merrily, this began . . . I don't know exactly *when* it began, but it did have a beginning.'

'Yes.'

'I started to hear him praying, very loud and . . . anguished. I would hear him through the walls: sometimes in what sounded like Latin – the words meant nothing to me. He would shout them into the night. And then, backwards and forwards from the Cathedral he'd go at all hours, in all weathers. I would hear his footsteps in the street at two, three in the morning. Going to the Cathedral, coming *from* there – sometimes rushing, he was, like a man possessed. I don't mean that in the . . .'

'I know.'

'And this was when he began cutting himself off: from men too, but especially from women. Would not even see his own sister. He would put her off – *I* was made to put her off – when she wanted to visit. He would not even speak to her on the telephone. Or to his granddaughters – he has two granddaughters. One of them brought her new baby to show him. He saw her coming down the street and made me tell her he was away. It made no sense to me. He'd been married for forty years.'

'Does it make sense now?'

'I have been reading,' Edna said, 'about St Thomas of Hereford.'

'Thomas Cantilupe?'

'He would not have women near him, either.'

She fell silent.

'But that was *then*,' Merrily said. 'That was the Middle Ages. Cantilupe was a Roman Catholic bishop. They weren't *allowed* to have . . .'

'I know that, but where did the Canon go when he went into the Cathedral? Where did he have his stroke?'

'Cantilupe's tomb.'

'I can't tell you any more,' Edna said. 'You had better do what you came for.'

In fact, the routine for this kind of situation usually involved blessing the entire house, room by room, starting at the main entrance, the blessing thus extended to all who passed in and out. But Susan Thorpe was hardly going to permit that.

If you couldn't tie down a haunting to a specific incident in the history of the house, then you at least should ask: What's causing it to happen *now*? Is it connected to the present function of the house, the kind of people living here? Old people feeling unwanted, neglected, passed-over? Confused, their senses fuddled . . .? Yet Susan Thorpe wouldn't accommodate that kind of client. '*Any signs of dementia, they have to go. We aren't a nursing home.*'

You could spend days investigating this, and then discover it was a simple optical illusion. Merrily moved a little closer to the dead bulb's bracket.

'I don't know what your son-in-law expected, but—'

'Stuffed-shirt, he is,' Edna said. 'I hope I die, I do, before I have to go into a place owned by people like them. Pretend-carers, they are.' Out of her daughter's earshot, Edna's accent had strengthened. 'Poor old souls. Grit my teeth, I will, and stay here until I can find a little flat, then you won't see me for dust.'

'Good for you,' Merrily said.

It was quiet. No wind in the rafters. They stood in silence for a couple of minutes and then Merrily called on God, who Himself never slept, to bless these bedrooms and watch over all who rested in them.

THIRTY-FIVE

Sholto

Her hands together, head bowed.

Even the piano was inaudible up here, and in the silence her words sounded hollow and banal.

'. . . and ask You to bless and protect the stairs and the landings and the corridors along which the residents and the workers here must pass to reach these rooms.'

She was visualizing the old ladies gathered around the piano two floors below, so as to draw them into the prayer.

'We pray, in the name of Our Lord, Jesus Christ, that no spirit or shade or image from the past will disturb the people dwelling here. We pray that these images or spirits will return to their ordained place and there rest in peace.'

This covered both *imprints* and *insomniacs*, although she didn't really think it could be an *insomniac*. There'd surely be some sign, in that case, some pervading atmosphere of unrest.

'Amen,' Edna said.

Merrily held her breath. It had been known, Huw Owen had said, for the spirit itself to appear momentarily, usually at the closing of the ritual, before fading – in theory for ever – from the atmosphere.

'Mind, it's also been known to appear with a mocking smile on its face and then – this is frightening – appearing again and again, bang-bang-bang, in different corners of the room . . .'

Although it was hard not to flick a glance over her

shoulder, Merrily kept on looking calmly in front of her under half-lowered eyelids, her body turned towards the darkness at the end of the passage. From which drifted a musty smell of dust and camphor which may not have been there before.

She waited, raising her eyes to the sloping ceiling with its blocked-in beams, and the filigree pouches of old cobwebs over the single curtained window. She straightened her shoulders, feeling the pull of the pectoral cross.

It was darker – well *seemed* darker. As though there'd been a thirty per cent decrease in the wattage of the bulbs. Possibly something was happening, something absorbing the energy – something which had begun as she ended her first prayer. A mild resistance was swelling now.

Merrily began to sweat, trying not to tense against the ballooning atmosphere. She wondered if Edna was aware of it, or if she herself was the only focus, her lone ritual beckoning it. When she spoke again, her voice sounded high and erratic.

'If there is a . . . an unquiet spirit . . . we pray that you may be freed from whatever anxiety or obsession binds you to this place. We pray that you may rise above all earthly ties and go, in peace, to Christ.'

That sounded feeble. It lacked something. It was too bloody *reasonable*.

Belt and braces, said the awful Chris Thorpe, stooped like a crane and sneering.

Yes, OK, there was something. Now that she was sure of that, there should perhaps be a Eucharist performed for the blessing of the house. It could be conducted by the local vicar, held under some pretext where all the residents could be invited. Those who were churchgoers would accept it without too many questions.

The atmosphere bulged. She felt a sudden urgent need to empty her bladder.

'May the saints of God pray for you and the angels of God guard and protect you . . .'

Either the air had tightened or she was feeling faint. Resist it. She fumbled at the mohair sweater to expose the cross. As she pulled at the sweater, her palms began to—

'Mrs Watkins.'

Merrily let go of the sweater; her eyes snapped open. Edna Rees was pointing to where, at the top of the three shallow steps, a figure stood.

'Please, there's really no need for this,' it said.

Angela turned over six cards in sequence and then quickly swept the whole layout into a pile.

But not before Jane had seen the cards and recognized three of them: *Death . . . The Devil . . . The Tower struck by lightning.*

'I can't do this,' Angela said. 'I'm afraid it's Rowenna's fault.'

It was the same pub where the psychic fair had been held, but this time they were upstairs in a kind of boxroom. Pretty drab: just the card table and two chairs. Rowenna had to perch on a chest of drawers, her head inches from a dangling lightbulb with no shade.

'I'm sorry, Angela,' she said. 'I really didn't realize.'

Angela looked petite inside a huge sheepskin coat with the collar turned up. She also looked casually glamorous, like a movie star on location. But she looked irritated, too.

'I suppose you weren't to know, but it's one of my rules in a situation like this to know only the inner person. I don't like to learn in advance about anyone's background or situation, because then, if I see a problem in the cards, I can know for sure that this information comes from the Source and is not conditioned by my personal knowledge, preconceptions or prejudices. I'm sorry, Jane.'

Jane heard the rumble of bar-life from the room below.

'Angela,' she said nervously, 'that's not because you turned up some really bad cards and you don't think I can take it?'

Angela looked cross. 'Cards have many meanings according to their juxtaposition.'

'Looked like a pretty heavy juxtaposition to me,' Rowenna said with a hint of malice. Angela had already done a reading for Rowenna – her future was bound up with a friend's, needing to help this friend discover her true identity – something of that nature. Rowenna had seemed bored and annoyed that the emphasis seemed to be on Jane.

Jane said, 'What was it Rowenna told you?'

'I told her what your mother was, OK?' Rowenna said. 'On the phone last night. It just came out.'

Priest or exorcist? Jane was transfixed for a moment by foreboding. 'That reading was telling you something about me and Mum, wasn't it?'

Angela straightened the pack and put it reverently into the centre of a black cloth and then folded the cloth over it. 'Jane, I'm not well disposed towards the Church. A friend of mine, also a tarot-reader, was once hounded out of a particular village in Oxfordshire because the vicar branded her as an evil infuence.'

'Vicars can be such pigs,' Rowenna said.

'However,' Angela looked up, 'I make a point of never coming between husbands and wives or children and parents.'

'Please, will you tell me what—?'

'Jane.' Angela's calm eyes held hers. 'When I look at your inner being, I sense a generous and uninhibited soul. But if your mother's burden is to be constrained by dogma and an unhappy tradition, you really don't *have* to share it.'

'Well, I know, but . . . mostly we get on. Since Dad died we've supported each other, you know?'

'Admirable in principle.'

'Like, she's pretty liberal about most things, but she's got this really closed mind about . . . other things.'

'All right, my last word on this . . .' Angela began to exude this commanding stillness; you found you were listening very hard. 'It might be wise, for both your sakes – your own and your mother's – for you to keep on walking towards the light. Don't compromise. Don't look back. Pray . . . I'm going to say it . . . pray that she follows in *your* wake.'

'You mean she needs to get out of the Church.'

'These are *your* cards, Jane, not hers.'

'Or what? What's going to happen to her if she stays with the Church?'

'Jane, don't put me in a difficult position. Now, how are things going at The Pod?'

The shadow on the stairs spoke in a surprising little-girly voice.

'Aren't you going to introduce me to your friend, Mrs Rees?'

'This,' Edna said with an overtone of resignation, 'is Miss Anthea White.'

'Athena!'

'Miss Athena White. Why aren't you at the party, then, Miss White?'

'At the piano with all those old ladies? One finds that sort of gathering *so* depressing.' Miss White moved out of the shadows. She was small, even next to Merrily, wearing a long blue dressing-gown which buttoned like a cassock.

Very tiny and elflike. Not as old as you expected in a place like this – no more than seventy.

'This is Mrs Watkins,' Edna said.

Miss White inspected Merrily through brass-rimmed glasses like the ones Lol Robinson wore, only much thicker. 'Ah, *there* it is. You keep the clerical collar well-hidden, Mrs Clergywoman. I say, you're very very pretty, aren't you?'

'Thank you,' Merrily said.

'One had feared the new female ministers were all going to be frightful leather-faced lezzies. Come and have a drink in my cell.'

'Now,' Edna said, 'you know you're not supposed to have alcohol in your rooms.'

'Oh, Mrs Rees, you aren't going to blab to the governor, are you? It's such a *frightfully* cold night.' Light seemed to gather in her glasses. '*Far* too cold for an exorcism.'

'Perhaps you could excuse me,' Edna said.

'Oh, do you *have* to leave?'

'I rather understand that I do,' Edna said tactfully.

'How did you guess?' Merrily asked, feeling tired now.

'Oh, don't be ridiculous.' Miss White handed her an inch of whisky in what seemed to be a tooth glass. 'You were hardly here to conduct a wedding.'

Her room was an odd little grotto up in the rafters, with Afghan rugs on the wall, an Aztec-patterned bedspread. And a strange atmosphere, Merrily sensed, of illusion. Twin bottles of Johnnie Walker lurked inside an ancient wooden radio-cabinet. There were several free-standing cupboards, with locks. The room was lit by an electrified pottery oil-lamp on a stand.

Athena White went to sit on the high wooden bed, her legs under her in an almost yogic position, her dressing-gown unbuttoned upwards to the waist. No surgical stockings needed here. Merrily was sitting uncomfortably on a kind of camping stool near the door. It put her head on a level with

Miss White's projecting knees. Miss White seemed relaxed, like some tiny goddess-figure on a plinth.

'Now then,' she said. 'What are you trying to do to Sholto?'

She let the name hang in the air until Merrily repeated it.

'Sholto?'

A mellower light gathered in Miss White's glasses. 'Weren't you able to see him?'

Merrily made no reply.

'Come on, young Mrs Clergyperson, either you did or you didn't.'

'Let's say I didn't.'

'That's a shame. Perhaps you were erecting a barrier? That's what your Church does though, isn't it? Very, very sad – throwing up barriers, wrapping itself in a blanket of disapproval. And yet' – Miss White's head tilted in mild curiosity – 'you are afraid.'

'I don't think so.'

'Oh yes, I can always detect fear. You're not afraid of Sholto, are you?'

'Am I to understand Sholto is your ghost?'

'How perceptive of you to apply the possessive,' said Miss White. 'I must say, it's an awful job you have, Mrs Clergyperson. I never thought to see a woman doing it.'

'Why not?'

'Is it a specialist thing, or have you simply been commandeered as Thorpe's prison chaplain?'

'Miss White—'

'Your Church is like some repressive totalitarian regime. Everyone has a perfectly good radio set, but you try to make sure they can only tune in to state broadcasts. Whenever the curtains accidentally open on some sublime vista, you rush in and snap them shut again. *That's* your job, isn't it?'

'The soul police,' Merrily said. 'You should meet my daughter.'

'Ye gods, are you old enough to have a daughter?'

'Let's drop the flattery, Miss White. What are you trying to tell me?'

'What I *am* telling you' – Miss White turned full-face to Merrily, and the light in her glasses became twin pinpoints – 'is to leave him alone.'

'Sholto?'

'Have you *any* idea what it's like in one of these places, where all is grey and faded, and romance resides solely in one's memory?'

'This room's hardly grey and faded.'

'You like my eyrie?'

'It's very cosy.'

'Cosy!' said Miss White in disgust. 'Pah!'

'But to get back to Sholto – that's your name for him, is it?'

'That, my dear clergyperson, *is* his name.'

'You know his history? Some things about him?'

'There's nothing I *don't* know about him. He's a randy sod sometimes, and a frightful lounge lizard, but very, very charming. A look of Ronald Colman, but I suppose you're too young—'

'No, I've seen some of those old films. And you . . . have seen him, I take it.'

'What a stupid question.'

'And the other residents?'

'Well, I can't speak for *all* the hags. Sholto's quite choosy – won't pinch the flabbier old buttocks.'

'What?'

'Oh, for heaven's sake, don't look like that, girl. He was a man of his time. Men *used* to pinch bottoms.'

'I'm sorry.' Merrily was feeling cramped on the stool. 'But

what exactly are we talking about here? Who . . . what exactly do you think Sholto is?'

'What do I think he is?' A vaguely malevolent elf now, white light spearing from her glasses. 'What do *you* think he is?'

An imprint? An insomniac? A volatile? This is the terminology of the Deliverance Age, Miss White.

'I'll tell you what he *isn't*, Mrs Clergygirl.' A finger wagging, the face narrowing, and the eyes almost merging behind the glasses. 'He isn't doing any harm. So you should go away and forget about him. In this museum of memories, Sholto is necessary.'

Merrily drank more whisky to moisten her mouth. 'Would you mind if I had a cigarette?'

'Certainly I would! Pull yourself together. If you don't realize the importance of willpower in *your* job . . .' Miss White's neck extended, birdlike. 'What *is* the matter with you, child?'

Willpower.

Merrily went cold. 'It was you, wasn't it?'

'I beg your pardon.'

'Something was trying to stop me administering the blessing. That was you, wasn't it? Exercising your . . . *willpower.*'

'Oh, what nonsense!' Miss White sniffed, delighted.

'Please,' Merrily said wearily, 'no more bullshit, Athena.'

A self-satisfied smile escaped beneath a little portcullis of teeth. 'Why don't you just ask yourself . . . What's your name, by the way?'

'Merrily.'

'Well, ask yourself, Merrily, was what you were doing appropriate? Was it polite?'

'Sorry?'

'Did you ask permission? No, you didn't. It was like a

police raid: the way they always go in at dawn and bash some-one's door down. It's disgraceful – we're not criminals, even if we are in prison. And what has Sholto done wrong?'

'Well, he . . . he's dead. He shouldn't *be* here.'

Miss White's magnified eyes glowed.

She's mad, Merrily thought. 'Look,' she said reasonably, 'shouldn't he be free to move on? That's what matters. And what keeps him here – that matters, too. Because if what keeps him here is only—'

'The undying pull of the flesh, one presumes. Perhaps we're part of his karma. Broke a lot of young hearts in his time, I'd guess. Now all he has to amuse him is a bunch of raddled old bags with their tits round their waists. For him, that's Purgatory, to use your terminology. But we're all of us far too old to be corrupted. Sholto is needed here to feed people's fantasies. He's not only harmless, he's essential, and that's an end to it. I'll keep him in order, don't worry. You can tell Thorpe you've got rid of him. Now . . . let's examine your own problem, which I would guess is a good deal less benign. What *are* you carrying around with you?'

'What?'

'Look at you, all hunched up against the cold. You're cowering.'

Merrily instinctively straightened as best she could on her camping stool.

'Oh, stop it! You're cowering *inside*. You can't hide that from me. Come here.'

Merrily found herself standing up.

'Come and sit on the bed. Come on, I'm not going to touch you up!' Athena White slid from the bed and leaned, in her tubular robe, over Merrily, peering closely into her eyes. 'Ye gods, you *are* buggered up, aren't you?'

Merrily's legs felt suddenly quite weak.

'Don't struggle,' Miss White said.

'This is not right.'

'It's not right at all. Look at me – no, *focus* on me, girl. That's better. I want to see the *inner* person. I feel you're normally quite strong, but he's certainly depleted you.'

'Who?'

'You tell me. Go on. Tell me his name.'

'I don't know what you—'

'Tell me his name: that ball of spiritual pus that's attached itself to you. What is his *name*?'

'Denzil Joy.'

'That's better,' said Miss White.

Crow Maiden

By 9:30, James Lyden and his band had been ejected from the cellar studio in Breinton Lane. Lol got out of there, too, before Denny's rage could do some damage. By the time the band had been packed into their Transit in the driveway, he was making his excuses – there was someone he needed to call.

Which was true.

'You can do it from here, man.' Denny's bald head was shining with angry sweat.

'I can't.' Lol was backing away out of the drive, pulling on his army-surplus jacket. No way he wanted to discuss this with Denny until he had some background.

'You . . .' Denny was stabbing at the fog. 'You know more than you're letting on. Where's this come from? What's this crow shit?'

'I'll call you tomorrow.'

'And you can tell that fucking Lyden he's finished!' Denny bawled after him down Breinton Lane.

The Transit van had reversed, and was alongside Lol now, James's Welsh friend, Eirion, at the wheel. It stopped.

'Mr Robinson,' Eirion shouted, 'for heaven's sake, what have we done?' He sounded shocked and frightened.

'Get your cocking head back in here, Lewis,' Lol heard James say lazily. 'The old man will sort it.'

'I'm sorry,' Eirion said, as the van pulled away. Lol wondered what his chances were of talking to Dick before James did.

'How old are you, Merrily?'

'Thirty-six.'

She sat at the bottom of the bed, feeling a little unconnected, slightly not-quite-here. She felt guilty because that was not unpleasant. Maybe the whisky . . .

Or not?

'When I was your age, I knew nothing,' Miss White said. 'Indeed, I knew very little even when I retired from the Civil Service. You would have been only a child then. I, however, was very high-powered in those days, or so I thought. In reality I knew nothing. It was only when I left London that I began to study in earnest.'

She unlocked one of the cupboards, threw open its double doors.

Merrily thought: *Oh . . . my . . . God . . .*

Books. Hundreds of books – many stored horizontally on the shelves, so as to stuff more in. Madame Blavatsky, Rudolph Steiner, Israel Regardie, Dion Fortune: recent paperbacks wedged against yellowing tomes on meditation, astrology, the Qabalah. If the other cupboards were similarly stocked, there must be several thousand books in this attic.

A lifetime's collection of esoteric reading. A witch's cave of forbidden literature. You wouldn't have prised Jane out of here this side of breakfast time.

'They know I have books in my cupboards,' Miss White said, 'but I rather imagine they consider me a subscriber to the lists of Messrs Mills and Boon.'

Merrily thought how wary she herself used to be of Jane's guru: the late folklorist, Lucy Devenish. God only knew what *this* old girl got up to when the lights were out.

One thing puzzled her.

'Miss White, I can't . . . What are you doing in a place like this?'

'Ah, yes . . . why not the bijou black-and-white cottage? Why not the roses round the door and the Persian cat in the window?'

'Something like that.'

'Because then, my little clergyperson, one would be obliged to prune the roses and feed the cat, to shop for food and employ workmen to preserve the ancient timbers. How much more space there is here . . . *inner* space, I mean. As well as beautiful hills to walk in, should one be overtaken by the need to commune with nature.'

'But how can you . . .? I don't know how to put this.'

'Be surrounded by twittering biddies, patronized by the dreadful Thorpe? That is simply the outer life. The Thorpes suspect I have enough money to buy the whole place, so they don't pressure me. All right, when one gets very, *very* annoyed with them, one can be . . . mischievous . . .'

'I bet.'

' . . . while at the same time' – Miss White smiled almost seraphically – 'giving one's fellow inmates a welcome, nostalgic *frisson* once in a while.'

His name drifted serenely in the air between them.

'Sholto,' Merrily said eventually.

'A-ha.'

'How did you do it?'

Miss White selected from the bookshelves what turned out to be a stiff-backed folder, and took out a yellowing photograph pasted on card.

'This is him?'

He wore a pinstriped suit with wide lapels. His hair was dark and kinked, his moustache trimmed to a shadow.

'I bought him in a print shop in Hay,' said Miss White. 'I

liked his little twist of a smile. No idea who he is or where he came from – there's no name on the photo. I thought he rather looked like a Sholto.'

Merrily said, 'I'm not going to ask you how you did this.'

'Good, because I should refuse to tell you. You could find out easily enough, if you studied. It's a very well established technique.'

'He isn't a ghost at all.'

'He's a projection. Do you know what I mean by that?'

Merrily said, 'Can I think about it?'

Projection?

Psychic projection, psychological projection – a grey area. Come on, Huw, what are we dealing with here?

'We don't fully understand this, but if we assume, to put it simply, that an imprint exists on a sensory wavelength or plane parallel to our own, then it follows that some people are capable of tuning into that wavelength, sometimes allowing the imprint to be transmitted in a way that renders it visible to others. They may be able, consciously or unconsciously, to lend it the energy it needs to manifest. They may even create their own imprint, projecting it like a hologram. If you come across one of these, you're unlikely to be able to get rid of it through prayer or ritual alone. You've got to stop the person from doing it.'

Merrily imagined, in the part of the passage where the bulb had blown, turning it into a black tunnel, a man in a double-breasted suit bringing a match to his cigarette, exhaling the smoke towards her – smoke which rose in a V, a grey, sardonic smile – before shrivelling up into his own vapour like a silently bursting balloon.

'You're thinking, is this devilry – aren't you?' The light through Miss White's glasses was intense and focused, like when as a kid you used the sun through a magnifying glass to burn a hole in a newspaper.

'I suppose I am.'

'Would you settle for *naughty*?'

'I'd love to, but I don't think I'd be allowed to. You see, the problem – as I see it – is that you've created an energy form separate from yourself, but possessing a few atoms of your transferred . . . intelligence?'

'Perhaps.'

'How far is that from it acquiring a level of existence of its own? A primitive level, perhaps, but then other – possibly negative – energies might be attracted to it. And then you could have trouble that's not so easy to control: a *volatile* – a poltergeist. Or worse.'

'Yes.' Athena White sat down next to Merrily. 'I follow your argument. It's unlikely, though, especially if *I'm* here.'

'But . . . I'm sorry, Athena, but you're not always going to be here, are you?'

'He'll die when I die.'

'You reckon?'

'Oh, you *are* a pain, Mrs Clergyperson. All right, I'll consider it. But it'll be a frightful wrench – for all of us.'

'I'm sure he'll live on in all your memories.'

'I've said I'll *consider* it,' Athena snapped. 'Now tell me about Denzil Joy.'

There was a rapping on the door, and Susan Thorpe said, 'Miss White, is there a woman in there with you?'

'I'm here, Susan,' Merrily said. 'Miss White's been helping me.'

'I hope she can keep her mouth shut.'

Miss White said loftily, 'You may, for once, count on it, Thorpe. Now leave us.'

'You know I can't drag the party out much longer.'

'Well, tell your husband to take his clothes off.'

'Oh!' said Susan Thorpe. They heard her footsteps recede.

'That makes me feel quite queasy,' Merrily said.

'Wait till you're as old as they are.' Mrs White stood up. 'Merrily, I'm very disturbed by this. I think he's feeding off you.'

'Don't.'

'If one doesn't face these things, one can't take remedial action. I suspect you haven't been yourself for some days. Tired? Depleted? Prone to emotional outbursts?'

'Well, yes, since you ask. And also flu-like symptoms: vaguely sore throat, blocked nose, temperature. I put it down to stress.'

'Losing the will to fight it?'

'Half the time I just want to run away. I mean . . . Well, to be quite honest, this was going to be my last job as Deliverance consultant . . . diocesan exorcist.'

'You were giving it up?' An eyebrow rose above the spectacles. 'While, under different circumstances, that is a decision one might wish to applaud—'

'I felt I couldn't cope. I felt under attack from all kinds of different directions.'

'As you may well be. This could be precisely what's happening. How many people know of your appalling experience with this man?'

'I don't know. The nurses involved . . . my daughter, Jane . . . my Deliverance course tutor. And Canon Dobbs, of course.'

'As he appeared to have arranged it for you? The sheer *ignorance* of the clergy dumbfounds me. Who else?'

'There's no one else I've told, I don't think. It's not something I enjoy talking about. What's the significance of that, anyway? If I mishandled the job in the hospital, and I've let him in, that's not their fault.'

'Admittedly, the idea of an unhappy spirit desperately clinging at the moment of death to a living person is not unknown, particularly in a sexually charged situation. But I think you must also consider the possibility of psychic attack by person or persons unknown. Which is far *far* more common than most people would imagine. Merely thinking ill of someone is its most basic form, but we may be looking at something more complex in this instance. If I were to lend you my copy of Dion Fortune's *Psychic Self-Defence* . . .'

'What are you trying to do to me? I'm a Christian.'

'As was Fortune herself, after her fashion. Merrily, how soon after the incident at the hospital did this unclean presence make itself apparent?'

'I felt tired afterwards, but that was natural; I'd been up all night. But I don't think I really became aware of it until I was called in to cleanse a desecrated church.'

'Interesting. This was during your service?'

'Well, I didn't actually . . . It was *before*.'

'When you entered the church?'

'I . . .' Merrily remembered standing outside the church talking to the policemen – with a stiffness and a clamminess in her vestments. Had she felt that in the car on the way there? Possibly.

'Think back, Merrily. Who were you with when you first experienced something amiss?'

'Policemen? I don't know, can't think. I'm mixed up and a bit anxious because I'm sitting here, a minister of the Church, unburdening myself to a practising occultist who, by force of willpower, has created a haunted house.'

'Who would you normally go to for spiritual help?'

'Huw, my course tutor, who was in the church with me when I exhibited what must have seemed to him like many of the symptoms of demonic possession.'

'In which case, why the blue blazes—?'

'It's complicated.'

'All right.' Athena White placed a hand on Merrily's knee.

It didn't feel like a cloven hoof. 'Go home, pull your bed into the centre of the room, and draw a pentacle . . .'

'You have *got* to be joking!'

'All right, a circle – in salt, or even chalk – around the bed. Perform whatever rite your religion allows, but supplement it, when you're lying in bed, by visualizing rings of bright orange or golden light around you and above you, so that you are enclosed in an orb of light. Keep that in your mind constantly until you fall asleep. If you awake in the night, visualize it at once, intact. This should bring you unmolested to the morning.'

'A circle?'

'Don't be afraid of it. There is but one God. Consider it heavenly light – angelic.'

Huw and Dobbs? Merrily frowned. She always knew it had to be something like this.

'Secondly, take the robes – vestments – you were wearing in the church when you were spiritually assaulted and burn them. You could try to bless them or sprinkle them with holy water, but it's really not worth it. Get rid of them.'

Merrily supposed this made sense.

'But that is not enough, and you know it, Merrily. Until you trace it to its source and eradicate it, you're always going to be a magnet for the obscene advances of this earthbound essence. This Denzil Joy. One can almost see him now, bloating your aura. You absolutely cannot afford to rest – indeed, you will *not* rest because of who you are – until you put *him* to rest.'

'Yes, I was going to ring you,' Dick Lyden said, agitated. 'The boy's back already, and he's not terribly happy.'

'*He's* not happy . . .' Lol dragged the phone over to the armchair.

Dick said, 'Laurence, it was my understanding that

Denny's studio was a proper professional operation – not some Mickey Mouse outfit. You know what this is costing me, don't you?'

Lol assured Dick that, while this was not the biggest studio around, it was one in which he personally would be delighted to record.

Dick said, 'As long as it didn't bloody well blow up, presumably.'

It didn't blow up, Lol told him. *Denny* blew up, pressured beyond reasonable resistance by the song they were laying on him. When Denny had heard enough of it, wires became detached.

'I'm not paying the man to be a bloody critic,' Dick said. 'I don't like *any* damned song they do either, and I haven't even heard them.'

Lol said, 'Do you and Ruth talk about your work much, over the family supper, comparing notes, that kind of thing?'

'What the hell has—?'

'For instance, did you talk much about Moon in front of James?'

Dick's voice dropped like it had been fast-faded. 'What are you saying?'

Lol said, 'James, as you may have gathered, isn't satisfied with an EP – he wants an album. Denny and me, we were a bit underwhelmed by the quality of what we'd heard so far. We suggested the boys run through the rest of their material, so we'd know what we were looking at. Most of it wasn't wonderful either.'

To be fair, it wasn't badly played, and the harmonies were as neatly dovetailed as you might expect from newly retired cathedral choirboys. It was the material – derived from the work of second-division bands which were already derivative of other second-division bands twenty years earlier – that didn't make it. Denny had, in reality, told Lol – behind the protection of thick glass – that they would make a recording of such pristine quality that the deficiencies in the area of compositional talent would stand out like neon.

'Well, James's mate Eirion isn't entirely insensitive.'

'Really?' Dick said. 'His old man runs Welsh Water.'

'Eirion can tell Denny isn't impressed, so after about three routine power-chord numbers he gets the band into a huddle, and then he and James sit down with acoustic guitars and they go into this quiet little ballad which James introduces as "The Crow Maiden". Perfect crystal harmonies – you could hear every word.'

'Get to the point.'

'I tend to remember lyrics – remembered the last verse, anyway, so I wrote it down.' Lol began to unfold a John Barleycorn paper bag. 'It's really subtle, as you can imagine – still you'll probably get the drift. You ready?'

'Oh, for heaven's sake—'

Lol held up the paper bag, and recited:

'*Found your refuge in the past*
'*You hid beneath its shade*
'*And when you knew it couldn't last*
'*You took your life with an ancient blade.*
'*CROW MAIDEN*
'*CROW MAIDEN*
'*YOU'RE FADIN'*
'*AWAY . . .*'

'Would you like that again?'

You could hear Dick's hand squeezing the phone.

'The little shit,' Dick said.

THIRTY-SEVEN

Faeces and Gangrene

Friday morning, 6.00 a.m. A cold morning moon through new glass. And a smell of putty in the vestry at Ledwardine, where Merrily stood before the wardrobe, frozen with indecision.

She had the Zippo. The Zippo would do it.

What are you waiting for?

She hadn't slept well, but she *had* slept until five, with – all right, yes – the bed in the middle of the room inside a circle of salt. All of which she'd swept into a dustpan before she left the vicarage, in case she didn't return before first light and Jane came looking for her, popped her head around the bedroom door and – God *forbid*!

She was half ashamed, half embarrassed – and had, as soon as she arose, knelt before the window and apologized to God, if He had been offended by the circle and the salt. But she was, in the end, helplessly grateful. For the first time in days, she had not awakened feeling ill, congested, soiled, or worse.

Grateful to whom, though? She'd prayed for a peaceful night, prayed for the soul of Denzil Joy. But it was, to her disquiet, the orange-gold orb of Athena White which had coloured her dreams.

She was balancing at the top of the slippery slope into New Age madness? Into Jane country? And if she burned the cassock and surplice?

361

Last night, in her state of compliance at The Glades, half hypnotized by the extraordinary Miss White, this had seemed entirely logical. This morning, she'd been dwelling on it with increasing horror – a bonfire of these vestments was wholly sacrilegious, the most explicit symbolic rejection of her vows.

She'd prayed hard over this one, kneeling under the window, summoning the blue and the gold. *Oh Jesus, give me a sign that this is acceptable in Your eyes.*

Please God, don't take it the wrong way. Infantile? God listened to your heart.

'*You will not rest – until you put him to rest.*'

Oh, Miss White, so plausible. This career civil servant – '*very high-powered*' – who had committed herself to an old folks' home to develop her inner life. '*Damned woman,*' Susan Thorpe had said afterwards, '*I could have sworn she was downstairs with the others. But you did manage to complete your exorcism?*' No problem, Merrily had assured her. Miss White was a surprisingly devout believer. '*One God. Angelic light.*'

A dabbler? A minister of God was following the advice of a mad dabbler all the way to New Age hell?

Now Merrily stood in the vestry, with no lights on and her torch switched off – after Sunday night's break-in, Ted probably had vigilantes watching out for signs of intruders. She felt like a thief: the taking and destruction of priest's vestments . . . wilful damage . . . and worse.

'*Burn them.*'

Where? On the drawing-room fire? In the garden, like a funeral pyre of her faith?

It was well meant. She had no bad feelings at all about Athena White as a human being. And the advice was . . . well meant.

And it was insidiously irresistible last night, after Jane had gone to bed, and Merrily had been standing at the sink, filling her hot water bottle and contemplating the night ahead . . . smelling *his* smell, feeling *his* fingers – *scritch-scratch* . . . hearing the ratchet wrench as *his* body snapped upright in its deathbed, the tubes expelled, *pip-pop!*

And now remembering how Ethel the cat – who, until this week, had habitually slept at the bottom of Merrily's bed – had once again padded discreetly and faithlessly up the stairs after Jane.

It was then that she'd reached into the cupboard for the drum of kitchen salt. Taking it with her into the scullery-office, where she'd followed the mad woman's next instruction – *'Trace it to its source'* – and called the Alfred Watkins Ward to ask Eileen Cullen for the address of the widow Joy.

And Eileen, puzzled, asking her, 'Is there a problem there, Merrily, you think? Would it not be a case of blessed relief for the poor woman?'

'Sometimes it doesn't work like that,' Merrily had said. 'She may even be feeling guilt that she wasn't there at the end.'

'That was my fault, so help me, for not telling the poor cow until it was over. All right, Merrily, whatever your secret agenda is, you made a good case. You know your way to Bobblestock district?'

She'd find it. As soon as Jane was off the premises, she would go and find Mrs Joy. She would take the whole Deliverance kit, and fresh vestments in the car boot.

But not these vestments.

She opened the wardrobe and pulled them down. They'd been washed, of course, since the night at St Cosmas. She hung the cassock and surplice over the arm that held the torch, still not switched on. She opened both doors wide and felt around to make sure she'd taken the correct garments.

Which was when she found the man's suit.

What?

She pushed the torch inside the wardrobe and switched it on. The suit was on a hanger, pushed to the end of the rail so that it was not visible if you opened only one door.

Merrily pushed her head inside to examine the suit. It was dark green, with a thin stripe of light brown, made of some heavyweight material, and well worn. She touched it. It felt damp.

Or moist, more like.

Merrily screamed. She now had her sign.

She stood, retching, in the moon-washed vestry.

The thin smell the suit gave off had reminded a doctor at the General Hospital of cat faeces and gangrene.

It was around eight, cloudy but fog-free, when Lol spotted the boy in Cathedral School uniform lurking below in Church Street. He went down, and the boy came over: a stocky dark-haired boy with an unexpectedly bashful smile. It was Eirion Lewis, son of the boss of Welsh Water.

'Hoped you might be about, Mr Robinson. I just . . . didn't really feel like going to school until I knew where we stood, you know?'

'Come on up,' Lol said.

Once inside, Eirion went straight to the guitar. 'Wow, is that a Washburn? Could I?'

Lol handed Eirion the Washburn and the boy sat down with it, picking out the opening riff to 'The Crow Maiden'.

'I have to play bass in the band because James is rather better on this than me.'

'Like McCartney,' Lol recalled.

'Really?'

'He was the worst guitarist in the band, so he wound up on bass.'

'Brilliant bass-player, actually. I . . . You know, I didn't mean what I said about how he should have been shot. You feel you've got to keep up with James's cynicism sometimes. Like, he's younger than me, you know?'

'Right,' Lol said.

'I . . . Mr Robinson, I really don't have much time. I just sort of . . .' Eirion hung his head over the guitar. 'I don't know what we did, but we did *something*, didn't we? I mean, this is really important to me, this recording. I don't want to blow it. You know?'

'Well, it was that song,' Lol said.

'*This* song? "The Crow Maiden"?'

'Which of you actually wrote it?'

'We both did. I do the tunes, James does the words. Like, he gives me a poem or something and I work a tune around it – or the other way about. You know?'

'It's a bit more, er, resonant than the other stuff, isn't it?'

'Yes, it is.'

'James tell you where he got the idea?'

'I assumed he made it up – or pinched it from some ancient Fairport Convention album or something. Actually, you know, what can I say? I mean . . . James is a shit, isn't he?'

'Oh?' Lol tilted his head. 'Why?'

'He just is, isn't he? He kind of tells lies a lot. Enjoys getting up people's noses. Does kind of antisocial things for the hell of it. Well, lately, anyway. God, this is stupid of me; you're his dad's mate, aren't you? You used to kind of work with him, right?'

'Oh, well, that's over now,' Lol said. 'Nothing you say will get back to James's old man, OK. "The Crow Maiden", it's about Denny's sister.'

'Sorry?'

'She committed suicide last weekend. She cut her wrists with an ancient blade.'

Eirion's fingers fell from the frets.

'Mmm,' Lol said, 'I can see you didn't know that.'

At the front door, Jane sniffed. 'What's burning out there?'

'I can't smell anything, flower. It's probably from the orchard. Gomer's been clearing some undergrowth.'

'Right.' Jane inspected her mum in the first bright daylight of the week. 'You're looking better.'

'Thanks.'

'Pressure off now?'

'Maybe. You're going to miss the school bus.'

Jane said casually, 'You know, if things have loosened up a bit, Mum, you really ought to take the opportunity to think about your long-term future.'

'It's not a problem, flower. I'll be going to heaven.'

'God,' said Jane, 'you Christians are so simplistic. 'Bye.'

'Work hard, flower.'

When the kid was out of sight, Merrily went around the side of the house to check out the garden incinerator. The vestments were ashes. She made the sign of the cross over them.

Then she burned the suit.

Merrily called directory enquiries for the Reverend Barry Ambrose in Devizes, Wiltshire. She rang his number.

'I'm sorry, he's just popped round to the church,' a woman said pleasantly. 'He'll be back for his breakfast any minute. I'm Stella, his long-suffering wife. Can I get him to call you?'

'If you could. Tell him I really won't keep him a minute.'

'That's no problem. He's talked a lot about you, Merrily, since you were on that course together. He thinks you're awfully plucky.'

'Well, that's . . . a common illusion. Has Barry done much in the way of Deliverance so far?'

'Only bits and bobs, you know. He's still quite nervous about it, to be honest. And you?'

'Still feeling my way,' Merrily said.

Waiting for Barry Ambrose to call back, she went to the bookcase in the hall where they kept the local stuff. She plucked out one she'd bought in the Cathedral shop: *St Thomas Cantilupe, Bishop of Hereford: Essays in His Honour.* She hadn't yet had time to open it.

'*I have been reading,*' Edna Rees had said, '*about St Thomas of Hereford.*'

In the book, several historians explored aspects of the saint's life and the effect he'd had on Hereford – enormous apparently. Merrily began to read about Cantilupe's final months, in 1282, after his dispute with the Archbishop of Canterbury, John Pecham.

This seemed to be a bureaucratic argument about one going over the other's head, further fired up by a clash of temperament. It had ended with Cantilupe being excommunicated and travelling to Italy to appeal personally to the Pope. On the way back, exhausted, he'd collapsed and died – at dusk on 25 August – while still in Italy. As was the custom (*Really? Christ!*) the body was boiled to remove the flesh from the bones. The flesh was buried at the monastery church of San Severo, the heart and bones were brought back to England by Cantilupe's steward, John de Clare. The heart was then kept at Ashridge, in Buckinghamshire, at a college of canons, while the bones came back to Hereford.

Where they began to attract pilgrims – thousands of them. When news of the miracles spread – cures of the crippled and the blind – it became the most important shrine in the West of England. And it made this comparatively remote cathedral very wealthy.

Although several of the bones seemed to have been removed as relics before this, it was not until the shrine was destroyed in the Reformation, on the orders of Henry VIII, that they were dispersed. The book recorded, without further comment, a story that during the journey from Italy the 'persecuted bones' had bled.

Barry Ambrose called back. She liked Barry: he was inoffensive, hamsterish, an old-fashioned vicar.

'Hey, Merrily . . . you heard about Clive Wells?'

The lofty old-money priest who'd sneered at Huw. 'Should I have?'

'He's packed it in,' said Barry.

'What, Deliverance?'

'The lot. He's apparently planning to emigrate to Canada with his family. Had some experience he wouldn't talk about to anybody – now he can't even go into the church. Can't even *pass* a church without going to pieces, so they say.'

'God.'

'Makes you think, doesn't it, Merrily. What can I do for you?'

It was, she admitted, a long shot. 'There's a girl moved into this area from Wiltshire . . . Salisbury.'

'Oh, they're very doubtful about me in Salisbury. You know what it's like.'

'Yeah. No, it's just . . . if you happened to hear anything. I don't even know what I'm looking for. This girl's called Rowenna Napier. They left the area earlier this year. It was suggested to me that there was something funny in her past which might not seem very funny to a church minister. I'm sorry, that's it, I'm afraid.'

Barry was unfazed. 'Well, I've got a name – that's a start, I suppose. I can only roll it along the Cathedral Close and see if anybody picks it up.'

'Could you?'

'Give me a day or two. So, how's it going, Merrily – really?' She heard the boxy sound of him covering the mouth-piece. 'I tell you, it scares seven shades out of me sometimes.'

'Thank God you said that, Barry. Stella gave me the impression you hadn't been doing too much.'

'All *she* knows,' Barry said with an audible shudder.

Viv arrived at the shop with a *Hereford Times*.

'Not too much about Moon, thank Gawd. They haven't picked up on her father's suicide, so that's a mercy. Maybe nobody's worked there long enough to remember.'

Or else Denny had refused to talk to them, Lol thought, and they were sitting on it till it all came out at the full inquest.

Viv said, 'Oh, yeah, I talked to my friend who still goes to The Pod. It's bizarre, but these two girls turn up out of nowhere: your friend's kid and an older one, right? Patricia, who is like mother superior in the group, says to make this Jane feel at home, she's a special person, they have to take care of her, she's got problems at home – this kind of stuff.'

'Problems *at home*?'

'I only mention this . . . like maybe you don't know as much as you think. You got something happening with the mother, is that it? Was that her the other day, when you ran outside?'

Lol didn't answer. Viv had tossed the *Hereford Times* on the counter, and he'd just noticed the lead headline.

> Crow sacrificed in County church horror

He snatched up the newspaper . . .

THIRTY-EIGHT

Nevermore

'Do you *know* how many messages I have left on your machine in the past two days?' Sophie demanded angrily. 'Surely, even if you were ill . . .'

Ill? Yes, she'd been ill. She saw that now. Merrily sat at the desk in the office with the 𝔇 on the door. Nothing had altered and yet everything had. The white winter sun lit the room. There were things to do.

'I'm very sorry, Sophie. I've behaved very badly.'

It could have been entirely psychological. If her vestments were tainted, however slightly, with Denzil's insidious musk, it would have a subliminal effect: expanding at moments of high emotional stress or extreme sensitivity – like the build-up to an exorcism in a country church – into a near manifestation. And it would then take root, and arise again at times – like emerging from sleep – when the subconscious was in free-flow.

Whatever, someone out there had tried to break her. But now, deep in her solar plexus, she was feeling the warm, pulsing thrill of redemption.

Sophie wore a royal-blue two-piece woollen suit. Her white hair was tightly bunned. She looked angry and perhaps overtired, but her eyes also displayed a small sparkle of hope. She'd become like a mother, Merrily realized.

'Merrily, about your resignation e-mail . . .'

'Oh, yes. Has the Bishop received that yet?' She heard the unconcern in her own voice. It didn't really matter any more whether or not she was the official Deliverance consultant. That was a spurious, manufactured title which conferred no special powers. It was just a beacon for the rat-eyes in the dark.

'The Bishop doesn't read his e-mail,' Sophie said. '*I* read his e-mail, and print out the relevant items and put them on his desk. This is yours, I think. What would you like me to do with it?'

She placed in front of Merrily a sheet of A4.

Dear Bishop, After long consideration . . .

Merrily saw what Sophie wanted – how she could make Sophie much happier. 'Could you wipe it?' she said easily. 'I wasn't really myself, was I?'

Sophie gripped the desk tightly, and then let go.

'Sophie?' Merrily stood up, took her arm.

'I didn't want you to go, and leave me alone here.' Sophie swallowed. 'Sometimes I feel I'm going mad.'

'That doesn't sound like you.'

'I know. Capable, reliable old Sophie – total commitment to the Cathedral. That's the *problem*, isn't it?'

'What is?'

'Something in the Cathedral's going wrong, and I'm afraid Michael . . .'

Merrily sighed. 'Might as well say it, Sophie. He can't see it, can he? He wouldn't feel it because he has no basic faith or spirituality? Isn't that what you're saying: that the Cathedral's not safe in Mick's hands?'

Treason.

'Sophie?'

Sophie brought a finger to her brow, as if to halt a fast-escaping thought. 'We have to talk, Merrily.'

The phone rang on her desk in the other office.

'Sure,' Merrily said. 'Whenever.'

She went in search of Lol. In John Barleycorn, the large, tribal-looking woman regarded her with some interest.

'You must be Jane's mum.'

'You *know* Jane?'

'Not personally,' the big woman said with an enigmatic smile. 'But I've got daughters, so I know the problem.'

'*Is* there a problem?' What the hell had Lol been saying? Merrily rocked inside with a blinding urge to wipe away all the rumours and gossip and deceit that had gathered in the days of the fog.

And, oh, there was so much to say to Jane and so much to bring out, after a week in which Merrily had felt so scared of her own daughter that the only way she'd been able to approach this issue was behind the kid's back.

The shop woman smiled to herself, heavy with superior knowledge.

'Where's Lol?' Merrily snapped.

'Oh.' The woman recoiled. 'I think he's over in the central library. That's where he said he was going.'

'Thank you.'

The day had taken a sharp dive into December dusk. She became aware, for the first time, of Christmas lights. Little golden Santas racing across Broad Street on their sleighs, and the warm red lanterns winking a welcome to wallets everywhere.

Christmas in three weeks: goodwill to all men . . . school Nativity play in the church . . . afternoon carol service . . . midnight eucharist. The churchwardens beadily monitoring those big festive collections. Courtesy visits: *Glass of sherry for the vicar, Celia. Not too much – don't want you falling out of the pulpit, ha-ha.*

And the core of cold and loneliness at the heart of it all. The huddling together, with drunken bonhomie and false laughter to ward off the dark.

She stopped outside the library, the lights still blinking universal panic over parties unorganized, presents unbought. For Merrily they emphasized a core of darkness in the little city of Hereford, deep and intense. She stood amid the rush-hour shoppers and she felt it in her solar plexus, where the ghost of Denzil Joy – the ghost that *wasn't* – had formed an interior fog. And now it was clear.

Lol was coming down the library steps, with a big brown book under his arm.

'Merrily!' Santa-light dancing across his gold-framed glasses.

Lol, she wanted to shout, *I'm all right. I'm clear.*

And rush into his arms.

And I still can't go to bed with you. We priests don't do that kind of thing.

'We have to talk, Merrily.'

Suddenly everybody wanted to talk.

'Me too,' she told him, still on that strange, sensitive high. 'Let's go to church.'

The vicar of All Saints had a bigger, more regular congregation than the Cathedral's.

This was because they'd cleared a big space at the rear of the medieval city-centre church and turned it into a restaurant. A good one too. It might not work in a village like Ledwardine, but it had worked here. This church was what it used to be in the Middle Ages, what it was built to be: the centre of everything. It was good to hear laughter in a church, see piles of shopping bags and children, who maybe had never been in a church before, gazing in half-fearful fascination down the nave towards the secret, holy places.

They carried their cups of tea to a table. Lol still had the big brown book under his arm. 'That's the Holy Bible, isn't it?' Merrily said. 'Go on, I can take it. Excite me.'

'Not' – Lol put down the book – 'exactly.'

On the spine it said, black on gold:

ROSS: PAGAN CELTIC BRITAIN

'Damn,' Merrily said. 'So close.'

'The crow,' Lol said.

'What?'

'You didn't tell me about the bloody crow they spread all over the altar at that little church.'

'Should I have?'

Lol opened the book. 'Didn't anyone give a thought to why they would sacrifice a crow?'

'Lol, we just want to keep the bastards out. We're not into understanding them. Maybe you should talk to the social services.'

'Crows and ravens,' Lol said. 'Feared and venerated by the Iron Age Celts. Mostly feared, for their prophetic qualities. But not like the you're-going-to-win-the-lottery kind of prophecy.'

' "Quoth the raven, *Nevermore*." '

'Right. *That* kind of prophecy – harbingers of darkness.'

'Being black. The persecution we still inflict on anything or anybody black, how bloody primitive we still are.'

'In Celtic folk tales, it says here, crows and ravens figured as birds of ill-omen or . . . as a form taken by anti-Christian forces.'

Merrily sat up.

'There's a story in here,' Lol said, 'of how, as late as the seventeenth century, a congregation in a house in the north of Scotland that was used for Christian worship . . . how the congregation was virtually paralysed by the appearance of a big black bird sitting on a pillar, emanating evil. Nobody could leave that house for over two days. They became so screwed up that it was even suggested the householder's son should be sacrificed to the bird. This *isn't* a legend.'

'Then why, if it inspires so much primitive awe, would anyone dare to sacrifice a crow?'

'Possibly to take on its powers of prophecy, whatever. That's been known to happen.'

'This makes me suspicious,' Merrily said. 'You're doing my job for me. Why are you doing my job?'

'Because of something that happened with Moon.'

And he told her about the disturbed woman standing on the Iron Age ramparts at Dinedor, with her hand inside a dead crow.

Merrily, thinking, drank a whole cup of tea, then poured more. She stared down the nave into the old mystery.

Lol said, 'The way she died – I don't believe she would have killed herself like that. I can't believe in the *reasons*. Like the psychological answer, that she was locked into this fatal obsession, so when she found out how her father died it all came to a head. Or the possible psychic theory that maybe Denny's been turning over in his mind: some lingering dark force which periodically curses his family with madness, and the only way you can make sure of avoiding it is to stay the hell away from Dinedor Hill.'

'That can happen, Lol. We believe that can happen. Psychology and parapsychology are so very close. But I don't necessarily buy a connection between what happened to Moon and the crow sacrifice at St Cosmas.'

'No,' Lol said, 'maybe you're right. Maybe I just saw the headline in the *Hereford Times* at the wrong time. Crows were on my mind then.' He closed the book. 'You look better, Merrily. Tired, but better.'

'Tired? I suppose I must be. I didn't realize. I've been dashing about. Oh, I took back my letter of resignation.'

'Figured you might.'

'Something . . . gave.'

'Like, you found out about this guy Huw and old Dobbs.'

'No, I . . . still don't know about that. But I will, very soon.'

'And Jane?'

'Inquiries are in hand.'

Lol said, 'I've had Viv in the shop looking into The Pod.'

'Ah . . . that explains *her.*'

'Apparently – you might find this interesting, not to say insulting – the women were told to look after Jane. That she was a special person with, er, a problem background.'

Merrily stiffened. 'A special person? She said that? *A special person with a problem background*? Where did that come from? Who told these women all this?'

'Don't know.'

Merrily breathed out slowly.

That night, Lol dreamed he awoke and went into the living room and stood at the window gazing down into Capuchin Lane, which was murky with pre-dawn mist, no lights anywhere.

He knew she was there, even before he saw her: grey and sorrowful, the dress meeting the mist in furls and furrows, her eyes as black as the eyes of the crumbling skulls she held, one in each hand.

I'd like to sleep now, Lol, she said. But the tone of it had changed; there was anguish.

He awoke, cold and numb, in Ethel's chair. He didn't remember going to sleep there.

THIRTY-NINE

One Sad Person

She slept through, incredibly, until almost ten, without any circles of golden light. Without, come to think of it, any protective prayers, only mumbles of gratitude as she fell into bed.

'Why didn't you *wake* me?'

'Because you were like mega-knackered,' Jane said. 'You obviously needed it.'

Merrily registered the toast crumbs. Jane had breakfasted alone. There was weak sunshine, through mist. It looked cold out there.

'Nobody rang?'

'Nobody.'

'Not even Ted? Not Huw Owen?' She'd called Huw four times last night, to keep herself in line for last-caller if he should try 1471.

'Uh-huh.' Jane shook her head. 'You need a new dressing-gown, by the way. You look like a bag-lady.'

'Not Annie Howe either?'

'The ice-maiden of West Mercia CID? You can't be that desperate for friends.'

'We commune occasionally.'

'Jesus,' said Jane, 'it'll be girls' nights out at the police social club next. And guest spots on identity parades.'

'Jane.'

'What?'

Merrily pulled out a dining chair. 'Sit down.'

'Why?'

'Because we need to talk.'

'I can't. I'm meeting Rowenna in town.'

'When?'

'For lunch at Slater's, then we're going Christmas shopping. But I wanted to get into town a couple of hours early because I haven't got *her* anything yet, OK?'

'You're spending a lot of time with Rowenna, aren't you?'

'Meaning like more than with you.'

'Or even boys,' Merrily said lightly.

Jane's eyes hardened. 'That's because we're lesbians.'

'You going to sit down, flower?'

'I have to *go*.'

'Sit *down*.'

Jane slumped sullenly into the chair. 'Why do you hate Rowenna?'

'I don't *know* Rowenna. I've only met her once.'

'She's a significant person,' Jane said.

'In what way?'

'In a way that I'd expect you to actually understand. Like she has a spiritual identity. She seeks wisdom. Most of the people at school, teachers included, think self-development is about A-levels and biceps.'

'Rowenna's a religious person?'

'I think we've had this discussion before,' Jane said loftily. 'Religion implies *organized* religion.'

'Anything else, therefore, must be *dis*organized religion.'

'Ah' – a fleeting faraway-ness in the kid's eyes – 'how wrong can you get?'

'So *tell* me.'

Jane looked at her, unblinking. 'Tell you what?'

'Tell me how wrong I can get. Tell me why I'm wrong.'

'Again?' Jane raised her eyes. 'It has to be a personal thing, right? You have to work at it. Make a commitment to yourself. I mean, going to church, singing a couple of hymns, listening to some trite sermon, that's just like, Oh, if I do this every week, endure the tedium for a couple of hours, God'll take care of me. Well, that's got to be crap, hasn't it? That's the sheep mentality, and when you end up in the slaughterhouse you're thinking: Hey, why didn't I just get under the fence that time?'

Merrily felt shadows deepening. 'So you're under the fence, are you, flower?'

Jane shrugged.

'Only I had this anonymous letter,' Merrily said.

'Was it sexy? Was it from one of those sad old guys who want to get into your cassock?'

'I'll show it to you.' Merrily went over to the dresser, plucked the folded letter out of her bag, handed the letter to Jane. Glimpsing the words brazenly endangering her Soul, as the kid unfolded it.

' "Brazenly endangering her soul and yours," ' Jane said, ' "by mixing with the Spiritually Unclean." Well, well. Unsigned, naturally. When exactly did this come?'

'Few days ago.'

'So you've been kind of sitting on it, right?'

'I've had one or two other things to think about, as you well know.'

Jane held the letter between finger and thumb as though it might be infected. 'Burn it, if you like,' Merrily said.

'Oh no.' Jane carefully folded the paper. Her eyes glowed like a cat's. 'I don't think so. I'm going to hunt down this scumbag, and when I find out—'

'I think,' Merrily said, more sharply than she intended, 'that you're missing the point. You went to this so-called psychic fair without even mentioning it.'

'Why? Would you have wanted to come along?'

'Maybe I would, actually.'

'Yeah, like some kind of dawn raid by the soul police.'

'I accept' – Merrily kept her temper, which would have gone out of the window long ago if they'd been having this discussion last night – 'that most of the self-styled New Age people at these events' – selecting her words like picking apples from an iffy market stall and finding they were all rotten – 'are perfectly nice, well-meaning . . .'

' . . . deluded idiots!'

'Jane—'

'I can't believe this!' Jane leapt up. 'Some shrivelled-up, po-faced old fart sends you a poison-pen letter and you secrete it away in your bag and save it up, probably sneaking the occasional peep to stoke up your holier-than-every-bastard-for-miles-around righteous indignation—'

'Sit down, flower.'

'No! I *thought* you were behaving funny. You're bloody terrified, aren't you? It's not, like: How dare this old fart point the finger at my daughter? Oh, no, you're crapping yourself in case this gets back to *Michael* and you get, like, decommissioned from the soul police! Jesus, you are one sad person, Mother.'

'Jane . . .' Merrily steadied herself on the Aga rail. 'Would you come back and sit down? Then we can talk about this like . . . adults?'

'You mean like priest and sinner. I don't think so, Merrily. I'm going upstairs to my apartment. I'm going to light some candles on my altar and probably offer a couple of meaningful prayers to my goddess. Then I'm going out. I'm not sure when I'll be back.'

'Light a couple of candles? I see.'

'Maybe four. They say it's always so much more effective,' Jane said, 'coming from a vicarage.'

'Really?'

Jane turned away and opened the door to the hall.

'That's what they say at The Pod, is it?' Merrily added.

The phone rang in the kitchen just then, and half a second later in the scullery-office. And it went on and on, and Merrily didn't dare answer it because she knew Jane would be out of the room before she reached the receiver.

'You'd better get that. It might be Annie Howe,' Jane said, and Merrily could see she was trembling with rage. 'She must . . . she must've already taught you everything she knows. About spying on people, undercover investigations . . . The soul police will never look back – you fucking nosy bitch.'

'Right! That's it!' Merrily bounced off the stove and into the middle of the room. 'You think you're incredibly cool and clever and in control of your own destiny, and all this crap. The truth is you're either a complete hypocrite or you're unbelievably naive, and has it never entered your head that the only reason this little . . . sect is interested in you is because of me and what I—'

'Me! *Me*, me, *me*!' Jane screeched. 'You are so arrogant. You are *soooo* disgustingly ambitious that you can't see the truth, which is that nobody gives a *shit* for your Church or the pygmies strutting around the Cathedral Close, not realizing what a total joke they are. Your congregations are like *laughable*. In twenty years you'll all be preaching to each other. You don't *matter* any more. You haven't mattered for years. I'm just like *embarrassed* to tell anybody what you do, you know that? You embarrass me to death, so just get off my back!'

The phone stopped. 'Get out,' Merrily said.

'Fair enough.' Jane smiled. 'I may be away some time.'

'Whatever you like. In fact, maybe you could go and stay at

Rowenna's for a few days. I'm sure there are lots of spare bedrooms in Colonel Napier's mansion.'

Jane paused in the doorway. 'Meaning what?'

'Only that you may not know as much about your very best friend as you thought you did.'

'You've been investigating her too? You've been checking up on *Rowenna*?'

Tears spurted into Jane's eyes, and Merrily took a step towards her. 'Flower, please—'

'You keep away from me. You keep *away*. You don't care how low you sink, do you, to protect your piddling little reputation?'

'Get a life, Jane.'

Jane's smile was horribly twisted. 'Oh, I will. I will certainly get a life.' She was whispering now. 'You see, there's no way I could ever trust you again, and if you can't trust somebody, what's the point? I don't have to stay at Rowenna's. There are loads of places I can live. I know lots of people now – like really *good* people.'

'That would be really stupid. You're sixteen years old.'

'That's right, at least you can count.'

'And these are not good people.'

'What the fuck would you know, Merrily?' Jane prodded a finger at the air between them. 'I'll tell you something. I'd rather sell my soul to the Devil than spend one more night in this mausoleum.'

'All right,' Merrily said. 'Stop right there. I don't care what you say about me, but don't ever say *that*. Just don't . . . ever . . . say it.'

Jane shrugged. 'Like . . . come and get me, Satan?'

She tossed back her hair, which wasn't really long enough to toss, and went out into the hall and Merrily heard her snatching her coat from the peg and then the creak and judder of the front door.

Merrily stood in the centre of the kitchen. After a while, she was aware of Ethel, the black cat, mewing pitifully at her feet. She picked up the cat, and saw that the mist outside was thickening.

The phone rang again.

She'd been hoping the first call would be from Huw. But now she hoped it was Lol. She needed to tell somebody.

'Merrily? It's Barry Ambrose.'

'Oh . . . Hello, Barry.' She sat down at her desk in the scullery-office, hoping, just at this moment, that he was calling to say he hadn't found out a thing.

'I found out about that girl, Merrily.'

'Rowenna?'

'I hope she's not too close to you, that's all,' Barry said.

Part Four

SQUATTER

FORTY

Dark Hand

The fog was worse in Leominster, which was why the bus was late, the driver explained. Fog, just when you thought you'd got rid of it!

Then again, if the bus hadn't been late, Jane would have missed it – thanks to the Reverend Bloody Watkins.

She slumped down near the back and felt sick. That was it, wasn't it? That was really *it*. There was no way she could go back there tonight. Outside the bus windows, the hills had disappeared, the view of fields extended about fifty yards, and then all you saw were a few tree-skeletons.

Why had she done this to herself? Why hadn't she just sat it out, mumbled a few apologies about going to the psychic fair and . . . but that wouldn't have worked, would it? Mum knew about The Pod. How the *hell* did she find that out? Was the Pod leaky? Had it been infiltrated by Christians?

This was just like so totally *unfair*. Jane felt sad and shabby in her old school duffel coat – hadn't even had a chance to find something else. If you're storming out, you had to do it, like, *now*! You couldn't blow the whole effect by going up to your apartment to change into your tight black sweater and your nicer jeans, or collect your new fleece coat.

Ironic, really. This morning, doing her salute to the *Eternal Spiritual Sun*, she'd thought: What is this really achieving? And thinking of the women in The Pod, how basically sad most of them looked. And yet the fact that they *were* so sad completely discredited Mum's crap about them only being interested in Jane because her mother was this big-time Church of England exorcist.

This was all so mega-stupid. If the bitch hadn't been so totally *offensive*, the two of them could have sorted this out. That remark about Jane having no boyfriend, that was just, like, well out of order. Boyfriend like who? Dean Wall? Danny Gittoes? The really humiliating aspect of this was that Mum herself – not long out of leather pants and tops made out of heavy-duty pond-liner – had been pregnant at nineteen, so presumably had been putting it about for years by then.

Life was *such* a pile of shit.

When they crawled into the bus station behind Tesco, Jane didn't want to get off. She had her money with her, but she didn't feel like shopping. Especially while walking around with Rowenna in all her designer items, and Jane in her dark-blue school duffel. What was she going to buy Rowenna, anyway, that wouldn't cause mutual embarrassment?

She made her way out of the bus station and across the car park, hoping there was nobody from school around – which was too much to hope for on a Saturday close to Christmas. Everybody came into Hereford on Saturday mornings – where else was there to go?

The fog was cold and she didn't even have her scarf. Tonight it would probably be *freezing* fog. Suppose Rowenna couldn't organize her a room, what would happen then? It was a lie, natch, that Jane knew loads of people; she didn't know anyone in The Pod well enough to beg a bed. Worst-case scenario, some shop doorway in the Maylords Orchard precinct? Or did they have iron gates on that? And then at 2.00 a.m. some dopehead comes along and rapes you.

OK, if it came to it, she probably had enough money to get a room in a hotel. Not The Green Dragon obviously, maybe something between that and the pubs where the junkies went to score. Funny how homely old Hereford took on this new and dangerous aspect when you were alone, and destined to stay alone, possibly for ever.

She turned down where the car park dog-legged and the path led through evergreen bushes to the archway under the buildings and into Widemarsh Street . . . and then Rowenna laughed lightly and said, 'Why don't we do it here? We'd be hidden by the fog. That would be pretty cool.'

Huh?

Jane stopped. There were cars parked fairly tightly here, with thick laurel bushes just behind them.

You could tell there were two people in the bushes, standing up, locked together. Jane backed up to the edge of the main car park. Vehicles were coming up out of the tunnel from the underground part, and one of them hooted at her to get out of the way. So she moved to the edge of the undergrowth and flattened herself against the wall.

They probably would never spot her from the bushes, as she couldn't see them properly either. She wouldn't have known it was Rowenna but for the voice. She could see the guy better, because he was pretty tall, and from here it looked like most of his tongue was down Rowenna's throat.

'Don't you think this has appalled me too?' Dick Lyden was raking his thick, grey hair. 'I can only offer you my profoundest apologies and assure you that it won't happen—'

'It fucking *has* happened,' Denny snarled, his back to the door of Lol's flat, as if Dick might make a break for it. 'It's done. It exists. If I hadn't been listening to the words – which I usually don't – *I'd* be down as producing it!'

'Denny, don't do this to me,' Dick pleaded.

'Don't do it to *you*?'

Lol was sitting on the window ledge. He had no mean-ingful contribution to make to this.

'How old is *your* boy?' Dick said to Denny.

'Eleven – and a half.'

'I'd like to think you didn't have this to come, Denny, but at some stage in his adolescent years you'll wonder what kind of monster you've foisted on the world – as well as trying to think what you did to become the object of his undying hatred.'

Sensing that Dick was actually close to tears, Lol said, 'Did you find out how he came to write that song?'

'Oh, well,' Dick escaped gratefully into anger, 'an artist . . . an *artist* gathers his inspiration wherever he may find it. Art is above pity. Art bows to no taboos. You know the kind of balls they spout at that age. I don't . . . I don't actually know what's the matter with him lately. He's become remote, he's arrogant, he sneers, he does small spiteful things. A com-plete bastard, in fact.'

Lol said, 'That's your professional assessment then?' and Denny finally smiled. 'The point is,' Lol continued, 'that the song isn't going to be heard any more, because Eirion Lewis says he'll refuse to play it. He's not a bad kid, it seems.' He glanced apologetically at Dick. 'A bit older than James, so perhaps he's come *through* the bastard phase.'

'In the final analysis,' Dick said, 'this is *my* fault. Ruth and I discuss cases, and quite often the boy's pottering about with his Walkman on and one thinks he's not interested. Little swine was probably making notes. It's a . . . I suppose a diverting tale, isn't it?'

'It's a family tragedy,' Denny growled.

'Denny, I *have* learned a lesson.'

'But the crows, man – how the fuck'd he know about the crows?'

'It's an old Celtic harbinger of death,' Lol said quickly, because he'd never actually told Denny about the crow.

Denny looked dazed for a second, then shook himself like he was trying to shed clinging shreds of the past. He moved away from the door, his earring swinging less menacingly. 'All right, I'll let them back in, so long as Lol turns the knobs.'

Dick looked at Lol.

'OK,' Lol said. Puzzled about what Denny had meant – *How the fuck'd he know about the crows?* – and still wondering how James could have been so crazy as to sing that song blatantly in Denny's face. Like the boy needed to see how far he could go, how much he could get away with, how badly he could hurt.

'Thanks,' Dick said humbly. 'Thank you both. You know I . . . This is going to sound a bit cranky coming from a shrink, but I *am* a *Christian* sort of shrink, and I feel that becoming Boy Bishop will somehow help to straighten the lad out.'

'What *is* this Boy Bishop balls, anyway?' Denny said. 'You hear about it, read bits in the *Times*, but I never take much notice.'

'More people ought to take notice or we'll lose it, like so many other things. It's a unique example of the Church affirming Christ's compassion for the lowly.'

'But it's always a kid from the Cathedral School,' Denny pointed out. 'How lowly is that?'

'It's symbolic – dates back to medieval times. The boy is Bishop until Christmas, but doesn't do much. Gives a token sermon on his enthronement, makes the odd public appearance – used to be taken on a tour of churches in the county, but I think they've dropped that. It also illustrates the principle of the humble being exalted. It's about the humble and the meek . . . something like that.'

'The humble and the meek?' Lol said. 'That's why they chose James?'

'All right, I know, I know. I suppose they chose James because he was a leading chorister. And he's a big lad, so the robes will fit. And, of course, he, ah, rather looks the part.'

'Like I said,' Denny shrugged, 'it's basically balls, isn't it?'

'I see it as a rite of passage,' Dick persisted. 'I don't think you can do something like that without experiencing a man's responsibility.'

Lol thought this was not the best time to talk about a man's responsibility in front of Denny.

But Denny didn't react. 'Listen,' he said. 'Tell the kid I can maybe do the studio Monday. I'll feel better tonight when the funeral's over.'

When Dick had gone, he said to Lol, 'I'm still looking for somebody else to blame for Kathy. He just got in the way.'

Lol nodded.

'I'm closing this shop, by the way,' Denny said.

'This afternoon – for the funeral, Viv said.'

'For good. We close at lunchtime, we don't open again.'

'Ever?'

'I'm shifting the records to the other place tomorrow. And big Viv, too. Extending the shop space into a store-room. If you're selling hi-fi, it makes sense to have a record department on the premises. This one was never big enough to take all the stock you need to really get the punters in. It was just . . . Kathy's shop. I don't ever want to come here again.'

'And this flat?'

'It won't affect you unless I can't manage to let the shop on its own, in which case I'll maybe sell the whole building.

Sorry to spring it on you, mate, but nothing's permanent. You're not a permanent sort of guy anyway, are you?'

Lol forced a smile.

'See you at the crem then,' Denny added. 'There won't be a meal or nothing afterwards. Won't be enough people – plus I'm not into that shit.'

'Denny,' Lol said, 'when you said to Dick, how did he know about the crows, what did you mean?'

'Leave it.' Denny opened the door. 'Like you said, it was nothing, a coincidence. Just the way some things cause you to remember other things. Some memory pops up, and you put it all together wrong.'

'What memory?'

'You don't let go of things, do you, Lol?'

'Some things won't let go of me. It's guilt, probably.'

'You didn't like her, did you?' Denny said.

'I liked her more towards the end.'

'You wouldn't fuck her because you didn't *like* her. That's the truth, isn't it?'

'I don't know.'

'That's kind of honourable, I suppose.'

'No, it isn't. Tell me about the crows.'

Denny came back in, shut the door. 'When she was a kid, they used to put her in her pushchair in the farmyard, to watch the chicks and stuff, yeah? And the crows would come. Crows'd come right up to her. They'd land on the yard and come strutting up to the pushchair. Or they'd fly low and sit on the roof, just over the back door. Sit there like vultures when Kathy was there. Only when she was there.'

Lol thrust his hands in the pockets of his jeans and stiffened his shoulders against the shiver he felt. 'How long did this go on?'

'Until the old man shot them,' Denny said.

*

'Do you remember Hilary Pyle?' Barry Ambrose asked her.

'I don't think so. Who was she?'

'He,' Barry said. 'It was in some of the papers, certainly the *Telegraph*, which always seems to splash Church crises. But they didn't know the whole story. Even I . . . I didn't know that was her name until this morning. Where's she now, the girl you asked about?'

'She's at my daughter's school.'

'Oh dear,' said Barry. 'But then people do sometimes change, don't they?'

'If they want to,' Merrily said, 'they have to *want* to. So what happened to this Hilary Pyle?'

'*She* did. He was a canon at the Cathedral, forty-five years old, married, with kids. I didn't know him particularly well, but I assumed he was a sound bloke. Certainly not the kind you'd imagine taking up with a schoolgirl.'

'Rowenna?'

'Soldier's daughter. Wasn't named in the papers – I think she was underage – in fact I'm sure she was. Fifteen or something. Also there was some question of rape when they first arrested Hilary, so the girl couldn't be named in the press, but he certainly was.'

'*Now* I remember. About two years ago? But he—'

'Yes. Poor bloke hanged himself in his garage. Leaving a note – rather a long note. Do you remember that? It was read out at the inquest – he'd apparently requested that.'

'Remind me.' Merrily felt a stab of foreboding.

'It was a rather florid piece of writing; he kept quoting bits of Milton. He said the girl was sent by the Devil, and this caused a bit of amusement in the press. Just the sort of thing some clergyman *would* say to excuse his appalling behaviour. "Sent by the Devil." She was a pale little thing, they said, but she knew which levers to pull, if you'll pardon the, er . . .'

Merrily found she was writing it all down on her sermon pad.

'You said there was more . . . other things that didn't get into the press.'

'Oh, yes, I'm frankly amazed it didn't get out. But I suppose the people who knew about it realized what the bad publicity could do. I think it was probably as a result of this that I, of all people, was asked to take on the Deliverance ministry here. They wanted an outsider, someone previously unconnected with the Cathedral. You see, it's so easy for a panic to spread. Look at Lincoln and the Imp. Look at Westminster. There are always people who'll look for the dark hand of Satan, aren't there?'

'Not us, of course.'

'Quite.'

'So what happened?'

'After Hilary committed suicide, two other canons confessed to the Bishop that they'd also had relations with this girl.'

'Jesus!' She hadn't been expecting that.

'It was thought there was another one, but he kept very quiet and survived the investigation. Not a *police* investigation, of course.'

'Did anybody talk to the girl herself?'

'Quite frankly, I don't think anybody in the Cathedral was prepared to go anywhere *near* the girl. What happened, I believe, was that the Army arranged for her father to be based somewhere else. Hereford, obviously, though no one here knew where they'd gone – nor wanted to. It cast quite a shadow for a while. Perhaps it still does: I know a number of previously stable marriages have gone down the tubes since then. Poor Hilary's suggestion of something evil had gathered quite a few supporters before the year was out.'

'Barry, I don't know how to thank you.'

'I don't know what you're going to tell your daughter, Merrily,' Barry said, 'but if she hangs around with Rowenna Napier she might start growing up a little too quickly, if you see what I mean.'

'I owe you one,' Merrily said.

Now she was frightened.

FORTY-ONE

Take Me

In Slater's, behind Broad Street, Jane had a deep-pan pizza and stayed cool – reminding herself periodically about Dean Wall, the slimeball, on the school bus in the fog, and what he'd said about Rowenna and Danny Gittoes.

Gittoes was Dean's best friend, and slightly less offensive, but the thought of Rowenna's small mouth around whatever abomination he kept in his greasy trousers was still pretty distasteful, especially when you knew it could be true.

'Calm down, kitten.' Rowenna had a burger with salad, mayonnaise all over it – *oh, please.*

'I just lost it completely.' Jane was sitting with her back to the door and the front windows, watching the cook at work behind a counter at the far end. The problem with Rowenna was that she was so incredibly charming; she gave you her full attention and you felt so grateful she wanted you as a friend.

'What did you say to her?'

'I slagged off the Church, rubbished everything that means anything to her. Said she was ambitious and arrogant – and that I'd rather sell my soul to the Devil than spend another night there. I guess this was not what Angela had in mind when she talked about leading Mum towards the light.'

Rowenna laughed. 'And you didn't mean a word of it, right?'

'I meant it at the time.' Jane cut another slice of pizza.

'She also said *we* were spending too much time together. She suggested I should be going out with boys, can you believe that?'

'That's uncommon,' Rowenna said. 'They're usually terrified you're going to get pregnant.'

'Like . . . there's nothing wrong with me,' Jane said experimentally. 'I don't have problems in that area. I've had relationships. It's just there aren't any guys around right now that I could fancy that much.' It occurred to her they'd rarely talked about men.

'The choice is severely limited.'

'Almost nonexistent.'

'Sure.'

'Like, I travel on the bus every day with Wall and Gittoes.'

'Don't,' Rowenna said. 'I may vomit.'

She grinned, shreds of chargrilled burger on teeth that were translucent like a baby's. *Come on*, Jane thought, *it might not have been her at all by the car park. It might not.*

'Could we perhaps lighten up now?'

'I keep thinking of those tarot cards,' Jane said seriously. 'You said it seemed like a pretty heavy layout, right?'

'Kitten, it's ages since I even looked at a tarot pack. You forget these things.'

'You don't forget. Those are like archetypal images. They're imprinted on your consciousness.'

'That guy in the denim jacket fancies you.'

'He's looking at *you*. He's just wondering how to get me out of the way. Death – that was the first of them.'

'Yeah, but the Death card can also just mean the end of something before a new beginning.'

'The Tower?'

'It's been struck by lightning. There's a big crack, with people falling off. That speaks for itself really: some really horrendous disaster, something wrenched apart.'

'Shit.'

'Or it could just mean a big clear-out in your life: throwing out the stuff that isn't important.'

'Like, if I don't get away, I'll go down with the Tower?'

'Say the Tower, in this instance, represents your mother's faith in this cruel Old Testament God, and you've got to help shatter it.'

'It could have been a prediction of what began this morning, though, couldn't it? Everything quiet, right? Me getting ready to go out. *She's* had this decent night's sleep for once – well rested, looking much better. And then like, out of nowhere, we're into the worst row for like . . . ages. It just blew up out of nothing – like the Tower cracking up. And then I say that thing to her about the Devil. It just came out; I wasn't thinking. And that . . . that was the *third* card.'

'Don't panic.' Rowenna put down her knife and fork. 'The Devil isn't always negative either, you know. The Devil was invented by the Christians as a condemnation of anybody who thought that they, the Christians, were a bit suspect. But actually the Devil's vital for balance in this world.'

'You reckon?'

'Living with a vicar, you're bombarded with propaganda. But when you look at the situation, all the Devil represents is doing what *you* want, not what you're told. Satan is just another word for personal freedom. So maybe Satanists are just people who don't like rules.'

'That's a bit simplistic, isn't it?'

'No, it's not.'

'OK, what about the low-lifes who killed that crow in the church?'

'So?'

'Well, that's got to be evil.'

'OK,' Rowenna said. '*One*, there's nothing to say they killed the crow. *Two*, it was a church nobody uses – a redundant church, right? *Three*, what's the difference between that and any normal protesters who disagree with what something stands for and go in and trash the place? Suppose these are just people who are seriously pissed off at how rich the Church of England is – and how totally useless, like the House of Lords . . . a complete con to keep people in order.'

'Well . . . maybe.'

'There's no *maybe*. That was your subconscious talking. Your inner self crying out to be free by coming out with the most outrageous thing possible in a vicarage, right?'

'Or I just wanted to get up her nose.'

'You're back-pedalling. You didn't plan what you wanted to say before it came out, so it has to be an expression of your innermost desire to be free. Listen, do it.'

'Are you crazy?'

'There you go again. Put up or shut up. So do it: give yourself to the Devil. You just stand up and open your arms, and you breathe, in your most seductive voice: *Lord Satan, take me . . .*' Rowenna giggled. 'It's just words, so it can't harm you . . . but it's also an invitation to your inner self to throw off the shackles. I reckon if you actually said that in a church, you'd get this *amazing* buzz.'

'No thanks.'

'See' – Rowenna pointed her knife – 'you're just completely indoctrinated. You will never escape.'

Jane was uncomfortable. She'd felt cool and superior when she'd first come in, but now Rowenna had turned the tables. She was a wimp again, a frightened little girl.

'Ro,' she said. 'Any chance of sleeping at your place tonight? I can't go back, can I?'

'Sure you can go back. Take Satan with you. By which I mean, go back with your head held high, with a new attitude.'

'It would just be one night.'

'Oh, kitten . . .' Rowenna sighed. 'That could really be a problem. We have this diplomat from the Middle East staying with us. I'm not supposed to even tell you this, because there are a lot of people want this guy dead. It's a security job – and we're the safe-house, you know what I mean? Armed guys in vans parked outside all night? It's really, really tedious.'

'Oh.'

'It happens to us quite often. It means that anybody wants to stay with us, they have to be vetted weeks in advance in case something crops up.'

'What am I going to do?'

Rowenna leaned over and squeezed Jane's wrist. 'You know your problem? You worry too much. You still have this deeply constricted inner-self. OK, The Pod will help sort that eventually – and I mean *eventually*.'

'What's wrong with The Pod?'

'Nothing. It's fine as far as it goes. It's merely a reasonable outlet for bored housewives too timid to have an affair. You must have realized that by now.'

'I thought it was quite heavy, actually.'

Rowenna smiled sympathetically. 'Listen, I have to go now. Go on, ask me where. You're gonna like this.'

'Huh?'

'The Cathedral.'

'I thought we were going shopping!'

'Yeah, me too,' Rowenna said ruefully. 'I just forgot what day it was. I have to meet my cousin, who—' Rowenna looked up. 'Who's this?'

'Where?'

'Guy looking at you through the window.'

'You tried that one earlier,' Jane said.

'He's not bad actually, if you're into older men. He's wearing black. He's *all* in black. I think he's coming in.'

'Yeah, I know.' Jane bit off a corner of pizza. 'It's fucking Satan, right?'

'He is. He's coming in for *you*.'

A draught hit the back of Jane's ankles as the door to the street opened.

Just when Merrily was in no mood to talk to him, Huw rang.

'How are you, lass?'

'I'm OK.'

'I've rung a few times,' Huw said. 'I've prayed, too.'

'Thanks.'

'What's been the problem?'

As though they'd spoken only last night and parted amicably.

'Rat-eyes,' Merrily said, 'probably.'

'Oh aye?' No change of tone whatsoever.

She told him calmly that she had been the subject of what seemed to be a psychic attack. She told him it had now been dealt with.

'This was what came with you into St Cosmas?' Huw said.

'I believe so.'

'And it's dealt with?'

'Yes.'

'You're clean, then?'

'I believe I am. How about you?'

Huw left a pause, then he said, 'About the hospital – I went in last night and I got a bollocking from an Irish nurse with a very high opinion of you. I said I shared that, naturally.'

'And explained to her why you and Dobbs were shafting me?'

'I assured her I would explain the situation fully to you at the earliest possible opportunity. Which is why I'm ringing. Can I meet you tonight?'

'I don't know,' Merrily said. 'I have other problems.'

'Happen I can help.'

'Happen I don't want you to.'

'Merrily . . .'

'What?'

'We have a crisis.'

'Who's *we*?'

'You, me, your Cathedral – the Christian Church.'

'Do you want to come here?'

'We'll meet in your gatehouse at six. We'll be alone then?'

'All right,' she said.

Lol held open the passenger door of the Astra for her. He slammed it shut and got in the other side.

Jane stared at him, coming down off her high. 'Where are we going?'

He started the engine, put on the lights, and booted the ancient heap out into the traffic. 'To a funeral, I'm afraid.'

'You're kidding.'

'Yeah, I'm kidding. I always wear a black suit on Saturdays.'

'Oh, Christ,' Jane said. 'It's Moon, isn't it?'

Lol turned right, towards Greyfriars Bridge. She was making a point of not asking him why he'd just swanned into the restaurant like that – looking quite smooth, for Lol. It had been cool, anyway, to play along. Cool, too, that the extreme warmth of her welcome appeared to have shocked him a little.

She grinned. 'I frightened you, didn't I?'

'There's effusive,' Lol said, 'and there's *effusive*.'

'Darling, as it happens I was mega-glad to see you.' There was no way Lol would let her spend the night in C & A's doorway. 'What was her face like?'

'Whose?'

'Rowenna's. I couldn't see, could I? I was busy expressing my delight at your arrival.'

'Yeah,' he said, 'I can still taste the mozzarella.'

'So how did she react?'

'She looked surprised.'

'Excellent,' Jane said.

Lol crossed four lanes of traffic at the lights, foot down. He must be running late. She suspected there were aspects of Lol's relationship with Moon she didn't fully understand. Of course, the problem here was that if he'd taken time to come and find her, in his funeral suit, that suggested he was acting on specific instructions from the Reverend Watkins. In the end you couldn't get away from her, could you?

'You weren't just passing, were you, Lol?'

'Your mum told me where you were having lunch.'

'Great,' Jane said dully.

'She said you'd had a row.'

'It was a minor disagreement.'

'Like between the Serbs and the Croats.'

'What else did she say?'

'She said a lot of things I'm inclined to let her explain to you personally.'

'Look,' Jane said, more harshly than she intended, 'tell her to fax it or something. I'm not going back.'

'You bloody are, Jane.'

'You can't make me do anything I don't want to.'

Lol turned left into the crematorium drive. 'You're right.' He sighed. 'I probably can't even trust you to stay in the car while I go inside.'

God, he looks so kind of desolate.

'Yes, you can,' she said. 'I'm sorry, Lol.'

Denny had been wrong. The modern crematorium chapel was at least half-full. Distant relatives, he explained to Lol –

nosey bastards whose faces he only half remembered. Also, a pair of archaeologist friends of Moon's from Northumberland, where she'd lived for a couple of years. And Big Viv and her partner, Gary. And the Purefoys, Tim and Anna. And Dick and Ruth Lyden.

And Moon, of course. Moon was here.

Denny had booked a minister. 'Though she'd probably have preferred a fucking druid,' he said, seeming uncomfortable and aggressive. He wasn't wearing his earring; without it he looked less amiable, embittered. He looked like he wanted to hit people. His wife Maggie was here, without the children. She was tall, short-haired and well dressed, and talked to the relatives but not much to Denny. He must be difficult to live with right now.

The minister said some careful things about Moon. He said she was highly intelligent and enthusiastic, and it was a tragic loss, both to her brother Dennis and his family and to the world of archaeology.

Denny muttered and looked down at his feet. Anna Purefoy wept silently into a handkerchief. They sang two hymns, during which Lol gazed at the costly oak coffin and pictured Moon inside it, with her strange, hard hands crossed over her breast. To intensify the experience in this bland place, to make it hurt, he made her say, *'I'd like to sleep now, Lol.'*

It hurt all the more because he knew that was wrong. She couldn't sleep. He kept thinking of his dream of the mist-furled Moon in Capuchin Lane, holding the broken heads of the ancestors as she'd held the crow. A dream . . . like the dreams she'd had of her father. Moon had joined not the ancestors but the grey ranks of the sleepless. When the curtains closed over the coffin, there were tears in Lol's eyes because he could not love her – had not even been able to help her. It was a disaster.

And it was not over.

Outside, in the foggy car park, Dick Lyden said to Lol, 'Never seen you in a suit before, old chap,' then he patted Denny sympathetically on the arm. Denny looked like he wanted to smash Dick's face in. Lol found the slender, sweet-faced Anna Purefoy at his side.

'I feel so guilty, Mr Robinson. We should have positively discouraged her. We should have seen the psychiatric problems.'

'They aren't always easy to spot,' Lol said.

'I taught at a further-education college for a year. I've seen it all in young women: manic depression, drug-induced psychosis. I should have *seen* her as she really was. But we were so delighted by her absorption in the farm that we couldn't resist offering her the barn. We thought she was perfect for it.'

'You couldn't hope to understand an obsession on that scale,' Lol said. He realized it was going to be worse for the Purefoys than for anyone else here, maybe even for Denny. They would have to live with that barn. 'What will you do with it now?'

'I suspect it will be impossible to find a permanent tenant. We'd have to tell people, wouldn't we? Perhaps we could revert to our original plan of holiday accommodation. I don't know, it's too early.'

'Well, good luck,' Lol said. He wondered if Merrily might be persuaded to go up there and bless the barn or something. He watched the Purefoys walk away to their Land Rover Discovery. Denny's wife, Maggie, was chatting to an elderly couple, while Denny stood by with his hands behind his back, rocking on his heels. A lone crow, of all birds, flew over his head and landed on the roof of the crematorium, and stayed there as though it was waiting for Moon's spirit to emerge in the smoke, to accompany it back to Dinedor Hill.

But nobody could *see* the smoke in this fog – and the way to Dinedor would be obscured. He imagined Moon alone in that car park, after everyone had gone. Moon cold in the tatters of her medieval dress – bewildered because there was nobody left. Nobody left to understand what had happened to her.

The Astra was parked about fifteen yards away. As he approached, Jane's face appeared in the blotched windscreen, looking very young and starved. He tried to smile at her; she looked so vulnerable. It was cold in the car as he started the engine.

She said, 'Lol, that woman you were talking to . . .'

'Mrs Purefoy?'

'The blonde woman.'

'That was Moon's neighbour and landlady, Anna Purefoy.'

He drove slowly out of the car park on dipped headlights.

Jane said, 'You mean Angela.'

'I thought it was Anna. I could be wrong.'

'Moon's neighbour?'

'On Dinedor Hill. They own the farm where she died.'

After a while, as the car crept back into the hidden city, Jane said, 'Help me, Lol. Things have got like horribly screwed up.'

The Invisible Church

The golden Santas drove their reindeer across a thick sea of mist in Broad Street. The lanterns glowed red like fog warnings. In the dense grey middle-distance, the Christmas trees twinkling above the shop fronts were like the lights of a different city.

And Merrily, alone in the gatehouse office, with the Cathedral on one side and the Bishop's Palace on the other, felt calmer now because Lol had called her before she left. Because Jane was with Lol in the flat above John Barleycorn, not three minutes' walk away, and maybe Lol would now find out how far it went, this liaison with the wan and wispy Rowenna, serial seducer of priests.

Scrabbling about under Sophie's desk, she found an old two-bar electric fire with a concave chrome reflector, plugged it in and watched the bars slowly warm up, with tiny tapping sounds, until they matched the vermilion of the lanterns outside.

Merrily stood by the fire, warming her calves and watching the lights. They were all part of Christmas, but anyone who didn't know about Christmas would not see them as linked.

She thought about that devil-worshipper pulled from the river not half a mile from here . . . the strings of crow-intestine on a disused altar . . . the inflicted curse of Denzil Joy . . . the old exorcist lying silent, half-paralysed – or faking it – in a hospital bed inside a chalked circle. And, inevitably, she thought of Rowenna.

Linked? All of them? Some of them? None of them?

After a while she spotted the untidy man – in bobble-hat, ragged scarf, RAF greatcoat – shambling out of the fog, with his exorcist's black bag, and wondered how many answers he could offer her.

Jane had decided to clean up Lol's flat: ruthlessly scrubbing shelves, splattering sink-cleaner about, invading the complexity of cobwebs behind the radiators.

A purge, Lol thought.

Just as they were hitting the city centre, she'd asked if they could go somewhere: the village of Credenhill, where the poet Traherne had been vicar in the seventeenth century. Where the SAS had, until recently, been based. And where, just entering dusk, he and Jane had found the perfectly respectable but undeniably small Army house where Rowenna's family lived. Until the last possible moment, Jane had been vainly searching for some rambling, split-level villa behind trees.

She'd stood for a long time at the roadside, looking across at the fog-fuzzed lights of the little house with the Christmas tree in its front window. 'Why would she lie? Why would she think it mattered to me if she lived in a mansion or bloody tent? Why does she *lie* about everything?'

On the way back, Lol considered what Merrily had said on the phone about Rowenna's sexual history. It had made him look quickly – but very hard – at the girl over Jane's shoulder in Slater's. Rowenna was pale, appeared rather fragile – fragile like glass.

Once they were back in his flat, he'd told Jane about the events in Salisbury.

Jane had listened, blank-faced, silent. Then she stood up. 'This flat's in a disgusting state.'

Lol sat with Anne Ross's *Pagan Celtic Britain* open on his knees, and let Jane scrub violently away at the kitchen floor and her own illusions. In the book, he read that crow-goddesses invariably forecast death and disaster.

At last, Jane came back from the kitchen, red-faced with exertion and inner turmoil.

Lol put the book down.

'I'm not going to be able to live with any of this,' Jane announced.

'But you still shafted me.'

Merrily was feeling her fury reignite – reflected in the red glow of the tinking electric fire, the sparky glimmerings from the Santas over Broad Street.

Trust in God, but never trust a bloody priest.

'You claimed you hardly knew him.'

Huw had taken off his scarf, but left his woolly hat on. They were sitting at opposite ends of Sophie's long desk under the window. Huw was just a silhouette with a bobble on top. You had to imagine his faded canvas jacket, his shaggy wolfhound hair.

'I *don't* know Dobbs,' Huw said, 'and I never tried to shaft you.'

She shook her head and lit a cigarette, staring out of the window. It was after six now and the traffic was thinning out. A granny and grandad kind of couple were walking a child down Broad Street towards All Saints, the child between them hopping and swinging from their hands under the decorations.

'I'm trying to explain,' Huw said. 'I want to give you a proper picture, as far as I can see it. They didn't want me to tell you, but there's no way round that now, so balls to them.'

'Who didn't?'

'The canons, the Dean's Chapter – well, not officially. None of this is *official*.'

'No kidding.'

'Two fellers came to see me. No,' raising a shadowy hand, 'don't ask. But they're honourable blokes.'

'As Mark Antony once said.'

'Jesus!' Huw thumped his forehead with the heel of his hand. 'Merrily, there is *no* conspiracy. These lads are scared. They didn't know what Dobbs was at, but it put the wind up them. Give us one of them cigs, would you?'

She slid the packet across the desk to him. 'Didn't know you did.'

'You know bugger all about me – nor me about you, when we cut to the stuffing. Ta, lass.' Huw shook the packet, extracted a cigarette with his teeth. 'The Devil, what's *he* like these days?'

'What?'

'The Devil, lass.'

Merrily said, 'Forked tail, cloven hooves, little horns – deceptively cuddly. And we invented him to discredit the pagan horned god Cernunnos. This is what Jane tells me, over and over.'

'Canny lass.' Huw extended his cigarette towards her Zippo, and in its flare she saw his grainy bootleather features flop into a smile. 'Like her mam.'

'Thank you.'

And then the smile vanished. 'So . . .' He drew heavily. 'What do *you* believe?'

'I do accept the existence of a dark force for evil,' Merrily said steadily.

Huw nodded. 'Good enough.'

When he had first arrived, she'd told him about the projection of the fouled phantom of Denzil Joy: how they'd done it, how well it had worked. She'd told him about the burning of the vestments, and the eucharist she planned for Denzil and Denzil's mute, abused wife. She was telling him because she needed him to know she was clean, able to deal with things.

Huw started now to talk about evil in its blackest, most abstract form. Evil, the *substance*. How it was always said that the deepest evil was often to be found in closest proximity to the greatest good. How Satanists would despoil churches for the pure intoxication of it, the dark high it gave them.

'And does that explain St Cosmas?'

'I don't know. I've not told Dobbs about that. He smelled it on me, mind, that night. Knew I'd just done an exorcism. Happen that's what got him talking.'

'Ah,' Merrily sat up, 'so Dobbs *has* talked to you.'

'Only in bits, till last night. The other times he were weighing me up, getting the measure of me. See, what he's done is he's shut himself down, boarded himself up, put himself into a vacuum. Working out whether he was going to snuff it or be fit enough to go back. I figured it was my job to give him the space he needed. To see he wasn't pestered – you know what I'm saying?'

'You sealed him into a kind of magic circle.'

'*Protective* circle: the invisible church. Magic is where you use your willpower to bring about changes in the natural pattern, to rearrange molecules. *We* ask God to do it, if He thinks it's the right thing – which is subtly different, as you know.'

'Protecting him from what? The Devil? What, Huw?'

'I wanted to bring you in on it, Merrily, honest to God I did. I *hated* going behind your back. But the Dean's lads are saying no way, no way. It's the last thing Dobbs'd want. They don't like the Bishop and you're the Bishop's pussycat.'

'Terrific.'

'You know that's not what I think, so stuff the Dean. Let's

talk about this; I really don't know how much time we've got. I've not come across it before in any credible situation.'

'*What?*'

A shadow had dropped over the room, like a cloth over a birdcage. Merrily saw that a line of golden Santas had gone out over Broad Street.

'We think there's a *squatter* in the Cathedral,' Huw said.

So, like, how could she go back to that school on Monday and be in the same room with the lying slag? The same building? *How?*

Lol said, without much conviction, that maybe it was best not to leap to too many conclusions.

'Yeah?' Jane collapsed on to the rug. 'Like which particular conclusions is it best to avoid, Lol? Should I maybe like hang fire on the possibility that Rowenna wants to be my best friend for reasons not entirely unconnected with my mother?'

'No, that's valid.'

'Is she real, Lol? Is she psychotic? Is there a word for women who need to shag priests?'

'Janey, If we were merely talking about a psychological condition, it would make it all so much simpler. She hasn't been anywhere near Merrily, has she?'

'Just the once.'

'All right,' Lol said, 'let's go back to when you first knew her. This must be before your mum became an exorcist. When did she make the first approach?'

'She didn't. It was me. This was when she first started at the school, right? Before her, the last new girl there was me, and I know what it's like when you come in from out of the area and they're all kind of suspicious of you. I went over to talk to her, and we just got on. That's it.'

'Did she know about Merrily?'

'Pretty soon she did. See, one of her most . . . attractive

qualities is she likes talking about *you*. She listens, she asks questions, she laughs at the things you say. She's sympathetic when you've got problems at home. *You* are the most interesting person in the world when you're with Rowenna.'

'You tell her everything.'

'Yeah,' Jane said gloomily. 'You tell her *everything*.'

'How soon before the psychic things, the New Age stuff?'

'I don't know. It just happened. You're talking all through the lunch hour, then you discover she's got her own car, so she gives you a lift home. But, yeah, when I found out she was interested in like otherwordly pursuits, that was the clincher. Soul-mates! It's just like so brilliant when you find somebody you can talk to about that stuff, and they're not going: *Yeah, yeah, but where do you go on Saturday nights*? It just never occurs to you to be suspicious, you're so delighted. And when she says, *Hey, there's this psychic fair at Leominster*, you don't go, *Oh, I'd better ask my mum*, do you?'

'What happened at the psychic fair?'

'We met Angela.'

'Mrs Purefoy?'

'If you say so. Although, when I look back, was she really *doing* the psychic fair? How do we know she read anybody *else's* cards? See, it was Rowenna who first mentioned the fair. It was Rowenna who, when we'd been there a while and it was getting cold and boring, suggested we consult a clairvoyant in the nice warm pub. It was Rowenna who said she'd had a call from Angela wanting to see us again. I will struggle for a long time against things I don't want to believe, Lol, but when the cracks start to appear . . .'

'What was Angela like?'

'Really, really impressive – not what you were expecting. Very smooth, very poised, very articulate and kind of upper-class. Like, you felt she had your best interests at heart at all times. And, of course, you believed every damn word she said.'

Lol smiled.

'She said I had extraordinary abilities.'

'Which, instinctively, you knew.'

Jane scowled.

'I suppose she recommended you should develop them.'

'She put me in touch with a group called The Pod.'

'Meeting over the healthfood caff in Bridge Street.'

'It *was* you then. I thought you hadn't spotted me.'

'If you'd been your usual friendly little self,' Lol said, 'I probably wouldn't have thought anything of it. So what happens at The Pod?'

'It's good actually. It's just about building up your awareness of like other realms.'

'Nothing heavily ritualistic?'

'Not at all. In fact – here we go – Rowenna's already suggesting it's kind of low-grade stuff. God, it's so transparent when you start seeing it from another angle.'

'It's not really. It seems quite sophisticated to me. They introduce you into a group full of nice, amiable women who mother you along, don't scare you off . . .'

'So The Pod are part of this?'

'I don't know. They seem fairly harmless. Somebody apparently suggested you'd be an asset. That's what I was told.'

'Because of Mum? What *is* all this?'

'It's just about women clerics, I think,' Lol said. 'They're still new and sexy, and it's the biggest and most disruptive thing to happen in the Church for centuries. Angela's involved with The Pod, right?'

'I don't actually think so. She's never's been to a meeting in the short time I've been going.'

'She mention your mum?'

'She said Rowenna'd told her. She said she was annoyed about that because she thought it was ethically wrong – some bullshit like that – to know things about people you were doing readings for. And, yeah, she's like, "Oh, I can't tell you anything tonight after all, I've probably got it all wrong" – until I'm begging her. And then all this stuff that I have to tease out of her and Ro, about needing to lead Mum into the light. And they're dropping what now seem like really broad hints that if I don't, some disastrous situation will develop. They just want to like . . . corrupt her, don't they?'

'I suppose so,' Lol said. 'And Merrily's right: they're getting at her through you. Whatever you might think, you're the most important thing in her life. That must be obvious to them – you being the only child of a single parent.'

'Who's them?'

'I don't know. The idea of all these evil Devil-worshippers targeting priests, it just sounds so . . . and yet . . .'

'We have to do something, Lol. I'm just like so boiling up inside. It's like I've been raped, you know? We . . .' Jane sprang up. 'Hey! Let's go and see *Angela*! Now we know who she is, let's just turn up on her doorstep and, like, demand answers.'

'No!'

'Why not?'

'Not yet, anyway.'

'*Why* not?'

'I've got to think about this.'

Jane frowned. 'This is about Moon again, isn't it?'

FORTY-THREE

Deep Penetration

Huw lifted his black bag up on to the desk, switched on the lamp, and took out a fat paperback.

Merrily recognized it at once. *The Folklore of Herefordshire* (1912) by Ella Mary Leather had been, for several months, Jane's bible, introduced to her by the late Lucy Devenish, village shopkeeper, writer of fairytales for children and a major source of the kid's problematic interest in all things New Age. It was a formidable collection of customs and legends, gathered from arcane volumes and the county's longest memories.

Huw opened it.

SECTION IV

SUPERNATURAL PHENOMENA

(1) WRAITHS

Visitors, it would have said now, in Huw-speak.

Mrs Leather revealed that all over Herefordshire it was accepted – at least in 1912 – that the wraith of a person might be seen by relatives or close friends shortly before or just after death. The departing spirit was bidding farewell to the persons or places most dear to it; this was stated as a matter of fact. It seemed amazing that it had taken less than a century for believers in ghosts to be exiled into crank country.

Huw turned the page and pushed the book directly under the desk lamp for Merrily to read.

He said nothing.

(3) DEMONS AND FAMILIAR SPIRITS

A Demon in the Cathedral

A very strange story of the appearance of a demon in the Cathedral is told by Bartholomew de Cotton. The event is supposed to have happened in AD 1290.

An unheard of and almost impossible marvel occurred in the Cathedral Church of the Hereford Canons. There a demon in the robes of a canon sat in a stall after matins had been sung. A canon came up to him and asked his reason for sitting there, thinking the demon was a brother canon. The latter refused to answer and said nothing. The canon was terrified, but believing the demon to be an evil spirit, put his trust in the Lord, and bade him in the name of Christ and St Thomas de Cantilupe not to stir from that place. For a short time he bravely awaited speech. Receiving no answer, he at last went for help and beat the demon and put him in fetters; he now lies in the prison of the aforesaid St Thomas de Cantilupe.

She looked up. 'Who was Bartholomew de Cotton?'

'No idea.'

'Where's the prison of St Thomas?'

'Don't know. Bishops *did* have their own prisons, I believe.'

'So what does it all mean?'

'I don't know,' said Huw. 'It could be an allegorical tale to put the knife in for one of the clerics. Could simply be some penniless vagrant got into the Cathedral and nicked a few vestments to keep himself warm, and it got blown up out of all proportion.'

'Or?'

'Or it could be the first recorded appearance of the *squatter*.'

Merrily became aware of a thin, high-pitched whine nearby. Possibly the bulb in the desk lamp, a filament dying.

She realized fully now why Huw used all these bloody silly words: *visitor, hitchhiker, insomniac.* It was because the alternatives were too biblical, too portentous.

And too ludicrous?

'So a *squatter*,' Merrily said, 'is your term for a localized demon – an evil spirit in residence.'

'If I were trying to be scientific I'd cobble summat together like *potentially malevolent, semi-sentient forcefield*. Or I might've called it a *sleeper*, but that doesn't sound noxious enough. You know what a sleeper is, in espionage?'

'It's a kind of deep-penetration agent, isn't it? Planted in another country years in advance, to be awoken whenever.'

Deep-penetration, Huw liked that. Made it sound, he said, like dampness. And it was *very* like that – in so deep, it was almost part of the fabric. It could be lying there for centuries and only the very sensitive would be aware of it.

'Like an *imprint*,' Merrily suggested.

'With added evil. Evil gathers *around* a holy place, like we said. The unholiest ground, they used to say, is sometimes just over the churchyard wall. But if it gets *inside*, you'll have a hell of a job rooting it out. It's got all those centuries of accumulated devotional energy to feed on, and it'll cause havoc.'

'But if you accept that this was an evil spirit, how could this canon beat it and put it in fetters? That argues for your first suggestion – that the canon caught some vagrant who'd stolen the vestments.'

'Or the entire story's metaphorical. It suggests he was able to bind this evil by ritual and the power of the Lord, and also . . .'

'St Thomas Cantilupe.'

'Aye,' said Huw, 'there we have the link – the key to it all.'

The whining in the bulb was making her nervous. It was like a thin wire resonating in her brain.

'Thomas Cantilupe.' Huw leaned back, and his chair creaked. 'Tommy Canty – now *there* were a hard bastard.'

The Norman baronial background, the years in government, the initial ambition to be a soldier. 'And you could still think of him as one,' Huw said. So he already had the self-discipline and, on becoming a bishop of the Church, had taught himself humility – and chastity.

'He went to Paris once and stayed wi' a feller, and the feller's wife – a foxy lady – contrives to get into bed wi' Tommy. Tommy rolls out t'other side, pretends he's still asleep. Next morning she asks him how he slept and he tells her he'd have had a better night if he hadn't been tempted by the Devil.'

Merrily thought of Mick Hunter under the aumbry light. And then she thought of herself and Lol: how close she'd come, in her near despair, to slipping into Lol's bed.

'Tommy Canty,' said Huw. 'No sleaze. No risks. Warrior for the Lord. What would your lad Hunter have made of him?'

Both fast-track, Merrily thought. Cantilupe had come straight in as bishop. No weddings and funerals for him, presumably. But, yes, in spite of that they'd probably have hated each other's guts.

'But think what Cantilupe did for this town,' Huw said. 'Most of the religious establishments along the border were well into debt during that period. After St Thomas's day, Hereford Cathedral never looked back. They were adding bits on to the building, all over the place. Pulling power of the shrine meant thousands of pilgrims, hundreds of accredited miracles, cripples brought in droves.

'If you were too sick to get to Hereford, you were measured on a length of string and they brought that instead. I don't know how it worked, but it did. You believe in miracles, Merrily, don't you? I bet Hunter doesn't.'

'Who can say? Look, the demon story – how long had Cantilupe been dead by then?'

'About eight years. And the shrine's power was near its peak. How could that demon get in? Was it brought in by one of the pilgrims? Was it already there and something activated it?'

'Like a *sleeper*?'

'Aye, exactly. But, thank God, the unnamed medieval canon, and the power of Christ channelled through the Cantilupe shrine . . . they contained it. *Imprisoned* is the word. Not killed or executed, but *imprisoned*.'

Merrily experienced one of those moments when you wonder if you're really awake. Mrs Straker, the aunt, had said Rowenna Napier lived in what she would call a fantasy world. But what would she call this? Where was it leading?

'Tommy Canty' – Huw liked saying that, maybe a Northerner's need for familiarity, as if he and the seven-centuries-dead St Thomas wouldn't be able to work together unless they were old mates – 'guardian and benefactor of Hereford. Must have been a mightily good man, or there'd be no miracles. Now his bones have all gone, but he's there in spirit. His tomb's still there' – Huw suddenly leaned towards her, blocking out the lamplight – 'except when it's *not* . . .'

'Oh.' She felt a tiny piece of cold in her solar plexus.

'Know what I mean?'

'Except when it's in pieces,' she said.

And the image cut in of Dobbs lying amid the stones,

arms flung wide, eyes open, breathing loud, snuffling stroke-breaths.

'I want to show you something else.' Huw bent over the bag, his yellowing dog-collar sunk into the crew-neck of his grey pullover. He brought out a sheaf of A4 photocopies and put them in front of Merrily. She glanced at the top sheet.

HEREFORD CATHEDRAL:

SHRINE OF ST THOMAS CANTILUPE

Conservation and Repair: the History

'You know what happened when he died?'

'They boiled his body, separated the bones from the flesh. And the heart—'

'Good, you know all that. All right, when the bones first arrived in Hereford, they were put under a stone slab in the Lady Chapel. You know about this, too?'

'Tell me again.'

'That was temporary. A tomb was built in the North Transept and the bits were transferred there in the presence of King Edward I – in, I think, 1287. The miracles started almost immediately, and petitions were made for Tommy to be canonized, but that didn't happen until 1320. That's when he got a really fancy new shrine in the Lady Chapel – which, of course, was smashed up during the Reformation a couple of centuries later, when the rest of the bones were divided and taken away.'

'So the present one is . . . which?'

'It appears to be the original tomb, which seems to have been left alone. According to this document, one of the first pilgrims wrote that he'd had a vision of the saint, which came out of the "image of brass" on top of the tomb. We know there *was* brass on this one, because the indent's still visible. Now, look at this.'

Huw extracted a copy of a booklet with much smaller print, and brought out his reading glasses.

'This is the 1930 account of the history of the tomb, and it records what happened the last time it was taken apart for renovation, which was in the nineteenth century. Quotes a fellar called Havergal, an archaeologist or antiquarian who, in his *Monumental Inscriptions*, of 1881, writes . . . can you read this?'

Merrily lifted the document to the light. A paragraph was encircled in pencil.

This tomb was opened some 40 years ago. I have an account written by one who was present, which it would not be prudent to publish.

Huw's features twisted into a kind of grim beam. 'You like that?'

'What does "not prudent" mean?'

'You tell me. I'd say the person who wrote that account was scared shitless.'

'By what they found?'

'Aye.'

'But the bones had all gone, right?'

'People aren't frightened by bones anyroad, are they? Least, they wouldn't be in them days.'

'You're presuming some . . . psychic experience?'

'The *squatter*,' Huw said. 'Suppose it was an apparition of the *squatter* in all his unholy glory.'

'Oh, please . . .' Merrily shuddered. 'And anyway, nothing happened when they opened it this time, did it?'

'No. And why didn't it?'

'How can I possibly . . .? Oh, Huw . . . Dobbs!'

'And backwards and forwards from the Cathedral he'd go, at all hours, in all weathers,' said Edna Rees. *'I'd hear his*

footsteps in the street at two, three in the morning. Going to the Cathedral, coming from there, sometimes rushing, he was like a man possessed.'

'Dobbs exorcized this thing?'

Huw shrugged. 'Contained it, he reckons – like that canon in the thirteenth century – with the help of St Thomas Cantilupe in whose footsteps *our* Thomas had so assiduously followed. Until he was struck down.'

Memories of that night snowballed her. Sophie Hill: *'He's just rambling. To someone. Himself? I don't know. Rambling on and on. Neither of us understands. It's all rather frightening . . .'* George Curtiss: *'My Latin isn't what it used to be. My impression is he's talking to, ah . . . to Thomas Cantilupe.'*

And the atmosphere in the Cathedral of overhead wires or power cables slashed through, live and sizzling.

'Dobbs modelling himself on his hero, Tommy Canty,' Huw said. 'Keeping his own counsel, thrusting away all temptation . . . keeping all women out of his life? Making sense now, is it, lass?'

The whining from the lamp was unbearable now, like the sound of tension itself. She was afraid of an awful pop, an explosion. Although she knew that rarely happened, she felt it would tonight.

'He fired his housekeeper of many years, did you know that? She didn't know what she'd done wrong.'

'Strong measures, Merrily, measuring up to Tommy Canty. Very strict about ladies – not only sexually. He kept *all* women at more than arm's length, with the exception of the Holy Mother. See, what you have, I reckon, is Dobbs inviting the mighty spirit of Cantilupe to come into him. Happen he thought they could deal with it together.'

'That's what he told you?'

'In not so many words. Not so many words is all he can manage.'

'You're saying that when it emerged that the Hereford Cathedral Perpetual Trust had finally managed to put enough money together to renovate the tomb, Dobbs was immediately put on his guard, suspecting something had happened when the tomb was last opened.'

'He *knew* it happened. He told me exactly where to find this document. He told me where to look in Mrs Leather's book. All right, it's not much, and that's the end of the documentation, but just because that eye-witness account was never published doesn't mean it hasn't been passed down by word of mouth.'

'Which is notoriously unreliable. All right, what *did* happen when they opened the tomb this time?'

Huw smiled. 'When you've been with that owd feller a while, you learn he doesn't like talking. And when he does, there are words he won't use. Me, I'll ramble on about *squatters* and *visitors* and the like, but Dobbs'll just give you funny looks.'

'Helpful.'

'I don't know, Merrily. I don't know that he's prepared to even think, at the present time, about what it was gave him the stroke. It's part of shutting down.'

'So who contained the' – she couldn't bring herself to use the word *demon*, either – '*squatter*, last century?'

Huw shook his head. 'Don't know. But if you carry on with this theory, you've got two explanations. *One* is that the then exorcist, or *somebody* at least, was ready for it. *Two* is that all you had was a single terrifying manifestation; that there wasn't sufficient energy around on that occasion for it to take up what you might call serious occupation.'

'So why should it now? What's changed?'

'Jesus Christ, Merrily, *you* can ask me that?' He held up a hand against the window, and began counting them off on his fingers. '*One*, the recent Millennium: two thousand years since the birth of Our Lord, and a time of great global religious and cosmic significance. *Two*, the appointment of a flash, smart-arse bishop who doesn't believe in anything very much . . .'

'You can't say that!'

'Have you questioned the slippery bastard in any depth, lass? Has anybody? *Three—*'

Merrily could stand it no longer and clicked off the whining lamp, dipping them back into reddened darkness. Outside, she noticed, a third row of golden Santas had gone out – as if the whole of this end of town was suddenly beset by destructive electrical fluctuations because of what they'd been discussing.

Madness! Stop it!

'And *three* is . . .'

Huw paused.

'You,' he said.

FORTY-FOUR

A Candle for Tommy

'I knew she was going to be trouble,' Sorrel said to Lol.

Patricia would have been the best, but Jane had no idea where she lived, didn't even know her last name. Sorrel was the one they got because there weren't many Podmores in the phone book. Sorrel who lived at Kings Acre, in the suburbs, but wouldn't let Lol come to see her there. She hadn't wanted to see him at all, until he mentioned police.

'How old *is* she?' Sorrel had finally agreed to meet him at the café in Bridge Street. They sat at one of the rustic tables, with the window blinds down. They sat under the Mervyn Peake etchings of thin, leering men and the fat witch with the toad.

'Thirteen,' he said, just to scare her.

Sorrel was plump and nervous. She closed her eyes on an intake of breath. 'We didn't know – no way we knew that. She said she was working. We thought she was seventeen at least.'

'Does she really look seventeen?'

'Oh God, I'm sorry.' Sorrel threw up her hands. 'This should not have happened. We're a responsible group. We have a strict rule about children.' She looked hard at Lol. 'You're Viv's friend, aren't you – the songwriter? She said—'

'And a friend of Jane's mother's,' Lol said. 'Her mother the vicar.'

Sorrel paled. Lol was starting to feel sorry for her.

'This could cause a lot of damage if it got out,' Sorrel said. 'I mean damage to the business. You know what people are like. They don't understand about these things. They'll think we're using children for weird rituals. It could close us down – I mean the café.'

'Mmm.' Lol nodded.

'I mean, I've got kids myself. And my husband, he doesn't . . . It's got out of hand, you see. They started calling it The Pod only because they were meeting here. It just grew out of healthy eating and Green issues. I'm not really that involved, but the name's linked now, and it's very hard for me to . . . to . . .'

'Look,' Lol said, 'I realize this is not your fault. You had pressure put on you, right?'

Sorrel didn't answer.

'So maybe it's whoever put on the pressure I need to talk to.'

'Please' – she was actually looking scared now – 'can't you just leave it?'

'I wish I could, but her mother's in the clergy. Things are difficult enough for women priests.'

'How did she find out?'

'An anonymous letter.'

'Bastards,' Sorrel said.

'You know what I think, Sorrel? I think you suspected Jane was quite young, but somebody else put the arm on you to take her into the group, and you weren't in a position to refuse. Who would that have been?'

Sorrel bit her lip.

'Was it Angela?'

'I don't know any Angela.'

'Anna Purefoy?'

'Oh Christ.' Sorrel stood up and walked to the counter,

picked up a cloth and began scrubbing Today's Specials from a blackboard, her back turned to Lol.

He stood up. 'I gather she's not actually in the group.'

'She doesn't need to be.'

'Why's that?'

She turned to face him. 'Because they own this building.'

'The Purefoys?'

'The building came up for sale when our lease had only about six months to run. The chemists next door were going to buy it to extend into, so it would've been . . . over for us. Then suddenly the Purefoys bought it. They knew one of our members . . .' Sorrel began to squeeze the cloth between her hands. 'Mr Robinson, I don't want to talk about this. I really do need this café. My husband's about to be made redundant, we've got a stupid mortgage . . . I'm sorry about Jane, but she's not been with us long, there's been no harm done. Nothing to interest the police, really.'

'Quite a bit to interest the press.'

'What do you *want*? I've said I'm—'

'How well do you know Rowenna?'

'I don't. No more than I know Jane. All right, a bit more. She's picked up messages here and things.'

'From whom?'

'We have a notice-board, as you can see. People leave messages.'

'And some that aren't on the board, maybe?'

'There are no drugs here,' Sorrel said firmly.

'I never thought there were. I don't even assume The Pod gets up to anything iffy. What I think is that maybe Jane will meet other people who aren't regular members, and she'll get invited to – I don't know – interesting parties. And Rowenna makes sure she goes to them, and at these parties there are maybe some slightly off-the-wall things going on, and before you know it her mother receives some pictures of Jane, well stoned and naked on a slab. Just call me cynical, but I used to be in a band.'

'That's ridiculous.'

'You know it's not.'

Sorrel threw the cloth down. 'So what do you . . . *want*?'

'I want to know about Anna Purefoy.'

'I don't know anything about her.'

'OK.' Lol stood up and moved towards the door. 'Thanks for all your help.'

'But I . . . I know somebody who might help you.'

He turned and waited.

'She used to be our teacher – before Patricia. When she heard the Purefoys had bought this building, she stopped coming. She may or may not need some persuading. But I can tell you where to find her.'

'In Hereford?'

'About twenty miles out,' Sorrel said. 'If she's still alive, that is.'

By the time they left the gatehouse, half the street's Santas and lanterns seemed to have gone out. You felt as though you were on the bridge of a ship leaving port at night, gliding slowly away from the lights.

'I'm sorry, lass,' Huw said, 'but think about it. What does the smart-arse iconoclast new Bishop do first? He breaks a two-thousand-year convention by appointing a female exorcist. In a city which history has shown to be periodically in need of a good guard dog, he . . .'

'Swaps his Rottweiler for a miniature poodle?'

'I've gone far enough down that road, luv. Don't want me throat torn out. All I'm saying is that the combination of all these factors – and maybe others we don't know about – could be felt to be having a dissipating effect. And a weakened body invites infection. Well, I'm telling you how Thomas Dobbs sees it.'

They walked across the green towards the huge smudge of the Cathedral.

'And you,' Merrily asked him, 'what do you believe?'

'Wait till we're inside.'

She was struck, as always, by the hospitality of the place: the stones of many colours, almost all of them warm; the simplicity of the arcade of Norman arches; the friendly modern glitter of the great corona, which always seemed to be hanging lopsided, although it probably wasn't. She knew nothing about medieval architecture, but it just felt right in here.

Ancient centre of light and healing.

They went directly to the North Transept, deserted except for one of the vergers, a tubby middle-aged man in glasses who looked across, suspicious, then relaxed when he saw Huw's collar and recognized Merrily.

He raised a hand to them. 'Anything I can do?'

'I've got a key, pal.' Huw indicated the partitioned enclosure. 'We'll be about ten minutes.'

'I'll have to stay in the general vicinity,' the verger said, 'if you don't mind. The Dean's been a bit on edge since that slab was reported stolen.'

Huw stopped. 'What was that?'

'I'd forgotten all about it,' Merrily said. 'A chunk of one of the side-panels, with a knight carved on it – it's missing.'

'Oh no,' the verger said, 'it isn't missing. Somebody must have made a mistake – miscounted. When the mason was in here this morning, he confirmed everything was there. Quite a relief, but it did make us think a bit more about security.'

Huw said, 'Do you know which piece it was? Which knight?'

'No idea, sir. The masons will be back on Monday. They'll now be able to put St Thomas together again. Too late, unfortunately, for the Boy Bishop ceremony. It'll be the first time he won't be able to pay his respects.'

'Boy Bishop?'

Merrily briefly explained about the annual ceremony and its meaning, while Huw unlocked the padlock with what apparently were Dobbs's keys. She saw where rudimentary repairs had been carried out since George Curtiss had kicked his way in.

Huw surveyed the dismantled tomb, looking more or less as it had the afternoon Merrily and Jane had stood in here with Neil, the young archaeologist. Segments of a stone coffin; knights in relief, with shields and mashed faces. 'What happens at this Boy Bishop ceremony then, lass?'

'Never been to one. Harmless bit of Church pageantry, I'd guess.'

'Is it?'

'Harmless? Any reason why it shouldn't be?'

'Everything worries me tonight.' Huw shoved his hands into the pockets of his greatcoat. 'Especially this missing stone business. First a stone's missing, then it's not. Church masons don't miscount.'

'Which means it's either still missing . . .'

'Or it's back. In which case, where's it been meanwhile?'

She wondered for a moment if he meant that the stone had been somehow dematerialized by the demon. Then she realized what he *did* mean.

'Hard to comprehend, especially seeing it like this,' he trudged around the rubble, 'that this box was once the core of it all. If you try and imagine the amount of psychic and emotional energy – veneration, desperation – poured into this little space over the centuries . . .'

'You can't. *I* can't.'

'And then imagine if – while it was away – that same stone had hot blood and guts spilled on it.'

'Huw!'

'And then it was brought back?' He shrugged. 'Just a thought.'

Merrily looked up at the huge, lightless, stained-glass window, and saw the dim figure of a knight pushing his spear down a dull dragon's throat.

'All right, what would happen if the balance tilted – if the dominant force in here was the force of evil?'

'Even a bit of evil goes a long way. Take all the aggro they've had over at Lincoln Cathedral. Terrible disruption, hellish disputes, and bad feeling and bitterness among the senior clergy. And consider the number of people who put all that down to evil influences emanating from this little old carving in the nave known as the Lincoln Imp. A thousand sacred carvings in that place – and one imp, know what I mean?'

'Yes.' Merrily was wondering what damage had been caused at Salisbury by Rowenna's sexual forays into the canonries.

'Had a few rows here too, mind,' Huw recalled. 'You remember – could be this was before your time – when the first contingent of Hereford women priests staged a circle-dance here in the Cathedral?'

'I read about it. They were supposed to have been gliding around trancelike, caressing the effigies on bishops' tombs, which some fundamentalists thought was a bit forward and rather too pagan.'

'Bloke who organized it, he said it were simply to introduce women to the Cathedral as an active spiritual force for the first time in its history. So as to make their peace with the old dead bishops. The Bishop at the time, he went along with it, but Dobbs went berserk, apparently. It were said he went round from tomb to tomb that night, like an owd Hoover, removing all psychic traces of the she-devils.'

'Devils?'

'I exaggerate.'

'*You* have a problem with circle-dancing?'

'Not especially. But I don't rule out there might *be* a problem. Cathedrals are just not places you bugger about with, without due consideration. You walk carefully around these old places.'

Merrily found herself wondering what a demon would look like. She tried to imagine one in canon's clothing, but all she could conjure was the crude cartoon image of a grinning skull, its exposed vertebrae vanishing into a dog-collar. What *was* the image with which Dobbs – if only in his own mind – had been confronted in the seconds before his stroke?

She thought of the lightning impression of Denzil Joy ratcheting up in her own bed. What if she'd been old, with a heart condition?

'What are we fighting here, Huw? Your *malevolent, semi-sentient forcefield* – and what else? Who else?'

'I wish I knew. But if Dobbs knew the significance of the dismantled tomb – and it's been in the newspaper enough times, so other folk did too. And we're not just talking about the headbangers now.'

He looked at Merrily.

'Who, then?' she asked.

Huw scratched his head. 'Happen the ones with know-ledge, and seeking more. *Higher* knowledge – the knowledge you can't get from other men. And you won't get it from God or His angels either, on account of you're not meant to have it. But demons are different: you can *command* a demon if you're powerful enough. Or you can bargain with it.'

'They found one headbanger floating in the Wye,' Merrily said. 'That's not been released by the police yet, so don't, you know . . . but a man whose body was found in the Wye, with head injuries, kept a satanic altar in his basement. With a big poster of the Goat of Mendes, and American stuff, dirty satanic videos, all that.'

'When was this, lass?'

'Couple of weeks ago. He was from Chepstow. The police are trying to identify his contacts in satanic circles – without conspicuous success.'

'Where in the Wye?'

'Just along the river from here, near the Victoria Bridge. Any relevance, do you think?'

He shook his head. He didn't know any more than she did. She needed to stop regarding Huw as the fount of wisdom, and start thinking for herself. If the possibility of arousing the demon of Hereford Cathedral had already become an occult cause célèbre, perhaps Sayer had been in here that night.

Merrily was cold and confused. This was all getting beyond her comprehension, and the sight of the empty, seg-mented tomb was starting to distress her.

She was glad when Huw said, 'Let's light a candle for Tommy,' and they moved out of the enclosure.

There was a votive stand which had previously been sited next to the tomb when it was intact. All its candles were out, so she passed Huw her Zippo and he lit two for them. The little flames warmed her momentarily.

He touched her elbow. 'Let's pray, eh?'

She nodded. They knelt facing the partition and the ruins of the shrine. One of the candles went out. She handed Huw the Zippo again, and he stood up and relit the candle. Merrily put out a hand, feeling for a draught from somewhere. No obvious breeze.

As Huw stepped back, the second candle went out.

He waited a moment then applied the lighter to the

second candle. As the flame touched the wick, the first candle went out.

A thin taper of cold passed through Merrily, and came out of her mouth as a tiny, frayed whimper.

Outside, in the fog-clogged and freezing night, Huw said, 'Watch yourself.'

Merrily was shivering badly.

'What I'm saying is, don't feel you've got summat to prove.'

'Li . . . like . . . like what?'

'You know *exactly* what. If anything happened, and you thought the sanctity of the Cathedral was at risk, you might just be daft enough to go in there on your own, to call on Tommy Canty and Our Lord to do the business.'

'I don't think I w . . . would have the guts.'

She felt naked, as though the fog was dissolving all her clothing like acid. She wanted Jane to be with her, and yet didn't want Jane anywhere near her.

'Listen to me: it were playing with us, then. It's saying, *I'm here. I'm awake.* You asked me what I believe. I believe there's an active squatter in there.'

'Suppose it was subjective . . . Suppose . . . the c . . . candles . . . Suppose that was one of us?'

'Then it was acting *through* one of us. You'll need extra prayers tonight, you know what I mean?'

'But what do we do, Huw?'

'A negative presence in the Cathedral itself? We might well be looking at a major exorcism, which in a great cathedral would require several of us, probably including – God forbid – the Bishop himself. Meanwhile, my advice to you, for what it's worth, is not to go in there alone.'

'Huw, I—'

'Not by night nor day. Not *alone.*'

Her forehead throbbed. She thought of what Mick Hunter had said that seemingly long-ago afternoon in The Green Dragon. *'I NEVER want to hear of a so-called major exorcism. It's crude, primitive and almost certainly ineffective.'*

She wished, at that moment, that Huw had taken the advice of the Dean's Chapter, and left the Bishop's pussycat well out of this. She felt she would never have the nerve to light a candle again.

'You know what you've got to do now, don't you, Merrily?'

'Go and talk to Mick.'

He put his big hand on her shoulder. 'He likes you. You're his favourite appointee. Tell him what's squatting in his Cathedral. Tell him what's got to happen.'

FORTY-FIVE

All There Is

For the first time, it looked like a real palace. There were many lights on, hanging evenly and elegantly in the foggy night. Several cars were parked tightly up against the deep Georgian windows.

Merrily hesitated.

Well, of course she did.

She remembered the end of day three of the Deliverance course in the Brecon Beacons – the lights in the chapel going off, the video machine burning out. Odd how all these power fluctuations seemed to occur around Huw.

First law of Deliverance: always carry plenty of fuse wire.

She'd wanted him to come with her to the Palace. '*Got to be joking, lass. A lowly rural rector from the Church in Wales creeps on to Hunter's patch and diagnoses a demonic presence in the man's own Cathedral? That would get me a big row, and a stiff complaint to the Bishop of Swansea and Brecon. And certainly no action. That would be the worst of it – no action at all. Best he doesn't know about me. That way, if he doesn't get involved, happen I can organize something on the quiet. Be a bit of a risk, mind, but it's a critical situation.*'

She'd wanted Huw to come and stay the night at Ledwardine vicarage, but he'd said he had to think. First put some mountains between himself and Hereford, then think and meditate – and pray.

She'd watched him walk away under the darkened Santas, into the fog, winding his scarf around his neck. And she wondered . . .

'*Fourth one in two years*,' Huw had said as she'd looked into the scorched mouth of the ruined video. '*It's a right difficult place, this.*'

And '*It were playing with us*,' he'd said just now, as the serial snuffing of votive candles threw shiver after shiver into her, convincing Merrily, without a second thought, of his claim that there was a squatter in the Cathedral.

She stood cold and doubt-haunted on the lawn before the Palace, her shopping bag full of supporting documents lying on the grass by her feet. The night seemed as heavy as Huw's greatcoat around her.

Suppose it was *him*? What, after all, was a priest but a licensed magician?

And where did this squatter story have its origins? Dobbs, perhaps – the man who had made a point of never once speaking to her directly; who had sent her that single cryptic note; who had made her a little present of Denzil Joy. A man, too, with whom Huw had spent long hours. Had they talked about Merrily? Huw hadn't said – but how could they have avoided it?

She looked up to where the sky began, below the tops of the chimney stacks.

Help me!

She was only aware that she must have shouted it aloud into the unyielding night when the white door opened, and there, against the falling light was . . .

'Merrily? Is that you?'

The Bishop himself, in tuxedo and a bow-tie of dark purple.

'Merrily!'

'I . . .' She started forward. 'Can I see you, Bishop?'

'Mick,' he reminded her softly. 'Come in, Merrily.'

She felt the pressure of his hand between her shoulder blades, and found herself in the chandeliered splendour of the Great Hall. Doric pilasters, a domed ceiling at the far end, like God's conservatory. She was blinded for a moment, disoriented.

The Bishop blurred past her to a table, pulling out two velvet-backed chairs.

'No,' she said, her nerve gone. 'This is terrible. I'm interrupting something. Could I come back early tomorow, perhaps? Oh, God, tomorrow's Sunday . . .'

'Merrily, relax. It's a perfect, timely interruption of a terminally tedious dinner party with some oleaginous oafs from the City Council and their dreary wives. Val will sparkle all over them until I return. Sit. You look terribly cold. A drink?'

'No, please . . .' She sat down, feeling like a tramp next to the Bishop, with his poise and his elegance. 'I just need your help, Mick.'

He listened without a word. Twenty minutes and no interruptions.

She talked and talked – except when she dried up.

Or fumbled in her bag for Mrs Leather – a book of local folklore: collected nonsenses.

Or for the report by the late Mr Havergal on the opening of the Cantilupe tomb in the mid-nineteenth century, an eye-witness description of which it had been considered imprudent to publish.

Or for her cigarette packet, which she gripped for maybe ten seconds, as though the nicotine might be absorbed through her stimulated sweat glands and made to flow up her arm, before she let it drop back into her bag.

It was an impromtu sermon given before an expert audience. A dissertation combining medieval theology with the elements of some Hollywood fantasy-melodrama. An exercise in semi-controlled hysteria.

'I can't . . . won't . . . ask you to believe the unbelievable. But I'm trying to do the job that you asked me to do . . . although . . . it's . . . led in directions I could never have imagined it would. Not so soon, anyway. Probably not ever, if I'm honest. But it's a job where you have to rely on instinct, where you never know what is truth and what's . . .'

Tests. Lies. Disinformation.

'And I'm reporting back to you in confidence, because those are the rules. And you're probably thinking what's the silly bitch doing disturbing me at home on a Saturday night, with dinner guests and . . .'

Looking up at him, wanting some help, but getting no reaction.

'You must wonder: is she overtired? Has she gone bonkers? The bottom line' – looking up at the twinkling chandelier, half wishing it would fall and smash into ten thousand crystal shards; that *something* would happen to make him afraid – 'is that I believe we should do this cleansing. And that you should be there. And the Dean, too. And as many canons as you feel you can trust.'

The Bishop's expression did not alter. He neither nodded nor shook his head.

'It could be carried out in total secrecy, late at night or, better still, early in the morning, at four or five o'clock. It would take less than a couple of hours. It's . . . Consider it a precaution. If nothing happens, then either it was successful or it wasn't necessary. I don't care if people say later that it wasn't necessary. It doesn't matter that . . .'

A door opened and Val Hunter stood there in black, dramatic. 'Michael?'

'Five minutes.' He lifted one hand.

With a single, long breath down her nostrils, Val went away without even a glance at Merrily.

The Bishop waited until his wife's footsteps had receded, then he spoke. 'Have you finished, Merrily?'

She nodded, dispirited.

'Who was it?' he said. 'Come on, it's either Dobbs, or the Dean – or, more likely, Owen. Who put you up to this?'

All three, she thought miserably. 'Circumstances,' she said at last. 'A lot of individually meaningless circumstances.'

He gave a small sigh. 'But I'd rather you didn't list them.'

'All I can say is I believe my suggestion is valid. We can't afford to take any risk.'

'Risk of what?'

'Of the Cathedral being contaminated.'

'Tell me, Merrily, who would conduct this major exorcism?'

'That would be your decision.'

'Ah,' he said, 'of course.' He shifted position, looking out through the long windows to the floodlight beams across the lawns, turned to milk chocolate by the fog. 'May I list once again your items of evidence? From the felling of Thomas Dobbs in the North Transept, to the apparently supernatural extinguishing of two votive candles.'

'I never said any of that was evidence.'

'Of course you didn't. You were merely reporting to me. The decision must be mine – on the advice of my female exorcist, the appointment of whom I was strongly advised against.'

'At the time, I didn't know that.'

'You didn't? You really didn't? Oh come, Merrily . . .'

'Silly of me. Arrogant, perhaps.'

'Yes,' the Bishop said, 'that's certainly how it's going to look when someone leaks to the media that, within weeks of your appointment, you advised me to have my cathedral formally exorcized.'

'I know.'

'If you want to go the whole hog, why not have the ceremony conducted entirely by – and in the presence only of – women priests? Obviously, that wouldn't offend *me*, being a radical.'

'Mick, you know there's nothing political—'

'Nothing political? Are you quite serious? Tell me, Merrily, do you *want* to become the subject of a hate campaign in the diocese, as well as receiving an unflattering profile in the *Observer* and any number of politely vitriolic letters to the *Church Times*? Do you *want* to move, quite quickly, to a new and challenging ministry on the other side of the country?'

'No.'

'And do you want to damage me?'

Silence. A dismal, head-shaking silence.

Merrily said, 'So you'd like me to resign?'

Mick Hunter grinned, teeth as white as the Doric pilaster behind him. 'Certainly not. I'd far prefer you to go home, have a good night's sleep, and forget this ill-advised visit ever occurred. It isn't the first time something like this has happened to me, and it won't be the last time it happens to you. Let it serve to remind you that people like us will always have opponents, enemies, within the Church.'

'Mick, don't you think this is far too complicated and too . . . bizarre to be a set-up?'

'Oh, Merrily, I can see your experience of being set up is really rather limited. My advice, if you're approached again by the source of this insane proposal, is that you tell him you questioned the wisdom of informing me and decided against it.'

'Making it *my* decision to say no to an exorcism.'

'It's a responsible role you now have, Merrily. Learning discrimination is part of it. Or you could go ahead with it, without informing me – which would, of course, were I or anyone else to find out, be very much a matter for resignation. But I don't think you'd do that, because you don't really believe any of this idiocy any more than I do. Do you, Merrily?'

'I don't know.' She put her face in her hands, pulling the skin tight. 'I *don't* know.'

Mick stood up and helped her to her feet. 'Get some sleep, eh? It's been a difficult week.'

'I don't know,' she repeated. 'How can I know?'

'Of course you don't know.' He put an arm around her shoulders, peered down into her face, then said, as if talking to a child, 'That's what they're counting on, Merrily, hmm? Look, if I don't go back and be pleasant to the awful councillors, Val will . . . be very unhappy.'

At the door, she sought out and held his famous blue eyes.

'Will you at least think about it?'

'I've already forgotten about it, Merrily,' he said. 'Good night. God bless.'

The fog seemed to be lifting, but the grass was already stiff with frost. The Cathedral was developing a hard edge. She crossed the green and walked into Church Street. The door in the alleyway beside the shop called John Barleycorn was opening as she reached it.

'Hi.'

'Hello, flower.'

Jane stood outside in the alley, no coat on, her dark hair pushed back behind her ears. Face upturned, she was shivering a little.

'I lied.'

They stood about five feet apart. Merrily thought: *We all lie. Especially to ourselves.*

'I don't have anywhere else to sleep,' Jane said. 'I don't actually know many people at all. I, uh, don't even know the people I thought I knew. So . . . like . . . the only friends I have are Lol and you. I . . . I hope . . .' She began to cry. 'I'm sorry, Mum. I'm really, really, really . . .'

Merrily's eyes filled up.

'I think there must be a whole load of things,' Jane snuffled, 'that I haven't even realized I did, yet. Like all the time I was doing this stuff – selling you up the river. I told the bitch everything. I told her about *everything*. And when I said that to you about selling my—'

'You didn't,' Merrily said very firmly. 'I didn't hear you say anything, flower.'

As they clung together on the already slippery cobbles, she thought: *This is all that matters, isn't it? This is all there is.*

FORTY-SIX

The Turning

She was like an elderly bushbaby in some ankle-length mohair thing in dark brown. She was waiting for him in the residents' lounge, where they were now alone – all the others at church, she said, 'bargaining for an afterlife'. She did not want to know anything about him.

'Waste of time at my age, Robinson; it's all forgotten by lunchtime.'

Lol didn't think so. Her eyes were diamond-bright behind round glasses a bit like his own.

'Anyway,' she said, 'I prefer to make up my own mind.' And she peered at him, eyes unfocusing. '*Oh*, what a confused boy you are. *So* confused, aren't you? And blocked, too. There's a blockage in your life. I should like to study you at length, but you haven't the time, have you? Not today. You're in a *frightful* hurry.'

Lol nodded, bemused.

'Slow down,' she said. 'Think things out, or you'll land in trouble. Especially dealing with the Purefoys. Do you understand me?'

'Not yet.' Presumably Sorrel Podmore had given her the background over the phone. Which was good: it saved time.

She'd collected all the cushions from the other chairs and had them piled up around her. She was like a tiny, exotic dowager.

'What do you know about the Purefoys?'

'Virtually nothing.'

'That's a good place from which to start. It's a very, very unpretty story.'

Jane had stood at the bedroom window for a long time, still feeling – in spite of everything – an urge to salute the Eternal Spiritual Sun.

Without this and the other exercises, without The Pod, there was a large spiritual hole in her life. She wasn't sure she was ready for Mum's God. Although part of her wanted to go to morning service, if only to show penitence and solidarity, another part of her felt it would be an empty gesture – hypocrisy.

And, anyway, she was, like, burning up with anger, and if the Eternal Spiritual Sun – wherever the bastard was these days – could add fuel to that, this was OK by Mystic Jane.

While Mum was conducting her morning service, Jane pulled on the humble duffel and walked into still-frozen Ledwardine, across the market square where, at close to midday, the cobbles were still white and lethal. She moved quickly, did not slip, fury making her surefooted. Rage at what they were trying to do to Mum – and what they'd already done.

They? Who? Who, apart from Rowenna?

With whom there was unfinished business.

Jane walked down to the unfashionable end of the village, where long-untreated timbers sagged and the black-and-white buildings looked grey with neglect.

She and Mum had sat up until nearly 2.00 a.m., hunched over this big, comfort fire of coal sweetened with apple logs. Like old times together, except it wasn't – because Mum was dead worried, and you could understand it. She'd talked – frankly, maybe for the first time – about the dilemmas constantly thrown up by Deliverance. The need to believe and also disbelieve; and the knowledge that you were completely on your own – especially with a self-serving, hypocritical bastard of a bishop like Mick Hunter.

But she wasn't alone now, oh no.

Jane stopped outside The Ox. The pulsing oranges and greens of gaming machines through the windows were brighter than the pub sign outside. This was as near as Ledwardine came to Las Vegas.

Jane went in. She was pretty sure they would be here. They'd been coming here since they were about thirteen, and they'd be coming till they were old and bald and never had a life.

There was just one bar: not big, but already half full. Most of the men in there were under thirty, most of the women under twenty, dregs of the Saturday-night crowd. Though the pub was old and timbered, the lighting was garish. A jukebox was playing Pearl Jam. It was loud enough, but the voice from halfway down the room was louder.

'WATKINS!'

Right.

Wall and Gittoes were at a table by the jukebox, hugging pints of cider. Jane strolled over to the fat, swollen-mouthed slimeball and the bony, spotty loser who had once, she recalled, expressed a wish to have unholy communion with her mother.

'I want to talk to you, Danny – outside.'

Danny Gittoes looked up slowly and blinked. 'I'm drinking. And it's cold out there.'

Jane took a chance. She'd gone to sleep thinking about this and she'd woken up thinking about it. If she was wrong, well . . . she just didn't bloody *deserve* to be wrong.

'Must have been cold in the church, too,' she said.

'What *are* you on about, Watkins?' Gittoes had this narrow face, dopey eyes.

Dean Wall rose and tucked his belly into his belt. 'If the lady wants to go outside, let's do it.'

'Siddown, Wall,' Jane snarled, indicated Gittoes. 'Just . . . *that*.'

'Got no secrets from Dean,' Gittoes said.

'I believe you.' Jane put on her grimmest smile. 'Rowenna and I, we don't have secrets either. For Christmas, I'm buying her a whole case of extra-strength mouthwash.'

'Fetch me a map,' demanded Athena White. 'There's a stack of them in the hall. Fetch me an OS map of Hereford. I want to locate this Dinedor Hill.'

Miss White seemed much happier now she knew precisely what this was about. And what *he* was about. The process of knowing him – and where he'd been and what made him afraid – had taken all of ten minutes. It would take Dick Lyden maybe four full sessions to get this far.

Lol was impressed – also disturbed. He sensed she could be, well, malevolent, when she wanted to. There was something dangerously alien about Athena White: unmoving, sunk into her many cushions, but her mind was darting; picking up the urgency of this.

Telling her about Katherine Moon had been the right thing to do.

He brought her the map. 'Spread it out on the floor,' she commanded. 'Move that perfectly awful table, there. Oh, dear, it's what one misses most stuck out here. The seclusion, the study time, yes, but there are things *going on* that one misses. OK, Dinedor Hill. Why Dinedor Hill? Put your finger on it, Robinson. Can't make out the damned map, but I can at least see your finger. Now give me your other hand.'

He found himself kneeling on the map, with the forefinger of one hand on Dinedor Hill, while she held his other hand, both of her small hands over his. They were frail and bony and very warm.

'Look at it, Robinson, look at the hill . . . no, not on the map, you fool. Picture it in your mind. Feel yourself there. Feel the wind blow, feel the damp, the cold. Think about Moon being there. She's coming towards you, isn't she? Now, tell me what you're seeing.'

'I'm seeing the crow,' he said at once. 'Her hand inside the crow. We're standing right at the end of the ramparts, with the city below us and the church spire aligned with the Cathedral tower.'

'Good.'

In the moments of quiet, he could hear crockery clinking several rooms away. Footsteps clumped outside the door, the handle creaked and Athena White let out a piercing squeak. 'Get away from that door! Go away!'

And the footsteps went away.

Miss White said, 'She killed that crow, you know.'

'I wondered about that.'

'I think she would have brought the crow down and killed it.'

Brought it down how?

Crow Maiden, he thought. '*And the crows would come,*' Denny had said. '*Crows'd come right up to her.*'

Lol opened his eyes. Through the window, the Radnor hills were firming up as the mist receded; you could see the underside of the sun in the southern sky.

'You see, it doesn't really work unless the blood is still warm,' Athena White explained.

Jane and Danny Gittoes stood in the alley alongside of The Ox. There were men's toilets here, the foul-smelling kind, and she was starting to get pictures of Danny Gittoes and Rowenna.

'Jane, I'm sorry, all right. I'm sorry about your mother's church, but I didn't take nothing, did I? And it was her idea, all of it.'

'Yeah, tell that to the police. "I did it for a blowjob, officer." Real mitigating-circumstances situation, that is. The magistrates will really like you for that, Gittoes.'

'I'll pay for it, all right? I'll pay for the window.'

'Tell me about the suit.'

'What about it?'

'What did she say about the suit?'

'She said it was a joke – on you and your ma. I didn't twig it. She had the suit in the back of her car, in one of them plastic suit-bags like you get from the cleaners, and I had to keep it inside the bag till I'd got it in the wardrobe – then take it out of the bag.'

'Did she go in with you?'

'She waited outside with the torch. She shone the torch in and she told me where to put the suit, and to make sure it was out of sight. Look, Watkins, this is between you and her, right? This en't nothing—'

'You're going down for it, Gittoes.'

'Nobody goes down for breaking a window.'

'It gets in the paper, though, and then everybody knows how pitiful you are. Everybody sees this redhaired stunner, and then they look at you. It does kind of test the imagination, doesn't it, Danny? It'll like follow you around for years – Beauty and the Sad Git.'

'What about *her*?'

'You really think she cares what anybody thinks? Hey – wow, I forgot.' Jane stepped away from him and began to smile. 'Isn't your stepfather up for a vacancy on the parish council?'

'Fuck you, Watkins.'

'Not even in your dreams.'

'What do you want? What you want me to do?'

'Tell me what happened when she first approached you. Was she on her own?'

'Course she was on her own.'

'I bet you thought she actually fancied you, didn't you?'

Gittoes blushed.

'Don't worry, she's good at that,' Jane said. 'Come on, don't stand there like a bloody half-peeled prawn. Talk to me.'

'I dunno what you *want*!'

'What do you know about her?'

'She's *your* friend!'

'Cooperate,' Jane hissed, 'or the first thing that happens – like tonight – is word gets to reach your stepfather.'

'*Please* . . . what you wanner know? You wanner know where she goes when you en't with her? You wanner know who her real boyfriend is? Cause I followed her – all right? – on the motorbike. Yeah, I thought I was in with a chance – how sad is that? I followed her around. I can give you stuff to, like, even the score . . . if you'll leave me alone.'

'Keep talking, hairball,' Jane said.

For quite a long time, Miss White continued, she did not really understand what a Satanist was. For a start, nobody would ever admit to being one. You had this absurd American self-publicist, La Vey, with his Church of Satan, following a poor variation of Crowley's Do What Thou Wilt philosophy. But that was a misnomer: there wasn't that quality of pure, naked hate which Satanism implied.

Black magic? Ah, not quite the same thing. Black magic was simply the use of magic to do harm. And, yes, Miss White had been tempted, too – was *often* tempted. Aware, of course, of the easy slope from mischief to malignity, but she had done worse things without the need for magic – hadn't everyone?

Miss White had practised ritual magic for a number of years before the robes and the swords and the chalices had begun to seem rather unnecessary and faintly absurd. It was during this period that she first encountered Anna Purefoy, or Anna Bateman as she was then.

'We were both civil servants at the time. Anna worked at the Defence Ministry – secretary to an under-secretary, quite a highly paid post for a girl her age. She never hid her interest in the occult – neither did I. There are a surprising number of senior civil servants practising the dark arts – by which, of course, I do *not* mean Satanism. To the vast, *vast* majority of ritual magicians, the idea of worshipping a vulgar creature with horns and halitosis is absolute anathema.'

The change came with Anna's persecution by Christians in the person of a junior Defence minister with a rigid Presbyterian background. A far more senior civil servant had been linked by a Sunday newspaper to an offshoot of Aleister Crowley's magical foundation, the O.T.O. In the resulting purge, Anna's resignation had been sought and bitterly given.

'I suppose her resentment and loathing of the Christian Church began there,' Miss White said, 'but it really developed when she met Tim.'

Timothy Purefoy: already a rich man and getting richer.

'Tim, like Anna, was blond and rather beautiful. Terribly charming and infinitely solicitous. Especially to elderly ladies in the area of Oxfordshire where he plied his trade. For in Tim's hands it was indeed a trade.'

'What did he do?' Lol asked.

'He was a minister of the Church of England, of course. First a curate and then a rector. I think he'd risen to Rural Dean by the time he was thirty. A throwback in many ways: what they used to call a "hunting parson": field sports and dinner parties, frightfully well connected, etc. And so he often got named – along with the Church itself, of course – in the published wills of wealthy widows. This is common practice, and the Church seldom bats an eyelid as long as it gets its share as well. Timothy was always terribly careful like that. Probably be a bishop by now, if he hadn't become fatally attracted to Anna, then reduced to a comparatively lowly post with Oxfordshire County Council.'

Miss White assumed that by this time Anna's bitter resentment of the Church, its prejudices, and the hold it retained on the British establishment had almost certainly become obsessively bound up with her continuing magical studies. The Church had destroyed her promising career, so she felt driven to wound the Church at every opportunity.

Lol was picturing the gentle, sweet-faced woman with flour on her apron in that mellow farmhouse kitchen. Then, later, dabbing her eyes at Moon's funeral.

'The destruction, humiliation or corruption of a priest is a great satanic triumph,' Miss White said. 'Everyone knows that. But the greatest triumph, the ultimate prize, is the defection, the *turning*, of an ordained minister.'

'Does that really happen?' He thought of big, bluff, jovial Tim Purefoy in his shiny new Barbour and cap. '*Come to the farmhouse . . . have a coffee.*'

'I don't know how often it actually happens,' said Miss White. 'Perhaps some of them remain ministers while practising their secret arts. How many churches have been clandestinely dedicated to the Devil – how can anyone know? What I do know is how very, very much it must have appealed to Anna, as an ex-MOD person – the idea of *turning* Tim. The Cold War was at its height, former British agents like Philby flaunted by the Soviets, so how wonderful, how prestigious – among her circle – to convert a priest to Satan? Especially such a recognizably establishment figure as Tim Purefoy.'

Of how it happened, Miss White had no specific knowledge.

'But one can imagine the Rural Dean's slow-burning obsession with the sensational blonde in the little cottage . . . those long, erotic Sunday interludes between Matins and Evensong. The subtler arts of sexual love come naturally to a magician,' she said enigmatically.

'But if he'd got such a good thing going, milking widows and being accepted by the county set, why would he give that all up?'

'Well, he didn't, of course – not voluntarily.'

Athena believed it was a new curate, some earnest evangelical practising an almost monastic self-denial, who blew the whistle on both of them. It was revealed that Anna had been giving regular tarot readings to villagers, in a cottage in the very shadow of Tim's parish church. And also once – famously – at the parish fête. It was Anna who was driven out of the village first, by a hate campaign drawing support from fundamentalist Christians for miles around.

'And meanwhile Tim was photographed leaving her cottage late at night. It rather escalated from there, but it never became a *very* big scandal, because the Church kept the lid on it. I don't know whether Tim was dabbling in Satanism by then, or whether that came later – but it did come. By which time both held a *considerable* grievance against the "witchhunting" Church itself. And the annexing of his spiritual baggage, no matter how corrupted it already was, due to his weak and greedy character, must have been an enormous boost for her own influence among her peers.'

Through the window, Lol could see a platoon of elderly ladies advancing up the drive.

'Damn,' Athena said. 'First they'll head off to their rooms to freshen up, if that's a suitable term, then they'll all come twittering in.'

'How did the Purefoys carry on making a living?'

'When a minister defects, he is treated – just like Philby in Moscow – as a great celebrity. He is presented at Court, as you might say.'

'What do you mean by "Court"?'

'Oh, Robinson, even *I* don't know who most of these people are. Very wealthy, very evil – actual criminals some of them. Certainly the narcotics trade, whatever they call it these days, has a very large satanic element, and has had for decades. The Purefoys had capital, they had contacts, they had a very *English* charm. With their patronage and advice, lucrative property deals followed, leading, for instance, to the purchase of that building in Bridge Street housing The Pod. I then simply could not continue working with that group any more, which was a great pity, as it did get me out of here once a week – they always sent a car for me. No, I knew what was going to happen, you see.'

'What?'

'They would use The Pod as – what do you call it? – a front. Anything from an innocent reception centre to a kind of spiritual brothel. Podmore already told me about your friend's daughter – but I want to ask you something about that. This friend herself wouldn't, by any chance, be Merrily Watkins?'

'How did you know that?'

'Ha! This clarifies certain small mysteries. Oh, *what* a target that woman must be for the Purefoys and their ilk. A *female* exorcist – and *such* a pretty girl.'

'Yes.' Lol began to fold the map.

'Ah,' said Athena calmly, 'I see.'

'Where've you been? I mean where *have* you been?' The kid just staring back at her, and Merrily taking a deep breath, gripping the Aga rail. 'I'm sorry. Christ, what am I *saying*?'

'I don't know, Mum.'

'I close my eyes in church, I see that lime-green Fiesta reversing into our drive. I come back from church, and you're not here. I'm sorry. There is no reason at all you have to be here all the time.'

'No, you're right,' Jane said. 'It was thoughtless of me.'

'Ignore me, flower. I'm badly, badly paranoid. Previously, I see a stranger in the congregation, and I think: *Yes. Wow. Another one!* Now, when I glimpse an unfamiliar face, I'm watching for a little sneer at some key moment; I'm watching their lips when we say the Lord's Prayer. I go round afterwards and sniff where they sat. Jesus, I shouldn't be saying this to you – you're only sixteen.'

'Yes, I am,' Jane said mildly. 'And I've just been to see Danny Gittoes. Rowenna gave him, like, oral sex in return for breaking into the church and contaminating your cassock with Denzil Joy's suit. Just thought you should know that.'

Merrily broke away from the Aga.

'Also – and I'm not qualified to, like, evaluate the significance of this – but Rowenna's been seeing – euphemism, OK? – *seeing* a young guy by the name of James Lyden. He goes to the Cathedral School and apparently tonight he's going to be enthroned in the Cathedral as something called – vomit, vomit – Boy Bishop. Does this mean anything to you?'

FORTY-SEVEN

Medieval Thing

She called Huw, but there was no answer. She didn't know his Sunday routine. Perhaps he drove from church to church across the mountains – service after service, until he was all preached out. If he had a mobile or a car-phone, it wouldn't work up there, anyway.

She next called Sophie at home. Sophie, thank God, *was* home. Merrily pictured a serene, pastel room with a high ceiling and a grandfather clock.

'Sophie, are you going to the Boy Bishop ceremony tonight?'

'I always do,' Sophie said. 'As the Bishop's lay-secretary, I consider my role as extending to his understudy.'

'That's not quite the right word, is it? As I understand it, the boy is a symbolic replacement – the Bishop actually giving way to him.'

'Well, perhaps. Should I explain it to you, Merrily?'

'Please.'

She listened, and made notes on her sermon pad.

'Shall I see you there?' Sophie asked.

'God willing.'

'I should like to talk to you. I've delayed long enough.'

An hour later, Merrily called Huw again, and then she called Lol but there was no answer there either, and no one else to call. When she put the phone down, she said steadily to herself, 'I shouldn't need this. I shouldn't need help.'

Jane, coming into the scullery with coffee, said, 'You can only ever go by what you think is right, Mum.'

'All right, listen, flower. Sit down. I'm going to hang something on you. And you, in your most cynical-little-bitch mode, are going to give me your instinctive reactions.'

Jane pulled up a chair and they sat facing one another, side-on to the desk.

'Shoot,' Jane said.

'It's a medieval thing.'

'Most of Hereford seems to be a medieval thing,' Jane said.

'In the thirteenth century, apparently, it was a fairly wide-spread midwinter ceremony in many parts of Europe. Sometimes he was known as the Bishop of the Innocents. It was discontinued at the Reformation under Henry VIII. The Reformation wasn't kind to the Cathedral anyway. Stained-glass windows were destroyed, statues smashed. Then there was the Civil War and puritanism. In most cathedrals, the Boy Bishop never came back, but Hereford reintroduced it about twenty-five years ago, and it's now probably the most famous ceremony of its kind in the country. The basis of it is a line from the Magnificat which goes: *He hath put down the mighty from their seat and hath exalted the humble and meek.*'

'That's crap,' Jane said. 'I don't know anybody my age who is remotely humble or meek.'

'How about if *I* tell you when to come on with the cynicism. OK, back to the ceremony. After a candlelit procession, the Bishop of Hereford gives up his throne to the boy, who takes over the rest of the service, leads the prayers, gives a short sermon.'

'Would I be right in thinking there aren't a whole bunch of boys queuing up for this privilege?'

'Probably. It's a parent thing – also a choir thing. The Boy Bishop is almost invariably a leading chorister, or a recently retired chorister, and he has several attendants from the same stable.'

'So, what you're saying is, Hunter symbolically gives up his throne to this guy.'

'No, it isn't symbolic. He actually does it. And then the boy and his entourage proceed around the chancel and into the North Transept, where he's introduced to St Thomas Cantilupe at the shrine.'

'Or, in this case, the hole where the shrine used to be.'

'Yes, I understand this will the first time since the institution of the ceremony in the Middle Ages that there's been no tomb.'

'Heavy, right?'

Merrily said, 'So you're following my thinking.'

'Maybe.' Jane pushed her hair behind her ears.

Merrily said, 'If – and this is the crux of it – you wanted to isolate the period when Hereford Cathedral was most vulnerable to . . . shall we call it spiritual disturbance, you might choose the period of the dawning of a millennium . . . when the tomb of its guardian saint lies shattered . . . and when the Lord Bishop of Hereford . . .'

She broke off, searching for the switch of the Anglepoise lamp. The red light of the answering machine shone like a drop of blood.

'Is a mere boy,' Jane supplied.

'That's the final piece of Huw's jigsaw. Is that a load of superstitious crap or what? You can now be cynical.'

'Thanks.'

'So?' Merrily's hand found the lamp switch and clicked. The light found Jane propping up her chin with a fist.

'How long do we have before the ceremony starts?'

'It takes place during Evensong – which was held in the late afternoon until Mick took over. Mick thinks Evensong should be just that – at seven-thirty. Just over three hours from now.'

'Oh.'

'Not very long at all.'

'No.' Jane stood up, hands in the hip pockets of her jeans. 'Why don't you try calling Huw Owen again?'

'He isn't going to be there, flower. If he is, it would take him well over an hour to get here.'

'Try Lol again. Maybe he can put the arm on James Lyden's dad.'

'The psychotherapist?'

'Maybe he can.'

'All right.' Merrily punched out Lol's number; the phone was picked up on the second ring.

'John Barleycorn.' A strange voice.

'Oh, is Lol there?'

'No, he's not. This is Dennis Moon in the shop. Sorry, it's the same line. I'm not usually here on a Sunday, but Lol's not around anyway. Can I give him a message if he shows before I leave?'

'Could you ask him to call Merrily, please?'

'Sure, I'll leave him a note.'

'Face it,' Merrily said, hanging up. 'This guy is not going to pull his boy out of the ceremony – thus forcing them to abort it.'

'I suppose not. Actually, it does seem quite scary. What if something did happen and we could have prevented it? But, on the other hand, what *could* happen?'

'Well, it won't be anything like thunder and lightning and the tower cracking in half.' She saw Jane stiffen. 'Flower?'

'Why did you say that?'

'What?'

'About the tower cracking in half.'

'It was the first stupid thing I thought of.'

'That's the tarot card Angela turned up for me: the Tower struck by lightning. It's just . . . Sorry, your imagination sometimes goes berserk, doesn't it?'

'Look.' Merrily stood up and put an arm around her. 'Thunder is not forecast, anyway. You don't get thunder at this time of the year, in this kind of weather. That tower's been here for many centuries. The tarot card is purely symbolic. And even if something like that *did* happen . . .'

'It did in 1786.'

'What did?'

'We did this in school. They had a west tower then, and it didn't have proper foundations and the place was neglected, and on Easter Monday 1786 the whole lot collapsed.'

Merrily moved away, looked down at the desk, gathering her thoughts. 'Look, even if it *was* likely, it's still not the worst disaster that could happen.'

'You mean the collapse of spirituality,' Jane said soberly.

'Whatever you say about the Church, flower, there's no moral force to replace it.'

'OK,' Jane said. 'So suppose all the people jumping off the Tower Struck By Lightning are the ones, like, abandoning Christianity as the whole edifice collapses. Suppose the final disintegration of the Church as we know it was to start *here*?'

Merrily said, 'Would you care?

FORTY-EIGHT

Blood

The crow.

As the crow flies: a straight line.

Dinedor Hill . . . All Saints Church . . . Hereford Cathedral . . . and two further churches, ending in . . .

'What's this place, Robinson? Can't make it out.'

'Stretford.' For a moment it stopped his breath. 'This . . . is the church of St Cosmas and St Damien.'

'Oh, Robinson,' Athena White said. 'Oh, yes.'

Once the old ladies had begun to gather in the lounge, she'd beckoned Lol away and up the stairs. In Athena's eyrie, with the Afghan rugs and all the cupboards, the OS map of Hereford had been opened out on the bedspread, and the line from Dinedor drawn in.

Athena's glasses were white light. 'It was in the *Hereford Times*, wasn't it? Was that last week, I can't remember? The crow . . . *the crow*. Why does one never see what is under one's nose?'

'They happened the same night. The crow sacrifice, and Moon's death . . . and a minister called Dobbs had a stroke in the Cathedral.'

'Yes!'

It all came out then, in strands of theory and conjecture which eventually hung together as a kind of certainty.

Tim Purefoy had said: *'That's one of Alfred Watkins's*

ley-lines. An invisible, mystical cable joining sacred sites. Prehistoric path of power. They're energy lines, you know. And spirit paths. So we're told. Probably all nonsense, but at sunset you can feel you own the city.'

Now, Athena White said, 'It doesn't matter whether it's there or not, Robinson. It's what the magician *perceives* is there. The magician uses visualization, driven by willpower, to create an alternative reality.'

Moon had said: *'The line goes through four ancient places of worship, ending at a very old church out in the country. But it starts here, and this is the highest point. So all these churches, including the Cathedral, remain in its shadow. This hill is the mother of the city. The camp here was the earliest proper settlement, long before there was a town down there.'*

'When the first Christian churches were built, Rome ordered them to be placed on sites of earlier worship, places already venerated, so as to appropriate their influence. But you see, Robinson, the pre-Christian element never really went away, because of the continued dominance of Dinedor Hill. So, if your aim was to destabilize the Cathedral and all it symbolizes, you might well decide to cause a vibration in what lies *beneath*.'

And Lol had said to Merrily – ironically in the café in the All Saints Church, on the actual line from St Cosmas to Dinedor Hill: *'In Celtic folk tales, crows and ravens figured as birds of ill-omen or . . . as a form taken by anti-Christian forces.'*

'At one end of the line,' Athena said, 'a crow is sacrificed. At the other – at the highest point – is your crow maiden.'

Lol said, 'Sacrificed?'

'Oh, yes.'

'They killed her?'

'Or helped her to take her own life? Probably, yes. I'm

sorry, Robinson, I don't know if this is what you wanted to hear.'

'It's just . . . are you sure about this?' *She's an old woman*, he thought. *She lives in a fantasy world.* 'You have to be sure.'

'And yet,' she said, 'these two deaths are so different. Calm down, Robinson, I won't let you make a fool of yourself. You see, as Crowley once pointed out, a sacrifice was once seen as a merciful and glorious death, allowing the astral body to go directly to its God. This essentially means a quick death, a throat cut . . . the way the crow presumably died. But your friend's blood was let out through the wrists. Not quick at all – a slow release . . .'

' "Crow maiden, you're fadin' away . . ." '

'What did you say?'

'Just a line from a song.'

Athena White's clasped hands were shaking with concentration. 'Robinson, have we discussed the power of blood?'

On the way back from The Glades, Lol kept glancing at the passenger seat – because of a dark, disturbing sensation of Moon sitting beside him.

'I'd like to sleep now.'

'I know,' he said once. 'I know you can't sleep. But I just don't know what to do about it.'

At the lectern in Ledwardine Church, with the altar behind them, candles lit, Merrily took both Jane's hands in hers, and looked steadily into the kid's dark eyes.

'You all right about this?'

'Sure.'

Merrily had locked the church doors – the first time she'd ever locked herself in. A church was not a private place; it should always offer sanctuary.

Merrily gripped the kid's hands more firmly.

'Christ be with us,' she said, 'Christ within us.'

'Christ behind us,' Jane read from the card placed in the open Bible on the lectern. 'Christ before us . . .'

'Hello, Laurence,' Denny said tiredly.

The shop was all in boxes around his knees. Despite the possible implications for his own domestic future, Lol had forgotten about Denny's decision to shut John Barleycorn for ever. The walls were just empty shelves now, even the bala-laika packed away. The ochre wall-lamps, which had lit Moon so exquisitely, did her brother Denny no favours. His face was grey as he wiped his brow with the sleeve of his bomber jacket.

'I haven't been totally frank with you, Lol. Another reason for all this is that I'm going to need all the money I can get' – he looked away – 'to pay Maggie off.'

Lol remembered the distance between them at Moon's cremation. 'You and Maggie . . .?'

'Aw, been coming a while. I won't explain now. Kathy's death could have saved it. At least, that's what *she* thought – Maggie. But the very fact she *thought* that . . .' Denny smashed a fist into a tall carboard box. 'That made it un-fucking-tenable.'

'I'm sorry,' Lol said awkwardly, the urge welling up in him to tell Denny what he believed had really happened to Moon. But could Denny, in his present state, absorb this arcane insanity? 'What about the kids?' he said instead.

'She'll have them.' Denny taped up the flaps of a box full of CDs. 'I'm hardly gonner fight *that*.' He looked across at the door to the stairs. 'Do something for me, Laurence. The bike.'

'Moon's bike?'

'Take it away, would you? It's oppressive. I dream about it.'

'How do you mean?'

'I *dream*. I have these fucking dreams. It starts with the bike and then it turns into this, like, cart with the same big wheels . . . like some old war chariot. I want to get into it, and I know if I do, it's gonna take me up there again. No fucking way.'

'To the hill.'

'No way, man. So, would you do that? Would you get rid of the bike? Somebody's gonner buy or lease this place, see, and then they'll make me take the bike out. I'm not touching it – it's like that fucking sword, you know? Take it away. Flog it, dump it . . . somewhere I don't know where it is.'

'All right. I'll do that tomorrow.'

'Thanks. Oh yeah, a woman rang for you. Mary?'

'Merrily?'

'Probably. She said could you call her. Look, Lol . . . I tried to use you to compensate for my brotherly inadequacies. I regret that now – along with all the rest.'

'There wasn't a lot you could do, Den. In the end, Moon's fate was in other hands.'

'No.' Denny's eyes narrowed. 'I don't buy this shit, Lol. I'm not buying any more than that she was sick. I'm not having anything else unloaded on me. I won't go down that road.'

Lol nodded. So he himself would have to go down that road alone.

'Hello, this is Ledwardine Vicarage. Merrily and Jane aren't around at the moment, but if you'd like—'

Lol put down the phone and went to sit down for a while in Ethel's chair, once-insignificant details crowding his mind.

Like the sword. The sword she'd just happened to find in a pit where it looked as though the Purefoys had been digging a pond. The sword sticking up for her to find – like it was meant. They'd put it there, hadn't they?

Perhaps they'd found it where Denny had buried it, or perhaps it wasn't the same sword at all – Denny's own memory refashioning it to fit the circumstances.

At the funeral, Anna Purefoy had said: *'We were so delighted by her absorption in the farm that we couldn't resist offering her the barn. We thought she was perfect.'*

Moon was perfect for them because – according to the tenets of Anna Purefoy's occultism – Moon's obsession was a passage to the heart of the hill's pagan past. By stimulating a resurgence of the once-dominant pagan energy, they were attempting to induce a spiritual reversion. Using the Celtic tradition of vengeful crow-goddess and blood ritual to link that holy hill with the pre-medieval Church at the terminus of the ley-line alignment. Thus feeding something old and corrupt inside the Christian Cathedral.

Belief was all, Athena White had said. It didn't matter how real any of this was, so long as *they* believed it. They hadn't even had to bend Moon to their will. She was already halfway there. But had they actually killed her? Had they used the Celtic sword as a sacrificial blade to cut her wrists? Because, if they hadn't done anything physical, it was an unprovable crime, bizarrely akin to euthanasia. Perhaps not even a crime at all.

He called Merrily again.

'Hello, this is Led—'

He put the phone down, then lifted it again and redialled, waiting for the message to end. 'Merrily,' he said. 'Look, I've got to tell somebody. It's about Moon and . . . and your desecration thing at the little church . . .'

He talked steadily about crows and sacrifice. After three minutes, the bleeps told him his time was up. He waited for a minute, then called back, waited again for the message to finish. This time he talked about projections. He knew why he was doing this: he had to hear himself saying it, to decide if he could believe it.

Moon's father: not a ghost but a *projection*, a transferred image. Transmitting a *projection* – Athena looking rather coy at this point – was not terribly difficult. Especially if the Purefoys had a photograph to work with. Photographs and memories, half-truth and circumstance – and the power of the ancestors, usurped.

'By some combination of projection, hypnosis, psychic-suggestion – maybe you have better words for this – they may have steered her to suicide.'

When the bleeps started again, he didn't call back. He took up his habitual stance at the window, looking down into Christmas-lit Church Street/Capuchin Lane. Moon's agitated shade was misting the periphery of his vision – Moon with her medieval dress and her rescue-me hair.

What did you do with information like this? What could you do but take it to the police, or try to get it raised at the inquest?

But the man to do this was Denny, the brother. At some stage, Denny – who wanted none of it – would have to be told. Lol went downstairs.

In the shop below, Denny was sitting, his back to Lol, on the last filled box. John Barleycorn was no more.

'Destroying something can be a very cleansing thing.' Denny had his hands loosely linked and he was rocking slowly on the box, his earring swaying like a pendulum: tick . . . tick . . . tick.

'You, er . . . you want to go for a drink?'

'Nah, not tonight, Laurence.'

'Only, you were right,' Lol said, 'about needing to talk.'

'Couldn't face it now, mate.' Denny stared out of the

window. 'Anyway. you wouldn't wanner be with me tonight.' He heaved himself down from the box and grinned. 'I'll be off. You look a bit shagged-out, Laurence. Get some sleep. It'll all seem much clearer in the morning.'

'It will?'

'Maybe.' Denny looked around the skeleton shop. 'Good night, mate.' He turned in the doorway. 'Thanks.'

There was a full moon. They hadn't seen it coming because of the fog, but tonight was a flawless, icy night and the moon hung over Broad Street – and the Christmas Santas couldn't compete, Jane thought.

> *Hail to Thee, Lady Moon,*
> *Whose light reflects our most secret hopes.*

Her only secret hope tonight was for Mum to come through this with everything intact: her reputation, her mind . . .

> *Hail to Thee from the Abodes of Darkness.*

There won't *be* any darkness, Jane thought, willing it and willing it. There *won't*.

They stood together on the green, watching people file into the Cathedral. The usual Evensong congregation, plus whatever audience the Boy Bishop ceremony pulled in with its pre-Christmas pageantry and extra choral element.

Mum had come in her long, black cloak – the winter-funeral cloak – wearing it partly because you couldn't turn up for a ceremony at the Cathedral in a ratty old waxed jacket. And partly because it was so much better for concealing—

Oh, please, no . . .

– the foot-long, gilt-painted, wooden cross she'd taken

from Ledwardine Church, prising it out of the rood-screen with a screwdriver, then immersing its prongs in holy water.

The whole bit! The complete, crazy Van Helsing ensemble. And Merrily had no plan. If the worst happened, if there was some indication of what she called *infiltration*, she was just going to, like, walk out, holding the cross high and shouting the magic words from the Deliverance handbook.

Madness? At the very least, professional suicide. Church of England ministers did not behave like this. She would be making her entire career into this minor footnote in ecclesiastical history, right under the bit about the female priests who circle-danced around the Cathedral touching up dead bishops.

And that was what you wanted, wasn't it? You always thought it was a wasted life.

No! Uncomfortable, Jane turned away from her mother. She didn't know. She didn't know any more. She began to feel helpless and desperate. They needed help and there was none.

She looked up at the Cathedral, warm light making its windows look like the doors in an advent calendar. She was aware of the timeless *apartness* of the place, even though it was surrounded by city. She thought about its possible future as a tourist attraction, or a carpet warehouse, or something. A rush of confused emotions were creating a panic-bomb, just as a woman came towards them. She wore an expensive suede coat and a silk headscarf – Sophie Hill, the Bishop's secretary and Mum's secretary too. Sophie who, Mum explained, didn't need a secretary's job, but *did* need to be part of the Cathedral. Sophie was looking apprehensive.

'Oh, hello, Jane,' she began awkwardly.

Which was like *Goodbye, Jane*. Mum said, 'Why don't you go in, flower, and find us a discreet pew with a good view – but not too near the front.'

'Sure,' Jane said meekly. She was wearing her new blue fleece coat and a skirt. Respectable. As she slipped away, the panic-bomb began to tick.

Walking quickly down towards the Cathedral porch, when she was sure they couldn't see her, she diverted along the wall and back across the green, running from tree to tree, to the access path, and down into Church Street. Seeing this big, bald guy come out of John Barleycorn and – *Thank you, thank you, God!* – Lol Robinson behind him in the doorway.

She started waving frantically at Lol as the bald guy vanished down the alley towards High Town.

'Jane?'

He looked seriously hyped up, nervous, but grateful to see her – all of those. With the overhead Christmas greens and reds strobing in his glasses, his hands making fists, and his mouth forming unspoken words – like he was full of stories that just had to be told.

But as Jane said, 'Oh, Lol, Mum is in such deep shit,' and her tears defused the panic, reduced it to mere despair, he just listened. Listened to all the stuff about what Mum and this loopy Huw called 'the Squatter'. And about the Boy Bishop, who was the weak point, like the fuse in an electric circuit.

This was when Lol finally cut in. 'How long? How long before the Boy Bishop gets . . .?'

'Enthroned?'

'Yeah. How long?'

He was out in the street now, pulling the shop door closed behind him, shivering in his frayed sweatshirt.

'I don't know. I don't know where in the service it comes. In half an hour? Maybe only ten minutes.'

She was asking him if he could get to this Dick Lyden first, and make him stop his son from going through with it, but Lol was just shaking his head, like she knew he would, and then he was pushing her away, up the street.

'Go back, Jane. Stay with her.'

'What about you?'

'I'm going to . . . going to do what I can.'

'You know what's going to happen, don't you? Lol, I want to come with you.'

'You can't.'

'You really *know* what's going to happen, don't you? At least, you have an idea?'

'I don't *know* anything, Jane. I just—'

'Lol . . .' She stumbled on the iced-up cobbles, clinging to his arm. 'Dobbs stood up against it, Dobbs put himself in the way – and he wound up as this paralysed, dribbling . . .'

'Dobbs was an old man in poor health.' He held her steady. 'Go back to her, Jane.'

'He was also . . .' Jane broke Lol's grip and spun to face him. 'He was also this really experienced exorcist. He knew all about this stuff; he'd been planning for ages. He knew exactly what he was facing, while Mum's just—'

'She wouldn't thank you for saying she was just a woman.'

'Oh, for God's sake, it's more than that.'

'Yes,' he said.

'Lol, who can we call? We can't raise Huw Owen. The Bishop's a total tosser. All those guys in dog-collars in there are just like . . . administrators and wardens and bursars and accountants. All this dark energy gathering, and . . .'

She flattened herself against a shop window as a bunch of young guys came past, hooting and sloshing lager at each other out of cans. They were lurching up the ancient medieval straight path to Hereford Cathedral – all huge and lit up like the *Titanic* – and none of them even seemed to notice it.

'Nobody really gives a shit, any more, do they?' Jane said.

FORTY-NINE

Costume Drama

When Jane reached the green again, Mum and Sophie were gone. Into the Cathedral, presumably. She looked behind her, hoping Lol would be there, that he'd changed his mind and would take her with him wherever he was going. But the night was hard and bright and empty; even the cackling lager crew had vanished.

She was alone now, with the frost-rimmed moon and the feeling of something happening, around and within the old rusty stones, that none of them could do a damned thing about.

She walked very slowly down to the Cathedral, hoping that something meaningful would come to her. But all she experienced was a stiffening of her face, as though the tears had frozen on her cheeks.

Should she pray?

And, if so, to whom? She reassured herself that all forms of spirituality were positive – while acknowledging that the Lady Moon looked a pitiless bitch tonight.

Jane went into the porch, and turned left through an ordinary wooden and glazed door into the body of the Cathedral. Always that small, barely audible gasp when you came out into the vaulted vastness of it. You were never sure whether it was you, or some vacuum effect carefully developed by the old gothic architects.

The organ was playing some kind of low-key religious canned music. Jane found herself on the end of a short queue of people. They were mostly middle-aged or elderly.

Which made Rowenna kind of stand out amongst them.

He remembered the last time he'd been up here at night, in the snow, with Moon beside him. *'I've changed my mind. I don't want you to come in.'*

What if he'd then refused to take no for an answer? What if he'd gone into the barn with her? What if he'd resisted the pushing of the darkness against him?

The pushing of the darkness? As he drove and fiddled vainly with the heater, he tried to re-experience that thin, frigid moment. There was a draught through a crack in the door, more chilling than blanketing cold outside. It felt like the slit between worlds.

He wished Denny was with him. Denny already had no love for the Purefoys – for taking advantage of Moon's fantasies so as to unload their crappy, bodged barn conversion. Incomers! Stupid gits! He needed the heat of Denny's honest rage. He needed this bloody heater to work – having run to the car without his jacket, because going back for it would have wasted crucial minutes.

Crucial minutes? Like he knew what he was going to do. Like only time might beat him: little four-eyed Lol, ex-psychiatric patient, shivering.

Ice under the wheels carried the Astra into the verge, the bumper clipping a fence post. Denny owned a four-wheel drive, had once done amateur rallying. But Denny wasn't here, so Lol was alone – with a little knowledge, a sackful of conjecture, and the memory of the draught through a thinly opened door.

He came to the small parking area below the Iron Age camp, and killed his headlights. There were no other vehicles there, but what did he expect – black cars parked in a circle, customized number plates all reading 666?

'You know what's going to happen. Don't you?'

Lol got out of the Astra and followed the familiar path. Big, muscular trees crowded him. Between them, he could see a mat of city lights – but none around him, none up here. None here since damp, smoky firelight had plumed within the cluster of thatched huts where families huddled against the dark beating of the crow-goddess's wings.

He'd never felt so cold.

Only the incense is missing, Merrily thought.

The warm colours of the soaring stone, the rolling contours of the Norman arches, the suspended corona – its daytime smiley, saw-tooth sparkle made numinous by the candles around it. And the jetting ring of red in the bottom of a giant black cast-iron stove near the main entrance.

Now a candlelight procession of choirboys singing plainsong, in Latin. One of the choirboys, the tallest of them, wore robes and a mitre, with a white-albed candle-bearer on either side.

There were about two hundred people in the congregation – not enormous, but substantial. They looked entirely ordinary, mostly over fifty, but an encouraging few in their twenties. Dress tending towards the conservative, but with few signs of the fuss and frothy hats such a service would once have produced.

Sophie sat next to Merrily, just the two of them on a rear central pew. Sophie's gloved hands were tightly clenched on her lap. What she'd said outside, her face white and pitted as the moon, had been banished to the back of Merrily's mind; not now, *not now*.

Her hands were underneath the cloak, clasped around the cross. She prayed it would never have to be revealed. She prayed that, in less than an hour's time, she and Jane would be walking out of here, relieved and laughing, to the car, where the cross would be laid thankfully on the back seat.

But where the hell *was* Jane? Not in the nave. Not *visibly* in the nave – but there were a hundred places in here to sit or stand concealed. But why do that?

Merrily studied James Lyden. He was a good-looking boy, and he clearly knew it. Could she detect an insolence, a knowing smirk, as the choirboy voices swirled and ululated around him? Perhaps not, though. It was probably James's idea of 'pious'.

And then there were two . . .

Here was Mick Hunter on a low wooden seat under the rim of the corona. It was not the first time she'd seen Mick in his episcopal splendour. He wore it well, like some matinée idol playing Becket. *'We're all of us actors, Merrily. The Church is a faded but still fabulous costume drama.'* She noticed the medieval touches, the fishtail chasuble, the primatial cross instead of the crozier; Mick was not going to be upstaged by a schoolboy. Sad, Jane would comment, wherever she was.

As the plainsong ended, the Boy Bishop turned his back on the congregation and knelt to face Mick Hunter on his throne.

Merrily's fingers tightened on the stem of the cross.

Jane had hidden in the little chantry chapel, where the stone was ridged like a seashell. She crouched where she supposed monks had once knelt to pray – though not ordinary monks; it was far too ornate. The medieval chant washed and rippled around her, so calming.

She must *not* be calm.

Rowenna stood not ten feet away, leaning against a pillar. Rowenna wearing a soft leather jacket, short black skirt, and black tights.

How would she react if Rowenna was to walk in here now? Go for her like a cat? Go for her eyes with all ten nails?

Uh-huh, better to keep quiet and watch and listen. Whatever was going to happen here, Rowenna would be central to it. She wasn't just here to watch her boyfriend – who would not be her boyfriend at all if he hadn't been the chosen as Boy Bishop.

And Jane suddenly remembered yesterday's lunch in Slater's, and Rowenna saying, *'Listen, I have to go. Go on, ask me where. You're gonna like this . . . the Cathedral.'* Then Jane expressing surprise because she'd understood they were going shopping, and Rowenna going, *'I just forgot what day it was. I have to meet my cousin'* – breaking off at this point because Lol had appeared. But it was obvious now: Rowenna would have gone with James to his dress rehearsal, so she'd know exactly . . .

The evil, duplicitous, carnivorous slag! Jane didn't think she'd ever hated anyone like she hated Rowenna right now.

But it was wrong to hate like this in a cathedral. It had to be wrong. She emptied her mind as the Bishop's lovely deep, velvet voice was relayed to the congregation through the speaker system. What Mum had once called his late-night DJ voice – so, like, *really* sincere.

'James, you have been chosen to serve in the office of Boy Bishop in this cathedral church. Will you be faithful and keep the promises made for you at your baptism?'

In the silence, Jane heard a small bleep quite close. It was such an un-cathedral noise that she flattened herself against the stones, and edged up to the opening and peeped out just once.

The Boy Bishop said, in a kind of dismissive drawl, 'I will, the Lord be my helper.'

Jane saw Rowenna slipping a mobile phone into a pocket of her leather jacket.

Mick Hunter said, 'The blessing of God Almighty – Father, Son and Holy Ghost – be upon you. Amen.'

Silence – as Jane held her breath.

The choir began to sing.

She relaxed. It was done. James Lyden was Boy Bishop of Hereford.

And nothing had happened.

Had it?

Amid the cold trees, below the cold moon, was a panel of light.

Lol stopped on the ice-glossed earthen steps. He thought at first it must be the farmhouse, and that he was seeing it from a different angle, seeing behind the wall of Leylandii.

But it was the barn.

The glazed-over bay was one big lantern.

Lol moved down the frozen steps and saw, behind the plate-glass wall, tall candles burning aloft on eight or ten holders of spindly wrought-iron.

A beacon! You would see it from afar, like a fire in the sky laying a flickering path towards the Cathedral tower.

It shocked him into stillness, as if the same candles had been burning on Katherine Moon's coffin. Behind their sombre shimmering, he was sure shadows were moving. All was quiet: not an owl, not a breath of wind. A bitter, still, rock-hard night.

He was scared.

'*Calm down, Robinson,*' Athena White said from somewhere. He ran from the steps to the rubble-stone barn wall and edged towards the lit-up bay. Rough reflections of the candlelight were sketched on to the ridged surface of a long frozen puddle, the remains of the pond-excavation where Moon had said she'd found the Celtic sword.

When he reached the front door, he realized it was lying open. He backed away, recalling the darkness pushing against him – the slit between worlds.

Tonight, however, the door was open, and – perhaps not only because he was so cold – the barn seemed to beckon him inside.

Merrily murmured to Sophie, 'What happens now?'

A hush as the Boy Bishop and his two candle-bearing attendants faced the high altar. Choristers were ranked either side, poised for an instant on a single shared breath.

As Mick Hunter walked away, smiling, the choir sailed into song, and the Boy Bishop approached the altar.

'Later,' Sophie whispered, 'the boy will lead us in prayer, and then he gives a short sermon. He'll say how important the choir's been to him, and that sort of thing. But first there'll be a kind of circular tour, taking in the North Transept.'

'The shrine?'

'I don't know quite how they're going to cope with that this time – perhaps they won't. What are you doing, Merrily?'

'I'm going to watch.' She edged out of the pew, holding the cross with one hand, gathering her cloak with the other.

'Are you cold, Merrily?'

'Yes.'

'Me too. I wonder if there's something wrong with the heating.'

The candle-led procession was leaving the chancel, drifting left to the North Transept. Merrily paused at the pew's end. She felt slightly out of breath, as if the air had become thinner. She looked at Sophie. 'Are you *really* cold, as well?'

Behind her, there was a muffled slap on the tiles.

Sophie rose. 'Oh, my God.'

Merrily turned and saw a large woman in a grey suit, half into the aisle, her fingers over her face, with blood bubbling between them and puddling on the tiles around her skittering feet.

FIFTY

Abode of Darkness

The barn was like an intimate church. Lol could sense it around him, a rich and velvety warmth. He could see the long beeswax candles, creamy stems aglow, and imagine tendrils of soft scented smoke curling to the rafters.

He stood for a moment, giving in to the deceptive luxury of heat – experiencing the enchantment of the barn as, he felt sure, Moon would have known it. Then catching his breath when the total silence gave way to an ashy sigh – the collapse of crumbling logs in the hearth with a spasm of golden splinters, the small implosion bringing a glint from a single nail protruding from the wall over the fireplace. A nail where once hung a picture of a smiling man with his Land Rover.

Which brought Lol out of it, tensing him – because another black-framed photo hung there now: of a long-haired woman in a long dress.

The candle-holders were like dead saplings, two of them framing a high-backed black chair, thronelike. And, standing beside the chair – Lol nearly screamed – was a priest in full holy vestments.

Merrily was gesturing wildly for a verger, a cleaner, anybody with a mop and bucket – people staring at her from both sides of the aisle, as though she was some shrill, house-proud harpy.

What she was seeing was the defiled altar at St Cosmas, blistered with half-dried sacrificial blood – while *this* blood was close to the centre of the Cathedral, and it was still warm and it was human blood, bright and pure, and there was so damned much of it.

The choir sang on. The Boy Bishop and his entourage were now out of sight, out of earshot, paying homage to Cantilupe in all his fragments.

She should be there, too. She should be with them in the ruins of the tomb, where the barrier was down, where Thomas Dobbs had fallen. Yet – yes, all right, *irrationally* maybe – she also had to dispose of the blood . . . the most magical medium for the manifestation of . . . what? *What?* Anyway, she couldn't be in both places, and there was no one else . . . absolutely nobody else.

Sophie was tending to the woman, the contents of her large handbag emptied out on the pew, the woman's head tilted back – Sophie dabbing her nose and lips with a wet pad, the woman struggling to say how sorry she was, what a time for a nosebleed to happen.

'She has them now and then,' a bulky grey-haired man was explaining in a low, embarrassed voice to nobody in particular. 'Not on this scale, I have to say. It's nerves, I suppose. It'll stop in a minute.'

Merrily said sharply, 'Nerves?'

'Oh,' he mumbled, 'mother of the Boy Bishop, all that. Stressful time all round.'

'You're Dick Lyden?'

'Yes, I am. Look, can't you leave the cleaning-up until after the service. Nobody's going to step in it.'

'That's not what I'm worried about, Mr Lyden. This is his

mother's blood?' She was talking to herself, searching for the significance of this.

'I don't want the boy to see the fuss.' Dick Lyden pulled out a white handkerchief and began to mop his wife's splashes from his shoes. 'He's temperamental, you see.'

Someone had given James Lyden one of the votive candles from near where the shrine had stood, and he waited there while they pushed back the partition screen.

'Not how we'd like it to be,' Jane heard this big minister with the bushy beard say. 'Still, I'm sure St Thomas would understand.'

'Absolutely,' James Lyden said, like he couldn't give a toss one way or the other.

There was no sign of Rowenna.

Pressed into the side of one of the pointed arches screening off the transept, no more than six yards away from them, Jane saw it all as the bearded minister held open the partition door to the sundered tomb.

Only the minister and the Boy Bishop went up to the stones – as though it was not just stone slabs in there, but Cantilupe's mummified body. The two candle-bearing boys in white tunics waited either side of the door, like sentries. One of them, a stocky shock-haired guy, saw Jane and raised a friendly eyebrow. She'd never seen him before and pretended she hadn't noticed.

The bearded minister stood before one of the side-panels with those mutilated figures of knights on it – their faces obliterated like someone had attacked them centuries ago with a hammer and a stone-chisel, and a lot of hatred.

The minister crossed his hands over his stomach, gazed down with closed eyes. He saw nothing.

'Almighty God,' he said, 'let us this night remember Your servant, Thomas, guardian of this cathedral church, defender of the weak, healer of the sick, friend to the poor, who well understood the action of Our Lord when His disciples asked of Him: which is the greatest in the Kingdom of God and He shewed to them a child and set him in the midst of them.'

Jane saw James Lyden's full lips twist into a sour and superior sneer.

The minister said, 'Father, we ask that the humility demonstrated by Thomas Cantilupe throughout his time as bishop here might be shared this night and always by your servant James.'

'No chance,' Jane breathed grimly, and the shock-haired boy must have seen the expression on her face, because he grinned.

'It is to our shame,' the minister went on, 'that Thomas's shrine, this cathedral's most sacred jewel, should be in pieces, but we know that James will return here when it is once again whole.'

Wouldn't put money on it. This time Jane looked down at her shoes, and kept her mouth shut.

Which was more than James did when he put down his candle on a mason's bench, and bent reverently to kiss the stone. Jane reckoned he must have spent some while dredging up this disgusting, venomous wedge of thick saliva.

When his face came up smiling, she felt sick. She also felt something strange and piercingly frightening: an unmistakable awareness, in her stomach, of the nearness of evil. She gasped, because it weakened her, her legs felt numb, and she wanted to be away from here, but was not sure she could move. She felt herself sinking into the stone of the arch. She felt soiled and corrupted, not so much by what she'd seen but by what she realized it meant, and she groped for the words she'd intoned with all the sincerity of a budgie – while Mum held her hands – before the altar at Ledwardine.

Christ be with us, Christ within us.

And then the electric lights went out.

'Look, darling,' he said, 'it's Mr Robinson. You remember Mr Robinson.'

Tim Purefoy held a large glass of red wine close to the tablecloth white of his surplice.

Anna wore a simple black shift, quite low-cut. She was a beautiful woman; she threw off a sensual charge like a miasma. Like an aura, Lol supposed.

'You know,' she said, 'I thought, one day, there would be somebody. I really didn't think it would be you.'

'The brother, perhaps.' Tim lowered himself, with a grateful sigh, into the chair. 'All rage and bombast, amounting, in the end, to very little – like most of them.'

'Or the exorcist,' Anna said, 'Jane's mother. I did so want to meet her before we moved on.'

'But not this little chap here. No, indeed. Hidden depths, do you think?' A bar of pewtery moonlight cut through the high window, reaching almost to the top of Tim Purefoy's pale curls. He held up a dark bottle without a label. 'Glass of wine, old son?'

'No thanks,' Lol said tightly. 'I . . . seem to be interrupting something.' Everything he said seemed to emerge slowly, the way words sometimes did in dreams, as though the breath which carried them had to tunnel its way through the atmosphere.

'Not at all.' Tim Purefoy took a long, unhurried sip of wine. 'It's finished now. It's done. We're glad to have the company, aren't we, darling?'

'Done?'

'Ah, now, Mr Robinson . . .' Tim put down his glass then used both hands to pull the white surplice over his head, letting it fall in a heap to the flags. 'You must have some idea of what we're about, or you wouldn't be here.'

Anna Purefoy brought Lol a chair and stood in front of him until he sat down – like he was going to be executed, sacrificed. Anna looked young and fit and energized, as if she'd just had sex. She must, he thought, be about sixty, however. 'Sure you won't have a glass of wine?'

Before you die?

'Communion wine?' Lol said.

Tim Purefoy laughed. 'With a tincture of bat's blood.'

'It's our own plum wine, silly.' Anna took the bottle from her husband and held it out to Lol. 'See? You really shouldn't believe everything you read about people like us.'

Lol remembered her patting floury hands on her apron. *'One can buy a marvellous loaf at any one of a half-dozen places in town, but one somehow feels obliged, living in a house this old.'*

He was almost disarmed by the ordinariness of it, the civility, the domesticity: candles like these, in holders like these, available in all good branches of Habitat. He blinked and forced himself to remember Katherine Moon congealing in her bath of blood – glancing across towards the bathroom door, holding the image of the dead, grinning Moon pickled like red cabbage. In *that* room over there, beyond *those stairs.* Behind *that door.*

Visualization, Athena White had said. *Willpower.*

'Thank you.' Lol accepted the stoppered wine bottle from Anna. He held it up for a moment before grasping it by the neck and smashing it into the stone fireplace. He felt the sting of glass-shards as the fire hissed in rage. Rivers of wine and blood ran down his wrist. And down over the hanging photo-graph of Moon.

'Now, tell me what you did to her,' Lol whispered.

The choir faded into trails of unconducted melody.

'Please remain in your seats.' The Bishop's voice, crisply from the speakers. 'We appear to have a power failure, but we're doing all we—' And then the PA system cut out.

Merrily spotted Mick in his mitre, by candlelight amid jumping shadows, before the candles began to go out, one by one, the air laden with the odour of cooling wax, until there was only the oval of light on the corona, like a Catherine wheel over the central altar – the last holy outpost.

She pulled the cross from under her cloak, standing close to the pool of blood on the tiles, though she couldn't see it now. A baby began to cry.

She looked across the aisle and the pews, towards the main door, to where the big black stove should have been jetting red, and saw nothing. The stove was out, too. The Cathedral gone dark – gone cold.

'*Jesus,*' – Merrily feeling the fear like a ball of lead in her solar plexus – '*may all that is You flow into me.*'

'James?' the bearded minister called out. 'Are you there?'

Jane stepped out from the archway and heard the swish of heavy robes as the Boy Bishop brushed past her in the dark. The candles held by the two attendants, the sentries, were also out. Only one small flame glowed – the two-inch votive candle given to James Lyden, now lying on the mason's bench. Jane ran and snatched it up, hid the flame behind her hand, and moved out into the transept, listening for the swish of the robes.

Lyden was going somewhere, being taken somewhere, escorted.

She heard him again – his voice this time. '*Yeah, OK.*' She followed quietly, though maybe not quietly enough, wishing she had her trainers on instead of her stupid best shoes.

She could see him now – a black, mitred silhouette against the wan light from the huge diamond-paned gothic windows in the nave.

Moonlight. Shadows of people, unmoving. Jane heard anxious whispers and a baby's cry mingling into a vast soup of echoes. Where was Mum? Where was Mum with the cross? Why wasn't she rushing for the pulpit, because, Christ, if there was a time for an exorcism, a time for the soul police to make like an armed response unit, this was it.

She could no longer see the mitred silhouette. Where had he gone, the sneering bastard who'd spat on the saint's tomb, and brought darkness? Although, of course, she knew it hadn't really happened like that. Somebody had hit a big fuse-box somewhere. It was all coincidence, theatrics.

Jane stumbled, stepped into space, groping for stone, nearly dropping her stub of a candle. Hearing quick footsteps receding ahead of her.

Steps. Stone steps going down.

The crypt? The Boy Bishop was going into the crypt.

Jane had never been down there, although it was open to visitors. Mum had seen it. Mum said it was no big deal. No, there weren't stacks of old coffins, nothing like that. Tombs at one end, effigies, but not as many as you might expect. It was just a bare stone cellar really, and not as big as you'd imagine.

Jane stayed where she was at the top of the steps.

Afraid, actually.

Admit it: afraid of being down there with Rowenna's creepy boyfriend in his medieval robes, afraid of what slime-ball stuff she might see him doing. The guy was a shit. Just like Danny Gittoes had broken into Ledwardine Church for Rowenna, James Lyden had spat on the tomb of the saint for her. Another sex-slave to Rowenna, who in turn was a friend of Angela. How long had Rowenna known Angela?

Aware of this long slime-trail of evil unravelling before her, Jane edged down two steps, listening hard.

Nothing.

She raised the stub of votive candle in its little metal holder. Perhaps she held the light of St Thomas, the guardian.

Could she believe that?

What did it matter? Jane shrugged helplessly to herself and went down into the crypt.

FIFTY-ONE

Sacrilege

'Blood,' Lol said. 'I've been learning all about blood.'

Feeling – God help him – the energy of it.

It had been the right thing to do. Another couple of minutes and the Purefoys would have had him apologizing for disturbing their religious observance.

Tim scowled. 'Mr Robinson, there are several ways we could react to your outburst of juvenile violence. The simplest would be to call the police.'

'Do it,' Lol said.

'If you think we would have any explaining to do,' Anna said, 'you're quite wrong. We have an interest in ritual magic. It's entirely legal.'

'I am an ordained priest of God,' Tim said. 'My God is the God of Abraham and Moses and Solomon, the God who rewards knowledge and learning; the God who shows us strength, who accepts that plague and pestilence have their roles . . .'

'Stop dressing it up.'

' . . . the God to whom Satan was a – an albeit occasionally troublesome – serving angel. Calling me a Satanist, as I suspect you were about to do, is therefore, something of an insult. For which' – Tim Purefoy waved a hand – 'I excuse you, because it was said in ignorance.'

'We were both brought up in the Christian tradition,'

Anna interrupted. 'It took us a while to realize that Christianity was introduced primarily as a constraint on human potential, which has to be removed if we are to survive and progress.'

'Let's say it's simply run its course,' Tim added, with the fervour of the converted. 'The Church has no energy left; it's riddled with greed and corruption. In this country alone, it's sitting on billions of pounds which could be put to more sensible use.'

'Even if we didn't lift a finger, it would destroy itself within the next fifty years. But the signs are there in the sky – too many to be ignored. We cannot ignore *signs*.'

'The signs are what brought us here to Hereford,' Tim said. 'But I don't think you want to know about that. I think you want to know about the death of Katherine Moon. I think you're here for reassurance that there was nothing you could have done to save her, am I right?'

'And we're happy to give you that.' Anna smiled and reached across the firelight for his bloodied hand. Her fingers were slim and cool.

George Curtiss had taken charge, talking to vergers, organizing people by sporadic candlelight, shouting from the pulpit, explaining.

As though he could.

Merrily noticed that candles had to be repeatedly relit; it was like last night, when she and Huw were at the saint's tomb. She stumbled past the central altar – only three candles left alight on the corona – looking around for Jane and the Bishop.

She found Mick Hunter eventually in the deep seclusion of his throne beyond the choir-stalls. The throne was of dark oak, many pinnacled, itself a miniature cathedral. He came out to join her, having removed the mitre. His sigh was like an audible scowl.

'Merrily, of all the people I could do without in this situation . . .'

'You really . . . really have to let me do it, Mick.' Keeping her voice low and steady. 'You can look away, you can grit your teeth – but you have to let me do it.'

'Do it?'

'You know exactly what I mean. You've got darkness and cold and spilt blood in your Cathedral. What you must do now is wind up the service, get the congregation out of here, lock the doors, and just . . . just let me do it.'

He stared down at her and, although it was too dark to see his face, she sensed his dismay and disbelief.

'All right,' she said, 'why don't you ask God? Why don't you go and kneel down quietly in front of your high altar and ask Him? Ask Him if He's happy about this?'

The Bishop didn't move. There were just the two of them here in the holiest place. She dropped the wooden cross and bent to pick it up.

'I made a mistake, didn't I?' Mick Hunter said. 'I made a big mistake with you.'

She straightened up. 'Looks like you did.'

'Do you remember what I said to you last night when you asked me if I wanted your resignation from the post of Deliverance Consultant?'

'You told me to get a good night's sleep and forget about it.'

'And?'

'I couldn't sleep.'

'Very well,' he said. 'Put it in writing for me tomorrow.'

'Mick—'

'Bishop,' he said, 'I think.'

*

Jane heard him breathing, so she knew roughly where he was
– like, somewhere in the crypt, because the breathing filled
the whole, intimidating blackness of it. She had her coat open
and the candle cupped in her hand inside. She caught a finger
in the flame and nearly yelped.

Christ be with me, she heard inside her head. In Mum's
voice. *Mum be with me* – that might be more use!

Just words, like a mantra – words to repeat and hold on to,
to try and shout down your fear, like those poor, doomed
soldiers in the First World War singing in the trenches. *Christ
within me*.

She walked towards the sound of breathing, which came
quicker now, with a snorting and a snuffling. Gross. What *was*
this? Maybe she should get back up the steps and shout for
help. But there was a power cut; and by the time she could get
someone with a lamp down here, it would be over, whatever
it was. Like she couldn't guess.

She shouted, 'Freeze!'

Bringing the candle out from under her coat, she held it as
high as she could reach.

A hundred quaking shadows broke out over the crypt, and
James Lyden's eyes opened wide in shock, his mouth agape.

'Oh!' Jane recoiled in disgust.

There he was, the Boy Bishop, with one gaitered leg on a
long-dead woman's stone face. His chasuble was tented over
Rowenna, now emerging – who for just a moment looked so
gratifyingly ridiculous on her knees that Jane laughed out
loud.

'You total slimeballs!'

But she was nervous, realizing this wasn't just some irrev-
erent stunt – the Boy Bishop in full regalia, except presumably
for his underpants. This was an act of deliberate sacrilege. It
was meant to have an unholy resonance.

Get out of here!

Jane turned and made a dash for the steps.

But crashed into a wall. In the dark you quickly lost any sense of direction.

When she turned back, Rowenna was already between her and the steps leading out. Suddenly James's arms encircled her from behind, his breath pumping against her neck.

Jane screamed.

Rowenna was easing the candle from between her fingers.

'Oh, kitten,' she said thickly. 'Oh, kitten, what *are* we going to do with you now?'

Jane glared at her with open hostility. 'Does our friend here know you do the same with Danny Gittoes?'

Holding the candle steady, between their two faces, Rowenna looked untroubled.

Jane said, 'Does he know about those clergymen in Salisbury?'

Rowenna shook her head sadly.

'I now know everything about you,' Jane continued. 'I know exactly what you are.'

Rowenna smiled sympathetically. 'You're not really getting any of this, are you? What *I* am is a woman, while *you* are still very much a child.'

Jane glared at her in silent fury, as Rowenna just shook her head. Looking at her now, you detected the kind of lazy arrogance in her eyes that you hadn't picked up on before – and the coldness.

'You must realize we were only friends because someone wanted your mother monitored, yeah?'

'Who?'

'And that sort of thing is how I make a bit of money sometimes.'

'Someone at The Pod? Angela? You set me up for Angela, didn't you?'

Annoyance contorted Rowenna's small mouth. 'Oh,

please. I was ahead of where The Pod are *years* ago. Though it was quite touching to think of you standing at the window in your little nightie, solemnly saluting the sun and moon, and thinking you were plugged into the Ancient Wisdom.'

'You bitch—'

'Pity it all went wrong, though. I could have really shown you things that would've blown you away.'

'Oh, you're just so full of shit, Rowenna. I—'

Rowenna suddenly slapped Jane's face, knocking her head back into James's chest. 'Don't push your luck with me any more. Given time, I could really do things to you. I could make you totally fucking *crazy*.'

Jane felt James Lyden's breath hot on her neck, and struggled vainly. 'You're even fooling yourself.'

'You don't know anything.' Rowenna held the candle very close to Jane's face, so that she could feel its heat. 'Remember that suit? The greasy old suit I had Danny hide in the vestry?'

'Yeah, who told you to do that?'

'*Nobody* told me. I don't take anyone's orders . . . unless I want to.' Rowenna wore a really sickly, incense-smelling scent that seemed to fill up the entire crypt. 'I just couldn't resist it after you'd told me how Denzil Joy had so badly scared your mother. I thought that would be really interesting – to see if I could make him *stick* to her.'

'What?'

Rowenna put her face very close to Jane's and *breathed* the words into her. For the first time, Jane knew what it meant to have one's skin crawl.

'I found his widow's name in the phone book, so I sent James round to collect any old clothes for charity. And next I got into *her*: the Reverend Merrily Watkins. I nicked some of her cigarettes when I was at the vicarage, and I smoked them slowly and visualized, and I did a few other things and . . . OK, maybe I asked for a little assistance. It's amazing what help you can get when you're working on the clergy – on the enemy. And it worked, didn't it? It really made her sweat; it made her ill. You told me she was ill. And I bet she didn't tell you the half of it.'

Jane felt sick. She must be lying. She *couldn't* have done all that.

'You're . . . just *evil*.'

'I'm special, kitten. I'm *very* special.' Rowenna moved away.

'No, you're not. You're just . . . maybe you *are* a lot older than me. You're, like, old before your time – old and corrupted.'

'Right.' Rowenna stepped away from her. 'That's it. James?'

James answered, 'Yes?' in this really subservient way.

'Hit her for me, would you? Hit her hard.'

James said, 'What?'

'*Hit* the little cunt!'

'No!' Jane turned and hurled herself against him. Turned in his arms and pushed out at his face.

Which made him angry, and he let go for an instant, and then he punched her hard in the mouth. And then Rowenna's hand came at her like a claw, grabbed a handful of her hair and pulled her forward. Jane felt a crippling pain in the stomach and doubled up in agony. Another wrench at her hair pulled her upright, so James could hit her again in the face – enjoying it now, excited.

'Yes,' Rowenna hissed. '*Yes!*'

As Jane's legs gave way, and the stone floor rushed up towards her.

Perhaps she passed out then. For a moment, at least, she forgot where she was.

'We can't!' she heard from somewhere in the distance.

'Go on, do it!'

Rowenna? Jane heard Rowenna's voice again from yesterday. *'Death can also just mean the end of something before a new beginning.'* She saw Rowenna pointing her knife across the table . . . *'Lord Satan, take me!'* . . . the Tower struck by lightning, people falling out of the crack . . . a long way down, on to the hard, cold stone floor.

Jane felt very afraid. *Must get up.* She opened her eyes once and saw, in a lick of light, another face right under her own, with dead stone eyelids.

They'd laid her out on one of the effigies.

She tried to lift her head from that stone face. But she couldn't, felt too heavy, as if all the stones of St Thomas's tomb were piled on top of her. Then the candlelight went away, as they pushed her further down against the stone surface. She felt stone lips directly under hers.

'Never go off on your own with an exposed flame,' Rowenna said. 'It's bad news, kitten. Night-night then.'

A stunning pain on the back of her head and neck.

Time passed. No more voices.

Only smoke.

Smoke in her throat. Her head was full of smoke – and words. And Mum whispering . . .

'Let me not run from the love that You offer
'But hold me safe from the forces of evil.'

But Mum was not here. It was just a mantra in her head.

'Thank God for that,' George Curtiss grunted from the pulpit, as the lights came back on.

There was laughter now in the nave – half nervous, half relieved – as George's words were picked up by the suddenly resensitized microphone.

'Well, ah . . . we don't know what caused this, but it was

most unfortunate, very ill timed. However, at least, ah . . . at least it demonstrates to our Boy Bishop that the life of a clergyman is not without incident.'

The Boy Bishop stood, head bowed, beneath the edge of the corona, in front of the central altar itself. Mick Hunter stood behind him, one hand on the boy's shoulder.

'We'd like to thank you all for being so patient. I realize some of you do need to get home . . .'

Merrily stood in the aisle, near the back of the nave, looking around for Jane, and very worried now. *This is all that matters, isn't it? This is all there is.'*

Something was wrong. Something else was wrong. The power seemed to be restored, but there was something missing. A dullness lingered – a number of bulbs failing to re-function, perhaps. The round spotlights in the lofty, vaulted ceiling appeared isolated, like soulless security lamps around an industrial compound.

'It's been suggested,' George said, 'that we now carry on with the ceremony, with the prayers and the Boy Bishop's sermon, but omit the final hymn. So, ah . . . thank you.'

And no warmth either. The warm lustre had gone from the stones; they had a grey tinge like mould, their myriad colours no longer separated.

George Curtiss stepped down.

An air of dereliction, abandonment, deadness – as though something had entered under the cover of darkness, and something else had been taken away.

Dear God, don't say that.

Under her cloak, the cross drooped from Merrily's fingers, as the choir began – a little uncertainly, it sounded – with a reprise of the plainsong which had opened the proceedings.

Sophie had appeared at her side. 'What happened?'

'Sophie, have you seen Jane?'

'I'm sorry, no. Merrily, what did Michael say to you?'

'Basically he sacked me.'

'But he can't just—'

'He can.'

She looked for the puddle of blood left by Mrs Lyden's nosebleed. It was hardly visible, carried off on many shoes into the darkness outside.

'Don't give in, Merrily.' Sophie said. 'You mustn't give in.'

'What can I do?'

Mick had melted away into the shadows. James Lyden, Bishop of Hereford, was alone, sitting on his backless chair, notes in hand, waiting for the choir to finish.

'I don't like that boy,' Sophie said.

The choristers ended their plainsong with a raggedness and a disharmony so slight that it was all the more unsettling. The sound of scared choirboys? By contrast, James Lyden's voice was almost shockingly clear and precise and confident: a natural orator.

'A short while ago, when I took my vows, the Lord Bishop asked me if I would be faithful and keep the promises made for me at my baptism.'

'You must stop him,' Sophie murmured.

'I can't. Suppose it . . . Suppose there's nothing.'

'Of course,' James said, 'I don't *remember* my baptism. It was a long time ago and it was in London, where I was born. I had no choice then, and the promises were made *for* me because I could not speak for myself.'

Sophie gripped her arm. '*Please*.'

'But now I *can*.' James looked up. Even from here, you could see how bright his eyes were. Drug-bright? 'Now I can speak for myself.'

'Don't let him. Stop him, Merrily – or I'll do it myself.'

'All right.' Merrily brought out the cross. It didn't matter now what anyone thought of her. Or how the Bishop might react, because he already had. The worst that could happen . . .

No, the best – the best that could happen!

. . . was that she'd make a complete fool of herself and never be able to show her face in Hereford again. Or in Ledwardine either.

Untying the cloak at her neck, she began to walk up the aisle towards James Lyden.

As James noticed her, his lips twisted in a kind of excitement. She kept on walking. The backs of her legs felt weak. *Just keep going. Stay in motion or freeze for ever.*

Members of the remaining congregation were now turning to look at her. There were whispers and mutterings. She kept staring only at James Lyden.

Who stood up, in all his majesty.

Whose voice was raised and hardened.

Who said, 'But, as we have all seen tonight, there is one who speaks more . . . eloquently . . . than I. And his name . . . his name is . . .'

'*No!*'

Merrily let the cloak fall from her shoulders, brought up the wooden cross, and walked straight towards the Boy Bishop, her gaze focused on those fixed, shining, infested eyes below the mitre.

FIFTY-TWO

A Small Brilliance

Lol was seeing himself with Moon down below the ramparts of Dinedor Camp. They were burying the crow, one of his hands still sticky with blood and slime . . . for him, the first stain on the idyll. He saw Moon turning away, her shoulders trembling – something reawoken in her.

'Did you ever watch her charm a crow?' Anna Purefoy asked. 'It might be in a tree as much as fifty, a hundred yards away, and she would cup her hands and make a cawing noise in the back of her throat. And the crow would leave its tree, like a speck of black dust, and come to her. I don't think she quite knew what she was doing – or was even aware that she was going to do it until it began to happen.'

It fell dead at my feet. Out of the sky. Isn't that incredible?

'It was simply something she could always do,' Tim added. 'Further proof that she was very special.'

Lol glanced at the red-stained photograph of Moon over the fireplace. Not one he'd seen before; they must have taken it themselves. Athena White had told him how they would use photographs, memorabilia of a dead person as an aid to visualization.

He turned back to the Purefoys. 'Why don't you both sit down.' He didn't trust them. He imagined Anna Purefoy suddenly striking like a cobra.

'As you wish.' She slipped into one of the cane chairs.

Tim hesitated and then lowered himself into the high-backed wooden throne.

'After she was dead,' Lol said, 'you left out that cutting from the *Hereford Times*, like a suicide note. She'd probably never even seen it, had she?'

'It doesn't matter.' Tim yawned. 'That's a trivial detail.'

Lol made himself sit in the other cane chair, keeping about ten feet between himself and them.

'How did you kill her?'

'Oh, really!' Anna leaned forward in the firelight, a dark shadow suddenly spearing between her breasts.

'Darling—'

'No, I won't have this, Tim. Murder is a crime. We did not kill Katherine. We showed her path she was destined to find, and she took it – according to the values of the Celtic ethos. We talked for hours and hours with Katherine. She could never relate to this era – this commercial, secular world, this erratic world, this panicking period in history. She knew she didn't want to *be* here, and she was looking for a way *back*.'

'Bollocks,' Lol said, although he realized it wasn't.

'And anyway,' Anna said, 'to the Iron Age Celt, death is merely a short, shadowy passage, to be entered boldly in the utter and total certainty of an afterlife. A Celtic human sacrifice was often a *willing* sacrifice. Katherine always knew she wouldn't enjoy a long life – I showed her that in the cards, though she didn't need me to – and therefore she was able to give what remained of it a purpose.'

'We helped her return to the bosom of her tradition,' Tim said comfortably.

'It was very beautiful,' Anna said softly. 'There was snow all around, but the bathroom was warm. We helped her put candles around the bath. She was naked and warm and smiling.'

'No!' Lol said.

But he saw again Moon's thin arms gleaming pale gold, lit by the four tall church candles, one at each corner of the white bathtub. Her teeth were bared. Her hands – something black and knobbled across Moon's open hands.

'But you didn't give her an afterlife, did you?'

He saw those sharp little teeth bared in excitement, Moon panting in the sprinkling light: energized, euphoric, slashing, gouging. And then lying back at peace, relieved to feel her lifeblood jetting from opened veins.

The tragedy and the horror of it made him pant with emotion. The Purefoys had done this, as surely as if they'd waylaid her like a ripper in a country lane. But it was actually worse than that . . .

Hands sweating on the edge of the chair seat, he flung at them what Athena White had explained to him.

'If a sacrifice is swift, the spirit is believed to progress immediately to a . . . better place. But if the death is protracted, the magician has time to bind the spirit to his will, so that it remains earthbound and subject to the commands of—'

'Oh, really' – Tim half rose – 'what nonsense . . .'

'It might well be,' Lol said, 'but *you* don't think it is. You think you still have her . . . and through her an access to her ancestors and to the whole pre–Christian, pagan Celtic tradition.'

He sprang up. He was sure Moon's image there on the wall was shining not with the candlelight, nor the moonlight, but with a sad grey light of its own.

'You just prey on inadequates and sick people like Moon, and attract little psychos like Rowenna and other people desperate for an identity and—'

'People like you,' Anna said gently.

'No.' He backed away, as she arose.

'Katherine told us about you, Laurence. She said you would often make her feel better because you were so insecure yourself, and had a history of mental instability.'

'That was a long time ago.'

Tim laughed. Anna held out her hands to Lol. Her face, in the mellow light, was beautiful and looked so exquisitely kind.

'It wasn't *such* a long time ago. And it doesn't go away, does it, Laurence? It's part of you. You have no certainty of anything, and you're drawn to people who do have.'

He stared into the explicit kindness of her, searching for the acid he knew had to be there, because this was the black siren, the woman who had moulded Moon into her own fatal fantasy and would have taken Jane too – to use as well.

Anna smiled with compassion, and he knew that if he let her touch him his resistance would be burned away.

She said softly, 'Laurence, think about this. What sent you to Katherine? Why did you come here tonight?'

Lol closed his eyes for just a moment. At once he saw a small, slim dark woman in black, with eyes that had to laugh at the nonsense of it all. He blinked furiously to send her away; this was no place for—

'Ah.' Anna was shaking her head, half amused – an infants' school headmistress with a silly child who would never learn. 'Why are you . . . why *are* you so obsessed with the little woman priest?'

'You can only . . .' His mind rebelled. Up against the far wall, facing this smiling Anna and the candles in the barn bay, he refused to be shocked, refused to believe she'd pulled the image of Merrily from his head. 'You can only think in terms of obsession, can't you? Love doesn't mean a thing.'

There were suddenly two bright orbs in the air.

'Love,' Tim Purefoy said, 'is the pretty lie we use to justify and glorify our lust. And the feeble term used in Christian theology to dignify weakness and sentiment.'

Both Purefoys were gazing with placid candour at Lol, as the bright orbs exploded, and Lol's ears were filled with roaring and the night went white.

A shadow fell across Merrily as she walked towards the altar with the cross in her hands.

The old priest stood next to her in the aisle. He wore a black cassock, stained, plucked and holed. He looked very ill, pale beyond pale. She had no idea how he came to be here – only why. His eyes looked directly into hers. His eyes were like crystals in an eroded cliff–face. They carried no apology. There was a bubble of spit in a corner of his mouth.

He held out a hand ridged and gnarled as a shrivelled parsnip.

Jesus Christ was the first exorcist – letters on a white page.

And Huw Owen on a mountainside in Wales. *'I don't want stuff letting in. A lot of bad energy's crowding the portals. I want to keep all the doors locked and the chains up.'*

Merrily nodded.

She put the cross into Thomas Dobbs's hand and stepped aside, with her back to a pew-end.

Jesus Christ was the first exorcist.

The Boy Bishop stood up, letting his notes flutter to the tiles. He held his crozier at arm's length, like a spear. His two candle-bearers had melted away, but Mick Hunter still stood a few paces behind him. Merrily saw a series of expressions blurring James's face. She thought of Francis Bacon's popes.

She thought that James's face was not now his own.

The Cathedral had filled with a huge and hungry hush.

Thomas Dobbs stopped about ten feet short of the boy – under the jagged halo of the corona. When he spoke, his voice was slurred and growly, dense with phlegm and bile, and the words tumbled out of him, unstoppable, like a rockslide.

'IN THE NAME OF . . . OF THE LIVING GOD, I CALL . . . I CALL YOU *OUT*!

'IN . . . NAME OF . . . GOD OF ALL CREATION . . .

' . . . NAME OF HIS SON JES . . . JESUS CHRIST . . . I CALL YOU *OUT* . . .

'I CALL YOU OUT AND . . .

'*BANISH YOU*.'

Merrily watched his pocked monument of a face, only one side of it working. She could almost feel the strength leaving his body, the despair at the heart of his struggle against his own weakness.

The Boy Bishop let his crozier fall, and ran down the aisle. Merrily saw Dick Lyden squeezing out of his pew, striding after his son. Where the boy had stood, she saw the slightly unclear figure of a slim woman in a long dress, with hair down to her waist, like dark folded wings, and then – as though Merrily had blinked – the woman was no longer there. She saw Dobbs clench his teeth so hard she felt they were going to split and fragment, and she saw his arm winching stiffly upward like a girder, pointing.

'*DEVIL . . . UNCLEAN SPIR . . . IT!*'

No more than a harsh rasp this time, and then he turned away, stumbling, and he and Merrily came face to face.

He put up a hand to her.

She didn't move. She didn't speak. There was nothing to say. She had no tradition.

Slowly, she bowed her head.

Felt the heat of his hand a second before his fingers touched her cheek.

Merrily looked up then, and saw in his old, knowing eyes, a small brilliance, before he died.

FIFTY-THREE

Silly Woman

Lol gazed into Anna Purefoy's pale eyes. There was no obvious expression in them: no fear, no alarm. Only perhaps the beginning of surprise, or was he imagining that?

There was dust in her fine, fair hair.

No blood at all – Anna's neck was simply broken. It wasn't obvious exactly what had done that, but it wasn't important, was it? Not important now.

He didn't touch her. He just stood up. Strangely, although part of the loft had come down, six of the ten candles were still alight. No shadows, other than his own, appeared to be moving.

He couldn't look for very long at Tim Purefoy, who was, mostly, still in his chair, the chair itself crushed into the stairs. The black bull-bars had torn Tim almost in half. One of his legs was . . .

God! Lol turned away, towards the car. The smell from Tim's body was hot and foul, and there was still running blood and what might be intestine over the windscreen of the Mitsubishi Intercooler Super-Turbo-whatever the hell it was called.

And something else, half across the roof, which he thought was Moon's futon fallen from the toppled loft. Making it impossible to see inside the vehicle. The steaming silence, though, was ominous.

Also, the old oak pillar. Nothing but old oak or steel would have stopped the bull-barred Mitsubishi. It had torn down the glazed bay like cellophane, exploded the urbane Tim Purefoy like a rotten melon. But the pillar had held.

He couldn't make himself go past Tim; he didn't want to know the details. Instead he squeezed around the back, stepping over the smashed pieces of the chair he'd been sitting in a few minutes ago. If he hadn't finally lost it . . . if Anna Purefoy hadn't pursued him, gleefully taunting him with her knowledge of his obsession for 'the little woman priest' . . . he would have been the first to be hit.

When he reached the other side of the car, he found the driver's window wound down. Right down – as if that was how it had been when the Mitsubishi rammed the glass-covered bay. As though the driver had needed to hear the impact – and the screams.

But there had been no screams audible above the engine's roar and the sounds of destruction. All too fast, too explosively unexpected.

Denny smiled out at him. 'Bodged job, eh? I always said it was a . . . bodged job. They never meant to . . . turn it into holiday 'commodation. Never planned to renovate it, till . . . till Kathy showed up. Dead, are they?'

'Mm,' Lol said.

'But *you're* all right. I never . . . I never thought you'd be here. I thought you were a . . .' Denny laughed out some blood. ' . . . a bit of a nancy, if I'm honest. No . . . no . . . you stay there. Don't fucking look down here, man. Not having you throwing up on my motor.'

'Shut up now,' Lol said. 'I'll have an ambulance here as soon as I can find the bloody phone.'

'I think on the table – bottom of the stairs. Be part of my fucking sump now.'

Lol tried the driver's door. 'Don't be stupid, mate,' Denny

said. 'You open that, I'll just fall out in several pieces. An Iron Age Celt dies in his chariot. I tell you about my dream? A mystic now, man – finally a fucking mystic.'

Lol saw that Denny's earring was gone. Or maybe the ear itself.

'You're so . . . indiscreet, Lol. That's your problem. You don't trust yourself – always got to tell somebody.'

Lol sighed. 'The extension. You heard me leaving that message for Merrily.'

'Been eavesdropping on your calls for weeks, Laurence. Needed to hear what you were saying to Lyden – about Kathy. Could never figure why you weren't all over Kathy. She attractive, this vicar?'

'Listen,' Lol said. 'I'm going over to the farm. I'll have to break in and use their phone.'

'If that makes you feel better. But if I've gone to the ancestors, time you get back . . .'

'I'll be less than five minutes. I'll smash a window in the kitchen.'

'Got a lot to say to those primitive fuckers,' Denny muttered. 'To the ancestors.'

'Don't go away,' Lol said.

'No. Cold in here, en't it? Must be the extra ventilation.'

Denny laughed his ruined laugh.

Headlights and warblers. *Déjà vu*. The ambulance cutting across the green again, directly to the north porch. A police car behind the ambulance. Behind that, a plain Rover: Howe.

'Later, Annie,' Merrily said, 'please? Is that all right? I need to see that Jane's . . .'

'Just don't go off anywhere,' Howe said.

'No further than the hospital.'

'No,' Jane protested, sitting up in the back of the ambulance, a paramedic hanging on to her arm. 'You're not coming. *I'm* not going. This is ridiculous. It's just like . . . mild concussion.'

'Could be a hairline fracture, Jane,' the paramedic warned.

'No way. This guy's just blowing it up on account of having his hands all over me.'

'I had my hands all over you,' the boy in white said patiently, 'because you were on fire.'

'Sure,' Jane said. Some of her hair was singed, and she had quite a deep cut on her forehead and bruising on the left side of her jaw and under her left eye. 'And, like, if you're wearing a dress and your name's Irene, you think nobody's going to suspect anything.'

'Eirion,' the boy said. There were black smuts all over his hands and his white alb.

'Whatever.'

'I'll be here for quite a while,' Annie Howe told Merrily. 'We have to talk in depth, Ms Watkins.' She pulled Eirion away from the ambulance. 'I think you need to tell me how she got on fire.'

'She was down in the crypt – with a candle. She said she must have tripped, but . . .' He hesitated. 'There was nobody else there when I got to her, OK? But she was face-down and her coat was on fire and . . . I really think you need to talk to James Lyden.'

'Who's he?'

'The Boy Bishop. His parents were looking for him. They've probably taken him home. They live in one of those Edwardian houses in Barton Street. And you need to talk to his girlfriend.'

'Oh, yes,' Merrily said, 'I think you definitely want to talk to James's girlfriend.'

'Name?'

'Melissa,' Eirion said. 'But she seems to have gone.'

Merrily said, 'Melissa?'

'I don't know her other name. James told me she lives with her foster-parents on a farm up on Dinedor Hill. He knows where it is – he's been up there a couple of times.'

'Jesus Christ,' Merrily said.

She went into the Cathedral and stayed away from everyone, even Sophie. Especially from Sophie – she mustn't be involved.

Merrily saw that there was a blanket over the body of Thomas Dobbs, and two uniformed policeman guarding it. The nave had a secular feel, like some huge market hall. Spiritual work to be done, here – but by whom?

Jane had absolutely refused to let Merrily go with her to the hospital, but in the end she had accepted Eirion's company. Merrily smiled faintly. The boy must have masochistic tendencies.

Across the nave, over by Bishop Stanbury's ornate chantry, she saw Huw Owen pacing about, hands deep in the pockets of his RAF greatcoat. She hadn't spoken to him yet, although George Curtiss had told her it had been Huw who'd brought Dobbs along, after helping him sign himself out of the General Hospital.

Dobbs's last stand. Where was the *squatter* now? Should James Lyden be exorcized, or merely counselled by his father? Where would they go from here? Who would work from the office with ☒ on the door? Not a woman, that was for sure.

A hand on her shoulder, but she didn't turn round. She knew his smell: light sweat, sex.

'A busy day, Merrily.'

'Indeed, Bishop.'

'Were you looking for me?'

'I don't know. Perhaps.'

He came round to face her. He'd changed into his jogging gear. His thick brown hair looked damp with sweat.

'I have to run sometimes, to clear it all away. It's very calming. I run through the streets and nobody knows who I am.'

'Oh, I think they do, Bishop. They've all seen your picture, running. But you can only run so far, can't you?'

Mick didn't smile. 'Let's go for a walk, shall we?'

'All right.'

She followed him out of the south door, towards the cloisters, along a narrow, flagged floor, dim and intimate. She'd left her cloak in the Cathedral and felt cold in her jumper and skirt, but was determined not to show it.

'This farce will be in the papers,' he said.

'*Something* will be in the papers.'

'What does that mean?'

'I imagine you're excellent at news management.'

'Said in a somewhat derogatory way.'

'Oh no,' she said. 'I'm impressed.'

'No, you aren't. You think I'm just an ambitious administrator, with few spiritual qualities.'

'If any,' Merrily agreed. *What the hell.* Jane was going to be all right, Huw was there in the Cathedral. *What the hell!*

The Bishop leaned against a door to his left, and the cold bit hard. They were almost outside.

This was the tourist part of the Cathedral – in summer, anyway. A stone-walled courtyard, a snackbar, steps and benches and tables. The Bishop held open the door for her and followed her out, pulling the door shut behind them. They were on a raised stone path bordered by flowerbeds and evergreen shrubs. There was a circular lawn with a dead fountain in the middle, a picturesquely ruined wall behind it, overhung by decorative trees and vines. Idyllic in summer: you could be miles from the city.

Deserted now under the icy moon.

'You,' Mick Hunter said mildly, 'are an unbelievable little bitch – an incredible cock-teaser.'

'Uh-huh.' Merrily shook her head, moving back to the door. 'This is not what I wanted to talk about.'

The Bishop placed himself in front of the door, shaking his head slowly. 'All right, what *do* you want to talk about?'

'Dobbs?'

'You want me to express regret? Very well, I regret it.'

Merrily folded her arms against the cold. There was no delicate way to put this. 'When Canon Dobbs was dying, he put out his arm and he pointed, and he managed to say, "Devil . . . unclean spirit." And everyone thought he was pointing at James Lyden. But I saw he was pointing at someone standing just to the left of James – in the shadows for once.'

Hunter didn't deny it. 'Does it surprise you that he hated me?'

'Under the circumstances, hardly. When you arrived, he was an old man in bad health. He was due to retire at any time, but *you* pushed him out. When he wouldn't resign voluntarily, you chose to humiliate him. Thus antagonizing the Dean and the Chapter and countless other people – people who really counted.'

'One can't be sentimental about these things.'

'This wasn't pragmatism, Bishop. This was lunacy. When you told me last night that you'd been advised against appointing a female Deliverance consultant, it didn't strike me at the time, but later I thought, that's not the kind of thing he does. He's a politician. He might appoint me later, when he's proved himself, but not . . . I mean, I bet the people who advised you against it were those people whose support you really needed.'

He said nothing.

'It had never really made obvious sense, but I thought –

and Sophie often said – that you were young and radical and a bit reckless. But you're also clever and cautious. You never put a foot wrong. How would some hot-headed revolutionary *ever* make bishop under the age of forty-five? How could he ever make bishop at all?'

'Merrily,' he said. 'Did it ever occur to you that I simply fancied the hell out of you?'

'God forgive me, it did. It occurred to me you were looking for a nice, safe legover, and what safer option than a female cleric with ambition and no husband? Sure, I thought that for quite a while. I even came to the conclusion I could handle it if we weren't alone too often.'

'How plucky of you.' He moved out of the doorway. His face was two-dimensionally gaunt – light and shadow – in the moonlight.

'But I still wondered why it was so important for Dobbs – the hardest, possibly the most uncompromising exorcist in the business – to be out of the way *now*? And *quickly*. Who could it possibly help to have a barely qualified novice floundering about? Someone who really didn't know the score on certain aspects of the situation. Someone whose appointment was politically sensitive. Someone who could be pushed around, blamed, bullied . . .'

'You're talking nonsense, Merrily. It's been an emotional few days for you, and you're—'

'Acting like a silly woman.'

He said, 'You know, frankly, I couldn't believe it when you wouldn't let me take you home and fuck you that night. It was such an *amazing* night . . . with the new snow and the ambulance and that wonderful charge in the air. We were all so *high*.'

'High?' She stared at him. 'High on an old man having a stroke? Wow! Even better tonight, then, Mick. This time he really died. I bet you nearly came in your episcopal briefs.'

The Bishop slapped her face.

She said, '*What?*'

He'd hardly moved his body, simply reached out and done it. Almost lazily, as if to show that if she really annoyed him he could knock her head from her shoulders without breaking more sweat than it took to circuit High Town.

'There are policemen in the Cathedral,' Merrily said.

'It's a cathedral, Merrily. It has very thick walls and windows which don't open. You aren't supposed to hear what goes on outside.'

'I can't believe you did that.'

'You can believe anything you want to believe. You can believe or disbelieve at will.'

'I think we should go, Bishop, before you do or say something else that won't help your glittering career.'

She was now realizing how stupid she'd been. She could have told Annie Howe. She could have called Huw over. Earlier, Sophie had offered to come with her. But, as usual, she hadn't been able to quite believe she wouldn't be making a complete fool of herself in front of others. And she had thought she'd be quite safe virtually anywhere in the shadow of the Cathedral.

He seemed quite relaxed, but he wasn't going to let her through the door. She found she was backing away on to the circular lawn.

'Do you know young James Lyden?' The Bishop put a foot on to the grass, already brittle with frost.

'Not really.'

'Not a popular boy. Even I don't like him awfully. He behaved rather badly today. What do you think's going to happen to him?'

'I don't know. His father's a psychotherapist. Perhaps *he'll* be able to handle it.'

'I don't think so – neither does James. Where do you think he is now?'

'I believe his parents took him home,' she said cautiously. What was *this* about?

'Wrong,' the Bishop said. 'James gave his old man the slip. The last thing James wanted was to go back home in disgrace – Hereford-cred is Dick Lyden's *raison d'être*. The boy's now undone all the good work for him. I told James he could hang out at the Palace for a while. Nobody knows he's there. Nobody there but me today, as Val left for the Cotswolds this morning. Rather an unpleasant, maladjusted boy, our James.'

'Yes.'

'He nearly killed your daughter.'

'Yes.'

'And who knows what he'll do now?' Mick said.

He came towards her, moving as an athlete, his arms loose. She knew that if she tried to run past him, towards the closed-down snackbar and the steps, he'd catch her easily. She stopped in the middle of the circular lawn, near the fountain with its stone pot on top. She put her hands up. He waited, a couple of yards away, moonlight on his hair.

'Look—' She tried to produce a laugh. 'How about we treat this like last night's conversation and pretend it never happened?'

Somewhere, over God knew how many intervening walls, she heard a car start up. That was the only sound.

'I don't think so,' he said quietly. 'I think you'd better carry on talking.'

'I think I've said all I want to say.'

'But not all I want to know.'

She found she'd now backed up against the ruined wall, far too high to get over. Probably the Bishop's Palace garden behind.

'There are people,' she said, 'who wish us ill. And I think – whether unwillingly, or because of blackmail, or something – you've been playing on *their* side.'

Her right shoulder rammed against a projecting stone, and she winced.

'All the signs for them . . . Cantilupe's shrine in pieces, I suppose, was the main one . . . I mean, if Dobbs had still been official, the spiritual defences would have been so much stronger, wouldn't they? Instead of him having to struggle alone and furtively at night, exposed to whatever psychic influences were at work.'

She began to edge, inch by inch, along the wall. There was a lower section further along, no more than three feet high. OK, she might wind up on the Palace lawn, but she could make it down to the river bank and . . .

Oh Jesus, that was wrong, wasn't it?

But what alternative was there? She kept moving – imperceptibly, she hoped.

'Try pinching yourself,' the Bishop said. 'It might all be a dream, a silly fantasy.'

'I don't think so. And I still don't know what you believe, if anything. I don't even know if you believe that what they're doing is likely to have any effect whatsoever.'

He smiled and stepped back from her. 'You know, I never wanted to be a bishop. There've been far too many in my family. From an early age I knew what unholy shits most of them were, so I never wanted to be one of them. No, I wanted to be a rock star – or a cabinet minister. I actually quite envied poor Tony, for a while, but politicians . . . everyone *suspects* them, don't they?'

'Do they?'

'Politicians are capable of anything, whereas bishops . . . bishops somehow are still seen as quite remarkably saintly. They might occasionally make some ill-advised remark about the fantasy of a virgin birth, but they don't embezzle large sums, fuck other people's wives or . . . what? What else don't they do, Merrily? What else don't bishops do?'

'Oh God,' she said. 'Don't make me say it.'

He straightened up, a foot taller than her.

'Let's go in now,' she said. 'You've already sacked me. I'm pretty stupid, really. A lousy exorcist, too.' She shook her head. 'I'll go away immediately. I'll apply for vicar of Penzance.'

'Merrily, what else don't bishops do?'

'I don't *know* that you did it. And if you did, I don't understand why – or even if it was an accident.'

'Go on.'

'Paul Sayer – the Satanist dragged from the river.'

'Ah,' he said.

'I think you know how he died,' she said.

And she dived for the low wall.

He caught her easily and threw her down, well away from the wall, into the frozen flowerbed under the central fountain. He slapped her hard, backwards, forwards, across both cheeks, shocking away her scream as he straddled her, pushing her skirt up and thrusting a hand between her legs.

He gave a long, ragged, rueful sigh.

Then took his hand away.

She froze up.

'The really unfortunate part, for me, Merrily,' he said, 'is that I cannot give you what you so richly deserve and would probably end up rather enjoying.'

She couldn't move. She heard herself panting in terror, panting so loud that it might have been coming from someone else lying next to her.

'DNA,' he said. 'D-N-bloody-A.'

Her spine was chilled, literally: the frost melting through

her jumper as he pressed her into the soil. She tried to pray, while at the same time looking to each side of her for a possible weapon.

'Because this isn't me, of course,' he told her. 'Bishops don't do this. It's never considered feasible for a bishop to even contemplate doing this to a woman. A bishop's where-abouts on the night in question are rarely – even in these suspicious times – ever questioned. Especially . . . if there's an unpleasant, arrogant, sociopathic teenager like young James Lyden on the loose. Having been found hiding in the Bishop's Palace and unceremoniously ejected therefrom by the understandably irate Bishop, he wanders the grounds . . .'

'You can't *possibly*—'

'My dear child, you have no *idea* of the things I've got away with . . . I really do believe I am . . . protected.'

'You're mad. I can't believe—' She panicked then, pushing against him, tossing her head from side to side, summoning a scream.

He jammed an arm into her mouth. 'No,' he said coldly, his other hand flattening a breast. 'Not that. *Never* that.'

Over his shoulder, she could see the Cathedral wall and one of the high, diamond-paned windows – with lights behind. With police, and perhaps a doctor summoned to examine Thomas Dobbs's body, or an electrician to find out what went wrong earlier? Vergers, canons, all within twenty feet – as the Bishop of Hereford placed his long, sensitive fingers round her throat.

'You rejected me, Mrs Watkins. On a personal level, that was the most insulting thing of all.'

'I want to pray,' she said.

He laughed.

'Does that really mean nothing to you?'

He took his hands from her throat.

'I don't believe in God,' he said, 'except as something

created by man in what he liked to believe was his image. I don't believe in Satan. I don't believe in saints – or demons. I accept the psychological power of symbolism, of costume drama.'

She said, 'You really don't see it, do you?' She squirmed to a sitting position, her back to the fountain. 'You don't see what you are!'

He recoiled slightly, puzzled.

'You don't realize . . . that a non-believer who manipulates—' she struggled to her feet as she spoke, ' . . . who manipulates the belief system to promote his own power and influence . . .' she snatched the stone pot from the top of the fountain; it was heavier than she expected; she almost let it fall; ' . . . is the most *satanic* . . . person of all.'

She was sobbing.

'Put it down,' the Bishop said.

She managed to raise the pot, with both hands, over her head. She backed on to the path.

Mick relaxed, spread his hands. 'You going to throw that at me?'

He was about four feet away from her. If she threw it at him with all her strength, he would catch it easily. If she came close enough to try to hit him with it, he would simply take it away from her.

His eyes caught the full moon. His eyes were at their wildest; she sensed enjoyment, a need to be at all times very close to the edge.

He shrugged.

'I was going to let you pray. I was going to let you kneel and pray. I accept the level of your faith. Very well, I'll use that pot, if you like. You can kneel and pray and, while you're talking to God, I can bring it down very hard, very cleanly, on the back of your head. Bargain?'

Her arms were aching, but she kept the pot raised, like an offering to the moon.

'It distresses me that you have to die,' Mick Hunter said. 'The way it's turned out with you, that leaves me sad. I do want you to know that I'm capable of feeling real distress.'

He walked towards her with his arms outstretched.

'Merrily?'

There was nothing more to say. She arched her back, feeling a momentary acute pain in her spine, and hurled the stone pot into the great gothic diamond-paned window.

Friends in Dark Places

You could see him sliding it into her. It was quite dark, but the camera came in close, and there was the beam of a torch or lamp on their fuzzy, shadowed loins. Candles wavered out of focus, balls of light in the background. You could make out the glimmer of a gothic window. Beneath the woman's buttocks was what might have been an altar-cloth.

'Is that him?' Annie Howe asked. 'Is it as simple as this?'

They knew from his parents that, for a period during his time at Oxford, he'd had long hair – though it was not fashionable at the time – and also a beard. But there seemed to be no actual pictures of him from those days.

'It could be him,' Merrily said. 'Then, again . . .'

'You going to invite his wife to look at this?' Huw wondered.

'If necessary,' Howe said. 'I'm advised it may not be entirely politic at this stage to expose a bishop's wife to pornography, and ask her if she recognizes her husband. She's coming back this afternoon from her parents' house in Gloucestershire. I've already spoken to her on the phone, and she didn't seem as shocked as she might be. Any reason for that?'

'It's a marriage,' Merrily said, 'and maybe a political marriage, at that. Put it this way, their kids go to boarding school, and Val seems to spend a lot of time away from home.'

'Interesting,' Howe said.

Her office at headquarters was no surprise. Minimalist was the word; the TV and video looked like serious clutter. Merrily found this calming for once; there were no layers here. She wondered if she dared light a cigarette. Perhaps not. Beyond the big window, the sky was grey and calm: one of those un-Christmassy mild days which so often precede Christmas.

'All right.' Howe stopped Paul Sayer's tape and rewound it. 'Let's look at it one more time.'

'Actually,' Lol said, 'that woman . . . Could I look at the woman?'

Howe glanced at him with tilted head, and set the tape rolling again.

The woman on the possible-altar wore a blindfold and a gag, but the more times you watched the scene, the less it seemed like rape. Too smooth. *She was ready,* Merrily thought.

'It's Anna Purefoy.' Lol leaned forward from the plastic chair next to Merrily's.

'Are you sure?' Howe asked him. 'This woman looks quite young. I'm told the film could be twenty years old. I thought we might be looking at the very early days of home-video, but my sergeant suggests it was transferred from something called Super Eight cine-film. Even so, Anna would have been in her late thirties, early forties.'

'It's her,' Lol insisted.

'Aye, they like to take care of themselves.' Huw Owen was occupying a corner of Howe's desk. He was the untidiest object in the immaculate room.

'I'm sorry, Mr Owen?'

'Secret of eternal youth, lass – sometimes you'd think they'd found it. Then they'll go suddenly to seed, or become gross like Crowley. Drugs were no help, mind, in his case.'

Howe stood with her back to the window. She appeared, for some reason, uncharmed at being addressed as 'lass'.

'Well, it's clear that this tape is never going to be usable in evidence, even if we could put our hands on the original. But it does prompt speculation. Would you like to speculate for us, Mr Owen?'

'I get the feeling *you* were at university,' Huw said. 'Did they have any kind of occult society at your place?'

'There were a hundred different societies, but I was never a joiner.'

'I can imagine,' Huw said. 'Well, you look at most universities, you'll find some kind of experimental mystical group – harmless enough in most cases, but one association leads to another.'

Merrily said, 'I have a problem with that. I can't see Mick having any interest at all in mysticism.'

'Happen a reaction against his solid clergy family?'

'His reaction, then, would be to avoid *any* kind of religious experience.'

'My knowledge of theology is limited,' Howe said, 'but what we've just been watching is not what I would immediately think of as religious.'

'No,' Merrily said, 'it's plain sex. If you're looking for serious motivating forces in Mick's life, you'd have to put sex close to the top. He'd be nineteen or twenty then, newly liberated from the bosom of what was probably a less-than-liberal family. Suppose he thought he was getting involved with people who could, I don't know, extend his experience in all kinds of interesting ways.'

'Very astute, lass.' Huw patted her shoulder. 'As you've been finding out, clergy and the children of clergy are always fair game.'

'Yes.'

'So we've got a lad from a high-placed clergy family, up at Oxford. What was he reading?'

'History,' Howe said, 'and politics.'

'He could have become anything,' Merrily said, 'yet winds up following his father into the Church. You just can't see him as a curate, somehow.' She looked up at Howe. 'It's like imagining Annie here directing traffic.'

Howe scowled.

'That's interesting,' Huw said. 'Why *did* he do it? You really want me to develop a theory, Inspector?'

'Go ahead.'

'All right. You've got this smart, handsome lad from a dog-collar dynasty, putting it around Oxford like a sailor on shore-leave. And he's drawn into summat – drawn in, to put it crudely, by his dick. He's having the time of his life – the best time ever. He doesn't see the little rat eyes in the dark.'

'Meaning what, Mr Owen?'

'There *is* a network. It might not put out a monthly news-letter, but it does exist. The general aim is anti-Christian. They might be several different groups, but that's their one rallying point – the destruction of the Christian Church.'

'I'd have thought,' Howe said drily, 'that they could simply sit back and watch the Church take *itself* apart.'

'She's got a point,' Merrily said, the need for a cigarette starting to tell.

'Merrily, lass, you'd be very naive if you thought the Church's problems were *entirely* self-generated.'

'Sorry, go on.'

''They've got a good intelligence network, the rat-eyes. The Internet now, more primitive then but, just like Moscow was head-hunting at Oxford and Cambridge in the Sixties, the rat-eyes had their antennae out.'

Lol said, 'Anna Purefoy was in Oxfordshire then. She worked for the county council. She'd been fired from the

MOD after some fundamentalist junior minister found out she was involved in magic, along with a few other people – a purge.'

'Part of the honey-trap then,' Huw said. 'Beautiful, experienced older woman. Aye, I think we can rule out rape in them pictures. Happen she said she enjoyed being tied up. If that *is* Hunter, it's an interesting connection, but I'd be looking for something harder. Suppose they stitched our lad up good? Suppose they had him full of drugs, and suppose he really did rape somebody – a young girl, say. Suppose they even arranged for him to kill somebody.'

Annie Howe began to look uneasy. 'That stuff's surely apocryphal.'

'That *stuff* happens all the time,' Huw told her. 'You coppers hate to think there's ever a murder you don't know about, but there's thousands of folk still missing. All right, say they've stitched him up – tight enough to have him looking at public disgrace and a long prison sentence.'

Howe sighed. 'Go on, then.'

'What do they want of him? I think they want him in the Church.'

'Oh, wow,' Merrily murmured.

'Make your father a happy man, they'd say. Repent of your evil ways. Make restitution. Join the family business. Either that or go down, all the way to the gutter. Well, he's in a panic, is our lad: self-disgust and a hangover on a grand scale. In need of redemption. So he goes home to his loving family, and the result, after the nightmares and the cold sweats, is the Reverend Michael Henry Hunter, a reformed character.'

'It's a brilliant theory, Huw. Is there a precedent?'

'Happen.'

'Meaning one you never proved.'

Huw looked down at his trainers. 'I once exorcised a young curate from Halifax who admitted celebrating a black mass. It was to get them off his back, he said. Blackmail again. I never met anybody more full of remorse.'

'You think Mick—?'

'It's sometimes what *they* do. They get in touch after he's ordained, with "Do us this one thing and we'll leave you alone for ever." Ha! You likely don't know this, Inspector, but having a reverse-eucharist performed by an ordained cleric is a *very* powerfully dark thing. And a fully *turned* cleric is . . . lord of all.'

'Like Tim Purefoy,' Lol said.

'There's one as is better dead, God forgive me.'

'Hold on,' Howe said. 'Are you saying these – whoever they are . . . possibly the Purefoys – might have been in touch with Hunter throughout his whole career?'

'Very likely smoothing his path for him. A satanic bishop? Some prize, eh?'

'Except he wasn't really,' Merrily said. 'He was a man with no committed religious beliefs at all. Perhaps that's how he could live with it. "I don't believe in the Devil" – he said that to me. Perhaps he really believed he was using *them*.'

'Very likely, lass.' Huw opened out his hands. '*Very* likely. But it doesn't change a thing.'

'But what a career, Huw! What an incredibly *lucky* career. He never put a foot wrong, said all the right things to all the right people, charmed everyone he met with his energy and his sincerity. He actually told me he believed he was pro-tected.'

'Obstacles would be moved out of his path. Look at how he got this job – his one rival has a convenient heart attack. Oh, aye, he could very well come to believe he was protected. But not by God, not by the Devil – by his own dynamism, his willpower, his bloody destiny. But what's the truth of it, Merrily? The truth is he's a demonic force, whether he believes in it or not.'

'He believed he was invulnerable, obviously.' Annie Howe switched off the TV and went to sit down behind her desk, behind a legal notepad. 'Certainly, if he seemed to think he could murder Ms Watkins in the actual Cathedral precincts, and we'd simply arrest James Lyden for it . . .'

'Do you think you would have, lass?'

'I hate to think so, but . . . well, we might have. As Lyden had already, that same evening, attacked Jane Watkins and left her unconscious in the crypt with her coat on fire. We're trying to persuade the CPS to go for attempted murder on that, by the way, but I don't suppose they will. Tell me your feelings on Sayer, Mr Owen.'

'Headbanger.'

'Meaning an amateur, a hanger-on.'

'If he possessed this tape, he might have been more than that – or not. Did he have a computer? Was he on the Internet?'

'He was, come to think of it.'

'You can dredge all kinds of dirt off the Net. If we assume he did know it was Mick Hunter on that tape, he might've tried a bit of blackmail. And Hunter sees the tape . . . or happen he's seen it before. He knows it looks bugger-all like him now, so he's not worried about the tape, but he doesn't like the idea of this lad Sayer walking round spreading bad rumours. Aye, he might well've bopped him over the head and dragged him down to the Wye. Cool as you like, popped him in a boat – I bet he had a boat, didn't he, athletic bugger like him wi' a river at the bottom of the garden. Then rowed him downstream. Who in a million years would ever look towards the Bishop's Palace . . .?'

'I don't think Hunter was even supposed to be here that night,' Merrily said. 'Out of town, as I recall.'

Huw snorted.

There was a long silence. Merrily looked at Lol,

remembering she hadn't been all that convinced when he'd first told her about Katherine Moon. And yet Lol himself had actually underestimated the full extent of it. They both needed a long walk – somewhere you could feel you weren't looking through a dirty spiderweb.

'There isn't a shred of evidence for any of this, Mr Owen, is there?' said Annie Howe.

'We're none of us coppers, lass. Just poor clergy and a lad wi' a guitar.'

'As for the other stuff: the ley-lines, the sacrifice of crows, the alleged *presence* in the Cathedral . . .' Howe pushed her notepad away. 'I don't want to know about *any* of it. I don't know how you people can pretend to . . . to do your job at all. To me, it's a complete fantasy world.'

Lol said, 'Have you talked to James Lyden?'

'I have *tried* to talk to James Lyden. He blames the girl – Rowenna Napier. We found her car, by the way – at the car park at the Severn Bridge motorway services. We've circulated a description. Her family seems to have given up on her. Lyden still thinks she's called Melissa, and that she lived with her now late foster-parents, with whom he'd spent many an interesting hour at their farmhouse on Dinedor Hill.'

'She seems to have used a number of identities,' Merrily said.

'But, in the end, just one,' said Huw.

Howe looked at him.

'The archetypal Scarlet Woman, lass. The temptress.'

Merrily thought, *What's he saying?* It was true that everything about Rowenna disturbed her: preying like a succubus on the Salisbury clergy, obviously dominating her own family – why *had* Mrs Straker suddenly clammed up? – and pulling off that insidiously effective psychic attack with the dregs of Denzil Joy. Rowenna was terribly dangerous – and still out there.

'She certainly seems to have acquired a considerable amount of money,' Howe said.

'For services rendered,' Huw told her.

'Certainly the basis for a few questions when we do find her. And I *do* want to find that girl – and Michael Hunter – before someone at Division decides to take this case out of my hands. Which is why I'm talking to . . . to people like you. Ms Watkins, when you suggested to Hunter that he knew something about the death of Paul Sayer . . .?'

'I'm sorry. I chose that moment to try and get away. Paul Sayer was never mentioned again.'

'But you raised it with him purely because your secretary told you she recognized Sayer from one of my photographs, yes?'

'It was the day you came into the Deliverance office. She recognized Sayer as a man who had actually come into the office asking for the Bishop – making Mick angry in a way Sophie says she'd never seen before – in a way that seemed to her . . . unepiscopal. Sophie's very discreet and very loyal, but also very observant.'

'This was not on the night he died, however.'

'No. A couple of days earlier.'

'Hold on.' Howe picked up a phone. 'Douglas, could somebody bring in Mrs Sophie Hill from the Bishop's office? . . . No, *now* . . . Thank you.'

'What you have to understand about Sophie,' said Merrily, 'is that the Cathedral is her life. She worried about this thing for days. She kept half-approaching me and then backing off.'

'Sure,' Howe said. 'Damn it, I think I'm going to have some divers in the Wye again.'

Huw slid from her desk. 'For Hunter?'

'What do you think?'

'Unlikely. He moves fast, that lad, in his jogging gear.'

Merrily closed her eyes for a moment, trying to remember

which way Hunter had gone after the stone pot had made
such a gloriously jagged, noisy hole in ancient glass. He'd
stared at her for a moment, then she'd turned and run away –
as lights were coming on everywhere, a verger and a policeman thrusting out of the door.

'And Hunter has friends,' Huw said. 'More friends than
even he knows. Friends in dark places.'

FIFTY-FIVE

Location Classified

They sat amongst the stones and they lit a candle for Tommy Canty.

Huw held the candle over each disfigured knight in turn, making a blessing for each. Merrily wondered if it had been the Bishop himself who had taken away the single knight and then brought it back, making sure that the tomb was still lying in pieces for the time of the Boy Bishop ceremony.

They would probably never know. Huw was convinced Mick Hunter would now be abroad. Italy, he thought; there were a number of dark sanctuaries in Italy. *How did he know that?*

So many questions.

DS Franny Bliss had been summoned back to St Cosmas and St Damien after reports from the two ornithologist ladies that a couple of people had been seen acting suspiciously close to the church, which the ladies apparently had been virtually staking out ever since. As a result, Craig the crow-catcher was in the cells, now suspected of greater involvement in the desecration than previously thought.

So, once again last night, simultaneous action along the Dinedor Line – with the Cathedral in the middle. Jane had seen Rowenna making a call on her mobile phone – perhaps to the Purefoys – as the Boy Bishop was about to be installed.

And then, coincidentally or not, a power failure. Its cause had still not been established.

Lol was convinced that, this time, the Purefoys – always assuming they were controlling the assault, which was by no means certain – believed they were using the very spirit, the element, the essence of Katherine Moon to try to awaken something agressively pre-Christian. They *believed* it, so at some level it was happening? And what form had their ritual – over by the time Lol arrived – actually taken? This all needed thinking about. Perhaps Merrily would be compelled to consult (Oh God!) Miss Athena White.

'But they were right, weren't they, lass?' Huw was stroking a stone.

'Mm?'

'The demon manifested in clerical clothing?'

'Yes, I suppose it did.'

And where was it now? Where was the *squatter*? Did it die with Dobbs? Did it flee with Mick? Was it over?

'Over?' Huw laughed a lot. 'The oldest war in the world, over? I'll tell you what, though . . .' He grew sober. 'We're up against it now. The Church is on its knees now, and the more we get weakened by public apathy, the more they'll put the boot in.'

'Jane thinks there's a new spirituality on the rise, replacing organized worship.'

'With all respect to the lass,' Huw said, 'it's people like Jane who'll turn religion into a minority sport.'

'She sees it more in terms of a period of cataclysmic psychic upheaval.'

'Could be,' Huw said. 'But if that happens, they'll still need somebody to police it. And, all the time, we're going to have folk like your Inspector Howe dismissing us as loonies. We're going to have battles with psychologists and social workers. We're going to be attacked by fellers like that Dick

Lyden, who thinks Dobbs was persecuting his poor mal-adjusted son. And, naturally, we're always going to be regarded with suspicion within the Church itself.'

Merrily stood up and dusted her knees. 'Hunter wanted me to draft a paper on New Deliverance. He suggested this would be an approach acceptable to psychologists and social workers.'

'For New Deliverance, read Soft Deliverance,' Huw said.

'I suppose that's right.'

'Happen that was going to be one of Mick's principal contributions: pioneer of Soft Deliverance. On the surface, decently liberal – exorcism by committee – but, underneath, the gradual dismantling of the final human barrier against satanic evil.'

Merrily shook her head, dubious, bewildered.

'Stick with it, lass,' Huw said. 'You've come too far now.'

'I don't know. The new bishop may not want me.'

'There's that,' Huw said.

'Anyway, there's a lot to think about. Lol and I are going to drive up into the Malverns, or somewhere – to do some walking and talking. He's very confused and spooked, after his showdown with the Purefoys. It's all going round in his head; he's realizing how close he came to winding up as dead as they are, and he's thinking: *What is this about?*'

'I gather that lad Denny Moon died this morning.'

'Yes.' She didn't want to talk about what Lol had heard from a porter in the Accident and Emergency unit at the General.

'Poor bugger. Always some casualties, Merrily, luv. Always.'

The porter said that, a few seconds after Denny was pronounced dead, a woman patient who'd been brought in after falling down some steps had begun to scream, and the nurses had had to open a window to let out a large black bird.

Huw was saying, 'Incidentally, I don't know who the

Purefoys have left their place to, and I don't like to think. But I reckon it could do with some attention smartish if we don't want yet more hassle.'

She shook her head. 'I don't think I could.'

Huw said, 'Oh, aye, I think you could.'

'You were the one who tried to talk me out of this whole thing!'

'That were because there was no tradition *then*,' Huw said. 'I think you've started one. Too late to back out now. You know what I'd do?'

'What?'

'Bugger the Malverns, they'll not go away. Take the lad up to Dinedor and do a little service of restitution for the spirit of this Katherine Moon. And for her brother. And their parents. See what happens.'

'I dread to think.'

'Don't dread,' said Huw. 'Second Law of Deliverance: *never* dread. Don't do it in the barn; it might be dangerous in there – I mean falling masonry and that. Go to the tip of the owd ramparts, and look out down the line, through All Saints and *this* place, to St Cosmas and St Damien.'

'Will you come?'

'I will not. It's not my patch.'

'What about the major exorcism? Who do we consult?'

'I think . . .' Huw looked up at the enormous stained-glass window, suddenly aglow with unexpected winter sunshine. 'I think we can leave it alone. Stand back, lass.'

He began to lug one of the stone panels of the Cantilupe tomb to one side, revealing a bundle of white and gold cloth about the size of a tobacco pouch. He bent down and gathered it up.

Merrily leaned over his shoulder. 'What on earth have you got there, Huw?'

'Picked it up before I fetched Dobbs from the hospital.

Planted it here before the service – with all due ceremony, naturally – so it was there throughout.'

He unrolled the cloth. There was a fragment of what looked at first like brick: dark red-brown, and brittle.

'Holy relics, lass.' Huw said. 'The undying power of holy relics.'

Dark red.

'Oh, my God,' Merrily said. 'His bones were supposed to have bled, weren't they?'

'Bit of the skull, apparently. Borrowed it from some monks. Location classified.'

'God.' She put out a finger.

'Aye, go on, lass. It's all right. You wouldn't have got within ten yards of the bugger when he were alive, mind, but there you go. Times change.'

He let her touch the piece of bone, and then rolled it up in its cloth again and slipped it into an inside pocket of his blue canvas jacket, next to his heart.

'Come on, then, Tommy,' he said.

Closing Credits

It's always difficult setting a novel in real locations without appearing to implicate real people ... which is why I've always avoided meeting the Bishop of Hereford.

However, the book would have been impossible without invaluable background information from the current Hereford Deliverance minister, who prefers, like Merrily, to keep a low profile; from the Director of the Hereford Cathedral Perpetual Trust, Sue Embrey, who provided crucial information on the Cathedral and the tomb of Thomas Cantilupe and was always really helpful and encouraging; from Ron Shoesmith, the archaeologist overseeing last year's renovation of the Canty tomb; from Richard Powell, of Capps and Capps, the mason who performed the actual renovation (without losing any bits) and from Brian Chave, who showed me Merrily's office and Mick's lair.

For information on Dinedor Hill and Cathedral-related hauntings, thanks to Hereford journalists Nicola Goodwin and George Children (whose excellent book, *Prehistoric Sites of Herefordshire*, co-written with George Nash, is published by Logaston Press).

Also thanks to Nick Whitehead, Andrew Hewson, Jill Dibbling, Penny Arnold and, of course, Pam Baker for the awful story of The Real Denzil Joy (oh, yes, there are some nurses who still have nightmares . . .). And Mark Owen thought it was time he got a mention, so here it is.

Finally, at the production end . . . mega thanks, as Jane would say, to my wife, Carol, who combined a massive, wide-ranging and detailed four-week professional (if unpaid) edit with some absolutely vital plot-surgery, and to Peter Lavery for hyper-sensitive fine-tuning of a quality you don't often get from publishers with the industry in the state it's in, but let's not go into all *that* . . . (Now, wasn't that a nice *long* sentence?)

A CROWN
OF LIGHTS

Part One

Goddess worshippers ... are particularly concerned with creativity, intuition, compassion, beauty and cooperation. They see nature as the outward and visible expression of the divine, through which the goddess may be contacted. They have therefore more to do with ecology and conservationism than with orgies and are often gentle worshippers of the good in nature.

Deliverance (ed. Michael Perry)
The Christian Deliverance Study Group

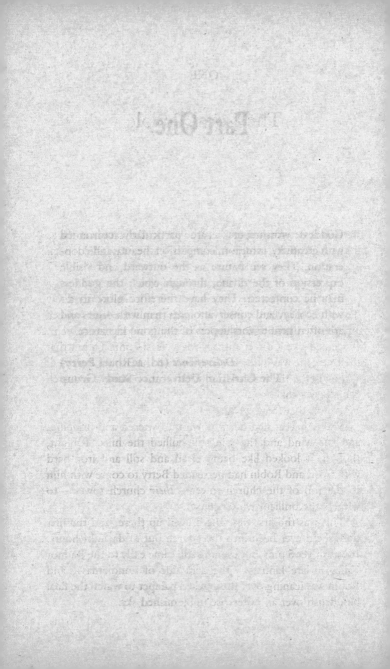

ONE

The Local People

Betty was determined to keep the lid on the cauldron for as long as possible, which might just – the way she'd been feeling lately – mean for ever.

The arrival of the old box was no help.

It turned up on the back step at St Michael's only a few days after they had moved into the farmhouse and a week after Betty turned twenty-seven. It wasn't her kind of present. It seemed like a direct threat – or at least confirmation that their new life was unlikely to be the idyll that Robin expected.

For Betty, the first inkling of this – if you could call such experiences inklings – had already occurred only minutes before on that same weird evening.

The new year had been blown in, battered and dripping, and the wind and the rain still bullied the hills. Tonight, though, it looked like being clean and still and iron-hard with frost, and Robin had persuaded Betty to come with him to the top of the church tower – *their* church tower – to witness the brilliant winter sunset.

This was the first time she'd been up there, and the first time she'd ever been into the church out of daylight hours. It wasn't yet 5 p.m. but evening still came early to the Radnor Valley in late January – the dark side of Candlemas – and Robin was leaning over the cracked parapet to watch the final bloodrush over an otherwise unblemished sky.

'I guess what we oughta do,' he murmured playfully, 'is shake down that old moon.'

The Forest was laid out before them: darkening storybook hills, bearded with bracken. There were few trees – misleadingly, it had been named forest in the medieval sense of a place for hunting. Betty wondered how much of *that* still went on: the lamping of hares, the baiting of badgers. Maybe some night Robin would be standing up here and would see a party of silent men with guns and dogs. And then the shit would fly.

'So, uh, how would you . . .' Robin straightened up, slapping moss from his hands, '. . . how would you feel about that?'

'You mean now, don't you?' With both hands, Betty pushed back her wild, blonde hair. She backed away from the edge, which had got her thinking about the death of Major Wilshire. Down below, about six feet out from the base of the tower, two flat tombstones had been exposed beneath a bush blasted back by the gales. That was probably where he'd fallen. She shivered. 'You actually mean *out here*?'

He shrugged. 'Why not?' He wore his orange fleece and his ludicrous flattened fez-thing with tiny mirrors around the side. The way Betty saw it, Robin Thorogood, having grown up in America, had yet to develop a functioning sense of the absurd.

'Why *not*?' Betty didn't remember exactly when 'shaking down the moon' had become his personal euphemism for sex, but she didn't altogether care for the term. 'Because this is, you know, January?'

'We could bring up blankets.' Robin did his abandoned puppy face.

Which no longer worked on Betty. 'Mother of God, I bet it's not even safe! Look at the floor . . . the walls! We wind

4

up down in the bloody belfry, in a cloud of plaster dust, with multiple fractures, what happens *then*?'

'Aw, come *on*. It's been here for six . . . *eight* centuries. Just because—'

'And probably falling apart for most of the last hundred years!'

Betty gripped one of the battlements, then let go quickly in alarm, convinced for a second that a lump of mortar, or whatever medieval mixture those old masons used, was actually moving underneath it. The entire tower could be crumbling, for all they knew; their funds had run to only a cursory survey by a local bloke who'd said, 'Oh, just make sure it doesn't fall down on anybody, and you'll be all right.' They ought to bring in a reliable builder to give the place a going-over before they contemplated even having a picnic up here. If they could ever afford a builder, which seemed unlikely.

Robin stood warrior-like, with his back to the fallen sun, and she knew that in his mind he was wearing animal skins and there was a short, thick blade at his hip. Very like the figure dominating his painting-in-progress: Lord Madoc the intergalactic Celt, hero of Kirk Blackmore's *Sword of Twilight*. 700 pages of total bollocks, but it was misty cover designs for the likes of Blackmore that were going to have to meet the mortgage premiums until Betty dared come out locally as a herbalist and healer, or whatever was socially acceptable.

'Just I had a sensation of what it would be like afterwards,' the great visionary artist burbled on, unabashed, 'lying here on our backs, watching the swirl of the cosmos, from our own—'

'Whereas I'm getting a real sensation of watching the swirl of tomato soup with croutons.' Betty moved to the steps, took hold of the oily rope, feeling about with a trainered foot for the top step. 'Come on. We'll have years to do all that.'

Her words lingered in a void as hollow as these ruins. Betty could not lose the feeling that this time next year they would not even be here.

'You know your trouble?' Robin suddenly yelled. 'You're becoming sensible before your time.'

'What?' She spun at him, though knowing that he'd spoken without thinking . . . that it was just petulance . . . that she should let it go.

'Well . . .' He looked uneasy. 'You know . . .'

'No, I don't.'

'OK, OK . . .' Making placatory patting gestures with his hands, too late. 'Wrong word, maybe.'

'No, you've said it now. In normal life we're not supposed to be sensible because we're living *the fantasy*. Like we're really not supposed to bother about everyday stuff like falling to our deaths down these bloody crumbling steps, because—'

'There's a guy over there,' Robin said. 'In the field down by the creek.'

'It's a brook.' Betty paused on the top step.

'He's looking up.' Robin moved back to the rim of the tower. 'He's carrying something.'

'A spear of light, perhaps?' Betty said sarcastically. 'A glowing trident?'

'A bag, I think. A carrier bag. No, he's not in the field. I believe he's on the footway.'

'Which, of course, is a public footpath – which makes him entitled to be there.'

'Naw, he's checking us out.' The sunset made unearthly jewels out of the tiny round mirrors on Robin's fez. 'Hey!' he shouted down. 'Can I help you?'

'Stop it!' Sometimes Betty felt she was a lot older than Robin, instead of two years younger. Whole lifetimes older.

'He went away.'

'Of course he did. He went home to warm his bum by a roaring fire of dry, seasoned hardwood logs.'

'You're gonna throw that one at me all night, I can tell.'

'Probably. While we're sitting with our coats on in front of a lukewarm stove full of sizzling green pine.'

'Yeah, yeah, the wood guy ripped me off. He won't do it again.'

'Dead right he won't. First rule of country living: show them, from the very start, that you're not an urban innocent.'

Robin followed her down the narrow, broken stone steps. 'While being careful not to antagonize them, right?'

Betty stopped on the spiral, looked back up over her shoulder. It was too dark to see his face.

'Sooner or later,' she said, 'there *is* going to be antagonism – from some of them at least. It's a phase we're going to have to go through and come out the other side with some kind of mutual respect. This is not Islington. This is not even Shrewsbury. In Radnorshire, the wheels of change would grind exceeding slow, if they'd ever got around to inventing the wheel.'

'So what you're saying, making converts could take time?'

'We won't live that long. Tolerance is what we aspire to: the ultimate prize.'

'Jeez, you're soooo— *Oh, shit—*'

Betty whirled round. He'd stumbled on a loose piece of masonry, was hanging on to the hand-rope.

'You OK?'

'Third-degree rope burn, is all. I imagine the flesh will grow back within only weeks.'

She thought of Major Wilshire again and felt unsettled.

'I was born just twenty miles from here,' she said soberly. 'People *don't* change much in rural areas. I don't want to cause offence, and I don't think we need to.'

'*You* changed.'

'It's not the same. I'm not *from* yere, as they say.' Betty stepped out of the tower doorway and onto the frozen mud of what she supposed had once been the chancel. 'My parents just happened to be working here when I was born. They were from Off. I am, essentially, from Off.'

'Off what?'

'That's what they say. It's their word. If you're an immigrant you're "from Off". I'd forgotten that. I was not quite eleven when we left there. And then we were in Yorkshire, and Yorkshire flattens all the traces.'

Curtains of cold red light hung from the heavens into the roofless nave. When Robin emerged from the tower entrance, she took his cold hand in her even colder ones.

'Sorry to be a frigid bitch. It's been a heavy, heavy day.'

The church was mournful around her. It was like a huge, blackened sheep skeleton, with its ribs opened out. Incongruously, it actually came with the house. Robin had been ecstatic. For him, it had been *the* deciding factor.

Betty let go of Robin's hand. She was now facing where the altar must have been – the English side. And it was here, on this frigid January evening, that she had the flash.

A shivering sense of someone at prayer – a man in a long black garment, stained. His face unshaven, glowing with sweat and an unambiguous vivid fear. He'd discovered or identified or been told something he couldn't live with. In an instant, Betty felt she was suffocating in a miasma of body odour and anguish.

No! She hauled in a cold breath, pulling off her woollen hat, shaking out her sheaf of blond hair. *Go away. Don't want you.*

Cold. Damp. Nothing else. Shook herself like a wet dog. *Gone.*

8

This was how it happened. Always without warning, rarely even a change in the temperature.

'And it's not officially a church any more,' Robin was reminding her – he hadn't, of course, sensed a thing. 'So this is not about causing offence. Long as we don't knock it down, we can do what we like here. This is *so cool*. We get to reclaim an old, pagan sacred place!'

And Betty thought in cold dismay, What kind of sacred is this? But what she actually said, surprised at her own calmness, was, 'I just think we have to take it slowly. I know the place is decommissioned, but there're bound to be local people whose families worshipped here for centuries. And whose grandparents got married here and . . . and buried, of course.'

There were still about a dozen gravestones and tombs visible around the church and, although all the remains were supposed to have been taken away and reinterred after the diocese dumped the building itself, Betty knew that when they started to garden here they'd inevitably unearth bones.

'And maybe,' Robin said slyly, 'just maybe . . . there are people whose distant ancestors worshipped here *before* there was a Christian church.'

'You're pushing it there.'

'I like pushing it.'

'Yeah,' Betty agreed bitterly.

They moved out of the ruined church and across the winter-hard field and then over the yard to the back of the house. She'd left a light on in the hall. It was the only light they could see anywhere – although if they walked around to the front garden, they would find the meagre twinklings of the village of Old Hindwell dotted throughout the high, bare hedge.

She could hear the rushing of the Hindwell Brook, which almost islanded this place when, like now, it was swollen.

There'd been weeks of hard rain, while they'd been making regular trips back and forth from their Shrewsbury flat in Robin's cousin's van, bringing all the books and stuff and wondering if they were doing the right thing.

Or at least Betty had. Robin had been obsessed from the moment he saw the ruined church and the old yew trees around it in a vague circle and the mighty Burfa Camp in the background and the enigmatic Four Stones less than a couple of miles away. And when he'd heard of the recent archaeological discoveries – the indications of a ritual palisade believed to be the second largest of its kind in Europe – it had blown him clean away. From then on, he *needed* to live here.

'There you go.' He bent down to the back doorstep. 'What'd I tell ya?' He lifted up something whitish.

'What's that?'

'It is a carrier bag – Tesco, looks like. The individual by the river had one with him. I'm guessing this is it.'

'He left it on our step?'

'House-warming present, maybe? It's kinda heavy.'

'Put it down,' Betty said quietly.

'Huh?'

'I'm serious. Put it back on the step, and go inside, put on the lights.'

'Jeeeeeeez!' Robin tossed back his head and howled at the newborn moon. 'I do not understand you! One minute I'm over-reacting – which, OK, I do, I overreact sometimes, I confess – and this is some harmless old guy making his weary way home to his humble fireside . . . and the next, he's like dumping ten pounds of Semtex or some shit—'

'Just put it down, Robin.'

Exasperated, Robin let the bag fall. It clumped solidly on the stone. Robin unlocked the back door.

Betty waited for him to enter first. She wouldn't touch the bag.

It was knotted at the top. She watched Robin wrench it open. A sheet of folded notepaper fell out. He spread it out on the table and she read the type over his shoulder.

Dear Mr and Mrs Thorogood,

In the course of renovation work by the previous occupants of your house, this receptacle was found in a cavity in the wall beside the fireplace. The previous occupants preferred not to keep it and gave it away. It has been suggested you may wish to restore it to its proper place.

With all good wishes,
The Local People

' "The Local People"?'

Robin let the typewritten note flutter to the tabletop. '*All* of them? The entire population of Old Hindwell got together to present the newcomers with a wooden box with . . .' He lifted the hinged lid, '. . . some paper in it.'

The box was of oak. It didn't look all that old. Maybe a century, Betty thought. It was the size of a pencil box she'd had as a kid – narrow, coffin-shaped. You could probably fit it in the space left by a single extracted brick.

She was glad there was only paper in there, not . . . well, bones or something. She'd never seriously thought of Semtex, only bones. Why would she think that? She found she was shivering slightly, so kept her red ski jacket on.

Robin was excited, naturally: a mysterious wooden box left by a shadowy stranger, a cryptic note . . . major, *major* turn-on for him. She knew that within the next hour or so he'd have found the original hiding place of that box, if he had to pull the entire fireplace to pieces. He'd taken off his fleece and his mirrored fez. The warrior on the battlements had been replaced by the big schoolboy innocent.

He flicked on all the kitchen lights – just dangling bulbs, as yet, which made the room look even starker than in daylight. They hadn't done anything with this room so far. There was a Belfast sink and a cranky old Rayburn and, under the window, their pine dining table and chairs from the flat. The table was much too small for this kitchen; up against the wall, under a window full of the day's end, it looked like . . . well, an altar. For which this was not the correct place – and anyway, Betty was not yet sure she wanted an altar in the house. Part of the reason for finding a rural hideaway was to consider her own future, which – soon she'd have to confess to Robin – might not involve the Craft.

'The paper looks old,' Robin said. 'Well . . . the ink went brown.'

'Gosh, Rob, that must date it back to . . . oh, arguably pre-1980.'

He gave her one of those looks which said: Why have you no basic romance in you any more?

Which wasn't true. She simply felt you should distinguish between true insight and passing impressions, between fleeting sensations and real feelings.

The basic feeling she had – especially since her sense of the praying man in the church – was one of severe unease. She would rather the box had not been delivered. She wished she didn't have to know what was inside it.

Robin put the paper, still folded, on the table and just looked at it, not touching. Experiencing the moment, the *here*ness, the *now*ness.

And the disapproval of his lady.

All right, he'd happily concede that he loved all of this:

the textures of twilight, those cuspy, numinous nearnesses. He'd agree that he didn't like things to be over-bright and clear cut; that he wanted a foot in two countries – to feel obliquely linked to the *old* worlds.

And what was so wrong with that? He looked at the wild and golden lady who should be Rhiannon or Artemis or Titania but insisted on being called the ultimately prosaic *Betty* (this perverse need to appear ordinary). *She* knew what he needed – that he didn't want too many mysteries explained, didn't care to *know* precisely what ghosts were. Nor did he want the parallel world of faerie all mapped out like the London Underground. It was the gossamer trappings and wrappings that had given him a profession and a good living. He was Robin Thorogood: illustrator, seducer of souls, guardian of the softly lit doorways.

The box, then . . . Well, sure, the box *had* been more interesting unopened. Unless the paper inside was a treasure map.

He pushed it toward Betty. '*You* wanna check this out?'

She shook her head. She wouldn't go near it. Robin rolled his eyes and picked up the paper. It fell open like a fan.

'Well, it's handwritten.' He spread it flat on the tabletop.

'Don't count on it,' Betty said. 'You can fake all kinds of stuff with computers and scanners and paintboxes. *You* do it all the time.'

'OK, so it's a scam. Kirk Blackmore rigged it.'

'If it was Kirk Blackmore,' Betty said, 'the box would have ludicrous runes carved all over it and when you opened it, there'd be clouds of dry ice.'

'I guess. Oh *no*.'

'What's up?'

'It's some goddamn religious crap. Like the Jehovah's Witnesses or one of those chain letters?'

'OK, let me see.' Betty came round and peered reluctantly

at the browned ink. ' "In the name of the Father, Son and Holy Ghost, amen, amen, amen . . ." Amen three times.'

'Dogmatic.'

'Hmmm.' Betty read on in silence, not touching the paper. She was standing directly under one of the dangling light-bulbs, so her hair was like a winter harvest. Robin loved that her hair seemed to have life of its own.

When she stepped away, she swallowed.

He said hoarsely, 'What?'

'Read.'

'Poison pen?'

She shook her head and walked away toward the rumbling old Rayburn stove.

Robin bent over the document. Some of it was in Latin, which he couldn't understand. But there was a row of symbols, which excited him at once.

$$ x \mathcal{I} \, 4 \, x \, \dot{\ominus} \, 4 \, x \, q \, 4 \, \triangle \, \dot{\ominus} \, \mathcal{I} \, \triangle \, 4 \, q $$

Underneath, the words in English began. Some of them he couldn't figure out. The meaning, however, was plain.

In the name of the Father Son and Holy Ghost Amen
Amen Amen . . .
    O Lord, Jesus Christ Saviour Salvator I beseech the
salvation of all who dwell within from witchcraft and
from the power of all evil men or women or spirits or
wizards or hardness of heart Amen Amen Amen . . .
Dei nunce . . . Amen Amen Amen Amen Amen.
    By Jehovah, Jehovah and by the Ineffable Names
17317 . . . Lord Jehovah . . . and so by the virtue of
these Names Holy Names may all grief and dolor and all
diseases depart from the dwellers herein and their cows

and their horses and their sheep and their pigs and
poultry without any molestation. By the power of our
Lord Jesus Christ Amen Amen . . . Elohim . . .
Emmanuel . . .

Finally my brethren be strong in the Lord and in the
power of His might that we may overcome all witches
spells and Inchantment or the power of Satan. Lord Jesus
deliver them this day – April, 1852.

Robin sat down. He tried to smile, for Betty's sake and
because, in one way, it was just so ironic.

But he couldn't manage a smile; he'd have to work on
that. Because this *was* a joke, wasn't it? It *could* actually be
from Kirk Blackmore or one of the other authors, or Al
Delaney, the art director at Talisman. They all knew he was
moving house, and the new address: St Michael's Farm, Old
Hindwell, Radnorshire.

But this hadn't arrived in the mail. And also, as Betty had
pointed out, if it had been from any of those guys it would
have been a whole lot more extreme – creepier, more Gothic,
less homespun. And dated much further back than 1852.

No, it was more likely to be from those it said it was from.

The Local People – whatever that meant.

Truth was they hadn't yet encountered any *local* local
people, outside of the wood guy and Greg Starkey, the
London-born landlord at the pub where they used to lunch
when they were bringing stuff to the farm, and whose wife
had come on to Robin one time.

Betty had her back to the Rayburn for warmth and
comfort. Robin moved over to join her. He also, for that
moment, felt isolated and exposed.

'I don't get this,' he said. 'How could anyone here *possibly*
know about us?'

TWO

Livenight

There were four of them in the hospital cubicle: Gomer and Minnie, and Merrily Watkins . . . and death.

Death with a small 'd'. No angel tonight.

Merrily was anguished and furious at the suddenness of this occurrence, and the timing – Gomer and Minnie's wedding anniversary, their sixth.

Cheap, black joke. *Unworthy of You.*

'Indigestion . . .' Gomer was squeezing his flat cap with both hands, as if wringing out a wet sponge, and staring in disbelief at the tubes and the monitor with that ominous wavy white line from a thousand overstressed hospital dramas. 'It's just indigestion, her says. Like, if she said it enough times that's what it'd be, see? Always works, my Min reckons. You *tells* the old body what's wrong, you don't take no shit – pardon me, vicar.'

The grey-curtained cubicle was attached to Intensive Care. Minnie's eyes were closed, her breathing hollow and some-how detached. Merrily had heard breathing like this before, and it made her mouth go dry with trepidation.

'It's rather a bad one,' the ward sister had murmured. *'You need to prepare him.'*

'Let's go for a walk.' Merrily plucked at the sleeve of Gomer's multi-patched tweed jacket.

She thought he glanced at her reproachfully as they left

the room – as though she had the power to intercede with God, call in a favour. And then, from out in the main ward, he looked back once at Minnie, and his expression made Merrily blink and turn away.

Gomer and Minnie: sixty-somethings when they got married, the Midlands widow and the little, wild Welsh-borderer. It was love, though Gomer would never have used the word. Equally, he'd never have given up the single life for mere companionship – he could get that from his JCB and his bulldozer.

He and Merrily walked out of the old county hospital and past the building site for a big new one – a mad place to put it, everyone was saying; there'd be next to no parking space except for consultants and administrators; even the nurses would have to hike all the way to the multi-storey at night. In pairs, presumably, with bricks in their bags.

Merrily felt angry at the crassness of everybody: the health authority and its inadequate bed quota, the city planners who seemed bent on gridlocking Hereford by 2005 – and God, for letting Minnie Parry succumb to a severe heart attack during the late afternoon of her sixth wedding anniversary.

It was probably the first time Gomer had ever phoned Merrily – their bungalow being only a few minutes' walk away. It had happened less than two hours ago, while Merrily was bending to light the fire in the vicarage sitting room, expecting Jane home soon. Gomer had already sent for an ambulance.

When Merrily arrived, Minnie was seated on the edge of the sofa, pale and sweating and breathless. *'Yow mustn't . . . go bothering about me, my duck, I've been through . . . worse than this.'* The TV guide lay next to her on a cushion. An iced sponge cake sat on a coffee table in front of the open fire. The fire was roaring with life. Two cups of tea had gone cold.

Merrily bit her lip, pushing her knuckles hard into the pockets of her coat – Jane's old school duffel, snatched from the newel post as Merrily was rushing out of the house.

They now crossed the bus station towards Commercial Road, where shops were closing for the night and most of the sky was a deep, blackening rust. Gomer's little round glasses were frantic with city light. He was urgently reminiscing, throwing up a wall of vivid memories against the encroaching dark – telling Merrily about the night he'd first courted Minnie while they were crunching through fields and woodland in his big JCB. Merrily wondered if he was fantasizing, because it was surely Minnie who'd forced Gomer's retirement from the plant hire business; she hated those diggers.

'. . . a few spare pounds on her, sure to be. Had the ole warning from the doc about that bloody collateral. But everybody gets that, isn't it?'

Gomer shuffled, panting, to a stop at the zebra crossing in Commercial Road. Merrily smiled faintly. 'Cholesterol. Yes, everybody gets that.'

Gomer snatched off his cap. His hair was standing up like a small white lavatory brush.

'Her's gonner die! Her's gonner bloody well snuff it on me!'

'Gomer, let's just keep praying.'

How trite did *that* sound? Merrily closed her eyes for a second and prayed also for credible words of comfort.

In the window of a nearby electrical shop, all the lights went out.

'Ar,' said Gomer dismally.

Through the hole-in-its-silencer roar of Eirion's departing car came the sound of the phone. Jane danced into Mum's grim scullery-office.

The light in here was meagre and cold, and a leafless climbing rose scraped at the small window like fingernails. But Jane was smiling, warm and light inside and, like, *up there*. Up there with the broken weathercock on the church steeple.

She had to sit down, a quivering in her chest. She remembered a tarot reader, called Angela, who had said to her, *'You will have two serious lovers before the age of twenty.'*

As she put out a hand for the phone, it stopped ringing. If Mum had gone out, why wasn't the answering machine on? Where *was* Mum? Jane switched on the desk lamp, to reveal a paperback New Testament beside a newspaper cutting about the rural drug trade. The sermon pad had scribbles and blobs and desperate doodles. But there was no note for her.

Jane shrugged then sat at the desk and conjured up Eirion. Who wasn't *conventionally* good-looking. Well, actually, he wasn't good-looking at all, in some lights, and kind of stocky. And yet . . . OK, it was the smile. You could get away with a lot if you had a good smile, but it was important to ration it. Bring it out too often and it became like totally inane and after a while it stopped reaching the eyes, which showed insincerity. Jane sat and replayed Eirion's smile in slow motion; it was a good one, it always *started* in the eyes.

Eirion? The name remained a problem. Basically, too much like Irene. Didn't the Welsh have some totally stupid names for men? Dilwyn – that was another. Welsh women's names, on the other hand, were cool: Angharad, Sian, Rhiannon.

He was certainly trying hard, though. Like, no way had he 'just happened to be passing' Jane's school at chucking-out time. He'd obviously slipped away early from the Cathedral School in Hereford – through some kind of upper-sixth privilege – and raced his ancient heap nine or ten miles to Moorfield High before the buses got in. Claiming he'd had to deliver an aunt's birthday present, and Ledwardine was on his way home. Total bullshit.

And the journey to Ledwardine . . . Eirion had really spun that out. Having to go slow, he said, because he didn't want the hole in his exhaust to get any bigger. In the end, the bus would've been quicker.

But then, as Jane was climbing out of his car outside the vicarage, he'd mumbled, 'Maybe I could call you sometime?'

Which, OK, Jane Austen could have scripted better.

'Yeah, OK,' she'd said, cool, understated. Managing to control the burgeoning grin until she'd made it almost to the side door of the vicarage and Eirion was driving away on his manky silencer.

The phone went again. Mum? Had to be. Jane grabbed at it.

'Ledwardine Vicarage, how may we help you? If you wish to book a wedding, press three. To pledge a ten-thousand-pound donation to the steeple fund, press six.'

'Is that the Reverend Watkins?'

Woman's voice, and not local. Not Sophie at the office. And not Mum being smart. Uh-oh.

'I'm afraid she's not available right now,' Jane said. 'I'm sorry.'

'When *will* she be available?'

The woman sounding a touch querulous, but nothing threatening: there was this deadly MOR computer music in the background, plus non-ecclesiastical office noise. Ten to one, some time-wasting double-glazing crap, or maybe the *Church Times* looking for next week's Page Three Clerical Temptress for dirty old canons to pin up in their vestries.

'I should try her secretary at the Bishpal tomorrow,' Jane said.

'I'm sorry?'

'The Bishop's Palace, in Hereford. If you ask for Sophie Hill . . .'

Most of the time it was a question of protecting Mum from herself. If you were a male vicar you could safely do lofty and remote – part of the tradition. But an uncooperative female priest was considered a snotty bitch.

'Look.' A bit ratty now, 'It *is* important.'

'Also important she doesn't die of some stress-related condition. I mean, like, important for me. Don't imagine *you'd* have to go off and live with your right-wing grandmother in Cheltenham. Who are you, anyway?'

Could almost hear the woman counting one . . . two . . . three . . . through gritted teeth.

'My name's Tania Beauman, from the *Livenight* television programme in Birmingham.'

Oh, hey! 'Seriously?'

'Seriously,' Tania Beauman said grimly.

Jane was, like, *horribly* impressed. Jane had seen *Livenight* four times. *Livenight* was such total crap and below the intelligence threshold of a cockroach, but compulsive viewing, oh yeah.

'*Livenight*?' Jane said.

'Correct.'

'Where you have the wife in the middle and the husband on one side and the toyboy lover on the other, and about three minutes to midnight one finally gets stirred up enough to call the other one a motherfucker, and then fights are breaking out in the audience, and the presenter looks really shocked although you know he's secretly delighted because it'll all be in the *Sun* again. That *Livenight*?'

'Yes,' Tania said tightly.

'You want her on the programme?'

'Yes, and as it involves next week's programme we don't have an awful lot of time to play with. Is she in?'

'No, but I'm Merrily Watkins's personal assistant, and I have to warn you she doesn't like to talk about the other stuff. Which is what this is about, right? The Rev. Spooky Watkins, from Deliverance?'

Tania didn't reply.

'I could do it, of course, if the money was OK. I know all her secrets. I'd be *very* good, and controversial. I'll call *anyone* a motherfucker.'

'Thank you very much,' Tania said drily. 'We will bear you in mind, when you turn twelve.'

'I'm sixteen!'

'Just tell her I called. Have a good night.'

Jane grinned. That was all Eirion's fault. Making her feel cool.

In the silence of the scullery, the phone went again.

'Jane?'

'Mum. Hey, guess wh—'

'Listen, flower,' Mum said, 'I've got bad news.'

THREE

Loved Like That

'So, like . . . how long will you be?'

'I just don't know, flower. We came here in Gomer's Land-Rover. It was all a bit of a rush.'

'She was never ill, was she?' Jane said. 'Like really *never.*' The kid's voice was suddenly high and hoarse. 'You can't count on anything, can you? Not even *you.*'

Merrily sighed. Everybody thought she could pull strings. Gomer and Minnie's bungalow had become like the kid's second home in the village, Minnie the closest she'd ever had to an adopted granny.

'Flower, I'll have to go. I'm on the pay phone in the corridor, and I've no more change. As soon as I get to know something . . .'

'She's not even all that old. I mean, sixty-something . . . what's that? Nobody these days—'

Jane broke off. Remembering, perhaps, how young her own father had been when his life was sliced off on the motorway that night. But that was different. His girlfriend was in the car, too, and the hand of fate was involved there, in Jane's view.

'Minnie's strong. She'll fight it,' Merrily said.

'She isn't going to win, though, is she? I can tell by your voice. Where's Gomer?'

'Gone back in, to be with her.'

'How's he taking it?'

'Well, you know Gomer. You wouldn't want him prowling around in your sickroom.'

Gomer, in retirement, groomed the churchyard, cleared the ditches, looked out for Merrily when Uncle Ted was doing devious, senior-churchwarden things behind her back. And dreamed of the old days – the great, rampaging days of Gomer Parry Plant Hire.

'He'll just smash the place up or something, if they let her die,' Jane concurred bleakly.

Meaning she herself would like to smash something up, possibly the church.

How many hours had they been here? Hospitals engendered their own time zones. Merrily hung up the phone and turned back into the ill-lit passage, teeming now: visiting hours. Once, she'd had a dream of purgatory, and it was like a big hospital, a brightly lit Brueghel kind of hospital, with all the punters helpless in operation gowns, and the staff scurrying around, feeding a central cauldron steaming with fear.

'Merrily?'

From a trio of nurses, one detached herself and came across.

'Eileen? I thought you were over at the other place.'

'You get moved around. We'll all end up in one place, anyway, if they ever finish building it, and won't that be a fockin' treat?' Eileen Cullen put out a forefinger, lifted Merrily's hair from her shoulder. 'You're not wearing your collar, Reverend. You finally dump the Auld Feller, or what?'

'We're still together,' Merrily said. 'And it's still hot.'

'Jesus, that's disgusting.'

'Actually, I had to leave home in a hurry.' Merrily spotted Gomer coming out of the ward, biting on an unlit cigarette, for comfort. 'I came with a friend. His wife's had a serious heart attack – unexpected. You won't say anything cynical, will you?'

'What's his name?' Sister Cullen was crop-haired and angular and claimed to have left Ulster to escape from 'bloody religion'.

'Gomer. Gomer Parry.'

'Well then, Mr Parry,' Cullen said briskly as Gomer came up, blinking dazedly behind his bottle glasses, 'you look to me to be in need of a cuppa – with a drop of something in there to take away the taste of machine tea, am I right?' She beckoned one of the nurses over. 'Kirsty, would you take Mr Parry to my office and make him a special tea? Stuff's in my desk, bottom drawer.'

Gomer glanced at Merrily. She moved to follow him, but Cullen put out a restraining hand. 'Not for you, Reverend. You've got your God to keep your spirits up. Spare me a minute?'

'A minute?'

'Pity you're out of the uniform . . . still, it's the inherent holiness that counts. All it is, we've got a poor feller in a state of some distress, and it'll take more than special tea to cope with him, you know what I'm saying.'

Merrily frowned, thinking, inevitably, of the first time she'd met Eileen Cullen, across town at Hereford General, which used to be a lunatic asylum and for one night had seemed in danger of reverting back.

'Ah no,' said Cullen, 'you only get one of those in a lifetime. This isn't even a patient. More like your man, Gomer, here – with the wife. And I don't know what side of the fence he's on, but I'd say he's very much a religious feller and would benefit from spiritual support.'

'For an atheist, you've got a lot of faith in priests.'

'No, I've got faith in *women* priests, which is not much at all to do with them being priests.'

'What would you have done if I hadn't been here?'

Cullen put her hands on her narrow hips. 'Well, y'*are* here, love, so where's the point in debating that one?'

The corridor had cracked walls and dim economy lighting.

'I'd be truly happy about leaving this dump behind,' Cullen said, 'if I didn't feel sure the bloody suits were building us a whole new nightmare.'

'What's his name, this bloke?'

'Mr Weal.'

'First name?'

'We don't know. He's not a man who's particularly forth-coming.'

'Terrific. He seen Paul Hutton?' The hospital chaplain.

'Maybe.' Cullen shrugged. 'I don't know. But you're on the spot and he isn't. What I thought was . . . you could perhaps say a prayer or two. He's Welsh, by the way.'

'What's that got to do with the price of eggs?'

'Well, he might be Chapel or something. They've got their own ways. You'll need to play it by ear on that.'

'You mean in case he refuses to speak to me in English?'

'Not Welsh like *that*. He's from Radnorshire. About half a mile over the border, if that.'

'Gosh. Almost normal, then.'

'Hmm.' Cullen smiled. Merrily followed her into a better lit area with compact, four-bed wards on either side, mainly elderly women in them. A small boy shuffled in a doorway, looking bored and aggressively crunching crisps.

'So what's the matter with Mrs Weal?'

'Stroke.'

'Bad one?'

'You might say that. Oh, and when you've said a wee prayer with him you could take him for a coffee.'

'Eileen—'

'It's surely the Christian thing to do,' Cullen said lightly.

They came to the end of the passage, where there was a closed door on their right. Cullen pushed it open and stepped back. She didn't come in with Merrily.

She was out of there fast, pulling the door shut behind her. She leaned against the partition wall. Her lips made the words, nothing audible came out.

She's dead.

Cullen shrugged. 'Seen one before, have you not?'

'You could've explained.'

'Could've sworn I did. Sorry.'

'And the rest of it?'

'Ah.'

'Quite.' What she'd seen replayed itself in blurred images, like a robbery captured on a security video: the bedclothes turned down, the white cotton nightdress slipped from the shoulders of the corpse. The man beside the bed, leaning over his wife – heavy like a bear, some ungainly predator. He hadn't turned around as Merrily entered, nor when she backed out.

She moved quickly to shake off the shock, pulling Eileen Cullen a few yards down the passage. 'What in God's name was he *doing*?'

'Ah, well,' Cullen said. 'Would he have been cleaning her up, now?'

'On account of the NHS can't afford to pay people to take care of that sort of thing any more?'

Cullen tutted on seeing a tea trolley abandoned in the middle of the corridor.

'Yes?' Merrily said.

Cullen pushed the trolley tidily against a wall.

'There now,' she said. 'Well, the situation, Merrily, is that he's been doing that kind of thing for her ever since she came in, three days ago. Wouldn't let anyone else attend to her if he was around – and he's been around most of the time. He asks for a bowl and a cloth and he washes her. Very tenderly. Reverently, you might say.'

'I saw.'

'And then he'll wash himself: his face, his hands, in the same water. It looked awful touching at first. He'd also insist on trying to feed her, when it was still thought she might eat. And he'd be feeding himself the same food, like you do with babies, to encourage her.'

'How long's she been dead?'

'Half an hour, give or take. She was a bit young for a stroke, plainly, and he naturally couldn't come to terms with that. At his age, he was probably convinced she'd outlive him by a fair margin. But there you go: overattentive, overpossessive, what you will. And now maybe he can't accept she's actually dead.'

'I dunno. It looked . . . ritualistic almost, like an act of worship. Or did I imagine that?' Merrily instinctively felt in her bag for her cigarettes before remembering where she was. 'Eileen, what do you want to happen here?'

Cullen folded her arms. 'Well, on the practical side . . .'

'Which is all you're concerned about, naturally.'

'Absolutely. On the practical side, goes without saying we need the bed. So we need to get her down to the mortuary soon, and that means persuading your man out of there first. He'd stay with her all night, if we let him. The other night an auxiliary came in and found him lying right there on the floor beside the bed, fast asleep in his overcoat, for heaven's sake.'

'God.' Merrily pushed her hands deep down into the pockets of Jane's duffel. 'To be loved like that.' Not altogether sure what she meant.

Cullen sniffed. 'So you'll go back in and talk to him?

Mumble a wee prayer or two? Apply a touch of Christian tenderness? And then – employing the tact and humanity for which you're renowned, and which we're not gonna have time for – just get him the fock out of there, yeah?'

'I don't know. If it's all helping him deal with his grief . . .'

'You're wimping out, right? Fair enough, no problem.'

Merrily put down her bag on the trolley. 'Just keep an eye on that.'

Well, she didn't know too much about rigor mortis, but she thought that soon it wouldn't be very easy to do what was so obviously needed.

'We should close her eyes,' Merrily said, 'don't you think?'

She put out a hesitant hand towards Mrs Weal, thumb and forefinger spread. The times she'd done this before were always in the moments right after death, when there was still that light-smoke sense of a departing spirit. But, oh God, what if the woman's eyelids were frozen fast?

'You will,' Mr Weal said slowly, 'leave her alone.'

Merrily froze. He was standing sentry-stiff. A very big man in every physical sense. His face was broad, and he had a ridged Roman nose and big cheeks, reddened by broken veins – a farmer's face. His greying hair was strong and pushed back stiffly.

Without looking at her, he said, 'What is your purpose in being here, madam?'

'My name's Merrily.' She let her hand fall to her side. 'I'm the . . . vicar of Ledwardine.'

'So?'

'I was just . . . I happened to be in the building, and the ward sister asked me to look in. She thought you might like to . . . talk.'

Could be a stupid thing to say. If there ever was a man who didn't like to talk, this was possibly him. Between them, his wife's eyes gazed nowhere, not even into the beyond. They were filmed over, colourless as the water in the metal bowl on the bedside table, and they seemed the stillest part of her. He'd pulled the bedclothes back up, so that only her face was on show. She looked young enough to be his daughter. She had light brown hair, and she was pretty. Merrily imagined him out on his tractor, thinking of her waiting for him at home. Wife number two, probably, a prize.

'Mr Weal – look, I'm sorry I don't know your first name . . .'

His eyes were downcast to the body. He wore a green suit of hairy, heavy tweed. 'Mister,' he said quietly.

'Oh.' She stepped away from the bed. 'Right. Well, I'm sorry. I didn't mean to upset you . . . any further.'

There was a long silence. The water bowl made her think of a font, of last rites, a baptism of the dying. Then he squinted at her across the corpse. He blinked once – which seemed, curiously, to release tension, and he grunted.

'J.W. Weal, my name.'

She nodded. It had obviously been a mistake to introduce herself just as Merrily, like some saleswoman cold-calling.

'How long had you been married, Mr Weal?'

Again, he didn't reply at once, as though he was carefully turning over her question to see if a subtext dropped out.

'Nine years, near enough.' *Yerrs*, he said. His voice was higher than you'd expect, given the size of him, and brushed soft.

Merrily said, 'We . . . never know what's going to come, do we?'

She looked down at Mrs Weal, whose face was somehow unrelaxed. Or maybe Merrily was transferring her own agitation to the dead woman. Who was perhaps her own age, mid to late thirties? Maybe a little older.

'She's . . . very pretty, Mr Weal.'

'Why wouldn't she be?'

Dull light had awoken in his eyes, like hot ashes raked over. People probably had been talking – J.W. Weal getting himself an attractive young wife like that. Merrily wondered if there were grown-up children from some first Mrs Weal, a certain sourness in the hills.

She swallowed. 'Do you, er . . . belong to a particular church?' Cullen was right; he looked like the kind of man who would do, if only out of tradition and a sense of rural protocol.

Mr Weal straightened up. She reckoned he must be close to six and a half feet tall, and built like a great stone barn. His eyebrows met, forming a stone-grey lintel.

'That, I think, is my personal business, thank you.'

'Right. Well . . .' She cleared her throat. 'Would you mind if I prayed for her? Perhaps we could—'

Pray together, she was about to say. But Mr Weal stopped her without raising his voice which, despite its pitch, had the even texture of authority.

'*I* shall pray for her.'

Merrily nodded, feeling limp. This was useless. There was no more she could say, nothing she could do here that Eileen Cullen couldn't do better.

'Well, I'm very sorry for the intrusion.'

He didn't react – just looked at his wife. For him, there was already nobody else in the room. Merrily nodded and bit her lip, and walked quietly out, badly needing a cigarette.

'No?' Eileen Cullen levered herself from the wall.

'Hopeless.'

Cullen led her up the corridor, well away from the door. 'I'd hoped to have him away before Menna's sister got here. I'm not in the best mood tonight for mopping up after tears and recriminations.'

31

'Sorry . . . whose sister?'

'Menna's – Mrs Weal's. The sister's Mrs Buckingham and she's from down south and a retired teacher, and there's no arguing with her. And no love lost between her and that man in there.'

'Oh.'

'Don't ask. I don't know. I don't want to know.'

'What was Menna like?'

'*I* don't know. Except for what I hear. She wasn't doing much chatting when they brought her in. But even if she'd been capable of speech, I doubt you'd have got much out of her. Lived in the sticks the whole of her life, looking after the ole father like a dutiful child's supposed to when her older and wiser sister's fled the coop. Father dies, she marries an obvious father figure. Sad story but not so unusual in a rural area.'

'Where's this exactly?'

'I forget. The Welsh side of Kington. Sheep-shagging country.'

'Charming.'

'They have their own ways and they keep closed up.'

The amiable, voluble Gomer Parry, of course, was origi-nally from the Radnor Valley. But this was no time to debate the pitfalls of ethnic stereotyping.

'How did she come to have a stroke? Do you know?'

'You're not on the Pill yourself, Merrily?'

'Er . . . no.'

'That would be my first thought with Menna. Still on the Pill at thirty-nine. It does happen. Her doctor should've warned her.'

'Wouldn't Mr Weal have known the dangers?'

'He look like he would?' Cullen handed Merrily her bag. 'Thanks for trying – you did your best. Don't go having nightmares. He's just a poor feller loved his wife to excess.'

'I'll tell you one thing,' Merrily said. 'I think he's going to need help getting his life back on track. That's the kind of guy who goes back to his farm and hangs himself in the barn.'

'If he had a barn.'

'I thought he was a farmer.'

'I don't think I said that, did I?'

'What's he do, then? Not a copper?'

'Built like one, sure. No, he's a lawyer, as it happens. Listen, I'm gonna have a porter come up and we'll do it the hard way.'

'A solicitor?'

Cullen gave her a shrewd look. She knew Sean had been a lawyer, that Merrily herself had been studying the law until the untimely advent of Jane had pushed her out of university with no qualifications. The *difficult* years, pre-ordination.

'Man's not used to being argued with outside of a court-house,' Cullen said. 'You go back and find your wee friend. *We'll* sort this now.'

Walking back towards Intensive Care, shouldering her bag, she encountered Gomer Parry smoking under a red No Smoking sign in the main corridor. He probably hadn't even noticed it. He slouched towards her, hands in his pockets, ciggy winking between his teeth like a distant stop-light.

'Sorry about that, Gomer. I was—'

'May's well get off home, vicar. Keepin' you up all night.'

'Don't be daft. I'll stay as long as *you* stay.'

'Ar, well, no point, see.' Gomer said. He looked small and beaten hollow. 'No point now.'

The scene froze.

'Oh God.'

She'd left him barely half an hour to go off on a futile

errand which she wasn't up to handling, and in her absence . . .

In the scruffy silence of the hospital corridor, she thought she heard Minnie Parry at her most comfortably Brummy: *'Yow don't go worrying about us, my duck. We're retired, got all the time in the world to worry about ourselves.'*

Instinctively she unslung her bag, plunged a hand in. But Gomer was there first.

'Have one o' mine, vicar. Extra-high tar, see.'

FOUR

Repaganization

Tuesday began with a brown fog over the windows like dirty lace curtains. The house was too quiet. They ought to get a dog. Two dogs, Robin had said after breakfast, before going off for a walk on his own.

He'd end up, inevitably, at the church, just to satisfy himself it hadn't disappeared in the mist. He would walk all around the ruins, and the ruins would look spectacularly eerie and Robin would think, *Yes!*

From the kitchen window, Betty watched him cross the yard between dank and oily puddles, then let himself into the old barn, where they'd stowed the oak box. Robin also thought it was seriously cool having a barn of your own. *Hey! How about I stash this in . . . the barn?*

When she was sure he wouldn't be coming back for a while, Betty brought out, from the bottom shelf of the dampest kitchen cupboard, the secret copy she'd managed to make of that awful witch charm. She'd done this on Robin's photocopier while he'd gone for a tour of Old Hindwell with George and Vivvie, their weekend visitors who – for several reasons – she could have done without.

Betty now took the copy over to the window sill. Produced in high contrast, for definition, it looked even more obscurely threatening than the original.

First the flash-vision of the praying man in the church, then this.

> O Lord, Jesus Christ Saviour Salvator I beseech the salvation of all who dwell within from witchcraft and from the power of all evil...Amen Amen Amen...Dei nunce... Amen Amen Amen Amen Amen.

Ritualistic repetition. A curious mixture of Catholic and Anglican. And also:

> By Jehovah, Jehovah and by the Ineffable Names 17317... Holy Names... Elohim... Emmanuel...

Jewish mysticism... the Kabbalah. A strong hint of ritual magic. And then those symbols – planetary, Betty thought, astrological.

It was bizarre and muddled, a nineteenth-century cobbling together of Christianity and the occult. And it seemed utterly genuine.

It was someone saying: *We know about you. We know what you are.*

And we know how to deal with you.

Inside the barn, the mysterious box was still there, tucked down the side of a manger. All the hassle it was causing with Betty, Robin had been kind of hoping the Local People would somehow have spirited this item away again. It was cute, it was weird but it was, essentially, a crock of shit. A joke, right?

The Local People? He'd found he was beginning to think of 'the local people' the way the Irish thought of 'the little people': shadowy, mischievous, will o' the wispish. A different species.

Robin had established that the box did originally come from this house. Or, at least, there were signs of an old hiding place inside the living-room inglenook – new cement, where a brick had been replaced. So was this the reason Betty had resisted the consecration of their living room as a temple? Because it was there that the anti-witchcraft charm had been secreted?

Betty's behaviour had been altogether difficult most of the weekend. George Webster and his lady, the volatile Vivvie, Craft-buddies from Manchester, had come down on Saturday to help the Thorogoods get the place together, and hadn't left until Monday afternoon. It ought to have been a good weekend, with loud music, wine and the biggest fires you could make out of resinous green pine. But Betty had kept on complaining of headaches and tiredness.

Which wasn't like her at all. As a celebratory climax, Robin had wanted the four of them to gather at the top of the tower on Sunday night to welcome the new moon. But – wouldn't you know? – it was overcast, cold and raining. And Betty had kept on and on about safety. Like, would that old platform support as many as four people? What did she think, that he was planning an orgy?

Standing by the barn door, Robin could just about see the top of the tower, atmospherically wreathed in fog. One day soon, he would produce a painting of it in blurry water-colour, style of Turner, and mail it to his folks in New York. *This is a sketch of the church. Did I mention the ancient church we have out back?*

And *ancient* was right.

This was the real thing. The wedge of land overlooking the creek, the glorious plot on which the medieval church of St Michael at Old Hindwell had been built by the goddamn Christians, was most definitely an ancient pagan sacred site.

George Webster had confirmed it. And George had expertise in this subject.

Just take a look at these yew trees, Robin, still roughly forming a circle. That one and that one ... could be well over a thousand years old.'

Red-haired, beardy George running his hands down the ravines in those huge, twisting trunks and then cutting some forks of hazel, so he and Robin could do some exploratory dowsing. What you did, you asked questions – Were there standing stones here? Was this an old burial place, pre-Christianity? How many bodies are lying under here? – and you waited for the twig to twitch in response. Admittedly, a response didn't happen too often for Robin, but George was adept.

No, there'd been no stones but perhaps wooden poles – a woodhenge kind of arrangement – where the yews now grew. And yes, there had been pre-Christian burials here. George made it 300-plus bodies at one time. But the area had been excavated and skeletons taken away for reburial before the Church sold off the site, so there was the possibility that some pagan people been taken away for *Christian* burial. The arrogance of those bastards!

What happened, way back when the Christians were moving into Britain, was some smart-ass pope had decreed that they should place their churches on existing sites of worship. This served two purposes: it would demonstrate the dominance of the new religion over the old and, if the site was the same, that might persuade the local tribes to keep on coming there to worship.

But that was all gonna be turned around at last. Boy, *was* it!

Robin stood down by the noisesome water, lining up the church with Burfa Hill, site of an Iron Age camp. He couldn't remember when – outside of a rite – he'd last felt so exalted.

Sure, it only backed up what he'd already instinctively known from standing up top of the tower the other night. But, hell, confirmation was confirmation! He and Betty had been meant to come here, to revive a great tradition.

It was about repaganization.

They hadn't talked too much about long-term plans, but – especially after the weekend's discoveries – it was obvious these would revolve around in some way reinstating the temple which had stood here before there ever was a Christian church. Physically, this process had already begun: the church had fallen into ruins; if this continued, one day only the tower would remain . . . a single great standing stone.

Beautiful!

So why wasn't Betty similarly incandescent with excitement? Why so damn moody so much of the time? Was it that box? He'd wanted to tell George and Vivvie about the box and what it contained, but Betty had come on heavy, swearing him to silence. *'It's no one else's problem. It's between us and them. We have to find our own way of dealing with it.'*

Them? Like who? She was paranoid.

And also, he knew, still spooked about what had happened to Major Wilshire, from whose widow they'd bought this place.

The Major had died after a fall from a ladder he'd erected up the side of the tower. Hearing the story, George Webster – who'd drunk plenty wine by then – had begun speculating about the site having a guardian and maybe needing a sacrifice every so many years. Maybe they could find out if anyone *else* had died in accidents here . . .

At which point Robin had beckoned George behind the barn and told him to keep bullshit ideas like that to himself.

Besides, if there *was* any residual atmospheric stress resulting from that incident, Robin figured the best answer would be to do something positive on the tower itself to put things right, and as soon as possible.

Some kind of ritual. Betty would know.

Back in the house, he placed the oak box on the kitchen table. Betty's sea-green eyes narrowed in suspicion.

'We have to deal with this, Bets,' Robin told her. 'Then we forget about it for ever.'

'But not necessarily now,' Betty said irritably.

But Robin was already reading aloud the charm again, the parts of it he could decipher. He suspected Betty could interpret some of those symbols – as well as being more psychically developed, her esoteric knowledge was a good deal deeper and more comprehensive than his own – but she was not being overhelpful here, to say the fucking least.

'OK,' he conceded, 'so it's probably complete bullshit. I guess these things must've been real commonplace at one time – like hanging a horseshoe on your gate.'

'Yes,' Betty said with heavy patience. 'I'm sure, if we make enquiries, we'll find out that there was a local wise man – they called them conjurors in these parts. They were probably still going strong in the nineteenth century.'

'Like a shaman?'

'Something like that. Someone who dealt in spells and charms. If a couple of dozen lambs went down with sheep-scab or something, the farmer would start whingeing about being bewitched and call in the conjuror. It was usually a man – probably because farmers hereabouts didn't like dealing with women. The conjuror would probably write out a charm to keep in the fireplace, and everyone would be happy.'

'There you go. We just happened to be exposed to this one when we were overtired and stressed-out and ready to leap to gross conclusions.'

Betty nodded non-committally. Against the murk of the morning, she was looking a little more vital, in her big, red mohair sweater and her moon talisman. She'd already gotten sweating piles of pine logs stacked up both sides of the Rayburn. Yesterday, she and Vivvie had hung Chinese lanterns on the naked bulbs and called down blessings. But when George had suggested consecrating the temple in the living room itself, Betty had resisted that. Not something to be rushed into. Give the house spirits time to get to know them. Which had sounded unusually fey, for Betty.

'You know, if I'd followed my first instinct when I spotted that guy from the tower, I'd've run down directly and caught him dumping the carrier bag.'

Betty shook her head. 'If whoever it was had come face to face with you on the doorstep, he'd just have made some excuse – like seeing lights in the house, coming over to check everything was OK. He'd have pretended the bag was his shopping and just taken it away with him.'

He didn't argue; she was usually right. He put his hands on the box, closed his eyes, imagined other hands on the box – tried for a face.

'I did that already,' Betty said, offhand. 'Nothing obvious.'

Robin opened his eyes. If she'd tried it and gotten nothing then there was nothing to be had. He had no illusions about which of them was the most perceptive in *that* way. He didn't mind; he still had his creative vision.

'Put it back, now huh, Rob?'

'In the fireplace?'

'In the *barn*, dickhead! Let's not take any chances. Not till we know where it's been.'

'Ha!' He sprang back. 'You just have to know, dontcha?'

'I'd quite *like* to know,' Betty said casually.

'Bets . . .' He walked over, took her tenderly by the shoulders. 'Look at me . . . listen . . . What the fuck's it matter

41

if someone *does* know we're pagans? What kind of big deal is that these days?'

'No problem at all,' Betty said, 'if you live in Islington or somewhere. In a place like this—'

'*Still* no problem is my guess. Bets, this is *not you*. It's me does the overreacting. Me who won't leave the house if there's only one magpie out in the garden. I'm telling you, this is a *good* place. We're *meant* to be here. We came at the right time. Meant, right? Ordained. Making the church site into a sacred place again. All of that.'

Betty gently disengaged his hands. 'I thought I might go and see Mrs Wilshire. The note says, "The previous occupant preferred not to keep it and gave it away." So presumably they're talking about Mrs Wilshire. Or more likely her husband.'

'He was an old soldier. He'd have thought this was pure bullshit.'

'Before he died,' Betty said.

'Whooo!' Robin flung up his hands, backed away, as if from an apparition. 'Don't you start with that!'

'They didn't even get to live here, did they? They get the place half-renovated and then the poor old Major is gone, crash, bang.'

Robin spread his arms. 'Bets, it's like . . . it's an ill wind. It's a big pile of ifs. If the Wilshires had gotten all the renovation work done, everything smoothed out and shiny, and then put the place on the market, it'd've been way out of our price league. If people hereabouts hadn't been put off by the tragic reasons for the sale, there might've been some competition . . . If it hadn't gone on sale in November, all the holiday-home-seekers from London woulda been down here. If . . . if . . . if . . . What can I say? All the ifs were in our favour. But, if it makes you feel better, OK, let's go see her. When?'

'What?'

'The widow Wilshire.'

'Oh. No, actually, I thought I'd go alone. She struck me as a timid kind of person.'

'And I would spook her?'

'We don't want to look like a delegation. Anyway, you've work to do.'

'I do. I have work.'

The Kirk Blackmore artwork was complete, and would now be couriered, by special arrangement, not to the publishers but to Kirk himself. But the idea of producing a painting of the church, fog-swathed, had gotten hold of Robin, and if he mentioned it to Betty she'd be like: *If you've got time for that, you've got time to emulsion a wall.* But while she was gone, he could knock off a watercolour sketch of the church. He was already envisioning a seasonal series . . . a whatever you called a triptych when there were *four* of them.

'Besides . . .' Betty walked to the door then turned back with a swirl of her wild-corn hair. 'I'm sure there are lots of new things you want to play with, without me on your back.'

Robin managed a grin. With Betty around it was sometimes like your innermost thoughts were written in neon over your head. Sometimes, even for a high priestess, this broad was awesomely spooky.

And so beautiful.

Face it: if he really thought there was an element of risk here, any danger of it turning into an unhappy place, they would be out of here, no matter how much money they lost on the deal.

But that wasn't going to happen. That wasn't a part of the package. How they'd come to find this place was, in itself, too magical to ignore: the prophecy . . . the arrival of the house particulars within the same week, the offer of the

Blackmore contract along with the possibility of a mega-deal for the backlist.

It was like the road to down here had been lit up for them, and if they let those lights go out, well that would really attract some bad karma.

The Local People?

Assholes. Forget them.

FIVE

Every Pillar in the Cloister

'Paganism.' The bishop spooned mustard on to his hot dog. 'What do we have to say about paganism?'

'As little as possible?' Merrily suggested.

The bishop put down his spoon on Sophie's desk. 'Exactly.' He nodded, and went on nodding like, she thought, one of those brushed-fabric boxer dogs motorists used to keep on their parcel shelves. 'Absolutely right.'

The email on the computer screen concluded:

> The programme will take the form of a live studio discussion and protagonists will probably include practising witches, possibly Druids, and 'fundamentalist' clergy. Would you please confirm asap with the programme researcher, Tania Beauman, in Birmingham?

'So, it's a "no", then. Fine.' Merrily stood up, relieved. 'I'll call them tonight. I'll say it's not a debate to which we feel we can make a meaningful contribution. And anyway, it's not something we encounter a particular problem with in this diocese. How does that sound?'

'Sounds eminently sensible, Merrily.' But the bishop's large, hairless face still looked worried.

'Good. Nobody comes out of an edition of *Livenight* with

any dignity left. The pits of tabloid TV – Jerry Springer off the leash.'

'Who is Jerry Springer?' asked the bishop.

'You really don't want to know.'

'One finds oneself watching less and less television.' He brushed crumbs from his generously cut purple shirt. 'Which is wrong, I suppose. It is, after all, one's pastoral duty to monitor society's drab cavalcade . . . the excesses of the young . . . the latest jargon. The ubiquity of the word "shag" in a non-tobacco context.'

'I'll get my daughter Jane to compile a glossary for you.'

The bishop smiled, but still appeared strangely apprehensive. 'So this . . .' he peered at the screen '. . . *Livenight* is not current affairs television?'

'Not as you know it. How would you describe *Livenight*, Sophie?'

'Like a rehearsal for Armageddon.' A shudder from the bishop's lay secretary, now permanently based in Merrily's gatehouse office. Sophie tucked a frond of white hair behind one ear and used a tissue to dab away a blob of English mustard which the bishop had let fall, appropriately, on the head of the burger-gobbling Homer Simpson on the computer's mouse mat. 'They begin with a specific topic, which is loosely based on a Sunday paper sort of news item.'

'Say you have a suburban husband who pimps for his wife,' Merrily said, 'is she being exploited, or is it a valid way of meeting the mortgage premiums?'

'Invariably,' Sophie said, 'they contrive to fill the studio with loud-mouthed bigots and professional cranks.'

Merrily nodded. 'And if you're insufficiently loud-mouthed, bigoted or cranky they just move on to the psycho sitting next to you who's invariably shaking at the bars to escape onto live television. Whole thing makes you despair for the future of the human race. I don't really think spreading despair is what we're about.'

'No,' the bishop said uncomfortably, 'quite. It's just that if you *don't* do it, we . . . we have a problem.'

Merrily stiffened. 'What are you saying exactly, Bernie?'

Bernie Dunmore had taken to wandering down to the Deliverance office on Tuesdays for a snack lunch with Merrily. He always seemed glad to get away from the Bishop's Palace.

Which was understandable. He was not actually the Bishop of Hereford although, as suffragan Bishop of Ludlow, in the north of the diocese, the caretaker role had fallen to him in the controversial absence of the Right Reverend Michael Hunter.

In the end, though, Mick Hunter's disappearance had not detonated the media explosion the diocese had feared, coinciding as it had with the resignation of two other Church of England bishops and the suicide of a third – all of this following calls for an outside inquiry into their personal expenses exceeding £200,000 a year, and the acceptance of unorthodox perks.

Questions had also been asked about Hunter's purchase of a Land-Rover and a Mercedes, used by his wife, and, as neither the press nor the police had been able to substantiate anything more damaging, the diocese had been happy to shelter behind any other minor scandal. Now the issue had been turned around: four bishops had spoken out in a *Sunday Times* feature – 'Keeping the Mitre on C of E Executive Stress' – about the trials of their job in an increasingly secular age. There was, inevitably, a picture of Mick Hunter in his jogging gear, 'escaping from the pressure'.

Was it better, under the circumstances, that the truth had not come out? Merrily wasn't sure. But she liked Bernie Dunmore, sixty-two years old and comfortably lazy. Prepared to hold the fort until such time as the search for a suitably uncontroversial replacement for Mick Hunter could begin. No one, in fact, could be less controversial than Bernie; the worst he'd ever said about Hunter was, 'One would have thought the Crown Appointments Commission would have been aware of Michael's personality problems.'

As Mick's appointee, Merrily had offered Bernie her resignation from his Deliverance role, citing the seasoned exorcist Huw Owen's warning that women priests had become a target for every psychotic grinder of the dark satanic mills who ever sacrificed a cockerel.

'All the more reason for you to remain, my dear,' Bernie had told her, though she couldn't quite follow his reasoning. She hoped it wasn't just because he enjoyed his Tuesday lunchtimes here sitting on the Deliverance desk with a couple of hot dogs and a can of lager.

'*You* explain, Sophie,' the bishop said.

His lay secretary sat up, spry and elegant in a grey business suit with fine black stripes, and consulted her memo pad.

'Well, as you know, this programme approached us some weeks ago, with a view to Merrily taking part in a general discussion on supernatural phenomena – which Merrily declined to do.'

'Because Merrily was afraid of what they might already know about recent events in Hereford,' added Merrily.

'Indeed. I then received a personal call from Ms Tania Beauman relating to this week's proposed paganism programme, again requesting Merrily.'

'They've obviously seen that understatedly sexy photo of you, my dear,' said Bernie.

Merrily sighed, looked at the clock: 1.35. She had to be back in Ledwardine by three for Minnie Parry's funeral.

Sophie said, 'You'll probably both recall the story in the

papers last Thursday about the pagan parents in Somerset who demanded that their child be allowed to make her own religious observances at the village primary school.'

The bishop winced.

'*Livenight*'s programme peg for this week,' Sophie explained. 'It's now claimed there are over 100,000 active pagans in Britain. Either belonging to groups – covens – or nurturing their beliefs independently.'

'Complete nonsense, of course.' The bishop sniffed. 'But figures like that can't be proved one way or the other.'

'The programme will discuss the pagans' claim that they represent the traditional old religion of the British Isles and, as such, should be granted rights and privileges at least equivalent to those accorded to Islam, Buddhism and other non-indigenous faiths.'

Bernie snorted. 'Most of their so-called traditions date back no further than the fifties and sixties. They're a sham. These people are just annoyed because they've been refused charity status.'

'In a secular state,' Merrily said, 'it could be argued that their superstitions are just as valid as ours – I'm doing my devil's advocate bit here.'

The bishop jutted his chins and straightened his pectoral cross. 'My question, though, is should we be actively *encouraging* people to strip off and have sex with each other's wives under the full moon while pretending it's religion? I think not. But neither do I think we should be engaging them in open battle – boosting their collective ego by identifying them as representatives of the Antichrist.'

'However,' Sophie said, 'that *does* reflect the general approach of one of our more . . . outgoing rural rectors: the Reverend Nicholas Ellis.'

'Oh,' Merrily said.

'In his sermons and his parish magazine articles, he's

tended to employ . . . quite colourful terminology. *Livenight*'s own kind of terminology, you might say.'

Sophie and the bishop both looked enquiringly at Merrily. She shook her head. 'I know of him only through the press cuttings. Loose-cannon priest who dumped his churches. Spent some years in the States. Charismatic. Direct intervention of the Holy Spirit . . . Prophecy . . . Tongues.'

'Split the community,' Bernie said, 'when he expressed disdain for actual churches and offered to conduct his charismatic services in community halls, barns, warehouses, whatever. So Mick Hunter agreed to appoint a regular priest-in-charge in the area, to appease the traditionalists, and let Ellis continue his roving brief.'

Merrily recalled that Ellis now belonged to a fast-growing Anglican anti-Church faction calling itself the Sea of Light.

'Awfully popular figure, this Nicholas, I'm afraid,' Bernie Dunmore said. 'Since we cut him loose, he's set up in some run-down village hall and he's packing it to the rafters with happy-clappies from miles around. Which makes him somewhat unassailable, and yet he's not a demonstrative bloke in himself. Quiet, almost reticent, apparently. But came back from America with a knowledge of agriculture and farming ways that seems to have rather endeared him to the Radnorshire people.'

Merrily grimaced, recalling what Eileen Cullen at the hospital had said about the piece of Wales just over the border: '*They have their own ways and they keep closed up.*'

Bernie flicked her a foxy smile. 'The man was after your job, did you know?'

Her eyebrows went up. 'Deliverance?'

'Wrongly assuming you'd be on the way out in the aftermath of Michael's, er, breakdown. Soon as I showed my face in Hereford, there was Nicholas requesting an audience.'

'Did he get one?'

'Showed him the door, of course, but tactfully. Good God, he's the last kind of chap you want as your exorcist. Sees the Devil behind every pillar in the cloister. Fortunately, Deliverance is rarely up for tender. Press-gang job, in my experience.' He beamed at Merrily. 'And all the better for that.'

'Is he currently doing any deliverance work?' she asked warily.

'Frankly, my dear . . . one doesn't like to enquire. Though if there are any complaints, I suppose we'll have to peer into the pond. Meanwhile . . . this *Livenight*.' The bishop snapped back the ringpull on his can of lager and accepted a tall glass from Sophie. 'Apparently, he *has* been mentioned as a possible – what do you call it? – front-row speaker.'

'Having already been approached by Ms Beauman,' Sophie said, 'and having apparently said yes.'

'But not on behalf of the diocese,' Merrily said. 'Just a lone maverick, surely?'

The bishop shrugged, spilling a little lager. 'One can't stop the man appearing on national television. And one can't be seen to try to stop him.'

'But if he starts shooting his mouth off about the invasion of sinister sects and child sacrifice and that kind of stuff, it's going to reflect on all of us.'

'In the wake of recent events here,' said the bishop, 'we were all rather looking for a quiet life for a while.'

Merrily looked into the big, generally honest face of the suffragan Bishop of Ludlow, a lovely old town in south Shropshire from which he was commuting and to which he clearly couldn't wait to get back.

'Well . . .' Sophie folded a square of green blotting paper into a beer mat for the bishop, giving herself an excuse not to look directly at Merrily. 'Ms Beauman did intimate to me that they might be prepared to consider rescinding their

invitation to the Reverend Mr Ellis . . . if they could recruit
for their programme the person they originally had in mind.'

There was an uneasy silence. The bishop drank some lager
and gazed out of the window, across Broad Street. It was
starting to rain.

'Shit,' Merrily said under her breath.

SIX

Unkind Sky

'A box?' Lizzie Wilshire looked vaguely puzzled. But more vague than puzzled, Betty thought.

'Inside the fireplace.'

'I did rather *like* that fireplace,' Mrs Wilshire recalled. 'It had a wonderful old beam across the top. It was the one emphatic feature of a rather drab room.'

'Yes, the living room.'

'You thought there ought to be beams across the ceiling too. Bryan said there still must be, underneath all the plaster. But I did like the fireplace, if precious little else.'

The fireplace to which Mrs Wilshire's chair was presently pulled close was forlornly modern, made of brownish dressed stone. It surrounded a bronze-enamelled oil-fired stove – undernourished flames behind orange-tinted glass.

Mrs Wilshire frowned. 'It also had woodworm, though.'

'The box?'

'The beam, dear. That worried me a little, until Bryan said, "Lizzie, it will take about 300 years for the worms to eat through it." I would still have wanted it treated, though.' She blinked at Betty. 'Have you had it treated, yet?'

'Not yet. Er, Mrs Wilshire . . . there was a box. It was apparently found in the fireplace, while you were having some repairs done to the walls. It contained a paper with a sort of . . . prayer. I suppose you'd call it a prayer.'

'Oh!' Understanding came at last to the bulging eyes of frail Lizzie Wilshire – big eyes which made her look like an extra-terrestrial or a wizened, expensive cat. 'You mean the *witch paper*!'

'Yes,' Betty said softly, 'the witch paper.'

It wasn't that she was particularly old, early seventies, Betty reckoned, but she had arthritis – obvious in her hands – and accepted her own helplessness. Clearly, she'd never been used to doing very much for herself or making decisions. 'It's so confusing now,' she said. 'So many things I know nothing about. Things I don't *want* to have to know about. Why should I?'

She was still living in this colonial-style bungalow on the edge of New Radnor, the tiny town, or big village, where she and the Major had lived for over fifteen years, since his retirement. Just a stopgap, the Major always said, until they found the right place . . . an interesting place, a place he could *play* with.

She told Betty how she thought he'd finally accepted that he was too old to take on something needing extensive refurbishment when, out on a Sunday drive, they'd found – not three miles away, at Old Hindwell – the house with which Major Bryan Wilshire, to the utter dismay of his wife, had fallen hopelessly in love.

'It was empty, of course, when we saw it. It had belonged to two reclusive bachelor farmers called Prosser. The last surviving one had finally been taken into a nursing home. So you can imagine the state it was in.'

Betty already knew all this from the estate agents, and from their own searches. Also she'd sensed a residual sourness and meanness in rooms left untouched by Major Wilshire. But she let his widow talk.

'And that awful old ruined church in the grounds. Some

would say it was picturesque, but I hated it. Who could possibly want a disused church? Except Bryan, of course.'

The Major had found the church fascinating and had begun to delve into its history: when it had last been used as a place of worship, why it had been abandoned. Meanwhile, the house was to be auctioned and, because of its poor condition, the reserve price was surprisingly low. This was when the market was still at low ebb, just before the recent property boom, and there was no rush for second homes in the countryside.

'There was no arguing with Bryan. He put in an offer and it was accepted, so the auction was called off. Bryan was delighted. It was so cheap we didn't even have to consider selling this bungalow. He said he could renovate the place at his leisure.'

A reputable firm of contractors had been hired, but Major Wilshire insisted on supervising the work himself. The problem was that Bryan was always so hands-on, climbing ladders and scaffolding to demonstrate to the workmen exactly what he wanted doing. Lizzie couldn't bear to look up at him; it made her quite dizzy. But Bryan had always needed *that* element in his life, serving as he had with *that* regiment in Hereford. The SAS, Betty presumed, and she wondered how an all-action man like Major Wilshire ended up with a wife who didn't like to look *up*.

At least that had spared Lizzie an eyewitness memory of the terrible accident. This had been brought about by the combination of a loose stone under a slit window in the tower, a lightweight aluminium ladder, and a freak blast of wind from the Forest.

At first they'd told her it was simply broken bones, and quite a number of them; so it would have taken Major Wilshire a long time to recover. Many months. But no internal injuries, so it could have been worse. He'd at least be home in a matter of weeks. Mrs Wilshire meanwhile had determined that he would never again go back to that awful place.

But Bryan had never come home again. The shock – or something – had brought on pneumonia. For this energetic, seemingly indestructible old soldier, it was all over in four days.

There was one photograph of the Major on the mantelpiece: a wiry man in a cap. He was not in uniform or anything, but in the garden, leaning on a spade, and his smile was only a half-smile.

'So quick. So bewilderingly *quick*. There was no time at all for preparations,' Mrs Wilshire said querulously. 'We'd always made time to prepare for things; Bryan was a great planner. Nothing was entirely unexpected, because he was always ready for it. Whenever he had to go away, my sister would come to stay and Bryan would always pay the bills in advance and order plenty of heating oil. He always thought ahead.'

How ironic, Betty thought, that a man whose career must have involved several life-or-death situations, and certainly some gruelling and risky training exercises, should have died after a simple fall from a ladder.

From a church? Was this ironic, too?

When it started to rain harder, Robin packed up his paints and folded the easel. A few stray drops on a watercolour could prove interesting; they made the kind of accidental blurs you could use, turned the painting into a *rain*colour. But if it came on harder, like now, and the wind got up, this was the elements saying to him: Uh-huh, try again.

He stood for a moment down below the church ruins, watching the creek rush down into a small gorge maybe fifteen feet deep, carrying branches and a blue plastic feedsack. Wild! There was a narrow wooden footbridge which people used to cross to get to church. The bridge was a little rickety, which was also kind of quaint. Maybe this even explained why the church had become disused. Fine when the congregation came on foot from the village, but when the village population had gotten smaller, and the first automobiles had arrived in Radnorshire . . . well, not even country ladies liked to have to park in a field the wrong side of the Hindwell Brook and arrive in church with mud splashes up their Sunday stockings.

In the distance, over the sound of the hurrying water, Robin could hear a vehicle approaching. It was almost a mile along the track to reach the county road, so if you heard any traffic at all, it had to be heading this way. Most often it was Gareth Prosser in his Land-Rover – biggest farmer hereabouts, a county councillor and also a nephew of the two old guys who used to own St Michael's. Robin would have liked if the man stopped one time, came in for a beer, but Gareth Prosser just nodded, never smiled to him, never slowed.

Country folk took time to get to know. Apparently.

But the noise wasn't rattly enough to be Prosser's Land-Rover, or growly enough to be his kids' dirt bikes. It was a little early to be Betty back from the widow Wilshire's, but – who knew? – maybe she at last had developed the hots again for her beloved husband, couldn't wait to get back to the hissing pine fires and into the sack in that wonderful damp-walled bedroom.

Sure.

Robin kicked a half-brick into the Hindwell Brook, lifting up his face to the squally rain. It would come right. The goddess would return to her. Just the wrong part of the cycle, was all. He offered a short, silent prayer to the spirits of the rushing water, that the flow might once again go their way. Winter was, after all, a stressful time to move house.

The vehicle appeared: it was a Cherokee jeep. When the driver parked in the yard and got out, Robin stared at him, and then closed his eyes and muttered, 'Holy shit.'

He didn't need this. He did not need this now.

'But we don't believe in those things any more, do we, my dear? Witches, I mean.'

How on earth had the wife of an SAS officer managed to preserve this childlike, glazed-eyed innocence? Betty smiled and lifted the bone china teacup and saucer from her knees in order to smooth her long skirt. Jeans would have been the wrong image entirely and, after the assault on the house over the past few days, she didn't have an entirely clean pair anyway.

Clean was paramount here. It was a museum of suburbia; it had actual trinkets. Betty guessed that the Major's wife had secretly been hoping that the renovation work at St Michael's would *never* be completed, that it would be simply a long-term hobby for him while they went on living here in New Radnor – which, although it was on the edge of the wilderness and still dominated by a huge castle-mound, was pleasant and open, with a wide main street, neat cottages, window boxes in the summer, a nice shop. Unlike Old Hindwell, it kept the Forest at arm's length.

Mrs Wilshire said, 'It was silly, it was slightly unpleasant. And, of course, it wasn't even terribly old.'

'About 1850, as I recall.'

'Oh,' said Mrs Wilshire. 'Have you found another one?'

'No, I think it's the same one,' Betty said patiently. 'Someone brought it back, you see.'

'Who in the world would do that?'

'We don't know. It was left on the doorstep.'

'What an odd thing to do.'

'Yes, it *was* odd, which is why we'd like to find out who

did it. I was hoping you might be able to tell me who you gave the box to when you . . . gave it away. Do you remember, by any chance?'

'Well, Bryan saw to that, of course. Bryan always knew where to take things, you see.'

'Would there perhaps have been . . . I don't know, a local historian or someone like that who might have had an interest in old documents?'

'Hmmm.' Mrs Wilshire pursed her tiny lips. 'There's Mr Jenkins, at the bookshop in Kington. But he writes for the newspapers as well, and Bryan was always very suspicious of journalists. Perhaps it was the new rector he gave it to.'

'Oh.'

'Not that he was terribly fond of the rector either. We went to one of his services, but only once. So noisy! I've never seen so many people in a church – well, not for an ordinary evensong. They must have come from elsewhere, like football supporters. And there were people with guitars. And candles – so many candles. Well, I have nothing against all that, but it's not for the likes of us, is it? Are you a church-goer, Mrs Thorogood?'

'Er . . . No. Not exactly.'

'And your husband? What is it your husband does for a living? I'm sure I *did* know . . .'

'He's an artist, an illustrator. He does book covers, mainly.'

'Bryan used to read,' Lizzie Wilshire said distantly. 'He'd go through periods when he'd read for days in his sanctum.' Her big eyes were moist; Betty thought of parboiled eggs.

'Look,' she said, 'is there anything I can do, while I'm here? Vacuum the carpet? Clean anything? Prepare you some-thing for tea? Or is there anywhere you need to go? You don't drive, do you?'

'Bryan never wanted me to use the car. He always said

rural roads were far more dangerous because of the tractors and trailers. And we have a local man, Mr Gibbins, who runs a sort of part-time taxi service. He takes me into Kington twice a week and carries my shopping for me. You mustn't worry about me, my dear, with all the work you must have on your hands, getting that old place ready to move into.'

'We moved in last week, actually.'

Mrs Wilshire's small mouth fell open. 'But it was an absolute hovel when—'

She stopped, possibly remembering that her own estate agent had preferred phrases like 'characterful and eccentric'.

'It's still got one or two problems,' Betty said, more cheerfully than she felt, 'but it doesn't let the rain in. Well, not in most of the rooms. Mrs Wilshire, is there anyone else apart from the rector that your husband might have handed that box to – or even told about it?'

Mrs Wilshire shook her head. 'He brought it back here to examine it, but he didn't keep it very long, I know that, because I wouldn't have it in the house – so dirty. I do rather remember something, but . . .'

Betty sighed. 'Look, let me wash up these cups and things, at least.'

'No dear, I can manage.' She fumbled her cup and saucer to the coffee table, but the cup fell over and spilled some tea, which began to trickle over the edge of the table onto the carpet. Betty snatched a handful of tissues from a box nearby and went down on her knees.

Mopping, she glanced up at Lizzie Wilshire and saw years of low-level pain there, solidified like rock strata. And then, as sometimes happened when observing someone from an oblique angle, she caught a momentary glimpse of Lizzie's aura. It was not intact and vibrated unevenly. This woman needed help.

Betty gathered up the cups and saucers. 'Are you having treatment for the . . . arthritis?'

'Oh, yes, Dr Coll. Do you know Dr Coll?' Betty shook her head. 'Dr Coll says I shall need a new hip, soon, and perhaps a new knee. But that may mean going all the way to Gobowen. Sixty miles or more! In the meantime, I'm on a course of tablets. Can't have new hands, unfortunately, but Dr Coll's been marvellous, of course. He—'

'Steroids?'

Mrs Wilshire looked vague again. 'Cortisone, I believe. And something else – some different pills. I have to take those *twice* a day. I haven't been taking them very long. Just since after Bryan died . . . It seems to have got so much worse since Bryan died. All the worry, I suppose.'

'Mrs Wilshire . . . I hope you don't mind me asking, but have you ever tried anything . . . alternative? Or complementary, as some people prefer to say.'

'You mean herbs and things?'

'Sort of.'

'I would be very wary, my dear. You never know quite what you're taking, do you?'

Betty carried the cups and saucers into a large kitchen – made pale, rather than bright, by wide windows, triple-glazed, with a limited view of a narrow garden, a steep, green hillside and a slice of unkind sky. At the bottom of the garden was a shed or summer house with a small verandah – like a miniature cricket pavilion.

Betty's compassion was veined with anger. Lizzie Wilshire was happily swallowing a cocktail of powerful drugs, with all kinds of side-effects. An unambitious woman who'd let her husband handle everything, make all her decisions for her, and was now willingly submitting to other people who didn't necessarily give a shit.

When Betty came back, Lizzie Wilshire was staring placidly into the red glow of the oil heater.

'Are you going to stay here?' Betty asked.

'Well, dear, the local people are so good, you see . . . You youngsters seem to flit about the country at whim. I don't think I could move. I'd be afraid to.' Mrs Wilshire looked down into her lap. 'Of course, I don't really like it at night – it's such a big bungalow. So quiet.'

'Couldn't you perhaps move into the centre of the village?'

'But I know Bryan's still here, you see. The churchyard's just around the hillside. I feel he's watching over me. Is that silly?'

'No.' Betty gave her an encouraging smile. 'It's not silly at all.'

She walked out to the car feeling troubled and anxious in a way she hadn't expected. That unexpected glimpse of the damaged aura suggested she was meant to come here today. Prodding the little Subaru out onto the long, straight bypass, under an already darkening sky, Betty decided to return soon with something herbal for Mrs Wilshire's arthritis.

It would be a start. And she was getting back that feeling of having come right round in a circle. It was as a child in Llandrindod Wells, fifteen or so miles from here, that she'd first become fascinated by herbs and alternative medicines – perhaps because the bottles and jars containing them always looked so much more interesting than those from the chemist. There was that alternative shop in Llandrindod into which she was always dragging her mother then – not that *she* was interested.

They were both teachers, her parents: her mother at the high school, her dad in line for becoming headmaster of one of the primary schools. Betty was only ten when he failed to get the job, and soon after that they moved to Yorkshire, where he'd been born.

Teaching? Until she left school, she didn't know there *was* any other kind of job. Her parents treated it like a calling to which they were both martyrs, and it was taken for granted that Betty would commit her life to the same kind of suffering. As for those 'flights of imagination' of hers . . . well, she'd grow out of all that soon enough. A teacher's job was to stimulate the imagination of others.

Her parents were unbelieving Anglicans. Their world was colourless. Odd, really, that neither of them was sensitive. If it was in Betty's genes, it must have been dormant for at least two generations. One of her earliest memories – from a holiday up north when she was about four – was her grandma's chuckled 'Go 'way wi' you' when she'd come up from the cellar of the big terraced house in Sheffield and asked her who the old man was who slept down there.

Betty drove slowly, *feeling* the countryside. The road from New Radnor cut through an ancient landscape – the historic church of Old Radnor prominent just below the skyline, like a guardian lighthouse without a light. Behind her, she felt the weight of the Radnor Forest hills – muscular, as though they were pushing her away. At Walton – a pub, farms, cottages – she turned left into the low-lying fertile bowl which archaeologists called the Walton Basin, suggesting that thousands of years ago it had been a lake. Now there was only the small Hindwell Pool, to which, according to legend, the Four Stones went secretly to drink at cockcrow – an indication that the Hindwell water had long been sacred.

To the goddess? The goddess who was Isis and Artemis and Hecate and Ceridwen and Brigid in all her forms.

It was at teacher-training college in the Midlands that Betty had been introduced to the goddess. One of her tutors there was a witch; this had emerged when Betty had confessed she found it hard to go into a particular changing room where, it turned out, a student had hanged herself. Alexandra had been entirely understanding about her reaction and had invited Betty home . . . into a whole new world of incense and veils, earth and water and fire and air . . . where dreams were analysed, the trees breathed, past and present and future coexisted . . . and the moon was the guiding lamp of the goddess.

The recent Walton Basin archaeological project had discovered evidence of a prehistoric ritual landscape here, including the remains of a palisade of posts, the biggest of its kind in Britain. Being here, at the centre of all this, ought to be as exciting to Betty as it was to Robin, who was now – thanks to George – totally convinced that their church occupied a site which too had once been very much part of this sacred complex.

So why had her most intense experience there been the image of a tortured figure frenziedly at prayer, radiating agony and despair, in the ruined nave of St Michael's? She'd tried to drive it away, but it kept coming back to her; she could even smell the sweat and urine. How sacred, how euphoric, was *that*?

Three lanes met in Old Hindwell, converging at an undistinguished pub. Across the road, the former school had been converted into a health centre – by the famous Dr Coll, presumably. The stone and timbered cottages had once been widely spaced, but now there were graceless bungalows slotted between them. In many cases it would be indigenous local people – often retired farmers – living in these bungalows, freed at last from agricultural headaches, while city-reared incomers spent thousands turning the nearby cottages into the period jewels they were never intended to be.

She didn't particularly remember this place from her

Radnorshire childhood, and she didn't yet know anyone here. It was actually pretty stupid to move into an area where you knew absolutely nobody, where the social structure and pattern of life were a complete mystery to you. Yet people did it all the time, lured by vistas of green, the magic of comparative isolation. But Betty realized that if there was to be any hope of their long-term survival here, she and Robin would have to start forming links locally. Connecting with the landscape was not enough.

Robin still had this fantasy of holding a mini fire festival at Candlemas, bringing in the celebrants from outside but throwing open the party afterwards to local people. Like a barbecue: the locals getting drunk and realizing that these witches were OK when you got to know them.

Candlemas – Robin preferred the Celtic 'Imbolc' – was barely a week away, so that was madness. Lights in the old church, chanting on the night air? Somebody would see, somebody would hear.

Too soon. Much too soon.

Or was that an excuse because Wicca no longer inspired her the way it did Robin? Why had she found George so annoying last weekend? Why had his ideas – truths and certainties to him – seemed so futile to her?

When she got home, Robin was waiting for her in the cold dusk, down by the brook. He wore his fez-thing with the mirrors, no protection at all against the rain. He looked damp and he looked agitated.

'We have a slight difficulty,' he said.

Robin was like those US astronauts; he saved the understatements for when things were particularly bad.

SEVEN

Possession

Even in embittered January, the interior of Ledwardine Church kept its autumnal glow. Because of the apples.

This was an orchard village and, when the orchards were bare, Merrily would buy red and yellow apples in Hereford and scatter them around: on the pulpit, down by the font, along the deep window ledges.

The biggest and oldest apple there was clasped in the hand of Eve in the most dramatic of Ledwardine's stained-glass windows, west-facing to pull in the sunset. Although there'd been no sun this afternoon, that old, fatal fruit was still a beacon, and its warmth was picked up by the lone Bramley cooking apple sitting plump and rosy on Minnie's coffin.

'Um . . . want to tell you about this morning,' Merrily said. 'How the day began for Gomer and me.'

She wasn't in the pulpit; she was standing to one side of it, in front of the rood screen of foliate faces and carved wooden apples, viewing the congregation along the coffin's shiny mahogany top.

'Somehow, I never sleep well the night before a funeral. Especially if it's someone I know as well as I'd got to know Minnie. So this morning, I was up before six, and I made a cup of tea, and then I walked out, intending to stroll around the square for a bit. To think about what I was going to say here.'

There must have been seventy or eighty people in the church, and she recognized fewer than half of them. As well as Minnie's relatives from the Midlands, there were several farmer-looking blokes who must have known Gomer when he was digging drainage ditches along the Welsh border. *'You wanner know why most of them buggers've come yere,'* he'd hissed in Merrily's ear, *'you watch how high they piles up their bloody plates with pie and cake in the village hall afterwards.'*

Now, she looked across at Gomer, sitting forlorn in the front pew, his glasses opaque, his wild white hair Brylcreemed probably as close to flat as it had ever been. Sitting next to him was Jane, looking amazingly neat and prim and solemn in her dark blue two-piece. Jane had taken the day off school, and had helped prepare the tea now laid out at the village hall.

'It was very cold,' Merrily said. 'Nobody else in the village seemed to be up yet. No lights, no smoke from chimneys. I was thinking it was true what they say about it always being darkest just before the dawn. But then . . . as I walked past the lychgate . . . I became aware of a small light in the church-yard.'

She'd approached carefully, listening hard – remembering, inevitably, the words of Huw Owen, her tutor on the Deliverance course. *'They'll follow you home, they'll breathe into your phone at night, break into your vestry and tamper with your gear. Crouch in the back pews and masturbate through your sermons . . . Little rat-eyes in the dark.'*

The light glowed soft in the mist. It was down at the bottom of the churchyard, where it met the orchard, close to the spot where Merrily had planned a small memorial for Wil Williams, seventeeth-century vicar of this parish and the vicarage's one-time resident ghost.

The light yellowed the air immediately above the open

space awaiting Minnie Parry. Merrily had stopped about five yards from the grave and, as she watched, the light grew brighter.

And then there was another light, a small red firefly gleam, and she almost laughed in relief as Gomer Parry, glowing ciggy clamped between his teeth, reached up from below and dumped his hurricane lamp, with a clank, on the edge of the grave.

'Oh, hell.' Gomer heaved himself out. 'Din't disturb you, nor nothing, did I, vicar? Din't think you could see this ole lamp from the vicarage. Din't think you'd be up, see.'

'I didn't see it from the vicarage. I was . . . I was up anyway. Got a lot of things to do before . . . Got to see the bishop – stuff like that.' She was burbling, half embarrassed.

'Ar,' said Gomer.

Merrily was determined not to ask what he'd been up to down there in the grave; if he was doing it under cover of darkness, it was no business of anyone else's. Besides, he'd made himself solely responsible for Minnie's resting place, turning up with his mini-JCB to attack the ice-hard ground, personally laying down the lining.

'Fancy a cup of tea, Gomer?'

Gomer came over, carrying his lamp.

'Bugger me, vicar,' he said. 'Catch a feller pokin' round your churchyard at dead of night and you offers him a cup o' tea?'

'Listen, pal,' Merrily said, echoing the asphalt tones of the verger of the Liverpool church where she'd served as a curate, 'I'm a bloody Christian, me.'

Gomer grinned, a tired, white gash in the lamplight.

'So . . . we went back to the vicarage.' Merrily's gaze was fixed on the shiny Bramley on Minnie's coffin. 'And there we were, Gomer and me, at six o'clock in the morning, sitting either side of the kitchen table, drinking tea. And for once I was at a bit of a loss . . .'

She heard light footsteps and saw a stocky figure tiptoeing up the central aisle; recognized young Eirion Lewis, in school uniform. He was looking hesitantly from side to side . . . looking for Jane. He must be *extremely* keen on the kid to drive straight from school to join her at the funeral of someone he hadn't even known.

It was, you had to admit, a smart and subtle gesture. But Eirion had been raised to it; his old man ran Welsh Water or something. Eirion, though you wouldn't know it from his English accent, had been raised among the Welsh-speaking Cardiff aristocracy: the *crachach*.

When he saw that Jane was in the front pew, a leading mourner, he quietly backed off and went to sit on his own in the northern aisle which was where, in the old days, the women had been obliged to sit – the ghetto aisle. Eirion was, in fact, a nice kid, so Jane would probably dump him in a couple of weeks.

Merrily looked up. 'Then, after his second mug of tea, Gomer began to talk.'

'All it was . . . just buryin' a little box o' stuff, 'fore my Min goes down there, like. So's it'll be underneath the big box, kind of thing. En't no church rules against that, is there?'

'If there are,' Merrily had said, lighting a cigarette, 'I can have them changed by this afternoon.'

'Just bits o' stuff, see. Couple o' little wedding photos. Them white plastic earrings 'er insisted on wearing, 'cept for church. Nothing valuable – not even the watches.'

She had stared at him. He looked down at his tea, added more sugar. She noticed his wrist was bare.

'Mine and Min's, they both got new batteries. So's they'd go on ticking for a year or so. Two year, mabbe.'

Don't smile, Merrily told herself. Don't cry. She remembered Gomer's watch. It was years old, probably one of the first watches ever to work off a battery. And so it really did tick, loudly.

'Dunno why I done it, really, vicar. Don't make no sense, do it?'

'I think, somehow . . .' Merrily looked into the cigarette smoke, 'it makes the kind of sense neither of us is clever enough to explain.'

'And I'm not going to try too hard to explain it now,' she said to the congregation. 'I think people in this job can sometimes spend too long trying to explain too much.'

In the pew next to Gomer, Jane nodded firmly.

'I mean, I *could* go on about those watches ticking day and night under the ground, symbolizing the life beyond death . . . but that's not a great analogy when you start to think about it. In the end, it was Gomer making the point that he and Minnie had something together that can't just be switched off by death.'

'Way I sees it, vicar, by the time them ole watches d'stop ticking, we'll both be over this – out the other side.' Gomer had pushed both hands through his aggressive hair. 'Gotter go on, see, isn't it? Gotter bloody go on.'

'Yeah.'

'What was it like when your husband . . . when he died?'

'A lot different,' Merrily said. 'If he hadn't crashed his car we'd have got divorced. It was all a mistake. We were both too young – all that stuff.'

'And we was too bloody old,' Gomer said, 'me and Min. Problem is, nothin' in life's ever quite . . . what's that word? Synchronized. 'Cept for them ole watches. And you can bet one o' them buggers is gonner run down 'fore the other.'

Gomer smoked in silence for a few moments. He'd been Minnie Seagrove's second husband, she'd been Gomer's second wife. She'd moved to rural Wales some years ago with Frank Seagrove, who'd retired and wanted to come out here for the fishing, but then had died, leaving her alone in a strange town. Merrily still wasn't sure quite how Minnie and Gomer had first met.

Gomer's mouth opened and shut a couple of times, as if there was something important he wanted to ask her but he wasn't sure how.

'Not seen your friend, Lol, round yere for a while,' he said at last – which wasn't it.

'He's over in Birmingham, on a course.'

'Ar?'

'Psychotherapy. Had to give up his flat, and then he got some money, unexpectedly, from his old record company and he's spent it on this course. Half of him thinks he should become a full-time psychotherapist – like, what mental health needs is more ex-loonies. The other half thinks it's all crap. But he's doing the course, then he's going to make a decision.'

'Good boy,' Gomer said.

'Jane still insists she has hopes for Lol and me.'

Gomer nodded. Then he said quickly, 'Dunno quite how to put this, see. I mean, it's your job, ennit, to keep us all in hopes of the hereafter: 'E died so we could live on, kinder thing – which never made full sense to me, but I en't too bright, see?'

Merrily put out her cigarette. Ethel, the cat, jumped onto her knees. She plunged both hands into Ethel's black winter coat.

The big one?

'Only, there's gotter be times, see, vicar, when you wakes up cold in the middle of the night and you're thinkin' to youself, is it bloody *true*? Is anythin' *at all* gonner happen when we gets to the end?'

From the graveside there came no audible ticking as Minnie's coffin went in. Gomer had accepted that his nephew, Nev, should be the one to fill in the hole, on the grounds that Minnie would have been mad as hell watching Gomer getting red Herefordshire earth all over his best suit.

Walking away from the grave, he smiled wryly. He may also have wept earlier, briefly and silently; Merrily had noticed him tilt his head to the sky, his hands clasped behind his back. He was, in unexpected ways, a private person.

Down at the village hall, he nudged her, indicating several tea plates piled higher with food than you'd have thought possible without scaffolding.

'Give 'em a funeral in the afternoon, some of them tight buggers goes without no bloody breakfast and lunch. 'Scuse me a minute, vicar, I oughter 'ave a word with Jack Preece.' And he moved off towards a ravaged-looking old man, whose suit seemed several sizes too big for him.

Merrily nibbled at a slice of chocolate cake and eaves-dropped a group of farmer-types who'd separated themselves from their wives and didn't, for once, seem to be discussing dismal sheep prices.

'Bloody what-d'you-call-its – pep pills, Ecstersee, wannit? Boy gets picked up by the police, see, with a pocketful o' these bloody Ecstersee. Up in court at Llandod. Dennis says, "That's it boy, you stay under my roof you can change your bloody ways. We're gonner go an' see the bloody rector . . ." '

'OK, Mum?'

Merrily turned to find Jane holding a plate with just one small egg sandwich. Was this anorexia, or love?

'What happened to Eirion, flower?'

'He had to get home.'

'Where's he live exactly?'

'Some gloomy, rotting mansion out near Abergavenny. It was quite nice of him to come, wasn't it?'

'It was incredibly nice of him. But then . . . he *is* a nice guy.'

'Yeah.'

Merrily tilted her head. 'Meaning he'd be more attractive if he was a bit of a rogue? Kind of dangerous?'

'You think I'm that superficial?'

'No, flower. Anyway, I expect he'll be going to university next year.'

'He wants to work in TV, as a reporter. Not – you know – *Livenight*.'

'Good heavens, no.'

'So you're going to do that after all then?' Jane said in that suspiciously bland voice that screamed *hidden agenda*.

'I was blackmailed.'

'Can I come?'

Merrily raised her eyes. 'Do I *look* stupid?'

'See, I thought we could take Irene. He's into anything to do with TV, obviously. Like, he knows his dad could get him a job with BBC Wales on the old Taff network, but he wants to make his own way. Which is kind of commendable, I'd have thought.'

'Very honourable, flower.'

'Still, never mind.'

'Sorry.'

'Sure. You told that – what was her name? Tania?'

'Not yet.'

'She'll be ever so pleased.'

And Jane slid away with her plate, and Merrily saw Uncle Ted, the senior churchwarden, elbowing through the farmers. He was currently trying to persuade her to levy a charge for

73

the tea and coffee provided in the church after Sunday services. She wondered how to avoid him. She also wondered how to avoid appearing on trash television to argue with militant pagans.

'Mrs . . . Watkins?'

She turned and saw a woman looking down at her – a pale, tall, stylishly dressed woman, fifty-fiveish, with expertly bleached hair. She was not carrying any food.

'I was impressed,' she said, 'with your sermon.' Her accent was educated, but had an edge. 'It was compelling.'

'Well, it was just . . .'

'. . . from the heart. Meant something to people. Meant something to me, and I didn't even know . . . er . . .'

'Minnie Parry.'

'Yes.' The woman blinked twice, rapidly – a suggestion of nerves. She seemed to shake herself out of it, straightened her back with a puppet-like jerk. 'Sister Cullen was right. You seem genuine.'

'Oh, you're from the hospital . . .'

'Not exactly.' The woman looked round, especially at the farmers, her eyes flicking from face to florid face, evidently making sure there was nobody she knew within listening distance. 'Barbara Buckingham. I was at the hospital, to visit my sister. I think you saw her the other night – before I arrived. Menna Thomas . . . Menna . . .' Her voice hardened. 'Menna Weal.'

'Oh, right. I did see her, but . . .'

'But she was already dead.'

'Yes, she was, I'm afraid.'

'Mrs Watkins,' the woman took Merrily's arm, 'may I talk to you?' Not a request. 'I rang your office, in Hereford. Sister Cullen gave me the number. She said you were probably the person to help me. The person who deals with *possession*.'

'Oh.'

74

'I rang your office and they said you were conducting a funeral here, so I just . . . came. It seemed appropriate.' She broke off. She was attracting glances.

'It's a bit crowded, isn't it?' Merrily said. 'Would you like—?'

'I'll come to the point. Would it be possible for you to conduct a funeral service for me?'

Merrily raised an eyebrow.

'For my sister, that is. I suppose I mean a memorial service. Though actually I don't. She should have . . . she should have a real funeral in church. A proper funeral.'

'I'm sorry, I'm not getting this.'

'Because I can't go, you see. I can't go to the . . . interment.'

'Why not?'

'Because . . . it's going to take place in that bastard's garden.' Her voice rose. 'He won't let her go. It's all about *possession*, Mrs Watkins.'

'I don't . . .' Several people were staring at them now, over their piled-up plates.

'Possession of the dead by the living,' explained Barbara Buckingham.

'I think we'd better go back to the vicarage,' Merrily said.

EIGHT

The E-Word

'Oh my God,' Betty said. 'The only time I go out on my own, in walks number one on the list of situations I wouldn't trust you to handle.'

Robin couldn't keep still. He was pacing the kitchen, touching walls and doors, the sink, the fridge – as if the permanence of this place in his life was no longer certain.

'So he's in this old green Cherokee, right? And he has on this well-worn army jacket with, like, camouflage patches. And it's unzipped, and all the time I'm hoping what's underneath is just gonna turn out to be some kind of black turtleneck. With, like, a thick white stripe around the neck.'

Betty took off her coat, hung it behind the door and came to sit down. It wasn't the vicar that worried her – every newcomer sooner or later had a visit from the vicar. It was how Robin had dealt with him.

'Pretty damn clear from the start he wasn't just coming to ask the way to someplace.' Robin went over to the kitchen table; there were two half-pint glasses on it and four small beer bottles, all empty. 'Guy wanted to talk. He was waiting for me to ask him in.'

'I don't suppose he had to wait long.'

'Soon's we get inside, it's the firm handshake. "Hi, I'm Nick Ellis." And I'm wondering do these guys drink beer? So I offer him a Michelob from the refrigerator.'

'Normal practice is to offer them tea, Robin.'

'No . . . wait . . . Transpires he spent some years in the States – which became detectable in his accent. And then – what can I say? – we . . .'

'You exchanged history. You drank beer together.'

'I confess, I'm standing there pouring out the stuff and I'm like . . .' Robin held up a glass with a trembling hand. 'Like, all the time, I'm half-expecting him to leap up in horror, pull out his cross . . . slam it in my face, like the guy in the Dracula movies. But he was fine.'

She looked sceptical. 'What did you tell him about us?'

'Well . . . this was hard for me. I'm a straight person, I've no time for deception, you know that.'

'What did you *tell* him?' Clenching her hands. 'What did you say about us?'

'Fucksake, whaddaya think I said? "Hey, priest, guess how *we* spent Halloween"?' Robin went over and pulled out a chair and slumped down. 'I told him I was an illustrator and that you were into alternative therapy. I told him you were British and we met when we were both attending a conference in New England. I somehow refrained from identifying the conference as the 1993 Wiccan International Moot in Salem, Mass. And although I did not say we were married I didn't mention handfasting either. I said we had gotten *hitched*.'

'Hitched?'

'Uh-huh. And when he brought up the subject of religion, as priests are inclined to do when they get through with football and stuff, I was quite awesomely discreet. I simply said we were not churchgoers.'

Betty breathed out properly for the first time since sitting down. 'All right. I'm sorry. I do trust you. I've just been feeling a little uptight.'

'Because you're not being true to yourself and your beliefs,' Robin said severely.

'So what was he like?'

'Unexceptional at first. Friendly, but also watchful. Open, but . . . holding back. He's of medium height but the way he holds himself makes him look taller. Rangy, you know? Looks like a backwoods boy. Looks fit. He drank just one beer while I appear to have drunk three. His hair is fairish and he wears it brushed straight back, and in a ponytail, which is cool. I mean, I have no basic problem with these guys – as a spiritual grouping. As a profession.'

'But?'

Robin got up and fed the Rayburn some pine. The Rayburn spat in disgust. Robin looked up at Betty; his eyes were unsteady.

'But, if you want the truth, babe, I guess this is probably a very sick and dangerous example of the species.'

Robin had been anxious the priest remained in the kitchen. He would have had problems explaining the brass pentacle over the living-room fireplace. Would not be happy to have had the Reverend Nicholas Ellis browsing through those books on the shelves. He was glad his guest consumed only one beer and therefore would be less likely to need the bathroom.

And when Ellis asked if he might take a look at the ancient church of St Michael, Robin had the back door open faster than was entirely polite.

Still raining out there. The priest wore hiking boots and pulled out a camouflage beret. They strolled back across the farmyard, around the barn into the field, where the ground was uneven and boggy. And there it was, on its promontory above the water, its stones glistening, its tower proud but its roofless body like a split, gutted fish.

'Cool, huh, Nick?' Robin had told the priest about St Michael's probably becoming disused on account of the Hindwell Brook, the problem of getting cars close enough to the church in the wintertime.

The priest smiled sceptically. 'That's *your* theory, is it, Robin?'

'Well, that and the general decline in, uh, faith. I guess some people'd started looking for something a little more progressive, dynamic.'

The Reverend Ellis stopped. He had a wide, loose mouth. And though his face was a touch weathered, it had no lines, no wrinkles. He was maybe forty.

'What do you mean by that, Robin?'

'Well . . . uh . . .' Robin had felt himself blushing. He talked on about how maybe the Church had become kind of hidebound: same old hymns, same old . . . you know?

The minister had said nothing, just stood there looking even taller, watching Robin sinking into the mud.

'Uh . . . what I meant . . . maybe they began to feel the Church wasn't offering too much in the direction of personal development, you know?'

And then Ellis went, 'Yeah, I do know. And you're dead right.'

'Oh. For a minute, I was worried I was offending you.'

'The Church over here *has* lost much of its dynamism. Don't suppose I need tell you that in most areas of the United States a far higher proportion of the population attends regular services than in this country.'

'So how come you were over there?' Robin had grabbed his chance to edge the talk away from religion.

'Went over with my mother as a teenager. After her marriage ended. We moved around quite a bit, mainly in the South.'

'Really? That's interesting. My mom was English and she

met my dad when he was serving with the Air Force in the North of England, and she went home with him, to New Jersey. So, like—'

'And it was there,' Nicholas Ellis continued steadily, 'that I first became exposed to what you might consider a more "dynamic" manifestation of Christianity.'

'In the, uh, Bible Belt?' *Snakes and hot coals?*

'Where I became fully aware of the power of God.' The priest looked up at the veiled church. 'Where, if you like, the power of the Holy Spirit reached out and touched me.'

No, Robin did *not* like. 'You notice how the mist winds itself around the tower? As a painter, that fascinates me.'

'The sheer fervour, the electric *momentum*, you encountered in little . . .' Ellis's hands forming fists for emphasis, 'little clapboard chapels. The living church – I knew what that meant for the first time. Over here, we have all these exquisite ancient buildings, steeped in centuries of worship . . . and we're losing it, *losing it*, Robin.'

'Right,' Robin had said neutrally.

Ellis nodded toward the ruins. 'Poets eulogizing the beauty of country churches . . . and they meant the *buildings*, the surroundings. Man, is that not beauty at its most superficial?'

'Uh . . . I guess.' Robin considered how Betty would want him to play this and so didn't rise to it. But he knew in his soul that what those poets were evoking, whether they were aware of it or not, was an *energy of place* which long predated Christianity. The energy Robin was experiencing right there, right this minute, with the tower uniting with the mist and the water surging below. Sure, the Christians picked up on that, mainly in medieval times, with all those soaring Gothic cathedrals, but basically it was out of their league.

Because, Robin thought, meeting the priest's pale eyes, this is a pagan thing, man.

And this was when he had first become aware of an agenda. Sensing that whatever the future held for him and this casual-looking priest in his army cast-offs, it was not going to involve friendly rivalry and good-natured badinage.

'Buildings are jewellery,' Ellis had said, 'baubles. When I came home, I felt like a missionary in my own land. I was working as a teacher at the time. But when I was subsequently ordained, ended up here, I knew this was where I was destined to be. These people have their priorities right.'

'How's that?'

Ellis let the question go by. He was now talking about how the States also had its *bad* side. How he had spent time in California, where people threw away their souls like candy wrappers, where the Devil squatted in shop windows like Santa Claus, handing out packs of tarot cards and runes and I Ching sets.

'Can you *believe* those people?' Robin turned away to control a grin. For, albeit he was East Coast raised, he *was* those people.

'Over here, it's less obvious.' Ellis shuddered suddenly. 'Far more deeply embedded. Like bindweed, the worst of it's underground.'

Robin hadn't reacted, though he was unsure of whether this was the best response or not. Maybe some normal person bombarded with this bullshit would, by now, be telling this guy he had things to do, someplace else to go, calls to make – nice talking with you, Reverend, maybe see you around.

Looking over at the rain-screened hills, Ellis was saying how, the very week he had arrived here, it was announced that archaeologists had stumbled on something in the Radnor Valley – evidence of one of the biggest prehistoric wooden temples ever discovered in Europe.

Robin's response had been, 'Yeah, wasn't that terrific?'

When Ellis had turned to him, there was a light in his eyes which Robin perceived as like a gas jet.

'He said it was a sign of something coming to the surface.'

'Them finding the prehistoric site?' Betty sat up, pushing her golden hair behind her ears.

'It was coming out like a rash, was how he put it,' Robin said. 'Like the disease under the surface – the disease which you only identify when the rash starts coming out?'

'What's he talking about?'

'Man with an agenda, Bets.' Robin detected a half-inch of beer in one of the Michelob bottles and drained it, laid down the bottle with a thump. 'If there's anything I can recognize straight off, it's another guy with an agenda.'

'Robin, *you* don't have an agenda, you just have woolly dreams.'

'You wanna hear this, or not?'

'Sorry,' Betty said, frayed. 'Go on.'

Robin told her that when Ellis had first come here, before the Church let him go his own way, he looked after four small parishes, on both sides of the border. New Radnor was the biggest. All the parishes possessed churches, except one of these was in ruins.

'But don't take this the wrong way. Remember this is a guy doesn't *go* for churches. He's into clapboard shacks. Now, Old Hindwell is a village with no church any more, not even a Baptist chapel. But one thing it does have is a clapboard fucking *shack*. Well, not exactly clapboard – more like concrete and steel. The parish hall in fact.'

'Is there one?'

'Up some steps, top of the village. Built, not too well, in the early sixties. Close to derelict, when Ellis arrived. He hacks through the brambles one day and a big light comes down on him, like that guy on the road to Damascus, and he's like, *"This is it. This is my church!"* You recall that film *Witness*, where the Amish community build this huge barn in, like, one day?'

'Everybody mucking in. Brilliant.'

'Yeah, well, what happens here is Christians converge from miles around to help Nick Ellis realize his vision. Money comes pouring in. Carpenters, plumbers, sundry artisans giving their work for free. No time at all, the parish hall's good as new . . . better than new. And there's a nice big cross sticking out the roof, with a light inside the porch. And every Sunday the place is packed with more people than all the other local churches put together.'

Robin paused.

Betty opened out her hands. 'What do you want me to say? Triumph of the spirit? You think I should knock that?'

'Wait,' Robin told her. 'How come all this goes down in a place with so little religious feeling they abandoned the original goddamn church?'

'Evangelism, Robin. It spreads like a grass fire when it gets going. He's a new kind of priest with all that American . . . whatever. If it can happen there, it can happen here – and obviously has. Which shows how right we were to keep a low profile, because those born-again people, to put it mildly, are *not* tolerant towards paganism.'

Robin shook his head. 'Ellis denies responsibility for the upsurge. Figures it was waiting to happen – to deal with something that went wrong. Something of which Old Hindwell church is symptomatic.'

Betty waited.

'So we're both moving in closer to the church, and I'm finding him a little irritating by now, so I start to point out these wonderful ancient yew trees – how the building itself might be medieval but I'm *told* that the yews in a circle and the general positioning of the church indicate that it occupies a pre-Christian site. I'm talking in a "this doesn't mean much to me but it's interesting, isn't it?" kind of voice.'

'Robin,' Betty said, 'you don't *possess* that voice.'

Ellis was staring at him. 'Who told you that, Robin?'

Robin floundered. 'Oh . . . the real estate agent, I guess.'

Furious with himself that, instead of speaking up for the oldest religion of these islands, he was scuttling away like some shamed vampire at dawn, allowing this humourless bastard to go on assuming without question that his own 2,000-year-old cult had established a right to the moral high ground. *So how did they achieve that, Nick? By waging countless so-called holy wars against other faiths? By fighting amongst themselves with bombs and midnight kneecappings, blowing guys away in front of their kids?*

'All right,' Ellis had then said, 'let me tell you the truth about this church, Robin. This church was dedicated to St Michael. How much do you know about him?'

Robin could only think of Marks and freaking Spencer, but was wise enough to say nothing.

'The Revelation of St John the Divine, Chapter Twelve. "And there was war in heaven. Michael and his angels fought against the dragon, and the dragon fought Michael and his angels." '

Robin had looked down at his boots.

' "And the great dragon was cast out . . . that old serpent called the Devil, and Satan, which deceiveth the whole world. He was cast out . . . into the earth." '

'Uh, right,' Robin said, 'I'd forgotten about that.'

'Interestingly, around the perimeter of Radnor Forest are several other churches dedicated to St Michael.'

'Not too much imagination in those days, I guess.'

Ellis had now taken off his beret. His face was shining with rain.

'The Archangel Michael is the most formidable warrior in God's army. Therefore a number of churches dedicated to him would represent a very powerful barrier against evil.'

'What evil would this *be* precisely, Nick?' Robin was becoming majorly exasperated by Ellis's habit of not answering questions – like your questions are sure to be stupid and inexact, so he was answering the ones you ought to have asked. It also bugged Robin when people talked so loosely about 'evil' – a coverall for fanatics.

Ellis said, 'I visit the local schools. Children still talk of a dragon in Radnor Forest. It's part of the folklore of the area. There's even a line of hills a few miles from here they call the Dragon's Back.'

Robin shrugged. 'Local place names. That so uncommon, Nick?'

'Not awfully. Satanic evil is ubiquitous.'

'Yeah, but is a dragon necessarily evil?' Robin was thinking of the fantasy novels of Kirk Blackmore, where dragons were fearsome forces for positive change.

Ellis gave him a cold look. 'It would seem to me, Robin, that a dragon legend and a circle of churches dedicated to St Michael is incontrovertible evidence of something requiring perpetual restraint.'

'I'm not getting this.'

'A circle of churches.' Ellis spread his hands. 'A holy wall to contain the dragon. But the dragon will always want to escape. Periodically, the dragon rears . . . and snaps . . . and is forced back again and again and keeps coming back . . .' Ellis clawing the air, a harsh light in his eyes, 'until something yields.'

Now he was looking over at the ruins again, like an army officer sizing up the field of battle. This was one serious fucking fruitcake.

'And the evil is now *inside* . . . The legend says – and

85

you'll find references to this in most of the books written about this area – that if just one of those churches should fall, the dragon will escape.'

Then he looked directly at Robin.

Robin said, 'But . . . this is a legend, Nick.'

'The circle of St Michael churches is not a legend.'

'You think this place is *evil*?'

'It's decommissioned. It no longer has the protection of St Michael. In this particular situation, I would suggest that's a sign that it requires . . . attention.'

'Attention?'

Robin put on a crazy laugh, but his heart wasn't in it. And Betty didn't laugh at all.

'What does he want?'

'He . . .' Robin shook his head. 'Oh, boy. He was warning me. That fruitcake was giving me notice.'

'Of what? What does he want?'

'He wants to hold a service here. He believes this church was abandoned because the dragon got in. Because the frigging dragon lies coiled here. And that God has chosen him, Ellis, given him the muscle, in the shape of the biggest congregations ever known in this area, given him the power to drive the dragon out.'

Betty went very still.

'All he wants, Bets . . . *all* he wants . . . is to come along with a few friends and hold some kind of a service.'

'What kind of a service?'

'You imagine that? All these farmers in their best suits and the matrons in their Sunday hats and Nick in his white surplice and stuff all standing around in a church with no roof singing goddamn "Bread of Heaven"? In a site that they stole from the Old Religion about 800 years ago and then fucking sold off? Jeez, I was so mad! This is *our* church now. On our farm. And we *like* dragons!'

Betty was silent. The whole room was silent. The rain had stopped, the breeze had died. Even the Rayburn had temporarily conquered its snoring.

Robin howled like a dog. 'What's happening here? Why do we have to wind up in a parish with a priest who's been exposed to the insane Bible-freaks who stalk the more primitive parts of my beloved homeland? And is therefore no longer content with vicarage tea parties and the organ fund.'

'So what did you say to him?'

'Bastard had me over a barrel. I say a flat "no", the cat's clean out the bag. So, what I said . . . to my shame, I said, Nick, I could not *think* of letting you hold a service in there. Look at all that mud! Look at those pools of water! Just give us some time – like we've only been here days – give us some time to get it cleaned up. How sad was *that*?'

Just like Ellis, she didn't seem to have been listening. 'Robin, what kind of service?'

'He said it would be no big deal – not realizing that any kind of damn service here *now*, was gonna be a big deal far as we're concerned. And if it's no big deal, why do it? Guy doesn't even *like* churches.'

'What kind of service?' Betty was at the edge of her chair and her eyes were hard.

'I don't know.' Robin was a little scared, and that made him angry. 'A short Eucharist? Did he say that? What is that precisely? I'm not too familiar with this Christian sh—'

'It's a Mass.'

'Huh?'

'An Anglican Mass. And do you know why a Mass is generally performed in a building other than a functioning church?'

He didn't fully. He could only guess.

'To cleanse it,' Betty said. 'The Eucharist is Christian disinfectant. To cleanse, to purify – to get rid of bacteria.'

'OK, let me get this . . .' Robin pulled his hands down his face, in praying mode. 'This is the E-word, right?'

Betty nodded.

An exorcism.

NINE

Visitor

The answering machine sounded quite irritable.

'*Mrs Watkins. Tania Beauman,* Livenight. *I've left messages for you all over the place. The programme goes out Friday night, so I really have to know whether it's yes or no. I'll be here until seven. Please call me . . . Thank you.*'

'Sorry.' Merrily came back into the kitchen, hung up her funeral cloak. 'I can't think with that thing bleeping.'

Barbara Buckingham was sitting at the refectory table, unwinding her heavy silk scarf while her eyes compiled a photo-inventory of the room.

'You're in demand, Mrs Watkins.' The slight roll on the 'r' and the barely perceptible lengthening of the 'a' showed her roots were sunk into mid-border clay. But this would be way back, many southern English summers since.

Walking through black and white timber-framed Ledwardine, across the cobbled square to the sixteenth-century vicarage, the dull day dying around them, the lights in the windows blunting the bite of evening, she'd said, 'How quaint and cosy it is here. I'd forgotten. And so close.'

Close to what? Merrily had made a point of not asking.

'Tea?' She still felt slightly ashamed of the kitchen – must get round to emulsioning it in the spring. 'Or coffee?'

Barbara would have tea. She took off her gloves.

Like her late sister, she was good-looking, but in a sleek

and sharp way, with a turned-up nose which once would have been cute but now seemed haughty. '*The sister's a retired teacher and there's no arguing with her*,' Eileen Cullen had said.

'I didn't expect you to be so young, Mrs Watkins.'

'Going on thirty-seven?'

'Young for what you're doing. Young to be the diocesan exorcist.'

'Diocesan deliverance consultant.'

'You must have a progressive bishop.'

'Not any more.' Merrily filled the kettle.

Mrs Buckingham dropped a short laugh. 'Of course. That man who couldn't take the pressure and walked out. Hunt? Hunter? I try to keep up with Church affairs. I was head-mistress of a Church school for many years.'

'In this area? The border?'

'God no. Got out of there before I was twenty. Couldn't stand the cold.'

Merrily put the kettle on the stove. 'We can get bad winters here,' she agreed.

'Ah . . . not simply the climate. My father was a farmer in Radnor Forest. I remember my whole childhood as a kind of perpetual February.'

'Frugal?' Merrily tossed tea bags into the pot.

Mrs Buckingham exhaled bitter laughter. 'In our house, those two tea bags would have to be used at least six times. The fat in the chip pan was only renewed for Christmas.' Her face grew pinched at the memories.

'You were poor?'

'Not particularly. We had in excess of 130 acres. Marginal land, mind – always appallingly overgrazed. Waste nothing. Make every square yard earn its keep. Have you heard of hydatid disease?'

'Vaguely.'

'Causes cysts to grow on internal organs, sometimes the size of pomegranates. Originates from a tapeworm absorbed by dogs allowed to feed on infected dead sheep. Or, on our farm, *required* to eat dead sheep. Human beings can pick it up – the tapeworm eggs – simply through stroking the sheepdog. When I was sixteen I had to go into hospital to have a hydatid cyst removed from my liver.'

'How awful.'

'That was when I decided to get out. I doubt my father even noticed I was gone. Had another mouth to feed by then. A girl again, unfortunately.'

'Menna?'

'She would be . . . ten months old when I left. It was a long time before I began to feel guilty about abandoning her – fifteen years or more. And by then it was too late. They'd probably forgotten I'd ever existed. I expect he was even grateful I'd gone – another opportunity to try for a son, at no extra cost. A farmer with no son is felt to be lacking in something.'

'Any luck?'

'My mother miscarried, apparently,' Mrs Buckingham said brusquely. 'There was a hysterectomy.' She shrugged. 'I never saw them again.'

'Where did you go?'

'Found a job in Hereford, in a furniture shop. The people there were very good to me. They gave me a room above the shop, next to the storeroom. Rather frightening at night. All those empty chairs: I would imagine people sitting there, silently, waiting for me when I came back from night classes. Character-building, though, I suppose. I got two A levels and a grant for teacher-training college.'

It all sounded faintly Dickensian to Merrily, though it could have been no earlier than the 1960s.

'So you never went back?' The phone was ringing.

'After college, I went to work in Hampshire, near Portsmouth. Then a husband, kids – grown up now. No, I never went back, until quite recently. A neighbour's daughter – Judith – kept me informed, through occasional letters. She was another farmer's daughter, from a rather less primitive farm. Please get that phone call, if you want.'

Merrily nodded, went through to the office.

'As it happens' – closing the scullery door – 'she's here now.'

'Listen, I'm sorry,' Eileen Cullen said. 'I couldn't think what else to tell her. Showed up last night, still unhappy about the sister's death and getting no cooperation from the doctor. I didn't have much time to bother with her either. I just thought somebody ought to persuade her to forget about Mr Weal, and go home, get on with her life. And I thought she'd take it better coming from a person of the cloth such as your wee self.'

'Forgive me, but that doesn't sound like you.'

'No. Well . . .'

'So she didn't say anything about holding a special service in church then?'

'Merrily, the problem is I'm on the ward in one minute.'

'Bloody hell, Eileen—'

'Aw, Jesus, all the woman wants is her sister laid to rest in a decent, holy fashion. She's one of your fellow Christians. Tell her you'll say a few prayers for the poor soul, and leave it at that.'

There was an unexpected undercurrent here.

'What happened with Mr Weal after I left the other night?'

'Well, he came out. Eventually.'

'Eventually?'

'He came out when *she* did. And he chose to accompany her down to the mortuary.'

'Is that normal?'

'Well, of course it isn't fockin' normal. We're not talking about a normal feller here! It was a special concession. Merrily, I really have to go. If the sister's tardy, how can you expect the nurses—'

'Eileen!'

'That's all I can tell you. Just persuade her to go home. She'll do no good for herself.'

'What's *that* supposed to—'

Cullen hung up.

It was dark outside now, and the thorns were ticking against the scullery window.

When Merrily returned to the kitchen, Barbara Buckingham was standing under a wall lamp, her silk scarf dangling from one hand as if she was wondering whether or not to leave.

'Mrs Watkins, I don't want to be a pain . . .'

'Merrily. Don't be silly. Sit down. There's no—'

'I try to be direct, you see. In my childhood, no one was direct. They'd never meet your eyes. Keep your head down, avoid direct conflict, run neither with the English nor the Welsh. Keep your head down and move quietly, in darkness.'

The woman had been too long out of it, Merrily thought, as the kettle boiled. She'd turned her spartan childhood into something Gothic. 'Tell me about the . . . possession.'

'In essence, I believe, your job is to liberate them. The possessed, I mean.'

Merrily carefully took down two mugs from the crockery shelf. 'Milk?' Through the open door, she could still hear that damned rosebush scratching at the scullery window.

'A little. No sugar.'

Merrily brought milk from the fridge. She left her own tea black, and carried both mugs to the table.

'It's a big word, Barbara.'

'Yes.'

'And often abused – I have to say that.'

'We should both be direct.'

'And I should tell you I've yet to encounter a valid case of possession. But then I've not been doing this very long.'

'It may be the wrong word. Perhaps I only used it to get your attention.' Looking frustrated, Barbara tossed her scarf onto the table. 'I've attended church most of my life. Much of the time out of habit, I admit; occasionally out of need. I have no time for . . . mysticism, that's what I'm trying to say. I'm not fey.'

Merrily smiled. 'No.'

'But Menna has been possessed for years. Do you know what I mean? Weal suffocated her in life; now he won't let her go after death.'

Cullen: *He asks for a bowl and a cloth and he washes her. Very tenderly, reverently you might say. And then he'll wash himself: his face, his hands, in the same water.'*

And followed her down to the mortuary. Did Barbara know about that?

Merrily heard a key in the side door, beyond the scullery, and then footsteps on the back stairs: Jane coming in, going up to her apartment.

'They were our family solicitors,' Barbara said. 'Everybody's solicitors, in those days, it seemed. Weal and Son . . . the first Weal was Jeffery's grandfather, the "and son" was Jeffery's father R.T. Weal. Weal and Son, of Kington, and their gloomy old offices with the roll-top desks and a Victorian chair like a great dark throne. I first remember Jeffery when he was fifteen going on fifty. A lumbering, sullen boy, slow-moving, slow-thinking, single-minded, his future written in stone – Weal and Son and Son, even unto the ends of the earth. I hated them, the complete *unchangingness* of them – same chair, same desks, same dark tweed suits, same dark car creeping up the track.'

'Eileen Cullen told me she thought he probably became a father figure,' Merrily said. 'After Menna had spent some years looking after her own father. Your dad was widowed, presumably.'

'Sixteen or seventeen years ago. I had a letter from Judith – my friend in Old Hindwell. My father wouldn't have told me; I no longer existed for him. And he was ailing, too. Later I learned that Menna never had a boyfriend or any social life, so she lost the best years of her life to her bloody father, and the rest of it to Weal. Who, of course, became the proverbial tower of strength when the old man died.'

'He looked after her then?'

'Seized his chance with a weak, unworldly girl. I . . . came to find her about two years ago. I'd recently taken early retirement. My daughter had just got married, my husband was away – I was at a *very* loose end. One morning, I simply got in my car and drove up here, and knocked on their door . . .' She stared into space. 'Menna seemed . . . unsurprised, unmoved, entirely incurious. I'd forgotten what these people can be like. She just stood there in the doorway – didn't even ask me in. Talked in an offhand way, as though I was a neighbour whom she saw occasionally but didn't particularly care for.'

'And you actually hadn't seen each other since she was a baby?'

The woman shook her head. There was distance now in her voice. 'She . . . wore no make-up. She was pale, in an unnatural, etiolated kind of way, like grass that's been covered up. And quite beautiful. But she didn't seem to either know or care who I was. She might as well already have been dead.'

Jane nicked the cordless from Mum's bedroom and took it upstairs to the trio of attic rooms that now made up her apartment: bedroom, sitting room–study and a half-finished bathroom. She put on the lights, took off her jacket, sat on the bed. Thinking about poor Gomer going home on his own to a house full of Minnie's things. It made her cry.

Fucking death!

Jane dried her eyes on a corner of the pillowcase. Gomer wouldn't cry. Gomer would get on with it. But how much in life was really worth getting on with? Where was it leading? Was Minnie any closer now to knowing the answer? *Oh God*.

Jane picked up the phone and looked at it and shrugged. If this didn't work, it didn't work. She rolled up her sleeve. The *Livenight* number was written in fibre-tip on the inside of her left arm. Jane pushed in the numbers, asked for Tania Beauman. The switchboard put her on hold and made her listen to Dire Straits – which could have been worse, though Jane would never admit it.

She leaned back against the headboard and contemplated the Mondrian walls, wondering if anyone else had ever had the idea of painting the squares and rectangles between sixteenth-century beams in different colours. She wondered what Eirion would think of it.

If she was ever to bring him up here.

If? Time was running out if she was going to fit in two *serious* lovers before she hit twenty. Serious could mean six months. Longer.

'Tania Beauman.'

'Oh, hi.' Jane sat up. 'You know who this is?'

'Oh,' said Tania.

'Hey, don't be like that. I may have cracked it for you.'

'Cracked . . . what?'

Jane swung her feet to the floor. 'I'm telling you, Tania, it wasn't easy. She really didn't want to know. *Livenight*? Pff! But I'm, like, "Look, Merrily, being elitist is what put the Church of England in the hole it's in today. You can't just turn a blind eye to paganism and pretend it isn't happening all over again. Or before you know it there'll be more of *them* around than you . . ." '

'That's a very cogent argument,' Tania said, 'but why aren't I talking to your mother?'

'Because I've, like, *nearly* got her convinced – but I'm not quite there yet.'

'Well, I have to tell you, you don't have much time.'

'But do I have the incentive, Tania? That's the point.'

'I wondered if there'd be a point.'

'To be blunt,' Jane said, 'I need a very, very small favour.'

Home burial. It was becoming, if not exactly commonplace, then less of an upper-class phenomenon than it used to be. Merrily tried to explain this to Barbara Buckingham: that it was a secular thing, or sometimes a green issue; that you often didn't even need official permission.

'The main drawback for most people is the risk of taking value off their house if and when it's sold. No one wants a grave in the garden.'

'He's not . . .' Barbara had picked up her scarf again; she began to wind it around her hands. 'He is not going to bury Menna; that's the worst of it. She's going into a . . . tomb.' She pulled the scarf tight. 'A mausoleum.'

'Oh.' *To be loved like that.*

'He has a Victorian house at Old Hindwell,' Barbara said. 'The former rectory. Do you know Old Hindwell?'

'Not really. Is it in this diocese, I can't remember?'

'Possibly. It's very close to the border, about three miles from Kington, on the edge of the Forest. Radnor Forest. Weal's house isn't remote, but it has no immediate neighbours. In the garden there's a . . . structure – wine store, ice house, air-raid shelter, I don't know precisely what it is, but that's where she's going to be.'

'Like a family vault?'

'It's sick. I went to see a solicitor in Hereford this morning. He told me there was nothing I could do. A man has a perfect legal right to keep his dead wife in a private museum.'

'And as a solicitor himself, your brother-in-law is going to be fully aware of his rights.'

'Don't call him that!' Barbara turned away. 'Whole thing's obscene.'

'He loved her,' Merrily said uncertainly. 'He doesn't want to be parted from her. He wants to feel that she's near him. That's the usual reason.'

'No! It's a statement of ownership. Possession is – what is it? – nine points of the law?'

'That word again. Do you mind if I smoke?'

'Go ahead.'

Merrily lit a Silk Cut, pulled over an ashtray.

'What about the funeral itself? Is it strictly private? I mean, are you kind of barred?'

'My dear!' Barbara dropped the scarf. 'It's going to be a highly public affair. A service in the village hall.'

'Not the church?'

'They don't have a church any more. The minister holds his services in the village hall.'

'Ah. And the minister is . . .?'

'Father Ellis.'

'Nick Ellis.' Merrily nodded. This explained a lot.

'I don't know *why* so many Anglicans are choosing to call themselves "Father" now, as if they're courting Catholicism. You know this man?'

'I know *of* him. He's a *charismatic* minister, which means—'

'Not happy-clappy?' Barbara's eyes narrowed in distaste. 'Everybody hugging one another?'

'That's one aspect of it. Nick Ellis is also a member of a

group known as the Sea of Light. It's a movement inside the Anglican Church, which maintains that the Church has become too obsessed with property. Keepers of buildings rather than souls. They claim the Holy Spirit flows through people, not stones. So a Sea of Light minister is more than happy to hold services in village halls, community centres – and private homes, of course.'

'And the same goes for burial.'

'I would guess so.'

'So Jeffery has an accomplice in the clergy.' Barbara Buckingham stood up. 'He would have, wouldn't he? It's such a tight little world.'

'Look,' Merrily said, 'I know how you feel, but I really don't think there's anything you can do about it. And if Nick Ellis is conducting a funeral service at the village hall and a ceremony in J.W. Weal's back garden, I'm not sure I can hold another one in a church. However—'

'Mrs Watkins . . . Merrily . . .' She'd failed with the solicitor, now she was trying the Church.

Merrily said awkwardly, 'I'm really not sure this is a spiritual problem.'

'Oh, but it *is*.' Barbara splayed her fingers on the table, leaned towards Merrily. 'She comes to me, you see . . .'

The bereavement ghost: the visitor. Maybe sitting in a familiar chair or walking in the garden, or commonly – like Menna – in dreams. Barbara Buckingham, staying at a hotel near Kington, had dreamt of her sister every night since her death.

Menna was wearing a white shift or shroud, with darkness around her.

'You'd prefer, no doubt, to think the whole thing is a projection of my guilt,' Barbara said.

'Perhaps of your loss, even though you didn't know her. Perhaps an even greater loss, because of all those years you *might* have known her, and now you realize you never will. Is your husband . . .?'

'In France on a buying trip. He has an antiques business.'

'How do you feel when you wake up?'

'Anxious.' Barbara drank some tea very quickly. 'And drained. Exhausted and debilitated.'

'Have you seen a doctor?'

'Yes. As it happens' – a mild snort – 'I've seen Menna's doctor, Collard Banks-Morgan. We were at the same primary school. "Dr Coll", they all call him now. But if you were suggesting that a little Valium might help to relax me, I didn't go to consult him about myself.'

'You wanted to know why she'd suffered a stroke.'

'I gatecrashed his surgery at the school in Old Hindwell. Made a nuisance of myself, not that it made any difference. Bloody man told me I was asking him to be unethical, pre-empting the post-mortem. He was like that as a child, terribly proper. If they'd had a head boy at the primary school, it would've been Collard Banks-Morgan.'

'*Did* you find out if there was a long-term blood pressure problem?'

'No.' Barbara Buckingham put on her scarf at last. 'But I will.'

'Look,' Merrily said, 'why don't we say a prayer for Menna before you go? For her spirit. Why don't we pop over to the church?'

'I've taken too much of your time.'

'I think it might help.' Fifth rule of Deliverance: whether you believe the story or not, never leave things without at least a prayer. 'I *would* like to help, if I can.'

And there was more to this. Merrily was curious now. Everything suggested there was more. Why should this woman feel robbed of a sister she'd never really known?

'Then come to the funeral,' Barbara said.

'Me?'

'Is that too much of an imposition?'

'Well, no but—'

'You were at the hospital with her.'

Merrily agonized then about whether she should tell Barbara Buckingham what she'd witnessed in the side ward. It was clear Cullen hadn't or Barbara would have mentioned that. She remembered the feeling she'd had then of something ritualistic about the way Weal was putting dabs of water on Menna's corpse and then himself. Refusing to let the nurses try to feed her. Refusing to let Merrily pray for her. Wanting to do everything himself. It was, she supposed, a kind of possession.

But she decided to say nothing. It might only inflame an already fraught situation.

'OK. I'll try to come. What day?'

'Saturday. Three thirty. Old Hindwell village hall.'

'That should be OK. If something comes up, where can I get a message to you?'

'Doesn't matter. If you aren't there, you aren't there.'

'I'll do my best. Have you . . . spoken to Mr Weal?'

'I'm not ready for that yet,' Barbara said. 'But I shall do. Thank you, Merrily.'

TEN

Nightlife of Old Hindwell

Robin had the map spread out under a wine-bottle lamp on the kitchen table, after they'd finished supper.

'Come take a look, Bets.' Holding his thick, black drawing pencil the way he held his *athame* in a rite. 'Whole bunch of churches around the Forest.'

The lamplight sheened his dense, Dark Ages hair. Betty leaned over him. He smelled sweet and warm, like a puppy. She felt an unexpected stirring; he was so lovably uncomplicated.

And so simplistic, sometimes, in his thinking. Why, since they'd arrived here, had any physical desire always been so swiftly soured by irritation? She gazed around the still-gloomy farmhouse kitchen. Why, with the stove on for over a week, was there still an aura of damp – always worse after sunset? She felt clammy and uncomfortable, as though she had the curse. If Robin had said, 'Let's give this place up, and leave now, tonight,' she wouldn't have hesitated.

But since that mention of the E-word, his attitude had unsubtly altered. A couple of seconds of trepidation then the male thing was kicking in. Robin wanted to find out precisely where Ellis was coming from, then get in his face. It hadn't been helped, Betty guessed, by Ellis wearing army gear. Combat gear? She was appalled to think that she might even once have shared Robin's zeal. If only this had been someone else's house, the home of a fellow pagan in need of moral support.

If only she wasn't already growing to hate their church too much to want to defend it.

She'd tried to remember her reaction on first seeing it, and couldn't. Probably because she was being practical at the time and paying more attention to the farmhouse, leaving Robin to moon over the ruins, take dozens of photographs.

He'd now finished ringing churches on the Landranger map. Although it didn't identify individual ones except by symbols, nearby place names sometimes would give a clue to the dedication. Betty could help him out there a little, from childhood knowledge of Welsh. She put a thumbnail to the southernmost symbol.

'That one: the village is Llanfihangel nant Melan. Llanfihangel's Welsh for "The Church of St Michael".'

'Cool.' Robin drew an extra ring around the church and then tracked around the others with the tip of his pencil until he came to the northern part of the forest perimeter. 'What's this? Same word, right?'

'Llanfihangel Rhydithon. That's another, yeah. And then ours, of course. Three St Michael churches around the Forest. He was right, I suppose.'

'Gotta be more. Three doesn't make a circle.'

With swift, firm pencil strokes, he redrew the plan on his sketch-pad. Graphics were important to Robin. Making a picture made things real.

'Of course,' Betty said, 'there's nothing to suggest all these churches were built at the same time. I vaguely remember going to Llanfihangel Rhydithon as a kid, and I don't think it's even medieval.'

'It's the site that counts. Come on, Bets, what are you, agnostic now? Look through Ellis's eyes. Guy thinks he's fighting an active Devil.'

'Or, more specifically, in the absence of people actually sacrificing cockerels and abusing children on his doorstep – against us,' Betty said bitterly.

'I'm still not sure he knows. Ellis was fishing. Like, who could've told him? Who *else* knows, or could've seen anything? We didn't even use removal men.'

Betty said, 'It scares me. I don't want this.'

'Aw, come on,' he said. 'You're a witch. Hey, you know, damn near all these churches have just gotta be on older sites, when you see how close they are to standing stones and burial mounds.' He leaned back in satisfaction. 'This valley's a damned prehistoric ritual freaking wonderland. Which explains everything.'

'It does?'

'You got all these sacred sites, right? It's a good bet most of them were still being used by surviving pagan groups well into medieval times, and probably long after that. This was a remote area with a small and scattered population. Closed in, secretive. I think it's fair to assume that even when they'd been brutally eradicated from most of the rest of the country, the Old Ways were still preserved here.'

'Possibly.'

'The Archangel Michael's the hard guy of the Church. It's them saying to the pagans, you bastards better come around, *or else*. Ellis, as a fundamentalist, relates to all of that. Plus, he's been influenced by insane Bible Belt evangelists who persecute snakes. Plus, his ego's already been blown up sky high by the size of congregations he's pulling when all the neighbouring churches are going down the tubes. I've decided the guy sucks. The only remaining question is how long we keep stalling before we tell him that he and his exorcism squad can go screw themselves.'

'I was going to say that if we don't make an issue of it, if we let it go quiet, then he'll probably forget about us,' Betty said lamely.

'Not gonna happen. Believe me, this guy's on some kind of crusade under the banner of St Michael. Hey! Would that explain the army surplus stuff? *Shit*.'

Robin smiled at his own flawed logic. Betty saw, with a plummeting heart, that he *wanted* to be a target of Christian fanaticism.

'When *we* look at those ruins,' he said, 'we see a resurgence of the true, indigenous spirituality. Whereas *he* sees a naked tower giving him and his religion the finger. He *so* wants to be the guy who killed the dragon and claimed it all back. It's an ego thing.'

'You and him both.'

The smile crashed. 'Meaning *what*?'

'You have a few beers together, you size each other up, and now you're both flexing your muscles for the big fight. You can't wait, can you? You love it that he's got this huge mass of followers and there's just the two of us here, newcomers, isolated . . .'

'Now listen, lady.' Robin was on his feet, furious. 'My instinct was to kick his ass, right from the off, but no . . . I play it the way I figure *you* would want me to! Mr Nice Guy, Mr Don't Frighten The Horses . . . Mr Take A Faceful Of Shit And Keep Smiling kind of guy!'

'No, you didn't. You thought you could play with him, lead him around the houses, take the piss out of him a little . . . when in fact he was playing with *you*.'

'You weren't even there!'

'And you've never given a thought to where this could leave us. We have to live here . . . Whatever happens, we have to live here afterwards. And we *will* have to live here, because – in case you haven't thought about this – who is going to buy a run-down house along with a ruined church which the local minister insists is infested with demonic evil?' She spun away from him. 'You shithead.'

Robin snatched in a breath that was halfway to a sob then threw his pencil down on the table. 'I need some air.'

'You certainly do!'

He turned his back on her, strode across the kitchen like Lord bloody Madoc and tore open the back door. Before he slammed it behind him, she heard the rushing of the rain-swollen Hindwell Brook in the night, like a hiss of glee.

Betty let her head fall into her hands on the tabletop.

What have we done? What have we walked into?

Robin stomped across the yard, hit the track toward the gate and the road. It was cold and the going wasn't so easy in the dark, but he was damned if he was going back for a coat and flashlight.

Why, *why* was whatever he said, whatever he did, whatever he tried to do, always the wrong fucking thing?

Four years he and Betty had been together and, sure, they were different people, raised in different cultures. But they'd previously come through on shared beliefs, a strong respect for natural forces and each other's destiny.

And he'd thought the road to Old Hindwell was lit for them both.

All the portents had been there, just as soon as they decided they would look for a place in the countryside where they might explore the roots of the old spirituality. They'd let it be known on the pagan network that they were looking for something rural and it didn't have to be luxurious. The Shrewsbury coven had worked a spell on their behalf and, before that week was out, they'd received – anonymously, but with a wellwisher's symbol and the message 'Thought you might be interested in this . . . Blessed Be!' – the estate agent's particulars of St Michael's Farm. And – in the very same post – a letter from Al Delaney at Talisman to say that Kirk Blackmore was impressed with Robin's work and would like him to design the new cover . . . with the possibility of a contract for the soon-to-be-rejacketed backlist of SEVEN VOLUMES!

Even Betty had to agree, it was like writing in the sky.

Robin joined the lane that led first past the Prosser farm and then on to the village. The farm was spread across the council roadway, like it owned it, sheds and barns on either side, mud from tractor wheels softening the surface of the road. A Land-Rover was parked under an awning. It had a big yellow sticker in the back window, and even at night you could read 'Christ is the Light!' in luminous yellow. Robin gave a moan, stifled it. He hadn't known about this. If Ellis denounced them, they'd have no support from their neighbours.

When he got clear of the farm he surveyed the night. Ahead of him, the moon lay on its back over a long hill bristling with ranks of conifers – a hedgehog's back, a dragon's back. Robin held out his arms as if to embrace the hill, then let them fall uselessly to his sides and walked on down the middle of the narrow lane, with ditches to either side and banks topped by hedges so savagely pleached they were almost like hurdles. Gareth Prosser was clearly a farmer who liked to keep nature under his thumb. *His farm, his land.* Robin wondered how Prosser had reacted to the team of archaeologists who'd moved in and sheared the surface from one of his fields to uncover postholes revealing that, 4,000 years ago, the farm had been a key site of ritual pagan worship. Maybe Prosser had gotten Ellis in to sanctify the site.

Whatever, there was virtually nothing to see there now. Robin had sent off to the Council for British Archaeology for the report on the Radnor Valley dig. A couple of weeks ago, when he and Betty had driven down with a vanload of books, he'd checked out the site but found just a few humps and patches where the soil had been put back and reseeded. The team had taken away their finds – the flint arrowheads and axes – and hundreds of photos, and given the temple back to the sheep.

And to the pagans.

Well, why not? The night before they moved in, they'd agreed there should be a sabbat here at Imbolc – which Betty preferred to call by its old Christian name, Candlemas, because it was prettier. They'd agreed there should be the traditional Crown of Lights, which Betty would wear if there was no more suitable candidate. At the old church above the water, it was all going to be totally beautiful; Robin had had this fantasy of the village people coming along to watch or even join in and bringing their kids – this atmosphere of joy and harmony at Imbolc, Candlemas, the first day of Celtic spring, the glimmering in the darkness.

But that had not been mentioned since, and he was damned if he was gonna bring it up again.

Robin walked on, uphill now. Presently, the hedge on the right gave way to a stone wall, and he entered the village of Old Hindwell. As if to mock the word 'Old', the first dwelling in the village was a modern brick bungalow. A few yards further on was the first streetlight, a bluish bulb under a tin hat on a bracket projecting from a telephone pole. Older cottages on either side now. At the top of the hill, the road widened into a fork.

On the corner was the pub, the Black Lion, the utility bulkhead bulb over its porch clouded with the massed corpses of flies. It was an alehouse, not much more; the licensee, Greg Starkey, had come from London with big ideas but not pulled enough customers to realize them.

Tonight, Robin could have used a drink. Jacketless, therefore walletless, he dug into his pockets for change, came up with a single 50p piece. Could you get any kind of drink for 50p? He figured not.

'Robin. Hi.'

'Jeez!' He jumped. She'd come out of an entrance to the Black Lion's back yard. 'Uh . . . Marianne.'

Greg's wife. She moved out under the bulb, so he could see she was wearing a turquoise fleece jacket over a low-cut black top. Standard landladywear in her part of London, maybe, but not so often seen out here. But Marianne made no secret of how much she'd give to get back to the city.

'Haven't seen you for days and days, Robin.'

'Oh . . . Well, lot of work. The house move, you know?'

The last time he'd seen her was when he'd driven down on his own with a vanload of stuff, grabbing some lunch at the Lion. She'd seemed hugely pleased that he was moving in, with or without a wife. *'Anything you wanna know about the place, you come and ask me; Wednesdays are best, that's when Greg goes over to Hereford market.'*

Yeah, well.

'Bored already, Robin? I did warn you.'

She was late thirties, disillusion setting up permanent home in the lines either side of her mouth.

Robin said, 'I, uh . . . I guess I just like the night.'

'Robin, love,' she said, 'this ain't *night*. This is just bleedin' darkness.'

She did this cackly laugh. He smiled. 'So, uh . . . you still don't feel too good about here.'

'Give the boy a prize off the top shelf.'

Her voice was too loud for this village at night. It bounced off walls. She moved toward him. He could smell that she'd been drinking. She stopped less than a foot away. There was no one else in sight. Robin kind of wished he'd turned around at the bottom of the street.

'This is the nearest I get to a night out, you know that? We got to *work*. We got to open the boozer every lunchtime and every bleedin' night of the week, and we don't get the same day off 'cause we can't afford to pay nobody, and we wouldn't trust 'em to keep their fingers out of the bleedin' till, anyway.'

'Aw, come on, Marianne . . .'

'They all hate us. We'll always be outsiders.'

'Come on . . . Nobody hates you.'

'So we take our *pleasures* separately. Greg whoops it up at Hereford market on a Wednesday. Me, I just stand in the street and wait for a beautiful man to come along who don't stink of sheep dip.'

'Marianne, I think—'

'Oh, sorry! I forgot – except for this Saturday when I'm going to a funeral. Because it is potilic . . . what'd I say? *Politic* – that's what Greg says: politic. I'm pissed, Robin . . .' Putting out her hands as if to steady herself, gripping his chest. 'And you're very appealing to me. I been thinking about you a lot. You're a different kind of person, aincha?'

'I'm an American kind of person is all. Otherwise just a regular—'

'Now don't go modest on me for Gawd's sake. I tell you what . . .' She started to rub her hands over his chest and stomach. 'You can kiss me, Mr American-kind-of-person. Think of it as charity to the Third World. 'Cause if this ain't the Third bleedin' World . . .'

'Uh, call me old-fashioned' – Robin gently detached her hands – 'but I really don't think that would be too wise.'

'Well, if anybody's watching . . .' Marianne's voice rose. 'If anybody's spying from behind their lace bleedin' curtains, they can *go fuck themselves*!'

Robin panicked; no way he wanted to be associated with this particular attitude. He backed off so fast that Marianne toppled towards him, clawed vaguely at the air and fell with her hands flat on the cindered surface of the pub's parking lot.

Where she stayed, on all fours, looking down at the road. *Oh shit.*

Robin moved to help her. She looked up at him and bared her teeth like a cornered cat. 'You pushed me.'

'No, no, I really didn't. You know I didn't.'

Marianne staggered to her feet, hands waving in the air for balance.

'How about we get you inside,' Robin said.

'You pushed me!' Backing towards the yard entrance, holding up her scratched hands like she was displaying crucifixion scars. If the people of Old Hindwell hadn't been watching from behind their curtains before, they sure were now.

'Fuck you!' Marianne said. '*Fuck you!*' she screamed and flew at him like a crazy chicken.

Robin backed off and spun around and found himself running any which way, until he was out of breath.

He stopped. Apart from his own panting, the place was silent again. He looked around, saw only night. The buildings had gone. He didn't know where he was.

And then he looked up and there, set into the partially afforested hillside, was the tip of a golden light, a shining ingot in the dense, damp, conifered darkness. It was, by far, the brightest light in Old Hindwell village and, as he stepped back, it lengthened and branched out. Became a cross, in golden neon.

Nick Ellis's clapboard church.

The cross hung there as if unsupported, like a big, improbable star.

The truth was, Robin found it kind of chilling. It was like

he'd been driven into a trap. Away in the darkness, he heard footsteps. He froze. Was she coming after him?

Too heavy, too slow. And the steps were receding. Robin walked quietly back the way he'd come and presently the light above the pub door reappeared. He moved cautiously into the roadway in case Marianne was still around, claws out.

A few yards ahead of him, passing the entrance to the school-turned-surgery, was a man on his own. A man so big he was like an outsize shadow thrown on a wall. *Must be a head taller than most of the farmers hereabouts.* But he hadn't come out of the pub. He was not drunk. He had a steady, stately walk and, as he passed the pub, Robin saw by the bulkhead light that the man was dressed in a dark suit and a white shirt and tie. The kind of attire farmers wore only for funerals.

The guy walked slowly back down the street, the same way Robin was headed. After a dozen or so paces, he stopped and looked over his shoulder for two, three seconds. Robin saw his face clearly: stiff, grey hair and kind of a hooked nose, like the beak of an eagle.

The guy turned and continued on his way down the street. Robin, having had to take the same route, hung around a while to put some distance between them; he didn't feel too sociable right now, but he did feel cold. He stood across from the pub, shivering and hugging himself.

The big guy was a shambling shadow against curtained windows lit from behind. Halfway down the street, he stopped again, looked back over his shoulder. *Looked*, not glanced. Robin only saw his face in silhouette this time. He was surely looking for someone, but there was no one there.

Robin shook his head, uncomprehending – a little more spooked.

The nightlife of Old Hindwell.

ELEVEN

No Ghosts, No God

Huddled in Jane's duffel coat, she walked past the village square, where the cobbles were glassy with frost. The moon was in the west, still hard and brighter than the security lamp beside the front door of the Swan.

It was 5.30 a.m. She clutched the church keys in a gloved hand. She planned to pray before the altar for Barbara Buckingham and for the soul of her sister, Menna.

Merrily walked in through the lychgate. Somewhere, beyond the orchard, a fox yelped. Down in the churchyard she saw a soft and now familiar glow.

'Last time, vicar. Honest to God.'

'Gomer, I don't mind, really.'

'Unnatural, sure t'be. Be thinkin' I'm some ole pervert, ennit?'

Merrily smiled. He was crouching by Minnie's grave, an area of raised earth, an elongated mole-tump, with the hurricane lamp on it. No memorial yet. No sound of underground ticking.

'I was just thinking, like,' Gomer said. 'I don't want no bloody stone. I got to have a stone?'

'Don't see why.'

'Wood. I likes wood. En't no good with stone, but I could carve out a nice piece of oak, see.' He looked up at Merrily, lamplight moons in his glasses. 'En't nothing to do with the money, like. Be a proper piece. We never talked about it, but her liked a nice bit of oak, my Min. I'll put on it about Frank as well, see.'

'Whatever you like, Gomer. Whatever you think she'd have wanted.'

'Summat to do, ennit? Long ole days, see, vicar. Long ole days.'

Merrily sat on a raised stone tomb, tucking her coat underneath her. 'What else will you do, Gomer?'

'Oh.' Gomer sniffed meditatively. 'Bit o' this, bit o' that.'

'Will you stay here?'

'Never thought about moving.'

'Jane thought you might go back to Radnorshire.'

'What for?'

'Roots?'

Gomer sniffed again abruptly. 'People talks a lot of ole wallop 'bout roots. Roots is generally gnarled and twisted. Best kept buried, my experience.'

'Yeah, you could be right.' She had a thought. 'You ever know a family called Thomas down on the border?'

'Knowed 'bout half a dozen families called Thomas, over the years. Danny Thomas, up by Kinnerton, he's a good ole boy. Keeps a 'lectric guitar and amplifiers in his tractor shed, on account his wife, Greta, she hates rock and roll. They was at Min's funeral.'

'Around Old Hindwell, I was thinking.'

'Ole Hindwell.' Gomer accepted a Silk Cut from Merrily's packet. 'Gareth Prosser, he's the big man in Ole Hindwell. Laid some field drainage for him, years back. Then he inherits another 200 acres and a pile o' cash, and the bugger buys hisself a second-hand digger at a farm sale. Always thought theirselves a cut above, the Prossers. County councillor, magistrate, all this ole wallop.'

'These particular Thomases had two daughters. Barbara was one?'

'Got you now. Her runned away?'

'That's right.'

'An' the other one wed Big Weal, the lawyer.'

'Menna.'

'Their ole man was Merv Thomas, Maesmawr, up by Walton. Never worked for 'em, mind – too tight, digged their own cesspits, never drained a field. Merv's dead now, ennit? Ar, course he is. Her'd never be wed otherwise.'

'You know Weal?'

'Always avoided lawyers,' Gomer said. 'Thieving bastards, pardon me, vicar. Weal's ole-fashioned, mind, but that don't make him any less of a thieving bastard. Looks after his wife, though, 'cordin' to what they says.'

'Menna's dead, Gomer.'

'Never!' Gomer was shocked enough to whip the ciggy out of his mouth.

'Died in the County, same night as Minnie.'

'But her was no more'n a kiddie!'

'Thirty-nine. A stroke.'

'Bugger me.' Gomer stared down at the soil. 'Big Weal must be gutted.'

'Could say that.'

Gomer put his ciggy back, shook his head. 'Ole Hindwell, eh? You know what they says about that place, don't you, vicar?'

'Tell me.' Merrily managed to get her cigarette going before the breeze doused the Zippo.

' "Place as God give up on",' explained Gomer.

'Lot of places like that.'

'With the church, see. Lets their church fall into ruin and never had another.'

'Until now.'

115

'Ar?'

'There's a kind of missionary minister who's holding services in the parish hall. Father Ellis?'

'Oh hell, aye.' Gomer puffed on his ciggy. 'Nutter.'

'That's what they say about him, is it? Nutter?'

'Had two or three proper, solid ole churches under his wing, and they says he favoured Ole Hindwell village hall above the lot of 'em. An' all this clappin' and huggin' and chantin' and stuff. Mind, in Ole Hindwell they wouldn't notice another bloody nutter if he was stark naked in the snow.'

'How do you mean?'

'Inbreedin'.' Gomer chuckled. 'We always says that. Some places gets that kind o' reputation for no reason at all other'n being a bit off the beaten track. And havin' its church falled into ruins.'

'Why *did* it fall into ruins? Apart from God giving up.'

'Now, there's a can of ole worms, ennit?'

'Is it?'

'Last but one vicar, they reckoned he went mad.'

'Like Ellis?'

'No, *mad* mad. All kinds o' rumours, there. Never come out, proper. You got a problem out there, vicar?'

'Well, erm . . . Mr Weal seems to be set on putting Mrs Weal into some kind of tomb in his garden.'

'Well, well,' Gomer said non-committally.

'And Barbara doesn't think that's a good idea. She doesn't think Weal's quite grasped the need to let go of the dead. And she wants me to go to the funeral with her, to hold her hand . . . or maybe to restrain her. And I think there's something odd about that whole situation. Would, er, would you happen to know anybody who might know the score there?'

Gomer nodded slowly. 'I reckon.'

'And maybe a bit about Barbara and why she hates that area so much.'

'Likely. Anythin' else?'

'Father Ellis? Seems to me that for everybody who thinks he's a nutter, there must be another five can't get enough, if you see what I mean.'

'No accountin' for the way folks is gonner go, them parts. Seen it before, oh hell, aye. Gimme a day or two.'

This time, Gomer declined the offer of tea and breakfast, said he'd got himself a nice, crusty cob needed using up. She could tell he was pleased to have something to occupy his time.

And *digging* was what Gomer did best.

Merrily went into church and prayed for Barbara and Menna and asked the Boss about another matter – kind of hoping she'd get a strong negative response.

Back at the vicarage just before seven, she punched out Tania Beauman's *Livenight* number. Waited for the answering machine to kick in.

'Oh . . . this is Merrily Watkins at the Hereford Diocese. Sorry for not getting back to you last night. I'll be in the office from about half nine, if you want to talk about . . . what I might be able to contribute to your programme. Thanks.'

No backing out now.

Be something different, anyway: bright lights, hi-tech hardware, the fast chat, the tat, the trivia, the complete, glossy inconsequentiality of it.

Jane came down for breakfast, all fresh and school-uniformed.

'Been up long, Mum?'

'Couple of hours. Couldn't sleep.'

'So, you rang *Livenight*, then?'

'Not much gets past you, does it, flower?'

'It'll be fun.'

'Be fun for *you*, watching at home.'

'Er . . . yeah,' Jane said airily.

That night, after a wedding rehearsal at the church for a couple whose chief bridesmaid would be their own grand-daughter, Merrily phoned Eileen Cullen from the scullery.

'I just got the feeling you might have heard from Barbara Buckingham again.'

'And why would you be thinking that, Reverend?' Cullen sounded more than usually impatient, as if she was carrying an overflowing bedpan in her other hand.

'She's keen to find out why Menna died.'

'High blood pressure.'

'Well, yes, sure. But why did she have high blood pressure at *her* age?'

'I told you why, and I haven't changed my mind. I reckon she'd been on the Pill for longer than she ought to've been. Years longer, that's my guess. Prolonged ingestion of synthetic oestrogen. Bad news – but then you'd know all that.'

'Eileen, I live the life of a nun. I've *forgotten* all that.'

'Well, it's not your problem, and it's not mine either and it's not poor Menna's any longer.' A pause, then she came back a little softer. 'Listen, if you've got the Buckingham woman on your back in a big way, I'm sorry. I'm sorry I sent her over, so I am.'

'You must have felt at the time that she had a valid problem.'

'Just wanted her out of me hair. You know what I'm like.'

'Mmm, that's why I don't think you're being entirely upfront.'

'Jesus Christ, I'm always upfront. Nobody in this fockin' job's got time to go round the side any more.'

'Did you by any chance tell her about Weal and that business with the water?'

'You mean so they could have a big row and disturb all my patients? Are you kidding? Did *you* tell her?'

'No.'

'Well, good.'

'Confidentially—'

'Merrily, when the hell do we ever talk any other way?'

'Barbara's getting troubled dreams.'

'Troubled, how?'

'Says she sees Menna.'

A pause. 'Does she?'

'Night after night.'

'Stress,' Cullen said. 'Look, I've got to—'

'Well, you would say that. No ghosts, no God. You think my whole life's a sorry sham.'

'Aye, but you're a well-meaning wee creature. Listen, I really do have to go.'

'So you haven't seen her then?'

'Of course I haven't fockin' seen her!' Cullen snapped. 'What the hell d'you think I am?'

Merrily's head spun. She stared at the circle of light thrown on the Holy Bible. The rosebush chattered at the dark window.

'I meant Barbara,' Merrily said.

'I have to go.' Cullen hung up.

Part Two

Witchcraft may be underestimated by Christians on the grounds that it is phoney and synthetic and that its covens are completely eclectic and belong to no national organization. There are, however, dangers . . .

Deliverance (ed. Michael Perry)
The Christian Deliverance Study Group

TWELVE

Bear Pit

She first became aware of him in the green room.

Her initial thought was that he must be a priest, because he was wearing a suit, though not a dog collar – well, how many *did* these days, outside working hours? And then, because he was so smooth and assured, and – perhaps, she thought afterwards, because his shirt was wine-coloured – she even wondered if he might be a bishop.

He brought her a coffee. 'This stuff could be worse,' he said. 'BBC coffee is *much* worse.'

'You do this kind of thing fairly often then?' she said. God, that wasn't quite, 'Do you come here often?' but it was dangerously close.

'When I must,' he said. 'Edward Bain, by the way.'

'Merrily Watkins.'

'I know,' he said.

He was, of course, attractive: lean, pale features and dark curly hair with a twist of grey over the ears. He'd made straight for Merrily across the green room – it sounded like some notoriously haunted, country house bedchamber, but was simply the area where all the participants gathered before the show. It was long and narrow and starting to look like a pantomime dressing room because of some of the costumes: Dark Age *chic* meeting retro-punk in a tangle of braids and bracelets.

The producer and his team mingled with the main guests and the support acts, observing and listening, picking out the potential stars-for-an-hour. Meanwhile the guests drank tea and coffee and spring water – no alcohol – and nibbled things on sticks, talking a lot, losing inhibitions, unblocking their adrenal glands, developing that party mentality. As if most of them hadn't brought it with them.

'Lord,' Edward Bain murmured, 'do they really *want* to be taken seriously?' He looked at Merrily with a faint, pained smile.

The smile chilled her. It was Sean's smile – her dead husband's. Boyish, disarming. Sean's smile when accused. She turned sharply away, as though distracted by an argument in progress between a tight-faced security officer and a ginger-bearded man wearing a short, white cloak over a red tunic with a belt. Into the belt was stuck a knife with a black handle.

'It's my fucking *athame*, man. It's a *religious* tool. You wouldn't ask a fucking bishop to hand over his fucking crozier!'

Edward Bain's smile became a wince, wiping away the similarity to Sean. If it had ever really been there. Merrily swallowed.

The security man turned to Tania Beauman for support. Tania wrinkled her nose. 'Oh, leave it, Grant. I suspect it looks more dangerous than it actually is.'

'Tania, it's a knife. If we start allowing weapons in the studio, we may as well—'

'It's a f—' The ginger guy blew out his cheeks in frustration, turned to Tania. 'This doorman is really hacking me off, you know? This is religious persecution.'

'Sure.' Tania was a short, capable bottle-blonde of about forty. 'If we just agree that it's purely ornamental – yeah, sorry, *religious* – and that you won't be taking it out of—'

'Of course I won't be fucking taking it out!'

'And if you use that word on camera before midnight, you realize you'll be excluded from the debate, yeah?'

The ginger man subsided in a surly kind of way, a semi-chastened schoolboy.

'That's *his* card marked,' Edward Bain told Merrily. 'He'll be used purely for decoration, now. Won't get asked a single question unless it starts to slow up and they're really desperate for confrontation.'

'I don't see that happening, somehow,' Merrily said, 'do you?'

'The boy's an idiot, anyway. If the *athame* is to have any potency at all it should hardly be displayed like some sort of cycling club badge.'

He smiled down at Merrily – instant Sean once more – and glided away, leaving her feeling clammy. And she thought, Oh my God. He's one of them.

'Oooooooooh.' Tania went into a sinuous shudder. 'Magnetic – and more.'

Over by the door, Edward Bain was into an intense conversation with a woman in a long, loose, classical kind of dress, like someone from rent-a-Muse. Merrily saw now that one of Bain's middle fingers wore a silver ring with a moonstone. She saw him and the woman clasp hands lightly and smile, and she imagined tiny blue electric stars crackling between their fingers. She wondered if they'd even met before tonight.

'Who is he?' Merrily muttered. 'I mean, *what* is he?'

'Don't you vicars ever read the *News of the World*?'

'Only if we're really desperate for a sermon.'

'He's the Man,' Tania said. 'If you call him something like King of the Witches, he'll look pained. He doesn't like the word "witch". He's a champagne pagan, if you like.

Works as a publishing executive and would rather be profiled in the *Observer* than the *News of the World* . . . and, yeah, he's getting there.'

'By way of *Livenight*?'

Tania frowned. 'Don't take this programme too lightly, Merrily. You can get deeply shafted out there. And we are watched by all kinds of people you wouldn't expect.'

Especially this week! By the acting Bishop of Hereford this week, and probably half of Lambeth Palace. Take it *lightly*? She'd had to put down her glass of spring water because she couldn't hold it still. Ridiculous; she conducted services every Sunday, she talked to hostile teenagers, she talked to God, she . . .

Sean was there, smiling in her mind. In getting here, she'd had to drive past where he died, on the M5, in flames. *Go away!*

She said, too loudly, 'Tania, can you . . . give me a run-down? Who else is here?'

'OK.' Tania nodded briskly. 'Well, we get the programme peg out of the way first, right? The couple who want their kid to be allowed to do his pagan prayers and whatnot at school.' She nodded towards a solemn, bearded man in a home-made-looking sweater. His partner had a waist-length plait. They might have been Muslims. They might even have been Christians.

Merrily said, 'Am I right in thinking you're not going to be spending very long on them?'

'Dead right. Boring, boring, boring. Actually, the head-master of the school's going to be better value. Born-again Christian. Actually talks like Sir Cliff, like he's got a boiled sweet in his cheek. OK, over there . . . Patrick Ryan – long hair, velvet jacket – Cambridge professor who's done a study of pagan practices. And shagged half the priestesses in the Home Counties by all accounts, but I doubt he'll be discussing *that*. If Ryan's too heavy, the little guy with the shaven head's Tim Fagan, ex-hack from the *Sun*, was sent out to do an exposé on some sexy coven and wound up joining them. Now edits a popular witchy magazine called – ha ha – *The Moon*.'

Edward Bain excepted, they all looked fairly innocuous.

'What about the other side?'

'Right. Well, we've got a really angry mother who claims paganism turned her daughter into a basket case. She is *very* strong. The kid got drawn into white witchcraft and ended up peeing in churches. Which leads neatly into you, I think.'

'Thanks.'

'You know what I mean.'

'Mmm.' Tania had revealed on the phone that she had seen news cuttings on last year's Herefordshire desecration case, involving the sacrifice of a crow in a country church. Not entirely appropriate, in Merrily's view.

'I mean, I can't say that was your orthodox paganism – if there is such a thing, which I doubt. It was a peculiar kind of black magic. It was a one-off.'

Tania Beauman shrugged.

'By "the other side",' Merrily said, 'I actually meant *us*, the Church. You said I wouldn't be on my own here.' How pathetic did *that* sound?

Tania looked mildly concerned. 'I didn't say that, did I? I'm sure I didn't say that.'

'You did, Tania.'

'Oh, well, what happened, the other bloke let us down. I think his wife had a miscarriage or something.' She was blatantly improvising. 'But if you're looking for back-up, the headmaster's brought along a few members of his church. See the guy in the white—'

'Which church would that be?'

'Well, Christian, obviously, but I suppose you'd probably call it more of a cult.'

'Wonderful.'

'They'll be doing some heavy apocalyptic stuff about the Antichrist walking the earth disguised as . . . Hang on – looks like Steve wants to do his pep talk.'

A bald man of about thirty, in white jeans and a crumpled paisley shirt, strode into the centre of the green room, lifted up his arms for silence, and went – Merrily guessed – into autopilot.

'OK, listen up, everybody, my name's Steve Ewing. I'm the editor of *Livenight*. I'd like to welcome you all to the programme and point out that we'll be on the air in about fifty minutes. You've all seen the show – if not, then that's your problem for sticking with boring old Paxman or the dirty movie on Channel 5. OK, now what I mainly want to stress to you is that *Livenight* is like life – you don't get a second chance.'

A woman cackled. 'All *you* know, mate.'

'Yeah, very good.' Steve Ewing smiled thinly. 'What I'm trying to get over here is that we don't hang around and neither should you. If you have something to say, don't hold back, because it'll be too late and we'll have moved on to another aspect of the debate, and you'll be kicking yourself all the way home because you missed your chance of getting your argument across on the programme.'

Merrily looked around for any exit sign. Wasn't too late to get the hell out of here.

'What I'm looking for,' said Steve, 'is straight talking and – above all – quick, snappy responses. There's a lot of choice material to get across, and we want to help you do that. So it's straight to the point, no pussyfooting, and if it's going to take longer than about thirty seconds, save it for your PhD thesis. John Fallon's the ringmaster. You won't meet him until you go in, but you've all seen John, he's a smart guy, a pro, and his bullshit threshold is zero. Any questions?'

There was some shuffling but no direct response.

'Why don't we get to meet Fallon before the programme?' Merrily whispered.

Tania Beauman hardly moved her lips. 'You'd know more about this than me, but I don't imagine they'd normally introduce the Christians to the lion.'

They called this the gallery. It was a narrow room with a bank of TV monitors, through which the director and the sound and vision mixers could view the studio floor from different angles. Once the show was on the air, the director would be in audio contact with the producer and the presenter, John Fallon, down in the bear pit. They actually called it that. In fact, Jane had found it a little disappointing at first. It was much smaller than it looked on the box – like a little theatre-in-the-round, with about six rows of banked-up seating.

'Does the whole audience have some angle on the debate?' she asked a white-haired bloke called Gerry, an ex-*Daily Star* reporter who was the senior member of Tania Beauman's research team.

'Nah,' he said. 'We've got a decent enough budget now, but it's not *that* big. The audience are just ordinary punters bussed in – tonight's bunch is from a paint factory in Walsall: packers, cleaners, management – a cross section of society.'

Gerry glanced at Eirion, who looked awfully young and innocent – and not happy. He had no stomach for subterfuge, Jane was realizing. He'd been appalled to discover that her mum, down there, did not know they were up here. Or, indeed, within sixty miles of *Livenight*.

Even in Eirion's car, with the patched-up silencer, it hadn't taken long to get here. The Warehouse studio complex had been quite easy to find, on the edge of a new business park, under a mile from the M5 and ten miles out of the central Birmingham traffic hell.

It was not until they'd actually left the motorway that Jane had revealed to Eirion the faintly illicit nature of this operation. 'Irene, I'm doing this for *you*. This could be your future. This is like cutting-edge telly. It's an *in*, OK. You might even get a holiday job.'

Eirion had looked appalled, like a taxi driver who'd just discovered he was providing the wheels in a wages snatch. He'd thought they were only driving up separately because Jane's mum might have to stay the night. He did not know how Jane came to have Tania Beauman in her pocket, and would probably not be finding out. Neither would Mum; the plan was, they'd clear off about two minutes before the programme ended, go bombing back down the motorway, and Jane would be up in her apartment with the lights out by the time Mum got home.

Tania Beauman had turned out to be actually OK. She'd told both Gerry and the grizzled director, Maurice, that Jane was her cousin, doing a media studies college course. Which could well be true, one day.

'How old is she?' Maurice had enquired suspiciously.

'Nineteen next month,' Jane said crisply. Eirion looked queasy.

'Stone me,' Gerry muttered. 'When the nineteen-year-olds start looking fourteen, you know you're getting too old for it.'

Maurice took off his cans. 'See, the problem with this particular programme is that we're not *Songs of Praise* and this is not the God Slot. What we do *not* want is a religious debate. We don't want the history of Druidism, we want to know what they get up to in their stone circles when the film crew's gone home. We don't want to hear about the people the witches've healed, we want to know about the ones they've cursed and the virgins they've deflowered on their altars. This is late-night TV. Our job – to put it crudely – is to send you off to bed with a hard-on.'

'I'll be interested to see how the little priest handles it,' Gerry said thoughtfully. 'She's got enough of her own demons.'

Jane stared at him.

'Marital problems,' Gerry said. 'Husband playing away . . . though what the hell possessed him, with that at home.'

'You never know what goes on behind bedroom doors.' Maurice shook his head, smiling sadly. 'You turned all that up, did you, Gerald?'

'And then, when it's all looking a bit messy . . . *Bang!* The husband goes and gets killed in the car, with his girlfriend. Merrily wakes up a widow . . . and soon after that she's become a priest. Interesting, do I detect guilt in there some-where, or do I just have a suspicious—'

'Christ!' Jane snarled. 'She didn't become a bloody nun! She—' She felt Eirion's hand on her arm and shook it off and bit her lip.

Gerry grinned. 'My, my. Women do stick together, don't they?'

'Lay off, Gerald.' Maurice slipped on his headphones, flipped a switch on his console. 'You there, Martin? Speak to me, son.'

'So.' Gerry leaned against the edge of the mixing desk. 'There you are, Jane. Now you know how easy it is to get people going. You just watch the monitors. Within about seven minutes, everybody's forgotten there are cameras.' He pencilled a note on a copy of the programme's running order; Jane made out the word *Merrily.* 'Be a lot of heat, tonight, I think. When it gets going, it's very possible one of those weirdos is gonna try some spooky stuff.'

Eirion stiffened. 'Spooky stuff?'

'I dunno, son. A spell or something, I suppose. Something to prove they can make things happen. I dunno, basically – it's all cobblers, anyway.'

Jane looked at Eirion. She was still shaking. They had a little file on Mum; if the show lost momentum, shafting her became an option.

THIRTEEN

A Surreal Memory

Betty's day clearly hadn't been too great either. You could tell not so much from her face as from her manner: no bustle.

'You don't tell me yours, and I won't tell you mine.' Robin didn't even lift his head from the kitchen table where he'd fallen into a sleep of dismay and frustration. 'We'll call it a shit amnesty.'

Ten fifteen on this cold, misty, moonless night. Betty had been out since mid-afternoon. She'd been to see the widow Wilshire in New Radnor again, taking with her an arthritis potion involving 'burdock and honeysuckle, garlic and nettle and a little healing magic'. Betty was good with healing plants; after pissing off her parents by walking out of teacher training, she'd worked at a herb garden and studied with a herbalist at nights for two and a half years. She'd gone to a whole lot of trouble with this potion, driving over to a place the other side of Hereford yesterday to pick up the ingredients.

'How is she now?'

'Oh . . . more comfortable. And happier, I think.'

Around six she'd phoned him to say she was hanging on there a while. Seemed Mrs Wilshire's home help had not made it this week and she was distressed about the state of her house and her inability to clean it up. So Betty would clean up, sure she would. Wherever she went, Betty added to her collection of aunts.

'OK,' Robin said, 'if she's so much better, I give up. Where's the bad stuff come in?'

'It isn't necessarily bad – just odd.' Betty took off her coat, hung it behind the back door, went to get warm by the stuttering Rayburn. 'So you first. It's Ellis, isn't it?'

'No, haven't heard a word from Ellis. This is Blackmore. He faxed. He doesn't like the artwork.'

'Oh.' Betty pushed her hands through her hair, letting it tumble. 'I did say it was a mistake, dealing with him directly. You should have carried on communicating through the publishers. If he can get hold of you any time he wants, he'll just keep on quibbling.'

'It was what he wanted. And *he* is Kirk Blackmore. And, frankly, quibbling doesn't quite reach it.'

'Not something you can alter easily?'

Robin laughed bleakly. 'What the asshole doesn't like is . . . everything. He doesn't like my concept of Lord Madoc – his face is wrong, his hair is wrong, his clothes are wrong, his freaking *boots* are wrong. Oh, and he walks in the wrong colour of mist.'

'I'm sorry.' Betty came round the back of his chair, put her hands on his shoulders, began to knead. 'All that work. What does it mean? What happens now?'

'Means I grovel. Or I take the one-off money and someone else's artwork goes on the book.'

'There's no way—'

'Betty . . . OK. I am a well-regarded illustrator. Any ordinary, midlist fantasy writer, they'd have to go with it. Blackmore, however, is now into a one-and-a-half-million-pound three-book deal. He walks with the gods. Different rules apply.'

Betty scowled. 'Doesn't change the fact that he writes moronic crap. Tell him to sod off. It's just one book.'

He sat up. 'It's not moronic. The guy knows his stuff. And it's not just one book. His whole backlist's gonna be rejacketed in the *Sword of Twilight* format, whoever's artwork that should be. Which is *seven* books – a lot of work. Face it, I *need* Blackmore. I need to have my images under his big name. Also, we need the money if we're gonna make a start on getting this place into any kind of good condition. We were counting on that money, were we not?'

'I suppose.'

'Right, end of story. Back to the airbrush.'

She bent and kissed his hair. 'You've gone pale.'

'Yeah, well, I didn't expect it. It was a kick in the mouth. Do me good – getting too sure of myself. All right, go ahead. Regale me with the unglad tidings you bring back from the big metropolis.'

They'd taken to calling New Radnor the big metropolis, on account of it having three shops.

'Well . . .' Betty sat down next to him. 'Mrs Wilshire was all worked up because she remembered she'd promised to get the home help to hunt out some of the Major's papers relating to . . . this place. He kept them in a wooden summer house in the garden. And of course, the home help didn't show up. Anyway, she gave me the key. That's why I'm so late. I was in there for over an hour. Quite a little field HQ the Major had there: lighting, electric heater, kettle, steel filing cabinet.'

'And she let you loose in there? Almost a stranger?'

'She needs somebody to trust.'

'Yeah.' People trusted Betty on sight; it was a rare quality.

'And she wanted it sorting out, but quite clearly couldn't face going down there, because of the extra responsibility it might heap on her, which she's never been good at. And also because there's a lot of him still there. You can feel him – a clean, precise sort of mind; and frustration because he couldn't find enough to do with it. So when he was buying a house, he was determined to know everything, get the very best deal.'

'Not like me, huh?'

Betty smiled. 'You're the worst kind of impulse buyer. You even hide things from yourself. You and the Major wouldn't have got on at all.'

'So what did you find?'

'Mrs Wilshire said I could bring anything home that might be useful. I've got a cardboard box full of stuff in the car.'

'But you didn't bring it in?'

'Tomorrow.' Betty leaned her head back. 'I've read enough for one night. No wonder he kept it in the shed.'

'What are you saying?'

'I mean, in one respect, Major Wilshire *was* like you – once he'd seen this place, he had to have it. But it also had to be at the right price. And of course he wasn't remotely superstitious. An old soldier, he wasn't afraid of anything that couldn't shoot him. But I suppose that if he happened to come up with certain information that might upset any *other* potential buyers . . .' Betty stopped and rolled her head around to ease tension. 'It's funny . . . the first time I ever went in those ruins, I thought, this is really not a happy place.'

'This is something the agent should've told us? We get to sue the agent?'

'How very American of you. No, I rather doubt it. All too long ago. Anyway, they told us about Major Wilshire's death, which was the main drawback, presumably, as far as they were concerned.'

'So what is this? The ruins are haunted?'

'We jumped to conclusions. We assumed the church was

abandoned because of flooding or no access for cars. Or at least *you* did.'

'I assumed. Yeah, assuming is what I do. All the time. OK.' Robin stood up. 'I can't stand it. Gimme the car keys, I'll go fetch your box of goodies.'

When he arrived back with the stuff, she had cocoa coming up. He slammed and barred the door. He was tingling with cold and damp.

'Whooo, it's turned into fog! Was it like that when you were driving home?'

'Some of the way.'

Just as well he'd fallen asleep earlier and hadn't known about the fog; he'd have been worried sick about her, with the ice on the roads and all.

He dumped the cardboard wine box on the table. 'Best not to go out at night this time of year, living in a place like this. Suppose it was so thick you drove into the creek?'

'Brook,' Betty said.

'Whatever.' Robin unpacked the box. Mostly, it seemed to be photocopies, the top one evidently from some official list of historic buildings.

CHURCH OF ST MICHAEL, OLD HINDWELL.
Ruins of former parish church. Mainly C13 and C14, with later south porch and chancel. Embattled three-stage tower of late C14, rubble-construction with diagonal buttresses to north-west and south-west . . .

And so on. There were a couple more pages of this stuff, which Robin put aside for further study.

'Like you said, looks like the Major built up a fairly comprehensive background file.'

He turned up some sale particulars similar to the one he

and Betty had received. Same agent – and same wording, give or take.

'A characterful, historic farmhouse with outbuildings and the picturesque ruins of a parish church, in a most unusual location . . .'

All true enough, as far as it went. Next, Robin found several pages ripped out of a spiral-bound notebook and bunched together with a bulldog clip. There was handwriting on them, not too intelligible, and a string of phone numbers.

'What's this?'

'Don't know. Couldn't make it out. There's all kinds of junk in there. Mrs Wilshire told me to take it anyway. I think she just wanted to get rid of as much as she could. Right, there you are . . . that's the start of it.'

He lifted out a news cutting pasted to a piece of A4. The item was small and faded. 'Rector Resigns due to Ill Health.'

It said little more than that the Reverend Terence Penney had given up the living of Old Hindwell and had left the area. A replacement was being sought.

'When was this?' A date had been scrawled across the newsprint but he couldn't make it out.

'1967.'

'*That* late? You mean the Old Hindwell church was still operational until '67?'

''68, actually.'

'Why did I have it in mind it must have been abandoned back in the thirties or forties?'

'Because you were sold on the idea that it was due to motor vehicles and the brook. Read the letter underneath. It's from the same woman who wrote the piece in the news-paper.'

It had been typewritten, on an old machine with an old ribbon.

Lower Lodge
Monkshall
Leominster
Herefordshire
18 May

Dear Major Wilshire,

Thank you for your letter. Yes, you are quite right, I did have the dubious honour of being appointed Radnor Valley correspondent of the *Brecon and Radnor Express* for a few years in the 1960s, receiving, if I recall correctly, something like one halfpenny a line for my jottings about local events of note!

My reports on the departure of the Reverend Penney were not, I must say, the ones of which I am most proud, amounting, as they did, to what I suppose would be termed these days a 'cover up'. But my late husband and I were comparatively recent incomers to the area and I was 'walking on eggshells' and determined not to cause offence to anyone!

However, I suppose after all this time there is no reason to conceal anything any more, especially as there was considerable local gossip about it at the time.

Yes, the Reverend Penney was indeed rather a strange young man, although I am still inclined to discount the rumours that he 'took drugs'. There were some hippy types living in the area at the time with whom he was quite friendly, so I suppose this is how the rumour originated.

In retrospect, I think Mr Penney was not the most appropriate person to be put in charge of St Michael's. He was a young man and very enthusiastic, full of ideas, but the local people were somewhat set in their ways and resistant to any kind of change. The church itself was not in very good condition (even before Mr Penney's arrival!), and the parish was having difficulty raising money for repairs – there were not the grants available in those days – and it was a big responsibility for such a young and inexperienced minister.

Yes, I am afraid that what you have been told is broadly correct, though I must say that I never found any signs of mental imbalance in Mr Penney, in his first year at least. He was always friendly, if a little remote.

My memories of THAT day remain confused. Perhaps we should have suspected something after the small fire, the slippage of tiles from the roof and the repeated acts of apparent vandalism (I realize no charges ever resulted from these continued occurrences, so I hope I can trust you, as a soldier, to treat this correspondence as strictly confidential), but no one could really have predicted the events of that particular October morning. It would not have seemed so bad had it not been raining so hard and the brook in such spate. Naturally, quite a crowd – for Hindwell – gathered and there was much weeping and wailing, although this was quickly suppressed and after that day I do not remember anyone speaking of it – quite extraordinary. It was as if the whole village somehow shared the shame.

No, as you note, the big newspapers never 'got on' to the story. Small communities have always been very good at smothering sensational events almost at birth. And what was I, the village correspondent, supposed to write? I was not a journalist, merely a recorder of names at funerals and prize-winners at the local show. Furthermore, later that day, I received a visit from Mr Gareth Prosser Snr, together with Mr Weal, his and our solicitor, who stressed to me that it would 'not be in the best interests of the local people' for this to be publicized in any way. Mr Prosser was the county councillor for the area and served

on the police committee and was a personage of considerable gravitas. It was not for me, a newcomer, to cross him
over an issue of such sensitivity!

The Church of England (the village is in Wales, but
the parish is in the Diocese of Hereford) chose not to take
any proceedings against Mr Penney. After his departure,
another minister was appointed but did not stay long and
thereafter the parish became part of a 'cluster' which is
not so uncommon these days! I suppose one could say
Old Hindwell 'lost heart' after the extraordinary behaviour
of Mr Penney.

I do hope I have been able to help you, but I am rather
'out of touch' with events in Old Hindwell. Although I
live no more than half an hour's drive away.

I seem never once to have revisited the village since we
moved house in 1983. Old Hindwell is one of those places
which it is easy to forget exists, except as a rather surreal
memory!

With very best regards,
Juliet Pottinger (Mrs)

'The Local People,' Robin said. 'Whoooeee! Those local
people sure like to wield power.'

'No more than in any small community.' Betty brought
over cocoa for them both. She knew he'd go for the cover-
up aspect first, rather than the significance of the event that
had been covered up. She almost wished she could have
censored the papers before letting him see them.

The idea of this panicked her. It was like the Wilshires in
reverse. Until they came here, she'd never even *thought* of
keeping secrets from Robin.

'And who is this Weal?' he said. 'Was the plan that they
might have to lean on this old broad legally?'

'She wouldn't have been an old broad then. She was probably quite a young broad.'

'Whatever, this smells of real redneck intrigue. Prosser Senior – that would be Gareth Prosser's old man?'

'Sounds like it,' Betty said. And then came to the point. 'But the main issue is, what happened to the Reverend Penney? What did he do that day that scandalized the community so much that he had to resign on so-called health grounds?'

'Didn't the widow Wilshire know any of this?'

'She'd never even seen the letter. Bryan would not have wanted to worry the little woman.'

'Well,' Robin said, 'it's clear that the Reverend Penney was under a lot of pressure and it drove him a little crazy. She talks about him feeling isolated. Maybe he came from some English city, couldn't cut it in the sticks. And the Local People resented him, gave him a hard time.'

'To the extent of vandalizing his church? Starting a fire? You don't think that sounds a little inner-city for a place like this?'

'Sounds like he was getting some hassle. Sounds like there could be something the Local People are a tad ashamed about, wouldn't you say?'

He looked pleased about this. He would make a point now of finding out precisely what had happened and what, if anything, the community had to hide. Betty, on the other hand, could sympathize with Juliet Pottinger's low-profile approach. Yes, it would be necessary to find out what had happened on what was now their property – but not to go about this in a conspicuous way. They were incomers and foreigners. And had a different religion, which may somehow have become known to certain people. Unspoken opinion might already be stacked against them; they must not be seen to be too nosy or too clever. They must move quietly.

'After Penney left,' she said, 'the church appeared to "lose heart". It was in full use until 1968 and now it's a ruin. In just over thirty years. Not exactly a slow decay.'

'Aw, buildings go to pieces in no time at all when they're left derelict. She implies in the letter that it was already falling apart. And maybe in those days the authorities weren't so hot on preserving old buildings. I'm more curious about what the Local People did to this Penney. Where's he now?'

'I don't know. And we're the last people to know anyone in the clergy who might be able to find out. We—'

'Look, I'll go find out the truth tomorrow. I'll go see Prosser. We're gonna need more logs – real logs. I'll go find out if Prosser knows a reputable log dealer and at the same time I'll ask him about Reverend Penney. See if he tries to lean on me, do the rural menace stuff.'

'I'll go, if you like,' Betty said, without thinking.

Robin put down his cocoa mug. 'Because I will rub him up the wrong way? Because I will be gauche and loud and unsubtle? Because I will say, you can't touch me, pal, I got the Old Gods on my side?'

'Of course not. I'm sorry. You're right. You should go. Men around here prefer to deal with other men.'

'What I thought.' He looked at her and grinned. 'This is nothing to worry about.'

'No,' Betty said.

Far from representing her and Robin's destiny and the beautiful future of the pagan movement in this country, she was now convinced that the old church of Michael was a tainted and revolting place that should indeed be left to rot. But how could she lay all this on him now, after his crushing disappointment over the Blackmore illustrations?

'Let's go to bed,' she said.

FOURTEEN

Armageddon

No way could she ever have imagined it was going to be like this.

She'd thought that it could never be worse than the pulpit that first time, up in Liverpool, when those three creaking wooden steps were like the steps to the gallows.

And may God have mercy on your soul.

She'd drunk very little of the spring water on offer in the green room, never once thinking of the fierce heat from the studio lights and what it might do to the irrigation of the inside of her mouth.

With ten minutes to go, she'd popped outside for a cigarette, sharing a fire-escape platform with two sly-smiling New Age warriors and their seven-inch spliff, shaking her head with a friendly, liberal smile when they'd offered it to her.

Never *really* imagining that the nerves wouldn't just float away once they were on the air. Because . . . well, because this was trivial, trash, tabloid television, forgotten before the first editions of tomorrow's papers got onto the streets.

This really mustn't be taken too seriously.

Merrily froze, 2,000 years of Christianity setting like concrete around her shoulders. The light was merciless and hotter than the sun. She was in terror; she couldn't even pray.

'Merrily Watkins,' he'd said, 'you're a vicar, a woman of God. Let's hear how you defend your creator against that kind of logic. Isn't there really a fair bit of sense in what Ned's saying?'

He was slight, not very tall. His natural expression was halfway to a smile, the lips in a little V. He was light and nimble and chatty. He earned probably six times as much as a bishop – the shiny-suited, eel-like, non-stick, omnipotent John Fallon.

'Well, Merrily,' he said. '*Isn't* there?'

And yet, there were no tricks, no surprises. It had started, exactly as Tania Beauman had said it would, with the parents Jean and Roger Gillespie, goddess-worshippers from Taunton, Somerset, who wanted their daughter's religion to be formally accepted at her primary school. They'd have a second child starting school next year; later a third one; they wanted new data programmed into the education machine, respectful references to new names: Isis, Artemis, Aradia. Roger was an architect with the county council; he maintained that his beliefs were fully accepted on the executive estate where the Gillespies had lived for three years.

They were both so humourless, Merrily thought, as Jean demanded parity with Islam and boring old Christianity, and special provision for her family's celebration of the solstices and the equinoxes, the inclusion of pagan songs, at least once a week, at the school assembly.

Fallon had finally interrupted this tedious monotone. 'And what do you do exactly, Jean? Do you hold nude ceremonies in your garden? What happens if the neighbours've got a barbecue going?'

'Well, that's just the kind of attitude we *don't* get, for a start.' Jean's single plait hung like a fat hawser down her bosom. 'Our rituals are private and discreet and are respected by our neighbours, who—'

'Fine. Sure. OK.' John Fallon had already been on the move, away from Jean, who carried on talking, although the boom-mic operator had moved on. Fallon had spun away through ninety degrees to his next interviewee: the elegant Mr Edward Bain, nothing so vulgar as King of the Witches.

'We're here to talk about religious belief,' Fallon had read from the autocue at the beginning of the show, 'and the right of people in a free society to worship their own gods. Some of you might think it's a bit loony, even scary, but the thousands of pagan worshippers in Britain maintain that theirs is the only true religion of these islands, and they want their ceremonies – which sometimes include nudity, simulated and indeed actual sex – to be given full charitable status and full recognition from the state and the education system . . .'

When he had his back to Merrily, she saw the wire to his earpiece coming out of his collar, like a ruched scar on the back of his neck. Relaying instructions or suggestions, from the programme's director in some hidden bunker.

'Ned Bain,' Fallon said, 'you're the high priest of a London coven – can we use the word "coven"? – and also a publisher and an expert on ancient religions of all kinds. I want you to tell me, simply and concisely, why *you* think paganism is, today, more relevant and more important to these islands than Christianity.'

And Edward Bain had sat, one leg hooked casually over the other like . . . like Sean had sat sometimes . . . a TV natural, expounding without pause, his eyes apparently on Fallon, but actually gazing beyond him across the studio. His eyes, in fact, were lazily fixed on Merrily's . . . and they – she clutched her chair seat tightly – they were *not* Sean's.

'Well, for a start, they've had their two millennia,' he said reasonably. '2,000 years of war and divison, repression and persecution, torture, genocide . . . in the name of a cruel, despotic deity dreamed up in the Middle East.'

From the seats tiered behind Merrily came the swelling sound of indrawn breath, like a whistling in the eaves. Part awe, part shock, part admiration at such cool, convincing blasphemy.

'2,000 years of the cynical exploitation, by wealthy men, of humanity's unquenchable yearning for spirituality . . . the milking of the peasants to build and maintain those great soaring cathedrals . . . created to harness energies they no longer even understand. 2,000 years of Christianity . . . a tiny, but ruinous period of Earth's history. A single dark night of unrelenting savagery and rape.'

There was a trickle of applause. He continued to look at Merrily, his mouth downturned in sorrow but a winner's light in his eyes. The space between them seemed to shrink, until she could almost feel the warm dusting of his breath on her face. On a huge screen above him was projected the image of a serene, bare-breasted woman wearing a tiara like a coiled snake.

'Now it's our turn,' he said softly. 'We who worship in woods and circles of rough stone. We who are not afraid to part the curtains, to peer into the mysteries from which Christianity still cowers, screaming shrilly at us to *come away, come away.* To us – and to the rest of you, if you care to give it any thought – Christianity is, at best, a dull screen, a block. It is *anti*-spiritual. It was force-fed to the conquered and brutalized natives of the old lands, who practised – as we once did, when we still had sensitivity – a natural religion, in harmony with the tides and the seasons, entirely beneficent, gentle, pacific, not rigid nor patriarchal. The Old Religion has always recognized the equality of the sexes and exalted the nurturing spirit, the spirit which can soothe and heal the Earth before it is too late.'

The trickle of applause becoming a river. John Fallon standing with folded arms and his habitual half-smile. Someone had dimmed the studio lights so that Ned Bain was haloed like a Christ figure, and when he spoke again it might have been Sean there, being reasonable, logical. Merrily began to sweat.

'The clock of the Earth is running down. We've become alienated from her. We must put the last 2,000 years behind us and speak to her again.'

And the river of applause fanned out into a delta among not only the myriad ranks of the pagans, but also the shop-floor workers and the wages staff and the middle and upper management of the paint factory in Walsall. The claps and cheers turned to an agony of white noise in Merrily's head and she closed her eyes, and when she opened them, there was the fuzzy boom-mic on a pole hanging over her head, and the camera had glided silently across like an enormous floor-polisher and John Fallon, legs apart, hands behind his back, was telling her and the millions at home, '. . . really a fair bit of sense in what Ned's saying? Well, Merrily . . . isn't there?'

She's frozen, Jane thought in horror, as two seconds passed.

Two entire seconds. . . . on *Livenight*! A hush in the bear pit.

'Come on, love.' Gerry's hands were chivvying at the monitors. 'You're not in the bloody pulpit now.'

Maurice, the director, said into his microphone, 'John, why don't you just ask her, very gently, if she's feeling all right?'

Jane wanted to haul him from his swivel chair and wrestle

him to the ground among the snaking wires. But then, thank Christ, Mum started talking.

It just wasn't her voice, that was the problem. She sounded like she'd just been awakened from a drugged sleep. Well, all right, it was going to be a tough one. Ned Bain was a class act, a cool, cool person, undeniably sexy. And Jane admittedly felt some serious empathy with what he was saying. Like, hadn't she herself had this same argument with Mum time and again, pointing out that paganism – witchcraft – was a European thing, born in dark woodland glades, married to mountain streams. It was practical, and Jane didn't even see it as entirely incompatible with Christianity.

The camera was tight on Mum – so tight that, *oh no*, you could see the sweat. And she was gabbling in that strange, cracked voice about Christianity being pure, selfless love, while paganism seemed to be about sex at its most mechanical and . . . feelingless.

Feelingless? Jesus, Jane thought, is that a real word? *Oh God.*

'This is bloody trite crap, especially after the pagan guy,' Maurice told John Fallon. 'Let's come back to her when, and if, she gets her shit together.'

'All right.' John Fallon spun away, a flying smirk. 'That's the, ah, Church of England angle.'

Someone jeered.

Oh God! When she was sure the camera was away from her, Merrily dabbed a crumpled tissue to her forehead, knowing immediately what she *should* have said, how she *could* have dealt with Bain's simplistic generalizations. Now wanting to jump up and tug Fallon back. But it was, of course, too late.

From halfway up an aisle between rows of seats, she caught a glance from Steve Ewing, the producer, his mouth hidden under a lip-microphone as used by ringside boxing commentators. It was as if he was ironically rerunning his pre-programme pep talk '... *you'll be kicking yourself all the way home because you missed your chance of getting your argument across on the programme.*'

From the adjacent seat to her left, a hand gently squeezed her arm: Patrick Ryan, the sociologist who was supposed to have shagged half the priestesses in the southern counties while compiling his thesis on pagan ritual practice. 'You'll get used to it,' he whispered.

She nodded. She sought out the eyes of Ned Bain, but they were in shadow now; he seemed to be looking downwards. He appeared very still and limp, as though his body was recharging. She thought, He was staring at me the whole time. And afterwards I couldn't do a thing.

'... gonna talk to Maureen now,' John Fallon was saying, back on the other side of the studio floor, just across the aisle from Ned Bain. 'Maureen, your teenage daughter was into all this peaceful, New Age nature worship. But that was only the start, because Gemma ended up, I believe, in a psychiatric unit.'

Oh, sure ... blame Bain for your own deficiencies. Merrily shook herself, furious. *Blame poor dead Sean.*

'She's still attending the unit, John.' Maureen was a bulky woman, early fifties, south London accent. 'Apart from that, she won't hardly leave the house any more, poor kid.'

'She became a witch, right?'

'She became a witch when she was about seventeen, when she first went to the tech college. There was a lecturer there like ... him.' Maureen jerked a thumb at Ned Bain, who tilted his head quizzically. 'Smooth, good-looking guy, on the make.'

Ned chuckled. *Really nothing like Sean. How could she have—*

'But let's just make it clear,' Fallon said, 'that this was *not*

Ned Bain here. So this other man recruited Gemma into a witch coven.'

Maureen described how her daughter had been initiated in a shop cellar converted into a temple, and within about six months her personality had completely changed. She'd broken off her engagement to a very nice boy who was a garage mechanic, and then they found out she was into hard drugs.

'But I never knew the worst of it till her mate come to see me one day. This was the mate she'd joined the coven with, and she told me Gemma had got involved with this other group what was doing black magic. She said Gemma went with the rest of them to St Anthony's Church – and I know this happened, 'cause it was in the papers – and they desecrated it.'

'Desecrated, how?'

'Well . . . you know . . . did . . . did their dirt.' The big face crumpled. 'Things like—'

'John, let me say . . .' Ned Bain was leaning forward. The camera pulled back, the boom-mic operator shifted position. 'This is satanism, and satanism is a specifically anti-Christian movement. It is entirely irrelevant to Wicca or any of the other strands of paganism. We do not oppose Christianity. We—'

'The hell you don't!' Merrily was half out of her seat, but well off-mic.

'We are an *alternative* to Christianity,' Bain stressed. 'And also, I should perhaps point out at this stage, a precursor, of the tired, politicized cult of Jesus. And I say precursor, because there's evidence that Christianity itself is no more than a fabrication, a modification of the cult of Dionysus, in which the story of the man-god who dies and is resurrected . . .'

'Yeah, yeah,' Fallon stopped him. 'Fascinating stuff, Ned, but I want to stay with satanism for a moment.'

'As you would,' Merrily muttered.

'Now, Ned, *you* would say that satanism is as much anathema to pagans as it is to the Christian Church. And yet young Gemma graduated – or descended – to some kind of devil worship after being initiated as a witch. I want to come back . . .' Fallon wheeled '. . . to Merrily Watkins . . .'

Merrily's hands tightened on the arms of her chair. *Please God . . .*

'Now, what we didn't say before about Merrily is that, as well as being one of the new breed of female parish priests, she's also the official exorcist – I believe Deliverance Minister is the correct term these days – for the Diocese of Hereford. That's right?'

'Yes.' *Ignore the camera, the lights. Don't look at Bain's eyes.*

'So what I want to ask you, do people like Maureen often come to you with this same kind of story?'

'I . . .' She swallowed. How could she say she hadn't been in the job long enough to have accumulated any kind of client base. 'I have to say . . . John . . . that what you might call *real* satanism is uncommon. What you have are kids who're playing old Black Sabbath albums and get a perverse buzz out of dressing up and doing something horribly anti-social. Quite often, you'll find that these kids will join a witch coven in the belief that it's far more . . . extreme, if you like, than it actually is. That they're entering a world of sex rites and blood sacrifice.'

'Which is *your* fault!' one of the pagans shouted. 'Because that's how the Church has portrayed us for centuries.'

'She's saying,' Maureen shrilled, extending a finger at Merrily, 'that my daughter only joined the witches because she thought they were evil?'

'No, what I'm—'

'She's sitting on the fence!' A heavy man bounded down one of the aisles. 'That's what she's doing.'

Two security heavies moved in from different directions. Fallon blocked the man's path. 'You are?'

'The Reverend Peter Gemmell.' He was grey-bearded and big enough to take on either of the two security men. 'You won't find me on your list. I'm an industrial chaplain, and I came with the factory group from Walsall. But that's beside the point. What I want is to tell you all the truth that my colleague here is too diplomatic, too delicate, too wishy-washy to introduce. And that is to say that Satan himself is present in this studio tonight.'

'Oh hell,' Jane said glumly, 'a fruitcake. Just when I thought she might be really cooking.'

'Lovely.' Gerry leaned back in his canvas chair with his hands behind his head.

Voice-crackle from Maurice's cans. He nodded, scanning the monitors to make sure Gemmell was alone. 'OK, Steve, thanks, will do. John, let's see where this one goes, OK?'

Eirion looked shell-shocked. 'Anything could happen down there, couldn't it? Suppose that guy had a gun?'

'Probably wouldn't be that much use against Satan, anyway,' Jane reasoned.

'Why don't you tell them?' The Rev. Peter Gemmell hissed at Merrily. 'Why don't *you* tell them that Satan is in our midst? That he's here now. Why don't you stand up and denounce him?'

Fallon saved her.

'Well, *you* tell us, Peter, since you're here. You point him out. Where exactly is Satan sitting?'

'I *shall* tell you.' Gemmell didn't hesitate. 'He's sitting directly behind you.'

Fallon stepped aside to reveal Ned Bain smiling and shaking his head, pityingly.

'That man . . .' Gemmell glared contemptuously at Bain. 'That man speaks from the Devil's script. From his lips spews the slick rhetoric of Satan the seducer.'

Sea of Light? Merrily wondered.

' "The satyr shall cry to his fellow!" ' Gemmell roared. ' "Yea, there shall the night hag alight, and find for herself a resting place!" Isaiah.'

Merrily thought of the number of interpretations you could put on that. In fact, she was sure there was a rather more innocent translation in the Revised English Bible. She just couldn't remember what it was. Couldn't remember anything tonight.

'The satyr,' Gemmell explained, 'is the so-called horned god of the witches – the god Pan. The night hag is the demon Lilith. And so the Bible tells us quite plainly that paganism invites the demonic to share its bed. And that is as true today as it was when it was written.'

'The Old Testament,' Bain said wearily. 'This guy comes down here and quotes at me from a hotchpotch of myth and legend and old wives' tales . . .'

'The voice of Satan!' Gemmell snarled, and Merrily was aware of Steve Ewing to her right, putting the bouncers on alert.

'Thank you, Peter.' John Fallon placed an arm on the big priest's shoulder. 'We're grateful for that, but I don't think we're quite ready for the battle of Armageddon tonight.'

'I have made my point,' Gemmell said with dignity and, with a baleful glance at Merrily, walked back up the aisle and then stopped and turned and, before the security men could reach him, roared out, 'We must – and *will* – put out the false lights in the night of filth!'

'Good man,' Fallon said. 'Well . . . Ned Bain's either the saviour of our planet or he's the Antichrist. But before that interruption, Merrily, you were saying so-called satanists are just a bunch of delinquent kids . . .'

'No, what I said was that real satanism is uncommon. I do know it exists. I *have* encountered the use of occult practices for evil purposes and I think Ned's being a bit optimistic if he thinks all pagans are in it to heal the earth.' Her mouth was dry again. She swallowed.

'Go on,' Fallon said.

'Well, I know for a fact that pagan groups are infiltrated by people with less . . . altruistic aims – whether it's money, or drugs or iffy sex.'

'Black propaganda!' a woman screeched. Fallon held up a hand for quiet.

'I do know a young girl,' Merrily said carefully, thinking of Jane watching at home. 'She's a girl who was very nearly ensnared by the people who were secretly running what appeared to be a fairly innocent mystical group for women. It's a minefield. In the glamorous world of goddesses and prophecy and . . . and nude dancing at midnight, it's very hard to distinguish between the people who truly and sincerely believe all this will heal the earth and free our souls . . . and the ones who are into personal power and gratification of their—'

'What group?' the woman shouted. 'She's making it up! John, you make her tell us where it was!'

'Ssssh,' Fallon said. 'OK, where was this, Merrily?'

'It was . . . around Hereford. Around the Welsh border. Obviously, I'm not going to name anybody who—'

'All right.' Fallon turned to the young woman who'd shouted out. 'It's Vivienne, right? And you're the priestess of a coven in Manchester. How do you know what kind of people you're initiating? How do you vet them?'

'You just . . . know.' Vivienne had cropped hair and earrings that seemed to be made from the bejewelled bodies of seahorses. 'The initiation process itself weeds out the scumbags and the weirdos. It's a psychic thing. You learn to pick up on it, and the goddess herself—'

'That is rubbish,' Merrily interrupted.

Vivienne paused. John Fallon smiled.

Merrily said, 'People *don't* get vetted before they're allowed to mess with other people's minds. You *don't* have any real organization or any fixed creed. Your rituals *don't* go back to pre-Christian times, they were all made up in the last half century. You're a complete ragbag of half-truths and good intentions and bad intentions and—'

'And that's any different from your Church?' Vivienne reared out of her seat. 'Half of you don't believe in a Virgin Birth! Half of you don't believe in the Resurrection! And you call *us* a ragbag. I'm telling you, lady, you'll have come to bits long before we do. It's happening right now. And you . . . you're part of the decay. We look at you and the blokes see a pretty face and nice legs, and that's just the Church's latest scheme to deflect attention from the rot in its guts.'

A build-up of cheers among the pagan ranks. John Fallon stepped back to let the camera catch it all.

'Your Church is dying on its feet!' Vivienne grinned triumphantly. 'It's not gonna see the new century out. You took our sacred sites from us, and we're gonna take them back. Your fancy churches will fall, and honest grass will grow up through their ruins, and towers will stand alone, like megaliths—'

'Whoah!' Fallon stepped back into the action. 'What *are* you banging on about?'

'All right,' Vivienne said. 'She's from the Welsh border, yeah? I can show you a church on her actual doorstep where that's already happened. I can show you a church with a tower and graves and everything ... which is now a *pagan* church. *You* don't know what's happening on your own doorstep. You don't know *nothing*!'

FIFTEEN

Fairground

'Move it!' Jane raced along the bright corridor, trailing her fleece coat over a shoulder. The building appeared to be still only half finished; there were lumps of plaster everywhere, and the panes of many windows still had strips of brown tape across them. 'Irene, move!'

'I was just trying to thank Maurice and Gerry.'

'We'll write them a letter! Come on. Believe me, she is not going to hang on here. She's going to be out of that bear pit before any of them can pin her in a corner. She'll be driving like a bat out of hell down the motorway, swearing that she'll never, never, never again . . .'

'I thought she did OK,' Eirion said, blundering behind her, 'in the end. She got that woman very annoyed.'

'*You* thought she did OK. *I* think she just about managed to rescue the situation. *She'll* think she was absolutely crap and like disgraced the Church and the bishop and . . . Jesus Christ!' Jane hit a pair of swing doors, still running. 'Can't you move any faster? I thought you were in the rugby team.'

'The chess team.' Eirion caught the doors on the rebound. 'You know it was the chess team.'

In the old Nova, with Jane leaning back, panting, against a peeling headrest, Eirion said, 'I wonder what Gerry meant, when that woman was going on about the pagan church.'

'Huh?'

'He said, "*That'll* flog, if I'm quick," and made a note on his script.'

'That church, you mean?'

'No, the story, I suppose.' Eirion drove out of the parking area, past a red and white striped barrier which was already raised. 'He means sell the story.'

'Who to?'

'Who would you normally sell a story to? To the papers. He was a tabloid journalist, wasn't he? And John Fallon didn't even follow it up on the programme, so . . .'

'He doesn't follow up anything that'll take longer than thirty seconds or won't lead to a fight. Irene, was that crass, meaningless and totally inconclusive, or what?'

'Bit like the Welsh Assembly without a vote.'

'You still want to do TV one day?'

'What? Oh . . . well, not quite that, obviously. Not exactly *that*. I want to be a TV news reporter.'

'So did those guys at one time, I expect. I mean, nobody starts out wanting to shovel shit for a living, do they?'

'That was you, wasn't it?' Eirion slowed for a roundabout. 'We're looking for M5 South, aren't we?'

'Huh?'

'Yeah, this one.' Eirion hit the slip road. 'That girl your mother was talking about. The girl who nearly got ensnared by those people running that women's mystical group in Hereford.'

'You already know it was me. You saw how it ended.'

'I wasn't sure.'

'Well, it was.'

'And yet you're still interested in paganism and all that. Because that's why we're here, isn't it? I mean, I know you did think *I* might get something out of it, career-wise . . .'

but you *are* kind of drawn to all that, aren't you? I mean, *still*.'

Jane snorted a laugh. A big motorway sign loomed up, wreathed in tendrils of mist: 'Worcester. The South West'. So many options. The motorway was romantic at night, despite those dark, blurred, nightmare memories that were more nightmare than memory, but fading.

'Like, despite everything,' Eirion persisted, 'you're still turned on by weird mystical stuff.'

'Irene, it's not "weird mystical stuff", it's about what we are and where we're going. Do you never lie in bed and wonder what we're part of and where it all ends?'

'I could lie awake all night and agonize about it, but it wouldn't make any difference, would it? I don't like the look of this fog, Jane.'

'But suppose it would? Suppose you could? I mean, suppose you could go places, deep into yourself and into the heart of the universe at the same time?'

'But I know I couldn't. I wouldn't have the – what is it? – the application. Neither would most of those people there tonight. They think they can discover enormous, eternal, mind-blowing truths by summoning gods and spirits and things, but they're just fooling themselves. I mean they were just . . . kind of sad tossers.'

'Ned Bain wasn't sad.'

'Course he was. He was just the tosser in the suit.'

Eirion drifted onto the motorway. It wasn't *too* foggy, but you couldn't see the sky. Jane hoped Mum wasn't feeling too choked about her performance to drive carefully.

She said, 'He was making the point that paganism is no longer a crank thing; that it has to be taken seriously as a major, continuing tradition in this country and a genuine, valid force for change. He was like . . . very controlled and eloquent. I'd guess he's quite a way along the Path.'

'You mean the garden path?'

'You know exactly what I mean.'

'He's manipulative. You couldn't trust him.'

'Because he's kind of good-looking?'

'Well,' Eirion said, 'that's obviously a small plus-factor with you.'

'Sod off. If I was that superficial, would I be going out with you?'

'Are you?'

'Superficial?'

'Going out with me?'

'Possibly. I don't know. I might be too weird for you.'

'Yeah, that's my principal worry, too,' Eirion said, dead-pan.

'Bastard.' Jane leaned her shoulder into his. 'I wish there'd been time to wait and grab that Vivienne when she came out.'

'She wouldn't have told you where that church is. You notice how quick she clammed up, as though she knew she'd said too much? Because if some witchcraft sect are secretly practising at a Christian church . . . well, I don't know. If they haven't actually broken in, is that some kind of crime? Probably not.'

'Well, there you go.'

'Your mother's going to have to find out about it, though, isn't she?'

'Probably.'

'And what will she do when she does find out?'

'Go in there with a big cross? How should I know?'

'You could be more sympathetic to her.'

'I *am* sympathetic.'

'You're also sympathetic to paganism.'

'I'm interested. I've had . . . experiences, odd psychic things I can't explain.'

'Like what?'

'I don't want to talk about it really.'

'Oh.' Eirion drove in silence. Yellow fog-warning lights signalled a 40 m.p.h. speed limit.

'I'm not being funny,' Jane said. 'This just isn't the time.'

'No.'

'Haven't you? Had things happen to you you can't explain? Feelings about places? Things you thought you saw? Times when your emotions and your, like, sensations are so intense that you feel you're about to burst through into . . . something else. Some other level? I mean, the Welsh are supposed to be like . . .'

'My gran's a bit spooky.'

'Tell me in what way.'

'No, you tell me about your mum. Tell me about your dad.'

'That bloody Gerry,' Jane said.

Eirion was hesitant. 'Was what he said . . .?' The rest of it was lost under the rattling of a lorry passing them in the centre lane, a low-loader without a load, fast and free in the night.

'Yeah,' Jane said. 'He had it more or less right. My dad met my mum at university, where they were both studying law, and she . . . got pregnant with me and left the university, and he carried on and became a bent solicitor.'

'There was a special course for bent solicitors?'

'Ha ha. They were both going to do legal aid stuff and defend people who couldn't afford solicitors and all kinds of liberal, crusading stuff like that, according to Mum. But Dad wanted money – because of me, maybe he'd have said. Because of the responsibility. Though Mum says she was already learning things about him she didn't like. And, anyway, he got into iffy deals with some clients and Mum found out about it and there was this big morality scene, not helped by him screwing his clerk.' Jane paused for breath. 'Around this time, Mum had been helping the local vicar with community work and also she had this quite heavy experience of her own.'

'What sort of experience?'

'This was when things were really, really bad, and she was desperately trying to sort things out in her own head. She drove off into the sticks and came across this tiny little church in a wood or something and there was, like, a lamplit path . . .'

'It was night?'

'No, it was daytime, dickhead. The lamplit path was, like, metaphorical or in her head or a visionary thing. And listen, if she ever asks, I didn't tell you this, because she hates . . . Can't you go any faster?'

'There's a speed limit.'

'I can't even see any fog now. Because if she catches us up . . .'

'There's still a speed limit. And so your dad was killed?'

'He hit a motorway bridge. They were both killed. I mean, Karen, too. I read some newspaper cuttings I wasn't supposed to find. It was horrible – a ball of fire.'

'I'm sorry.'

'It was years ago,' Jane said without emotion.

'Which motorway?'

'The M5. I suppose this is the M5, isn't it?'

'It's a long motorway.'

'Well, it wasn't on this stretch, I don't think. I don't quite know where it was. I didn't read that bit. You don't want to keep looking out for a certain bridge all your life, do you?'

'No, you don't.'

'What Gerry said about a guilt trip, that's bullshit. I mean, why should *she* feel guilty? She was never mixed up in any of those crooked deals. Well, all right, it's easier for a widow to get into the Church than a newly divorced woman. Maybe she did feel guilty at the way that decision was so neatly taken out of her hands.'

'How do you feel about your dad?'

'He was kind of fun,' Jane said, 'but I was very little. Your dad's always fun when you're little. What was your home like? Did you all speak Welsh? I mean, *do* you?'

'Only when we have certain visitors. As everybody can speak English and English is a much bigger language and more versatile, you don't *have* to speak Welsh to anybody. But there are some people it's more *correct* to speak Welsh to. If you see what I mean.'

'Wow, minefield.'

'It's a cultural minefield, yeah. But I like Welsh. It's not my first language, but it's not that far behind.'

'Do you swear in Welsh? I mean you could swear in Welsh at school, in front of the teachers, and nobody would know.'

'That's an interesting point,' Eirion said. 'Actually, most Welsh people, when they swear, revert automatically to English. They're walking along the street conversing happily in Welsh, then one trips over the kerb and it's, like, "Oh, shit!" '

'Oh shit.' Jane whispered.

It was sudden – like a grey woollen blanket flung over your head.

'Oh, dear God,' Jane said.

It was like they'd entered some weird fairground. Red lights in the air. Also white lights, at skewed angles, inter-secting across all three carriageways.

She heard Eirion breathe in sharply as he hit the brakes and spun the wheel. Spun into a carnival of lights. Lights all over the place. *False lights in the night of filth.* Grabbed by her seatbelt, Jane heard screams, dipping and rising like the screams of women on a roller coaster.

The engine stalled. The car slid and juddered.

And stopped? Had they stopped?

Under the fuzzed and shivering lights, there was a moment of massive stillness in which Jane registered that Eirion had managed to bring the car to a halt without hitting anything. She breathed out in shattered relief. 'Oh, Jesus.'

'It's a pile-up,' Eirion said. 'I don't know what to do. Should we get out?'

'We might be able to help someone.'

'Yeah.'

There was fog and there was also steam or something. And the silhouettes of figures moving. Even inside the car, there was a smell of petrol. Jane scrubbed at the windscreen, saw metal scrunched, twisted, stretched and pulled like intestine. The fog swirled like poison gas, alive with shouting and wailing and the waxy, solidified beams of headlights.

Jane screamed suddenly and thudded back into the passenger seat. Eirion frenziedly unbuckled his seatbelt, leaned across her. 'Jane?'

'I saw an arm. In the road. An arm sticking out. With a hand and fingers all splayed out and white. Just an arm, it was just—'

Brakes shrieked behind them.

Behind.

You never thought about behind. Jane actually turned in time to see it, the monster with many eyes, before it reared and snarled and crushed them.

SIXTEEN

Lurid Bit

Gareth Prosser was loading hay or silage or whatever the hell they called it in these parts onto a trailer for his sheep out on the hills. He was panting out small balloons of white breath. He didn't even look up when Robin strolled over, just muttered once into the trailer.

''Ow're you?'

Robin deduced that his neighbour was enquiring after his health.

'I'm fine,' he said, although he still felt like shit after the Blackmore put-down. 'Nice morning. Specially after all that fog last night.'

'Not bad.'

Gareth Prosser straightened up. He wore a dark green nylon coverall and an old discoloured cap. Behind him, you could hardly distinguish the grey farmhouse from the barns and tin-roofed shacks. There was a cold mist snaking amongst a clump of conifers on the hillside, but the sun had risen out of it. The sun looked somehow forlorn and out of place, like an orange beachball in the roadway. It was around 8.15 a.m.

'Wonder if you can give me some advice,' Robin said.

Gareth Prosser looked at him. Well, not in fact *at* him, but at a point just a couple degrees to his left, which was disconcerting – made you think there was someone behind you with an axe.

'Firewood,' Robin said. 'We need some dry wood for the stove, and I figured you would know a reputable dealer.'

Gareth Prosser thought this over. He was a shortish, thickset guy in his fifties and now well overweight. His face was jowly, the colour and texture of cement.

Eventually, he said, 'Mansel Smith's your man.'

'Ah.' Robin was unsure how to proceed, on account of, if his recollection was accurate, the dealer who had sold them the notorious trailerload of damp and resinous pine also answered to the name of Mansel Smith.

'You get your own wood from, uh, Mansel?'

Prosser slammed up the tailgate on the trailer.

'We burns anthracite,' he said.

'Right.' If Mansel Smith was the only wood dealer around, Robin could believe that. And yet somehow he thought that if Gareth Prosser did ever require a cord of firewood from Mansel it would not be pine and it would not be wet.

'Well, thanks for your advice.'

'No problem,' Prosser said.

Right now, if this situation was the other way about, Robin figured he himself would be asking his neighbour in for a coffee, but Prosser just stood there, up against his trailer, like one of those monuments where the figure kind of dissolves into uncarved rock. No particular hostility; chances were this guy didn't know or didn't care that Robin was pagan.

Well, this was all fine by Robin, who stayed put, stayed cool. If there was one thing he'd learned from the Craft it was the ability to become still, part of the landscape like an oak tree. Prosser stayed put because maybe he *was* part of the landscape, and Robin figured they could both have stood there alongside that trailerload of winter fodder until one of them felt hunger pains or he – unlikely to be Prosser – burst out laughing.

But after about five seconds, the farmer looked up when a woman's voice called out, 'Gareth! Who was that?'

Prosser didn't reply, and she came round the side of one of the sheds onto the half-frozen rutted track.

'Oh,' she said.

'Hi there,' Robin said.

The woman was a little younger than Gareth, maybe fifty, and a good deal better preserved. She wore tight jeans and boots and a canvas bomber jacket. She had a strong, lean face and clear blue eyes and short hair with, possibly, highlights.

'Good morning,' the woman said distinctly. 'I'm Councillor Prosser's wife.'

'Hi. Robin Thorogood. From, uh, next door.'

'Judith Prosser.'

They shook hands. She had a firm grip. She even looked directly into his eyes.

'I've got some coffee on,' she said.

'That would be wonderful.'

'I'll be in now,' Gareth said.

Robin had learned, from Betty, that when they said 'now' they meant 'in a short while'. So he smiled and nodded at Gareth Prosser and gratefully followed Judith up the track toward the farmhouse complex. In the middle distance, their two teenage sons were wheeling their dirt bikes out to the hill. There was a sound like a chainsaw starting up and one of the boys splattered off.

'Be an international next year, our Richard,' Judith Prosser said proudly. 'Had his first bike when he was four. All Wales Schoolboy Scrambling champion at eleven. Perfect country for it, see.'

'Doesn't it mess up the fields?'

'Messes up the footpaths a bit.' Mrs Prosser smiled ruefully. 'We gets complaints from some of the rambling groups from Off. But not from the local people.'

Robin nodded.

'Councillor Prosser's boys, see,' Mrs Prosser said, like it was perfectly reasonable that being a councillor should automatically exclude you from certain stifling social impositions. Robin didn't detect any irony, but maybe it was there.

'I see,' he said.

'This is Juliet Pottinger.' An efficient and authoritative Scottish voice. *'I'm afraid I am away this weekend, but you may wish to leave a message after the tone. If you are a burglar uninterested in thousands of books which are essentially old rather than antiquarian, then I can tell you that you are almost certainly wasting your time.'*

Betty thought she sounded like a woman who would at least give you a straight answer – if not until Monday.

Bugger. She cleared away the breakfast things, ran some water for washing-up. Whatever Robin learned about the Reverend Penney from the Prossers, she didn't trust him not to put some pagan-friendly spin on it, and it was important to her now to find out the truth. What had Penney done to cause 'weeping and wailing' in the village? Why had the local people hushed it up? Did the priest, Ellis, know the full story and did this explain why he was so determined to subject the site to some kind of exorcism? She'd never settle here until she knew.

The phone rang, had her reaching for a towel before the answering machine could grab the call.

'Oh, my dear, I'm sure it's working already!'

'Mrs Wilshire?'

'I have had what, without doubt, was the best night's sleep I've had in months!'

'That's, er, wonderful,' Betty said hesitantly, because the likelihood of her arthritis remedy kicking in overnight was remote, to say the least.

'I can bend my fingers further than . . . Oh, I must show you. Will you be in this area today?'

'Well, I suppose . . .'

'Marvellous. I shall be at home all day.'

'Er . . . you didn't stop taking your cortisone tablets, did you? Because steroids do need to be wound down slowly.'

'Oh, I wouldn't take any chances.'

'No.'

It was psychological, of course, and Betty felt a little wary. Mrs Wilshire was a woman who could very easily become dependent on people. If Betty wasn't careful, she'd wind up having to call in to see her every other day. Still, if it hadn't been for Mrs Wilshire they would never have got onto the Penney affair.

'OK, I'll drop in later this morning if that's all right. Er, Mrs Wilshire, the papers you kindly let me take – about the church? There was one from a Mrs Pottinger, relating to the Reverend Penney. Do you know anything about that?'

'Oh, there was a lot of trouble about him, my dear. Everyone was very glad when he left, so I'm told.'

'Even though the church was decommissioned and sold soon afterwards?'

'That was a pity, although I believe it was always rather a draughty old place.'

'Er, do you remember, when you bought the house – and the church – did the Reverend Ellis come to visit you there?'

'Oh, I don't know. I was hardly ever there. It was Bryan's project. Bryan's house, until it was finished. Which I confess I really rather hoped it never would be.'

'So you don't know if the Reverend Ellis went to see Bryan there?'

'I'm afraid I don't. Though I'm sure he would have mentioned it. He never mentioned Mr Ellis in connection with that house. I don't *remember* him ever mentioning Mr Ellis.'

'No suggestion of Mr Ellis wanting to conduct a service in the church?'

'A church service?'

'Er . . . yes.'

'Oh no, my dear. I'm sure I would have remembered that.'

Just us, then.

The first thing Mrs Judith Prosser asked him was if they would be keeping stock on their land. Robin replied that farmers seemed to be having a hard enough time right now without amateurs creeping in under the fence. Which led her to ask what he did for a living and him to tell her he was an artist.

'That's interesting,' Mrs Prosser said, though Robin couldn't basically see how she could find it so; there wasn't a painting on any wall of the parlour – just photographs, mainly of men. Some of the photos were so old that the men had wing collars and watch chains.

As well as chairman's chains. Robin wondered if 'Councillor' was some kind of inherited title in the Prosser family – like, even if you had all the personality of a bag of fertilizer, they still elected you, on account of the Prossers knew the way to County Hall in Llandrindod.

Mrs Prosser went through to the kitchen, leaving the door open. There was a black suit on a hanger behind the door.

'We have a funeral this afternoon,' she explained.

'I guess councillors have a lot of funerals to attend.'

She looked at him. 'In this case, it's for a friend.'

'I'm sorry.'

'We all are. Sit down, Mr Thorogood.'

The furniture was dark and heavy and highly polished. The

leather chair he sat in had arms that came almost up to his shoulders. When you put your hands on them, you felt like a dog begging.

Funerals. Was this an opening?

'So it's, uh, *local*, this funeral?' Boy, how soon you could grow to hate one simple little word.

'In the village, yes.'

'So you still have a graveyard – despite no church?'

Mrs Prosser didn't reply. He heard her pouring coffee. It occurred to him she hadn't commented on him being American. Maybe 'from Off' was all-inclusive; how far 'Off' was of no major consequence.

He raised his voice a little. 'I guess there must've been problems with funerals when the old St Michael's Church was in use. What with the creek and all.' OK, it might not be in the best of taste to keep on about funerals, but it was his only way into the Reverend Penney, and he wasn't about to let go.

'Because of the brook, no one's been buried there in centuries.' She came back with two brown cups and saucers on a tray.

'Thank you, uh, Judith. Hey, I met the vicar. He came round.'

'Mr Ellis is a good rector.'

'But not local,' Robin said.

'You don't get local ministers anywhere any more, do you? But he brings people in. Very popular, he is. Quite an attraction.'

'You like to see new people coming in?'

She laughed: a good-looking woman, in her weathered way. 'Depends what people they are, isn't it? Nobody objects to churchgoers. And the collections support the village hall. They're always very generous.'

'Just Nick doesn't seem your regular kind of minister,' Robin said.

'He suits our needs,' said Mrs Prosser. 'Father Ellis's style of worship might not be what we've been used to in this area, but a breath of something new is no bad thing, we're always told. Jog us out of our routine, isn't it?'

'I guess.' He tasted the coffee. It was strong and surprisingly good. Judith Prosser put the tray on a small table and came to sit on the sofa opposite. She was turning out to be unexpectedly intelligent, not so insular as he'd figured. He felt ashamed of his smug preconceptions about rural people, *local* people. So he went for it.

'From what I hear, this area seems to attract kind of off-the-wall clergy. This guy, uh . . . Penney?'

'My,' she said, 'you *have* picked up a lot of gossip in a short time.'

'Not everybody finds themselves buying a church. You feel you oughta find out the history.'

'Or the lurid bits, at least.'

'Uh . . . I guess.' He gave her his charming, sheepish smile.

'Terry Penney.' Judith sipped her coffee. 'What's to say? Quiet sort of man. Scholarly, you know? Had his study floor to ceiling with books. Not an unfriendly person, mind, not reclusive particularly. Not at first.'

'He didn't live at the farmhouse – our house?'

'Oh, no, that was always a farm. No, the rectory was just out of the village, on the Walton road. Mr Weal has it now – the solicitor.'

Robin recalled the name from someplace. Juliet Pottinger's letter?

'So . . .' He put down his coffee on a coaster resting on the high chair arm. 'The, uh, lurid bit?'

'Restrain yourself, Mr Thorogood, I'm getting there.'

Robin grinned; she was OK. He guessed the Christ is the Light sticker was just the politically correct thing to do in Old Hindwell.

'Well, it was my husband, see, who had the first inkling of something amiss – through the county council. Every year Old Hindwell Church would apply for a grant from the Welsh Church Acts Committee, or whatever they called it then, which allotted money to old buildings, for preservation. Although the church was in the Hereford diocese it's actually in Wales, as you know. However, this particular year, there was no request for money.'

She turned on a wry smile. She was – he hadn't expected this – enjoying telling this story.

'The Reverend Penney had been yere . . . oh, must have been nearly eighteen months by then. Thought he must have forgotten, we did, so Councillor Prosser goes to see him. And Mr Penney, bold as you please, says, oh no, he hasn't forgotten at all. He doesn't want a grant. He doesn't think the church should be preserved!'

Robin widened his eyes.

'The church is *wrong*, says Mr Penney. It's in the wrong place. It should never have been built where it is. The water's not healthy. The fabric's rotten. Parking's difficult. Oh, a whole host of excuses. He says he's written to the diocese and whoever else, suggesting that they dispense with St Michael's at the earliest possible opportunity.'

Robin was fazed. 'He called for them to get rid of his own church? Just like that?'

'*Just* like that. No one could believe it.'

'Wow.' Robin was thinking furiously. Had Penney realized this was a powerful pagan site? Was it that simple? Had he made some kind of discovery? He tried to hide his excitement. 'Was he mad?'

'Perhaps he'd always been a little mad,' said Mrs Prosser. 'But we just never saw it until it was too late.'

'So, like . . . what did he do?'

Judith Prosser put down her coffee. 'No one likes to talk about it. But, as the owner now, I suppose you have a right to be told.'

One of the few good things about living here was that the post usually arrived before nine; in some rural areas you couldn't count on getting it before lunchtime.

Today's was a catalogue from a mail order supplier of garden ornaments – how quickly these people caught up with you – and a letter addressed to *'Mrs' Thoroughgood* with a Hereford postmark.

That 'Mrs' told her what this was going to be.

She sat down at the table with the letter in front of her. Usual cheap white envelope. They'd received two when they were living in Shrewsbury. They said things like: *We Know About Your Dirty Nude Ceremonies Worshipping Heathen Gods. The Lord Will Punish You.*

How had they found out? Who'd told them? Had Robin been indiscreet?

Betty felt gutted. The sick irony of this was that she hadn't practised as a witch since they moved here and, the way she was feeling now, never would again – at least, not in any organized way.

She contemplated tossing the letter in the stove unopened. But if she did that it would dwell in her, would be twice as destructive.

With contempt, Betty slit the envelope.

She read the note three times. Usual capitals, usual poor spelling.

But otherwise not quite what she'd expected.

YOU HAD BETTER TELL THAT LONG HAIRED
LOUT THAT IF HE WANTS TO GO HELPING
HIMSELF TO THE FAVOURS OF THE
BIGGEST HORE IN THE VILLAGE HE OUGHT
TO BE MORE DISCREAT ABOUT IT.

SEVENTEEN

Revelations

It was incredible! So wonderfully bizarre that, walking back to St Michael's Farm, Robin forgot all about agonizing over that asshole Blackmore who thought bestsellerdom had conferred upon him an art critic's instincts.

On the footbridge over the Hindwell Brook, he stopped a moment, evoking the incredible scene on that October morning back in the sixties when the brook was in flood. Had anyone photographed it? Could there be pictures still around?

Naw, anyone who'd pulled out a camera would probably have been compelled by some local by-law to hand over the film to Councillor Prosser – whichever Prosser happened to be the councillor at the time.

Judith Prosser had let him out the front way, through a dark-beamed hallway with some nice oak panelling. Up against the panelling there had been an outsize chair with a leather seat and a brass plate on the back. The chairman's chair, Judith had explained when he asked about it, from the Old Hindwell Community Council, disbanded some years ago under local government reorganization. And, yes, Gareth had been its chairman – twice.

Robin wondered if Judith Prosser called her husband by his title. Maybe got a little bedtime buzz out of it: *Oh, oh . . . give it to me harder, Councillor . . .*

He grinned at the winter sun. He felt a whole lot lighter. Holy shit, he'd actually spoken, in a meaningful way, to a Local Person! It was a seminal thing.

Indeed, when he looked across at the church on its promontory he even had the feeling that the Imbolc sabbat could go back on the schedule. He could see it now – using his visualization skills to cancel the brightness, and paint the sky dark, he could see lights awakening in the church, its ruins coming alive. He conjured the sound of Celtic drums and a tin whistle. *Son et lumière.* He saw, in the foreground, Betty's graceful silhouette – Betty in her pale cloak and a headdress woven from twigs. And, in the headdress, a ring of tiny flames, a sacred circle of candle-spears, a crown of lights.

He came in through the back door of St Michael's farmhouse so much happier than when he'd gone out of it. Returning with the breeze behind him.

'Siddown, babe,' he told her. 'You should hear this.'

'Should I?' She was already sitting down.

Robin halted on the stone flags. His mood fell, like a cooling meteor, to earth.

Her voice was flat as nan bread. At gone ten in the morning she was still in her robe. She looked pale and swollen-eyed, sitting at the kitchen table with a glass of the hot water she sometimes drank early in the day.

'You OK?'

Her hair also looked flat, like tired barn-straw. She'd been sleeping when he'd slipped out of bed around seven. He'd first made some coffee and toast for himself, not keeping especially quiet, and left a note for her on the table before he went over to the Prosser farm. He was half suspecting then that it was going to be one of *those* days, the kind he'd hoped there wouldn't be any more of after they moved to the country. In fact, since they'd moved here those days had accumulated one after the other, sure as sunrise. It was now reaching the point where it seemed they could never, simultaneously, be in a good mood. Like the sun would only shine on one of them at any one time.

Is this a psychic malaise? Could this be solved?

'Bets?' He was burning to bring her comfort, but he didn't know how. There were always going to be areas of her he could not reach; he accepted this. He also accepted that in some ways he was no more than her attendant. This was not *necessarily* sad, was it?

'I'm sorry. Time of the moon.' She gave him the palest smile he could recall. 'Tell me what you learned at the farm.'

She was evidently not going to talk about whatever it was. He sat down opposite her and, in a voice from which the oil of narrative enthusiasm had now been well drained, told her what he'd learned about the Reverend Penney.

It was obviously his change of mood, but now he saw beyond the bizarre; he saw the sadness of it all.

'It's like early in the morning, still only half light and a mist down by the water, so not everyone sees it. Just the Prossers, that's the two brothers who lived here, and their older brother – Gareth's father – and his wife. And Gareth himself, who'd have been in his twenties back then. And this Mrs Pottinger, she was there soon enough, in her role as the eyes and ears of Old Hindwell for the *Brecon and Radnor Express*. Because she'd seen a . . . what do you call that thing they kneel on to pray?'

'Hassock,' Betty said. 'I think.'

'Yeah. Pottinger was out for an early walk with the dog and she'd seen a hassock floating down the brook. Maybe her first thought was that this was the vandals she talked about in her letter to Major Wilshire. Seems she wanted to call the cops, but she ran into the Prossers, and the Prossers stopped her. They knew it was an inside job.'

'Yes,' Betty said, like she knew it would have to be.

'Well, the brook was already high, with all the rain, and close to bursting its banks, and that's what they think's happened at first. It's overflowed into the field by the barn and it's halfway up the promontory where the church is. It's like there's a dam – like a tree or something fell into the brook – but as the day gets lighter they can see the full extent of what's going down here.'

While he told her, he was seeing it so clearly, hearing the voices over the rushing and roaring of the water. Shrieks of shock from the women, Pottinger's dog barking in excitement. Judith Prosser hadn't been there, of course; it would be another fifteen years before she and Gareth were married, but she must have heard the story many times since.

'Everything!' Robin said. 'Everything that wasn't part of the fabric or nailed down. All the pews, the lectern, a big tapestry from the wall, the choir stalls . . . all floating down the Hindwell Brook. Until the first stuff reaches the bend and gets snagged on some branches and it all starts to pile up.'

He could see the great dam, one of the pews on end, wood groaning and splintering like the wreck of a sailing ship on the rocks, the water rising all around. He wanted so much to paint it, like Turner would have painted it, all mist and spray.

Betty said, 'The altar?'

'Oh yeah, that too. He'd stripped off the cloth and dragged it out through the doors and out to the end of the promontory, like he'd done with all the pews, and just . . . just tipped it into the water.'

Visualizing the great spout of water as the altar crashed into the brook.

'He was apparently a big guy. Played rugby. Very strong. His most impressive feat was to rip out the stone font. He must've rolled it out the double doors. They found it sticking out of the water, like a big rock.'

Betty glanced bleakly across at him, then picked up her glass and drank the rest of the warm water like it was a double Scotch.

'And where was he? Where was Penney?'

'Gone. They never saw him again. The Prossers and some other guys they could trust salvaged what they could. Took about four of them to get the font out – they waited nearly a week till the water level dropped down, and draped tarpaulin and stuff over it meantime. Couple of weeks later, the diocese gets a cheque for several thousand. Whole damn thing was hushed up.'

'They never found out why he did it?'

'Just he'd grown to hate the church, was all. There was no further explanation. He'd cleaned it out. Musta taken him hours, working at it through the night, by the oil lamps – no electricity in there. Trashing his own church like a maniac. When they went inside, it was all bare. Just the Bible from off of the lectern. The Bible lying there in the middle of the nave. Lying open.'

Betty waited a long time before she asked him.

'Open at?'

Robin smiled, shaking his head.

'The Book of Revelations, wouldn't you guess? About Michael and his angels taking on the Devil and *his* angels? The great dragon getting cast out into the earth? All of this underlined in ink.'

'I see.' Betty stood up.

'Shows us where Ellis is coming from, doesn't it? He's clearly heard about Penney and the dragon fixation that gets him so screwed up he trashes his own church. Well, OK, maybe the poor guy experiences some pre-Christian energy on that site which is so awesome it shakes his Christian faith, scares the shit outa him. To Penney it's devilish. It blows his mind . . . he wrecks the joint.'

'Thereby becoming a *vehicle* for this energy, I suppose,' Betty said wearily.

'Holy shit!' A big light came on in Robin's head. 'Hey, that's so cool! The priest is unwittingly helping the church to cast off Christianity – to revert.'

Betty took her glass to the sink, not looking at him, like she didn't want to hear what was coming next. But, hell, he had to say it. It was staring them right in the face.

'Bets . . . it's down to us, now, isn't it? To, like, finish the job. It puts us hard against Ellis, but . . . like, is this fate, or what?'

He was tingling with excitement. This was their clear future.

At the sink, Betty put down the glass, turned both taps on full. She was staring into the water running out of the taps. 'I doubt this is as simple as you imagine.'

'Or maybe it just *is*. Maybe it's also fate that the local people weren't so attached to the church the way it was that they wanted to fight to save it.'

'It was in a poor state, anyway. It was going to cost a fortune in repairs. That's what the Pottinger woman said.'

'And maybe Ellis was right about something coming to the surface. Bad news for him . . . but not for us, babes.'

'Oh, don't be so bloody simplistic! Just for a moment stop trying to make *everything* fit into your dream scenario.'

'Well, sure . . . OK.' He felt hurt. 'I mean let's talk this thing through.'

'I have to go out. I have to go and see Mrs Wilshire.'

'Again? What the fuck *is* this?'

'It's not your problem.'

'Oh really?' Hell, this needed saying, this was long overdue. 'Well what *is* my problem is why you always have to find excuses to get out of here. Like going in the *car*. Why don't you ever even go into the village? The place we live next to? Why don't you get to know the people *here*? People like Judith Prosser next door. OK, Gareth might be a dumb bastard, but she's OK, not what I imagined. Maybe we were wrong to start condemning the local people as total redneck bigots, purely on your flawed fucking childhood memories.'

Betty didn't flare up. She just stared hard at him for a couple of seconds, and he stared back.

And then she said, 'I never said that. I'm sure there are some decent, liberal, perceptive, outward-looking people down there.' She went to the table, picked up a piece of white notepaper, pushed it at him. 'Like, for instance, the person who sent that.'

EIGHTEEN

Cold, Earthly, Rational . . .

The Gothic letter D was still on the office door, but hanging loose now, at an angle. D for Deliverance – Bishop Hunter's idea.

As had been the Reverend Watkins becoming Deliverance Consultant.

She stood on the stone stairs, in front of the closed door, and decided, after all, to go back home. Her head ached. What the hell was she doing here? As she turned to creep back down the stairs, the office door opened.

'I *thought* it was!'

Merrily stopped, and slowly and sheepishly turned around again.

'I *thought* it was your car.' Sophie was expensively casual in a blue and white Alpine sweater. 'What on earth are you doing here? Nobody would have expected you to come in today.'

She'd spoken briefly to Sophie on the phone, asking her to put the bishop in the picture.

'Merrily, you look—'

'Yeah, I know.'

'Starved.' Sophie stood aside for her.

Merrily slung Jane's duffel coat on the back of her chair, and slumped into it. 'If I hadn't come in *today*, I might never have come in again.'

Sophie frowned and began making tea. Through the gate-house window, above Broad Street, the late morning sun flickered unstably in and out between hard clouds. The air outside had felt as though it was full of razor blades. The weather forecast had said there might be snow showers tonight – which was better than fog.

'The bishop tried to ring you.' Sophie laid out two cups and saucers. 'He said if I spoke to you to tell you there was no need to phone back.'

'Ever.'

'Don't be silly, Merrily. On reflection, I'm glad you did come in. Are you listening to me?'

'I'm listening.'

'You *cannot* drive to Worcester.'

'I'll be perfectly—'

'You will not. *I* shall drive you. Leave your car here. I don't want an argument about this, do you understand?'

'Well, I can take a bit of a rest this afternoon. They're not releasing her until after five.'

'She should stay there another night,' Sophie said stiffly. 'Concussion's unpredictable.'

'I think, on the whole, I can probably do without her discharging herself and stalking the streets of Worcester at midnight.'

'I should have thought that she'd be sufficiently penitent not to dare to—'

'Sophie' – Merrily cradled her face in cupped hands, looked up sorrowfully – 'this is Jane we're talking about.'

'If she were *my* daughter . . .'

'Don't give yourself nightmares.' Merrily dropped her hands, trying not to cry from exhaustion, anxiety, confusion and a terror which seemed to be lodged deep inside her, which every so often would pulse, hot-wiring her entire nervous system.

'Delayed shock, Merrily.'

'If you tell me I need trauma counselling, I'll put this computer through the window.'

Sophie brought over a chair, sat down opposite Merrily.

'Tell *me* then.'

The sun had put itself away again. Sophie added two sugars into Merrily's tea and switched on the answering machine.

Sophie? Sophie in her incredibly expensive Alpine sweater. Sophie who served the cathedral and all it represented. Yeah, why not?

'When you really contemplate the nature of this job,' Merrily said, 'you can start to think you're more than half mad. When the line between reality and whatever else there is . . . is no longer distinct. When it's no longer even a *line*.'

And when you swerve around a crashed lorry in the fog, and there's a figure staggering in the road that you just know you're going to hit, and in the last second, while you're throwing yourself around the wheel, you see her face.

'I'm starting actually to understand the Church's conservatism on the supernatural. Shut the door and bar it. Block the gap at the bottom with a thick mat. Let no chink of unnatural light seep in, because a chink's as good as a . . . whatever you call a big blast of light that renders you blind.'

'As in Paul on the road to Damascus?' Sophie said.

'Not exactly. Paul was . . . sure.'

'You *are* tired.'

'I mean, *I'm* sure . . . I'm just not quite sure what I'm sure *of*. It's only by being dull and conservative that the Church remains relatively intact. Bricks and mortar and *Songs of Praise*. Leave the weird stuff to Deliverance. It's a dirty job, and they've never been totally convinced someone has to do it.'

'I did watch the *Livenight* programme,' Sophie said. 'I didn't really see how else you could have handled it. Without coming over as a . . . crank.'

'Or a bigot. Both of which are probably better than a drowning wimp.' Merrily drank her tea, both hands around the cup, like someone pulled out of the sea and wrapped in a blanket. 'You spend an interminable hour making a fool of yourself on TV, you walk out thinking all religion's a joke. You're unhappy and ashamed and cynical all at the same time. You get in your car, you drive maybe not quite as carefully as you ought to, given the ubiquitous fog warnings and the fact that your husband just happened to have died horrifically on this same stretch of motorway. You drive into a fog bank. You become aware of two dull specks of red that you think must be a hundred yards away and which turn out to be this bloody great crashed lorry dead in your path. You spin the wheel in panic. You become aware of a figure dragging another figure across the road in front of you. The second figure stares full into your headlights, and you see . . . you see the face of your daughter who you know for a fact is at home in bed fifty-odd miles away. Your daughter's face . . . blank, white, expressionless. Like the face of a corpse.'

Sophie shuddered. 'It must have been . . . I can't imagine what that must have been like.'

'Like . . . Nemesis,' Merrily said. 'You know what I was thinking about in the few minutes before? I was thinking about this woman who believes she's seeing her sister's ghost. I was just deciding she really didn't have a psychiatric problem— Oh *no!*'

'What's the matter?'

'I told her I'd go with her to her sister's funeral. It's this afternoon. It's in about two hours. Or less.'

'Oh, Merrily, nobody could possibly expect—'

'I've got to.'

'You've had no *sleep*.'

'Oh, I've had . . . had an hour on the sofa. Fed the cat, grabbed a slice of toast, rung Worcester Infirmary twice to make sure Jane's not . . . worse. No, look, I've got to go, because . . .' *Because if I don't and something awful happens* . . . 'Beause it's something I can't just leave in the air.'

'Then you must lie down for a while first. I'll find somewhere in the palace. Look at you – you're trembling. Are you saying this pile-up actually happened in the same area where your husband was killed?'

'Well, that was on the other side, the northbound lanes. He was . . . I suppose he was on my mind, when . . .'

When she'd walked into that studio? Was Sean stalking her then? Was he already deep-harboured in her head when she'd entered the TV building? Having driven along the same stretch of the M5, under the very same bridge against which his car had balled on impact and bounced in its final firedance, while he and Karen were torn and roasted.

Couldn't tell Sophie any of that. Couldn't tell her about the eloquent pagan, Ned Bain, sitting there with his lazy, knowing Sean-like eyes, and even his legs crossed à la Sean. *Just stay with the main event.*

'And, you think . . . what you think is that this can't be happening. And if it can't be happening then it's a hallucination. And you *know* you're not hallucinating. Therefore – click, click – it has to be a paranormal experience, just like all the paranormal experiences other people have told you about and you've nodded sagely and given your balanced opinion.'

'But only you would think that. Only someone in your—'

'Only someone in my weird, cranky job.'

'But you didn't hit her,' Sophie said intensely. 'Did you? You did not hit Jane.'

'No. There was no impact. I didn't hit anyone. But still a complete nightmare – I mean dreamlike. You haven't physically driven into your daughter, therefore it must be a premonition: a vision of *killing your own child*.'

'But it wasn't, was it?'

'I could see Sean in her face . . . that little bump in the nose, the twist of the lips. I could see Sean in her, like I'd never seen him there before.'

'Juxtaposition of ideas,' Sophie said, 'or something.'

'I swerved, violently. Stopped the car and got out, terrified out of my mind. Only to discover . . .' Sophie reached across the desk, squeezed Merrily's cold right hand. '. . . that this really was Jane. The actual Jane, being pulled away by a terrified Eirion after being very nearly killed when this speeding low-loader smashed into the back of his car. She was pale and expressionless not because she was dead, but because she was semi-concussed. This is the mind-blowing perversity of it, that there is *an absolutely cold, earthly, rational explanation* . . . for everything. For every aspect of it. Why do I find that even more frightening? The most horrifying moment in my life, and there is, in the end, a simple, rational explanation.'

'You're afraid that you've stopped looking for simple rational explanations? Is that what you mean?'

'Maybe.'

'How many people were killed?' Sophie asked. 'In the end.'

'Three. And one critical in hospital. I think about four slightly hurt, including Jane. There were about six cars involved, and a couple of lorries. Seemed like the parameds and the fire brigade were on the scene before I was out of my car. There was one poor woman . . .'

Merrily shook her head, blinked away the unbelievably horrific image of a torn-off arm on the central reservation.

'You were very lucky, both of you. And the boy?'

'Eirion. His car was a write-off.'

'He's not injured, that's all that matters.'

'Some whiplash. They kept him in for the night, too, but I think his father picked him up this morning. Or his father's chauffeur. I talked to his stepmother on the phone. Eirion seems to be blaming himself for what happened. *Nice* kid.'

'So, altogether . . .'

'What I keep coming back to is, suppose I'd arrived one second earlier? Suppose I'd killed her? In one of those one-in-a-billion freak family tragedies? What would I have done with the rest of my life? What would any of it be worth?'

'But you didn't. Someone didn't want to lose you – and didn't want you forever damaged either.'

Merrily leaned back, shook out a cigarette. 'You ever thought of getting ordained, Sophie?'

'God forbid.' Sophie stood up. 'Put that thing away and get your coat.'

'It's Jane's coat. What for?'

'Jane's coat, then. I'm going to drive you to this funeral. You can perhaps sleep on the way. If we leave now, we might even stop for a sandwich.'

'Sophie, it's Saturday. You can't . . . You have things to do.'

'Oh,' Sophie said, 'I think Hereford United can manage without me for one week.'

Merrily blinked. Sophie unhooked a long, sheepskin coat and a woollen scarf from the door. It did rather look like the sort of outfit you would wear to a football match in January. Bizarre?

'This is above and beyond, Soph.' Merrily got unsteadily to her feet.

'I should be grateful if you didn't smoke in my car,' Sophie said.

NINETEEN

Abracadabra

The main road from Old Hindwell to New Radnor passed through the hamlet of Llanfihangel nant Melan. The church of St Michael was right next to the road and, although it didn't actually look very old, there were indications of a circle of ancient yew trees, which suggested it had been rebuilt.

Although there were a number of other cars nearby, Betty stopped the Subaru. She was in no mood to talk to Mrs Wilshire or anybody else right now. She would check out the atmosphere of the church. It might even calm her down.

She was still furious with Robin. If he'd been accosted the other night by the drunken wife of Greg Starkey, feeling him up in the street, why hadn't he told Betty when he arrived home? Old Hindwell wasn't exactly known for its red-light quarter. So why had he kept quiet?

Why? Because they'd just had a goddamn row over his handling of Nick Ellis. Because he'd slammed out of the house and didn't think she'd be speaking to him anyway. Because he was cold and tired. *Because.*

So why hadn't he mentioned it the next day, even?

Because . . . Jeez, was it important? Did she think he *enjoyed* it? Did she think he'd snatched this chance to feel Marianne's tits?

Actually, she didn't think that. What she thought was that Robin hated to tell her anything that might make her think less of Old Hindwell. *Why don't you get to know the people here? Like Judith Prosser – she's OK, not what I imagined.*

Dickhead.

Betty walked over to the church. The stonework suggested extensive Victorian renovation. Did anything remain of the church built as part of some alleged St Michael circle? How would this one feel inside?

Sooner or later, when Robin was not around, she would have to go back into the Old Hindwell ruins to face the question now looming large: the stained and sweating, fear-ridden man at prayer – was that him? Was that the Reverend Terry Penney? Was he dead now?

But this wasn't an exercise in psychic skills. Before she went back there, she wanted to know all there was to be known about *all* the churches in the St Michael circle.

However, in Llanfihangel Church, she was immediately accosted by a man in a light suit who asked her if she was on the bride or the groom's side. So much for standing there in the silence and feeling for the essence of the place. Betty apologized and escaped with a handful of leaflets, which she inspected back in the Subaru.

And just couldn't believe it. One, apparently produced as a result of a community tourism initiative, was blatantly entitled, 'Where sleeps the Dragon on the trail of St Michael's churches'.

Betty slumped back in her seat, broke into a peal of wild, stupid laughter. A tourist leaflet. Was that how all this had started?

The text explained that there were four St Michael churches around Radnor Forest – at Llanfihangel nant Melan, Llanfihangel Rhydithon, Cefnllys and Cascob. It presumably didn't mention Old Hindwell because it was a ruin, now on private land.

An inside page was headed: 'St Michael and the Dragon of Radnor Forest'.

It referred to the introduction by Jewish Christians of 'angelology'. Angels guarded nature and local communities. St Michael guarded Israel and was named in the Book of Revelations, etc., etc. Most Welsh churches dedicated to him had appeared in the tenth and eleventh centuries.

The specific Radnor reference had been pulled from a book called *A Welsh Country Parson* by D. Parry-Jones, who recounted a legend that the last Welsh dragon slept in Radnor Forest and, to contain it, local people had built four St Michael churches in a circle around the Forest. It was said that if any of these churches was destroyed, the dragon would awaken and ravage the countryside once more.

This was it? This was the source of Nicholas Ellis's paranoia?

Crazy!

Still, it did look as though Robin and Ellis were right. Assuming there was no fire-breathing elemental beast locked into the landscape, this appeared to be a simple metaphor for paganism, the Old Religion.

'. . . *if any one of these churches is destroyed . . .*'

Old Hindwell *had* been virtually destroyed . . . and initially by its rector, which didn't make any obvious sense. Why would a clergyman make a gesture which was bound to be adversely interpreted by anyone superstitious enough to give any credence to the dragon legend?

Unless Penney had been a closet pagan. Was that likely?

Not really. Something was missing. For a moment, Betty smelled again the rich, sickening stench from the praying man in the skeletal nave.

She drove off too quickly, the Subaru shuddering.

*

Lizzie Wilshire greeted her with a spindly embrace.

'I don't know whether it's your herbal mixture or just *you*, my dear, but I feel *so* much better.' Holding out her right hand and making it into a claw, the fingertips slowly but effectively closing on the palm.

'Gosh,' Betty said.

'I haven't been able to do that for months!' Those ET eyes shining like polished marbles. 'You're a wonder, my dear!'

'I wouldn't quite say that.'

Psychological? The potion couldn't possibly have had such a spontaneous and dramatic effect unless her problem was essentially, or to an extent, psychosomatic.

And yet . . . Betty caught an unexpected sidelong glimpse of Lizzie's aura. It was, without a doubt, less fragmented. And she was talking constantly, garrulous rather than querulous now.

'Were you originally called Elizabeth? Like me?'

'A long time ago,' Betty admitted, as they sat down.

'A *long* time ago, my dear, you weren't even born.' Lizzie Wilshire laughed hoarsely. 'Now, were those papers useful? If not, just throw them away. I'm in a clearing-out mood. Clutter frightens me. I'm even thinking of selling the summer house. Every time I look out at it, I expect to see Bryan walking across the garden. Do people buy summer houses second-hand like that? Can they take them away?'

'I should think so. You could advertise it in the paper. I could do that for you, if you want.'

'Oh, would you? That's terribly kind. Yes. I told Dr Coll – I hope you don't mind . . .'

'About the summer house?'

'About you, of course! About your wonderful herbal preparation. He called in this morning, even though it's Saturday

– such a caring, caring man – and said how much better I was looking, and naturally I told him about you.'

'Oh.' In Betty's experience the very last thing a doctor liked to be told was that some cranky plant remedy had had an instantaneous effect on a condition against which powerful drugs had thus far failed to make a conspicuous impact.

'He was delighted,' Lizzie said.

'He was?'

'Far be it from him, he said, to dismiss the old remedies. Indeed, he's often suggested I might benefit from attending one of the Reverend Ellis's services – but that's all too brash and noisy for me.'

'He must be a very unusual doctor.'

'Simply a very caring man. I didn't realize how *pastoral* country doctors could be until Bryan died. Bryan had a thing about the medical profession, refused to call a doctor unless in dire emergency. He'd have liked *you*. Oh, yes. His army training involved finding treatments in the hedgerows. A great believer in natural medicine, was Bryan. Although, one does need to have a fully qualified medical man in the background, don't you think?'

'Yes,' Betty said. 'I suppose so. Shall I make some tea?'

She knew now where everything was kept. She knew on which plate to arrange which biscuits. On which tray to spread which cloth. All of which greatly pleased Mrs Wilshire. When it was done, Betty sat down with her and they smiled at one another.

'You've brightened my life in such a short time, Betty.'

'You've been very helpful to me, too.'

'I won't forget it, you know. I never forget a kindness.'

'Oh, look . . .'

'We never had children, I've no close relatives left. At my age, with my ailments, one doesn't know how long one has left . . .'

'Come on . . . that's daft.'

'I'm quite serious, my dear. I said to Dr Coll some time ago, is there anything I can do to help you after my death? Is there anything you need? New equipment? An extension to the surgery? Of course, he brushed that aside, but I think when you've been treated so well by people, by a community, it's your *duty* to put something back.'

'Well . . .'

'In the end, the most he would do was give me the name of a local charity he supports, but . . . Oh dear, I've embarrassed you, I'm so sorry. We'll change the subject. Tell me how you're getting on with that terrible old place. Have you been able to do anything with the damp?'

'These things take time,' Betty said, careful not to mention the need for money.

Getting into the car, she felt deeply uncomfortable. It might be better if she didn't return to Mrs Wilshire's for a while. The old girl probably wasn't aware of trying to buy attention, even if it was only with compliments about a very ordinary herbal preparation, but . . . Oh, why was *everything* so bloody complicated, suddenly?

She leaned back in the seat, rotating her head to dispel tension. She noticed the dragon leaflet on the passenger seat. Where, out of interest, was the next church on the list?

Cascob.

Nestles in the hills near the head of the Cas Valley . . . village appears in the Domesday Book as Casope – the mound overlooking the River Cas.

Promising, she supposed. And was about to throw the leaflet back on the seat, when another word caught her eye.

It was 'exorcize'.

*

196

A couple of miles into Radnor Forest, Betty became aware of an ominous thickening of cloud . . . and, under it, a solitary signpost.

She must have passed this little sign twenty times previously and never registered it, perhaps because it pointed up that narrow lonely lane, a lane which didn't seem to lead anywhere other than: Cascob.

Strange name. Perhaps some chopped-off, mangled Anglicization of a Welsh phrase which meant 'obscure-church-at-the-end-of-the-narrow-road-that-goes-on-for-ever'. Or so it seemed, perhaps because this was the kind of road along which no stranger would dare travel at more than 20 m.p.h. It was deserted, sullen and moody. Robin would be enchanted.

There wasn't much to Cascob. A bend in a sunken, shaded lane, a lone farmhouse and, opposite it, a few steep yards above the road, the wooden gate to the church itself, tied up with orange binder twine. Betty left the Subaru in gear, parked on the incline, untied the twine around the gate.

Sheep grazed the sloping, circular churchyard among ancient, haphazard gravestones and tombs that were crumbly round the edges, like broken biscuits. There was a wide view of a particularly lonely part of the Forest, and the atmosphere was so dense and heavy that Betty couldn't, for a while, go any further.

Some places, it was instantaneous.

The old man in the cellar at Grandma's place in Sheffield . . . that had probably been the first. None of them had frightened her for quite a while, not until she'd learned from other kids that you were *supposed* to be afraid of ghosts. Until then, she'd been affected only by the particular emotions specific to each place where something similar happened: fear, hatred, greed and – the one emotion she hadn't at first understood – lust.

She steadied her breathing. Cascob Church squatted

under low, grey cloud. It looked both cosy and creepy. To what extent had the present sensations been preconditioned by what she'd read in the leaflet?

'. . . to exorcize a young woman . . .'

She walked on, towards the church.

The stone and timbered building, like many this old, seemed to have grown out of the site organically. There were oak beams in its porch and under the pyramid-cap of the tower. It snuggled against an earthmound which was clearly not natural, possibly a Bronze Age tumulus. From the base of the mound grew an apple tree, spidery winter branches tangled against the cold light. There was a gate across the porch – more twine to untie.

Betty stepped inside. There were recent posters on the wall and a framed card invited all who entered to say a prayer before they left. She would not be so crass as to offer a prayer to the goddess. When she put out a hand to the oak door, Cascob Church seemed to settle around her, not unfriendly, certainly ancient and comfortably mysterious.

And locked.

She wondered for a moment if this was a sign that she was not supposed to enter this place. But then, all churches were kept locked these days, even – perhaps especially – in locations this remote.

She walked back across the churchyard and the narrow road to the farmhouse to enquire where she might borrow a key. The bloke there was accommodating and presented her with a highly suitable one, about six inches long. It made her right hand tingle with impressions, and she twice passed it quickly to her left hand and back again before reaching the porch.

The lock turned easily. She went in and stood tensely, with the door open behind her.

The church inside was dark and basic. Betty stood poised

to banish anything invasive. But there was nothing. It was quiet. So far removed from the foetid turmoil swirling in the Old Hindwell ruins that she banished *that* from her thoughts, lest she somehow infest Cascob.

The place was tiny and probably little changed since the fourteenth or fifteenth century. A farmers' church, with a font for christenings but no room for gentry weddings.

There was a wooden table with literature on it, including the sleeping dragon leaflet and a similar one about Cascob Church itself. A collection box had Betty fumbling for a fiver, an offering to appease the God of the Christians. She stood for a moment behind one of the back pews, not touching its dark wood, her head hanging down so as not to face the simple altar. It was not *her* altar, it faced the wrong direction, and she'd turned away from all this eight years ago.

Betty closed her eyes. It had been her decision. She'd turned from the east to face the north: a witch's altar was always to the north. There was no turning back . . . was there?

When she reopened her eyes, she was facing the white-washed north wall, where a document hung in a thin, black frame.

Betty looked at it, breathed in sharply. The breathing came hard. The air around her seemed to have clotted. She stared at the symbols near the bottom of the frame.

And saw, with an awful sense of déjà vu:

She felt almost sick now, with trepidation. There was nothing coincidental about this.

At the top of the document, under the funeral black of the frame, was something even more explicit.

ABRACADABRA
ABRACADABR
ABRACADAB
ABRACADA
ABRACAD
ABRACA
ABRAC
ABRA
ABR
AB
A

Betty spun away from the wall, snatched up one of the leaflets about the church and ran outside.

Under the Zeppelin cloud, she opened the leaflet to a pen and ink drawing of the church and a smaller sketch of the Archangel Michael with wings outstretched and a sword held above his head.

Under the drawing of the church, she read:

'. . . the Abracadabra charm, dated from the seventeenth century, purported to have been used to exorcize a young woman. Heaven knows what she went through, but it sheds an interesting light on the state of faith in Radnorshire at the time.'

Betty stilled herself with a few minutes of chakra breathing, then went back into the church and up to the document itself, again leaving the door open for light.

What she'd read was a transcript of the original charm produced, it said in a tiny footnote, by an expert from the British Museum. The original was at the bottom: a scrap of paper with the ink faded to a light brown and now virtually indecipherable. There were no details about exactly how or when it had been found in the church.

But there was no inglenook fireplace where a box might be placed.

Hands clenched in the pockets of her ski jacket, Betty read the transcript. The two charms might be a century or more apart, but the similarities were obvious.

In the name of the Father, Son and of the Holy Ghost
Amen X X X and in the name of the lord Jesus Christ I
will delive Elizabeth Loyd from all witchcraft and from all
Evil Spirites and from all evil men or women or wizardes
or hardness of heart Amen X X X

It went on with a mixture of Roman Catholic Latin – *pater noster, ave Maria* – and cabbalistic words of power like 'Tetragrammaton', the name of God. At the bottom were two rows of planetary symbols. The sun, the moon and Venus were obvious. The one that looked like a '4' was Jupiter.

Wizards . . . spirits . . . hardness of heart. All too similar. Another solid link, apart from St Michael, between the two churches.

There was more obsessive repetition:

I will trust in the Lord Jesus Christ my Redeemer and
Saviour from all evil spirites and from all other assaltes of
the Devil and that he will delive Elizabeth Loyd from all
witchcraft and from all evil spirites by the same apower as
he did cause the blind to see, the lame to walke and that
thou findest with unclean spirites to be in thire one mindes
amen X X X as weeth Jehovah Amen. The witches com-
passed her abought but in the name of the lord i will
destroy them Amen X X X X X X X

It was signed by Jah Jah Jah.

Poor Elizabeth Loyd. A 'young woman'. How old?

Twenty? Seventeen? Was she really possessed by evil? Or was she schizophrenic? Or, more likely, simply epileptic?

Heaven knows what she went through, but it sheds an interesting light on the state of faith in Radnorshire at the time.

Had it been carried out here, in the church? If so, Betty wasn't picking up anything. What kind of minister had mixed this bizarre and volatile cocktail of Anglicanism, Roman Catholicism, paganism, cabbalism and astrology?

Or was it the local wise man, the conjuror?

Or were they one and the same?

Betty was glad the charm lay behind glass, that she wouldn't have to force herself to touch it, where it had been held by the exorcist, didn't even like to look too hard at the original manuscript, was glad that the ink had faded to the colour of soft sand.

She walked back outside into the churchyard and was drawn back – felt she had no choice – to that spot amongst the graves where she'd previously felt the weight of something. She wondered what had happened if, after the exorcism, the epilepsy or whatever persisted? There was something deeply distasteful about the whole business – and there had probably been villagers at the turn of the eighteenth century who also found it disturbing. But they'd have to keep quiet. Especially if the exorcism was performed by the minister.

She was gazing out towards the Forest – yellowed fields, a wedge of conifers – when the pain came.

It was so sudden and so violent that she sank to her knees in the long, wet grass, both hands at her groin. There was an instant of shocking cold inside her, and then it was over and she was crawling away, sobbing, to the shelter of a nearby gravestone.

She stayed there for several minutes, her breathing rapid

and her heart rate up. She pushed her hair back out of her eyes and found that it was soaked with sweat.

When she was able to stand again, she was terrified there might be physical damage.

She stumbled back to the church wall and, trembling, wrote a huge banishing pentagram, clockwise on the air.

And then followed it with the sign of the cross.

TWENTY

Blessed Beneath the Wings of Angels

Been a while since he was here last, but it might as well have been yesterday. Nothing changed, see. A new bungalow here, a fancy conservatory there. A few new faces that started out bright and shiny and open . . . and gradually closed in, grew cloudy-eyed and worried.

Like this boy in the pub. Londoner, sounded like. Gomer had seen it before. They came with their catering certificates and visions of taking over the village inn and turning it into a swish restaurant with fiddly little meals and vintage wine, fifty quid a time. Year or so later, it was back to the ole steak pie and oven chips and a pint of lager – three diners a night if they was lucky, at a fiver apiece.

Gomer sucked the top off his pint of Guinness. Ole Hindwell, he thought, where city dreams comes to die.

'Not seen you around before,' the London boy said.

'That's on account you en't been around yourself more'n a week or two,' Gomer told him.

'Two years, actually. Two years in March.' The boy had dandruffy hair, receding a bit, greying a bit. You could tell those two years had felt to him like half a lifetime. He'd be about forty years old; time to start getting anxious.

'Bought the place off Ronnie Pugh, is it?'

'That's right.'

'Ar.' Gomer nodded, spying the creeping damp, already

blackening walls they must have rewhitewashed when they moved in. 'Tryin' to get rid for six year or more, ole Ronnie.'

'So it appears,' the boy said, regrets showing through like blisters.

As well they might. Never fashionable, the Forest. No real old money, see. Radnorshire always was a poor county: six times as many sheep as people, and you could count off the mansions on one hand. Not much new money, neither: the real rich folk – film stars, pop stars, stockbrokers, retired drug dealers and the like – went to the Cotswolds, and the medium-rich bought theirselves some rambling black-and-white over in Herefordshire.

While Radnorshire – no swish shops, no public schools, no general hospital, no towns with much over 3,000 people – collected the pioneer-types. Trading in the semi in Croydon or Solihull for two scrubby acres, a dozen sheep and a crumbly old farmhouse with rotting timbers, loose slates and stone-lice.

And the pensioners. Radnorshire got them too, by the thousand. Couples like Minnie and Frank, buying up the old farm cottages and the cheap bungalows. And then one of them dies and the other's stuck, all alone in the middle of nowhere, on account of Radnorshire property prices don't rise much year to year, and the poor buggers can't afford to move away.

'Not going up the funeral?' the boy said. Though the car park was full, there was only himself and Gomer in the Black Lion. Mourners for Menna Weal had parked up outside, stopped in for one drink, and trailed off to the village hall. Funny old set-up, doing church services at the village hall. But that was Radnorshire – lose your church and you makes do.

Gomer shook his head. 'Well, I never knowed her that well, see.' Truth was, with Min only days in the ground, he couldn't face it, could he? Good to help the little vicar, but he realized the vicar was only giving him something to do to take his mind off his own loss; she wouldn't want him attending no funeral.

'Nor me,' the boy said. 'Mrs Weal never came in here. Her husband comes in occasionally.'

'Picks up his business in the pub, what I yeard. Folks from Off. Friendly local lawyer, sort o' thing.' Gomer had heard this from a few people. He didn't say much, Big Weal, played his cards close, but he put himself about in all the right places.

The boy came over bashful. 'He picked *us* up, actually. He was in here when we were looking over the place. Knew the agent, wound up doing the conveyancing.' He laughed, a bit uncomfortably. 'Bloke's so big you don't feel you dare refuse, know what I mean?'

'Likely it was the same with poor Mrs Weal,' Gomer said.

He'd gathered a fair bit of background about Menna from Danny Thomas, the rock-and-roll farmer at Kinnerton who, it turned out, was a distant cousin. Danny had fancied her himself at one time, but Merv Thomas kept her out of the way of men. Selfish bastard, old Merv, especially after his wife passed on; he had to have another woman around doing the things women had been put on God's earth to do.

Frail, pale little person, Menna, it seemed. All right for washing and cleaning, but too frail for farming, definitely too frail for Merv Thomas's farm. Sons was what Merv had needed, but never got. So now the Thomas farm had gone to folk from Off, the deal sorted by J.W. Weal who then married the profits. '*What a bloody waste,*' Danny Thomas had said, guitar on his knee in the barn, crunching Gomer's eardrums with something called 'Smoke on the Water'.

'Like I said, he never brought her in here.' The boy leaned over his bar, confidentially. 'You never saw her round the village neither. We used to wonder if she had agoraphobia or somefing, but I never liked to ask.'

'Ar.' Wise attitude. Nobody liked a new landlord nosing into the affairs of local people. 'Her never had no friends yere, then?'

'Mrs Prosser, Councillor Prosser's wife, she used to go there once or twice a week, apparently.'

Judy Prosser. This figured. Judy Prosser was born and raised the other side of the quarry, no more than half a mile from Merv Thomas's farm. She'd have known the Thomas girls, likely Barbara better than Menna, being nearer her age. Judy Prosser would know the score. Smart girl that one; not much got past her, whereas most everything got past that dull bugger Gareth.

Well, Gomer had always got on well enough with Judy, in the days before Gareth bought his own digger. Likely he'd hang around here, see if she came in the pub after the funeral.

'My missus went across there once,' the boy continued.

'To visit Menna?'

'They'd be about the same age, near enough, and she reckoned maybe they could be friends. But she got short shrift. Never got further'n the doorstep.'

'This is the ole rectory?'

'Blooming great big place for just the two of them. Never seemed to have guests to stay or anyfing, even in the summer. Never went on holidays either.'

'Solicitor, see,' Gomer said. 'Gotter have hisself a big house. Status in the community. Plus, his ole man likely got a good deal on it when they ditched the church. You drinking . . .?'

'Greg. Fanks very much,' the boy said. 'I'll have a half. So you were from round here, originally, Mr—'

'Gomer Parry Plant Hire,' Gomer said. 'Radnor Valley born an' bred. Used to run a bunch o' diggers and bulldozers.

We done drainage, soakaways, put roads in, all over the valley. My nephew, Nev, he does it now, see.'

'Oh, yeah, *I* know. He was filling in after the archaeological digs, yeah? Used to come in for a sandwich and a pint at lunchtime?'

'Sure t'be.'

'They were digging all over the place. We all got excited when it came out they'd found an old temple. We fought it was gonna be like Stonehenge and we'd get thousands of tourists. But all it was – it was just a few holes in the ground where there'd been like wooden posts what rotted away centuries ago. Noffing to see, apart from all the stone axe-heads and stuff they dug up. Terrible disappointment.'

'Ar. Typical Radnorshire tourist attraction, that is.' Gomer took out his tin to roll a ciggie. 'Sounds good till you sees it.'

Crossing the Welsh border, you came, unexpectedly, out of darkness into light, Merrily thought, raising herself up in the passenger seat of Sophie's Saab. The last English town, Kington, with its narrow streets and dark surrounding hills, had been more like a Welsh country town. The hills beyond were densely conifered until the trees thinned to reveal a rotting cathedral of fissured rocks.

And then, suddenly, the Radnor Valley opened up and the whole landscape was washed clean under a sandy sky, and Merrily sank back again, just wanting to go on being driven through the winter countryside, not having to make any decisions . . . not having to answer difficult questions with a boom-mic hanging over her like a club.

Sophie took a left, and the car began to burrow under high banks and high, naked hedges. As the lanes narrowed, Old Hindwell began to be signposted, but by now they might just as well have followed any vehicle on that road;

every car and Land-Rover seemed to contain people dressed in black.

'One forgets,' Sophie mused, 'that rural funerals are such social events.'

The lanes seemed to have brought them in a loop, back into conifer country. The official Old Hindwell sign was small and muddied. Just beyond it, set back into a clearing, sat a well-built, stone Victorian house with a small, conical turret at one end. In most of its windows, curtains were drawn; the others probably didn't have curtains.

'The old rectory, do you think?' Sophie said.

'Weal's house? You could be right. There's obviously nobody about. If it is the rectory, we ought to be able to see the old church nearby.'

She peered among the trees, an uneasy mixture of leafless, twisted oaks and dark, thrusting firs.

'I suppose it must have occurred to you,' Sophie said, 'that the old church here might have been the one referred to by that woman on your TV programme.'

'The pagan church, mmm?' The road took them through a farm layout – windowless buildings on either side. 'But let's not worry about that until someone asks us to.'

The first grey-brown cottages appeared up ahead.

And the cars. The village was clogged with cars.

The pub car park was full, as was the yard in front of what had once been a school. Cars and Land-Rovers also lined the two principal lanes, blocking driveways and entrances, until the roads became so narrow that another parked vehicle would have made them impassable. Could it possibly be like this every Sunday?

Sophie slowed for a drab posse of mourners. They crossed the road and filed into a tarmac track between two big leylandii.

'The village hall,' Merrily said, unnecessarily.

It stood on what she judged to be the western edge of the village, partly concealed a little way up a conifered hillside, and was accessed by a footpath and steps. Sophie wondered aloud how they got any wheelchairs up there, for all the disabled people who thought Nicholas Ellis's prayers might cure them.

'So it's true then?' Merrily said. 'He does healing, too?'

'I copied cuttings from the local papers onto your computer file.' Sophie reversed into a field entrance to turn round again in the hope of finding a space. 'I don't suppose you had time to read them yet. I don't know how many people he's actually supposed to have healed.'

'You don't usually get statistics on it.'

Sophie frowned. 'That sort of thing is just not Anglican, somehow.'

'No? What about the shrine of St Thomas, in the cathedral?'

'*Not* the same thing.'

'What – because Ellis spent some time in the States?'

'My information is that he learned his trade with the more extreme kind of Bible Belt evangelist.' Sophie shuddered. 'Would you like to borrow my coat? It may not be exactly funereal, but it's at least . . .'

'Respectable?'

'I'm sorry,' Sophie said. 'I didn't mean—'

'Of course you didn't.' When Merrily smiled her face felt so stiff with fatigue that it hurt. 'If anyone does notice me, I could pretend to be a poor single-parent whom Mr Weal defended on a shoplifting charge.'

When the strangers came in, Gomer was getting the local take on the planting of Menna Weal in the rectory garden.

'Most people couldn't equate it wiv him being a lawyer and into property,' Greg said. 'Who's gonna wanna buy a house wiv a bleedin' great tomb? They say he'll leave it to his nephew who's started in the firm, but would you wanna live in a house wiv your dead auntie in the garden?'

Gomer wondered how he'd feel if his Min was buried in the back garden, and decided it wouldn't be right for either of them. In the churchyard she wasn't alone, see. Not meaning the dead; it was the coming and going of the living.

'But what I reckon . . .' Greg said. 'That building's right down the bottom of the garden, OK? You could lop it off, make it separate. A little park, with a footpath to it. The Weal memorial garden. I reckon that's what he's got in mind.'

'Nobody ask him?'

'Blimey, you don't ask *him* nothing. Not even the time – you'd get a bleedin' bill. It's like there's a wall around him, wiv an admission charge. And no first names. It's Mr Weal. Or J.W., if you're a friend.'

'He got many friends?'

'He knows a lot of people. That's the main fing in his profession.' Greg turned to his two new customers. 'Yes, gents . . .'

They wore suits – but not funeral suits. Both youngish fellows, in their thirties. One was a bit paunchy, with a half-grown beard; he ordered two pints.

'Not here for the funeral?' Greg said.

'Ah, that's what it is.' The plump, bearded one paid for their drinks. 'Must be somebody important, all those cars.'

'Oh, that's not unusual. There's a mass of cars every Sunday. Popular man, our minister. You get people coming from fifty miles away.'

Gomer looked up, gobsmacked. Most of these folks were not here for Menna at all, but part of some travelling fan club for the rector? Bloody hell.

'Hang on,' the plump feller with the beard said. 'Are there *two* churches, then?'

'Kind of,' Greg said. 'Our minister uses the village hall for his services.'

'But the old one, the old church – that's disused, right?'

'Long time ago. It's a ruin.'

'Can you still get to it?'

'You probably can,' Greg said, 'but it's on private land. It's privately owned now.'

'Only my mate wanted to take some pictures. With permission, of course. We don't want to go sneaking about. Who would we ask? Who owns it?'

'Well, it's new people, actually – only been moved in a week or so. There's a farmhouse, St Michael's. If you go back along the lane, past the post office, and on out of the village, you'll see a big farm, both sides of the road, then there's a track off to your left. If you go over a little bridge and you get to the old rectory, on your right, you've gone too far.'

'They all right, the people?'

'Sure,' Greg said. 'Young couple. He's American, an artist – book illustrator. Yeah, they're fine.'

'What's the name?'

Gomer was suspicious by now. Gomer was always suspicious of fellers in suits asking questions. Not Greg, though; suspicious landlords didn't sell many drinks.

'Oh blimey, let me think. Goodfellow. Goodbody? Somefing like that.'

The paunchy bloke nodded. 'Thanks, mate, we'll go and knock on their door.'

'You can take a picture of my pub, if you like,' Greg said. 'What is it, magazine, holiday guide?'

The two men looked at each other, swapping grins.

'Something like that,' said the one who did the talking.

*

The village hall was like one of those roadside garages built in the 1950s, with a grey-white facade and a stepped roof. From its summit projected a perspex cross which would obviously light up at night. Conifers crowded in on the building, so you had the feeling of a missionary chapel in the jungle.

It was coming up to 3.45 p.m., the sky turning brown, the air raw. As Sophie drove away, Merrily felt unexpectedly apprehensive. From inside, as she walked up the steps, came the sound of a hymn she didn't recognize.

Below her, Old Hindwell was laid out in a V-shape. Beyond one arm arose the partly afforested hump which, Sophie had told her, was topped by the Iron Age hill fort, Burfa Camp. The northern horizon was broken by the shaven hills of Radnor Forest. The small, falling sun picked up the arc of a thin river around the boundary, like an eroded copper bangle.

Across the village, divided from it by a fuzz of bare trees, she could see the tower of the old church. She wondered if Nicholas Ellis would have made Old Hindwell his main base if that church had still been in use. Arguably not, since using the community hall was a good demonstration of his personal creed: the Church was people, ancient churches were museums.

The hymn she didn't know, sung unaccompanied by organ or piano, came to an end, and then there was the sound of a communal subsidence into rickety chairs. Merrily pushed open the double doors and went in.

Into darkness. Into a theatre with the house lights down. But the stage – she stifled a gasp – was lit, as though for a Nativity play. *Just not Anglican, somehow.* Gently, she pulled the doors together behind her and stood under a cracked green exit sign.

There was a row of shadowed heads and shoulders no

more than four feet in front of her. The chairs were arranged like theatre-in-the-round under the girdered ceiling. The industrial window blinds were all lowered.

It was alarmingly like the *Livenight* studio, and the audience must have been at least as big: maybe 200 people, some on wooden benches pushed back to the walls. Spotlights in the ceiling lit the stage where stood a man in a white, monkish robe, head bowed, eyes cast down to hands loosely clasped on his stomach.

Merrily's first, disappointing glimpse of the Reverend Nicholas Ellis was a definite *so-what* moment.

'. . . is a particularly poignant occasion for me,' she heard. 'It's only weeks since Menna came to me, with her loving husband, to be baptized again, to pledge herself to the Lord Jesus in the presence of the Holy Spirit. I wonder . . . if somehow . . . she knew.'

His face was bland and shining, his mouth wide, like a letter box. His light brown hair was brushed straight back, a modest ponytail disappearing into the folds of his monk's cowl. Monastic gear was less unorthodox than it used to be for Church of England ministers, but in dazzling white this was hardly a sign of humility. Too messianic for Merrily. His words rang coldly in the factory acoustic.

'I conducted the solemn but joyful service of rebaptism at their home. And on that day the very air was alive with hope and rejoicing, and these two souls were blessed beneath the wings of angels.'

From the shadows, someone, a man, cried out – involuntarily, it seemed, like a hiccup – 'Praise God!' As though the heavenly host had suddenly burst through the ceiling.

Nicholas Ellis was silent for a moment. Merrily couldn't make out his expression because the spotlights in the ceiling were aimed not at him but at the uncovered coffin.

Lidless! In the American style, Menna Weal lay in an open

casket. Wrapped in her shroud. Her face looked like marble under the lights. A curtain of shadows surrounded her.

Merrily didn't like this, found it eerie. She looked for Barbara Buckingham in the congregation, but in this light it was hopeless. How could Barbara, wherever she was, stand this performance? How could any of them?

Eerie – what a funeral should *never* be.

Nicholas Ellis said, 'And it is to that same loving home that, in a short time, Menna's body will return. The final laying to rest of these earthly remains will be a small private ceremony which, in the context of that loving relationship, is as it should be.'

Merrily saw the seated figure of J.W. Weal, hunched like a big rock, gazing steadily at the body of his wife. Her thoughts were carried back to the county hospital, that first sight of him with his bowl of water and his cloth. An act of worship?

'Let us thank God for love,' Ellis said, 'when the black dragon wings of evil beat above our heads and the night air carries the stench of Satan.'

Merrily wrinkled her nose.

'. . . let us remember that only the strong light of love can bring us through the long hours of darkness. Now let us all rise and, with Menna and Jeffery together in our hearts, sing number two on our hymn sheet, 'Take Me, Lord, To Your Golden Palace'.

The lights blinked on, so that they could all read the words. Everyone rose, with a mass scraping of metal chair legs that was almost a shriek, and Merrily saw, at the front, one broad head thrust above all the others. J.W. looking down on the remains of his wife.

'*A statement of ownership*,' Barbara had said. '*Possession is nine points of the law*.'

*

Merrily found herself outside in the cold again, feeling slightly shocked.

She stopped about halfway down the steps, with her back to a Scots pine tree. The sand colour in the sky had all but disappeared, washed under the rapid, grey estuary of dusk. Below her, Old Hindwell settled into its umbered shadows. Merrily stood watching for the lights of Sophie's Saab, listening for its engine.

Just not Anglican, somehow.

You could say that again. She sank her hands far into her coat pockets.

It had been a singalong, gospelly, country-and-western hymn. It was cloying, trite – no worse but certainly no better than the stilted Victorian hymns which Merrily had been trying for months to squeeze out of her services. She'd had no hymn sheet, but the dipping of the house lights told her when the last verse had finished. Then words that were not on the hymn sheet took over – when, in the darkness, the tune and the rhythm disappeared but the singing itself did not stop.

Merrily stood silent, not having been exposed for quite some years to this phenomenon: the language of the angels according to some evangelists. Nonsense words, bubbling and flowing and ululating between slackened jaws.

Tongues. The gift of. The sign that the Holy Spirit was here in Old Hindwell village hall.

Right now, she was in no position to dispute this. It wasn't the hymn or its ghostly coda which had brought her out here, nor the sight of the silent, sombre Jeffery Weal, his gaze still fixed on his wife while the congregation summoned angels to waft her spirit into paradise.

It was just that, during the hymn, while the lights were on, she'd had an opportunity to investigate the congregation, row by row, and Barbara Buckingham was definitely not there. And while that meant she hadn't had to listen to Ellis's Gothic nonsense and stand in fuming silence while all around her sang themselves into a religious stupor, it did raise a possible problem.

Barbara was a determined woman. She had a serious grudge against this area, arising from a deprived childhood, which had become narrowed and focused into a hatred of the lumbering, sullen, slow-moving, single-minded Jeffery Weal.

Suppose she was already at Weal's house? Outside somewhere, waiting for the mourners at the small private ceremony that would follow.

Merrily hurried down the rest of the steps. After what she'd seen in there, she too wanted very much to know how this was going to end.

TWENTY-ONE

Lord Madoc

'Robin, it's Al.'

But this was *not* Al. Al was so cheerful that if he called you too early in the morning it hurt.

And this was not early morning, it was late afternoon and Betty had gone to see the goddamn widow Wilshire again and the voice on the phone was like the voice of a relative calling to say someone close to you was dead.

As art director handling Talisman, the fantasy imprint of the multinational publisher, Harvey-Calder, Al Delaney did not know any of Robin's relatives; he kept his dealings strictly to artists and writers and editors. So Robin was already feeling sick to his gut.

'Hi,' he said. 'How's it going?'

With the light failing fast, he stood by the window in his studio. Or, at least, the north-facing room that was to go on serving as his studio until they'd gotten enough money together to convert one of their outbuildings. The room had two trestle tables, one carrying his paints and his four airbrush motors, only two of which now worked. Airbrushes seemed to react badly to Robin. Must be all that awesome psychic energy.

Haw!

'I'm calling you from home,' Al said.

'That would be because it's Saturday and the offices are closed, right?'

'And because I've just heard from, er . . . Kirk Blackmore.'

'Uh-huh.' Robin moistened his lips.

'And I'd rather say what I want to say from home. Like that Blackmore's an insufferable egomaniac who'd stand there and tell Botticelli he couldn't draw arses, and that there are a few of us who'd like to use the Sword of Twilight to publicly disembowel him. But, tragically—'

'Tragically, he is also the hottest fantasy writer in Britain, so it would be unwise to say that to his face. Yeah, yeah. OK, Al, just listen for one minute. Since I got Blackmore's fax, I've been giving it a whole lot of thought and I've come up with something which I think he's gonna like a whole lot more. I accept that the purple mist was too lurid, the lettering too loud, so what I propose, for starters—'

'Robin, he now doesn't want you to do it at all.'

On the second table, the work table, lay Robin's preliminary watercolour drawings for the proposed new Kirk Blackmore format, the one which would run down the backlist like gold thread. The one, in fact, which would launch the fund which would finance the restoration of the outbuildings – providing Betty with her own herbal haven and Robin, in a year or two, with the most wonderful, inspiring, *sacred* studio.

'He just . . . he just said he didn't like the painting,' Robin said. His whole body seemed very light. 'He said he . . . he said there were *elements* of the painting he didn't like, was all.'

Al said, 'He wants someone else to do it, Robin.'

'Who?' Robin couldn't feel his hands.

'It doesn't matter who. Nobody in particular – but not you. Mate, I'm sorry. I was so convinced you were the man for this, I would've . . . I had to tell you today. I didn't want you spending all weekend working out something that wasn't even going to get—'

'And the backlist?'

'The backlist?'

'What I'm saying, this isn't just the one cover he doesn't like . . .?'

'It *is* the one cover he doesn't like, obviously, and you'll get paid in full for that, no problem at all. But it's also . . . How many ways can I put this? He wants . . . he wants another artist. He doesn't want you.'

Robin held up the core design which Blackmore should have loved, took a last look into the eyes of Lord Madoc who, in times of need, would stand in his megalithic circle and summon the Celtic Ray.

Robin's Madoc – who would not now be Blackmore's Madoc. A lean, noble, beardless face, its hairstyle – or glorious *neglect* of style – shamelessly modelled on Betty's own delicious profusion. Sympathetic magic: Madoc's hair was full of electricity and pulsed in the mist around him; Madoc, the hack fantasy hero, had been permitted to reflect the bright essence of Betty's holy power. How could frigging Blackmore have failed to respond to that?

And what were they gonna live on now?

Maybe not love. He recalled Betty's face before she had gone out, the light gone from her eyes, the shine from her skin. And her hair all brushed. She'd brushed her hair flat!

She also wore a skirt he didn't even remember her owning, a dark, mid-length skirt – a very ordinary skirt. This was the true horror of it. When she left the house she was looking like *an ordinary person.*

And it was his fault. Ever since they got here, everything he did was wrong. And everything he didn't do – or say.

Jeez, he'd never even thought much about what had

happened with Marianne outside the pub. That whole sequence was like a dream – the glowing cross in the sky, the big, weird guy looking over his shoulder at no one right behind him. Robin had gone home and he'd slept, and tomorrow had been another lousy day.

He felt cold to his gut. Lately, Betty had lain with her back to him in bed, feigning sleep, a psychic wall between them.

Very tired, she would say, with the move and all.

'Fuck!' Robin tore the Madoc drawings end to end and let the strips fall to the floorboards. 'Fuck, oh fuck, oh *fuck.*'

Trying to picture Blackmore as he was ripping them, but he'd never seen the guy. The face that came to him was the smug, unlined, holy face of the Reverend Nicholas Ellis. Ellis had done this. Ellis who had made Robin his devil, focused his smug, holy Christian hatred on the ruins of St Michael's, the lair of the dragon. Ellis had brought down bad luck on them.

And they were innocent.

He broke down and wept in frustration and despair, his head among the scattered paint tubes. Robin Thorogood, illustrator, seducer of souls, guardian of the softly lit doorways? What a fucking joke.

By seed, by root, by bud and stem, by leaf and flower and fruit, by life and love, in the name of the goddess, I Robin, take thee, Betty, to my hand, my heart and my spirit at the setting of the sun and rising of the stars.

A handfasting. None of this till-death-do-us-part shit.

In the fullness of time we shall be born again, at the same time and in the same place as each other, and we shall meet and know and remember and love again.

It made you cry. Every time you thought of that it made you cry. How much of the prosaic Christian marriage ceremony could do that to you?

Robin cried some more. He saw her in her wedding dress. He saw her slipping out of the dress, when they were left alone, for the consummation, the Great Rite.

How could it be that their souls were sailing away from each other? How could this happen in the sacred place which, it had been prophesied – it had been fucking *prophesied* – was their destiny?

Robin rose from the table. He figured what he would do now was take a walk down to the barn.

And from the barn he would retrieve the box containing the charm which promised to protect this house and all the chickens and pigs and local people therein from the menace of the Old Religion.

And he, Robin Thorogood, guardian of the softly lit doorways, would take this box and carry it to the edge of the promontory on which the Christians had built their church and, with due ceremony and acknowledgement to the Reverend Penney, hurl the motherfucker into the hungry torrent of the Hindwell Brook.

Robin wiped his eyes with a paint cloth. He thought he heard a knocking at the front door.

Local people. It was probably only *Local People*. Like the deeply local person who wrote the anonymous letter to his wife, shafting him good.

Well, these local people could just remove themselves from off of his – and the building society's – property. Robin's fists bunched. They could very kindly evacuate their asses from said property right now.

The guy said, 'Mr Thorogood?'

Not a local person. Even Robin was getting so he could separate out British accents, and this was kind of London middle class.

Two of them, and one carried a biggish metal-edged case.

When Robin saw the case, he thought sourly, Whaddaya know, it's another local person bringing us another box with another charm to guard us against ourselves and thus turn our idyllic lives into liquid shit.

'Mr Thorogood, my name's Richard Prentice. This is Stuart Joyce.'

Robin flicked on the porch light. Overweight guy with a beard, and a thinner, younger guy in a leather jacket. Double-glazing, Robin figured; or travelling reps from some company that would maximize your prospects by investing the contents of your bank account in a chain of international vivisection laboratories.

'We both work for the *Daily Mail* newspaper,' Prentice said. 'If it's convenient, I'd like a chat with you – about your religion.'

'About my . . .?' Robin glanced at the case. Of course, a camera case.

'I understand you and your wife are practising witches.'

Robin went still. 'How would you have come to understand that?'

Relax. No camera around the thin guy's neck.

Prentice smiled. 'You didn't happen to watch a TV programme called *Livenight*, by any chance?'

'We don't have a TV.'

'Oh.' The man smiled. 'That would certainly explain it. Well, Mr Thorogood, you and your wife were referred to on that programme.'

'What?'

'Not by name – but your situation was mentioned. Now, it sounds as though we're the first media people to approach you. And that's a good thing for both of us, because—'

'Hold on a moment,' Robin said. 'If, as you say, we *are* witches – which, in these enlightened times, I'm hardly gonna deny . . . Why are you interested? There are thousands of us.

It's, like, the fastest growing religion in the country right now. What I'm saying is, what kind of big deal is that for a paper like yours?'

'Well, I'll be straight with you, Robin, it's primarily the church. How many witches have actually taken over a Christian church for their rituals?'

'Well, Richard,' Robin said, 'if I can reverse that question, how many Christian churches have taken over pagan sites for *their* rituals?'

Richard Prentice grinned through his beard. '*That*, my friend, is an excellent point, and we'd like to give you the opportunity to amplify it.'

'I don't think so, Richard.'

'Could we come in and talk about it? It's perishing out here.'

'I really don't think so. For starters, my wife—'

'Look,' Prentice said. 'You were more or less outed – if I can use that term – on a TV programme watched by millions of viewers. I'd guess you're going to be hearing from a lot of other journalists over the next few days. And I mean tabloid journalists.'

'Isn't that what you are?'

'We like to call ours a *compact* paper. There's a difference.'

'Don't make me laugh, Richard.'

'Robin . . . look . . . what we have in mind – and this would be for Monday's paper, so we'd have a whole day to get it absolutely right – is a serious feature explaining exactly what your plans are for this church, and why you believe you're no threat to the community.'

'Somebody say we're a threat to the community here?'

'You know what local people are like, Robin.'

'Out,' Robin said.

'I'm sorry?'

'Go, Richard.'

'Robin, I think you'll find that we can protect you from the unwanted intrusion of less responsible—'

'Leave now. Or I'll, like, turn you into a fucking toad.'

'That's not a very sensible attitude. Look, this was probably a bad time. I can tell something's happened to upset you. We're going to be staying in the area tonight. I suggest we come back in the morning. All right?'

Robin stepped out of the porch. Through the trees, he could hear the racing of the Hindwell Brook.

'OK,' Prentice said, 'that's your decision.'

And if they'd gone at that moment, things might all have been so much less fraught.

Unfortunately, at this point the porch and Robin were lit up brightly, and Robin realized the younger guy suddenly had a camera out.

The rushing of the brook filled his head. *Cold white noise.* Robin thought of silent Betty with her back to him in the sack. He thought he heard, somewhere on the ether, the rich sound of Kirk Blackmore laughing at his artwork.

Robin made like Lord freaking Madoc.

TWENTY-TWO

Wisp

Merrily could see the battlemented outline of Old Hindwell church tower over the bristle of trees, and the spiteful voice cawed in her head.

'I can show you a church with a tower and graves and everything . . . which is now a pagan church. You don't know what's happening on your own doorstep.'

If these pagans had been around for a while, it would explain why Ellis had adopted Old Hindwell – extremes attract extremes. The only other abandoned Anglican church she could think of in the diocese was at Llanwarne, down towards Ross-on-Wye, and that was close to the centre of a village and open to the road, a tourist attraction.

But whether this was or wasn't the alleged neo-pagan temple was not the issue right now. What she needed to make for was the former rectory, which was not ruined, far from abandoned . . . but about to accommodate its first grave.

She would probably encounter Sophie's car along the way. And Barbara Buckingham?

That grumbling foreboding in her stomach – that was subjective, right? Merrily walked faster, aware that the only sound on the street was the soft padding of her own flat shoes. She walked into the centre of the village, where there was a small shop and post office – closed already – and the pub had frosted windows and looked inviting only compared with everywhere else.

In one of the cottages, a dog howled suddenly, a spiralling sound; maybe it had picked up a distant discordant wailing emanating from the village hall. Something which was not, perhaps, quite human.

The pub car park was still full. With the cars – of course – of outsiders. The singing in tongues should have given it away: many people in today's congregation were not, in fact, family mourners or friends or long-time clients of J.W. Weal, but core members of Nicholas Ellis's church.

And the tongues was not a spontaneous phenomenon; for them it had become routine, a habit, almost an addiction, a Christian trip. She'd learned that while at theological college when a bunch of students, well into the born-again thing, had persuaded her to join them at a weekend event known as the Big Bible Fest, held in a huge marquee near Warwick. Two long days of everybody smiling at everybody else and doing the '*Praise Him!*' routine like kids with a new school-yard catchphrase, and by the end of the first day Merrily had been ready to swing for the next person who addressed her as 'sister'.

It had been Jeremy, one of the faithful, who'd told her that the cynical bitch persona was simply concealing her fear of complete surrender to the Holy Spirit. He was challenging her to go along that night with an open mind, without prejudice, without resistance. Praise Him! So, OK, she'd attended a service where all the hymns had been simple, rhythmic pop anthems, sung by happy people in Hawaiian shirts and sweatpants – and all ending in tongues.

Tongues was the gift of Christ, originally granted to a select few. The Bible did not spell out what tongues actually sounded like, its linguistic roots, its grammatical structure, but modern evangelical Christians insisted it was a way of talking directly to God, who Himself did not necessarily speak English.

Not entirely convincing, but for the first two hymns she'd held out. After all, hadn't her own formative mystical moment occurred in total silence, lit by the blue and the gold, alone in a little hermit's cave of a church?

And then – *Praise Him, praise God!* – her mouth had been open like everyone else's, and out it all came like those flimsy coloured scarves produced by conjurers. Words which were flowing and lyrical and meant nothing, but sounded as if they ought to. Lush, liquid worship. Dynamic, wordless prayer. A disconnecting of the senses. A transcendent experience, up there around the marquee's striped roof.

She could, in fact, still bring it on when she wanted to, could summon that wild Christian high, simple as popping a pill, as though just doing it that once had been a lifetime's initiation. It was easy.

Maybe too easy.

She wondered to what extent the locals had joined in. Were slow-speaking farmers now singing in tongues? Did they say 'Praise God' when they met by the sheep pens on market day, instead of the time-honoured ''Ow're you?'

You couldn't rule that out. After all, it was in Wales that traditional church worship had been massively abandoned in the rush to build stark, spartan Noncomformist chapels. So how far down the charismatic road did Old Hindwell go? Was it like the Toronto Blessing, with people collapsing everywhere? Were they discovering Galilean sand in the palms of their hands and gold fillings in their teeth?

But how appropriate was this at a funeral?

Merrily scanned the cars by the pub. Was one of them Barbara's? What make had Barbara been driving? Merrily didn't know.

She turned and walked on down the darkening street, a

headache coming on, although it was dulled by the cold. Beyond the village shop and a lone bungalow with a 1970s-style rainbow-stone porch, the grass verge came to an end, so Merrily walked in the road, down into a conifered valley which would eventually open out to the hill country of Radnor Forest.

Soon afterwards, she heard the low mutter of approaching vehicles, and then dipped headlights began to cast a pale light on the road, and she pressed close to the hedge as the cortège came past.

As the mourners had started coming for their cars, Gomer had moved to the pub window to look out for Gareth and Judy Prosser. Chances were the Prossers would be on foot, but they'd still have to come this way. Most of the people picking up their vehicles Gomer didn't recognize.

'There a funeral tea up the hall?' he asked Greg.

'If there is, we weren't asked to provide it. Nah, they say Father Ellis don't go for eating and drinking in church.'

'It's a bloody village hall!'

'Not when he's there it ain't.'

Gomer looked over his shoulder at Greg polishing glasses for the customers that didn't come in. 'You're not a church-goer, then, boy?'

'Never was. But the bloody pressure's on now.' The anxious look flitted across Greg's face again. 'Lot of people've started going. He don't look much, Ellis, but they reckon you come out feeling on cloud nine. I mean, whatever it is, I'm not sure I wanna catch it. The wife's gone to this funeral. And I let 'em use the car park – all his fans from miles around. Not that many of 'em drop in for a pint or anyfing afterwards. Don't need drink when you're high on God.'

'You got a few yere now, boy,' Gomer observed. 'Stand by your pumps.'

Two men and three women came in, all in black. One of the men was Tony Probert, farmer from Evenjobb – Gomer knew him to speak to, just about – and one of the women was . . .

'Gomer Parry!'

'Greta,' Gomer said, ''ow're you?'

Greta Thomas, wife of Danny, the rock-and-roll farmer from Kinnerton. She was little and busty, with a voice Nash Rocks could've used for blasting. Used to be receptionist for Dr Coll.

'I hope you're lookin' after yourself, Gomer,' Greta yelled. 'Not goin' back to the wild?' Never one to make a meal of the ole condolences; once the funeral was over Greta believed it was time to start cheering you up.

'I'm doing fine, Gret.'

''Cause if Min thought you was on the bevvy . . .'

'Moderation in all things, you know me, girl. I dunno, I seen bloody Danny earlier, he never said you was goin' to see Menna off.'

'Never remembers nothing, 'cept his bloody chords. Tony and Julie was coming, so I had a lift.' Greta pulled Gomer towards a table. 'Reckoned *somebody* ought to represent Danny's side of the family.'

'Nothin' to do with wantin' to see the famous Reverend Ellis in action without goin' to a reg'lar service, like?'

Greta looked sheepish. 'No harm in that, is there?'

'Worth it, was it?'

'Well . . . strange, it is, actually, Gomer.'

'Ar?'

'Specially the funny singing. Like a trance – beautiful really, when it gets going. The voices are like harmonizing natural, the men and the women. Really gets you. It's quite . . . I don't know . . . sexy. That's a stupid thing to say, ennit?'

'Better get you a drink, Gret.'

He went to Greg at the bar, bought Greta a brandy. He might learn something here, and it beat going home to an empty bungalow with no fire, no tea, nothing but crap Saturday night telly and then a cold bed.

Greta looked up at him from under a fringe of hair dyed the colour of Hereford clay.

'I didn't mean that how it sounded, Gomer. I mean, I've never been that religious, but it makes you think. A lot of people's saying that. Dr Coll – even Dr Coll – reckons Mr Ellis is the best thing ever happened to this area.'

'Why do he reckon that?' Clergy, in Gomer's experience, came and went and never got noticed much, unless they started messing with people's wives – or they were little and pretty.

'The way it's bringing the community together,' Greta said. 'You'd never get that with an ordinary parson and an ordinary church. When did you ever see local people and folk from Off hugging each other?'

'En't natural,' Gomer conceded.

'And they also reckons you can get a private consultation.'

'What for?'

'Anything, really. Sickness, emotional problems . . .'

'What's he do for that?'

'Fetches them out of you, Gomer. Lays his hands on you, fetches it all out.'

'Bloody hell, Gret.'

'There's folk swears by it.'

'Bloody hell.'

He leaned back and thought for a bit. Doctor's receptionist for what – ten years? Her'd have been no more than a young girl when her first went to work for Dr Coll's old feller. Still . . .

'How well did you actually know Menna Thomas, Gret?'

Doctors' receptionists, it was easier for them to talk about the dead than the living, and Greta Thomas was still talking when Tony Probert and his wife and the other couple had finished up their drinks and looked a bit restive, so Gomer told them it was OK, he'd take Greta home himself.

On the way, he said, 'And how well did you know her sister Barbara?'

Which was how he found out the truth about the hydatid cyst.

Behind the hearse came an old-fashioned taxi, like a London black cab. Merrily saw brake lights come on about a hundred yards down the lane and she moved quietly towards them. Stone posts stood stark against the last of the light and she heard the grating of metal gates.

Silhouettes now. Someone in a long overcoat pushing a bier. Merrily watched the coffin sliding onto it under the raised tailgate of the hearse, saw the bier pushed through the gates. It was followed by several people fused into one moving shadow.

Against the band of light below the grey roller blind of evening, she could see the roof of the old rectory. No lights on there. The taxi started up, rolled away down the lane. No sign of another car.

No sign of Barbara Buckingham.

Suppose Barbara had accosted Weal, made a nuisance of herself, and Weal – as a solicitor, able to expedite these things – had responded with some kind of injunction to restrain her. In which case, why hadn't Barbara told Merrily? Why hadn't she left a message?

At the gates, peering down an alley of laurels, Merrily was pulled sharply back by the realization that this whole situation was entirely ridiculous. Only Jane would do something like this. But then more headlights were glaring around the bend behind her, and she slipped inside the gates to avoid them.

The vehicle went past on full beams: not Sophie's Saab but a fat four-wheel drive with two men in it. Leaving Merrily standing on the property of J.W. Weal as, somewhere beyond the laurels, a single warm light was anointing the bruised dusk with an amber balm.

She followed the laurel alley towards the house, now only half expecting the dramatic eleventh-hour appearance of Barbara Buckingham like the dissenting wedding guest with just cause for stopping the service.

By the house, the drive split into a fork, one prong ending at a concrete double garage, the other dropping down a step and narrowing into a path, its tarmac surface fragmenting into crazy paving to cross the lawn – which was wedge-shaped and bordered by spruce and Scots pine. At the narrow end of this wedge stood a conical building, the source of the light.

The wine store . . . the ice house . . . Menna's waiting tomb.

Merrily stood by the last of the laurels, on the edge of the lawn, and looked up at the Victorian house – substantial, grey and gabled, three storeys high. The light from the open door of the tomb, maybe forty yards away, was bright enough to outline the regular stone blocks in the back wall of the house. She could see the shadows of heavy, lumpen furniture in the room immediately behind a bay window on the ground floor. This house was very J.W. Weal.

At its end of the lawn, the mausoleum was a squat Palladian temple. Victorian kitsch, its interior was creamed with electric light from two wrought-iron hanging lanterns. Then the light was suddenly blocked and diffused . . . two men looming. Merrily backed up against the house wall, laurel leaves wet on her face.

'Mind the step, George.'

'He could use a light.'

'Knows his way down yere in his sleep, I reckon.'

The undertakers maybe? Must be the departure of the last outsiders.

Feeling very much on her own now, Merrily moved down the lawn, stopping about fifteen yards from the door of the mausoleum. From an oblique angle, she could see inside, to where mourners were grouped around a stone trough set into the middle of the floor. She saw Ellis, in his white robe. She saw a wiry bearded man, a squat bulky man, and a woman. They were still as a painted tableau, faces lit with a Rembrandt glow. And she thought, aghast, *This is intrusion, this is voyeurism, this is none of my business!*

This was about a man – not an affable man, not an immediately likeable man, but a man who had loved his wife, who had treated her with great tenderness till the last seconds of her life. Who had – whatever you thought of rebaptism, rebirth in the faith – come with her to Christ. Who could not bear to be entirely parted from her. Who had chosen to gaze out every morning from their bedroom window, prob-ably for the rest of his life, across to where she lay.

That's it. I'm going. She turned abruptly away.

And walked into the man himself.

Her face was suddenly buried in the cold, crisp shirt-front in the V of his waistcoat.

It smelled of camphor.

For a moment, she was frozen with shock, let out a small 'Oh' before his big arms came around her, lifting her off her feet. For a flowing second, she was spun in space through the path of light from the tomb, and then put down in shadow and held.

'Men-na,' he breathed.

The great body rigid, compressing her. Camphor. Carbolic. She was gripped for a too-long moment, like a captured bird, and then the arms sprang apart.

'I'm sorry . . .' she whispered.

He was silent. Neither of them moved.

A small night breeze had arisen, was rippling the laurels and sighing in the conifers. The firs and pines were like sentries with spears. J.W. Weal was just another shadow now; she didn't feel that he was looking at her. The line of light shivered, and Merrily saw figures standing in the doorway of the mausoleum. Nobody spoke, nobody called to her. It was dreamlike, slow-motion.

She turned and walked away – trying not to run – across the lawn, in and out of the path of light, her arms pressed into her sides, as though his arms were still around her. The strong light from the mausoleum haloed the old rectory, illuminating the inside of the bay-windowed room on the ground floor.

And then, as she was looking up at that same window, it became dark all round. The door of the mausoleum had been closed. They'd been waiting for Jeffery Weal to return from the house, and now they'd shut themselves away for the finale, leaving darkness outside. The lawn was black, the track of light from the tomb having vanished. Merrily felt small and bewildered and ashamed, like a child who should be in bed but had peered through the bannisters into an unknown, unknowable, grown-up world.

'Men-na.'

What was he *thinking* then?

She searched for the entrance to the drive. Without light, she would need to go carefully.

Yet there *was* light: a dull, diffused haze behind the bay window, where the backs of chairs threw rearing shadows up the interior walls. She now hated that room. She knew it was very cold in there, colder than it was out here. She didn't want to be looking in. She didn't want to see . . .

. . . the pale figure flitting across the wide windows, from pane to pane.

The slight, moth-like thing, the wisp of despair.

She didn't want to see it. She *couldn't* see it.

But as the room came out to her, enclosing her in its pocket of cold, she could almost hear the flimsy, flightless, jittering thing beating itself against the glass in its frenzy, with a noise like tiny crackling bones.

Merrily flailed and stumbled into the laurels, slipped on numbed legs and grabbed handfuls of leaves to keep from falling. Only these weren't the laurels; they had thorns, winter-vicious. Still she clutched them in both hands, almost relishing the entirely physical pain, then she scrambled up and onto the drive, hobbling away towards the gateposts.

Part Three

The vast majority of charismatic churches are aware of the dangers of confusing demonic attack with psychological problems . . . There are, however, some charismatic groups which are inclined to carry out a ministry of deliverance which concerns most other charismatic churches and which leads to 'casualties'.

Deliverance (ed. Michael Perry)
The Christian Deliverance Study Group

Tango with Satan

Since coming home to her apartment at the vicarage, Jane had . . . well, just slept, actually. Longer, probably, than she'd ever slept before. She woke up briefly, thought of something crucially important, went back to sleep, forgot about it. Just like that for most of a day.

It was the hospital's fault. Hospitals were, like, totally knackering. Unless you were drugged to the eyeballs, you *never* slept in a hospital – be more relaxing bedding down on a factory floor during the night shift. Naturally, Jane had tried telling them this, but no, they'd insisted on keeping her in, in case her skull was fractured or something worse. Which she knew it wasn't, and *they* knew really, but it was, like – yawn, yawn – procedure, to forestall people suing the Health Service for half a million on account of her having gone into a coma on the bus.

Sleep was all you really needed. Real sleep, home sleep. Sleep was crucial, because it gave the body and the brain time to repair themselves, and because it was a natural thing.

And, also, in this particular case, because it postponed that inevitable Long Talk With Mum.

The Long Talk had not taken place, as expected, in the car coming home from Worcester Royal Infirmary last night, because it was Sophie's car and Sophie was driving it, and Sophie – to Jane's slight resentment – seemed more concerned about Mum, who had herself at one point fallen asleep in the passenger seat and awoken with a start – like a really *seismic* start – which made Sophie judderingly slam on the brakes going down Fromes Hill. Mum had shaken herself fully awake and said – in that flustered, half-embarrassed way of hers when lying – that something must have walked over her grave.

And, like, trod on her hands? Why were both her hands clumsily criss-crossed with broad strips of Elastoplast, like *she* was the motorway pile-up casualty?

Fell among thorns, was all Mum would say when they finally got home, must have been around ten. Bewilderingly, she'd hugged Jane for a long time before they'd staggered off to their respective bedrooms, without mention of the impending Long Talk.

Odd.

Jane slept through most of Sunday morning, venturing downstairs just once for a bite to eat from the fridge – lump of cheese, handful of digestive biscuits – while Mum was out, doing the weekly pulpit gig. Then leaving her plates conspicuously on the draining board so that Mum would know she'd eaten and wouldn't come up to ask about lunch and initiate the Long Talk.

She vaguely remembered awakening to see Mum standing by the bed in her clerical gear, like a ghost, but she must have fallen asleep again before either of them could speak. She kept half waking to hear the ting of the phone: a lot of calls. *A lot of calls.* Was this about the accident? Or *Livenight* – Mum apologizing to half the clergy for screwing up on TV?

For Sunday lunch, alone with Ethel the cat, Merrily had just a boiled egg and a slice of toast. Which was just as well because, before 2 p.m., the bishop was on the phone, enquiring after Jane and revealing himself to be a worried man.

The *Daily Mail* had phoned him at home. Did he know that a former church in his diocese had become a temple for the worship of pagan gods?

Well, of course he did. He'd seen the damned TV programme like everyone else, but he was hoping that either nothing more would be heard of it or it would turn out to be safely over the border in the Diocese of Swansea and Brecon.

Not that he'd told the *Mail* that. He'd told the *Mail* he was 'concerned' and would be 'making enquiries'.

And this was one of them.

'As it happens,' Merrily said, 'I was in Old Hindwell yesterday.'

Bernie Dunmore went quiet for a couple of seconds.

'That's an extraordinary coincidence,' he said.

'It is. But nothing more than that.'

'Did you see the church?'

'Only the tower above the trees. I didn't see any naked figures dancing around a fire, didn't hear any chanting. Is it really true? Who are they?'

'Witches, apparently. People called Thorogood, ironically enough. Young couple, came from Shrewsbury, I think. But he's American.'

'In parts of America, witchcraft is awfully respectable these days.'

'Merrily, this is Radnorshire.'

'Er . . . quite.'

'As for the church – well, strictly speaking it isn't a church at all any more. Did all the right things when they let it go. Took away the churchyard bones to a place of suitable sanctity. Virtually *gave* it to the farming family whose land had surrounded it for generations. Stipulating, naturally, that

241

relatives of people whose names were on the graves should be able to visit and lay flowers, by arrangement.'

'Why *did* they let it go? It's not as though the village has an alternative church.'

'Usual reasons: economics coupled with a very convenient period of public apathy.'

'You could dump half the parish churches in Britain on that basis.'

'Also, this isn't a building of any great architectural merit,' Bernie said. 'Old, certainly, but the only *history* it seems to have is one of more or less continuous major repairs and renewals, dating back to the fifteenth century or earlier. The dear old place never seems to have wanted to stay up, if you get my meaning. Close to a river or something, so perhaps built on ground prone to subsidence. Things apparently came to a head when the rector at the time actually suggested it should be decommissioned.'

'Really?'

'Anyway, all that's irrelevant. The unfortunate fact is, if it's got a tower or a steeple and a handful of gravestones, the general public will still see it as holy ground, and there'll be protests.'

'But there's nothing you can do about that, is there? You can't actually vet new owners.'

'The Church *can* vet them, obviously, when the Church is the vendor. And the Church does – we're not going to sell one to someone who wants to turn it into St Cuthbert's Casino or St Mary's Massage Parlour. But when it's being sold on for the second or, in this case, third time, you're right, it's more or less out of our hands.'

'So is there any reason for this to escalate into anything?'

'Merrily, this is Nicholas Ellis's patch. This is where he holds his gatherings . . . in the village hall.'

'I know. I was there for a funeral. The congregation was singing in tongues over the coffin.'

The bishop made a noise conveying extreme distaste.

'But the point I was about to make, Bernie, is that Ellis is Sea of Light. He doesn't *care* about churches.'

'Oh, Merrily, you don't really believe the bugger isn't going to start caring very deeply – as of now?'

'You've spoken to him?'

'Never spoken to the man in my life, but the press have. They didn't tell us what he said, but I expect we'll all be reading about it at length in the morning.'

'Oh. Anything I can do?'

Bernie Dunmore chuckled aridly. 'You're the Deliverance Consultant, Merrily, so what do *you* think you could do?'

'That's not fair. Look, I'm sorry I messed up so badly on TV, if that's what—'

'Not at all. No, indeed, you were . . . fine. As well as being probably the only woman on that programme who looked as if she shaved her armpits. Was that sexist? What I'm trying to say . . . you're the only one of us who officially knows about this kind of thing and is able to discuss it in a balanced kind of way. Not like Ellis, that's what I mean. Obviously, I can't forbid the man to speak to the media, but I'd far rather it were you . . .'

'The only problem, Bishop—'

'. . . and if all future requests for information could be passed directly to our Deliverance Consultant. As the official spokesperson for the diocese on . . . matters of this kind.'

Merrily felt a tremor of trepidation. And recalled the whizz and flicker, the crackle and tap-tap on the window of a room full of shadows.

'But, Bernie, this job . . . deliverance—'

'I know, I know. It's supposed to be low-profile.' He

paused, to weight the punchline. 'But you have, after all, been on television now, haven't you?'

Ah.

'I won't dress it up,' Bernie said. 'You'll probably have problems as a result. Extremists on both sides. The pagans'll have you down as a jackboot fascist, while Ellis is calling you a pinko hippy doing the tango with Satan. Still, it'll be an experience for you.'

She stripped off the plasters Sophie had bought from the pharmacy at Tesco on the way to Worcester last night – a fraught journey, from the moment she'd stumbled into the Saab's headlight beams somewhere on the outskirts of the village.

She then changed out of her clerical clothes and went up to the attic to check that Jane was OK.

The kid was asleep in her double bed under the famous Mondrian walls of vermilion, Prussian blue and chrome yellow. Merrily found herself bending over her, like she hadn't done for years, making sure she was breathing. Jane's eyes fluttered open briefly and she murmured something unintelligible.

Merrily quietly left the room. They'd assured her at the hospital that her daughter was absolutely fine but might sleep a lot.

Downstairs, the phone was ringing. She grabbed the cordless.

It was Gomer. He'd just been to the shop for tobacco for his roll-ups and learned about the motorway accident.

'Her's all right?'

'Fine. Sleeping a lot, but that's good.'

'Bloody hell, vicar.'

'One of those things.'

'Bloody hell. Anythin' I can do, see?'

'I know. Thanks, Gomer.'

'So you wouldn't've gone to Menna's funeral then? I never went to look for you. One funeral's enough . . . enough for a long time.'

'You were in Old Hindwell yesterday?'

'Reckoned it might be a good time. Found out a few things you might wanner know, see. No rush, mind. You look after the kiddie.'

'In the morning?'

'Sure t'be,' Gomer said.

Good old Gomer.

'Mum.'

'Flower!'

Jane was standing in the kitchen doorway in her towelling dressing gown. She looked surprisingly OK. You wouldn't notice the bruise over her left eye unless you were looking for it.

'You hungry?'

'Not really. I just went to the loo and looked out the window, and I think you've got the filth.'

'What?'

'He's outside in his car, talking on his radio or his mobile. Overweight guy in a dark suit. I've seen him before. I think it's that miserable-looking copper used to tag around after Annie Howe, the Belsen dentist. I'll go for another lie-down now, but just thought I'd warn you.'

Merrily let him in. 'DC Mumford.'

'DS Mumford, vicar. Amazingly enough.'

'Congratulations.'

'They have accelerated promotion for young graduates like DI Howe,' Mumford said heavily. 'For plods like me, it can still take twenty-odd years. How's your little girl?'

'You're just a late starter,' Merrily assured him. 'You'll

whizz through the ranks now. Jane's doing OK, thanks. But that's not why you're here?'

Andy Mumford's smile was strained as he stepped into the kitchen. Another two or three years and he'd be up for retirement. Merrily had coffee freshly made and poured him one. She'd left the door open for Jane, for once hoping she was listening – a strong indication of recovery.

'You've been in contact with Mrs Barbara Buckingham,' Mumford said. 'We traced her movement back through the hospital. Sister Cullen says she referred her to you.'

Merrily stiffened. 'What's happened?'

'She's been reported missing, Mrs Watkins.'

'Barbara? By whom?'

'Arranged to phone her daughter in Hampshire every night while she was here. But hasn't rung for two nights. Does not appear to have attended her sister's funeral.'

'Oh my God.'

'Checked with Hampshire before I came in. No word there. It's an odd one, Mrs Watkins. Teenagers, nine times out of ten they'll surface after a while. A woman Mrs Buckingham's age, middle class, we start to worry.' Mumford sipped his coffee. 'You saw her last when?'

'Tuesday evening, here. It was the only time. How much did Eileen Cullen tell you?'

'She said Mrs Buckingham was very upset, not only over her sister's premature death but the fact that she wouldn't be getting buried in the churchyard like normal people. She said she thought you'd be the minister most likely to give the woman a sympathetic hearing.'

'I'm just the only one Eileen knows.'

Mumford smiled almost shyly. 'To be honest, Mrs Watkins, I got the feeling there might have been another reason she put the lady on to you, apart from this objection to the burial. But that might just be promotion making me feel I ought to behave like a detective. Of course, if you don't think that would throw any light on our inquiry . . .'

'Well . . . there was another reason, relating to my other job. You can put this down to stress if you like but don't go thinking she was nuts because I don't think she was – *is*.'

'Not my place, Reverend.'

'She was having troublesome dreams – anxiety dreams probably – about her sister. Barbara left home in Radnorshire when Menna was just a baby, and they'd hardly seen each other since. Anybody would feel . . . regrets in that situation. She's a Christian, she was headmistress at a Church school. Eileen thought she might appreciate some spiritual, er, counselling.'

'She explain *why* she was alone? Why her husband wasn't with her?'

'She said he was away – in France, I think. He deals in antiques.'

'Didn't say anything about him leaving her, then?'

'Oh God, really?'

'For France, read Winchester.' Mumford pulled out his pocketbook. 'Richard Buckingham moved out two months ago.'

'Another woman?'

'That's the information we have from the daughter. So, were you able to ease Mrs Buckingham's mind? I mean, if I was to ask you if you thought there was any possibility of her taking her own life . . .?'

'Oh no. She was too angry.'

'Angry.'

'Yeah, I'd say so.'

'At anybody in particular?'

'At J.W. Weal, I suppose. Know him?'

'Paths have crossed in court once or twice. He used to do

quite a bit of legal aid work, maybe still does. I don't get out that way much these days.'

'Really?' She'd made a joke out of it to Sophie, but she couldn't imagine Weal defending small-time shoplifters and car thieves and dope smokers; that would mean he'd have to *talk* to them. 'I had him down as a wills and conveyancing man.'

'Place like that, a lawyer has to grab what he can get,' said Mumford. 'Mrs Buckingham didn't care for her brother-in-law, I take it.'

'Not a lot. You have a situation where Menna spends her young life looking after her widowed father and then gets married to a much older bloke, in the same area. No life at all, in Barbara's view. And then can't even get away when she dies.'

'You don't like him either then, Mrs Watkins?'

'I don't know him.'

Mumford considered. 'You'd wonder, does anybody? So, when you spoke to her, did Mrs Buckingham give you any idea what she was going to do next?'

'She wanted me to go to the funeral with her. I went along, but she apparently didn't.'

'*You* were there?'

'We were supposed to meet.'

'Seems an unusual arrangement, if you don't mind me saying.'

'I thought she needed somebody.'

'You didn't know Mrs Weal, then?'

'Well, I was actually at the county hospital, with a friend, just after she died. But, no, I didn't actually know her. I don't really know why I said I'd go along. It's not like I don't have enough to do. Maybe . . .' Why did coppers always make you feel unaccountably guilty? 'Maybe I thought Barbara might do something stupid if I wasn't there, which I might have been able to prevent. It's hard to explain.'

'Stupid how?'

'Maybe cause some kind of scene. Start hurling accusations at J.W. Weal, or something, at the funeral.'

'But you didn't find her there?'

'To be honest, it was a difficult day. I had Jane to pick up from hospital in Worcester. If I'd known Barbara had been reported missing, I'd have . . . tried harder.'

She returned from seeing Mumford out to find Jane at the kitchen table. The kid was dressed in jeans and her white fluffy sweater. She looked about ten. Until, of course, she spoke.

'He thinks she's dead.'

'Police always think that, flower.'

'I think you think she's dead, too.'

'I don't think that, but I do feel guilty.'

'You always feel guilty,' Jane said.

TWENTY-FOUR

Against the World

Old Hindwell post office was a brick-built nineteenth-century building a little way down from the pub, on the opposite side of the street. Betty was there by eight fifteen on this dry but bitter Monday morning. The newsagent side of the business opened at eight. There were no other customers inside.

'*Daily Mail*, please.'

The postmistress, Mrs Eleri Cobbold, glanced quickly at Betty and went stiff.

'None left, I'm sorry.'

'You've only been open fifteen minutes.' Betty eyed her steadily. It was the first time she'd been in here. She saw a thin-faced woman of about sixty. She saw a woman who had already read today's *Daily Mail*.

'Only got ordered copies, isn't it?' Mrs Cobbold swallowed. 'Besides two extras. Which we've sold.'

Betty was not giving up. She glanced at the public photocopier at the other end of the shop. 'In that case, could I perhaps borrow one of the ordered papers and make a copy of one particular page?'

Mrs Cobbold blinked nervously. 'Well, I don't . . .'

Betty sought her eyes, but Mrs Cobbold kept looking away as though her narrow, God-fearing soul was in danger.

She glanced towards the door and seemed very relieved when it was opened by a slim, tweed-suited man with a neat beard.

'Oh, good morning, Doctor.'

'A sharp day, Eleri.'

'Yes. Yes, indeed.' Mrs Cobbold bent quickly below the counter and produced a *Daily Mail*. She didn't look at Betty. 'You had better take mine. Thirty-five pence, please.'

'Are you sure?'

'Yes,' Mrs Cobbold whispered.

This was ridiculous.

'Thank you.' Betty also bought a bottle of milk and a pot of local honey. She took her purse from her shoulder bag. She didn't smile. 'And if I could have a carton of bat's blood as well, please.'

This, and the presence in the shop of the doctor, seemed to release something.

'Take your paper and don't come in here again, please,' Mrs Cobbold said shrilly.

The doctor raised a ginger eyebrow.

Betty started to shake her head. 'I really can't believe this.'

'And' – Mrs Cobbold looked at her at last – 'you can tell that husband of yours that if he wants to conduct affairs with married women, we don't want to have to watch it on the street at night. You tell him that.'

Betty's mouth fell open as Mrs Cobbold stared defiantly at her. The doctor smiled and held open the door for her.

Robin paced the freaking kitchen.

She wouldn't let him fetch the paper. She didn't trust him not to overreact if there were any comments . . . to behave, in fact, like a man who'd been cold-shouldered by his wife, told his artwork was a piece of shit and then stitched up by the media.

She'd been awesomely and unapproachably silent most of

yesterday, like she was half out of the world, sealing herself off from the awful implications of the whole nation – worse still, the whole *village* – knowing where they were coming from. Implications? Like *what* implications? A lynch mob? The stake? Their house torched? Was this the twenty-first century or, like, 1650?

Later in the day he'd actually found her sunk into a book on the seventeenth-century witch-hunts. The chapter was headed 'Suckling Demons'; it was about women accused of having sex with the Devil. But she wouldn't talk about it. He just wanted to snatch away the book and feed it to the stove.

She'd hardly moved from the kitchen for the rest of the morning, drinking strong herbal tea and smoking – Robin counted – eleven cigarettes. And still he hadn't told her the *truly* awful news, about Blackmore, because things were bad enough. He'd just spent the entire day trying to persuade her just to talk to him, which was like trying to lure a wounded vixen from her lair.

Was she blaming *him* for the truth leaking out – like he'd been down the pub handing out invitations to their next sabbat. And the journalists . . . well, how *was* he supposed to have handled them? Invite the bastards in to watch them perform the Great Rite on the hearthrug?

Some chance.

If he'd had the brains he was born with, she'd told him, her voice now inflected with hard Yorkshire – this was while they were still speaking – he'd've kept very quiet, not answered the door. There was no car there, so they could quite easily have been away from home.

What? This had made him actually start pulling at his hair. Like, how the fuck was he supposed to know it was the goddamned media at the door? Might have been insurance salesmen, the Jehovah's freaking Witnesses. How *could* he have known?

No reply. No reply either when he'd twice called George Webster and Vivvie, up in Manchester, to see if they knew anything about this damn TV show. He'd left two messages on their answering machine.

And then yesterday, after a lunch of tomato soup and stale rolls, Betty had said she needed time to think and went outside to walk alone, leaving Robin eking out the very last of the sodden pine wood. Maybe she went to the church to try and communicate with the Reverend freaking Penney. Robin wasn't interested any more. When she came back, she started moving furniture around and drinking yet more herbal tea.

Maybe there was something on her mind he didn't know about. Dare he ask? What was the damn use?

It was like she was waiting for something even worse to happen.

This was all down to Ellis. No question there. It was Ellis sicked the press on them.

Goddamn Christian bastard.

She came in from the post office and laid a newspaper on the kitchen table. She didn't even look at Robin. 'I'm going to change,' she said and went out. He heard her going upstairs.

The room felt cold. The colours had faded.

This was bad, wasn't it? It was going to be worse than he could have imagined, although he accepted that he maybe hadn't endeared himself to the *Mail* hacks by going for their camera like that.

He looked at the paper. At least it wasn't on the front. Nervously, he turned over the first page.

Holy shit . . .

Just the whole of page three, was all.

Down the right-hand side was a long picture of St Michael's Church, in silhouette against a sunset sky, the tower starkly framed by winter trees. It was a good picture, black and white. The headline above it, however, was just crazy: 'Witches possess parish church. "Nightmare evil in our midst," warns rector'.

'Evil?' Robin shouted. 'They really *listened* to that crazy motherfucker?'

But it was the big picture, in colour, that made him cringe the most.

It was a grainy close-up of a snarling man, eyes burning under long, shaggy black hair. On his sweat-shiny cheeks were streaks of paint, diluted – if you wanted the truth – by bitter tears, but who was ever gonna think that? This was blue paint. It had obviously come off the cloth he'd used to wipe his eyes. In the picture, it looked like freaking woad. The guy looked like he would cut out your heart before raping your wife and slaughtering your children. Aligned with the picture, the story read:

> This is the face of the new 'priest' at an ancient village church.
>
> Robin Thorogood is a professional artist. He and his wife, Betty, are also practising witches. Now the couple have become the owners of a medieval parish church – while the local rector has to hold his services in the village hall.
>
> 'This is my worst nightmare come true,' says the Rev.

Nicholas Ellis. 'It is the manifestation of a truly insidious evil in our midst.'

Now the acting Bishop of Hereford, the Rt Rev. Bernard Dunmore, is to look into the bizarre situation. 'It concerns me very deeply,' he said last night.

It is more than thirty years since the church, at Old Hindwell, Powys, was decommissioned by the Church of England. For most of that time, it stood undisturbed on the land of farming brothers John and Ifan Prosser. When the last brother, John, died two years ago it passed out of the family and was bought by the Thorogoods just before Christmas.

Robin Thorogood, who is American-born, says he and his wife represent 'the fastest-growing religion in the country'. He claims that many of Britain's old churches were built on former pagan ritual sites – one of which, he says, he and his wife have now repossessed.

However, when invited to explain their plans for the church, Mr Thorogood became abusive and attacked *Daily Mail* photographer Stuart Joyce, screaming, 'I'll turn you into a f—ing toad.'

Now villagers say they are terrified that the couple will desecrate the ruined church by conducting pagan rites there. They say they have already seen strange lights in the ruins late at night.

The Thorogoods' nearest neighbour, local councillor Gareth Prosser, a farmer and nephew of the former owners, said, 'This has always been a God-fearing community and we will not tolerate this kind of sacrilege.

'These people sneaked in, pretending to be just an ordinary young couple.

'Although this is a community of old-established families, newcomers have always been welcome here as long as they respect our way of life.

'But we feel these people have betrayed our trust and that is utterly despicable.'

'Trust?' Robin exploded. 'What did that fat asshole ever trust us with?' Jeez, he'd hardly even spoken to the guy till a couple days ago, and then it was like Robin was some kind of vagrant.

He sat down, beating his fist on the table. It was a while before he realized the phone was ringing. By that time, Betty had come down and answered it.

When she came off the phone she was white with anger.

'Who?' Robin said.

She didn't answer.

'Please?'

She said in low voice, 'Vivvie.'

'Good of them to call back after only a day. *Did* they know anything about that programme? For all it matters.'

'She was on the programme.'

He sat up. '*What?*'

'They were both there in the studio, but only Vivienne got to talk.' Betty's voice was clipped and precise. 'It was a late-night forum about the growth of Dark Age paganism in twenty-first-century Britain. They had Wiccans and Druids, Odinists – also some Christians to generate friction. It's a friction programme.'

Robin snorted. TV was a psychic drain.

'Vivienne was one of a group of experienced, civilized Wiccans put together by Ned Bain for that programme.'

'Jesus,' Robin said, 'if she was one of the civilized ones, I sure wouldn't like to be alone with the wild children of Odin.'

And Ned Bain? Who, as well as being some kind of rich, society witch, just happened to be an editorial director at Harvey-Calder, proprietors of Talisman Books. Robin had already felt an irrational anger that Bain should have allowed Blackmore to dump a fellow pagan – although, realistically, in a big outfit like that, it was unlikely Bain had anything at all to do with the bastard.

Betty said, 'She claims she lost her cool when some woman priest became abusive.'

'She doesn't *have* any freaking cool.'

'This priest was from Hereford. Ned Bain had argued that, after 2,000 years of strife and corruption, the Christian Church was finally on the way out and Vivienne informed the Hereford priest that the erosion had already started in her own backyard, with pagans claiming back the old pagan sites, taking them back from the Church that had stolen them.'

Robin froze. 'You have *got* to be fucking kidding.'

She didn't reply.

'She . . . Jeez, that dumb bitch! She *named* us? Right there on network TV?'

'No. Some local journalist must have picked it up and tracked us down.'

'And sold us to the *Mail*.'

'The paper that supports suburban values,' Betty said.

The phone rang. Robin went for it.

'Mr Thorogood?'

'He's away,' Robin said calmly. 'He went back to the States.' He hung up. 'That the way to handle the media?'

Betty walked over and switched on the machine. 'That's a better way.'

'They'll only show up at the door.'

'Well, *I* won't be here.'

He saw that she was wearing her *ordinary person* outfit, the one with the ordinary skirt. And this time with a silk scarf around her neck. It panicked him.

'Look,' he cried, 'listen to me. I'm sorry. I'm truly sorry about that picture. I'm sorry for looking like an asshole. I just . . . I just lost it you know? I'd just had . . . I'd just taken this really bad call.'

'From your friend?' Betty said.

'Huh?'

'From your friend in the village?'

The phone rang again.

'From Al,' he said. 'Al at Talisman.'

The machine picked up.

'*This is Juliet Pottinger,*' the voice told the machine. '*You appear to have telephoned me over the weekend. I am now back home, if you would like to call again. Thank you.*'

'Look' – Robin waved a contemptuous hand at the paper – 'this is just . . . complete shit. Like, are we supposed to feel threatened because the freaking Bishop of Hereford finds it a matter warranting *deep concern*? Because loopy Nick Ellis sees us as symptoms of some new epidemic of an old disease? What is he, the Witchfinder freaking General, now?'

He leapt up, moved toward her.

Betty's hair was loose and tumbled. Her face was flushed. She looked more beautiful than he'd ever seen her. She always did look beautiful. And he was losing her. He'd been losing her from the moment they arrived here. He felt like his heart was swollen to the size of the room.

'We're not gonna let them take us down, are we? Betty, this is . . . this is you and me against the world, right?'

Betty detached her car keys from the hook by the door.

'Please,' Robin said. 'Please don't go.'

Betty said quietly, 'I'm not *leaving* you, Robin.'

He put his head in his hands and wept. When he took them down again, she was no longer there.

TWENTY-FIVE

Cyst

Ledwardine sat solid, firmly defined in black and white under one of those sullen, shifty skies that looked as if it might spit anything at you. Just before nine Merrily crossed the square to the Eight-till-Late to buy a *Mail*.

A spiky white head rose from the shop's freezer, its glasses misted.

'Seems funny diggin' out the ole frozen pasties again, vicar.'

They ended up, as usual, in the churchyard, where Gomer gathered all the flowers from Minnie's grave into a bin liner.

'Bloody waste. Never liked flowers at funerals. Never liked cut flowers at all. Let 'em grow, they don't 'ave long.'

'True.' She knotted the neck of the bin liner, spread the *Daily Mail* on the neighbouring tombstone and they sat on it.

'Barbara Buckingham's missing, Gomer. Didn't show up for Menna's funeral. Never got back to me, and hasn't been in touch with her daughter in Hampshire either.'

'Well,' Gomer said, 'en't like it's the first time, is it?'

'She just go off without a word when she was sixteen?'

'Been talkin' to Greta Thomas, vicar. No relation – well, her man, Danny's second cousin twice removed, whatever.'

'Small gene pool.'

'Ar. Also, Greta used to be secertry at the surgery. Dr

Coll's. En't much they don't find out there. Barbara Thomas told you why her was under the doctor back then?'

'Hydatid cyst.'

Barbara had talked as though the cyst epitomized all the bad things about her upbringing in the Forest – all the meanness and the narrowness and the squalidness. So that when she had it removed, she felt she was being given the chance to make a clean new start – a Radnorectomy.

Gomer did his big grin, getting out his roll-up tin.

Merrily said, 'You're going to tell me it wasn't a hydatid cyst at all, right?'

Gomer shoved a ready-rolled ciggy between his teeth in affirmation.

'I never thought of that,' Merrily said. 'I suppose I should have. What happened to the baby?'

'Din't go all the way, vicar. Her miscarried. Whether her had any help, mind, I wouldn't know. Even Greta don't know that. But there was always one or two farmers' wives in them parts willin' to do the business. And nobody liked Merv much.'

'Hang on . . . remind me. Merv . . .?'

'Merv Thomas. Barbara's ole feller.'

'Oh God.'

Gomer nodded. 'See, Merv's wife, Glenny, her was never a well woman. Bit like Menna – delicate. Havin' babbies took it out of her. Hard birth, Menna. Hear the screams clear to Glascwm, Greta reckons. After that, Glenny, *her* says, that's it, that's me finished. Slams the ole bedroom door on Merv.'

Merrily stared up at the sandstone church tower, breathed in Gomer's smoke. She'd come out without her cigarettes.

'Well, Merv coulder gone into a particlar pub in Kington,' Gomer said. 'Even over to Hereford. Her'd have worn that, no problem, long as he din't go braggin' about it.'

'But Merv thought a man was entitled to have his needs met in his own home.'

It explained so much: why Barbara left home in a hurry, also why she had such a profound hatred of Radnor Forest. And why Menna had invaded her conscience so corrosively – to the extent, perhaps, that after she was dead, her presence was even stronger. When Menna no longer existed on the outside, in a fixed place in Radnorshire, she became a permanent nightly lodger in Barbara's subconscious.

'But the bedroom door musn't have stayed closed, Gomer. Barbara said her father was determined to breed a son, but her mother miscarried, and then there was a hysterectomy.'

Gomer shrugged.

'But then his wife died. Hang on, this friend of yours . . .' Merrily was appalled. 'If she knew about Barbara, then she must've known what might have been happening to Menna.'

'Difference being, vicar, that Menna had protection. There was a good neighbour kept an eye on Menna, specially after her ma died. Judy Rowland. Judy Prosser now.'

Judy . . . Judith. 'Barbara said she had letters from a friend called Judith, who was looking out for Menna. That eased her conscience a little.'

'Smart woman, Judy. I reckons if Judy was lookin' out for Menna, Menna'd be all right. Her'd take on Merv, would Judy, sure to.'

'She still around?'

'Oh hell, aye. Her's wed to Gareth Prosser – councillor, magistrate, on this committee, that committee. Big man – dull bugger, mind. Lucky he's got Judy to do his thinkin' for him. Point I was gonner make, though, vicar, I reckon Judy was still lookin' out for Menna, seein' as both of 'em was living in Ole Hindwell.'

'You mean after her marriage?'

'No more'n five minutes apart, boy at the pub told me.'

'So if she also still kept in touch with Barbara, maybe Barbara went to see her, too, while she was here.'

'Dunno 'bout that, but her went to see Greta, askin' questions 'bout Dr Coll.'

Gatecrashed his surgery. Made a nuisance of myself. Not that it made any difference. Bloody man told me I was asking him to be unethical, pre-empting the post-mortem.

'What did Barbara want to know about Dr Coll?'

'Whether he was treatin' Menna 'fore she died, that kind o' stuff.'

'What's he look like, Dr Coll?'

'Oh . . . skinny little bloke. 'Bout my build, s'pose you'd say. Scrappy bit of a beard, like that political feller, Robin Cook.'

'He was at Menna's funeral. The private bit.'

'Ar, would be.'

'So where's Barbara then, Gomer? Where is Barbara Thomas?'

'I could go see Judy Prosser, mabbe. Anybody knows the score, it's her. I'll sniff around a bit more. What else I gotter do till the ole grass starts growin' up between the graves again?'

It was colder now. The mist had dropped down over the tip of the steeple. Gomer's roll-up was close to burning his lips. He took it out and squeezed the end. He looked sadly at the grave, his bag of frozen pasties on his knees and his head on one side like a dog, as if he was listening for the ticking of those two watches under the soil.

'I've got to go back there today.' She told him about Old Hindwell seemingly metamorphosed into Salem, Mass. 'You, er, don't fancy coming along?'

Gomer was on his feet. 'Just gimme three minutes to put these buggers in the fridge, vicar.'

*

Jane was not happy. Jane was deeply frustrated. She telephoned Eirion from the scullery.

'They've found out where that church is! The pagan church? I had *completely* forgotten about it! The one that woman was going on about on *Livenight*? I'd *forgotten* about it. Like, you apparently lose all these brain cells when you have a bump, and I just didn't *remember* that stuff, and then bits started coming back, and I knew there was something vital, but I couldn't put my fing— Anyway, it's all over one of the papers. It's somewhere just your side of the border. And she's just raced off over there . . . on account of there's this *major* scene going down.'

'Major scene?' Eirion said.

'And I'm, like, I have *got* to check this out! But would she let me go with her? Like, she's even taken Gomer with her. But not me – the person who is profoundly interested in this stuff? And, like, because of the other night there is, of course, not a thing I can do about it. She just puts on this calm, sorrowful expression and she looks me in the eyes, and she's like, "You're going to stay here, this time, aren't you, flower?" I am completely, totally, utterly *stuffed*.'

Eirion said calmly, 'So how are you now, Eirion? How's the whiplash? Is there any chance your car isn't a complete write-off?'

'Ah.' Jane sat down at the desk. 'Right. Sorry, Irene. You have to understand that self-pity is, like, my most instinctive and dominant emotion.'

'You OK?'

'Yeah, slept a lot. Still feel a bit heavy when I first get up, but no headaches or anything. No scars at all. Like I said, some things I can't remember too clearly. About that programme and stuff. But . . . yeah. Yeah, I'm OK.'

'My stepmother spoke to your mother. I've been feeling

I ought to ring her, too. Do you think she'd be OK about that?'

'With you she'd be fatally charming. So *is* it a write-off?'

'Interesting you should ask about the car before asking about me.'

'I know *you're* OK. Your stepmother told Mum you were OK.'

'I might have subsequently suffered a brain haemorrhage in the night.'

'Did you?'

Eirion paused. 'Yes, it *is* a write-off. A car that old, if you break a headlamp, it's a write-off.'

'I'm sorry.'

'I loved that car. I worked all summer at a lousy supermarket for that little Nova. I should get just about enough on the insurance to replace it with a mountain bike.'

'Irene, I'm really, really sorry.' Jane felt tears coming. 'It's all my fault. Everything I touch these days I screw up. I don't suppose you want to see me ever again, but one day – I swear this on my mother's . . . altar – I'll get you another car.'

'What, you mean in fifteen years' time I'll come home one day in my Porsche and find a thirty-year-old Vauxhall Nova outside my penthouse?'

'In my scenario,' Jane said, 'you're actually trudging home to your squat.'

'Let's forget the car,' Eirion said. 'You can sleep with me or something instead.'

'OK.'

Silence.

Eirion said, 'Listen, I'm sorry. That just came out. That was a joke.'

'I said it was OK.'

'You don't understand,' Eirion said. 'I don't want it to be like that.'

'You don't want to sleep with me?'

'I mean, I don't want it to be like . . . like you shag first and then you decide if you want to know the person better. I don't want it to be like that. It never lasts. Most of the time that's where it all ends.'

'You've done a lot of this?'

'Well . . . erm, I was in a band. You get around, meet lots of people, hear lots of stories. It's just not how I want it to be with us, OK?'

'Wow. You don't mess around on the phone, do you?'

'Yeah, I'm good on the phone,' Eirion said. 'Listen . . . It's been weird. I can't stop thinking about that stuff. I've just been walking round the grounds and turning it all over and over—'

'Oh, the *grounds* . . .'

'I can't help my deprived upbringing. No, I was thinking how close we came to being like—'

'Dead?'

'Well . . . yeah, it really bloody shakes you up when you start thinking about it.'

'Brings your life into hard focus. Unless you've had concussion, when it seems to do the opposite most of the time.'

'I started thinking about your mum, what that would've done to her, with both her husband and her daughter – and it doesn't matter what kind of shit he was, he was still her husband and your dad – like, both her husband and her daughter wiped out on the same bit of road. And maybe her, too, if she hadn't stopped in time – these pile-ups can just go on and on in a fog. And . . . I don't know what I'm trying to say, Jane . . .'

'I do. It was like when I said to you in the car – I remember this because it was just before it happened. I said, do you never lie in bed and think about where we are and how we relate to the big picture?'

'I just don't lie in bed and think about it, I tramp around the grounds and the hills and think about it.'

'That's cool,' Jane said.

'And I was thinking how, when we were talking to Gerry earlier . . . you remember Gerry, the researcher?'

'Gerry and . . . Maurice?'

'That's right. You remember Gerry saying, before the show started, that he wouldn't be surprised if one of them – one of the pagans in the studio – tried some spooky stuff, just to show they could make things happen?'

'He said that?'

'He said *spooky* stuff. And I said, "What? What would they do?" And Gerry said a spell or something, just to prove they could make things happen. It was just after he was going on about your mum, and how your dad was killed and maybe she felt guilty—'

'Oh *yeah* – the bastard.'

'And you jumped down his—'

'Sure. I mean, where *did* he get that stuff?'

'He got it from that guy Ned Bain.'

'Ned . . .? Oh, the really cool—'

'The smooth-talking git,' Eirion said. 'But that whole thing was getting to me. Because they *didn't* do anything, did they? There was no spell, no mumbo-jumbo, no pyrotechnics; they were all actually quite well behaved. But somehow Gerry had got it into his head that they were going to pull some stunt. So, anyway, I rang him this morning. You know . . . how I'm that bloke who wants to be a TV journalist? So I'm writing a piece on my adventures in the *Livenight* gallery for the school magazine . . .'

'You're not!'

'Of course I'm not. It's just what I told Gerry to get him

talking. I told him I was explaining in my piece how the programme researchers get their information, and there were things I didn't have a chance to ask him there on the night.'

'And where *do* they get it?'

'Cuttings files, obviously. But they also talk to the guests beforehand. Like this Tania talked to your mum . . . and Gerry talked to Ned Bain and a few others. But Gerry reckoned it was Bain had provided all this detailed background on the Church of England's first woman diocesan exorcist.'

'Gerry just told you that?'

'It took a bit of digging, actually, Jane. After which Gerry said how he thought I had a future in his profession; said to give him a call when I get through college.'

'Wow, big time.'

'Sod off.'

'So he was genned up on Mum? Like *know thine enemy*?'

'But is that sort of stuff about your dad going to be readily available from the *Hereford Times* or something?'

'She won't do interviews about herself.'

'So where did he get it?'

'It's no big secret, Irene. Maybe it's all floating around on the Internet.'

'Exactly. I'm going to check it out, I think.'

'Who told Gerry they were going to pull a stunt? That from Ned Bain too?'

'Gerry claimed he'd never said that. He said I must've misunderstood. But he bloody *did* say it, Jane. He just didn't want it going in a school magazine that they were happy for stuff like that to happen on a live programme.'

'Stuff like what?'

'I don't know, it just—'

'I mean, OK, let's spell it out, bottom line. Are you suggesting the evil Ned Bain and his satanic cronies did some kind of black magic resulting in a fog pile-up which caused the deaths of several people? Is that what you're saying?'

'Not exactly that . . .'

'What are you, some kind of fundamentalist Welsh Chapel bigot?'

'Unfair, Jane.'

'So what *are* you suggesting?'

'I don't know, I just . . . I mean no, it would be ridiculous to suggest that those tossers in fancy dress could do anything like that, even if they *were* evil, and I don't think they are. Not evil, just totally irresponsible. They're like, "Oh, can we work hand in hand with nature to make *good* things happen and save the Earth?" How the fuck can *they* know that what they're going to make happen is going to be *good* necessarily?'

'You sound like Mum.'

'Well, maybe she's right.'

'Don't meddle with anything metaphysical? Throw yourself on God's mercy?'

'Unless you know what you're doing, maybe yes. And they don't, they *can't* know what they're doing. How can they, Jane?'

'It never occurred to you that by working on yourself for, like, years and years and studying and meditating, you can achieve wisdom and enlightenment?'

'But most of those people haven't, have they? It's just, "Oh, let's light a fire and take all our clothes off . . ." '

'That is a totally simplistic *News of the World* viewpoint.' Jane's head was suddenly full of a dark and fuzzy resentment. 'You haven't the faintest idea . . .'

'At least I'm not naive about it.'

'So I'm *naive*?'

'I didn't say that.'

There was a moment of true, sickening enlightenment. 'You've been talking to her, haven't you?'

'Who?'

'My esteemed parent, the Reverend Watkins. She didn't just speak to your stepmother on the phone, she spoke to you as well, didn't she?'

'No. Well only at the hospital. I mean you were *there* some of the time.'

'*That's* why there's been no big row. Why she hasn't asked me what the hell I was doing on the M5 at midnight. Why she's so laid-back about it.'

'Look, Jane, I'm not saying Gwennan didn't also fill her in on some of the details, but I've never even—'

'I've been really, really stupid, haven't I? It really *must* have destroyed some of my brain cells. While I'm sleeping it off, you're all having a good chat. *You* told her how I'd rigged the whole trip, making you think she knew all about us going. Then she's like, "Oh, you have to understand Jane found it hard coming to terms with me being a priest, has to go her own way." This cosy vicar-to-cathedral-school-choirboy tête-à-tête. Gosh, what are we going to *do* about that girl?'

'Jane, that is totally . . .'

'And you're like, "Oh, I'm trying to understand her too, Mrs Watkins. If you think I'm just one of those reprehensible youths who only want to get inside her pants, let me assure you—" '

'For Christ's sake, Jane . . .'

'That is just *so* demeaning.'

'It would be if it—'

'You are fucking well dead in the water, Irene.'

'J—'

TWENTY-SIX

Demonstration of Faith

Merrily pulled the old Volvo up against the hedge.

'I'm sure *that* wasn't there on Saturday.'

A cross standing in a garden.

'Mabbe not,' Gomer said.

It wasn't any big deal, no more than the kind of rustic pole available from garden centres everywhere, with a section of another pole nailed on as a horizontal. It had been sunk into a flowerbed behind a picket fence in the garden of a neat, roadside bungalow about half a mile out of Walton, on the road leading to Old Hindwell. There were three other bungalows but this was the only one with a cross. Although it was no more than five feet high, there was a white light behind it, leaking through a rip in the clouds, and the fact that it was out of context made you suddenly and breathlessly aware of what a powerful symbol this was.

The bungalow looked empty, no smoke from the chimney. Merrily drove on. 'You know who lives there?'

'Retired folk from Off, I reckon.'

'Mmm.' Retired incomers were always useful for topping up your congregation. If the affable local minister turned up to welcome them, just when they were wondering if they were going to be happy here among strangers, they would feel obliged to return the favour, even if it was only for the next few Sundays. But if the friendly minister was the

271

Reverend Nicholas Ellis, drifting away after a month or so could be more complicated.

This was what Bernie Dunmore had been afraid of. She'd received a briefing on the phone from Sophie before they left.

'Apparently there was something of a record turn-out at the village hall yesterday. The bishop understands that a number of people were out delivering printed circulars last night, and bulletins were posted on Christian websites, warning of pagan infestation. Today there's to be what's been described as "a Demonstration of Faith", which the bishop finds more than a little ominous.'

'I wonder what he said to them in his sermon. You know any regular churchgoers in the village, Gomer?'

'We'll find somebody for you, vicar, no problem.'

'The bishop's in conference all day . . .'

Unsurprisingly.

'. . . but what he wants you to do initially, Merrily, is to offer advice and support to the Reverend Mr Ellis. By which I understand him to mean restraint.'

What was she supposed to do exactly? Put him under clerical arrest?

But if Merrily felt a seeping trepidation about this exercise, it clearly wasn't shared by Gomer, who was hunched eagerly forward in the passenger seat, chewing on an unlit ciggy, his white hair on end like a mat of antennae. Describing him to someone once, Jane had said: 'You need to start by imagining Bart Simpson as an old man.'

The lane dipped, darkening, into a channel between lines of forestry. The old rectory appeared on the left, in its clearing. Merrily kept her eyes on the narrowing road. How would she have reacted if she'd turned then and seen a pale movement in a window? She gripped the wheel, forestalling a shudder.

'Not a soul, vicar,' Gomer observed ambivalently.

'Right.' Her voice was huskier than she would have liked. The towering conifers were oppressive. 'This must be the only part of Britain where you plunge into the trees when you *leave* the Forest.'

'Ar, we all growed up never thinkin' a forest had much to do with trees.'

Merrily slowed at the mud-flecked Old Hindwell sign. A grey poster with white lettering had been attached to its stem.

'Christ is the Light!'

That hadn't been there on Saturday either. She accelerated for the hill up to the village. Halfway up, to the right, the tower of the old church suddenly filled a gap in the horizon of pines. It was like a grey figure standing there.

The manifestation of a truly insidious evil in our midst.

A seriously inflammatory thing to say – Ellis playing it for all it was worth.

She'd read the *Daily Mail* story twice. Robin Thorogood sounded typical of the type of pagan recruited for *Livenight*. Primarily political, and an anarchist – what they used to call in Liverpool a tear-arse – but not necessarily insidiously evil. She wondered what his wife was like; no picture of her in the paper.

Sophie had said, *'The bishop would like you to point out to whoever it might concern that, while this might have previously been a church, it is also now this couple's private property, and they do not appear to be breaking any laws – which the Reverend Ellis and his followers might well be doing if any of them sets foot inside it.'*

Merrily slowed to a crawl at the side road to the church and farm. This was where you might have expected to find a lychgate. There was a small parking area, and then an ordinary, barred farm gate. She saw that, while St Michael's

Church had never been exactly in a central position, trees and bushes had been allowed to grow around what was presumably the churchyard, hedging it off from the village. Somewhere in there, also, was the brook providing another natural barrier.

They moved on up the hill. 'I wouldn't mind taking a look at that place without drawing attention. Would that be possible, Gomer?'

'Sure t'be. There's a bit of an ole footpath following the brook from the other side. They opened him up a bit for the harchaeologists last summer, so we oughter be able to park a good way in.'

'You know everything, don't you?'

'Ah, well, reason I knows this, vicar, is my nephew, Nev, he got brought in to shovel a few tons o' soil and clay back when the harchaeologists was finished. I give Nev a bell last night. Good money, he reckoned, but a lot o' waitin' around. Bugger me, vicar, look at *that* . . .'

Merrily braked. There was a cottage on the right, almost on the road. It had small windows, lace-curtained, but in one of the downstairs ones the curtains had been pushed back and a candle was alight. Although the forestry was thinning, it was dark enough here for the flame to be visible from quite a distance. Power cut?

Not exactly. The candle was fixed on a pewter tray, which itself sat on a thick, black book, almost certainly a Bible. *Christ is the Light.*

'Annie Smith lives there,' Gomer said. 'She's a widow. Percy Smith, he had a little timber business, died ten year ago. Their boy, Mansel, he took it over but he en't doin' too well. Deals mostly in firewood now, for wood-burners and such.'

Merrily stopped the car just past the cottage. 'She overtly religious, this Annie Smith?'

'Never made a thing of it, if she is. But local people sticks together on things, see. Gareth Prosser goes along with the rector, say, then the rest of 'em en't gonner go the other way. It's a border thing: when the Welsh was fightin' the English, the border folk'd be on the fence till they figured out which side was gonner be first to knock the ole fence down, see. And that was the side they'd jump down on. But they'd all jump together, see.'

'Border logic.'

'Don't matter they hates each other's guts the rest o' the time, they jumps together. All about survival, vicar.'

'And *does* Gareth Prosser go along with the rector?'

'They d'say he's got one o' them Christ stickers in the back of his Land-Rover.'

'What does that mean, then?'

'Means he's got a sticker,' said Gomer.

Before they reached the village centre, they'd passed five homes with candles burning in their windows, and two of them with Bibles stood on end, gilt crosses facing outwards. A fat church candle gleamed greasily in the window of the post office. Merrily, usually at home with Bibles and candles, found this uncanny. *'We don't do this kind of thing any more.'*

'It's medieval, Gomer. One couple. One pagan couple – OK, young, confrontational, but still just one couple. Then it's like there's a contagious disease about, and you put a candle in the window if it's safe to go inside. Is this village . . . I mean, is it normally . . . normal?'

'Just a village like any other yereabouts.' He pondered a moment. 'No, that en't right. Ole Hindwell was always a bit set apart. Not part o' the Valley, not quite in the Forest. Seen better times – used to 'ave a little school an' a blacksmith. Same as there used t'be a church, ennit? But villages around yere, they grows and wanes. I never seen it as not normal.'

A big, white-haired man was walking up the hill, carrying something on his shoulder.

'They d'say he does a bit o' healin',' Gomer said.

'Ellis? Laying on of hands at the end of the services?'

At the Big Bible Fest in Warwickshire, the spiritual energy generated by power prayer and singing in tongues would often be channelled into healing, members of the congregations stepping up with various ailments and chronic conditions and often claiming remarkable relief afterwards. It was this aspect Merrily had most wanted to believe in, but she suspected that, when the euphoria faded, the pain would usually return and she hated to hear people who failed to make it out of their wheelchairs being told that their faith was not strong enough.

'They reckons he does a bit o' house-to-house. And it en't just normal sickness either.'

'Know any specific cases?' A snatch of conversation came back to her from Minnie's funeral tea at Ledwardine village hall. *Boy gets picked up by the police, with a pocketful o' these bloody ecstersee. Up in court . . . Dennis says, "That's it, boy, you stay under my roof you can change your bloody ways. We're gonner go an' see the bloody rector . . ."*

When the big man stepped into the middle of the road and swung round, the item on his shoulder was revealed to be a large grey video camera. He took a step back, to take in the empty, sloping street, where the only movement was the flickering of the candles. He stood with his legs apart, recording the silent scene – looking like the sheriff in a western in the seconds before doors flew open and figures appeared, shooting.

No doors opened. Clouds hung low and heavy; there was little light left in the sky; the weather was cooperating with the candles. The cameraman shot the scene at leisure.

'TV news,' Merrily said. 'There'll be a reporter around

somewhere, too. I'm supposed to make myself known to them.'

Gomer nodded towards the cameraman. 'Least that tells you why there's no bugger about. Nobody yere's gonner wanner explain on telly about them candles.'

Even if they could, Merrily thought.

'What you wanner do, vicar?'

'It's not what I *want* to do,' Merrily said, 'but I do have to talk to the Reverend Nick Ellis. He lives on the estate. Would that be . . .?'

Past the pub, about a hundred yards out of the village centre, were eight semi-detached houses on the same side of the road.

'That's the estate.' Gomer pointed, as they approached.

Merrily parked in front of the first house. Though these were once council houses, fancy gates, double glazing and new front doors showed that most of them had been purchased.

They all had candles in the windows.

Only one house, fairly central, kept its maroon, standard-issue front door and flaking metal gates. It was the only one still looking like a council house. Except for the cross on the door: wood, painted gold, and nailed on.

There was a large jeep crowding the brief drive. A sticker over a nameplate on the gate announced that Christ was the Light. In the single downstairs window, two beeswax candles burned, in trays, on Bibles.

Merrily had heard that Ellis was living in a council house because, when he'd given up his churches, he'd also given up his rectory. The Church paid the rent on this modest new manse. A small price to pay per head of congregation, and it wouldn't do Ellis's image any harm at all, and he would know that.

She felt a pulse of fury. From singing in tongues to

erecting a wall of silence, this man had turned a whole community, dozens maybe hundreds of people, against a couple who hadn't yet been here long enough for anyone really to know them. The Thorogoods would need to be very hard-faced to survive it.

TWENTY-SEVEN

Spirit of Salem

'This is no coincidence,' George said on the phone. 'This is fate. We all know what tomorrow is.'

'Probably the last day of my freaking marriage.'

'You have to go with it, Robin. We can turn this round. We can make it a triumph.'

Robin wanted to scream that he couldn't give a shit about Imbolc; he just wanted things to come right again with his wife, some work to bring in some money, his religious beliefs no longer to be national news. He just wanted to become a boring, obscure person.

In the background, the old fax machine huffed and whizzed. He watched the paper emerge.

Thou shalt not suffer a witch to live

Poison faxes? Creepy Bible quotes? Someone had unleashed the Christian propaganda machine. The spirit of Salem living on.

'It's all our fault, man,' George said.

'Not your fault. Vivvie's fault.'

'I share the blame. I was there too. I also now share the responsibility for getting you and Betty through this.'

'We could maybe get through this, George, if people would just leave us the fuck alone.'

He wasn't so sure about that, though, the way Betty was behaving.

By 9 a.m. the answering machine had taken calls from BBC Wales, Radio Hereford and Worcester, HTV, Central News, BBC Midlands and 5 Live. And from some flat-voiced kid who said he was a pagan too and would like to pledge his support and his magic.

Already they were starting to come to the front door. By 11 a.m., there'd been four people knocking. He hadn't answered. Instead he'd closed the curtains and sat in the dimness, hugging the Rayburn. He'd listened to the answering machine, intercepting just this one call from George.

The whole damn story was truly out; it had been on all the radio stations and breakfast TV. Was also out on the World Wide Web, with emails of support – according to George – coming from Native Americans in Canada and pagans as far away as India. George claimed that already this confrontation was being seen as a rallying flashpoint for ethnic worshippers of all persuasions. Strength and courage were being transmitted to them from all over the world.

'We don't want it,' Robin told George. 'We came here for a *quiet* life. Pretty soon I'm gonna take the phone off the hook and unplug the fax.'

'In that case,' George said, 'surely it's better that the people you know—'

'You mean people *you* know. Listen, George, just hold off, can you do that? I would need to talk to Betty.'

'When's she going to be back?'

'I don't *know* when she's gonna be back. She's mad at me. She thinks I screwed up with the *Mail* guys. *I* think I screwed up with the *Mail* guys. *I'm* mad at me.'

'You need support, man. And there's a lot of Craft brothers and Craft sisters who want to give you some. I tell you, there's an unbelievable amount of strong feeling about this. It'll be very much a question of *stopping* people coming out there.'

'Well you fucking *better* stop them.'

'Plus, the opposition, of course,' George said. 'We don't know how many they are or where they're coming from.'

Robin peered round the edge of the curtain at the puddles in the farmyard and along the side of the barn. It looked bleak, it looked desolate. In spite of all the courage and strength being beamed at them, it looked lonely as hell. Sure he felt vulnerable; how could he not?

When he sighed, it came out rough, with a tremor underneath it.

'How many were you thinking?'

'Well, we need a coven,' George had said. 'I'll find eleven good people which, with you and Betty makes . . . the right number. We could be there by nightfall. Don't worry about accommodation, we'll have at least two camper vans. We'll bring food and wine and everything we need to deck out the church for Imbolc. Be the greatest Imbolc ever, Robin. We'll set the place alight.'

'I dunno. I dunno what to do.' For George this was cool, this was exciting. If you'd put it to Robin, even just a few days ago, he'd have said yeah, wow, great. It was what he'd envisaged from the start: the repaganized church becoming a centre of the old religion at the heart of a prehistoric ritual landscape. *The idyll.*

But this was not Betty's vision any more – if it ever had been.

'Leave it with me, yeah?' George said. 'Blessed be, man.'

'I'm quite psychic, you know.' Juliet Pottinger had what Betty regarded as a posh Lowland Scottish accent. 'I was about to go into town, and then I thought, no, if I go out now I shall miss something interesting.'

Which was a better opening than Betty could have hoped for.

Lower Lodge was an extended Georgian cottage on the edge of a minor road about two miles out of Leominster and a good twenty-five miles east of Old Hindwell. Once away from Old Hindwell, Betty's head had seemed to clear. The day was dull but dry, the temperature no worse than you could expect in late January. Out here, she felt lighter, less scared, less oppressed.

Mrs Pottinger's house was full of books. Six bookcases in the hall, with two piles of books beside one of them, propped up by an umbrella stand. In the long kitchen, where she made Betty tea, the demands of reading and research seemed to have long since overtaken the need for food preparation. Books and box-files were wedged between pans on the shelves and under cups and plates on the dresser. The only visible cooker was a microwave, and an old Amstrad word processor with a daisywheel printer took up half the kitchen table. There was – small blessing – no sign of a *Daily Mail*.

Juliet Pottinger was about sixty-five, with a heavy body, layered in cardigans, and what you could only call wide hair. Her seat was a typist's chair, which creaked when she moved. She was working, she said, on a definitive history of the mid-border.

'I'm sorry I didn't phone first,' Betty said. 'I just happened to be . . . passing.'

'But you live at Old Hindwell, you say?'

'At St Michael's.'

'Oh,' said Mrs Pottinger. 'Oh . . . .'

It meant Betty didn't have to spend too long explaining her interest in the church, and no need to make reference either to her religion or the ruined building's palpable residue of pain.

'The widow sold it, then?' said Mrs Pottinger. 'Thought

she would. It was in the *Hereford Times* about Major Wilshire . . . old regiment man. The SAS. He wrote to me – as you know, of course.'

'Mrs Wilshire passed over to me some documents relating to the house and the church, and your letter was one of them. That's how we learned about Mr Penney.'

'Oh, I feel such a terrible wimp about that, Mrs Thorogood. I wanted to write up the whole story, but I doubt the *Brecon and Radnor* would have printed it, for legal reasons. Also, I ramble so, become over-absorbed in detail – always been more of a historian than a journalist. And, of course, the local people were against *anything* coming out.'

'Why do you think that was?'

'In case it reflected poorly on them, I suppose. In case it drew attention to *their* affairs. Gareth Prosser the elder was the councillor then, upholding the family's local government tradition of conserving the community in whatever ways are most expedient and saying as little as possible about it in open council. My brief, as local correspondent for the paper, was to report nothing that everyone didn't already know. Except, of course, in the case of poor Terry, when I was instructed *not* to report what everyone already knew. Oh dear, it really has not been a happy place, I'm afraid.'

'You felt that?'

'I always knew that. However, I don't want to depress you. You do, after all have to . . .'

'Live with it? That's why I need to know about its true history. It oppresses me otherwise.'

'Does it?' Mrs Pottinger's eyes became, in an instant, shrewdly bird-like.

'Yes, it . . . I . . .' Betty's banging heart was confirming that it was too late for subterfuge. 'I'm, I suppose you'd say, sensitive to atmosphere – acutely sensitive.'

'*Are* you indeed?'

'The first time I saw that ruined church, I had a very negative reaction, which I kept to myself because my husband loved it . . . was enraptured. For some time I kept trying to tell myself we could, you know, do something about it.'

'You mean feng shui or something?'

'Or something,' Betty said carefully. 'The place upsets me. It unbalances me in ways I can't handle. After we moved in, that became stronger, until I could feel it almost through the walls of the farmhouse. I hope I don't sound like an idiot to you, Mrs Pottinger.'

She was amazed at what she'd just said – all the things she hadn't been able to say to Robin. Mrs Pottinger did not smile. She pulled off her half-glasses and thought for a few moments, tapping one of the arms on a corner of the Amstrad.

'While we were living in Old Hindwell,' she said at last, 'we acquired for ourselves a dog. It was a cocker spaniel we called Hopkins. My husband would take him for walks morning and evening. By using the footpath which follows the brook past the church, it was possible almost to circumnavigate the village. Have you walked that particular path yet?'

'I haven't, but I think my husband has.'

'It's a round trip of about a mile and a half, a perfect evening walk. But would Hopkins follow it? He would *not*. Within about twenty yards of the church – approaching from either direction – that dog would be off! Disappeared for a whole night once. Well, after this had happened two or three times, Pottinger tried putting him on a lead. But when they reached some invisible barrier – as I say, about twenty yards from the church, where the yew trees began – Hopkins would start tugging in the opposite direction with such force that he almost strangled himself. Pottinger used to say he was afraid the poor creature would choke himself to death rather than continue along that path.'

Mrs Pottinger replaced her glasses.

'As you can imagine, that's another story I didn't write for the *Brecon and Radnor Express*.'

Betty found the story chilling, but not surprising. The only time she'd ever seen anyone on that path was the night the witch box was delivered.

'Did you try to find out what might have scared your dog?'

'Naturally, I did. I was fascinated, so I went to visit Terry.'

Betty registered that Penney was the only male – not even her own husband – whom Mrs Pottinger had referred to by his first name.

'It was the first time I'd actually been up to the rectory, as he never seemed to invite people there. Normally I'd collect his notes and notices for the *B and R* at the church, on Sundays after morning service. The rectory was far too large for a bachelor, of course – or even for a married clergyman with fewer than four children. One can understand why the Church is now shedding so many of its properties, but in those days it was still expected that the minister should have a substantial dwelling. Terry, however, was . . . well, it was quite bizarre . . .'

Betty remembered how Mrs Pottinger's letter to Major Wilshire had ended, with the suggestion that Old Hindwell existed for her now as little more than a 'surreal memory'.

'His appearance, I suppose, was becoming quite hippyish – although this was the mid-sixties, when that term was not yet in circulation. He'd seemed quite normal when he first arrived in the village. But after a time it began to be noticed that he was allowing his hair to grow and perhaps not shaving as often as he might. And when I arrived at the rectory that day – it was about this time of year, perhaps a little later –

Terry showed me into a reception room so cold and sparsely furnished that it was clear to me that it could not possibly be in general use. I remember I put my hand on the seat of an old armchair and it was actually damp! "Good God, Terry," I said, "we can't possibly talk in *here*." I don't know about you, Mrs Thorogood, but I can't even *think* in the cold.'

Betty smiled. The book-stuffed kitchen was stiflingly warm.

'And so, with great reluctance, Terry took me into his living room. And when I say *living* room . . . it contained not only his chair and his writing desk, but also his bed, which was just a sleeping bag! He told me he was repainting his bedroom, but I wasn't fooled. This single room was Terry's home. He was camping in this one room, like in a bedsitter, and, apart from the kitchen, the rest of the rectory was closed off. I doubt he even used a bathroom. Washed himself at the sink instead, I'd guess – when he even remembered to. Not terribly . . . Is there something the matter, Mrs Thorogood?'

Betty shook her head. 'Please go on.'

'Well, he'd chosen this room, I guessed, because of the built-in bookshelves. He might not have had much furniture or many private possessions, but he had a good many books. I always examine people's bookshelves, and Terry's books included a great deal of theology, as one would expect, but also an element of what might be termed the *esoteric*. Do you know the kind of thing I mean?'

'The occult?'

'That word, of course, merely means hidden. There was certainly a *hidden* side to Terry. He was perfectly affable, kind to the old people, good with children. But his sermons . . . I suppose they must have been beyond most of the congregation, including me occasionally. They were sometimes close to meditations, I suppose – as though he was still working out for himself the significance of a particular biblical text. When I told him about our dog Hopkins, he didn't seem in the least surprised. He asked me how much I knew about the history of the area. At that time not a great deal, I admit. He asked me, particularly, if I knew of any legends about dragons.'

Betty cleared her throat. 'Dragons.'

'In the Radnor Forest.'

'And did you?'

'No. There's very little recorded folklore relating specifically to Radnor Forest. The only mention I could find was from . . . Hold on a moment.'

Mrs Pottinger jumped up, her hair rising like wings, an outstretched finger moving vaguely like a compass needle. 'Ah!' She crossed the room and plucked a green-covered book from the row supported by tall kitchen weights on a window ledge. 'You *are* enlivening my morning no end, Mrs Thorogood. So few people nowadays want to discuss such matters, especially with a garrulous old woman.'

She laid the book in front of Betty. It was called *A Welsh Country Parson*, by D. Parry-Jones. It fell open at a much-thumbed page.

'Parry-Jones records here, if you can see, that a dragon had dwelt "deep in the fastnesses" of the Forest. And he records – this would be back in the 1920s or '30s – a conversation with an old man who insisted he had heard the dragon *breathing*. All rather sketchy, I'm afraid, and somewhat fanciful. Anyway, it soon became clear to the people he was involved with on a day-to-day basis that Terry was becoming quite *obsessed*.'

Betty looked up from the book, shaken.

'As a symbol of evil,' Mrs Pottinger said, 'a satanic symbol, the dragon from the Book of Revelation represents *the old enemy.* My impression was that Terry thought he was in some way being tested by God – by being sent to Old Hindwell, where the dragon was at the door. That God had a mission for him here. Well, English people who come to Wales sometimes do pick up rather strange ideas.'

Mrs Pottinger put on a rather superior smile, as though Scots were immune to such overreaction. Ignoring this, Betty said, 'Did he believe there were so-called satanic influences at work in the Forest? I mean, is there a history of this . . . of witchcraft, say?'

'If there was, not much is recorded. No famous witchcraft trials on either side of the border in this area. But, of course' – a thin, sly smile – 'that doesn't mean it didn't go on. Quite the reverse, one would imagine. It may have been so much a part of everyday life, something buried so deep in the rural psyche, that rooting it out might have been deemed . . . impractical.'

'What about Cascob?'

'Cascob? Oh, the charm.' Mrs Pottinger beamed. 'That is rather a wonderful mixture, isn't it? Do you know some of those phrases are thought to have been taken from the writings of John Dee, the Elizabethan magus, who was born not far away, near Pilleth?'

'Do you know anything about the woman, Elizabeth Loyd?'

'Some poor child.'

'Could *she* have been a witch? I mean, the wording of the exorcism suggests she was thought to be possessed by satanic evil. Suspected witches around that time were often thought to have . . . relations with the Devil.'

. . . *some women are known to have boasted of it,* Betty had read yesterday. The Devil's member was described as being *long and narrow and cold as ice* . . .

'Nothing is known of her,' Mrs Pottinger said, 'or where

her exorcism took place, or who conducted it. The historian Francis Payne suggests that the charm was probably *buried* to gain extra potency for the invocation.'

'Buried?'

'It was apparently dug up in the churchyard.'

Betty sat very still and nodded and tried to smile, and felt again the weight of a certain section of Cascob's circular churchyard, and the chill inside the building.

'Mrs Pottinger,' she said quickly, 'what finally happened to Terry Penney?'

'Well, he'd virtually destroyed his own church – an unpardonable sin. He had effectively resigned. He'd already left the village before the crime was even discovered, taking with him his roomful of possessions in that old van he drove.'

'You suggested in your letter to Major Wilshire that there'd been previous acts of vandalism.'

'Did I? Yes, minor things. A small fire in a shed outside, spotted and dealt with by a churchwarden. Other petty incidents, too, as though he was building up to the main event.'

'Where did he go after he left?'

'No one knows, or much cared at the time. Except, perhaps, for me, for a while. But the Church was very quickly compensated for the damage done, so perhaps Terry had more money than it appeared. Perhaps his frugal lifestyle was a form of asceticism, a monkish thing. Anyway, he just went away – after setting in train the process which ultimately led to the decommissioning of Old Hindwell Church. And the village then erased him from its collective – and wonderfully selective – memory.'

'You really didn't like the place much, did you?' Betty said bluntly.

'You may take it that I did not feel particularly grateful to some of the inhabitants. We left in '83. My husband had been unwell, so we thought we ought to live nearer to various amenities. That was what we told people, at least. And that's . . .' Mrs Pottinger's voice became faint. 'That's what I've been telling people ever since.'

She sat back in her typing chair, blinked at Betty, then stared widely, as if she was waking up to something.

Betty returned the stare.

'You're really rather an extraordinary young woman, aren't you?' Mrs Pottinger said in surprise, as though she'd ceased many years ago to find young people in any way interesting. 'I wonder why it is that I feel compelled to tell you the truth.'

'The truth?'

'Tell me,' Mrs Pottinger said, 'who's your doctor?'

TWENTY-EIGHT

A Humble Vessel

There was no doorbell, so she knocked twice, three times. She was about to give up when he answered the door.

'Ah,' he said, 'Reverend Watkins.' Registering her only briefly before bending over the threshold, apparently to inspect the candles in the neighbouring windows. 'Good.'

Meaning the candles, she guessed.

'I'm sorry to bother you, Mr Ellis . . .'

'They told me you'd be dropping in.' He shrugged. 'I accept that.'

'I feel a bit awkward . . .'

'Yes,' he said, 'you must do. Do you want to come in?'

She followed him through a shoebox hall which smelled of curry, into a small, square living room which had been turned into an office. There was a steel-framed desk, two matching chairs. A computer displayed red and green standby lights on a separate desk, and there was a portable TV set on a stand with a video recorder underneath.

'The war room,' Nicholas Ellis said with no smile.

His accent sounded far more transatlantic than it had during Menna's funeral service. He wore a light grey clerical shirt, with pectoral cross, and creased grey chinos. His long hair was loosely tied back with a black ribbon. His face was wind-reddened but without lines, like a mannequin in an old-fashioned tailor's shop.

He waved her vaguely to one of the metal chairs.

'Not much time, I'm afraid. I'll help you all I can, but I really don't have much time today, as you can imagine. Events kind of caught up on me.'

When he sat down behind his desk, Merrily became aware of the aluminium-framed picture on the wall behind him, over the boarded-up fireplace. It was William Blake's *The Great Red Dragon and the Woman Clothed with the Sun*. Sexually charged, awesomely repulsive. Ellis noticed her looking at it.

'Revoltingly explicit, isn't it – shining with evil? I live with it so that when they look in my window they will know I'm not afraid.'

They? The war room?

Merrily sat down, kept her coat on.

'So . . .' he said, as if he was trying hard to summon some interest. 'You are the, uh . . . I'm sorry, I did write it down.'

'Diocesan Deliverance Consultant.'

It had never sounded more ludicrous.

'And the suffragan Bishop of Ludlow has sent you to *support* me. Well, here I am' – he opened his arms – 'a humble vessel for the Holy Spirit. Have you ever truly experienced the Holy Spirit, Merrily?'

'In my way.'

'No, in other words,' he said. 'It doesn't happen in *your* way, it happens in *His* way.'

'Damn,' Merrily said, prickling. 'You're right.'

He looked at her with half a smile on his wide lips. 'Diocesan . . . Deliverance . . . Consultant. I guess you're like one of those young female MPs . . . what did they call them . . . Blair's Babes? I suppose it was only a matter of time before we had them in the Church.'

'Like woodworm.'

He didn't reply. He'd lost the half-smile.

'Meaning I look vaguely presentable,' Merrily said, 'even though I must know bugger all.'

'And you feel you *must* throw in the odd swear word to show that the clergy doesn't have to be stuffy and pious any more.'

'Gosh,' Merrily said, 'it doesn't take you long to get the measure of a person, does it?'

Ellis smiled at last. 'My, we really aren't getting along, are we? You aren't going to want to "support" me at all, are you? Well, other priests tend not to, as I'm a fundamentalist. That's what the Anglican Church calls someone who truly believes in the living God.' He leaned back. 'I'm sorry. Let's start again. How do you propose to support me?'

'How would you like to be supported?'

'By being left alone, I guess.'

'That's what I guessed you'd say.'

'Aren't you clever?'

He was looking not at her, but through her, as though she was, for him, without substance – or at least insufficiently textured to engage his attention. It made her annoyed, but then it was designed to.

She pressed on, 'Um . . . you said "war room".'

'Yes.'

'And, obviously, quite a few people here seem to agree with you on that.'

'Yes.'

'And it all *looks* quite dramatic and everything.'

'You make it sound like a facade. It's an initial demonstration of faith in the Lord. It will spread. You'll see twice as many candles on your way out.'

'Isn't it a bit . . . premature to call this a war zone? One story in a newspaper? Two amateur witches in a redundant church? Unless . . .'

He gave her just a little more attention. 'Unless?'

'Unless this goes back rather further than this morning's *Daily Mail*.'

'It goes back well over 2,000 years, Merrily. "The satyr shall cry to his fellow. Yea, there shall the night hag alight, and find for herself a resting place." '

'Isaiah.' Merrily remembered the taunts of the industrial chaplain, the Rev. Gemmell, in the *Livenight* studio, inviting her to stand up and denounce Ned Bain as an agent of Satan in front of seven million viewers. 'Meaning that, whether they accept it or not, all followers of pagan gods are actually making a bed for the Devil.'

'In this case,' Ellis said, 'to reflect the imagery of the Radnor Forest, a nest for the dragon.'

'Because the former church here is dedicated to St Michael?' Merrily glanced up at the Blake print, in which the obscene and dominant dragon, viewed from behind, was curly-horned and not really red but the colour of an earthworm. It was hard not to believe that William Blake himself must have seen one.

'One of five churches positioned around Radnor Forest and charged with the energy of heaven's most potent weapon. Cefnllys, Cascob, Llanfihangel nant Melan, Llanfihangel Rhydithon, Old Hindwell.'

'The Forest is supposed to be a nest for the dragon? Is that a legend?'

'No legend is *simply* a legend,' Ellis said. 'We have the evidence of the five churches dedicated to the warrior angel. If one should fall, it creates a doorway for Satan. You see merely two misguided idiots, I see the beginnings of a disease which, unless eradicated at source, will spread until all Christendom is a mass of suppurating sores. This is what the Devil wants. Will you deny that?'

'Hold on . . . You say there's a legend that if one of the churches falls, etcetera . . . Yet you're not interested in preserving churches, are you? I mean, as I recall, when the Sea of Light group was inaugurated, someone said that the only way faith could be regenerated was to sell off all the churches as museums and use the money to pay more priests to go out among the people.'

'Correct. And in the village here, a resurgence of faith has already restored a community centre which had become derelict, a home for rats. Look at it now. Eventually, the church will move out, put up its illuminated cross somewhere else. But in the meantime, God has chosen Old Hindwell for a serious purpose. I can see you still don't understand.'

'Trying.'

'You see a ruined church, I see a battleground. Look . . .'

He stood up and strode to the computer, touched the mouse and brought up his menu, clicked on the mailbox icon. His in-box told him he had two unread emails. One was: *From: warlock. Subject: war in heaven.* He clicked. The message read, 'I am a brother to dragons and a companion to owls.'

'Book of Job,' Merrily said.

Ellis reduced and deleted it. 'There's one every day.'

'Since when?'

'They like to use that Internet provider, Demon. Today's is a comparatively mild offering.'

'You reported this to the police?'

'The police? This is beyond the police.'

'They can trace these people through the server.'

'It'll only turn out to be some fourteen-year-old who received his instructions anonymously in a spirit message from cyberspace, and the police are gonna laugh. I would hardly expect them to understand that there's a chain of delegation here, leading back, eventually, to hell. That, of course – ' he nodded at the computer – 'is Satan's latest toy. I keep one here, for the same reason I have that repulsive picture on the wall.'

Masochism, Merrily thought. A martyrdom trip.

'I'm a defiant man, Merrily. Don't go thinking this began with the arrival of the Thorogoods. I've been set up for this. I've been getting poison-pen letters for months. And phone calls – cackling voices in the night. Recently had a jagged scratch removed from my car bonnet: a series of vertical chevrons like a dragon's back.'

'Maybe you *do* need support.'

He hit the metal desk with an open palm. 'I *have* all the support I will ever need.'

'What do you plan to do?'

'God shall cast out the dragon – through Michael. I made a civilized approach to Thorogood. I told him I wanted to perform a cleansing Eucharist in the church. He put me off. He can't do that now. He faces the power of the Holy Spirit.'

'And the cold shoulder from the people of Old Hindwell.'

'You mean our Demonstration of Faith? You disagree with that?'

She shrugged. 'Candles are harmless. I just hope that's where it ends.'

'My dear Merrily' – Ellis walked to the door – 'this is where it *begins*. And, with respect, it's not your place to *hope* for anything in relation to my parishioners.'

'Aren't the Thorogoods also your parishioners?'

He expelled a mildly exasperated hiss.

'And if they're trying to make a point about reclaiming ancient sites, hasn't it occurred to you that you're just helping to publicize their cause?'

'And what's Bernard Dunmore's policy on the issue?' Ellis demanded. 'Say nothing and hope they won't be able to maintain their mortgage repayments? Try to forget they're there? Is that, perhaps, why the Church is no longer a force in this country, while evil thrives unchallenged? Perhaps *you* should find out for yourself what kind of people the Thorogoods really are. Maybe you could visit their property. Under cover of darkness again?'

Damn! She stood up. 'OK, I'm sorry. It was a private funeral, and I had no right. But I was looking for someone. Someone who, as it happens, has now been reported missing from home.'

'Oh?' For the first time, he was thrown off balance.

'Barbara Buckingham, née Thomas? Menna's sister?'

'I've never heard of her. I didn't even know Menna had a sister.'

Merrily blinked. 'Didn't you ever talk to Menna about her background?'

'Why should I have probed into her background?'

'Just that when I have kids for confirmation we have long chats about everything. Rebaptism, I mean. I'd have thought that was something much more serious.'

'Merrily, I don't have to talk about this to you.'

She followed him into the hall. 'It's just I can't believe you're one of those priests who simply goes through the motions, Nick.'

'I do have an appointment. I'm sorry.'

'Splish, splash, you're now baptized?'

When he swiftly lifted a hand, she thought, for an incredible moment, that he was going to hit her and she actually cringed. But all he did was twist the small knob on the Yale lock and pull open the front door, but when he noticed that momentary cower, he smiled broadly and his smooth face lit up like a jack-o'-lantern.

She didn't move. 'I still don't fully understand this, Nick.'

'I know,' he said. 'And you must ask yourself why.'

'I mean I don't understand why you're using the enviable influence you've developed in this community to put people in fear of their immortal souls. You didn't have to make that inflammatory statement to the *Mail*.'

He looked at her as if trying, for the first time, to bring her into focus and then, finding she was too flimsy to define, turned away. 'I can't believe,' he said, 'that *you* have somehow managed to become a priest of God.'

She walked past him through the doorway, glanced back and saw a man with nothing much to lose. A man who had stripped himself down to the basics: cheap clothes, a small council house, a village hall for a church, and even that impermanent. There was something distinctly medieval about him. He was like a friar, a mendicant.

'Of course,' she said from the step, '*they're* also helping to publicize *you*. And maybe the villagers aren't afraid for their immortal souls at all, they're just assisting their rector to build his personal reputation. If you were in a town, virtually nobody would think this was . . . worth the candle.'

'This is a waste of time,' Nick Ellis said. 'I have people to see.'

The door closed quietly in her face.

Merrily stood on the path. She found she was shaking.

She hadn't felt as ineffectual since the *Livenight* programme.

TWENTY-NINE

Dark Glamour

As Merrily got back into the car, Gomer pointed to the mobile on the dash.

'Bleeped twice. Third time, I figured out how to answer him. Andy Mumford, it was, that copper. Jane gave him your number. He asked could you call back.'

'He say what about?'

'Not to me.'

She picked up the phone, entered the Hereford number Gomer had written on a cigarette paper, having to hold the thin paper close to the window because it was beyond merely overcast now – and not yet 1 p.m. Three fat raindrops blopped on the windscreen. This was, she told herself, going to be positive news.

'DS Mumford.'

'It's Merrily Watkins.'

'Ah.'

'Has she turned up?'

'Afraid not, Mrs Watkins.'

'Oh.' She heard Ellis's front door slam, and saw him coming down the path. He was carrying a medium-sized white suitcase. He walked past her Volvo without a glance and carried on towards the village centre.

'But I'm afraid her car has,' Mumford said. 'You know the Elan Valley? Big area of lakes – reservoirs – about thirty miles west of Kington? They've pulled her car out of one of the reservoirs.'

'Oh God.'

'Some local farmer saw the top of it shining under the water. Been driven clean through a fence. Dyfed-Powys've got divers in there. When I checked, about ten minutes ago, they still hadn't found anything else. Don't know what the currents are like in those big reservoirs. I'm sorry to have to tell you this, Reverend, but I thought you'd want to know.'

'Yes. Thank you.'

'If I hear anything else, I'll get back to you. Or, of course, if *you* hear anything. It's been known for people to . . .'

'What, you think she might have faked her own death?'

'No, I'm a pessimist,' Mumford said. 'I tend to think they'll pull out a body before nightfall.'

It began as a forestry track, then dropped into an open field with an unexpected vista across the valley to the Radnor Forest hills of grey green and bracken brown, most of which Gomer knew by name.

And strange names they were: the Whimble, the Smatcher, the Black Mixen. Evocative English-sounding names, though all the hills were in Wales. Merrily and Gomer sat for a moment in the car and took in the view: not a farm, a cottage or even a barn in sight. There were a few sheep, but lambing would come late in an area as exposed as this: hill farming country, marginal land. She remembered Barbara Buckingham talking about her deprived childhood – the teabags used six times, the chip fat changed only for Christmas. As they left the car at the edge of the field, she paused to say a silent prayer for Barbara.

She caught up with Gomer alongside a new stile which, he said, had been erected by Nev for the archaeologists. This was where the track became a footpath following the line of the Hindwell Brook, which was flowing unexpectedly fast and wide after all the rain. It had stopped raining now, but the sky bulged with more to come. Gomer pointed across the brook, shouting over the rush of the water.

'Used to be another bridge by yere one time, but now the only way you can get to the ole church by car is through the farm, see.'

'Where was the excavation?'

'Back there. See them tumps? Nev's work.' He squinted critically at a line of earthmounds, where tons of soil had been replaced. 'Boy coulder made a better job o' that. Bit bloody uneven, ennit?'

She went to stand next to him. 'You'd like to get back on the diggers, wouldn't you?'

'Minnie never liked it,' Gomer said gruffly. 'Her still wouldn't like it. 'Sides which, I'm too old.'

'You don't think that for one minute.'

Gomer sniffed and turned away, and led her through an uncared-for copse, where some of the trees were dead and branches brought down by the gales had been left where they'd fallen.

'Prosser's ground, all of this – inherited from the ole fellers. But he don't do nothin' with it n'more. Muster been glad when the harchaeologists come – likely got compensation for lettin' 'em dig up ground the dull bugger'd forgotten he owned.'

'Why's he never done anything with it?'

'That's why,' Gomer said, as they came out of the copse.

And there, on a perfect promontory, a natural shelf above the brook, on the opposite bank, was the former parish church of St Michael, Old Hindwell.

'Gomer . . .' Merrily was transfixed. 'It's . . . beautiful.'

The nave had been torn open to the elements but the tower seemed intact. A bar of light in the sky made the stones shimmer brown and grey and pink between patches of moss and lichen.

'It's the kind of church townsfolk dream of going to on a Sunday. I mean, what must it be like on a summer evening, with its reflection in the water? How could they let it go?'

Gomer grunted, rolling a ciggy. 'Reverent Penney, ennit? I tole you. Went off 'is trolley.'

'Went off his trolley how, exactly?' She remembered that Bernie Dunmore had made a brief allusion last night to the rector at the time actually suggesting that Old Hindwell Church should be decommissioned.

Now, with a certain relish, Gomer told her what the Reverend Terence Penney, rector of this parish, had done with all that ancient and much-polished church furniture on an October day in the mid-1960s.

'Wow.' She stared into the water, imagining it foaming around the flotsam of the minister's madness. 'Why?'

'Drugs,' Gomer said. 'There was talk of drugs.'

'Where is he now?'

Gomer shrugged.

She gazed, appalled, at the ruin. 'I bet we can find out. When we get back to the car, I'll call Sophie. Sophie knows everybody in a dog collar who isn't a dog.'

They went back through the dismal, dying copse.

'Not many folks walks this path n'more,' Gomer said, ''cept a few tourists. Place gets a bad reputation. Then this feller fell off the tower, killed hisself.'

Merrily stopped. 'When?'

'Year or so back? Bloke called Wilshire, army man, lived New Radnor way. Falls off a ladder checkin' the stonework on the ole tower. That's how come these Thorogoods got it cheap, I reckon.'

'I see.'

At the car, despite the extensive view, the mobile phone

signal was poor and she had to shout at Sophie, whose voice kept breaking up into hiss and crackle, shouting out the name Penney.

Gomer said, 'You wanner go talk to the witches, vicar?'

'Dare we?' She thought about it. 'Yeah, why not.'

But when they drove back to the farm gate, there was a TV crew videotaping a thirtyish couple with a 'Christ is the Light' placard. You could tell by their outward bound-type clothing that they were not local. Merrily found herself thinking that some people just didn't have enough to do with their lives.

She was confused. She didn't *know* this place at all. It was like one of those complicated watches that did all sorts of different things, and you had to get the back off before you could see how the cogs were connected. Problem was, she didn't even know where to apply the screwdriver to prise off the back.

'Black Lion?' Gomer suggested. 'I'll buy you a pint and a sandwich, vicar.'

At the Black Lion there were no visible candles – no lights at all, in fact.

Merrily saw Gomer glance at his wrist, before remembering he'd buried his watch. 'About a quarter to two,' she said.

Gomer frowned. 'What's the silly bugger playin' at, shuttin' of a lunchtime with all these TV fellers in town?'

Merrily followed him up a short alley into a yard full of dustbins and beer crates. There was a door with a small frosted-glass window and Gomer tapped on it. Kept on tapping until a face blurred up behind the frosted glass, looking like the scrubbed-over face of one of the suspects in a police documentary. 'We're closed!'

'Don't give me that ole wallop, Greg, boy. Open this bloody door!'

'Who's that?'

'Gomer Parry Plant Hire.' Sounding like he was planning to take a bulldozer to the side of the pub if he couldn't gain normal access.

Bolts were thrown.

The licensee was probably not much older than Merrily, but his eyes were bagged, his mouth pinched, his shirt collar frayed. He'd shaved, but not well. Gomer regarded him without sympathy.

'Bloody hell, Greg, we only wants a pot o' tea and a sandwich.'

The man hesitated. 'All right . . . Just don't make a big fing about it.'

They followed him through a storeroom and an expensive, fitted kitchen with a tomato-red double-oven Aga, and the sound of extractor fans.

'Busy night, boy?'

'Yeah.' But he didn't sound happy about it. 'Go frew there, to the lounge bar. I won't put no lights on.'

'Long's we can see what we're eatin'.'

The lounge bar, grey-lit through more frosted glass, looked to have been only half renovated, as if the money had run out: new brass light fittings on walls too thinly emulsioned. Also a vague smell of damp.

'I can make you coffee, but not tea,' Greg said without explanation.

'We'll take it.' Gomer pulled out bar stools for Merrily and himself.

Greg threw out the dregs of a smile. 'Hope this is your daughter, Gomer?'

'En't got no daughter,' Gomer said gruffly. 'This is the vicar of our church.' As Greg's smile vanished, Gomer sat down, leaned both elbows on the bar top. 'Who made you close the pub, then, boy?'

'The wife.'

'And who made *her* close it?'

'Look,' Greg said, 'I'm not saying you're a nosy git, but this is your second visit inside a few days, asking more questions than that geezer from the *Mail*. What are you, Radnorshire correspondent for *Saga* magazine?'

Merrily was quietly zipping up her coat. It was freezing in there. 'Well, Mr . . .'

'Starkey.'

'Mr Starkey, the nosy git's me. I'm with the Hereford Diocese.'

Greg's eyes slitted. 'Wassat mean?'

'It means . . . Well, it means I'm interested, among other things, in what the Reverend Ellis is getting up to – you know?' Greg snorted; Merrily unwound her scarf to let him see the dog collar. 'This seems to be one of the few places without a candle in the window.'

Greg pushed fingers through his receding hairline. He looked as if there wasn't much more he could take.

'You wanna know what he's getting up to? Like *apart* from destroying marriages?'

'No, let's include that.' Merrily sat down.

Greg said there'd been a full house last night.

'First time in ages. Folks I ain't never seen before. Not big drinkers, but we got frew a lot of Cokes and shandies and if you know anyfing about the licensing trade you'll know that's where the big profit margins lie, so I got no complaints there.'

'Thievin' bugger,' Gomer said. 'So what brought this increase in trade, boy?'

'Wife went to church, Gomer. That funeral. Mrs Weal.

Never come back for a good while after you'd left. I mean hours. Said she'd got talking to people. First time she'd really talked to anybody since we come here.' He scowled. 'Including me.'

'She'd never been before?' Merrily said. 'To church – to the hall?'

'Nah. Not to any kind of church. See, what you gotta realize about Marianne – and I've never told a soul round here, and I would bleedin' hate for anybody—'

'Not a word, boy,' Gomer said. 'Not a word from us.'

'She got problems.' Greg's voice went down to a mutter. 'Depression. *Acute* depression. Been in hospital for it. You know what I mean – psychiatric? This is back in London, when we was managing a pub in Fulham. She was getting . . . difficult to handle.'

Merrily said nothing.

'Wiv men and . . . and that.' Greg waved it away with an embarrassed shake of the head. 'Ain't a nympho or noffink like that. It was just the depression. We had a holiday once and she was fine. Said she was sure she'd be fine the whole time if we went to live somewhere nice, like in the country.' He snorted. 'Country ain't cheap no more. Not for a long time.'

''Cept yere, mabbe,' Gomer said.

'Yeah.'

'It's a trap, Greg, boy.'

'Tell me about it. I've had people in here – incomers, you can pick 'em out from the nervous laughter – still lookin' for strawberries and cream on the village green and the blacksmith tap-tappin' over his forge. Be funny if it wasn't so bleedin' tragic.'

'That was you, was it?' Merrily said softly. 'When you first came here?'

'Her – not me. I ain't a romantic. I tried to tell her . . .

yeah, all right, maybe I did fink it was gonna be different. I mean, there's noffink *wrong* with the local people, most of 'em . . .'

'I coulder tole you, boy,' Gomer said. 'You come to the wrong part o' the valley. Folks back there . . .' he waved a hand over his shoulder, back towards New Radnor. 'They're different again, see. Bit of air back there. Makes a difference.'

'So your wife went to church again yesterday?' Merrily prompted.

'Yeah. Off again. Up the village hall. Couldn't get out this place fast enough. I didn't want *this*. Sure I wanted her to make friends, but not this way. I said, come on, we ain't churchgoers and it'd be hypocritical to start now.'

'Without the hypocrites, all our congregations would be sadly depleted,' Merrily admitted. 'But she went anyway. And came back all aglow, right?'

Greg didn't smile.

'Made lots of new instant friends,' Merrily said. 'People she'd only nodded to in the village shop hugged her as she left. She realized she'd never felt quite so much at home in the community before.'

'Dead on,' Greg said sourly.

'And she wants you to close the pub and go to church with her next week.'

'Says it's the only way we're gonna have a future. And I don't fink she meant the extra business. It won't . . .' He looked scared. 'It won't *last*, will it, Miss . . .?'

'Merrily.'

'It can't last. Can it? She's not a *religious* person. I mean . . . yeah, I coulda foreseen this, soon as people starting whispering about the new rector, what a wonderful geezer he was, how their lives was changed, how he'd . . . I dunno, helped them stop smoking, straightened out their kids, this kind of stuff. All this talk of the Holy Spirit, and people fainting in church. And Marianne kind of saying, "Makes you fink, don't it? Never had no luck to speak of since we moved in. Wouldn't do no harm, would it?" ' Greg looked at Merrily's collar. 'Not your style, then, all this Holy Spirit shite?'

'Not my style, exactly . . .'

Gomer said, 'Don't do any good to let your feet get too far off the ground, my experience.'

'Why did they want you to close the pub today?' Merrily asked.

'Aaah.' Shook his head contemptuously. 'You seen the paper. He told 'em all yesterday this was coming off. Got bloody Devil-worshippers in the village and they gotta be prepared. Bleedin' huge turnout. Standing room only up the hall, 'cording to Marianne, when I could get any sense out of her. People hanging out the doors, lining the bloody steps.'

'This is local people or . . . newcomers?'

'Mainly newcomers, I reckon. A few locals, though, no question. And apparently Ellis is going . . .' Greg threw up his arms. ' "There's a great evil come amongst us! We got to fight it. We are the chosen ones in the battle against Satan!" ' Satan is this Robin Thorogood? All right, a Yank, a bit loud – in your face. But *Satan*? You credit that?'

'You know him, then?'

He shrugged. 'Americans. Talk to 'em for half an hour, you know 'em. His wife's more down to earth. I didn't know they was witches, though. They never talked about that. But why should they?'

'You were going to tell us why you'd closed the pub.'

'He don't want any *distractions*. He wants *concentration of faith*.'

'I don't understand,' Merrily said. 'Why?'

'Mondays he holds his healing sessions,' Greg said. 'Up the village hall.'

'So?'

There was a lot of pain and bewilderment in his eyes.

'I can help,' Merrily said. 'Just tell me.'

Greg breathed heavily down his nose. 'Last night, she says to me, "I'm unclean." Just like that – like out the Bible. "I've been tempted by Satan," she says.'

'En't we all, boy?' Gomer said.

'By *Thorogood*. Suddenly, she's being frank all the time. She's telling me stuff I don't wanna know. Like she was . . . tempted sexually by Robin Thorogood, agent of Satan. She was possessed by his "dark glamour". She wanted to sh— sleep wiv him. She comes out wiv all this. To *me*.'

'*Wanted* to sleep with him?'

'Ah, noffink bleedin' happened. I'm sure of that. He ain't been here two minutes. Plus she's ten years older than what he is, gotta be, and if you seen his wife . . . Nah, I doubt he even noticed Marianne. It's just shite.' Greg shook his head, gutted. 'I'll go get your coffee.'

'Greg, hang on . . . "Possessed by his dark glamour?" ' This wasn't his wife speaking, this was Ellis. 'Did she actually use the word "possessed"?'

'I reckon, yeah. To be honest, I couldn't take no more. I was knackered out. I went to bed. This is totally stupid. This don't happen in places like this. This is city madness, innit?'

'And she's up at the hall now?'

Merrily slid from her stool, picked up her scarf.

THIRTY

Handmaiden

Out in the pub car park, she was ambushed.

'Mrs Watkins – Martyn Kinsey, BBC Wales. I gather you're speaking for the diocese today.'

'Well, I am, but—'

'We'd like to knock off a quick interview, if that's OK.'

He'd probably recognized her from *Livenight*. She asked him if there was any chance of doing this stuff later. From where she stood she could see the top of the cross on the village hall, and it was lit up, and it hadn't been lit before.

'Actually' – Kinsey was a plump, shrewd-eyed guy in his thirties – 'if we don't do it now, I suspect we could be overtaken by events. Nick Ellis is over there in the hall, having a meeting with some people. We're expecting him to come out and announce plans for a march to St Michael's Church, probably tonight.'

'That's what he's doing in there, is it?' The cross was lit up for a policy meeting? *I don't think so.*

'Isn't that going to be too late for your programme?'

'Oh sure – much too late. We might get a piece in the half nine slot, though that'll be only about forty seconds. But I think it's going to be a damp squib anyway, with no one there to protest at. The Thorogoods have been smart enough to vacate the premises.'

'You've not been able to speak to them?'

Kinsey shook his head. 'That's why we're going to have to make do – if you don't mind me putting it like that – with people like you. Just tell us where the Church stands on this issue. A straightforward response. Won't take more than a couple of minutes.'

Of course, it wasn't straightforward. And, with the positioning and the repositioning and the *cutaways* and the *noddies*, it took most of twenty minutes. Kinsey asked her if the diocese was fully behind Ellis; Merrily said the diocese was *concerned* about the situation. So would she be joining in tonight's protest? Not exactly; but she'd be going along as an observer.

'So the diocese is actually sitting on the fence?'

Merrily said, 'Personally, I don't care too much for witch-hunts.'

'So you think that's literally what this is?'

'I just wouldn't like it to turn into one. The Reverend Ellis has a perfect right – well, it's his job, in fact – to oppose whatever he considers evil, but—'

'Do *you* think it's evil?'

'I haven't met the Thorogoods. I wouldn't, on face value, condemn paganism any more than I'd condemn Buddhism or Islam. But I *would*, like everyone else, be interested to find out what they're proposing to do in Old Hindwell Church.'

'You'd see that potentially as sacrilege?'

'The significant point about Old Hindwell Church is that it's no longer a functioning church. It's been decommissioned.'

'What about the graveyard, though? Wouldn't relatives of dead people buried there—'

'There never were all that many graves because the proximity of the brook caused occasional flooding. What graves there were are quite old, and only the stones now remain.

Obviously, we're concerned that those stones should not be tampered with.'

'What about the way the village itself has reacted? All the candles in the windows . . . how do you feel about that?'

Merrily smiled. 'I think they look very pretty.'

'What do you think they're saying?'

'Well . . . lots of different things, probably. Why don't you knock on a few doors and ask?'

Kinsey lowered his microphone, nodded to the cameraman. It was a wrap. 'Out of interest, Martyn,' Merrily said, 'what *did* people have to say when you knocked on their doors?'

'Sod all,' said Kinsey. 'Either they didn't answer or they backed off or they politely informed us that Mr Ellis was doing the talking. And in some cases not so politely. Off the record, why *is* Ellis doing this? Why's he going for these people – these so-called pagans?'

'You tell me.'

'I can't. He's not your usual evangelical, all praising God and bonhomie. He's quiet, he chooses his words carefully. Also he gets on with the locals . . . which is unusual. They're canny round here, not what you'd call impressionable. Anyway, not my problem. You going to be around, if we need anything else?'

'For the duration,' Merrily said.

'Well, good luck.'

'Thanks.'

She ran all the way to the village hall, meeting nobody on the way, bounding up the steps and praying she wasn't too late, because if it was all over . . . well, hearsay evidence just wasn't the same.

At the top, she stopped for breath – and to assess the man in the porch, obviously guarding the closed doors to the hall. Slumped on a folding chair like a sack of cement. He was an unsmiling, flat-capped bloke in his fifties. She didn't recognize him.

He didn't quite look at her. ''Ow're you?'

'I'm fine. OK if I just pop in?'

'No press, thank you. Father Ellis will be out in a while.'

'I'm not press.'

'I still can't let you in.'

Merrily unwound her scarf. He took in the collar, his watery eyes swivelling uncertainly.

'You're with Father Ellis?'

'Every step of the way,' Merrily said shamelessly.

He ushered her inside. 'Be very quiet,' he said sternly, and closed the doors silently behind her.

Suddenly she was in darkness.

She waited, close to the place where she'd stood at Menna's funeral service, until her eyes adjusted enough to reassure her there was little chance of being spotted. Here, at the end of the hall, she stood alone.

All the window blinds had been pulled down tight, and it seemed to have a different layout, no longer a theatre-in-the-round. Whatever was happening was happening in a far corner, and all she could see of it was a white-gold aura, like over a Nativity scene, a distant holy grotto.

And all she could hear was a sobbing – hollow, slow and even.

Merrily slipped off her shoes, carried them to the shelter of a brick pillar about halfway down the hall. It was cold; no heating on.

She waited for about half a minute before peering carefully around the pillar.

The glow had resolved into two tiers of candles. The sobbing had softened into a whispery panting. Merrily could make out several people – seemed like women – some sitting or kneeling in a circle, the others standing behind them, all holding candles on small tin or pewter trays, like the ones in the windows of the village.

Women only? This was why the guy on the door had let her in without too much dispute.

The scene, with its unsteady glow and its umber shadows, had a dreamlike, period ambience: seventeenth or eighteenth century. You expected the women to be wearing starched Puritan collars.

'In the name of the Father . . . and of the Son . . . and of the Holy Ghost . . .'

Ellis's voice was low-level, with that transatlantic lubrication. User-friendly and surprisingly warm.

But only momentarily, for then he paused. Merrily saw him rise up, in his white monk's robe, in the centre of the circle, the only man here. Next to him stood a slender table with a candle on it and a chalice and something else in shadow, probably a Bible.

His voice rose, too, became more distinct, the American element now clipped out.

'O God, the Creator and Protector of the human race, Who hast formed man in Thine own image, look upon this Thy handmaiden who is grievously vexed with the wiles of an unclean spirit . . . whom the old adversary, the ancient enemy of the earth, encompasses with a horrible dread . . . and blinds the senses of her human understanding with stupor, confounds her with terror . . . and harasses her with trembling and fear.'

Merrily's feet were cold; she bent and slipped on her shoes. She wouldn't be getting any closer; from here she could see and hear all she needed. And she was fairly sure this was a modified version of the Roman Catholic ritual.

Ellis's voice gathered a rolling energy. 'Drive away, O Lord, the power of the Devil, take away his deceitful snares.'

At some signal, the women held their candles high, wafting out the rich and ancient aroma of melted wax.

With a glittering flourish, Ellis's arm was thrust up amid the lights.

'Behold the Cross of the Lord! Behold the Cross and flee, thou obscene spirits of the night!'

His voice dropped, became intense, sneering.

'Most cunning serpent, you shall never again dare to deceive the human race and persecute the Holy Church. Cursed dragon, we give thee warning in the names of Jesus Christ and Michael, in the names of Jehovah, Adonai, Tetragrammaton . . .'

Merrily stiffened. *What?*

She leaned further out to watch Nick Ellis standing amongst all the women, brandishing his cross like a sword in the light, brandishing words which surely belonged originally to the Roman Church, to Jewish mysticism, to . . .

The candles lowered again, to reveal a single woman crouching.

More like cringing?

Ellis laid the cross on the tall table and bent down to the woman.

'Do you embrace God?' His voice had softened.

The woman looked up at him, like a pet dog.

'You must embrace God,' he explained, gently at first. 'You must embrace God, embrace Him, embrace Him . . .' His right arm was extended, palm raised, the loose sleeve of his robe falling back. 'Embrace *Him*!'

Shadows leaping. A short expulsion of breath – *'Hoh!'* – and a sound of stumbling.

Merrily saw he'd pushed the woman away; she lay half on her back, panting.

'Say it!' Ellis roared.

'I . . . embrace Him.'

'And do you renounce the evil elements of this world which corrupt those things God has created?'

'Yes.' She came awkwardly to her feet. She was wearing a white shift of some kind, possibly a nightdress. She must feel very cold.

'Do you renounce all sick and sinful desires which draw you away from the love of God?'

She began to cry again. Her London accent said this had to be Greg Starkey's wife, Marianne, the sometime sufferer from clinical depression, not a nympho in the normal sense, but tempted by the dark glamour of the witch Robin Thorogood. Was that it? Was that really the extent of her possession?

And, oh God, even if there was a whole lot more, this was not right, not by any stretch.

'Say it!'

Her head went back. She started to sniff.

'Say, "I so renounce them"!'

'I s . . . so . . . renounce them.'

'And do you, therefore, wish with all your heart to expel the lewd and maleficent spirit coiling like a foul serpent within you?'

Her head was thrown right back, as if she expected to be slapped, again and again.

'I ask you once more . . .' Softly. 'Do you wish, with all your heart . . .?'

'*Yes!*'

'Then lie down,' Father Ellis said.

What? Merrily moved away from the pillar. She could see now that Ellis was pointing at a hessian rug laid out on the boarded floor. Marianne drew an unsteady breath and went to stand on the rug. The watching women kept still. But she caught a movement from a darkened doorway, with a 'Toilets' sign over the top, and moved back behind her pillar.

There was a man in that doorway, she'd swear it.

Ellis said, 'Don't be afraid.'

He turned to the table and took up another cross from a white cloth. Merrily saw it clearly. About nine inches long, probably gold-plated. He held it up to the candlelight, then lowered it again. One of the women leaned forward, handed him something.

Involuntarily, Merrily moved closer. The woman held up her candle for Ellis. Merrily saw a yellow tube, then an inch of pale jelly was transferred to Ellis's forefinger. She saw him smearing the jelly along the stem of the crucifix.

What?

Ellis nodded once. Marianne Starkey crumpled to her knees then went into an ungainly squat, holding the night-dress up around her thighs.

'Be calm now,' Ellis said. 'Sit. Relax.'

The woman sat still. Ellis raised his eyes from her. 'O God of martyrs, God of confessors, we lay ourselves before Thee . . .' He glanced at Marianne, whispered, 'Lie back.'

Merrily watched Marianne's body subside onto the rough matting, her knees up, the nightdress slipping back. Ellis knelt in front of her.

'I ask you again,' he whispered. 'Is it your heart's wish that the unclean spirit might be expelled for ever?'

'Yes.'

'And do you understand that a foul spirit of this nature may effectively be purged only through the portal of its entry?'

'Yes . . .' Marianne hesitated then let her head fall back over the edge of the mat and onto the boarded floor with a dull thump. She closed her eyes. 'Yes.'

Ellis began to pray, a long, rolling mumble, slowly becoming intelligible.

'Let the impious tempter fly far hence! Let thy servant be defended by the sign . . .' Ellis rose and put the cross swiftly on Marianne's forehead. '. . . of Thy Name.' He placed the cross against her breast. 'Do Thou guard her inmost soul . . .'

Merrily thought, 'He won't. He can't. It isn't possible, not with all these women here.'

Ellis reared over Marianne. 'Do Thou rule . . .' Then he bent suddenly. '. . . her inmost parts.'

Marianne gave a low and throaty cry, then Ellis sprang up, kissing the cross, tossing it to the table, and it was over. And women were hugging Marianne.

And Merrily was frozen in horror and could no longer see a man in the doorway.

THIRTY-ONE

Jewel

The converging lanes were filling up with vehicles – like last Saturday. When Ellis and the women – but not Marianne – came down the steps, they were joined by more people. By the time they all reached the road there were about thirty of them, with Ellis seeming to float in their midst, glowingly messianic in his white monk's habit.

The sick bastard.

Merrily turned away, found her hands were clenched together. Shame. Fury. When she could stand to look again, she saw that someone was bearing a white wooden crucifix aloft, in front of Ellis. At the apex of the village hall roof, the neon cross became a beacon in the rain. Like it was all a crusade.

She didn't recognize anyone in Ellis's group, but why should she? She guessed they were not locals anyway. A couple of the men wore suits but most others were casually but warmly dressed, like members of a serious hiking club. Nobody was speaking. Shouldn't they be singing some charismatic anthem, swaying, clapping?

Killing the shakes, Merrily walked erratically along the lane to the corner where a bunch of reporters stood under umbrellas and Gomer was waiting for her in the rain, an unlit ciggy drooping from his mouth.

'Vicar . . . you all right, girl?' Following her behind a

Range Rover parked under some fir trees, he regarded her gravely. 'You looks a bit pale.'

'Don't fuss, Gomer.' Merrily dropped a cigarette in the process of trying to light it.

Gomer straightened his glasses.

'Sorry.' She touched his arm. 'It's *me*. I'm furious with me, that's all.'

'Happened in there, vicar?'

'Exorcism – of sorts. I ought to have stopped it. I just' – she thumped her thigh with a fist – 'stood there . . . let it happen.'

'Hexorcism?' Gomer said, bewildered. 'This'd be Greg's missus?'

'Must've been.'

'The bugger hexorcized Greg's missus for fancyin' a feller?'

'For embracing the dark,' Merrily said, with unsuppressible venom. 'For letting herself become possessed by most unholy and blasphemous lust.'

'Load of ole wallop. You gonner tell Greg?'

'Perhaps not.'

'Boy oughter know,' said Gomer, 'whatever it was.' He nodded towards a man getting into the Range Rover. 'Dr Coll,' he observed.

The cameramen were backing away down the street ahead of Ellis and his entourage. Dr Coll drove away in his Range Rover, leaving Merrily and Gomer exposed.

'I can't believe I let it happen,' she said. 'I couldn't believe it *was* happening. I can't tell Greg. You saw the state he was in. He'd go after Ellis with a baseball bat. That . . . *bastard*.'

Ellis walked without looking to either side. When a couple of the reporters tried to get a word with him, his anoraked minders pressed closer around him – the holy man. Merrily and Gomer walked well behind, Merrily turning things over and over.

Internal ministry, it had been called when the phenomenon had first been noted in the North of England. Mostly it was for supposed incidents of satanic child abuse – a number of allegations, but not much proven. It was a charismatic extreme, an evangelical madness: the warped and primitive conviction that demonic forces entered through bodily orifices and could only be expelled the same way.

It had all happened too quickly, clinically, like a doctor taking a cervical smear. The fact that it was also degrading, humiliating – and, as it happened, amounted to sexual assault – would not be an issue for someone who had convinced himself of it being a legitimate weapon in the war against Satan. Someone invoking the power of the Archangel Michael against a manufactured dragon.

When, in fact, *he* was the monster.

Got to stop him.

But if she spoke out there would be a dozen respectable women ready to say she was a liar with a chip on her shoulder; about a dozen women who had watched the ritual in silence. Then, afterwards, tears and hugs and 'Praise God!'

'Gomer . . . those women over there, who are they?'

Gomer identified Mrs Eleri Cobbold, the village sub-postmistress, Mrs Smith whose cottage they'd passed, Linda Llewellyn who managed a riding stables towards Presteigne. The others he didn't know. Mostly from Off, he reckoned.

Marianne wasn't among them.

'No back way out of the hall, is there?'

'Yes, but not without comin' down them steps, vicar, less you wants to squeeze through a fence and lose yourself in the forestry.'

So she was still up there. That made sense; they'd hardly

want to bring her out looking like a road casualty, not with TV crews around.

Ellis had reached the car park of the Black Lion. He was evidently about to hold a press conference.

'Gomer, could you kind of hang around and listen to what he says? I need to go back in there.'

All eyes were fixed on Ellis as Merrily walked inconspicuously back through the rain towards the steps.

Nobody on the door this time. Inside the hall, all the blinds were now raised, the chairs were spread out and a plain wooden lectern stood in the centre of the room. This time, one corner looked very much like another and only a vague smell of wax indicated that anything more contentious than an ad hoc meeting of the community council had taken place.

No, there *was* something else: the atmosphere you often caught in a church after a packed service – tiny shivers in the air like dust motes waiting to settle.

A black coat slung over one of the chairs suggested someone was still around, if only a cleaner. Presently, Merrily became aware of voices from beyond the door with the 'Toilets' sign above it – where that solitary man had stood. She crossed the hall, not caring about the sound of her shoes on the polished floorboards.

The door opened into an ante-room leading to separate women's and men's lavatories. It contained a sink and one of the chairs from the main room – Marianne sitting in it. A woman was bending over her with a moistened paper towel, patting her brow. Marianne didn't react when the door swung shut behind Merrily, but the other woman looked up at once, clear blue eyes unblinking.

'We can manage, thank you.'

The voice echoed off the tiles: cold white tiles, floor to

ceiling, reminding Merrily of the stark bathroom at Ledwardine vicarage.

'How is she?'

'She's much better, thank you. Had problems at home, haven't you, my love?'

The woman wore jeans and a black and orange rugby shirt. She had a lean, wind-roughened face, bleakly handsome. A face which had long since become insensitive to slaps from the weather and the world. A face last seen lit by the lanterns in Menna's mausoleum.

The woman dabbed at Marianne's cheek, screwed up the paper towel and looked again at Merrily, in annoyance. 'You want the lavatory, is it?'

'No. I'd just like a word with Marianne – when you've finished.' Merrily unwound her scarf. 'Merrily Watkins. Hereford Diocese.'

'Oh? Come to spy on Father Ellis, is it? We're not stupid. We know what the diocese thinks of him.'

Marianne looked glassy-eyed. *She* didn't care one way or the other.

'And anyway,' the woman said, 'Mrs Starkey hasn't been through anything she didn't personally request. Father Ellis doesn't do a soft ministry.'

'Obviously not.'

'Practical man who gets results. She'll be fine, if people will let her alone. If you want to talk to anybody, you can talk to me. Judith Prosser, my name. Councillor Prosser's wife. Come outside.'

She gave Marianne's shoulder a squeeze then went and held open the door for Merrily, ushering her out and down the central aisle of the hall, past Ellis's lectern. She picked up the black quilted coat from a chair back, and they went out through the main doors.

The rain had stopped. At the top of the steps, Judith

Prosser didn't turn to look at Merrily; she leaned on the metal railings and gazed over to the village centre, where Ellis and his entourage were assembling for the media.

'And was it the diocese sent you to Menna's funeral, too, Reverend Watkins?'

Above Old Hindwell, a hopeless sun was trying vainly to burn a hole in the clouds. Mist still filigreed the firs on Burfa Hill but the tower of the old church was clear to the north.

'I didn't think you'd recognized me,' Merrily said.

'Well, of course I recognized you.'

This was the intelligent woman who Gomer seemed to admire. Who did her husband's thinking for him. Who could sit and watch another woman physically invaded in the name of God.

'For what it's worth, that was nothing at all to do with the diocese,' Merrily told her. 'I'd arranged to meet Barbara Buckingham at her sister's funeral. You remember Barbara?'

Judith Prosser's head turned slowly until her eyes locked on Merrily's.

'*Had* you now?'

'She was referred to me by a nurse at Hereford Hospital, after her sister died there. I do . . . counselling work, in certain areas.'

'Didn't come to the funeral, though, did she?'

'She's disappeared,' Merrily said. 'She spent some days here and now she's disappeared. The police are worried about her safety.'

'Oh, her *safety*? An eyebrow arched under Judith's stiff, short hair. 'And what are we to assume they mean by that?'

'We both know what they mean, Mrs Prosser.'

The sun had given up the struggle, was no more than a pale grey circle embossed on the cloud.

'Poor Barbara,' Judith said.

Merrily did some thinking. While she hadn't come up here to discuss Barbara and Menna, as soon as the conversation had been diverted away from Ellis himself, Judith Prosser had become instantly more forthcoming.

'Barbara told me you used to write to her.'

'For many years. We were best friends for a time, as girls.'

'So you know why she left home.'

'Do *you*?'

'I know it wasn't a hydatid cyst.'

'Ha. Good informants you must have. What else did they tell you?'

'That you were looking out for Menna, and keeping Barbara informed. Menna was a source of . . . disquiet . . . for Barbara. Especially after their mother died.'

'Ah.' Judith Prosser nodded. 'So that's it.' She leaned back with her elbows against the railings. 'Well, let me assure you right now, Mrs . . . *is* it Mrs? Let me assure you emphatically that Mervyn Thomas never touched Menna. I know that, because I warned him myself what would happen to him if he ever did.'

'But you'd have been just a kid . . . or not much more.'

'This was not when Menna was a child. Good heavens, Merv was never a child-molester. He'd wait till they filled out. Ha! No, there was never anything for Barbara to worry about there. *Nothing*. She could go on living her rich, soft, English life without a qualm.'

'Hasn't she been to see you in the past week or so?'

Judith sniffed. 'I heard she was around, pestering people – including you, it seems. Evidently she couldn't face me.'

'Wasn't it you who told her about Menna's stroke?'

'I sent her a short note. Somebody had to.'

'But not her husband.'

Mrs Prosser smiled and nodded. 'Let me also tell you, Mrs Watkins, that Jeffery Weal was the best thing that could have happened to Menna. If you knew her – which Barbara, lest we forget, never really *did* – Menna was a wispy, flimsy little thing. Insubstantial, see, like a ghost. She— Are you all right?'

'Yes.' Merrily swallowed. 'I'm fine. Why was Mr Weal so good for her?'

'If you knew her, you would know she would always need someone to direct her life. And while he was not the most demonstrative of men, he adored her. Kept her like a jewel.'

In a padded box, Merrily thought, in a private vault.

'Anyway,' Judith said, 'I do hope the Diocese of Hereford is not going to interfere with Father Ellis. He suits this area very well. He meets our needs.'

'Really? How many other people has he exorcized?'

Judith Prosser sighed in exasperation. 'As far as local people are concerned, he's giving back the church the authority it *used* to have. Time was when we had a village policeman and troublesome youngsters would get a clip around the ear. Now they have to go up before people like my husband, Councillor Prosser, and receive some paltry sentence – a conditional discharge, or a period of community service if they're *very* bad. Time *was* when sinners would be dealt with by the Church, isn't it? They weren't so ready to reoffend *then*.'

'The way Father Ellis deals with them?'

Judith smiled thinly. 'The way God deals with them, he would say, isn't it? Excuse me, I must go back and minister to Mrs Starkey.'

Halfway down the steps, Merrily encountered Gomer coming up. There were now a lot of things she needed to ask him. But, behind his glasses, Gomer's eyes were luridly alive.

'It's on, vicar.'

'The march?'

'Oh hell, aye. Tonight. No stoppin' the bugger now. Somebody been over to St Michael's, and they reckons Thorogood's back. En't on his own, neither.'

Merrily felt dejected. All she wanted was to get home, do some hard thinking, ring the bishop to discuss the issue of *internal ministry*. She didn't want to even have to look at Nicholas Ellis again tonight.

'Bunch o' cars and vans been arrivin' at St Michael's since 'bout half an hour ago. One of 'em had, like, a big badge on the back, 'cordin' to Eleri Cobbold. Like a star in a circle?'

'Pentagram,' Merrily said dully.

'Ar,' said Gomer, 'they figured it wasn't the bloody RAC.'

'How's Ellis reacted?'

'Oh, dead serious. Heavy, grim – for the cameras. Man called upon to do God's holy work, kind o' thing.'

'Yeah, I can imagine. But underneath . . .'

'Underneath – pardon me, vicar – like a dog with two dicks.'

'I don't need this,' Merrily said.

THIRTY-TWO

Potion

Betty left Mrs Pottinger's lodge in weak sunshine, wanting nothing more than to collapse in front of that cranky farm-house stove and pour it all out to Robin.

Except that Robin would go insane.

She called for a quick salad at a supermarket cafe on the outskirts of Leominster. By the time she reached the Welsh border, it was approaching an early dusk and raining and, in her mind, she was back in the shop with Mrs Cobbold and the slender man with the pointed beard.

'Oh, good morning, Doctor.'

'A sharp day, Eleri.'

Dr Coll.

She needed to tell somebody about Dr Coll and the Hindwell Trust. She wished it could be Robin. Wished she could trust him not to go shooting his mouth off and have them facing legal action on top of everything else.

The Hindwell Trust, Juliet Pottinger had explained, was a local charity originally started to assist local youngsters from hard-pressed farming families to go on to higher education. To become – for instance – doctors and lawyers, so that they might return and serve the local community.

A *local people's* charity.

Juliet Pottinger had come to Old Hindwell because of her husband's job. Stanley had been much older, an archaeologist with the Clwyd-Powys Trust, who had continued to work part-time after his official retirement. He was, in fact, one of the first people to suspect that the Radnor Basin had a prehistory as significant as anywhere in Wales. His part-time job became a full-time obsession. He was overworking. He collapsed.

'Dr Collard Banks-Morgan was like a small, bearded, ministering angel,' Mrs Pottinger had said wryly. 'Whisked poor Stanley into the cottage hospital. Those were the days when anyone could occupy a bed for virtually as long as they wished. Stanley practically had to discharge himself in the end, to get back to his beloved excavation.'

And while Stanley was trowelling away at his favoured site, a round barrow at Harpton, Dr Coll paid Mrs P. a discreet visit. He informed her, in absolute confidence, that he was more than a little worried about Stanley's heart; that Stanley, not to dress up the situation, had just had a very lucky escape, and he could one day very easily push the enfeebled organ . . . just a little too far.

'Oh, don't *tell* him that. Good heavens, don't have him carrying it around like an unexploded bomb!' said Dr Coll jovially. 'I shall keep tabs on him, myself.' Chuckling, he added, 'I believe I'm developing a latent interest in prehistory!'

Dr Coll had been discretion itself, popping in for a regular chat – perhaps to ask Stanley the possible significance of some mound he could see from his surgery window or bring him photocopies of articles on Victorian excavations from the *Radnorshire Transactions*. And all the time, as he told Juliet with a wink, he was observing Stanley's colour, his breathing, his general demeanour. *Keeping tabs*.

She thought the man's style was wonderful: perfect preventative medicine. How different from the city, where a GP could barely spare one the time of day.

And Betty was rehearing Lizzie Wilshire: *'Dr Coll's been marvellous . . . such a caring, caring man.'*

Juliet Pottinger had said as much, without spelling anything out, to their most solicitous solicitor, Mr Weal, who was handling their purchase of a small strip of land – 'for a quite *ludicrous* amount' – from the Prosser brothers. How could she possibly repay Dr Coll's kindness?

Oh, well, said Mr Weal, when pressed, there *was* a certain local charity, to which Dr Coll was particularly attached. Oh, nothing *now*, he wouldn't want that, he'd be most embarrassed. But something to bear in mind for the future perhaps? And please don't tell Dr Coll that he'd mentioned this – he would hate to alienate a client.

It was two years later, while they were on holiday in Scotland – a particularly hot summer – that Stanley, exhibiting symptoms of what might be sunstroke or something worse, was whisked off by his anxious wife to a local hospital. Where two doctors were unable to detect a heart problem of any kind.

'Stanley died three and a half years ago of what, in the days before everything had to be explained, would have been simply termed old age,' said Mrs Pottinger.

'And did you ever take this misdiagnosis up with Dr Coll?' Betty was imagining Juliet waking up in the night listening for his breathing, monitoring his diet, being nervous whenever he was driving. It must have been awfully worrying.

'I took the coward's way out, and persuaded Stanley to move somewhere else, a bit more convenient. I said I was finding the village too claustrophobic, which was true. By then I'd discovered that Dr Coll had . . . well, *appeared* to have created a . . . dependency among several of his patients, and all of them, as it happened, incomers to the area. People who might be feeling a little isolated there, and would be overjoyed to find such a friendly and concerned local GP.'

'Making up illnesses for them, too?'

'I don't know. People don't like to talk about certain things. People are only too happy to praise their local doctor, to boast about what a good and caring GP they have. Perhaps ours was an isolated case. Certainly, some of them did die quite soon. One rather lonely elderly couple, childless and reclusive, died' – her voice faded – 'within only months of each other.'

'And did they by any chance leave money,' Betty asked her, 'to this . . .?'

'The Hindwell Trust. Yes, I rather believe there was a substantial bequest.'

'Did you never say anything?'

'Don't look at me like that,' Mrs Pottinger snapped. 'Was I supposed to go to the police? I'd have been a laughing stock. I believe Dr Coll even helped out as a police surgeon for some years. Yes, I did, when we were about to leave the village, suggest to the Connellys, who'd bought a rather run-down smallholding . . . but . . . No, it was a waste of time. Dr Coll is a very popular man: he has five children, he hosts garden parties at his lovely home on the Evenjobb road. Even now, I don't necessarily believe—'

'What about the solicitor?'

'Oh, Mr Weal and Dr Coll go *right* back. Fellow pupils at the Old Hindwell Primary School. In fact, Mr Weal administers the Hindwell Trust – and its trustees include Councillor Gareth Prosser. You see?'

I see. Oh yes, I do see.

Such a caring, caring man.

Driving out of the hamlet of Kinnerton, Betty felt a rising panic, an inability to cope with this news on her own. The Radnor Valley was all around her, a green enigma. Abruptly, she turned into a lane which she already knew of because it led to the Four Stones.

She stopped the car on the edge of a field beyond Hindwell Farm – Hindwell, not *Old* Hindwell. Different somehow – placid and open and almost lush in summer. She could see the stones through the hedge. She loved this place, this little circle. She and Robin must have been here ten or fifteen times already. It was still raining, but she got out of the car and climbed eagerly over the gate. It felt like coming home.

The Four Stones were close to the hedge, not high but plump and rounded. Betty went down on her knees and put her arms around one and looked across the open countryside to the jagged middle-distant hillside where stood the sentinel church of Old Radnor. She hugged the stone, surrendering to the energies of the prehistoric landscape.

This was the religion – and the Radnorshire – that she understood.

The rain intensified, beating down on her out of a blackening sky. Betty didn't care; she wished the rain would wash her into the stone. When she stood up, she was pretty well soaked, but she felt better, stronger.

And angry. Bitterly angry at the corruption of this old and sacred place. Angry at the bloody *local people*, the level to which they appeared to have degenerated.

She drove to the end of the lane and, instead of turning left towards Walton and Old Hindwell, headed right, towards New Radnor, against the rain.

Even if the woman's bungalow was strewn with copies of the *Daily Mail*, she would charm Lizzie Wilshire around to her side. She would ask her directly if the Hindwell Trust was mentioned in her will.

'Above all,' Max said, pouring himself a glass of red wine, 'we can challenge them intellectually.'

Max had this big, wildman beard. You could've lost him

at a ZZ Top convention. But any suggestion of menace vanished as soon as he spoke, for Max had a voice like a one-note flute. He was a lecturer someplace; he liked to lecture.

'St Michael equates with the Irish god Mannon, of the Tuatha de Danaan. Mannon was the sea god, and also the mediator between the gods and humankind and the conductor of souls into the Otherworld. In Coptic and cab-balistic texts, you will find these roles also attributed to Michael. Therefore, every "Saint" Michael church is, regard-less of its origins, in essence a pagan Celtic temple. Which is why this reconsecration is absolutely valid.'

Normally, even coming from Max, Robin would have found this amazing, total cosmic vindication. Right now he really couldn't give a shit.

Because it was close to dark now, and still Betty had not returned, had not even called.

He walked tensely around the beamed living room, which *they* had taken over, stationing candles in the four corners, feeding gathered twigs to a feeble fire they'd gotten going in the inglenook where the witch-charm box had been stored. When George and Vivvie had come down, the first weekend, Betty had stopped them establishing a temple in this room. But now, in her absence, they'd gone right ahead.

Altar to the north – some asshole had cleared one of the trestle tables in Robin's studio and hauled it through. Now it held the candle, pentacle, chalice, wand, scourge, bell, sword.

There had to be a power base, George said. There would be negative stuff coming at them now from all over the country. It was about protection, George explained, and Betty would understand that.

If she was here. She'd never been away this long before, without at least calling him. Robin imagined the cops arriving, solemn and sympathetic and heavy with awful news of a fatal car crash in torrential rain.

Never, for Robin, had a consecration meant less. Never had a temple seemed so bereft of holiness or atmosphere of any kind.

'She'll be back, Robin.' A plump middle-aged lady called Alexandra had picked up on his anxiety. She'd been Betty's college tutor, way back, had been present at their handfasting. Her big face was mellow and kind by candlelight. 'If anything had happened to her, one of us would surely know.'

'Sure,' Robin said.

'I just hope she'll be happy we've come.'

'Yeah,' Robin said hoarsely. See, if she'd only called, he'd have been able to prepare her for this. He knew he should have held them off until he'd consulted with her. But when George had come through on the mobile, Robin had been already majorly stressed out, beleaguered, and it hadn't immediately occurred to him that they would have to accommodate a number of these people in the farmhouse, with sleeping bags being unrolled in the kitchen, and more upstairs.

And kids, too. Max and Bella's kids: two daughters and a nine-year-old son called Hermes – Robin had already caught the little creep messing with his airbrushes. At least *they* weren't gonna sleep in the house; the whole family were now camped in the big Winnebago out back. It had a pentagram in the rear window, the same place Christians these days liked to display a fish symbol.

Robin went over to the window again, looking out vainly for small headlights.

Sometimes suspicion pierced his anxiety. He wondered if this whole thing had been in some way planned. While George was into practicalities like dowsing and scrying, Vivvie was essentially political. For her, Robin sometimes thought, paganism might just as easily have been Marxism. And it was Vivvie who had accidentally, in the heat of the moment, let it out on TV. He never had entirely trusted Vivvie.

And now they were looking at a serious showdown with some seriously fanatical fundamentalist Christians. Two of the Wiccans, Jonathan and Rosa, had been down to the village to take a look, and had seen a gathering of people around a man in white. Ellis? This confrontation, Max said, must not be allowed to get in the way of the great festival of light. But George had grinned. George loved trouble.

'What is terrific about this,' Max piped, waving his wineglass, 'is that only two deities were directly filched from the Old Faith by Christianity. One was Michael, the other was the triple-goddess, Brigid, who became associated with Saint Brigid, the Abbess of Kildare – who was, in all probability, herself a pagan worshipping in an oak grove. So, as we know, Imbolc is the feast of Brigid, Christianized as Candlemas – the feast of *Saint* Brigid . . .'

Max beamed through his beard in the candlelight. There was no particular need for him to go on; they all knew this stuff, but Max was Max and already a little smashed.

'Therefore . . . it is absolutely fitting that this church should be reconsecrated on that sacred eve, in the names of both Mannon and Brigid, with a fire festival, which will burn away . . .'

Jesus. Robin stared out of the window into the uninterrupted night. He wondered if Betty, once away from here, had decided never to come back.

There was a green Range Rover parked in front of Lizzie Wilshire's bungalow, so Betty had to leave the car further down the lane, under the outer ramparts of the New Radnor castle mound, and run through the rain. It didn't matter now; this was the same rain that was still falling on the Four Stones.

When she reached the Range Rover, the clear, rectangular sign propped in its windscreen made her stop. Made her turn and walk quickly back to her car.

The sign said, 'DOCTOR ON CALL'.

She had to think. Was this a sign that she was supposed to go in there, tackle Dr Coll face to face?

Betty sat in the driving seat, thankful for the streaming rain obscuring the windscreen and her face from any passers-by.

She went over it all again in her head. Dr Coll, who was here. Mr Weal, the solicitor whose home was not so far from St Michael's Farm and whose wife had recently died.

'*So how did Mr Weal become your solicitor?*'

'*He's simply there. He becomes everyone's solicitor sooner or later. He's reliable, it's an old family firm, and his charges are modest. He draw up wills virtually free of charge.*'

'*I bet he does.*'

'*I don't suppose any of this will affect you at all. You're too young: you'll see both of them out. It probably wouldn't have affected Major Wilshire, either. He was ex-regiment, a fit man with all his wits about him.*'

Lizzie Wilshire: '*Bryan had a thing about the medical profession, refused to call a doctor unless in dire emergency. A great believer in natural medicine, was Bryan.*'

All his wits about him.

'*. . . it was, unfortunately, entirely in character for Bryan to attempt such a job alone. He thought he was invulnerable.*'

A light tapping on the rain-streaming side window made Betty jump in her seat. She was nervous again, and the nerves had brought back the uncertainty. She could be getting completely carried away about this. She hurriedly wound down the window.

'Mrs Thorogood?'

Betty was unable to suppress a gasp.

Raindrops glistened in the neat, pointed beard under his rugged, dependable face.

'I'm sure Mrs Wilshire wouldn't want you hanging around out here in the rain. Why don't you come into the house?'

'I didn't want to intrude,' Betty said. 'I was going to wait till you'd gone.'

'Nonsense,' said Dr Collard Banks-Morgan. 'As much as anything, I'd very much like to talk to you about the herbal medicine you so generously prepared for Mrs Wilshire.'

He held open the car door for her. He was wearing the same light-coloured tweed suit, a mustard-coloured tie. On his head was a tweed hat with fishing flies in it. He had an umbrella which he put up and held over her, guiding her briskly past his green Range Rover and up the path to the bungalow.

For a moment, it was almost like an out-of-body experience – she'd experienced that twice, knew the sensations – and she was watching herself and Dr Coll entering the porch together. As though this was the natural conclusion to a sequence of events she'd set in motion when she'd decided she had to leave Robin at the mercy of the media and seek out Juliet Pottinger.

She was now being led into a confrontation with Collard Banks-Morgan, in the presence of Mrs Wilshire. Bright panic flared, she was not ready! She didn't know enough!

But something evidently had taken over: fate, or something. Perhaps she was about to be given the proof she needed.

Betty could hardly breathe.

'Won't be a jiff.' Dr Coll stood in the doorway, shaking out his umbrella. 'Go through if you like. Mrs Wilshire's in the sitting room, as usual.'

Betty nodded and went through. Though it was not yet

three o'clock, the weather had made the room dark and gloomy, so that the usually feeble-looking flames in the bronze-enamelled oil stove were brazier-bright, making shadows rise around Mrs Wilshire, in her usual chair facing the fireplace. She didn't turn when Betty came in.

'I'm sorry about this, Mrs Wilshire,' Betty said. 'I wasn't going to come over until the doctor had left.'

Mrs Wilshire still didn't turn round.

The shadows leapt.

The force of her own indrawn breath flung Betty back into the doorway.

'Oh, Jesus Christ!'

Not, *Oh, Mother!* which she only said, still self-consciously, at times of minor crisis.

Her hand went to her mouth. 'Oh no . . .'

There was a small click and wall lights came on, cold and milky blue.

'Go and look at her, if you like,' said Dr Coll. 'I think you ought to.'

He walked over to the fireplace, stood with an elbow resting on the mantelpiece.

'You aren't afraid of death, are you, Mrs Thorogood? Just a preliminary to rebirth, isn't that what you people believe?'

Betty found she was trembling. 'What happened to her?'

Dr Coll raised an ironic eyebrow. 'Among other things, it seems *you* happened to her.'

Betty edged around the sofa, keeping some distance between her and the doctor. When she reached the window, a movement outside made her look out. Another car had parked next to the Range Rover. A policeman and a police-woman were coming up the path.

Betty spun and saw Lizzie Wilshire, rigid and slightly twisted in her chair with a little froth around her bluing lips and her bulbous eyes popped fully open, as if they were lidless.

Dr Coll stepped away from the fireplace. He was holding up a round, brown bottle with a half-inch of liquid in the bottom.

'Is *this* your herbal potion, Mrs Thorogood?'

THIRTY-THREE

The Adversary

From Off, they were, nearly all of them, Gomer reckoned. He'd told Merrily he could never imagine too many local people sticking their heads above the hedge, and he was right. There were maybe fifty of them – not an enormous turnout under the circumstances – and the ones Merrily could hear all had English accents.

Two TV crews had stayed for this; they were pushing microphones at the marchers as they came to the end of the pavement, a line of lamps, moving on into the lane past Annie Smith's place, bound for the Prosser farm and St Michael's. Telly questions coming at them, to get them all fired up.

'But what are you really hoping to achieve here?'

'Do you actually believe two self-styled white witches can in some way curse the whole community?'

'Don't people have the right, in the eyes of the law, to worship whatever they want to?'

And the answers came back, in Brummy, in Northern, in cockney London and posh London.

'This is not about the law. Read your Bible. In the eyes of God they are profane.'

'Why are there as many as five churches around the Radnor Forest dedicated to St Michael, who was sent to fight Satan?'

A woman in a bright yellow waterproof holding up five fingers for the camera.

There was a central group of hardcore Bible freaks. This was probably the first demonstration most of them had ever joined, Merrily thought. For quite a number, it was probably the first time they'd actually been closely involved with a church. It was the isolation factor: the *need to belong* which they never realized they'd experience until they moved to the wild hills. And the fact that Nicholas Ellis was a quietly spoken, educated kind of fanatic.

'It's true to say,' a sprightly, elderly woman told HTV Wales, 'that until I attended one of Father Ellis's services I did not truly believe in God as a supernatural being. I did not have faith, just a kind of wishy-washy wishful thinking. Now I have more than faith, I have *belief*. I exult in it. I *exult*. I love God and I hate and despise the Adversary.'

For a moment, Merrily was grabbed by a sense of uncertainty that recalled her first experience of tongues in that marquee near Warwick. Whatever you thought about Ellis, he'd brought all these people to God.

Then she thought about his slim, metal crucifix.

Ellis himself was answering no questions tonight; gliding along, half in some other world, no expression on his unlined, shiny face. Self-belief was a great preserving agent.

Hanging back from the march, Merrily rang to check on Jane, walking slowly with the phone.

'It was on the radio,' the kid said. 'That Buckingham woman's probably dead, isn't she?'

'Not necessarily.'

'But if she is, you don't think she topped herself, do you?'

'That's something the police get to decide, flower.'

Jane made a contemptuous noise. 'The police won't do a thing. They don't have the resources. The only reason this area has the lowest level of crime in southern Britain is because half the crimes don't even get discovered, everybody knows that.'

'So cynical, so young.'

'I read the story in the *Mail*. Totally predictable right-wing stitch-up.'

'You reckon?'

'Yeah. Mum . . . Listen, the truth, OK? Have you spoken to Irene since we were in Worcester? Like, him telling you all about me conning him into taking me to *Livenight* by saying you knew all about us going and it would help his career. And then – like, in his role as a Welsh Chapel fundamentalist bigot – asking if you knew how seriously interested I was in alternative spirituality, and maybe that what I secretly wanted was to get to know some of those people – the pagans – and then you both agreeing that this was probably a spiteful teenage reaction against having a mother who was a priestess and into Christianity at the sexy end.'

The kid ran out of breath.

Merrily said, 'Was this before or after Eirion said to me, "Oh God, I'm so sorry, this is all my fault, what if she's got brain damage?" And I said, "No, it's all *my* fault, I should never have agreed to do the bloody stupid programme"? Was it *after* that?'

Jane said nothing.

'Look,' Merrily said, 'after the initial blinding shock of seeing you in the middle of the motorway, it didn't take a lot of creative mental energy to form what looked like a complete picture of how you and Eirion came to be in the neighbourhood of Birmingham anyway. Complete enough to satisfy me, anyway, without any kind of tedious, acrimonious inquest. I mean, you know, call me smug, call me self-deluded, but the fact is – when you really look at it – I'm actually not *that* much older than you, flower.'

Silence.

'Shit,' Jane said at last. 'OK, I'm sorry.'

'I know.'

'Er, might that have been the Long Talk, by any chance?'

'I think it might.'

'Phew. What time will you be back?'

'Hard to say.'

'Only, that nurse phoned.'

'Eileen?'

'Said whatever time you get back, could you ring her? She sounded weird.'

'Weird how?'

'Just not the usual "Don't piss me about or I'll take your bedpan back" voice. Kind of hesitant, unsure of herself.'

'I'll call her.'

'Yeah,' Jane said. 'Somehow, I would if I were you.'

When the procession reached the Prosser farm, Merrily saw two people emerge discreetly from a gate and join it without a word: Judith Prosser and a bulky, slab-faced man.

'That's Councillor Prosser, Gomer?'

'Impressive, en't he? Wait till you hears him talk. Gives whole new meanin' to the word orat'ry.'

'Not that you don't rate him or anything.'

'Prince among men,' said Gomer.

By the time the march reached the track to St Michael's Farm, a police car was crawling behind. That figured: even good Christians these days had short fuses. They walked slowly on.

'That reminded me,' Gomer said. 'Learned some'ing about the Prossers and this Ellis 'fore I left the Lion. Greg yeard it. One o' the boys – Stephen? – got pulled over in a nicked car in Kington. Joyridin', 'e was. 'Bout a year ago, this'd be. Woulder looked real bad for a magistrate's boy.'

'It happens.'

'Not yere it don't. First offence, mind, so Gareth talks to Big Weal, an' they fixes it with the cops. Gareth an' Judy promises the boy won't put a foot out o' line again. Just to make sure of it, they takes him to the Reverend Ellis, gets him hexorcized . . .'

Merrily stopped in the road. 'I'm not hearing this.'

The mobile bleeped in her pocket. She pulled it out, hearing Judith Prosser's words: *Time was when sinners would be dealt with by the Church, isn't it?*

'Merrily?'

'Sophie!' She hurried back along the lane to a quieter spot.

'Is this convenient? I tracked down a Canon Tommy Long, formerly the priest in charge of St Michael's, Cascob. He was more than glad to discuss something which he said had been puzzling him for many years. Shall I go on?'

'Please.'

'Seems that, in the late summer of 1965, he had a visit from the Reverend Mr Penney. A very odd young man, he said – long-haired, beatnik-type, and most irrational on this occasion – who suggested that, as Cascob was a remote place with no prospect of other than a slow and painful decline in its congregation, the Reverend Long might wish to seek its decommissioning by his diocese.'

'Bloody hell.'

'Once he realized this was far from a joke, the Reverend Long asked Mr Penney to explain himself. Mr Penney came out with what was described to me as a lot of nonsensical gobbledegook relating to the layout of churches around Radnor Forest.'

'St Michael churches?'

'In an effort to deflect it, the Reverend Tommy Long pointed out a folk tale implying that if one of the churches were destroyed it would allow the, ah, dragon to escape. Mr Penney said this was . . . quite the reverse.'

'Why?'

'Mr Long wasn't prepared, at the time, to hear him out and now rather wishes he had.'

'What happened then?'

'Nothing. Mr Long pointed out that the Church in Wales would hardly be likely to part with a building as historic and picturesque as Cascob, especially as it contains a memorial to William Jenkins Rees, who helped to revive the Welsh language in the nineteenth century. The Reverend Mr Penney went somewhat sullenly away and, some months later, committed his bizarre assault on St Michael's Old Hindwell.'

'When he went away, where did he go? Does Mr Long know?'

'There's no happy ending here, Merrily. Mr Long says he was told some years later that Terry Penney died in a hostel for the homeless in Edinburgh or Glasgow, he isn't sure which. The poor man had been a heroin addict for some time. I think I shall go home now, Merrily.'

Robin spotted some lights, but they were the wrong lights.

He saw them through the naked trees, through the bald hedgerow further along from the barn. They were not headlights.

George came to stand alongside him at the window.

'What do you want to do, Robin? Shall we all go out and have a few words with them – in a civilized fashion?'

Vivvie dumped her glass of red wine and came over, excited. 'Is it them?' She had on a long red velvet dress, kind of Tudor-looking, and she wore those seahorse earrings that Robin hated. The bitch was ready to appear on TV again. 'What I suggest is we—'

'What *I* suggest,' Robin said loudly, 'is *we* don't do a

goddamn thing. This is still my house . . . mine and . . . Betty's.'

The whole room had gone quiet, except for the damp twigs crackling in the hearth.

'*I'm* gonna go talk to them,' Robin said.

George smiled, shaking his head. 'You're not the man for this, Robin. You tend to speak before you've thought it out, if you don't mind me saying so.'

'I *do* mind, George. I mind like *hell* . . .'

'And you're tired,' Alexandra said kindly. 'You're tired and you're upset.'

'Yeah, well, damn freaking right I'm upset. I've been accused by that bastard of being a manifestation of insidious evil. How upset would *you* feel?'

'That's not what I meant.'

Robin backed up against the window, gripping the ledge behind him with both hands. 'So, I'm gonna go out there on my own.'

'That's really not wise,' Vivvie said, appealing to the coven at large.

Max cleared his throat. 'What I would suggest—'

'Don't you . . .' Robin threw himself into the room. 'Don't any of you tell me what's wise. And you . . .' He levelled a shaking finger at Vivvie. 'If it hadn't been for you and your goddamn big mouth—'

'Robin . . .' George took his arm, Robin shook him off.

Vivvie said, 'Robin, I'll thank you not to use the expression *God*-damned . . .'

'Shut the fuck *up!*'

Robin saw that it had begun to rain again. He saw the lights curling into rivulets on the window.

He took off his sweater.

*

The gate to St Michael's Farm was shut.

Through the bare trees you could see lights in the house, you could see the black hulk of what seemed to be a barn. But you could not see the church. The itinerant congregation formed a semicircle around Nicholas Ellis at the gate. The two men with garden torches stood either side of the gate.

A white wooden cross was raised – five or six feet long, like the one in the bungalow garden on the road from Walton.

Merrily felt an isolated plop of rain. Umbrellas went up: bright, striped golf umbrellas. A cameraman went down on one knee on a patch of grass, as if he'd found God, but it was only to find a low angle, to make Ellis look more like an Old Testament prophet.

Disgracefully, Ellis responded to it. A kind of shiver seemed to go through him, like invisible lightning, and his wide lips went back in a taut grimace.

'My friends, can you feel the *evil*? Can you feel the evil here in this place?' And then he was crying to the night sky. 'Oh Lord God, we pray for your help in eradicating this disease. You who sent Your most glorious warrior, Michael, to contain the dragon, the Adversary, the Old Enemy. Oh Lord, now that this infernal evil has once again returned, we pray that You will help us drive out these worshippers of the sun and the moon and the horned gods of darkness. Oh Lord, *help us*, we pray, *help us*!'

And the chant was taken up. 'Help us! *Help us, Lord!*' Faces were turned up to the rain.

Merrily winced.

Ellis cried, '. . . You who send Your blessed rain to wash away sin, let it penetrate and cleanse this bitter earth, this soured soil. Oh Lord, wash this place clean of Satan's stain!'

His voice rode the slanting rain, his hair pasted to his forehead, the hissing torchlight reflected in his eyes. *Until I attended one of Father Ellis's services I did not truly believe in God as a supernatural being.*

Now Ellis was spinning round in the mud, his white robe aswirl, and putting his weight against the gate and bellowing, 'Come out! Come out, you snivelling servants of the Adversary. Come out and face the sorrow and the wrath of the one true God.'

'Fuck's sake, Nick . . .'

Ellis sprang back.

The weary, American voice came from the other side of the gate. The TV camera lights found a slightly built young guy with long, shaggy hair. He wore a plain T-shirt as white as Ellis's robe, but a good deal less suited to the time of year. He was just standing there, arms by his side, getting soaked. When he spoke, the tremor in his voice indicated not so much that he was afraid but that he was freezing.

'Nick, we don't need this shit, OK? We never touched your lousy church. There's no dragon here, no Satan. So just . . . just, like, go back and tell your God we won't hold you or your crazy stuff against him.'

The man with the cross stood alongside Ellis, like a sentinel. One of the garden torches fizzed, flared and went out. There was a gasp from the crowd, as though the flame had been a casualty of demonic breath. To charismatics, everything was a sign. Merrily moved in close to the gate. She needed to hear this.

Ellis put on a grim smile for the cameras. 'Let us in, then, Robin. Open the gate of your own free will and let us – and Almighty God – be readmitted to the church of St Michael.'

He waited, his white habit aglow. 'Praise God!' a man's voice cried.

Robin Thorogood didn't move. 'I don't think so, Nick.'

He was watching Ellis through the driving rain – and fighting just to keep his eyes open. To Merrily, he looked bewildered, as if he was struggling to comprehend the motivation of this man who was now his enemy on a level he'd never before experienced. He finally hugged himself, bare-armed, his T-shirt soaked, grey and wrinkled, into his chest. Then, defiantly, he let his arms fall back to his sides, still staring at Nick Ellis, who was now addressing him sorrowfully and reasonably in a low voice which the TV people might not pick up through the splashing of the rain.

'Robin, you know that we cannot allow this to go on. Whether you understand it or not – and I believe you fully understand it – if you and your kind proceed to worship your profane, heathen deities in a temple once consecrated in His holy name, you commit an act of gross sacrilege. You thereby commend this church into the arms of Satan himself. And you curse the community into which you and your wife were innocently welcomed.'

'No.' Robin Thorogood shook his sodden hair. 'That is bullshit.'

'Robin, if you don't recognize it, I can't help you.'

The big cross was shaking in the air. One of the men screamed out. *'Thou shalt not suffer a witch to live!'*

Merrily tensed, expecting an invasion – when something struck Ellis in the chest.

THIRTY-FOUR

Kali

Jane agonized for a while, cuddling Ethel the cat, and then rang Eirion at what she always pictured as a grim, greystone mansion beyond Abergavenny. The line was engaged.

She went back to the sitting room, still holding the cat, and replayed the tape she had recorded of the Old Hindwell story on the TV news.

There was a shot of the church from across a river. The male voice-over commented, *'The last religious service at Old Hindwell Parish Church took place more than thirty years ago. Tomorrow night, however, this church could be back in business.'*

Cut to a shot of a dreary-looking street, backing onto hills and forestry.

'But the people of this remote village close to the border of England and Wales are far from happy. Because at tomorrow night's service, the ancient walls will echo to a different liturgy.'

Ancient black and white footage of naked witches around a fire, chanting, 'Eko, eko, azarak . . .'

'And to one local minister, this is the sound of Satan.'

Talking head (Eirion had taught her the jargon) of a really ordinary-looking priest, except that he was wearing a monk's habit. The caption read: 'Father Nicholas Ellis, Rector'.

This Nicholas Ellis then came out with all this bullshit about there being no such thing as white witchcraft. His voice was overlaid with pictures of candles burning in people's windows – *seriously* weird – and then they cut back to Ellis saying, 'It's out of our hands. It's in God's hands now. We shall do whatever he wants of us.'

Over shots of their farmhouse, the reporter said that Robin and Betty – Betty, Jesus, whoever heard of a witch called Betty? – were in hiding today, but 'a member of their coven' had confirmed that the witches' sabbath would definitely be going ahead tomorrow at the church, to celebrate the coming of the Celtic spring.

'The Diocese of Hereford says it broadly supports Father Ellis, but seems to be distancing itself from any extreme measures.'

Then up came Mum: 'Personally, I don't care too much for witch-hunts.'

On the whole, Jane felt deeply relieved.

She called Eirion again. This time it rang, and she prepared to crawl.

Eirion's stepmother, Gwennan, answered – a voice to match the house, or maybe it just sounded that way because she answered in Welsh. Jane almost expected her to hang up in disgust when she found it was someone who could only speak English, but the woman was actually quite pleasant in the end.

'He's in his room, on the Internet. Seventeen years old and still playing with the Internet, how sad is that? Hold on, I'll get him.'

'OK. I'm sorry,' Jane said when he came on. 'I am so totally sorry. Everything I said . . . I'm brain-damaged. I make wrong connections. I don't deserve to live.'

'I agree, but forget that. Listen . . .'

'Charming.'

'Are you online yet?'

'No, I keep telling you. Mum's got the Internet at the office in Hereford. If there's anything I need, I look it up there. Too much surfing damages your—'

'I was going to give you a web site to visit.' Eirion sounded different, preoccupied, like something was really getting to him. 'I'd like you to see it for yourself, then you'll know I'm not making it up.'

'Why would I think that?'

'I mean, the Web . . . sometimes it's like committing yourself into this great, massive asylum.'

'Irene . . .?'

'I was checking out pagan web sites, trying to find out what I could about Ned Bain and these other people, OK?'

'Why?'

'Because I'm off school and I got fed up with walking the grounds contemplating the infinite.'

'And where did it get you?'

'To be really honest, into places I didn't think existed. You start off on the pagan web sites, which are fairly innocent, or at least they *seem* innocent afterwards, compared with the serious occult sites you get referred to. It's like you're into a weeding-out process and after a while it's kind of, only totally depraved screwballs need apply, you know? Like, you can learn, among other things, how to effectively curse someone.'

'What's the address for that one? Let me grab a pen.'

'Jane,' he sounded serious, 'take my word for it, when you actually see it on the screen it suddenly becomes less amusing. It's like getting into some ancient library, where all the corridors stink of mould and mildew. All these arcane symbols.'

'Sounds like Dungeons and Dragons.'

'Only for real. You start thinking, Shit, suppose I pick up some . . . I don't know . . . virus. And periodically you get casually asked to tap in your email address or your name and your home address . . . or maybe just the town. And sometimes you almost do it automatically and then you think, Christ, they'll know where to *find* me . . .'

'Wimp.'

'No. Even if you put in a false name, they can trace you, and they can feed you viruses. So, anyway, I got deeper and deeper and eventually I reached a site called Kali Three.'

'You mean, like . . .'

'Like the Indian goddess of death and destruction. *That* Kali.' Eirion paused. 'And that was where I found her.'

Found her? For some reason, Jane started thinking about Barbara Buckingham. A shadow crossed the room and she sat up, startled.

It was Ethel. Only Ethel.

Jane said, 'Who?'

'Your mum,' Eirion said. 'Merrily Watkins, Deliverance Consultant to the Diocese of Hereford, UK.'

'Wha—'

'She came up on Kali Three pretty much immediately. There was a picture of her. Black and white – looked like a newspaper mugshot. And then inside there was kind of a potted biography. Date of birth. Details of the parish in Liverpool where she was curate. Date of her installation as priest-in-charge at Ledwardine, Herefordshire. Oh . . . and "daughter: Jane, date of birth . . ." '

'Picture?' Jane said bravely.

'No. But there's a picture of your dad.'

'*What?*'

'Another black and white. Bit fuzzy, like a blow-up from a group picture. Sean Barrow. Date of birth. Date of . . . death. And the place. I mean the exact place, the flyover, the nearest junction. And the circumstances. All of what Gerry said at *Livenight* and more. It says "Sean and Merrily were estranged at the time, which explains why she afterwards retained the title Mrs but switched back to her maiden name." It says that "She is" . . . hang on, the print goes a bit funny here . . . yeah, that "she is still vulnerable" . . .

353

something . . . "the death of her husband. Without which she might have found it harder to enter the Church." '

Jane exploded. 'Who *are* these bastards?'

'I don't know. There are several names, but I don't think they're real names. I think it'd take you a long time to find out who they are – if you ever could. They could be really heavy-duty occultists or they could just be students. That's the problem with the Net, you can't trust anything on there. A lot of it's lies.'

'But . . . why? What kind of . . .?'

'That's what scares me. There's a line at the bottom. It says, "The use of the word 'Deliverance' is the Church's latest attempt to sanitize exorcism. Having a woman in the role, particularly one who is fairly young and attractive, is an attempt to mask what remains a regime of metaphysical oppression. This woman should be regarded as an enemy.'

Jane felt herself going pale. 'Mum?'

'And there are all these curious symbols around the bottom, like runes or something – I've no idea what a rune looks like. But it – this is the worrying bit – it points out that "Anyone with an interest can see Merrily Watkins on the *Livenight* television programme", and it gives the date, and it says that the programme will be coming live from a new Midlands studio complex, just off the M5. So that's out of date now, but it must have been there before the pro-gramme took place, obviously. And it says that if anyone is interested in further information, they can get it from . . . and then there's a sequence of numbers and squiggles which I can't make any sense of, but I don't think it's another web site, more like a code, so . . . Jane?'

'Yeah.' A whisper.

'I'm sorry. I didn't want you to hear it like this, because I could be making it up, couldn't I? To support the stuff you were rubbishing this morning.'

'Irene . . . what am I going to do?'

'I don't know. What happened . . . happened to other people. It's not even a good coincidence. I mean, who believes in any of this crap?'

'*You* do.'

'I don't know whether I do or not. And anyway, I'm just a fundamentalist Welsh Chapel bigot.'

'Were there any other people mentioned on this web site, apart from Mum?'

'Probably. I didn't look, to be honest. What if there'd turned out to be a whole bunch of names and biographies of people and they were all recently dead or . . .? Shit, that's how it's supposed to work, isn't it? Preying on your mind?'

'Like, suppose there was this big hex thing and people . . . all over the country . . . the world . . . were being invited to, like, tune in and focus on Mum, the enemy, to put her off. Because, we both know how rubbish she was on that programme. I mean, she was fine on TV tonight, wasn't she? Kind of cool, almost. Suppose it wasn't just nerves that night. Suppose there were hundreds – thousands – of people sending her hate vibes or something. And then they all started focusing on that piece of road, where Dad . . . It's *horrible*!'

'It's also complete crap, Jane. We're just stretching things to fit the facts. We're playing right into their hands.'

'*Whose* hands?'

'Anybody who frequents the web site – including, presumably, Ned Bain, if he was the one putting it round about your mum. That doesn't mean he's behind any of it. It just tells us where he got his information.'

'It's still creepy.'

'It's meant to be creepy.'

'Can you tell when it was originally pasted on the site?'

'Somebody else might be able to, but not me. For all I know, somebody could have pushed it out *after* the show, to make it look . . . I don't know. It's all crap, and it makes me mad.'

'Irene, I'm going to have to tell her.'

'I think you should. I'll try and find out some more.'

'You're wonderful,' Jane said. *Whoops*. 'Er . . . how's the whiplash?'

'Well, it just kind of hurts when I look over my shoulder.'

Jane instinctively looked over hers and shivered, and it wasn't an exciting frisson kind of shiver. Not now.

THIRTY-FIVE

This is History

'A martyr?' The rain had eased. Merrily pushed back the dripping hood of her saturated, once-waxed jacket. 'With his chest all splattered. Perhaps that was what he wanted.'

When the police had gone in, she'd walked away from it all. Her first instinct had been to stay on Robin Thorogood's side of the fence, maybe go and talk to him, but now the cops were doing that. Journalists and cameramen were together in another group by the gate at St Michael's Farm, waiting for someone to emerge.

Ellis had been driven away in a white Transit van, the cross and the torches packed away in the back. His followers watched the white van's tail lights disappear along the end of the track, talking quietly in groups. There was an air of damp anticlimax.

'For just one moment,' Merrily said to Gomer, 'I thought—'

'Coppers thought that, too. Out o' their car in a flash.'

'It looked like blood.'

'Shit does, in a bad light.'

'It really was?'

'Sheepshit, or dogshit more like, stuck on a bloody great lump o' soil. He din't smell too fragrant then. Likely the real reason he's buggered off so quick.'

'Whoever threw it . . . that wasn't a great idea. Thorogood was winning their argument.'

'Young kiddie, it was. 'E had it on the end of a spade. Seen him come up behind the boy in the T-shirt.'

'Still look good in the press, though,' Merrily said glumly. 'On their pictures he *will* look like a martyr. I . . .' She glanced over the gate to where two police were still talking to Thorogood.

'Look out, vicar,' Gomer murmured.

Judith Prosser was heading over, without her Gareth. She wore a shiny new Barbour, a matching wide-brimmed hat.

'They've found Barbara's car, then, Mrs Watkins.' She spotted Gomer. 'Ah . . . I see you have your *informant* with you.'

''Ow're you, Judy?'

'Gomer. I heard your wife died. I'm sorry.'

'Things 'appens,' Gomer said gruffly. He shook his head, droplets spinning from his cap.

Judith nodded. 'So what about Barbara, Mrs Watkins? She down there, in Claerwen Reservoir, is it?'

'Well, I don't *know* those reservoirs, Mrs Prosser. But I think if Barbara's body was in there, they'd have found it by now. I reckon the answer to that mystery's much more likely to be found here.'

'Do you indeed?'

'Don't you?'

'You like a mystery, do you?'

'How's Marianne?' Merrily said.

'Mrs Starkey is quite well' – wary now – 'I assume.'

'Those lustful demons can be difficult to extract.'

The caution was suddenly discarded as Judith laughed. 'Don't you believe all you hear.'

'Like what?'

'All kinds of nonsense gets talked about, Mrs Watkins. Be

silly for you to start passing on rumours, isn't it? I certainly haven't heard anything to upset me.'

She smiled; she had good teeth.

'In that case, you must have a strong constitution, Mrs Prosser,' Merrily said.

Left to himself, Robin would have kicked the kid's ass.

Hermes, nine years old, brother of Artemis, twelve, and of Ceres, six and a half.

Max and Bella did not kick Hermes's ass. They were not the ass-kicking kind. They would, presumably, explain to him later, in some detail, what effect having tossed shit at the Christian priest might have on him karmically.

No hassle from the cops for Hermes, either. Soon as they found out this was a kid, and that they didn't get to lean on a grown pagan, they didn't hang around. Soon as the cops had gone, the media went off too, back to the Black Lion. None of them came to the house.

Robin peeled off his sodden T-shirt, towelled himself dry, stood in front of the cheery fire with a bath towel around his shoulders.

'They'll be back tomorrow night,' George said with a good lashing of relish, 'when we're in the church. And this time there'll be hundreds of them. It's going to get really, really interesting, man.'

Robin said, 'Did she call?'

'Betty? Er, no.'

'That car's old, Robin,' Vivvie said. 'Maybe it's just broken down.'

'I listened to the weather forecast,' George said. 'The rain's likely to have passed by morning. It'll get colder, but tomorrow looks like being dry, so we'll have all day to prepare the site.'

Robin shivered under the towel. 'You guys don't get it,

do you? This is not gonna happen without Betty. If Betty doesn't come back . . . no Imbolc.'

'You're tired, man,' George said.

'She *will* come back,' Vivvie promised with intensity. 'She won't want to miss this.' Her eyes glowed. 'Imbolc . . . the glimmering of spring. This really is the start of an era. This is history. Like Max was saying while you were outside, it's going to be the biggest thing since the Reformation. But whereas that was just Henry VIII plundering the riches of the Catholic Church, this is about the disintegration and decay of pride and vanity . . . and the regrowth of something pure and organic in the ruins. This is so beautifully symbolic, I want to cry.'

'Well, I'll tell you,' Robin said. 'I'm starting not to give a shit.'

'You don't mean that. You did a terrific job tonight.'

'I most likely looked a complete asshole. I just wasn't gonna cringe in front of that creep in his monk's robes, was all. I was gonna look as white as he was.'

And maybe less pretentious. He wasn't gonna go out there swinging a gold pentacle. He'd wanted to handle the confrontation with simple human dignity. Because what he'd really hoped for was that Betty would be out there watching – that she'd gotten home OK, but had been unable to come through the gate on account of the march, so was out there watching her *tactless, thoughtless, irresponsible* husband handling a difficult situation with some kind of basic human dignity.

And then fucking Hermes had blown it all away.

If you were looking for omens, you sure had one there. What kind of headlines were they gonna get tomorrow? 'Witches Hurl Shit at Man of God'. The perfect follow-through to Robin looking like a freaking cannibal that last time.

'Robin . . .' The motherly Alexandra smiled a tentatively radiant candlelight smile at him across the room.

'Sorry?'

'Robin, there's a small car just come into the yard.'

'Huh . . .?'

He shot to the window, the bath towel dropping to the flags. He shaded his eyes with his cupped hands, up against the glass, hardly daring to hope that he'd see . . .

A little white Subaru Justy.

Oh God. Oh God. Robin sagged over the big, wide window sill, staring down between his hands and working on his breathing until he no longer felt faint with relief.

He straightened up. 'Look, would you mind all staying here? I have to do some explaining.'

The Black Lion was packed, the air in the bar full of damp and steam, coming off journalists, TV people, even a few of the Christian marchers – all wet through, starved, in need of a stiff whisky. Greg was run off his feet. No sign of Marianne yet.

Gomer fetched Merrily a single malt and one for himself. There was nowhere to sit except in a tight corner by the window next to the main door. Whenever the door opened, they had to lean to one side, but at least they weren't overheard as Merrily told Gomer the plain truth about Marianne's exorcism.

Gomer didn't blink. He weighed it up, nodding slowly. He laid out a row of beer mats on the table – and, with them, Merrily's dilemma.

'Gotter be a problem for you, this, girl. Question of which side you're on now, ennit?'

'Yes.' Merrily lit a cigarette. She'd taken off her wet coat, but still had the scarf wound round her neck. She was still seeing Robin Thorogood there on his own, vastly outnumbered, not wearing anything witchy, not countering Ellis's talk of Satan and sacrilege with any pagan propaganda. It could have been an act, to appear ordinary in the face of all the cross-waving – and yet it was *too* ordinary to be feigned.

'What you gonner do, then, vicar?'

'Gomer, how could Judith Prosser and those other women sit there and watch it? Can they really believe in him to that extent?'

Gomer took out a roll-up. 'Like I said, it's about stickin' together, solid. Ellis's helped the right people, ennit? Judy and Gareth with their boy. And who knows what else he done.'

'Oh my God.'

'Vicar?'

Merrily drank the rest of her whisky in a gulp.

'Menna,' she murmured. *'Menna . . .'*

Robin turned on the bulkhead lamp. It was no longer raining, but the wind had gotten up. A metal door creaked rhythmically over in the barn; it sounded like a sailing boat on the sea making him wish he and Betty were alone together, far out on some distant ocean.

Still naked to the waist, he stood on the doorstep and watched her park next to one of the Winnebagos. She stepped out of the car and into a puddle. The whole of the yard was puddles tonight.

She didn't seem to care how wet her feet got. Her hair was frizzed out by the rain, uncombed.

Oh God, how he loved this woman. He tried to send this out to her. *I take thee to my hand, my heart and my spirit at the setting of the sun and the rising of the stars . . .*

He saw her standing for a moment, entirely still, taking in the extra cars in the yard, the two Winnebagos.

Then she saw him.

He came out of the doorway, walked towards her. She still didn't move. If it was cold out here, he wasn't feeling it yet.

'Bets, I . . .'

He stopped a couple of yards from his wife. The back of his neck felt on fire.

'Bets, I couldn't stop them. It was either them or . . . or all kinds of people we didn't know. It had all gotten out. You just couldn't imagine . . . It was all over the Internet. We were getting hate faxes and also faxes from people who were right behind us – like, religious polarization, you know, over the whole nation? Or so . . . so it seemed.'

Betty spoke at last, in this real flat voice.

'Who are they?'

'Well, there . . . there's George and Vivvie, and . . . and Alexandra. And Stuart and Mona Osman, who we met at some . . . at some sabbat, someplace. And Max and Bella . . . Uh, Max is kind of an all-knowing asshole, but they're OK where it matters. I guess. And some other people. Bets, I'm sorry. If you'd only called . . .'

There was no expression at all on her face; this was what scared him. Why didn't she just lose her temper, call him a stupid dickhead, get this over?

'See, we always said there was gonna be a sabbat at Imbolc. Didn't we say that? That we were gonna bring the church alive with lights? A big bonfire to welcome the spring? So like . . . maybe this was destined to come about. Maybe there was nothing we could do to get in the way of it. Like it's meant to be – only with more significance than we could ever have imagined.'

Why did this all sound so hollow? Why was she taking a step back, away from him?

There was a splish in a puddle. Her car keys? She'd

dropped the car keys. Robin rushed forward, plunged his hand and half his arm into the puddle, scrabbling about in the black, freezing water, babbling on still.

'Look . . . Ellis was here, with his born-again buddies. Chances are they're gonna be back tomorrow – only more of them. There was like this real heavy sense of menace. You and me, we couldn't've handled that on our own, believe me.'

He hated himself for this blatant lie, but what could he say? He pulled out the dripping keys, hung on to them.

Betty said, 'Give me the keys, Robin.'

'Why? *No!*'

'I can't stay here tonight.'

'Please . . . you don't know . . . Bets, it's gotten bigger than us two. OK, that's a cliché, but it's true. What's happening here's gonna be . . .'

'Symbolic,' a voice said from behind him. He turned and saw Vivvie on the step. Vivvie had come out to help him. Vivvie alone.

The worst thing that could've happened.

'Symbolic of the whole struggle to free this country from two millennia of religious corruption and spiritual stagnation. He's right, Betty. We have to play our part. We have to reconsecrate the church and it has to be tomorrow night. It's why we're here.'

Betty started to shake her head, and the light from the bulkhead caught one side of her face and Robin saw the dark smudges, saw she'd been crying hard.

'Bets!' He almost screamed. 'Look, I know things haven't been right. I know you never connected with this place. Honey, please . . . once this is over we'll sell up, yeah? I mean, like, Jeez, from what I've been hearing there's gotta be about a hundred pagans ready to take it off our hands. But this . . .

Imbolc . . . this is something we have to go through – together, yeah? Please let it be together.'

'Give me those keys.'

'I will not let you leave!'

'You will not stop me,' Betty said. 'And *she* certainly won't.'

She turned away, walked across the yard toward the track.

Robin ran after her, managed four paces before the cold, suddenly intense, bit into his chest and his breathing seemed to seize up. But that was nothing to the pain right dead centre of his heart chakra.

His eyes flooded up.

'Don't follow me,' Betty said. 'I mean it, don't take one more pace.'

THIRTY-SIX

The Atheist

'You're back home?' Eileen Cullen's relief was apparent, even over hospital corridor echo and clattering trays.

Merrily switched on the engine, turned the heater up all the way and shook a cigarette into her lap. 'I'm in my car on a pub car park in Old Hindwell, and wet and cold.'

'You're still *out* there? Oh hey, one of the porters saw you on the box tonight, said he fancied the hell out of you. Listen, you've heard about Buckingham? The car in the reservoir?'

'It doesn't mean she's dead, Eileen.'

'It's scary, Merrily. Civilized woman like that, if she wanted to do away with herself, why not a bottle of Scotch and a handful of pills?'

'I still can't believe she has.'

'Aye, well, sometimes you . . .' Cullen hesitated. 'Sometimes there's things you just don't want to believe, no matter what. What are the alternatives, after all? It's suicide, face it. And don't you go feeling guilty. There's nothing you could've done.'

'How can you say that?'

'Because, Reverend, that's the official motto of the National Health Service. Listen, will you be in town tomorrow?'

'Probably not tomorrow.'

'I need to talk to you.'

'Are we not talking now?'

'What I want to talk about, you don't on the phone. Well you don't at all if you've got any sense. I could come and see you . . . at your home.'

'Eileen?' Jane was right; Cullen, hard as a hospital potato, had never sounded less assured.

'Truth is . . . I've not been frank with you, Merrily – or with meself, come to that. There's things I ought to've said.' She dropped her voice to just above a whisper. 'About the night Menna Weal died. And I can't talk here, I'm on the public phone.'

'You've got an office, haven't you?'

'It's open house in there, so it is. Anyway, I *won't* talk in this place, and I don't get off now until the morning. You've got my home number, so call me when you can.'

'Eileen, don't . . . do *not* hang up. Let's just talk about Menna, OK? The stroke could have been brought on by stress, right? Severe emotional stress?'

'Hypertension due to emotional trauma. Distended arteries, then a clot gets shunted into the brain. What kind of trauma you thinking about?'

'Exorcism,' Merrily said.

'Oh, terrific,' Cullen said drably.

'The expulsion of an evil entity. *Intended* expulsion.'

'I know what it *is*, I was raised a Catholic. But, excuse me, Reverend, would not someone in your job be seeing it everywhere you bloody look?'

'Just . . . bear with me, OK? You get some ministers – of an evangelical or charismatic persuasion – who believe that demonic forces . . . and angelic forces, come to that . . . are all around us in all kinds of guises. Like there are probably a few in California who'd offer to exorcize me in order to expel the demon nicotine.'

'You mean eejits.'

'So here's poor Menna – withdrawn, maladjusted maybe, communication problems. OK, I won't go into details, but there's good reason to think she was abused by her dad.'

'Is that a fact,' said Cullen, who'd heard it all many times before.

'Probably over a long period. But not necessarily when she was a kid.'

'So you could be talking about more of an unnatural *relationship*.'

'If she was as naive and immature as I've been told, I think we're still talking about abuse.'

Merrily lit another cigarette and gathered her thoughts, staring out along the village street. From here, she could count candles in nine separate windows. The street lighting was so meagre and widely spaced that some of the candles seemed disproportionately bright through the rain-blobbed windscreen and unintentionally jolly, like Christmas lights.

She just wanted to air this stuff, to another woman.

'I don't want to speculate too much about the state of the Weal marriage . . . but it seems likely the obsessive love there was fairly one-sided. And Weal must have realized that – that the father was still very much in the background, even though dead.'

'You mean Weal's thinking he might be having a happier time altogether if he can remove whatever emotional block's been left behind in Menna by her having a sex beast for a father.'

'I doubt the concept of happiness means much to him, but yeah . . . And he wouldn't have her seeing a psychiatrist or a therapist because that's not the kind of thing you're seen to do in Old Hindwell. So, after a lot of agonizing and soul-searching, perhaps, he goes to the priest.'

'Who you say's not your regular kind of priest, yeah?'

'Mmm. At the funeral, Ellis disclosed that Weal and

Menna were baptized *together*, not long before she died. I think *that* means she was exorcized. Historically, baptism's always been linked with exorcism. In the medieval Church, it was more or less believed that until it was baptized, a baby was the property of the Devil and if it died before baptism it would be consigned to the fires of hell.'

'No offence to you, personally,' Cullen said, 'but how I hate the Church.'

'So, suppose Weal believed that having Menna rebaptized into the faith would free her from the influence of her father . . . from the effects of her childhood. And suppose the ceremony – conducted in the privacy of their home – involved . . . well, something considerably more stressful than a sprinkling of holy water. And I *mean* more stressful.'

'Then, sure, you *could* be into stroke country.'

'That's what I thought.'

'And . . .' Cullen hesitated, 'as you've mentioned baptism, the anointing of the forehead with water, if we cast our minds back to a certain wee side ward . . .'

'Mmm.'

'I always thought any anointing of a corpse was down to the priest.'

'Me, too.'

Long silence.

'Possession is nine points of the law,' Merrily said. 'That was what Barbara Buckingham said.'

'Possession?' Cullen said.

'Possession of the dead by the living, was how she put it, ostensibly meaning the private tomb. But I think there were other things she wasn't prepared to put into words, maybe even to herself.'

'Ah, Merrily . . .'

'Pretty much like you, really. Why don't you just tell me the rest?'

Cullen said, 'This is a pressure job, you know? You get overtired, so you do.'

'And imagine things.'

'That's true.'

'Like?'

'Like things you don't believe in.'

'Did something happen when you went down to the morgue?'

Cullen sighed. 'Maybe.'

'He went along with you – which is not usual.'

'Not only that, he sent the porters away. He asked could he spend some time with her, say his goodbyes.'

'How long?'

'A clear hour. To cut a long story short, they sent for me, in the end, to exercise my fabled diplomacy on the man. When I get down there, I'm delighted to see he's finally leaving. Has on his hat and coat, a big dark solicitor's overcoat, like he's on his way to court. I didn't approach him, but I thought it was as well to follow him, to make quite sure he left the premises. So I did that. I followed him.'

Cullen broke off. There was the sound of someone calling from a distance, then Cullen said, 'Two minutes, Josie, all right?'

'Bloody hell,' Merrily said, 'don't stop now.'

'Ach, normal way of things you wouldn't get this out of me with thumbscrews. All right. Weal goes out by one of the back doors near the consultants' car park. You can get across the yard there to the temporary visitors' car park. It's the quickest way, if you don't mind there being no lights. Which I wish to God there had've been, then I could've said it was a reflection.'

Merrily revved the engine to blow more heat into the Volvo.

'I could still say it was,' Cullen said defiantly. 'I can say any damn thing I want to, as I'm an atheist. I do not believe in God, I do not believe in angels or demons.'

'And you don't believe what you saw. A lot of people say that. That's OK.'

'Feel free to be patronizing, Reverend. I've woken up about seven times in the night since then. Gets into me fockin' dreams, the way you get a virus in your computer. And everything freezes on you.'

'I know.'

'Oh, *you* know everything, so you do!'

'I'm sorry.'

'I'm standing in the doorway, just the other side of the big plastic doors, and I'm watching him walk across to the visitors' car park, which is all but empty now. Nobody about but him and this . . . Jesus.'

Merrily's eyes turned this way and that, determinedly counting nine candles in nine windows, banishing all wildly flickering thoughts of the old rectory garden, while Cullen kept her waiting.

Until, at last, over the sound of footsteps in the hospital corridor and a woman squealing, she whispered, 'Just a hovering thing, you know? Like a light. Not a bright light . . . more kind of greyish, half there and half not. That's as best as I can tell you. You could see it and then you couldn't. But you knew . . . you bloody *knew*. I went very cold, Merrily. *Very* cold, you know?'

'Mmm.'

'And him . . . Oh, he knew it was there, all right. I swear to God he knew it was there. Twice, he looked back over his shoulder. I . . . Aw, hell, I can't believe I'm saying this out loud. It made me go cold, you know?'

'I *do* know,' Merrily said.

THIRTY-SEVEN

Night Hag

Gomer was standing up at the bar with Greg Starkey, talking to him between other customers buying drinks. Greg glanced at Merrily through bloodshot eyes, trying to keep his voice muted, not succeeding.

'I'm on eggshells, trying to run a boozer, while she's up inna bedroom, sitting on the edge of the bed, staring into space. If I put a hand on her it's like I've hit her, you know? Like she got no skin? That's what it does to them, is it? A blessing?'

A *blessing*? 'How much did she tell you about it?' Merrily asked.

'Not a lot. I fought it was all gonna be "Praise the Lord" and that. I was geared up for that. Woulda been better than the battered wife routine. Who's that bastard fink he is?'

'Thinks he's St Michael,' Merrily said soberly. 'Greg, do you think she'd talk to *me*?'

'I just told Gomer I'll put it to her. Soon's I get a minute, which could be closing time. How long you got?'

'As long as it takes.'

'I'll do what I can. *Yes*, sir . . . Carlsberg, is that?'

Merrily beckoned Gomer back to the cold place nobody else wanted, near the door. She told him what she'd discussed with Eileen Cullen, about the reasons they figured J.W. Weal might have wanted Menna cleansed.

Gomer said shrewdly, 'You reckon Barbara Thomas knew?'

'About the baptism? It's possible, isn't it?'

The steamy light pooled in Gomer's glasses. 'Likely what Barbara Thomas found out got her killed then, ennit?'

'Good God, Gomer!'

Gomer sniffed. 'Reckoned I'd say it 'fore you did. Mind your back, vicar.'

A young woman had come in alone. She stood on the mat, shaking back wild, corn-coloured hair that somehow looked not only out of place in Old Hindwell, but out of season. She drew a breath, scanned the crowd in the bar and then walked through.

'Until there's a body,' Merrily said, 'she hasn't been killed. Until there's a body she isn't dead.'

'Who you got lined up for it, then? Big Weal hisself?'

'Shhhh!'

Gomer looked around, unconcerned. 'He en't yere.'

'OK,' Merrily whispered, 'considered objectively, it seems ridiculous. I mean, if Barbara found out Weal arranged to have his wife exorcized by Ellis, as some kind of primitive pyschological therapy . . . well, he might not want that out in the open, but it's only slightly dirty washing. And it *is* Christianity, of a sort. It's no reason to kill somebody. And would he really expect to get away with it in a place like this?'

Gomer threw up his hands. 'Place like *this?* Nowhere bloody easier, vicar! Local people protects local people. Might keep any number o' secrets from each other, but if they gets a threat from Off, they'll close in real tight till it's over and gone. They thought J.W. Weal *had* done it, they'd be happy to shovel shit over his tracks, ennit?'

'The other thing that struck me,' Merrily said, 'is that the doctor who kept prescribing all that oestrogen that sent Menna's blood pressure up . . .'

'Dr Coll, eh? Now *there's* a respected man.'

'If Menna did develop dangerously high blood pressure, furred arteries, serious danger of fatal clotting, why didn't he warn her? Why wasn't he monitoring her? If she was on the Pill for . . . I don't know, twenty years or more . . .'

Gomer said, 'What you wanner do is you wanner talk to Judy. Proper, though. None o' this circlin' round each other. Talk to her straight.'

'Tonight?'

'As well as Mrs Starkey? Busy ole night you got lined up there.'

'OK, tomorrow.' She pulled out her cigarettes and then put them back. 'I don't know why I'm doing this. Why am I doing this, Gomer?'

'Because . . . 'ang about.' Gomer turned towards the bar. Merrily saw Greg Starkey frantically beckoning them over. 'I think the boy wants you,' Gomer said.

Greg opened the solid wooden gate in one side of the bar, to allow Merrily and Gomer through.

'Just walks in like noffink's happened, asks for a room for the night. Well, I've only got two rooms, ain' I, and they've both gone to reporters. I can't turn her away, but what if the wife comes out, nursing her Bible, and finds the bleedin' spawn of Satan under a blanket on the settee?'

'Gomer,' Merrily said, 'just don't call me vicar in front of her, OK?'

Greg led them into the well-fitted kitchen with the tomato-red Aga. A woman stood next to it, gripping the chromium guard rail, as though she was on the deck of a small boat in a gale.

The night hag.

Couldn't be more than late twenties. Pleated skirt, dark sweater, ski jacket, all that blond hair.

'This is my friend,' Greg said, 'wiv the accommodation. Merrily Watkins.'

Merrily watched the young woman's eyes. No recognition at all. Clearly not a *Livenight* viewer, not even that particularly relevant edition.

'*OK,*' she'd said to Greg, in a snap decision, '*just tell her I'm someone with a big house who does B and B sometimes.*'

B and B? Sanctuary? What a vicarage was for.

Good Samaritan. The good Samaritan, who went to the aid of someone from a different culture, a different ethos.

'It's only for one night,' Betty Thorogood was saying. 'Probably.'

'And this is Gomer Parry,' Greg said.

''Ow're you?' Gomer flashed the wild-man grin.

Gotter be a problem for you, this, girl. Question of which side you're on now, ennit?

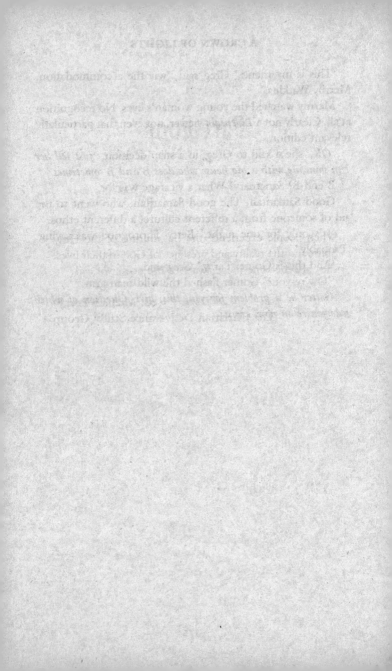

Part Four

When people experience the outpouring of the Holy Spirit and the reality and presence of God in their lives, they also become more aware of the power of evil.

Deliverance (ed. Michael Perry)
The Christian Deliverance Study Group

THIRTY-EIGHT

The Real Thing

Merrily flashed her headlights twice and then pulled out to the end of the car park and waited for the young woman to come over.

'Funny how things turns out, ennit?' Gomer said mildly, from the back seat.

'You think this is a terrible mistake?'

'Bit late to worry 'bout that, vicar.'

The blonde came warily out of the short alley leading to the Black Lion's yard, and got into the Volvo. Merrily eased the car into the main street, glancing into her wing mirror; nobody was following them.

'Just put my mind at rest,' Betty Thorogood said. 'You're really *not* from the media, are you?'

'I'm really not.' Merrily felt deeply uneasy about this now but, at the same time, curiously elated. She drove carefully along the village street, past all the little candles glowing brightly. 'Actually, Betty, it's much worse than that.'

She was getting uncomfortable, anyway, driving with the scarf on.

Jane had called Eirion back. 'I'm getting obsessed about this. The more you think about it, the more things occur to you.'

'Then stop thinking about it. Go to bed.'

'I'd just lie awake, getting spooked. I keep thinking how

keen they were to get Mum on that programme, all those calls from Tania. Why *would* they go to all that trouble for just one person who's not very controversial.'

'Nice legs, nice face – tabloid television?'

'But they told Bain about her – or somebody did – well beforehand. So they'd have plenty of time to prime Kali Three.'

'I doubt anyone at *Livenight*'s even heard of Kali: the web site *or* the goddess. When you're putting a programme together you must make all kinds of deals to get people to come on. I don't really think we're looking at any kind of big conspiracy – it's just the way things turned out. However . . .'

'What?'

'Just I hit on another site. It's called Witchfinder. It's for people who want to contact a coven. Wherever you are in Britain, it'll put you in touch with your nearest group: email addresses mainly.'

'Any around here?'

'Loads . . . well, two. But that's not the point. From Witchfinder, I clicked on another site, which was a kind of pagan *Who's Who?*'

'The *Which Witch* guide?'

'Very good, for somebody with brain damage.'

'It's *because* of the brain damage. Normally I'm serious and pedantic.'

'I got it to search for Ned Bain. Turned up a surprising amount. I assume it's true, but anybody can put anything on the Net.'

'Unflattering stuff?'

'Not particularly. Biographical stuff, mainly. He's a writer and publisher, now in charge of Dolmen Books, the New Age imprint at Harvey-Calder. Been married twice, high priest of top people's coven in Chelsea. A champagne pagan, that's what he gets called.'

'Sham-pagan?'

'I wouldn't say that, since he's been into it a long time – since he was at university and possibly before. But what's really significant is that we suddenly have an explanation of why he hates the Church so much.'

'He never *said* that,' Jane said crossly. 'He insisted his lot were an alternative to Christianity. He didn't say anything about—'

'Well, it's pretty obvious, when you read about his background. His father was an academic – a professor of English literature at Oxford, and also a fairly acclaimed poet, though I've never heard of him. Edward Bainbridge?'

'Bain*bridge*?'

'That's also Ned's real name. His father died back in the mid-seventies. He was . . . I wish you could see this stuff. I don't want you to think I'm jumping to the wrong conclusions.'

'Just tell me.'

'It's just that his father was stabbed to death.'

Jane gripped the phone. 'Ned Bain's father was *murdered*?'

'It's complicated.'

'Spill it. No, hang on a sec.' She pulled the phone from her ear. Sound of a car in the drive. 'Mum's here. I'll call you back – if not tonight, first thing tomorrow.'

'I'll go back online,' Eirion said. 'See what else I can discover before midnight.'

'Anorak.'

'Don't lie there getting spooked, Jane. Think of me, think of my strong body.'

'In your dreams, Welshman.'

The headlights exposed Ethel trickling across the lawn – a black cat, witch-friendly, crossing the beam of the sensor which then activated the lantern on the porch, spraying light up the 400-year-old black and white facade of Ledwardine vicarage.

Merrily switched off the engine. How would Nicholas Ellis react if he could see her giving sanctuary to the spawn of Satan, a child of the dragon, a worshipper of profane, heathen deities . . . filth, scum, spiritual vermin. How, come to that, would the bishop react? *'The pagans'll have you down as a jackboot fascist, while Ellis is calling you a pinko hippy doing the tango with Satan.'*

The elation was long over. Merrily's head was choked with contradictions. The twenty-five-minute journey through deserted country lanes had been, at best, awkward, their conversation sparse and stilted. It was evident that there was far more wrong in the life of Betty Thorogood than Nicholas Ellis and the *Daily Mail*, but very little had come out. What was she supposed to say to this woman: *'Trust me, I'm a priest'*?

Gomer, sensing the tension, opened his side door. 'How 'bout you gives me your key, vicar? I could put the ole kettle on, and explain a few things to young Jane first, if she's still up.'

'Brilliant.' Gomer could be uncannily perceptive.

They watched him let himself into the vicarage. When he opened the door, a light came on in the hall.

'I promise I won't be sick as I walk in,' Betty Thorogood said drily.

Merrily leaned her head on the back of her seat. 'Is it that obvious?'

'I can tell you're having second thoughts.'

'Being psychic.'

'I'm not psychic that way.'

At the first sight of the dog collar, Betty Thorogood had not screamed or hurled herself at the passenger door. This was not a Hammer film. This was not *Livenight*.

'I'm sorry,' Merrily said. 'It was a stupid remark.'

'Aye, well. Nearly as stupid as mine about being sick.' Something – tiredness, probably – had brought out a Northern accent. Yorkshire? 'Look, I realize what you did was a spur-of-the-moment thing. You couldn't have known I'd walk into that pub.'

Merrily said, 'What actually brought you there?'

'Couldn't go back home.' Mirthless laugh. 'Place was full of witches.'

The porch light went out. Merrily could no longer see Betty's face.

'Also,' Betty said tonelessly into the darkness, 'I'd just been virtually accused of murder.'

Despite *Livenight*, Jane still always thought of *them* as dark-haired, dark-complexioned. Celtic. But this was an English rose, and a wild rose at that. She had a subdued energy about her. Or maybe that was just a subjective thing, because, thanks to Gomer, Jane *knew*.

Wow!

'This is Betty,' Mum had said casually. 'She's staying the night. This is my daughter, Jane. Brew some tea, flower. We'll be down in a few minutes.'

Under normal circumstances, this would have been an ultra-cool moment, a significant chapter in the liberalization of the Anglican Church.

But the chances that the Thorogood woman was *not* involved with Ned Bain were pretty remote. Pagans stuck together, so clearly Mum could have invited in more than she knew.

'We keep a room *fairly* ready,' she was saying. 'It's not very grand, but the bedding should be aired.'

'Anything, please,' Betty Thorogood said.

Jane forgot about the tea, followed them upstairs. The

blonde, it had to be admitted, did not *look* like a threat. Instead she looked done in. By now, most people who'd never been here before would be commenting on the atmosphere and the obvious antiquity of the place – the twisting black beams, the bulging walls, the tilted ceilings. This woman might have been climbing the stairwell of a concrete apartment block.

Mum said, 'If you need a change of clothes I'm sure we can sort something out. I'm a bit on the stunted side, but Jane's got a lot of stuff from the days when you were supposed to buy everything a couple of sizes too big.'

The self-styled witch and Mum were standing on the landing, near the second staircase leading to Jane's apartment. 'Bathroom's that one.' Mum indicated the one door that was slightly ajar. 'It's bleak and cold and horrible, but one day, when we get the money . . .' She broke off.

From six stairs down, Jane witnessed this clearly. Betty Thorogood quivered for just an instant before tossing back her mass of hair and, almost absently, shaking out a word.

'Apples?'

Mum froze; Jane saw her eyes grow watchful.

Mum said, 'I'm sorry?' As though she hadn't heard, which of course she had.

She and Jane both had. And they knew what it meant. For a moment, the air up here seemed almost too thick to breathe.

'I'm sorry,' Betty said. 'I just . . . you know . . . Sorry.'

Jane marched up four steps. 'You had a feeling of apples?'

Mum frowned. 'Jane . . .'

'What kind of apples?'

'I . . .' Betty shook her head again, as if to clear it, her hair tumbling. 'I suppose not apples as much as blossom. White, like soft snow.'

'Oh, wow,' Jane breathed.

'I'm sorry,' Betty said. 'It just came out.'

Mum bit her lip.

Jane said, 'And we thought Wil had *gone* . . .'

Mum started flinging lights on. 'Betty, if you want to just check out your room . . .'

Betty Thorogood nodded and followed her.

She wasn't getting away that easily.

'Wil was our ghost,' Jane called after them. 'Wil Williams, vicar of this parish. Found dead in the orchard behind the church in 1670. Hanging from an apple tree – when the blossom was out.'

'I'm sorry,' Betty Thorogood said again. 'It's a problem I have.'

'Wow,' Jane said, in serious awe. Nobody knew about the apple blossom. Not even Kali Three. 'You're the real thing, aren't you?'

THIRTY-NINE

Witches Don't Cry

The kid brought them tea at the kitchen table and then started filling the kitchen with the seductive scent of toast. It was ten thirty. As far as Jane was concerned, Betty Thorogood had proved herself.

Merrily had stopped agonizing about this stuff. Where sensitives were concerned, seeking the cold, earthly, rational explanation could be wastefully time-consuming. Life was too short to question it too hard; it just *was*. It would have been less impressive in Betty's case if she hadn't, in other respects, appeared defeated, demoralized, broken. As though she'd looked into her own future and seen black water.

'Is Wil still here?' demanded Jane, galvanized – knowing nothing about the death of the elderly woman, Mrs Wilshire. 'I mean as a spirit, not just an imprint?'

'I don't know,' Betty said. 'Sometimes it's hard to qualify what I feel. I just get images sometimes. Fragments, incomplete messages.'

The apple blossom. Last year, when they'd first moved in, Merrily had been sensing an old distress locked into the upper storeys of the vicarage, the timeless dementia of trapped emotions. Jane, under the influence of Miss Lucy Devenish, folklorist and mystic, claimed to have actually smelled the blossom, felt it on her face like warm snow.

It was this undismissable haunting and the Church's

general disinterest which had prodded Merrily in the general direction of Deliverance. There needed to be someone around to reassure people that they weren't necessarily losing their minds.

Jane was saying, 'Were you like sensitive *before* you became a witch?'

Betty looked uncomfortable. 'It's why I became one. If you exclude spiritualism, Wicca's one of the few refuges for people who are . . . that way. My parents are C of E, which doesn't encourage that kind of thing.'

An apologetic glance at Merrily, who also caught a triumphant glance from Jane, little cow, before she went greedily back into the interrogation. 'But, like, who do you actually *worship*?'

'That's probably the wrong word. We recognize the male and female principles, and they can take several forms. Most of it comes down to fertility, in the widest sense – we don't need more people in the world, but we do need expanded consciousness.'

'And you, like, draw down the moon?' The kid showing off her knowledge of witch jargon. 'Invoke the goddess into yourself?'

'Kind of.'

Betty was reticent, solemn in the subdued light of the big, cream-walled kitchen. Maybe having a vicar in the same room was an inhibiting factor, but this woman was certainly not *Livenight* material. Merrily sat down at the table and listened as Betty, pressured by Jane, began explaining how she'd actually got into Wicca at teacher training college, before dropping out to work for a herbalist. How she'd saved up to go with a friend to an international pagan conference in New England, where she met the American, Robin Thorogood, making a film with some old art school friends. So Robin had found Betty first, and *then* Wicca, in that order. Betty's face momentarily shone at the memory. Her green eyes were clear as rock pools: she must literally have bewitched Robin Thorogood.

The phone rang. Jane dropped the cheese grater and carried the cordless into a corner.

'You have a disciple,' Merrily said softly.

'Kids only find Wicca exotic because it's forbidden. When it becomes a regular part of religious education they'll find it just as boring as . . . anything else.'

'Don't feel you have to talk it down on my account.'

'Merrily' – Betty pushed back her hair – 'there doesn't need to be conflict. There's actually a lot of common ground. Spiritual people of any kind have more in common than they do with total non-believers. In the end we want the same things, most of us. Don't we?'

'Maybe.'

Jane said loudly, 'No, I'm sorry, she's not here. I was kind of expecting her back, but in her job you can't count on anything. Sometimes she spends, like, whole nights battling with crazed demonic entities and then she comes home and sleeps for two days. It's like she's in a coma – really disturbing. Sure, no problem. Bye.'

'Flower,' Merrily said, 'you do realize that little exercise in whimsy might be lost in the transition to cold print.'

'In the *Independent*?'

Merrily nodded. 'So just don't say it to the *Daily Star*.'

She went over to switch on the answering machine. When she came back Betty was saying, 'In Shrewsbury, we were members of a coven containing quite a few . . . pagan activists, I suppose you'd have to call them. Teachers, mainly. They're good people in their way, but they'd be more use on the council. They're looking for organized religion, for structure.'

'These are the people who've moved in on your house?' Merrily asked her.

'Some of them. It's what I wanted to come down here and get away from. You don't *have* to work in a coven. The only structures I'm really interested in now are the ones you build for yourself. But Robin will go along with anybody, I'm afraid.'

'Why don't you phone him?'

'I will. I just don't want to speak to any of the others. We came down here to work alone. At least, I did. Robin just wanted to live somewhere inspiring and to show it off to his friends. He'd tell you we were sent here because of a series of omens. All that was irrelevant to me.'

Interesting. What was slowly becoming apparent to Merrily was that Betty had come to Old Hindwell in a state of personal spiritual crisis. She'd been drawn into witchcraft by the need to understand the psychic experiences she'd been having from an early age. But maybe paganism hadn't come up with the answers she'd sought.

'Omens?' Merrily brought out her cigarettes. To Jane's evident disgust, Betty accepted one.

'Estate agent particulars arriving out of the blue, that kind of thing. When Robin saw the church, he was hooked. Just like Major Wilshire.'

'Tell me about *Mrs* Wilshire again,' Merrily said.

The police had questioned Betty for almost an hour at Mrs Wilshire's bungalow. A detective constable had arrived who probably had never had a suspicious death to himself before.

'I'd no idea she suffered angina,' Betty had told them. 'I just concocted something harmless for her arthritis.'

No, she could not imagine why Mrs Wilshire would stop taking the Trinitrin tablets prescribed for her angina, a full, unopened bottle of which had been discovered by Dr Banks-

Morgan. No, she would never in a million years have advised Mrs Wilshire to stop taking them. She had only suggested a possible winding-down of the steroids if and when the herbal remedy had any appreciable effects on the arthritis.

'She told me Dr Coll knew all about me, and he was very much in favour of complementary medicines for some complaints.'

'You know that's not true, Mrs Thorogood,' the CID man had said. 'Dr Banks-Morgan says he has no respect at all for alternative medicines and he makes this clear to all his patients.'

It got worse. If Mrs Wilshire was not becoming unduly influenced by Mrs Thorogood and her witch-remedies, why would she tell Dr Banks-Morgan she needn't bother coming to visit her again?

Betty could not believe for one minute that Mrs Wilshire had told her caring, caring GP not to come back. But she knew which of them was going to be believed.

'What a bastard,' Jane said. 'He's trying to fit you up.'

'Where did they leave things?' Merrily said. 'The police, I mean.'

'They said they might be in touch again.'

'They probably won't be. There's nothing they can prove.'

Betty said, 'Do you believe me?'

'Course we do,' Jane said.

'Merrily?'

'From what little I know of Dr Coll, I wouldn't trust him too far. Gomer?'

Gomer thought about it. 'Smarmy little bugger, Dr Coll. Always persuading folk to 'ave tests and things for their own good, like, but it's just so's he can pick up cash from the big drug companies – that's what Greta reckons.'

'Then I'll tell you the rest,' Betty said.

And she told them about Mrs Juliet Pottinger and what she'd said about the Hindwell Trust.

'En't never yeard of it,' Gomer said when she'd finished.

Merrily didn't find that too surprising if the trust was administered by J.W. Weal.

'Lot of incomers is retired folk,' Gomer confirmed. 'Like young Greg says, they comes out yere in the summer, thinks how nice it all looks and they're amazed at how low house prices is, compared to where they comes from. So they sells up, buys a crappy ole cottage, moves out yere, gets ill . . .'

'Fair game?'

'Like poor bloody hand-reared pheasants,' Gomer said.

Merrily asked Betty, 'Is it your feeling Mrs Wilshire's left money to the Hindwell Trust?'

Betty nodded.

'This stinks,' Merrily said.

'Works both ways, see,' said Gomer. 'Patient needs their will sortin', mabbe some poor ole biddy goin' a bit soft in the head, and Dr Coll recommends a good lawyer, local man, trust him with your life. Big Weal turns up, you're some little ole lady, you en't gonner argue too much. 'Sides which, it's easy for a lawyer to tamper with a will, ennit? Get the doctor to witness it. All local people, eh?'

Betty explained why she'd gone to see Mrs Pottinger in the first place. Talking about that particular atmosphere she'd perceived in the old church, but hesitating before finally describing the image of a stricken and desperate man in what might have been a stained cassock.

'Wow,' said Jane.

Merrily tried not to react too obviously, but she was becoming increasingly interested in the Reverend Terence Penney. 'What year was this, again?'

'Sixty-five,' Betty said. 'He seems to have been turning into a hippy.'

Gomer looked up. 'Loads o' hippies round yere, late sixties. You could get an ole cottage, no electric, for a few 'undred, back then, see, and nobody asked no questions. More drugs in Radnor them days than you'd find the whole o' Birmingham.'

'But you never actually ran into Penney yourself?' Merrily lit another cigarette.

'No, but I been thinkin' of Danny Thomas. That boy knew all the hippies, see. Most locals they didn't have nothin' to do with 'em, but Danny, 'e was right in there. Up in court for growin' cannabis, the whole bit. You want me to get Danny on the phone?'

'It's a bit late,' Merrily suggested.

'Boy don't keep normal farmin' hours,' Gomer said.

Danny Thomas had now turned down the music. In Danny's barn there were speaker cabinets the size of wardrobes, all covered with chicken shit. Gomer also recalled an intercom on the wall. Bawling down it at Danny when he was wanted on the phone was how most folk reckoned Greta's voice had reached air-raid siren level.

It must be cold tonight out in Danny's barn, but Danny would jump around a lot to the music before collapsing into the hay with a joint. Gomer pictured him sitting on a bale, straggly grey hair down the back of his donkey jacket, with Jimi at his feet – Mid-Wales's only deaf sheepdog.

Gomer sat on the edge of the vicar's desk and waited while Greta had summoned Danny back to the farmhouse.

'What's goin' down, Gomer, my man? You become a private eye, is it? Every bugger I meet these days, they just been grilled by Gomer Parry.'

'All right, listen to me, boy,' Gomer said. 'Give your

ole drug-raddled memory a rattle on the subject of Terry Penney.'

A few seconds of quiet. Bit of a rarity around Danny unless he'd had a puff or two.

'Poor bugger,' he says at last.

'Come to a sad end, what I yeard.'

'I liked ole Terry.'

'You go to 'is church?'

'Din't like him *that* much. But he was all right. He lent me his Dylan albums.'

'When?'

'Sixty-four, sixty-five. This to do with that bugger Ellis? Tricky bastard, he is. Blew poor ole Gret's mind. Gets 'em all in a bloody trance.'

'Why'd he do it, Danny? Why'd Penney fill up the ole brook with good pews?'

'Dope, ennit?'

'Ar, well, that's what they all says. Don't mean bugger all.'

Danny went quiet again.

'What you know about Penney, Danny? What you know about Penney you en't sayin'?'

'Long while back, Gomer. Terry's dead. Let the poor bugger lie.'

'Can't.'

'It's that vicar o' yours, ennit? Diggin' the dirt.'

'We needs to know, boy.'

'Gimme a day or so to think about it.'

'Can't. C'mon, Danny, who's it gonner harm?'

'Me.' Danny's voice went thin. 'I'm as guilty as any bugger, Gomer. It was me got Terry into it. Well . . . me and Coll.'

'Dr Coll?'

'*Me* and Dr Coll,' Danny says. 'And the bloody sixties

that promised us the earth. And here we all are nigh on forty year later and further in the shit.'

'Stay there,' Gomer said. 'Don't move.'

When Betty Thorogood started to cry, it turned everything around.

Until now, talking about a world she knew, she'd been cool and assured. The otherworldly – visions and gods and archetypes – did not scare her, any more than neuroses scared a psychologist. In the everyday world, implicated in the death of a harmless widow, Betty came apart.

'I just wanted to help her. I was *sorry* for her . . . that's all there was to it.'

Jane had moved her chair back, appalled. Witches don't cry! Merrily leaned across the table, put a hand over Betty's.

Betty parted her hair, peered at Merrily through her tears. 'What if their tests show up something nasty in that potion I gave her? Something I didn't put there.'

'What are they going to find? Henbane? Deadly nightshade? Rat poison? He doesn't need all that. He's got natural causes, apparently hastened by her overreliance on you.'

'I just don't understand why she would stop taking the pills he'd prescribed. She thought he was wonderful. She thought . . .' Betty's eyes filled up again. 'She thought *everyone* was wonderful. Everyone who tried to help her. The local people were *so good*. Because she was from Off, anyone local who didn't actually spit on her front step seemed wonderful and caring. I was so sorry for her. And dying there, in her chair, in front of that lukewarm fire . . . Perhaps he *is* telling the truth. Perhaps poor, fuddled Mrs Wilshire thought my little herbal remedy, bottled under the moon, was some sort of cure-all.'

'There's an experienced nurse I know,' Merrily said. 'Perhaps I'll give her a call.'

She stopped as Gomer returned. His glasses shone like twin torch-bulbs.

'Come and talk to Danny, vicar.'

FORTY

Key to the Kingdom

As Danny talked, the picture formed for Merrily in ragged, fluttering colours. Radnor Forest in the 1960s: hippy paradise.

The flower children had wandered in from Off and settled in this border country in their hundreds because it was cheap and remote. They rented or even bought half-ruined cottages far from the roads. Thin boys in yellow trousers chopping wood from the hedges. Beautiful, long-haired girls in ankle-length medieval dresses fetching water from the well.

In spite of the electricity supply being at best intermittent, they brought the new music – why, The Incredible String Band even lived for a while near Llandegley towards the north-western end of the Forest.

And the dope. The hippies also brought the dope.

The local people were amused rather than hostile – the hippies didn't do any damage and they were always a talking point.

And for some – like Danny Thomas, dreamy, faraway farmer's boy – this was what they'd been waiting for all their lives. When it was really happening Danny was good and ready; he figured he must've been born a hippy – growing up on Elvis, then the Beatles, popping purple hearts to groove all night and still be awake in time to milk the cows.

Merrily smiled.

And then cannabis. Danny had acquired his first joint at a dance in Llandod in 1963, with another to smoke in the top field after sunset. He did a bit of dealing for a while, but he was never much good at that and, besides, there was a much more reliable dealer emerging in the area. Better just to grow the stuff – nice, sheltered spot, in Bryncot Dingle – and then give it away. Danny was so excited by the dawning of this incredible new world that, by the summer of 1965, he was wanting to turn on the whole Forest.

'Who was this "more reliable dealer"?' Merrily asked. 'Can I take a guess?'

Danny was talking freely now, his voice hoarse but liquid, like wet ash. Dr Coll had been the son of a surgeon at Hereford Hospital with a house in New Radnor. Still a medical student back then, in need of a few quid, like all your students. 'Medical students always got their sources, ennit?' Danny said.

'He was a hippy, too?'

'Lord, no. Dr Coll en't never been a hippy, not even as a boy. Just a feller with a eye to a few quid. Course when he qualified as a doctor, that all come to an end. Gotter keep 'is nose clean. Or at least keep it *lookin'* clean.'

And there would have been better ways of making money by then, Merrily thought. 'What about Terry Penney? When did he appear?' From what Betty had learned from Mrs Pottinger and from what Sophie had passed on to Merrily, Penney had emerged as a bright boy, but impressionable, and not too well-off. But what Danny was saying produced a different picture: Terry was an upper-middle-class radical with a posh, wealthy girlfriend who everyone thought was his wife, until she found life in Radnor seriously lacking and went back to the Smoke, leaving the vicar of Old Hindwell to grow his hair and smoke dope with the likes of Danny Thomas.

Terry, like Danny, was finding the sixties life-enhancing and life-changing. But Terry also saw it from a religious perspective: drugs opening the doors of perception, the gates of the soul. Terry was a fan of the seventeenth-century poet, Thomas Traherne, who had found secrets of the universe in Herefordshire meadows.

The dope had certainly elevated and coloured Terry's faith in God. Today, perhaps he'd be all happy-clappy and singing-in-tongues, like Ellis, and perhaps the drugs would have represented a passing phase. But it was a never-ending inner journey, then. Terry and Danny, untroubled by the law, would smoke dope supplied at very reasonable rates by young Dr Coll, and Danny discovered that he loved the whole world and Terry loved the world and God. Terry believed that the time was coming when all mankind would be herbally awakened to the splendour of the Lord.

Then Dr Coll brought the acid along.

'What you gotter remember,' Danny said, 'is that this was before the Beatles was admitting to doin' drugs. En't nobody hardly'd yeard of LSD, 'specially in Radnorshire.'

Merrily nodded. Acid had been something different. Not just another drug, but the key to serious religious experience, a direct line to God. To Aldous Huxley, Timothy Leary, all those guys, LSD was the light on the road to Damascus, and anyone could get there.

So, one fine, warm day in the summer of 1965, Terry Penney and Danny Thomas and Dr Coll had found a shady corner of a Radnor Valley field, overlooking the Four Stones. They had their lumps of sugar and Dr Coll brought out the lysergic acid. An experiment, he said. He wouldn't take any himself; he'd supervise, make sure they came to no harm.

Danny's trip lasted for ever. Under the perfumed, satin sky, he went through whole lifetimes in one afternoon. He found that the Radnor Valley was in his blood . . . *really in his blood* – the whole landscape turning to liquid and jetting through his veins. When he looked at the inside of his wrist he could see through the skin and into that fast-flowing land. He *was* the land, he was the valley, he was the forest. He walked through the silken grass down to the Four Stones, which he now understood to hold the mind of the valley, and Dr Coll said afterwards he had to stop Danny beating his head on the prehistoric stones to get inside them because the stones knew the secret.

The Reverend Penney, meanwhile, came to believe he'd been granted access to the very kingdom of heaven.

He saw an angel, a giant angel with his feet astride the valley. Merrily imagined a great William Blake angel with the red sun in his wings and a raised sword which cleaved the hills.

Life was never going to be the same again for either Terry or Danny. Danny was still tripping when he got home to the farm and he walked down the yard and saw the depth of sorrow in the eyes of the beautiful pigs and realized how much he loved those pigs. To this day, Danny Thomas said, he wouldn't see a pig ever killed.

He and Terry took four more trips together. Terry told Danny that he knew now that he had seen the Archangel Michael, who had been appointed to guard the forest and the Radnor Valley, because this was a great doorway through which you could enter the kingdom. Terry found a book by the Reverend Parry-Jones who'd been vicar at Llanfihangel Rhydithon back in the 1920s and he too thought the Forest was special, but he also mentioned a dragon that you could hear breathing in the night, and Terry said this was no surprise because places of great spiritual power were equally attractive to devilish forces.

Terry considered it no accident that he had been brought here, now, at this time of spiritual awakening, to be the priest of one of St Michael's churches. He had told Danny he was going to call a meeting of all the other St Michael clergy around the Forest because they were destined to work together. But this never happened, because the other ministers had all heard about Terry Penney.

Still Terry insisted he was being groomed by God for the Big Task. Every day, before dawn, he'd kneel before his altar in Old Hindwell Church and beg God and St Michael that his mission might be revealed to him.

But God held out on him.

Terry decided he was not yet worthy, did not yet know enough, was not yet pure enough. He stopped smoking cannabis and concentrated on reading the Book of Revelation a hundred times. He wrote out important verses from it on sheets of white card and hung them around his room at the old rectory. His sermons became impenetrably apocalyptic. He began to research St Michael and the lives of those saints and mystics who had become obsessed by the warrior archangel. He made solemn pilgrimages to all the St Michael churches around Radnor Forest . . . approaching each from the direction of the last, walking the final mile barefoot after a day's fasting.

'Local people was startin' to go off him in a big way,' Danny said. 'Local people don't like it when their vicar gets talked about in other parishes.'

Terry Penney had walked barefoot across the bridge to the church of St Michael, Cefnllys – an awesome setting, where an entire medieval town had been laid out under its castle. Then Terry had hiked unshod across the bleak Penybont Common to Llanfihangel Rhydithon. Next, he'd come down from the Forest to the yews encircling the rebuilt roadside church at Llanfihangel nant Melan. And finally he'd tramped on calloused feet along the sombre, narrow road to Cascob, where he'd stood before the old *Abracadabra* charm.

It was three weeks after this that Terry had that visit from Councillor Prosser, wondering why he hadn't applied for a grant towards the upkeep of the old building.

Two weeks later, Terry trashed the church.

What had happened, Danny said, was that one night Terry came to the conclusion that God wanted him to go alone into St Michael's, Old Hindwell, and open himself to revelation.

In fact, drop some acid.

Danny had obtained the LSD for Terry from Dr Coll. The price had gone up by then, acid being in demand, but Terry didn't care. In fact, the idea of the priest taking a trip in his own parish church bothered Danny more than Terry.

'This would be about the time,' Merrily said, 'that Timothy Leary first promoted acid as a religious experience.' She'd once done a paper on that at college.

'A great religious man, vicar,' concurred Danny. 'Studied the use of peyote in the ole American Indian churches.'

'What about the Old Hindwell Church experiment?' she probed.

'Well,' said Danny. 'For starters, he wouldn't 'ave nobody with him. Dr Coll was back home at the time, but Terry wouldn't 'ave him to supervise – nor me. Had to be just him an' God, see. Terry reckoned nothin' bad was gonner happen to him in the house of God. But me, I wouldn't've gone in there alone at night in a million year, with or without drugs – creepy ole place like that.'

'Bad trip?'

'Had a bad one meself, few months later,' Danny said. 'Kept gettin' flashbacks for bloody weeks. Scared the shit out o' me. Anyway, the next time I seen Terry, the boy was a mess. Hadn't shaved, din't smell too good. Smelt of *fear*, you know?'

'Yes.'

'*I* don't know what 'appened to Terry Penney that night. I just sits in yere, hammering buggery out o' the ole Les Paul and I remembers the good times.'

'You must have asked him about it?'

'Terry din't wanner talk about it at all, vicar. Kept 'isself to 'isself. And then they finds bits o' church floatin' down the brook, and Terry's gone. I used to wonder whether the boy seen the carvings on the wood screen come alive, or whether he seen . . . I dunno . . .'

'The dragon?' Merrily said.

'He seen St Michael out in that field. Mabbe 'e seen the dragon in 'is own church?'

Merrily recalled the William Blake print in Nick Ellis's war room. *The Great Red Dragon and the Woman Clothed with the Sun* – relating to an image from Revelation about the dragon waiting for the woman to give birth so that it could devour the child. The dragon was said to have seven heads and ten horns. It was not a nice dragon, and Blake's painting throbbed with a transcendent evil.

'I don't know how much of this Ellis knows,' Merrily said, telling them as they sat around the kitchen table, 'but it would account for a lot. If he believes Penney had a black vision of the dragon inside that church – Satan rising, or in his view paganism rising – and if we believe what he told me about being the subject of some kind of hate campaign, forecasting a return of the dragon . . .'

Poison-pen letters for months. And phone calls – cackling voices in the night. Recently had a jagged scratch removed from my car bonnet. Series of chevrons . . . like a dragon's back.

'. . . then, to him, Betty, you and Robin are the embodiment of something that already exists in those ruins on a metaphysical level.'

'It's not true, though,' Betty said. 'We didn't know any-thing about Penney. We didn't even know for certain that the church had been built on an ancient site until we'd bought it.'

'How do you know that now?'

'Well, after we learned about all the prehistoric archae-ology in the area, it seemed like it was on the cards. Also – this probably won't cut much ice with you – a friend of ours went round with a dowsing rod and pendulum.'

'Jane, do we have an Ordnance Survey map handy?'

'Brilliant!' Jane leapt up.

Mr Penney came out with what was described to me as a lot of nonsensical gobbledegook relating to the layout of churches around Radnor Forest.

Betty said that Robin had tried to work out a pattern on the map, but they had been aware of only three St Michael churches at the time.

'OK.' Jane had returned with the map, spread it out on the table. 'You'll have to help me out here, Gomer. Where's Cascob?'

Gomer found it after a bit of peering. He also found St Michael's, Cefnllys, then Llanfihangel Rhydithon and Llan-fihangel nant Melan. Jane encircled them – along with Old Hindwell (ruins of).

'Five now.' Jane drew a ring round the last one. 'And they do go right around the Forest.'

Betty was silently contemplating the map. 'It's too big, this,' she said at last. You wouldn't have anything smaller scale?'

'Only a road map.' Jane bounced up again. 'I'll get it.'

'And some paper?' Betty said.

Neither Cascob nor Cefnllys was marked on the road map, but she put circles on the approximate spots, and pushed the map and the paper and a pencil towards Betty.

Betty copied the pattern onto the paper. 'It's not perfect, but it's there.'

'It's a five-pointed star,' Merrily said. 'A pentagram.' She looked at Betty. 'Can you explain?'

Betty swallowed. 'Could I have another cigarette?'

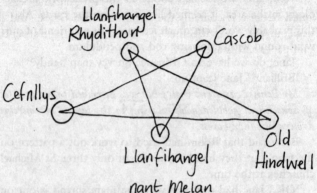

Merrily lit it for her. Betty was now looking uncertain, perhaps worried.

'If these churches were built to form not a circle but a five-pointed star, that would represent a defensive thing, OK? The pentagram's a powerful protective symbol. It's used in banishing rituals. Like if you're faced with . . . an evil entity . . . and you draw a big pentagram in the air, it ought to go away. So the medieval Christians might have wanted to enclose Radnor Forest in a giant pentagram of St Michael churches for the purpose of containing the dragon. Or whatever the dragon represented for *them*.'

'It's hardly a perfect pentagram,' Merrily pointed out. 'It could be purely coincidental.'

But then, she thought, in Ellis's ministry, nothing is coincidental.

'There's another connection here,' Betty said, 'with Cascob. The word "abracadabra" is used in a charm – an exorcism – which was found buried in the churchyard. The word "abracadabra" has become devalued because of all those stage conjurors using it, but it's actually very, very old and very powerful, and it's believed to represent the pentagram because it contains the letter "A" five times. And if you put the "A"s together . . .' Betty pulled Jane's pencil and paper across and drew:

'Cool,' Jane said.

'Actually, it's not,' Betty said soberly. 'The defensive, white magic pentagram has the point at the top. What you've just found on the map is an *inverted* pentagram.' She put down the pencil and looked at Merrily. 'I don't think I need to explain what that means.'

'No.' Merrily pulled out a cigarette. 'Probably not.'

Jane looked mystified. 'You mean it's like an aggressive thing?'

Betty said, 'It tended to be used in black magic. See the horns? Even pagans accept that horns are not *invariably* a good sign. Look . . . I went to Cascob the other day. That exorcism's displayed on the wall, in a frame. It dates back to about 1700, and was used to purge a woman called Elizabeth Loyd of evil spirits and alleged assaults of the Devil. I . . . got a bad feeling from it.'

'In what way?'

Betty looked embarrassed.

'You mean the exorcism itself?'

'I don't know. My first thought was that Elizabeth Loyd was just some poor epileptic or schizophrenic girl who somebody decided must be possessed. Then I . . . got the feeling that maybe she did have something . . . satanic . . . inside her. I don't know. The wording was a mixture of Roman Catholic and pagan and cabbalistic references.'

'Oh?'

'A combination of religion and magic, therefore. I suppose what really scared me was that the words were so very similar to the ones used in a charm that was found in a box concealed in an old fireplace at our house. And that one was dated over a century later. Nothing had changed.'

Nothing had changed.

Nothing changes. Merrily tried to focus. There was something very important here.

'*You* found this charm?'

'No, it was delivered to us. The box was placed on our doorstep just after we moved in. It spooked us quite a bit, because it was a charm against witchcraft. It seemed to be saying, "We know what you are and we know how to deal with you." There was a note with it, signed "The Local People".'

'Nasty,' Jane murmured.

'The wording of this exorcism,' Merrily said, 'do you remember how it went?'

'It invoked God and the Trinity. It said it would deliver Elizabeth Loyd from all witchcraft and spirits and hardness of heart. It had Roman Catholic stuff, kind of Ave Maria, and it used these cabbalistic names of power – Tetragrammaton, the mighty name of God.'

'Did it really?'

'That means something?'

'I don't know. OK, something else . . . Cascob. Apparently, Penney approached the then vicar or rector of Cascob and suggested he get his church decommissioned. He talked about the St Michael churches around Radnor Forest. The vicar reminded him of a folk tale implying that if one of those churches were destroyed it would allow the *dragon* to escape.'

'Right.'

'Penney said it was . . . quite the *reverse*.'

'Wow,' Jane said, 'like the reverse pentagram. I don't get it.'

'Nor me.' Merrily stared at the irregular star of churches. 'Whether the churches were intended to be a circle and just happened to fall into this rather vague star shape . . . or whether it's all complete coincidence. And, when you think about it, if you turn the map upside down, it's not inverted any more, is it?'

'*Wrong!*' Jane cried. 'Because pagans always work to the north, right, Betty? Their altars are *north-facing*. The two prongs, the horns, are pointing north.'

Merrily nodded, with reluctance. 'Yeah, OK. I think it's at least fair to say that Penney became convinced this was bad news. If his LSD experience – and in those days, the early Leary days, the feeling was that this wasn't just another drug – if his experience convinced him that the unfortunate layout of the churches invited the old serpent to slither in . . . then that would explain why he was so determined to destroy the pattern by taking out one of the churches.'

'I wonder how much of this Ellis knows?' Betty said.

Possibly quite a lot, Merrily thought. She was considering the distinctly medieval aspects of Ellis's unnecessary exorcism of Marianne Starkey.

She dreamed, through most of that night it seemed, in colour.

Deep velvet purples and wild, slashing yellows. Abstract images, and then the church at Old Hindwell, vibrating blue against a pink evening sky. White-clad Ellis and his followers walking like pilgrims through the woods with their Bibles and bottles of holy water to exorcize the pagan place by night. Betty, in a robe of pale mauve.

Jesus Christ screaming on the cross.

Fire sizzling. Yellow fire in the kindling. The robe shrivelled and blackened. Betty's golden hair alight.

At the foot of the cross, Marianne Starkey in a torn white nightdress, blood-flecked.

Out of a dream full of savage heat, Merrily awoke into the cold. The sizzling became the metallic rattle of night hail on the bedroom window. Merrily wrapped herself in the too-thin duvet and prayed for the blue and the gold, but they wouldn't come.

FORTY-ONE

The Kindling in the Forest

It was dawn.

Max led Robin out, through his own house, through the mingled aromas of incense and marijuana, out through the kitchen, past the Rayburn on which sat the remains of a pot of fragrant stew tended last night by Alexandra, past sleeping people in sleeping bags.

Robin, as if sleepwalking, his mind disconnected.

He followed Max across the cold yard, in between the oily pools, past the barn, five cars as well as the Winnebagos parked in front of it now, including the Subaru Justy. There was an intermittent sleet.

'I thought it was meant to be cold and sharp and fine.'

'Give it time,' said Max.

In fact, the sky was not so dark: there was a curdled-milk moon under thin cloud and a pale, muddy glow in the east. It was February, and the blackest night of Celtic winter was supposed to be over.

The fuck it was over. Robin stared, for the first time with resentment, at the church: big and bare. The tower was lamp black. The sky in the north and west was burnt umber.

Robin had spent the night in his studio, but had hardly slept. He hadn't shaved for two days. He didn't want to be here any more, not without Betty. Without Betty there could be no light.

A short while ago, he'd been aroused from a miserable doze by a tapping on the door, and there was big, beardy, flutey-voiced Max, and he said, 'Oh, Robin, I'm sorry to disturb you so early, but we have to discuss tonight.'

'Max, how many ways can I say this? If there was *no* tonight, I would not be awfully gutted.'

Max was nodding solemnly, the asshole. 'I understand. I do understand, Robin. I would give anything to have Betty back, but if she has a problem with all this, it's perhaps as well she stays away, and she probably knows that.'

'Oh, that's what you think, is it?'

Betty had to be someplace close. She couldn't have gone far, unless she'd called for a cab. And then where? Back to Shrewsbury? Back to her parents in Yorkshire, who'd barely spoken to her since she gave up her career for the Craft? Maybe she was staying with the widow Wilshire.

He'd thought she would at least've phoned. He'd had the phone and the answering machine in his studio all night, but all he heard were good wishes from supporters he didn't know, threats from enemies he didn't know, offers from media people – even one call from some private TV production company suggesting the Thorogoods might like to discuss the possibility of a docusoap series about the day-to-day lives of witches. What did these guys think their average day was like, for Chrissakes – they had breakfast in their ceremonial robes, went down to the shops hand in hand, skyclad, then sang 'The Witches' Rune' together in the tub before having tantric sex in front of an open fire?

Max was bleating on, '... *would* have been a problem with numbers but, as usually happens when something is meant, it's been solved.'

'Solved?' Robin said vaguely.

'I want you to come and meet someone.'

A Tilley lamp stood on one of the old tombstones in what had been the chancel, about where the Christian altar was originally located. Presumably the Reverend Penney had hurled the altar in the creek with the rest of the stuff – or had he baulked at that?

When Max and Robin walked into the nave, George Webster was saying to someone, 'Yeah, I see your point. The problem is, this whole building, being Christian, is oriented on the east. We can either go with that or we can just pretend the building isn't here at all and work with the site geophysically. You know what I mean?'

'So which do *you* think, George?' A man's voice, smooth. 'You're the geomancer.'

'I think there's got to be a compromise somewhere.'

'No,' the man said firmly. 'Oh no, no compromise. We either use their altar and change the current, or we build our own to the north and work, as you say, with the site'

'Ah . . . Ned.' Max sounded like a hesitant owl. 'I've brought Robin Thorogood.'

Ned Bain, pagan publisher, king-witch in all but title, came out into the lamplight. Robin had never seen him before. His face looked white in the gaseous Tilley light, but it was strong and lean and kind of genial. His hair was tight and curly. He had on a dark suit with a dark shirt underneath, kind of priesty – like *church* priesty.

'Hi.' He gripped Robin's arm.

'Hello.'

'I do like your name. It evokes Robin Goodfellow, the hobgoblin. Is it your given name?'

'Sure.'

'Someone's prescience? And I very much like your work.'

411

'Well, uh . . . thanks.' Despite the temperature, Robin's arm felt warm all the way to the shoulder, even after Bain let it go.

'This place inspires you?'

'I guess.'

'It should do. It's an important site. It's an axis.' Bain's voice was one peg down from smooth and refined, maybe a tad camp, but not enough to deter the ladies, Robin guessed. He felt faintly uncomfortable about the heat in his arm.

'Listen, Robin, I'm grateful for what you're doing. I know this has *got* to be a strain. I mean physically, psychically, domestically.'

'Uh . . . yeah, domestically, sure.'

'But I can't tell you how important it is, mate.' Bain was standing on the tombstone next to the lamp, casual, on someone's grave. His eyes found Robin's. Couldn't see those eyes but they'd found him and they held him. 'This *is* our religion. We *are* the religion of the British Isles. All these church sites are *our* sites.'

'Right. Uh, I've been kind of out of it . . . You just drive over here or were you here last night?'

'No, I was in a hotel last night. I think you were already crowded enough, weren't you? I drove over this morning. I wanted to watch the sun rise here. And to see the place in the dark. I'm sorry, I should've asked your permission.'

'Uh, no, that's . . .'

Max said, 'The point is, we have to get this right. Old Hindwell's a crucial test case, and if we're seen to back down before this man Ellis, it'll set the Craft back years . . . decades, even.'

Robin glanced at George. George was looking up over the walls of the nave towards the moon. Robin guessed George had told Ned Bain all about Betty walking out and Robin coming to pieces. He'd been set up for a pep talk.

Trouble was, it was working. Bain had magnetism, even in the dark – maybe especially in the dark. Also he had a certain instant gravitas: when Max talked, you thought *bullshit*; but if Ned laid something on you, you were inclined to accept its importance.

'You've done Imbolc before, of course, Robin?'

'Sure.'

'It *is* very appropriate.' Ned picked up the Tilley lamp by its wire handle. He looked like a modern, clean-shaven Christ out of Holman Hunt's *The Light of the World*. 'It's the first fire festival of the year. The kindling in the forest of winter.'

'Like, the winter of Christianity?'

'Well perceived,' Bain said very softly. Robin felt stupidly flattered. 'It *is* the winter of Christianity.'

'And Ned's devised a rite reflecting that,' George said.

'Didn't take many modifications. Which shows how essentially right it is.' Ned Bain raised the lamp so that there was a core of light in the centre of what had been the chancel. 'For instance, when we chant, "Thus we banish winter, thus we welcome spring", we'll be banishing rather more than winter. Or, in this case, a spiritual winter which has lasted 2,000 years. And we'll be welcoming, into this temple, a new light stronger than any one spring.'

'Right,' Robin said.

The lamp sputtered. Around Ned, as he lowered it, shadows grouped and divided again.

'What I'm saying, Robin, is that for the duration of our rite, Old Hindwell will be the centre of . . . everything.'

Robin was awed, no longer reluctantly.

George said, 'She'll be sorry she missed out on this.'

'Betty?'

'Yeah. Can't you get her back, man? She's the priestess for this. She's got more' – George opened his hands like he was letting out a cloud of smoke – 'than any of us.'

'I *was* very much looking forward to meeting her,' Ned Bain said. 'Word gets around.'

'Well, uh . . .' Robin looked down into the dark around his feet. 'I guess the pressure got too much, is all. Things haven't been going so very right for either of us.'

'Yes. I heard about Blackmore.'

Robin looked up.

'He's an awkward sod.' Ned shrugged. 'But personally . . . you know . . . I *liked* that design.'

'You did?'

'A lot. I mean . . . Well, I still think Kirk could be persuaded to listen to reason.'

For Robin, the volatile light seemed to leap up the walls. 'Even at this stage?'

'The central motif's there, isn't it?'

'Well, sure, I . . . I could have all seven covers . . .' Robin's heart raced. 'I mean I could have them completed inside a month.'

'Well, you know, I can't make any promises. Except to talk to him. But we go back quite a long way.'

'There you are, man,' George said. 'Ned talks to this Blackmore, you talk to Betty.'

Robin breathed out ruefully. 'My part is not gonna be easy.'

'Do your best.' Ned Bain clapped Robin on the back. That heat again. Bonding. 'We're going to need all the psychic energy we can produce.'

Robin was elated. The electricity of fate. After the blackest night, the last night of winter, his personal lowest point for years, this guy just shows up without warning and things start coming together. Holism? Interconnection? The central premise in Wicca.

There was some kind of psychic energy here today all right. The kindling in the dark forest. Robin's inner vision projected it onto the church walls like the airbrush mist around Lord Madoc. He could see it all coming together, like a beautiful painting. Betty would inevitably be drawn back. It was how these things worked.

Imbolc: it would be *their* rebirth, too. Robin tried to conceal some of his delight. He mustn't look naive.

'Well . . .' He grinned. 'I guess the whole thing would be easier if Ellis and his . . . flock . . . Like, if he just gave up and left us alone.'

George glanced at Ned Bain.

Ned Bain smiled broadly, shaking his head.

George felt it was safe to laugh.

Max said, 'I don't think you quite get this, do you, Robin? This *is* the energy. The surrounding hostility, the negativity from the village, all helps to create a rather special kind of tension. What you have is the whole struggle in microcosm. With those fanatical, fundamentalist Christians the other side of the gate singing their simplistic hymns, throwing everything at us, everything they've got left.'

'Friction, man.' George Webster rubbed his hands together and then did that smoke thing. 'The combustion. It's a fire festival. The dragon rises.'

FORTY-TWO

Raising the Stakes

'Christ be with me, Christ within me, Christ behind me, Christ before me . . .'

In the not-quite-silence of Ledwardine Parish Church, amid dusty skitterings at mouse and bat and early-bird level, Merrily was kneeling near the top of the chancel steps, asking for clarity of mind, clearance of all nightmares. Murmuring the ancient Celtic prayer, 'St Patrick's Breastplate'.

> 'I bind unto myself the Name,
> The Strong Name of the Trinity . . .'

Today was Candlemas – known to pagans as Imbolc. It concerned the quickening of life in Mother Nature's belly. The Catholic Church blessed its candles on this day. The Church of Nicholas Ellis kept them in its windows to ward off witchcraft.

When the 'Breastplate' was around her, Merrily went and sat in the front pew. She was wearing jeans and a sweater and Jane's duffel coat. She was still recalling details of Ellis's exorcism of Marianne Starkey.

'Cursed dragon, we give thee warning in the names of Jesus Christ and Michael, in the names of Jehovah, Adonai, Tetragrammaton . . .'

In the half-light, she was granted clarity. What became

clear was that Ellis was following a tradition of exorcism accepted there on the border for many centuries. Betty had written out for her what she could remember of the charm found in the fireplace at St Michael's farmhouse and also the one in Cascob Church: a mongrel exorcism, a cunning cocktail of Catholicism, Anglicanism, paganism and ritual magic. Precisely what you would expect to find in an area where cultures and languages and religions overlapped and survival often depended on juggling in the dark. This litany of names of power and magical repetition was a blunt instrument, a club. Merrily imagined Elizabeth Loyd 300 years ago, kneeling cowed and emptied on the stone flags of St Michael's Cascob.

When you found an adversary or an obstacle, you demonized it and then, powered by the sacred names, you beat it into the stones. Hard, practical . . . tested over centuries. *'Father Ellis doesn't do a soft ministry.'*

'It's hardly Jeffery Weal, is it?' Barbara Buckingham had said of Ellis's happy-clappy evangelism. Hardly. But happy-clappy was only the surface of it. Happy-clappy could unite the population, ensnaring the hearts and minds of local and incomer alike.

But under the surface, as Judith had said, Ellis suited the village. A quiet evangelist, neither ebullient, nor charismatic in the popular sense, but practical – dressed like an army chaplain. And he could, when required to, put the fear of God into people: the councillor's boy who took a car, threatening to bring dishonour to his respected family . . . the kid with a pocketful of Ecstasy . . . the repressed solicitor who only wanted his love for his wife to be reciprocated . . . the bored and lascivious licensee's wife who, sooner or later, might tempt a *local* man.

Ellis had earned his support by dealing with ripples on the normally dark and stagnant waters of Old Hindwell, while focusing, beyond them, on some bigger, darker, more nebulous objective. In the village hall, he had been rooting out some imagined, petty demon of desire. But also, through Marianne, attacking Robin Thorogood and what he represented.

But what *did* he represent? The Thorogoods had made no threats, taken no particular stance – Betty even appeared unsure that witchcraft was the right and only way for her. Yet Ellis had lost no time in demonizing them.

'Gotter be a problem for you, this, girl. Question of which side you're on now, ennit?'

Merrily stood and approached the altar. The stained-glass windows were coming alive with the dawn. She spoke the last verse of the 'Breastplate', the address to Jesus.

'Let me not run from the love that you offer
But hold me safe from the forces of evil.
On each of my dyings shed your light and your love.
Keep calling me until that day comes
When with your saints I may praise you for ever.
Amen.'

Merrily walked, blinking, out of the church. It was going to be a cold, bright, hard day.

When she got home, Jane had breakfast ready. The radio was turned to 5 Live, the news station.

'Mum, they've just trailed a report from Old Hindwell. It's coming up within the next ten minutes. That was about five minutes ago.'

'Better turn it up then.'

'And . . .' Jane cleared her throat, 'there's some stuff I need to tell you.'

'Any chance it could wait? It's just I seem to have got more to think about than at any time since my A levels.'

'No,' Jane said, 'it can't wait. It's about a web site, called Kali Three. Kali as in the goddess of death and destruction?'

'Not one of ours.' Merrily helped herself to a slice of toast. She was thinking about how best to approach Marianne Starkey. Marianne was crucial now, if Merrily was going to restrain Ellis. 'Not even one of Betty's.'

'Are you listening?'

'Sure. Sorry.'

'There's this obscure web site. A really heavy occult thing. A kind of like a hit list of people who are considered a threat to the, er . . . to, like, the expansion of human consciousness through magic, that kind of thing. Anyway, you're included on it.'

'You're kidding! Still . . . shows I must've got something right.'

Jane said, 'Sometimes you just make me sick, you know that?'

Merrily put down her toast. 'Jane, any other time I might be mildly affronted to think a bunch of loonies had put out a fatwa on me on the Internet, but right now . . . hold on, turn it up.'

Jane angrily turned up the radio far too loud. A woman said, '. . . *remote Welsh border village of Old Hindwell, where the local rector has declared holy war on a community of witches occupying a one-time parish church. In Old Hindwell is our reporter, Tim Francis. Tim, what's happening there?'*

'Well, not too much at the moment, Melissa, but I suspect this is merely the calm before the storm, because tonight is when the witches are proposing to actually reconsecrate this former Christian church to their own gods. Tonight is, in fact, the pagan festival known as Imbolc – I think I pronounced that

right – which is apparently the first really important witches' sabbath of the year.'

'Gosh, that sounds rather sinister.'

'Well, apparently it commemorates the start of the Celtic spring, which is not terribly sinister . . . However . . . what is seen by the rector, Nick Ellis, as a provocative gesture is the witches' intention to celebrate that festival tonight inside the former St Michael's Church, which in effect will make it into a pagan temple again.'

'And are they going to dance in the nude, Tim?'

'God,' said Jane, 'this woman is so sad.'

'I would say that is, um, a strong possibility. Now, last night we saw the new owner of the church, Robin Thorogood, clearly trying to calm down the situation when he confronted Nick Ellis here at the entrance to his farm, also leading to the church.'

Clip of Robin Thorogood over rain: *'We never touched your lousy church. There's no dragon here, no Satan. So just . . . just, like, go back and tell your God we won't hold you or your crazy stuff against him.'*

Tim said, *'However, Melissa, last night's placatory attitude was to be short-lived. We believe about a dozen witches are now residing at the farm here, and their leader, the latest to arrive, is a former official of the British Pagan Federation and an outspoken proponent of pagan religion. That's Ned Bain . . .'*

Jane gasped.

'. . . who joins me now. Ned Bain, the impression we all get is that you're raising the stakes here. The very fact that you, a leading pagan activist, have come all the way from London—'

'I think, Tim, that the stakes have already been raised enormously by Nicholas Ellis. He's a driven man, a fanatic, who's made life hell for two people who just wanted to be left alone to practise their religion.'

'In a Christian church.'

'In an abandoned church built on a site of ancient worship. Nicholas Ellis made the preposterous suggestion last night that he and his cronies should be allowed access to the site to carry out what amounts to an exorcism. Well, let's not forget this land now belongs to Betty and Robin Thorogood. They've been faced with an army of militant Christians who've promised to turn up in even greater numbers. We're here to support the Thorogoods.'

'And you'll be welcoming the Celtic spring with them tonight.'

'Indeed.'

'At the church itself?'

'At a site of established ancient sanctity.'

'And how many of you will be involved in that?'

'A full coven. Thirteen members.'

Melissa said from the studio, *'Ned, you going to be dancing in the nude?'*

'We shall probably be skyclad, yes, unless the weather is particularly inclement.'

'You'll be freezing!'

'Melissa, our beliefs will keep us warm.'

'Well, rather you than me. Thank you, Ned Bain, and Tim Francis. And we'll keep you up to date with whatever happens. Now, here on 5 Live . . .'

Jane switched off. When she turned round, her face had darkened.

'They're not taking any of it seriously.'

'Vicars and witches? What did you expect?'

'How can you *sit* there and—'

'Because I'm used to it. It's a secular society and we've become a quaint anachronism. Of course they're not taking it seriously.' Unfortunately, they would do soon, if it came out that the police had interviewed Betty regarding Mrs Wilshire.

Jane pulled out a chair and sat down directly opposite Merrily. 'You have *got* to listen to me, do you understand?'

'I'm listening.'

'Ned Bain—'

'He's a smooth operator. A clever man.'

'It goes deeper. Up in the gallery, at *Livenight*, we found the researcher already knew all about you and Dad and how Dad died and where it happened and everything, and he told Irene he got that information from Ned Bain, and it's all there on the Kali Three web site with suggestions that you should be regarded as an enemy, like, by pagans and occultists everywhere.'

'How do you know all that?' The kid had her full attention now.

'Because Irene spoke to Gerry, the researcher, afterwards.'

'About your dad? They had all *that*?'

For an awful moment, she was back in that stifling, oppressive studio, dry-mouthed, with Bain lazily watching her through what appeared, for just a moment, to be Sean's eyes.

'Everything,' Jane confirmed.

And earlier that man smiling Sean's pained, 'Isn't it all so tedious?' smile. All of it following a Sean-haunted drive up the M5, and then, when returning home, on that same stretch of motorway, on the way back.

'What we figured it means,' Jane said, 'is that people all over the world were probably sending you ill will at that point.'

'Down their computers?'

'Don't try and laugh it off. You were *crap* on telly.'

'Thanks.'

'Maybe that wasn't all your fault, you know? There's a lot of really heavy people out there. They knew your weaknesses: your guilt trip about Dad and the Church.'

'That's . . . silly.'

'And now Ned Bain's in Old Hindwell.'

'OK, not good.'

Two religious fanatics facing each other across the ruins of a church that was spiritually suspect. Both sides raising the stakes.

Betty Thorogood came down, wearing a sloppy old baseball sweater of Jane's. She declined an egg, but accepted toast and honey.

She'd heard the radio report from upstairs.

She said she was going back to St Michael's.

'I don't want that church reconsecrating – not in anybody's name. I'm not forecasting some apocalypse scenario, I just don't want it to happen. I'm stopping it.'

'You've got thirteen people to persuade. All determined to celebrate Candlemas.'

'They can bloody well do it somewhere else,' Betty said flatly.

Merrily brought coffee. 'Tell me exactly what happens at Candlemas.'

'It's the festival of Brigid, the triple goddess.'

'Three stages of womanhood,' Jane translated, 'maiden, mother, hag.'

'Imbolc means belly. It's about Mother Earth giving birth to spring, so in Wicca we put the emphasis on the mother. Three women are involved in the rite, but the mother wears the crown of lights . . . that's a headdress of candles. This is a festival of light and new awakening. Of all the sabbats, it's probably the one closest to Christianity, I'd guess.'

Merrily nodded.

'Normally, it would be an especially good time to consecrate a church or temple, simply because it's coming out of a long period of darkness, reawakening to spring.'

'Everything perfect, then,' Merrily said neutrally, 'for giving back Old Hindwell to the old gods.'

'No, everything's utterly wrong – take it from me. If there were good omens before, it all reversed when we moved in. I've become snappy and irritable and . . . alienated from Robin. We've hardly even, you know, touched each other since we arrived. And even regarding money. Robin had the possibility – almost the *certainty* – of a very lucrative contract, to do seven book covers for Kirk Blackmore, the fantasy writer.'

'Wow,' Jane said. 'I used to read his stuff, when I was a kid.'

'And then the rug seems to have been pulled. Blackmore's decided he doesn't like Robin's concept, and it's Blackmore calls the shots. That's just the latest thing to go wrong.'

Jane said, 'Maybe *you* need the new light.'

Betty shook her head. 'There won't be any. We won't bring that place out of the darkness; it'll suck us in.' She looked vaguely around, from face to face. 'Whatever you may think about this, I've called out to the goddess in the night, and the goddess won't come to me. I'm not being emotional or hysterical about this. I just don't see a good future.'

'OK, so you go back,' Merrily said, 'and you try to stop it. How do you do that?'

Betty shrugged. 'If necessary I can just tell them all to get out. It'll cause another row with Robin, but the house is half mine. That's only a last resort. If I play along for a while, something subtler might occur. I don't want to create negative vibrations, if possible. What about you?'

'I'm going to have to try and cool Ellis. One or two ideas occur. Well, one anyway.' Merrily's throat was dry from too much smoking, not enough sleep. 'Maybe we can meet somewhere, late afternoon, and see where we stand.'

'There's a footbridge,' Betty said, 'that leads from the church to the other side of the brook.'

'I know it. Four o'clock?' Part of her was saying this was whimsy, that the only really important things were to, first, find Barbara Buckingham, and second, persuade the police to investigate the Hindwell Trust. 'Betty, what do you think, seriously, is likely to happen if we can't stop this tonight?'

Betty shook her head quickly, non-committally.

'The dragon gets out,' Jane said, 'whatever that means.'

'I've been thinking.' Betty looked at Merrily. 'The problem with this place is nothing really to do with us. But it *is* to do with you, I suspect – with what you do. Ellis thought it needed exorcizing. I'm not sure he was wrong.'

'But not by him.'

'No,' Betty said, 'not by him.'

'You mean . . . by me?' Merrily felt obscurely honoured and immediately guilty about that.

'I wondered about tonight,' Betty said. 'Candlemas is Candlemas. I suppose it's a good time, wherever you stand. I mean, I'd go in *with* you, if you thought that would help. Or, if you thought that would be spiritually wrong, I'd stay out of the way.'

'I don't know.'

'Would you think about it, Merrily? It's become kind of central to everything, hasn't it?'

'But . . . exorcizing a church . . .'

'Like you keep saying,' Jane said, 'it isn't a church any more.'

'All right, I'll talk to the bishop.'

'Please don't do that,' Betty said. 'He might suggest you have other priests along. That would bother me. I don't want it to look like a *formal* sellout.'

Merrily nodded. 'OK.'

'Wow,' Jane said.

FORTY-THREE

Mitigating Circumstances

Jane had called Eirion at the rotting mansion and there was no answer. Well, there *was* an answer . . . on a machine, and in Welsh.

Like she wasn't already feeling excluded enough. Gomer had collected Betty and taken her back to Old Hindwell, Mum had gone off on her own. Little Jane had been given the really important job of relaying any messages to Mum on her mobile.

Bastards!

'I can't *speak* bloody Welsh!' she howled over the message. 'Just tell Irene . . . Eirion . . . to call me. It's very urgent. It's Jane Wat—'

She shut up. The message was being translated.

Dafydd and Gwennan Lewis are unable to take your call. Please leave your message after the tone. Diolch yn fawr.

'OK. Please, please, tell Eirion to ring me. It's Jane Watkins. It's very urgent. Please?' Realizing she'd ended on a kind of strangled sob. Maybe that would underline the urgency, or maybe just the existing suspicions of the wealthy and powerful Dafydd Lewis about the hysterical English. It was not bloody *fair*, because she now had, like, *masses* of new data to lay on Eirion. He could hit the Net, and they could crack this thing wide open.

Jane paced the kitchen. Actually, she was quite proud of

Mum this time, agreeing to undertake an exorcism on behalf of a witch. Like, it was a really heavy decision to have to make. But had she accepted the significance of Kali Three? It really was a pity they hadn't got a decent computer.

Ah!

Jane went rapidly round the house, doing what had to be done – laying a fire in the drawing room, putting out dried cat food for Ethel, and all the time thinking hard. She didn't need Irene; she just needed an online computer.

Sophie!

Sophie had one in the Deliverance office. It was only right that the diocese should pay for this research.

There should be a bus to Hereford passing through Ledwardine within the hour. Jane ran a brush through her hair, tugged on her fleece coat and was out of there. There'd be some resistance from Sophie, sure, but nothing Jane couldn't handle with the usual combination of pathos and rat-like cunning.

She bought a Mars bar from the Eight-till-Late and stood on the square munching it, relishing the freedom to *do* things. Back at bloody school next week, with dismal GCSEs looming. Although the public school system was this, like, totally disgusting anachronism, she wished she was at the cathedral school with Eirion; at least it was in the middle of town.

It was bright but unexpectedly cold on the square. Jane chewed and stamped her feet on the cobbles. A silver BMW went past, then slowed suddenly and backed up and stopped on the edge of the square. The window glided down on the passenger side. Some sex beast wondering if she was in need of a lift.

'Excuse me, little girl.' Creepy voice sibilating from the bourgeois, tinted interior. Eyes narrowing, Jane pocketed the Mars bar and sashayed over. 'Looking for somewhere, I am, see?' he oozed. 'Wonder if you can point me in the right direction. Little place called . . . if I can just see it on the map . . . Ah, got it . . .' The passenger door was thrown wide open. '*England!*'

Jane glared in delight. 'You bastard!'

'Good morning, Eirion,' Eirion said. 'How's the whiplash? Well, it's quite a bit more comfortable, thank you, Jane.'

Jane got in. The leather seat creaked luxuriously. 'Where'd you steal the flash Kraut wheels?'

'Gwen's, it is. She owes me. Don't ask. Are you doing the decent thing and going to school?'

'Well, I *was*, naturally. But, on second thoughts, I think we'll go to Hereford Cathedral. I can show you the Deliverance office, in the gatehouse.'

'Jane . . .' Eirion snatched off his baseball cap and his dark glasses. 'Half the school goes past there.'

'You won't be spotted, you'll have your head bent over a keyboard. By lunchtime your eyes will be so terminally weakened you'll be regretting you ever left the land of Druids and sad male voice choirs.'

Eirion sighed and let out the clutch. He handed her a brown A4 envelope. 'Read this.'

'What is it?'

'What do you think it is?'

Jane pulled out a thin sheaf of printouts.

'Kali Three.'

She read about her mother and her father.

At home with a young child, Merrily Watkins was horrified to discover that her husband was 'representing' Gerald McConnell, a West Midlands businessman who would later be jailed for four years for fraud and money-laundering. It was this . . .

Jane looked across at Eirion. She felt embarrassed.

Eirion drove serenely on. 'There but for the grace of God, Jane. When my father was on the board of the Welsh Development Agency . . . Never mind, he'd have been out by now even if the charges had stuck.'

'You're just saying that to make me feel better.'

'I wish. Read the other stuff, on Bain and his old man. Start at the top of page five.'

Jane read:

Ned was ten years old when his mother, Edward Bainbridge's first wife, Susan, walked out on her husband. They were quietly divorced and, soon afterwards, Bainbridge formed a relationship with Mrs Frances Wesson, the widow of a chaplain at his college. Mrs Wesson had remained a strong, even fanatical Christian, although the extent of this did not become apparent to Bainbridge or his son until after the marriage.

Strange how formally this was written. Like out of a real biography, not the usual chatty crap you got off the Net. It drew you into what, even though it was then the mid-1970s, seemed like a Victorian kind of world.

Thus Ned entered his teenage years in a stifling High Church household dominated by the beautiful but austere Frances Wesson, whose own two children seemed to be accorded special privileges. To please his new wife, Bainbridge, hitherto a lukewarm Christian at most, began to attend church services twice every Sunday. Ned was soon glad to be sent away to public school, where he was free to pursue an interest in subjects which would certainly have been forbidden at home.

During school holidays, he became aware of his father's slide into depression. Edward Bainbridge had given up writing poetry after his latest volume had been derided as maudlin, self-pitying and, indeed, pitifully inept. Unsurprisingly, his academic reputation was crumbling and his drinking had become a problem. All of this was concurrent with the dissolution of the Bainbridge marriage, with the couple living increasingly separate lives. If Edward now no longer attended church, his wife had inflicted all its trappings and symbolism on what remained of their domestic life. The house in Oxford had become heavy with icons and crucifixes; its drawing room had a constant and pervading smell of incense, and Frances had even set up a private chapel in a pantry next to the kitchen.

The summer of 1975 brought a severe and life-changing shock for Ned. Edward Bainbridge's brother, David, arrived at the school to break the news that his father was dead. Ned learned, to his horror, that his father had bled to death on the floor of the private chapel, and that his stepmother had already been charged with murder.

Some days later, to the eighteen-year-old Ned's outrage, the charge was reduced to manslaughter, to which Frances Bainbridge had agreed to plead guilty. There was, she had claimed, a strong element of self-defence. According to Mrs Bainbridge, her husband, who had been drinking heavily for most of the day, had come hammering on the door of the chapel while she was at prayer and, when she refused to admit him, had kicked in the door, burst into the tiny chapel and proceeded to tear down drapes and overturn the altar. When she screamed at him to get out, he began to slash viciously with a kitchen knife at a Victorian picture of Christ, until he stumbled and dropped the knife – whereupon Mrs Bainbridge snatched it up. Edward Bainbridge then attacked his wife, tearing at her dress, and in her struggle to get away she stabbed him fatally in the throat.

The original murder charge was reduced to manslaughter after Frances Bainbridge's description of the events – somewhat unconvincing to Ned – was supported by her son Simon, aged fifteen, and her twelve-year-old daughter Madeleine, both of whom said they had witnessed the struggle. Frances Bainbridge pleaded guilty to manslaughter, but walked free from the court after being given a two-year suspended sentence because of the mitigating circumstances.

Ned Bainbridge returned to school to sit his A levels before going up to Oxford, to his father's old college where, with fellow students, he formed his first coven.

Eirion drove into Hereford via Whitecross. 'Quite a significant family skeleton, isn't it?' he said. 'You can understand that guy not being over-fond of the Church.'

FORTY-FOUR

Feel the Light

Greg had shaved. He wore a clean shirt. He stood in the back doorway at the end of the yard and made rapid wiping movements with his arms.

'No, no, *no*.'

Merrily stopped about four yards away. 'She's worse?'

'She's better,' Greg said. 'That's the point, innit? I'm grateful for you taking the witch away and everyfing, but I'm not having you upsetting my wife.'

The day, like Greg, had hardened up. Merrily dug her hands into the pockets of Jane's much-borrowed duffel coat. She nodded, resigned, looking down at all the crushed glass ground into the pitted concrete yard.

'I'm sorry, Reverend,' Greg said. 'I said I'd ask her if she'd talk to you, but I didn't in the end. I don't want noffink bringing it back. These past two days – bleedin' nightmare. You understand, don't you?'

'You think she's coming out of it?'

'She's talking to me. That's enough for now.'

'Right, well . . .' Merrily shrugged. 'Thank you. I'll see you, Greg.'

It was nearly 11 a.m. Martyn Kinsey, of BBC Wales, had spotted her going into the yard, and given her a conspiratorial wink. Martyn was going to be her last resort, if she got nowhere with Marianne Starkey. Martyn Kinsey and a big, unchristian lie: *Entirely off the record, the diocese has received two complaints, of a very serious nature, against Father Nicholas Ellis. Yes, of course from women.*

Last resort, though.

Merrily had reached the entrance to the alley which led from the Black Lion yard to the village when she heard the wobble and slide of a sash window. 'Who's this?' a woman called down.

''S all right,' Greg rasped. 'I dealt wiv it. Just go back and siddown, willya?'

'Hey!' Marianne leaned out of the upstairs window. 'I saw you, din' I?'

Merrily paused. *Please, God* . . .

'Inna toilets,' Marianne said, 'with Judy Prosser. 'Cept you was wearing a . . . whatsit round your neck.'

Merrily put a hand to her throat. 'Day off today.'

Greg said nervously, 'Marianne, just leave it, yeah?'

'You wanna cuppa tea, love?'

'That would be really very nice,' Merrily said. 'It's quite cold again today, isn't it?'

Greg hung around, restive, breathing down his nose. Marianne waved him away. 'It'll be OK. You go and replace your kegs.'

They were upstairs in the living room of the flat above the pub. The furniture looked inexpensive, but it was all newish, as if they'd ditched all their old stuff when they moved here. For a bright new start.

Greg waved a finger at his wife. 'You just say what you wanna say.'

Marianne was in a cream towelling robe, and she wore no make-up. She slid back into a big lemon sofa opposite the television. The sound was turned down on two young women ranting at Robert Kilroy-Silk.

'Slept late,' Marianne said. 'Must have a clear conscience.'

'Good.'

'You reckon it can really do that? Wipe the slate clean?'

'Why not?'

'Siddown . . . please.' Marianne picked up a cigarette packet from the sofa. 'Ain't taken everything away, mind. I still need these. Don't suppose you do?'

'Actually . . .' Merrily slipped off her coat, let it fall to the carpet. She sat on the edge of an armchair beside the TV, and accepted one of Marianne's menthol cigarettes.

'Blimey, you'll go to hell, love. In spite of it all.'

'I prefer to think I'll just go to heaven a bit sooner. How do you feel now, Marianne?'

'Bit weird. Bit hollow.'

'All happened kind of suddenly, hasn't it?'

'Can't believe it. I feel like a little girl. All nervous. Need me hand held.'

Probably why she'd been so glad to see Merrily. A lady priest. Someone who would know, would understand.

'I mean, you shouldn't be feeling like that at someone's funeral, should you?' Marianne said. 'Ain't right.'

'You mean feeling good?'

'Yeah.'

Merrily lit their cigarettes. 'Finding yourself joining in the singing?'

'The singing. Sure.'

'Mmm. I know what that's like.'

'I should think you do, Reverend.'

'Merrily.'

'Nice name. Yeah, that's what happens, Merrily. I only went along for a laugh. No, not a laugh, I was hacked off with everybody, with this place, with Greg. Like, Greg's sayin', one of us oughta go, put in an appearance. It's the way they are, the locals, innit? God-fearing? So, yeah, OK,

I'll do it – 'cos they all reckon I'm a slapper – I'll be down that hall with me hat on and I'll put on a real show for 'em.'

Merrily smiled. 'And in the middle of the show . . . wow, it turns into the real thing.'

'Cloud nine, love. Like after half a bottle of vodka? Nah, not really. I mean, I was so ashamed. Joyful, yet ashamed. Ashamed of *me*. I was horrified at me – what I was, what I'd been. I wanted . . . what's the word . . .?'

'Redemption?'

'That's a bleeding big word.'

'Big thing.'

'Do you know, I went out the back afterwards, and I was sick over the fence? Sick as a dog, with all that hating of meself pouring out. After that, I felt very . . . light, you know? Cut loose. Then this lady come over, I don't know her name, but she lives in a bungalow on the road out of here, and that's where we went. Some other ladies come too, and they was all really kind. I cried most of the time.'

Merrily smoked and nodded. It was difficult to believe it could happen so quickly until you encountered it, but it did happen. It happened particularly to people in crisis, depressed people and – unexpectedly – to angry, cynical people.

'Found I could talk to them. Talked about stuff I never talked about since I left London. Personal stuff, you know? One of the ladies, she says, "I knew you was in trouble when I seen you and that feller." '

'Robin Thorogood.'

Marianne shivered. 'I thought it was *me* invited *him*. But he was playing with me. He's a dark person, he is, Merrily. He brought out the bad and lustful part of me.'

'Who told you he was a dark person?'

'In the paper, wannit? They come round with the paper . . . yesterday.'

'Who did?'

'Eleri, from the post office. And Judy Prosser. I'd been to church – to the hall – on Sunday, and it was wonderful, I was blown away all over again, really. And afterwards I was introduced to Father Ellis, and he's like, "I can tell you been deeply troubled. I feel you been exposed to a great evil." And it sets me off crying again, and he takes my hand and he says, in this lovely soft voice, he says, "You come back to me when you feel ready to have the disease taken away." And the next day Eleri come round with the paper, and there *he* is, that Robin, his face – like I never seen it before, I mean you could *see* the evil in him, snarling, vicious. I went a bit hysterical when I seen that picture. He was like they said he was.'

'What happened then?'

'They took me up the hall. Father Ellis was there.'

'Did they tell you *why* you were going to the hall?'

'What?'

'Doesn't matter. Father Ellis . . .?'

'He was dressed all in white, as usual. He was like a saint, and I felt so comforted. I felt I was in the right hands, the hands of a living saint. And we sits down and Father Ellis explains about the demon what Robin had put inside of me.'

'Those were his words?'

'Once he'd given me the demon, he didn't wanna know me no more, he just pushed me away.'

'Robin?'

'Pushed me away, and I fell down in the street. The demon did that. That was the demon. After the pub closed, Greg and me, we had this terrible ding-dong. I'm insulting him, I'm like *belittling* him, you know what I mean? I'm screaming, "Go on, do it to me, you got any bottle." Poor Greg. Turns him off like a light, you talk dirty. But that wasn't *me*. I know now that wasn't me. That was the *demon*.'

'Is that what Father Ellis said?'

'He said he could take it away, but it wouldn't be easy, and it was not to be gone into lightly and I would have to understand that I would be giving myself to the Holy Spirit. He said it was a foul entity, the demon, and it was gonna have to come out . . . like a rotten tooth.'

Merrily said. 'You mean . . . out of your mouth?'

Marianne's eyes narrowed, lines appeared either side of her mouth. She looked accusingly at Merrily. 'Judy said you come to spy on Father Ellis.'

'I was sent to support him,' Merrily said. 'From the bishop, remember? The bishop thought he needed some help.'

Marianne looked confused. 'That Judy, she took you outside, din't she? I was glad when she did that.'

'We hadn't met before. I think she was a bit suspicious of me.'

'She took you outside,' Marianne said. 'I was very glad.'

'We had a good chat,' Merrily assured her. 'We worked things out. Marianne, do you remember what Father Ellis did . . . to exorcize the demon of lust?'

Marianne blinked, affronted. 'He said the Church has strict rules about the exorcizing of demons. They don't just *do* it. You could wind up exorcizing someone who was mentally ill, couldn't you?'

'Er . . . yes. Yes, you could.'

Ellis told her this? Merrily's heart sank a little. This was established Deliverance procedure. You didn't even contemplate exorcism until all the other possibilities, usually psychiatric, had been eliminated.

'Don't get me wrong, love, he could've done what he liked without a word, the way I was feeling, long as he took it away. But he explained it was a *disease*. I needed checking over by a doctor, and what he was doing should be medically supervised.'

'He *said* that?'

'Dr Banks-Morgan was there for the whole thing,' Marianne said. 'That's the kind of man Father Ellis is.'

The male figure in the doorway.

She sat in her car for a while.

Then she rang Hereford Police, asked for Mumford. He was out, so she rang Eileen Cullen at home, hoping she wasn't asleep. A man answered; Merrily realized she knew nothing about Cullen's domestic situation. When she came on the line, she sounded softer, a bathrobe voice.

'Before you say a word, Merrily, there is one incident I will never talk about again, not to you, not to anyone.'

'Angina,' Merrily said.

'Ask away,' Cullen said.

'The pills you take for angina. Tri-something?'

'Trinitrin. You feel it coming on, you stick one under your tongue.'

'Becomes automatic?'

'Long-term sufferers, they practically do it in their sleep.'

'Take a hypothetical case. Person on Trinitrin for angina becomes converted to herbal remedies. Says I'm going to stop filling myself up with these nasty drugs. Then she feels an attack coming on, so what does she do?'

'Reaches for the Trinitrin. Says I'll stop fillin' meself up with these awful drugs *tomorrow.*'

'All right.' No time for the subtle approach. 'Hypothetically, if, in circumstances like this, a doctor saw an opportunity to do away with a patient in a way which might throw blame on someone else, say for instance the herbalist . . . how would he go about it?'

'Jesus, Merrily, what *is* this?'

'It's, er . . . a question. Just a question.'

'Well here's your answer – a hundred ways. Could casually

swap her Trinitrins for blanks, for starters. Who's gonna know? It's easy for a doctor. Always has been.'

Robin had been gazing from his studio window when he saw her walking, like some grounded angel, across the yard, and he'd gone running wildly through the farmhouse, like some big, stupid kid, knocking a bowl of cornflakes out of the hands of a mousy, pregnant witch from Gloucester, called Alice.

Now he held Betty's hand, and he was breathing evenly for the first time in many hours. They shared this big cushion they used to have in their previous apartment. Only now it was on the floor of the parlour, the room with the inglenook which was now the house temple.

They'd been left alone in here, just Robin and Betty and the altar and the crown of lights.

The kindly, mature witch, Alexandra, Betty's one-time tutor, had made it. Alexandra was a twig-weaver, or whatever you call it, and this was a tight wreath of hedgerow strands, like a crown of thorns without the thorns. Across the top of the wreath was shaped a kind of skullcap made out of one of those foil trays you got around your supermarket quiche. The candles which ringed its perimeter were the kind you had on birthday cakes, though not coloured.

'A *Blue Peter* job,' Betty had said with a wistful smile, referring to some TV show she used to watch as a kid, where you were taught how to make useful artefacts from household debris. Foil trays apparently featured big.

'I love you,' Robin said. 'I want you to wear it tonight.'

Outside on a calm night, with all the candles lit around the head of a beautiful woman, the crown of lights looked awesome.

'It's the mother wears the lights,' Betty said.

'This is special.'

'What would Ned say?'

'He'll be cool.'

Everything was cool, coming together, happening just like he'd known it would. He hadn't asked where she'd spent last night. That didn't matter. She sometimes needed time to think things out. He recalled how one moonlit night she'd gone out walking from Shrewsbury into the countryside, hadn't returned until dawn, had covered maybe twenty miles and hadn't noticed the time go by. He'd been frantic, but she was her own person. She was his priestess. He would trust her for ever, through life after life after life.

'Ned's even gonna fix things with Kirk Blackmore, I tell you about that?'

'Yes,' Betty said, 'I'm sure he will.'

'Bets, things are really turning around. It's Imbolc. I can feel the light coming through.'

'Yes,' Betty said.

Down the hill, into the forestry land, until she came to the point where there were farm buildings either side of the road and a Land-Rover with a 'Christ is the Light' sticker. Oh, he had his uses, did Jesus Christ: the very name served as a disinfectant.

Merrily turned in to a rutted track between two stone and timbered barns, and there was the farmhouse, grey brown, black windows. No garden, just a yard of dirt and brown gravel, where she parked the Volvo. There was a glazed front porch, its door hanging ajar. She saw the interior door swing open before she was even into the porch, and Judith Prosser standing there, cool and rangy in her orange rugby shirt.

'You're late, Mrs Watkins. Had you down for an early riser, I did.'

The banter was wrapped around Judith's need always to

be ahead of the situation. This visit must, on no account, be seen as a surprise.

'Late night, Mrs Prosser.'

'I've coffee on.'

'That would be good . . . Erm, I felt there were things left in the air from last night.'

'No bad thing, sometimes,' Judith replied swiftly. 'Left in the air, they have a chance to blow away.'

'But sometimes they stick around and the air goes sour, and that's not a good thing in my experience.'

'Oh, *your* experience.' Holding open the door for Merrily. 'Profound today, is it, Mrs Watkins?'

'You have a problem with profound?' Merrily blinked. It was dark inside and the hulking furniture made it darker.

'Life's too short to tolerate problems.'

'Life's too short for cover-ups, Mrs Prosser,' Merrily said.

Judith turned to face her. They were standing in a square hall dominated by a huge, over-ornate chair with a nameplate on the back. It looked like the seat of a council chairman or a presiding magistrate. Judith leaned an elbow on one of its carved shoulders.

'As I said last night, it would be stupid for you to react to silly rumours.'

'Here's the situation,' Merrily said. 'I was there, I saw the whole thing: the cross, the petroleum jelly. Also Dr Coll standing in the doorway – and didn't *that* explain why a bunch of local matrons were able to sit there and watch Ellis violate a woman with a metal cross? Because there was a *doctor* present. This, of course, makes everything all right, above board, entirely respectable, clinically proven.'

Judith Prosser flicked a speck of dust or ash from the point of the chairman's chair.

'I'm not sure how far from being a police matter this is,' Merrily continued, 'but we're very close to finding out.'

FORTY-FIVE

Stupid Wires

Jane typed in the word 'charismatic'. The usual, mainly irrelevant list appeared. She grabbed the mouse, dithered over 'Charismatic Q and A'.

'Try it,' Eirion suggested. 'Might lead somewhere better.'

On the screen: 'The Charismatic Movement: what in the name of God is it all about?'

'Click,' Eirion said.

> The Charismatic Movement (from the Greek *charismata*, meaning 'spiritual gifts') developed in the 1950s and '60s from the Pentecostal movement, crossing over the denominations, embracing the sphere of angelology and the gifts of healing, prophecy, speaking in tongues and power-prayer. It reached a new peak worldwide in the 1990s . . .

There was a list of options. Jane clicked on 'Yes, I want to talk to God.'

They needed all the help they could get.

Sophie had said she shouldn't be allowing this, before shutting them in the Deliverance office with the computer.

And she wanted copies of anything they found.

Jane had said, 'This is awfully good of you . . . Mrs Hill.'

Collecting a contemptuous frown and, 'Jane, you are not

among the people with whose patronage I can cope. Try "evangelism".'

On the way here, Jane had told Eirion virtually everything she'd learned so far – about Terry Penney, about pentagrams . . . The poor little Chapel boy had seemed unnerved, regaining his cool only when he saw the computer. Smiling his famous smile at Sophie, who wore a checked woollen skirt with a grey twinset and pearls – Sophie, who might one day be the last person in the entire universe still wearing a twinset and pearls.

Jane clicked again, losing enthusiasm for talking to God. When it was working fast and well, the Internet could give you the illusion of *being* God – you could imagine Him operating like this, constructing human situations with a click of the mouse, running programs, consigning icons to the dumpbin.

'Evangelism', though, had been a bummer. There were background articles on St John the Evangelist. There were four web sites about some kind of computer software with that name. There were no obvious links into crank preachers in the American South who might have known Nick Ellis; and 'Charismatics' proved little better.

'I could try "Bible Belt",' Eirion offered.

'You'd probably get suppliers of religious fashion accessories,' Jane said gloomily.

' "Cults?" '

'No chance. People never think of themselves as being in a cult. "Just off to the cult, don't wait up" – doesn't happen.'

'What we need is a Christian search engine.'

'What we need is divine intervention.' Jane walked over to the window which overlooked the forecourt of the Bishop's Palace. No good searching for it out there.

'OK,' Eirion said. 'What are we *really* asking for?'

'Some big, rattling skeleton in Ellis's vestment closet.

Something that maybe caused him to leave America, come back here in a hurry. When you think about it, most Brits who go over to the States tend to stay there, making piles of money. So it's reasonable to think Ellis came back because something happened to make him kind of persona non grata. Like he was the leader of a mass suicide cult who contrived not to go down with the rest.'

'We'd have heard about it.'

'We're stuffed.' Jane angrily keyed in 'loony fundamentalist bastards', and the Web found, for some no doubt entirely logical reason, a bunch of science fiction and fantasy writers including David Wingrove, David Gemmell and Kirk Blackmore.

'We're just not asking the right questions.'

'Kirk Blackmore . . . where did I hear that?'

Sophie came in then, with a piece of paper, a name written on it. 'Try this.'

'Ah,' Jane said, as Blackmore came up on the screen. 'This was the guy whose covers Robin Thorogood was going to design, but they pulled the plug.'

Eirion was staring up at Sophie, bewildered.

'I used the telephone.' Sophie inclined her neck, swan-like. 'It's rather old-tech, it involves the less-exact medium of human speech, but it does tend to be more effective when dealing with the clergy.'

' "Marshall McAllman",' Eirion read.

'Before the Reverend Nicholas Ellis came to New Radnor and then Old Hindwell, he was a curate for just over a year at a parish outside Newcastle-upon-Tyne. I've talked to his former vicar, the Reverend Alan Patterson, who only found out after the Reverend Mr Ellis had been with him for several months that he'd previously been a personal assistant to the Reverend Mr McAllman – which did not entirely please him.'

'Let's put it in, Jane.' Eirion keyed in the name, while the computer was still showing:

KIRK BLACKMORE ORACLE.
The reclusive Celtic scribe returns with a
remarkable new Lord Madoc novel which . . .

'Found,' Eirion said, after a few seconds. ' "The Mobile Ministry of Marshall McAllman".'

He clicked. Kirk Blackmore vanished.

'There you are.' Sophie peered. ' "Angelweb Factfile. The journeys of Reverend Marshall McAllman were directed by the Will of God and took him from Oklahoma . . ." '

' ". . . to South Carolina",' Eirion read from the screen, ' "via Arkansas and Tennessee, dispensing a low-key but extremely potent evangelism effectively tailored to the needs of small towns and simple folk. He developed a loyal following after several witnessed instances of prophecy, divine inspiration and angelic" blah blah blah . . . "Reverend McAllman retired in 1998, a disillusioned man, after surviving a campaign by an unscrupulous journalist on a Tennessee newspaper, the *Goshawk Talon*. Although there remains considerable debate about Reverend McAllman's ministry, his name is still revered in" blah, blah—'

'There you have it, then,' Sophie interrupted. 'Your next port of call must surely be the, ah, *Goshawk Talon*.'

'Does that mean it's in a place called Goshawk?' Jane wondered.

'Doesn't matter, let's just put it in,' Eirion said. 'This is very fast, Mrs Hill, are you on ISDN?'

'I wouldn't know. It's all stupid wires to me. Go *on*.'

' "Found". Some stuff on birds of prey. And . . . "The *Goshawk Talon* and Marshall McAllman" . . . OK.' Eirion clicked, waited. 'Oh.'

The file you are seeking is unavailable.

Jane's face fell. 'What do we do now?'

'A technical brick wall.' Sophie sighed. 'Hard to imagine how we survived for so long without all this.' Then she did something most un-Sophie-like – stamped her foot. '*Phone* them, child! They presumably *have* telephones in Goshawk, Tennessee. If this publication still exists, it shouldn't take long to find the number. If it doesn't, we shall have to think of something else. Get on to international directory enquiries.'

'I don't know how.'

Sophie sighed in mild contempt. 'Leave it to me.' She stalked out.

'Wow,' Jane said. 'The turbo twinset.'

Eirion smiled his Eirion smile. It did things to her, but this was not the time. There never seemed to be a time. The sudden urgency manifested by Sophie made Jane quite tense. What if someone was ringing home with information far more important than anything they could hope to find on the Net, and she wasn't there to relay it. Paranoid, she rang the vicarage answering machine. One message for Mum to call Uncle Ted. *Sod that.*

'We seem to be drifting a long way from Kali Three,' Eirion said. He started to key it in.

'No, don't.' Jane leapt up and stood at the window, staring down at the wood pile below. There was a sense of being very close to something, but it was too indistinct, ghostly. She felt that invoking Kali Three would somehow bring bad luck. She turned back to the room.

'We have to go there.'

'Old Hindwell?' Eirion said. 'I'm not sure about that. Why?'

'We just *do*.'

'Absolutely not.' Sophie was in the doorway.

'Sophie, there's some really heavy—'

'Don't you think your mother has enough to worry about? Sit down and speak to the man from the paper. Or would you prefer me to do it? Perhaps it might be better if I did.'

'She's right,' Eirion said. 'She's going to sound so much more authoritative than either of us. Especially to Joe-Bob McCabe, of the *Goshawk Talon*.'

'Ah sure lerve your *ac*cent, ma'am,' said Jane. The only person from Tennessee she'd ever heard talk was Elvis.

'The man's name,' said Sophie, 'is Eliot Williams. He's busy at the moment, but his editor's getting him to call me back. I think he rather senses a story.'

'Wow,' Jane said, 'you're, like, incredible.'

But Sophie had already returned to her office, where the phone was ringing.

FORTY-SIX

Nine Points

A dark, Victorian living room. Merrily imprisoned in the lap of a huge, high-sided leather armchair, coat folded on her knees, cup and saucer on top of that.

Judith Prosser was adept at disadvantaging her visitors.

'And since when is religion a matter for the police, Mrs Watkins?'

'When it's sexual assault.' Merrily drank some of the coffee. Perversely, it was good coffee.

'Do you know what I think?' Judith's own chair put her about a foot higher than Merrily. 'I've been enquiring about you, and do you know what I think? I think that Father Ellis has dared to intrude into what you consider to be your back yard. He is doing what you think only you should be doing.'

'You think *I'd* do—?'

'How would I know *what* namby-pamby thing you would do these days, when the Church is like a branch of the social services?' A withering contempt for both.

'Now we're getting to it,' Merrily said.

'*Are* we, Mrs Watkins?'

Merrily tried to sit up in the chair. She felt like a child. Around the walls were dozens of photographs, mostly of men wearing chains of office, although a group of more recent ones showed boys with motorbikes and trophies.

'What *are* "we" getting to?' Judith leaned back, arms folded.

'The question of Old Hindwell preferring to do its own thing. Which is kind of admirable in one sense, I suppose.'

Judith reared up. 'It is *entirely* admirable, my girl. This is an independent part of the world. What do we need with the mandarins in Cardiff and London and Canterbury? The English. Even the Welshies . . . they all think they can come out yere and do what they like. When Councillor Prosser was on the old Radnor District Council, they used to have to employ young officials, trotting out their fancy ideas – hippies and vegetarians, half of them. It was, "Oh, you can't build *there* . . . you have to use *this* colour of slate on your roofs . . . you can't do *this*, you can't do *that*." Well, they were put in their place soon enough. The *local* people, it is, who decides. *We* know what's needed, *we* know what works. And Father Ellis, even though he's not from yere, is a man with old values and a clear, straightforward, practical approach, based on tradition. He *understands* tradition.'

Merrily was tired of this. 'How many people has he exorcized so far?'

'I can tell you that all of them have come freely to him and asked for it to be done.'

'Like your son?'

A pause. 'Gomer Parry again, I suppose.'

'Doesn't matter where it came from. I just wondered if your son actually went along to Ellis and asked to be cleansed of the taking-and-driving-away demon.'

'His parents took him.' Judith scowled. 'Another problem in today's world is that parents don't take responsibility. *We* took him to Father Ellis, Councillor Prosser and I. It was our duty.'

'And you really think he had a demon inside him that demanded the full casting-out bit?'

'Oh . . . Mrs . . . Watkins . . .' Exasperated, Judith stood and went to lean an arm on the high mantelpiece. 'They *all* have demons in them, whether it's mischievous imps or worse. In the old days, the demons were beaten out of them at school. Now, if a teacher raises a hand to a child, he's in court for assault, and nothing the poor magistrate can do to help him.'

'I see.' There was an awful logic to this: exorcism as a tool of public order. Evidently the local women had decided that the wanton demon in Marianne Starkey – which perhaps made some local men a little restless, a touch frisky – should be eradicated before it led to trouble. Marianne's reaction to the male witch adding a piquantly topical flavour to the exercise.

'Menna,' Merrily said. 'What about Menna?'

Judith brought her arm slowly down to her side, stiffening ever so slightly.

'Judith, did Menna herself go to Father Ellis and beg for exorcism, to get rid of the molesting spirit of Mervyn Thomas?'

Judith was silent.

'Or was it J.W.'s idea? In his role as husband. And father figure.'

Judith said, eyes unmoving, 'How do you know she was cleansed?'

'Wasn't she?'

'Is that any business of yours or mine?' First sign of a significant loss of cool. 'What would *I* know about the private affairs of Mr and Mrs J.W. Weal? Was I supposed to be her guardian and her keeper *all* her life?'

'You were obviously still concerned about her. You went to visit her regularly. You were still, by all accounts, her only real friend. You were the best person to realize she was . . . still a victim.'

'He loved her!'

'He *suffocated* her, Mrs Prosser. When she was in hospital, he tended her, he washed her, hardly let the nurses near her. I saw him with a bowl of water, as if he was baptizing her all over again. As if he was somehow confirming and reinforcing what Father Ellis had done.'

'You see everything, don't you?'

'Look, I just happened to be there, with Gomer the night his Minnie died. J.W. was like a priest, giving his wife the last rites. But she was already dead. Ellis said at the funeral that he'd baptized them together. Was that a public thing? Were you present?'

Judith came away from the fireplace. There was a large, iron coal stove in it, closed up. She walked to the small window and stood looking out. She was thinking. And she evidently did not want Merrily to see her thinking.

'No,' she said eventually. 'No, I was not there, as such.'

'Am I right in thinking that Menna was still felt to be . . . possessed, if you like, by her father?'

'He was not a pleasant man,' Judith said.

And did you get Menna on the Pill from an early age because you were afraid that what happened to Barbara might happen to her, too? Merrily didn't ask that. It perhaps didn't need asking, not right now.

'You couldn't *really* be sure that Merv was leaving her alone, could you?'

Judith didn't reply.

'And whatever he was like, she was still dependent on him. Dependent on a strong man? Which Weal realized, and lost no time in exploiting.'

Judith kept on looking out of the window. 'He was too old for her, yes. Too rigid in his ways, perhaps. But she *was* a flimsy, delicate thing. She would always need protection.

She was never going to have much of a life with Jeffery, but she would at least be protected.'

'Like a moth in a jar,' Merrily said – and Judith turned sharply around. Merrily met her clear gaze. 'When exactly did you begin to think that J.W. Weal, in his way, might be as bad for Menna as her father had been?'

'It was not my business any more.'

'Oh come on, you'd known that girl all her life. Did it really not occur to you that Weal might think he was somehow still in competition with the dead Mervyn Thomas for Menna's affections? If that's the right word? That maybe he didn't think he was getting . . . everything he was entitled to.'

Judith came back to the fireplace. 'Who is this going to help now?'

Merrily thought back to Barbara Buckingham. *Possession is nine points of the law.'* Perhaps there was still a chance to help Barbara.

But that wouldn't matter much to Judith Prosser.

'Menna,' Merrily said softly. 'Perhaps it will help Menna.'

And so it came out.

The big room at the back of the house. The dining room in which probably no one ever dined. The bay-windowed room with rearing shadows. The room facing the mausoleum.

'This was where it was actually done?' Merrily said. 'How do you know that?'

'Because I watched, of course. I stood in the garden and I spied, just as you did on the night of Menna's funeral. I was in our yard when I saw Father Ellis's car go past slowly. I followed on foot. I saw him enter the old rectory with the medical bag he carries for such occasions. It was towards evening. I saw Menna dressed in white. I saw Father Ellis. I did not see Jeffery.'

Something had snapped. Something had fallen into place. Perhaps something which, even to a *local person*, was no longer defensible.

Merrily said cautiously, 'And did what happened bear comparison with what took place at the village hall yesterday?'

'I don't know,' Judith said. 'It was not possible to see what was happening below the level of the window.'

Merrily's palms were damp. 'You're saying she was on the floor at some point?'

'I'm saying she wasn't visible.'

'When was this?'

'About three . . . four . . . weeks ago? I can't remember exactly.'

'Not that long before she had her stroke, then.'

'I'm making no connection, Mrs Watkins.'

'Do you believe she was possessed and needed exorcism?'

'I think she needed help.'

'Was Dr Coll there?'

'I have no reason to think so.'

'So just Ellis and Menna.'

'I imagine Jeffery was somewhere in the house. His car was there anyway.'

'But you didn't see him in the room?'

'No. What do you want, Mrs Watkins? How can *you* knowing any of this possibly help Menna now?'

'She haunted Barbara,' Merrily said.

'Haunted?'

'I'm using the word loosely. Like memories haunt, guilt haunts.'

'Yes, we know all about that.'

'And spirits haunt.'

'Do they really?' Judith said. 'Do you seriously believe that?'

'Wouldn't be much good in this job if I didn't.' What did

Judith herself believe? That Ellis was an effective psychologist or an effective and useful con man?

Merrily said, 'Barbara wanted me to do a kind of exorcism in reverse, to free Menna's spirit from Weal's possession. Possession of the dead by the living.'

'Do you seriously believe—?'

'*She* believed. And *I* believe we may have a tormented and frantic . . . essence which can't find peace. Like a moth in a jar, except—'

'A moth in a jar doesn't live long.'

'Exactly. That's the difference.'

'And how would you deal with this, Mrs Watkins?' Judith placed her hands on her narrow hips. 'How would you deal with it *now*? How would you go about it? Explain to me.'

'Well, it wouldn't be an exorcism, because this is not an evil spirit. If we think of her perhaps as still a victim, needing to be rescued. Which is normally done by celebrating a Requiem Eucharist in the appropriate place, in the company of people close to the dead person. In this case it could be you. And Mr Weal, obviously.'

'Then it will never be done, will it?'

Merrily heard Eileen Cullen, with the echoes of hospital clatter. *'Swear to God he knew it was there. Twice, he looked back over his shoulder.'*

'He *won't* let her go.' She sank into the chair, clutching the bundled coat to her chest. 'That's what this is about: possessing her in death as he never fully did in life. And knowing that . . . how can I let it go on?'

'Suppose . . .' Judith's voice had risen in pitch. 'Suppose I could get you into that house, into that room – or into the tomb – to perform your ceremony? You wouldn't be doing it with his compliance, but you wouldn't be doing it against his will either, since he wouldn't know about it. Wouldn't that be better than nothing from your point of view, Mrs Watkins?'

'How could you fix that?'

'I have keys, see – keys to the house and also to the tomb. Menna was often taken unwell, so Jeffery gave me a key to get in and attend to her. When she died, he needed someone to let the masons in, to work on the tomb.'

'Why would you want to risk letting *me* in?'

'Perhaps,' Judith said, 'it's a question of what is right – the right thing to do. I cared for Menna when she was alive. Perhaps it's the last thing I can do for her.'

'But it's not right for *me* to go into someone's house without permission.'

'Well . . .' Judith shrugged. 'That's your decision, isn't it?' She bent over and released a valve on the iron stove; there was a rush of air and a slow-building roar of fire. 'I was about to say, Mrs Watkins, that Jeffery won't be there tonight. It's his lodge night. He never misses it, unlike Councillor Prosser. It'll be even more important to him now. Always a great comfort to a man, the Masons.'

Merrily said, 'Perhaps it's a job for Father Ellis instead.'

Judith looked at her with severity. 'Does that mean you are afraid, Mrs Watkins?'

Part Five

...

and when I raised for right there came darkness

I stood up and I cried in the congregation.

Book of Job, Chapter 30, v. 26-8

Part Five

When I looked for good, then evil came unto me;
and when I waited for light there came darkness . . .
I stood up and I cried in the congregation . . .
I am a brother to dragons and a companion to owls.

Book of Job, Chapter 30, v. 26–9

FORTY-SEVEN

Breath of the Dragon

Merrily had arranged to meet Gomer in the Black Lion for a sandwich around two thirty. She was early, but the pub was already filling up with those civilized rambling-club types – anoraks and soft drinks – who seemed to constitute Ellis's core congregation.

More of them today, substantially more. You looked at them individually and they seemed worryingly genuine: young people with a vision of a new day, elderly people with a new and healthy approach to the evening of the day. There was a buzz of energy in the dispirited, part-painted Black Lion bar, each hug, each 'Praise God' passing on a vibration.

Merrily found herself standing next to a white-bearded man of about sixty, one of the few with a glass of beer. She asked him where he was from. Wolverhampton, he said, West Midland Pentecostal.

'How far've you come, sister?'

'Oh, just from Ledwardine, just over the border. How many of you are there?'

'About . . . what, fifty-five? Hired ourselves a coach. Luckily, there's a lot of retired people in our church, but quite a few youngsters've taken a day off work.' He grinned, relaxed. 'It's a question of whose work you put first, isn't it? We're going to walk down to this satanist place after lunch and hold some Bible readings outside the gate. I've not actually seen Father Ellis yet, but I'm told he's a very inspiring man.'

'So they say.'

'Praise God,' said the man from Wolverhampton.

Merrily saw Gomer coming in and pointed to the table near the door. She ordered drinks and cheese sandwiches at the bar. Greg Starkey avoided her eyes.

Gomer was wearing his bomber jacket over a grey sweatshirt with 'Gomer Parry Plant Hire' on it in red.

'Three bloody coaches on the car park, vicar.'

'Mmm. It's what happens these days – everything goes to extremes. Fastest growing movement in the Church and, hey, they're going to prove it.'

'En't the only ones. Bunch of ole vans backed into a forestry clearing up towards the ole rectory. Lighting camp fires, bloody fools.'

'Travellers?'

'Pagans, they reckons.'

Merrily sighed. 'All we need.'

'Two police vans set up in the ole schoolyard – Dr Coll's surgery. Another one in Big Weal's drive – the ole rectory. Makes you laugh, don't it? Two biggest bloody villains in East Radnor, both well in with the cops.'

Merrily dumped her cigarettes and lighter on the table. 'You find out some more?'

'Been over to Nev's.'

'Your nephew, yes?'

'Ar. Drop in now and then, make sure the boy's lookin' after the ole diggers. Anyway, Nev's with a lawyer in Llandod, plays bloody golf with him. He gave him a ring for me, off the record, like. Word is Big Weal's favourite clients is *ole* clients, specially them not too quick up top n'more.'

'Going senile?'

'Worries a lot about their wills when they gets like that,

see. Who's gonner get what, how it's gonner get sorted when they snuffs it. What they needs is a good lawyer – and a good doctor. Puts their mind at rest, ennit?' 'Specially folk as en't had a family lawyer for generations, see.'

'Incomers? Refugees from Off, in need of guidance?'

'Exac'ly it, vicar. This boy in Llandod, he reckons Weal gets a steady stream of ole clients recommended by their nice, kindly doctor. That confirm what you yeard, vicar?'

'Fits in. And if we were to go a step further down that road, we might find a nice kindly priest.'

'Sure t'be,' Gomer said. 'Church gets to be more important, the nearer you gets to that big ole farm gate.'

Two bikers came in. One wore a leather jacket open to a white T-shirt with a black dragon motif. The dragon was on its back, with a spear down its throat. It was hard to be sure which side they represented.

At four o'clock, the ruined church of St Michael looked like an old, beached boat, waiting for the tide of night to set it afloat.

'Going to be lit up like a birthday cake,' Betty said with distaste. 'You can't spot them from here, but there are clusters of candles and garden torches all over it. In the windows, on ledges, between the battlements on the tower. It'll be visible for miles from the hills.'

'Making a statement?'

'Yeah. After centuries of holding ceremonies discreetly in the woods and behind curtains in suburban back rooms, we're coming out.'

They'd met in the decaying copse, Merrily walking from the old archaeological site, where Gomer had parked, Betty coming across the bridge from the farmhouse and joining the footpath.

The sky had dulled, low clouds pocketing the sunken sun,

and you could feel the dusk, carrying spores of frost. Betty looked cold. Merrily tightened her scarf.

'Bain still wants to do it naked?'

'Possibly. They'll light a small fire inside a circle of stones in the open nave. Dance back to back with arms linked behind. Not as silly as it sounds. After a while you don't feel it. You're aglow.'

Like singing in tongues, Merrily thought. A long, flat cloud lay over the church now, like a wide-brimmed hat. From the other side of the ruins, beyond the pines and the Sitka spruce, they could hear the sounds of a hymn: straggly singing, off-key. The Christians at the gate.

'They're going to keep that up all night long, aren't they?' Betty said.

'You've heard nothing yet. There are scores more in the village now.'

'Bad.' Betty shivered. 'Ned believes the spiritual tension will fuel the rite. He says we can appropriate their energy. That is way, way out of order.' She shook herself. 'I need to get them out of here, lock the gates and . . . try and save my marriage.'

'Will you stay here . . . afterwards?'

Betty shook her head. 'We won't survive this. We'll lose everything we've got with that house, but I don't care if we're destitute. Only problem is, I'm going to feel guilty about anyone else living here. I wish we could sell it to a waste disposal firm or something.'

'But we're going to deal with that,' Merrily said firmly.

'No. It was very stupid of me to ask you.' Betty looked at her, green eyes sorrowful, without hope. 'I wasn't thinking. This is part of a prehistoric ritual complex. We don't know who or what those original inhabitants were, but they chose their sites well. They knew all the doorways. Can't you feel the earth and the air fusing together as it gets dark? This is a place that knows itself – but we don't know it. Can't you hear it?'

'Just the singing,' Merrily admitted.

'I can hear a constant low humming now. I know it's in my head, but it's this *place* that's put it there. We don't know what went on here, nobody does. There are no stones left standing, only the holes where they were . . . and that church. And whatever – metaphorically, if you like – is underneath that church. And whatever it is, it's much older than Christianity.'

'And much, much older than Wicca?' Merrily said.

'Sure. We were invented in the fifties and sixties by well-meaning people who knew there was no continuous tradition. Most of Wicca's either made up or culled from Aleister Crowley and Dion Fortune. It has no *tradition*. There. I've said it. Is that what you wanted?'

The singing was already louder; more Christians had arrived.

'There's a tradition here,' Merrily said, 'of sorts. A strand of something that goes back at least to medieval times. Unfortunately, it seems to have been preserved by *my* lot.'

'Yeah. You can certainly feel it in Cascob. Oh, and St Michael's, Cefnllys. I meant to tell you – I looked this up – that when they eventually built a new church at Llandrindod the rector had the roof taken off Cefnllys Church to stop people worshipping there.'

'He did?'

'It was in a book. I suddenly remembered it from when I was a kid in Llandrindod. So I looked it up. I mean, was *he* thinking like Penney? Did they both feel the breath of the dragon? Probably didn't understand any of it, but something scared them badly. Now people like Ned Bain are coming along and saying: it's OK, it's fine, its cool . . . because *we're* the dragon. Do you still want to go in there with your holy water?'

'What time?'

'Any time after . . . I dunno, nine? If you don't come, I'll understand. Who's that?'

It was a vehicle, creaking over the footpath, where it had been widened by the archaeologists. Merrily ran to the edge of the copse. She could see Gomer's ancient Land-Rover parked the other side, with Gomer leaning on the bonnet, smoking a roll-up, watching the new vehicle trundling towards him. It was Sophie's Saab.

FORTY-EIGHT

Black Christianity

No candles? The candles had gone from the windows. Not just gone out, but *gone*: the trays, the Bibles, everything.

At first, it seemed an encouraging sign, and then Merrily thought, It isn't. It isn't at all. In the face of the invasion, the local people had withdrawn, disconnected; whatever happened tonight would not be their fault.

It was about 5.50 p.m. The post office and shop had closed, there were few lights in the cottages. Only the pub was conspicuously active; otherwise Old Hindwell, under dark forestry and the hump of Burfa Hill, had retracted into itself, leaving the streets to them from Off.

The multitude!

In the centre of the village, maybe 300 or 400 people had gathered in front of the former school. They had Christian placards and torches and lamps. They were not singing hymns. They seemed leaderless.

Gomer put the Land-Rover at the side of the road, in front of the entrance to the pub's yard, where it said 'No Parking'. The car park was so full that none of the coaches would get out until several cars were removed. Two dark blue police vans lurked inside the school gates. Four TV crews hovered.

The minority of pagans here seemed to be the kind with green hair and eyebrow rings. Maybe twenty of them, in

bunches – harmless probably. One group, squatting outside
the pub, were chanting 'Harken to the Witches' Rune', to the
hollow thump of a hand drum.

'Sad,' Jane commented. She and Eirion were in the back
of the Land-Rover; Merrily sat next to Gomer in the front.
'They're just playing at it, just being annoying.'

'You'll be joining the Young Conservatives next, flower.'

'But those so-called Christians *really* make me sick.
They're tossers, holier-than-thou gits.'

'Phew,' Merrily said. Through the wing mirror, she saw
Sophie's Saab pulling in behind them. Sophie didn't get out.

Eirion said, 'What do you want us to do, Mrs Watkins?'

'Just stay with Gomer and Sophie. Perhaps you could get
something to eat in the pub?'

Jane was dismayed. 'That's all the thanks we get? A
mouldy cheese sandwich and a can of Coke?'

'Don't think I'm not *immensely* grateful for what you two
and Sophie've uncovered. Just that I need to put it to Ellis
by myself. If there are any witnesses, he won't even talk to
me.'

They'd talked intently for over an hour in the Land-Rover,
listened to a cassette recording of a phone call involving
Sophie and some journalist in Tennessee, and then Merrily
had watched as Betty, now armed with many things she
hadn't known about Ned Bain, had walked away into the
last of the dusk, not looking back.

Merrily leaned against the Land-Rover's passenger door,
and it opened with a savage rending sound.

'How long will you be?' Jane asked.

'As long as it takes. He hasn't even shown yet. An hour
and a half maybe?'

'And then we come looking for you?'

'And then do whatever Gomer tells you.'

The crazy violence seemed to start as soon as Merrily's feet touched the tarmac: lights flaring, a woman's scream, a beer can thrown. A black cross reared out of a mesh of torch beams amid a tangle of angry voices.

'. . . *finished*, you fuckers. Had your time. Christ was a wanker!'

'. . . your level, isn't it? The gutter! Get out of my—'

Sickening crunch of bone on flesh. Blood geysering up.

'Oh dear God—'

'So why don't you just fuck off back to your churches, 'fore we have 'em *all* off you?'

'Stand back!'

'Reverend?' A hand pulling Merrily back, as the police came through.

'Marianne?'

She was pushed. 'Stand back, please. Everybody, back!'

Headlights arriving. Then Collard Banks-Morgan with his medical bag. Next to him, a man in a dark suit. *Not a white monk's habit, but a dark suit.*

A woman shrieked, 'You'll be damned for ever!' and started to cry.

'Listen, Reverend,' Marianne said calmly. 'I'm better now.'

'Good.'

'Things you oughta know.' She pulled Merrily into the yard.

She followed when they took the man with the broken nose into the surgery. A woman too, spattered with his blood, wailing, Ellis's arm around her. 'He's in good hands, sister. The best.'

In the waiting room, the lighting was harsh, the seats old and hard, the ceiling still school-hall high, with cream-painted metal girders. A woman receptionist smiled smugly through a hatch in the wall. 'Come through,' Dr Coll sang, voice like muzak. 'Bring him through, that's right.'

Doors slammed routinely. There were health posters all over the walls: posters to make you feel ill, paranoid, dependent. No surprise that Dr Coll had taken over the school, a local bastion of authority and wisdom.

'I'd like to talk to you,' Merrily said to Ellis.

'I'm sure you would, Mrs Watkins,' he said briskly, 'but I don't have the time or the interest to talk to you. You're a vain and stupid woman.' Under his suit he wore a black shirt, no tie, no clerical collar.

'What happened to your messiah kit?'

'Libby, tell Dr Coll I'll talk to him later,' Ellis said to the receptionist.

Merrily said, 'There's going to be trouble out there.' She waited as Ellis dabbed with a tissue at a small blood speck on his sleeve. 'Are you going to stop them marching to the church?'

'Who am I,' he said, 'to stop anyone?'

'You started it. You lit the blue touchpaper.'

'The media started it. As you say, it's already out of hand. It'd be highly irresponsible of me to inflame it further. Now, if you don't mind . . .'

'You *could* stop them. You could stop it *now*. It isn't worth it for a crumbling old building with a bad reputation.'

'I'd lock the door after us if I were you, Libby,' Ellis said to the receptionist.

'I'll do that, Father.'

Ellis held open the main door for Merrily, looking over her head. 'After you.' She didn't move. 'Don't make me ask the police to come in,' Ellis said.

'Could you clear up a few points for me, Nick?'

'Good*night*.'

She had no confidence for this, still couldn't quite believe it.

' "I am a brother to dragons",' Merrily said.

'Go away.' He didn't look at her, opened the door wider. 'Book of Job.'

'I do *know* the Book of Job.'

The sounds of the street outside came in, carried on cold air, sounds alien to Old Hindwell – shouts, jeers, a man's unstable voice, on high, *'May God have mercy on you!'*

'I think your real name is Simon Wesson,' Merrily said. 'You went out to the States with your mother and sister in the mid-seventies, after the death of your stepfather. Over there, your mother married an evangelist called Marshall McAllman. You later became his personal assistant. He made a lot of money before he was exposed and disgraced and your mother divorced him – very lucratively, I believe.'

She couldn't look at him while she was saying all this, terrified that it was going to be wrong, that Jane and Eirion had found the wrong person, that the journalist whose voice Sophie had so efficiently recorded was talking about someone with no connection at all to Nicholas Ellis.

'McAllman concentrated on little backwoods communities. His technique was to do thorough research before he brought his show to town. He'd employ investigators. And although he would appear aloof when he first arrived . . .'

'None of your good-old-boy stuff from Marshall,' the journalist had told Sophie on the tape. *'Marshall was cool, Marshall was laid-back, Marshall would target a town that was hungry and he'd spread a table and he'd check into a hotel and sit back and wait for them to come sniffing and drooling . . .'*

'. . . his remoteness only added to his mystique. They came to him – the local dignitaries, the civic leaders, the business people – and he passed on, almost reluctantly, what the Holy Spirit had communicated to him about them and their lives and their past and their future . . . and he convinced them that they and their town were riddled with all kinds of demons.'

Merrily focused on a wall poster about the symptoms of meningitis. She spoke in a low voice, could see Libby the receptionist straining to hear while pretending to rearrange leaflets behind the window of her hutch.

'Time and time again, the local people would pull Marshall into the bosom of the community, everyone begging him to take away their demons, and their children's demons . . . especially the daughters, those wayward kids. A little *internal ministry* . . . well, it beats abortion. He was a prophet and a local hero in different localities. He only went to selected places, little, introverted, no-hope places with poor communications – the places that were gagging for it.'

The print on the meningitis poster began to blur. She turned at last to look up at Ellis, his nose lifted in disdain, but she could see his hand whitening around the doorknob.

'He taught you a lot, Nick, about the psychology of rural communities. And about manipulation. Plus, he gave you the inner strength and the brass neck to come back to this country and finally take on your hated, still-vengeful stepbrother.'

She stood in the doorway and waited.

Ellis closed the door again.

In the Black Lion, Jane saw Gomer was talking at the bar to a fat man of about thirty in a thick plaid shirt that came down halfway to his knees. At their table by the door, Sophie gathered her expensive and elegant camel coat over her knees to protect them from the draught.

'I'd take you two back to Hereford with me, if I thought you'd stay put in the office.'

'No chance.' Jane ripped open a bag of crisps, stretched out her legs.

'Nothing's going to *happen* here, Jane,' Sophie said. 'The whole thing comes down to two obsessive men settling a childhood grudge.'

'But what a grudge, Sophie. Serious, *serious* hatred fermenting for over a quarter of a century. A fundamentalist bigot and a warlock steeped in old magic. A white witch and a black Christian.'

'Jane!'

'He *is*. If you, like, *subvert* Christianity, if you use it aggressively to try and hurt or crush people of a different religion . . . or if you go around exorcizing demons out of people who haven't actually got demons *in* them, just to get power over them – like this guy McAllman – then you're using Christianity for evil, so that's got to be *black* Christianity.'

'I wouldn't exactly call Bain a *white* witch, either,' Eirion murmured.

Sophie said, 'Jane, your grasp of theology—'

But Gomer was back with them, thoughtfully rolling and unrolling his cap. 'That's Nev,' he said, watching the man in the plaid shirt go out. 'My nephew, Nev, see. Er, some'ing's come up, ennit? Mrs Hill, if there's a chance you could stay with these kids till the vicar gets back . . .'

'Uh-huh.' Jane shook her head. 'Mum said to stick with Gomer.'

Gomer sighed. He opened the pub door, peered out. Jane got up and leaned over his shoulder. There were still a lot of people out there and more police – about seven of them. Also, the guy in the plaid shirt standing by a truck. In the back of the truck was a yellow thing partly under a canvas cover.

'What's that?' Jane demanded.

'Mini-JCB.'

'Like for digging?'

'Sure t'be,' Gomer admitted gruffly.

Ellis took her into the second surgery: a plain room with a big, dark desk, Victorian-looking. Authority. A big chair and a small chair. Ellis sat in the big chair; Merrily didn't sit down. She was thinking rapidly back over the history of her faith, the unsavoury aspects.

In the Middle Ages, Christianity was still magic: charms and blessings indistinguishable. The Reformation was supposed to have wiped that out but, in seventeenth-century Britain, religious healers and exorcists were still putting on public displays, just like modern Bible Belt evangelists. And when it was finally over in most of Britain, here in Radnorshire – inside the inverted pentagram of churches dedicated to the warrior archangel – it continued. In a place with a strong tradition of pagan magic, the people transferred their allegiances to the priests . . . the more perspicacious of whom took on the role of the conjuror, the cunning man.

Few more cunning than Nicholas Ellis, formerly Simon Wesson. His face was unlined, bland, insolent – looking up at her but really looking down.

'Where's your mother now, Nick?'

'Dead. Drowned in her swimming pool in Orlando, four years ago. An accident.'

'Your sister?'

'Still out there. Married with kids.'

'You came back to Britain because of what happened over Marshall McAllman and this Tennessee newspaper?'

'I've told you I *won't* discuss that.' He brought a hand down hard on the desk. He was sweating. 'And if you say a word about any of this outside these walls, I shall instruct my solicitor to obtain an immediate injunction to restrain you and make preparations to take you to court for libel. Do you understand?'

'This is Mr Weal, is it?'

'Never underestimate him.'

'I wouldn't. He'll do anything for you, won't he? After what you did for him. And for his wife – before she died.'

Ellis kept his lips tight, his face uplifted to the lights and shining.

'You must have investigated this parish pretty thoroughly before you applied for it. Or were you looking specifically for a parish that suited your kind of ministry? Or was it just luck?'

'Or the will of God?'

'From what I gather, your mother was into a particularly mystical form of High Church—'

He turned his chair away with a wrench. 'No. No. *No!* I will *not*.'

'Perhaps *she* found the connections. Perhaps she was a particular influence on McAllman's ministry.' Merrily stood with her back to the door. 'Any point in asking you if you *did* actually help to cover up a less-than-hot-blooded murder?'

His eyes burned.

'All that matters is Ned Bain thinks you did,' Merrily said.

'Edward is a despicable nonentity.'

'Not in pagan circles he isn't. I mean, I suppose it's easy to say that's *why* he became a pagan. It's rough, natural, wild . . . very much a reaction against your mother's suffocating churchiness.'

He rose up. 'Blasphemer!'

Merrily lost it, bounced from the door. 'Do you know what *real* blasphemy is, Nick? It's a man with a nine-inch cross.'

'I will *not*—'

'Do you sterilize it first?'

'May God have mercy on you!'

'Only, I was there when you exorcized Marianne Starkey. Who . . .' Merrily prayed swiftly for forgiveness. 'Who's now prepared to make a detailed statement.'

A lie. But she had him. He stared at her.

'We've prepared a press release, Nick. Unless she hears from me by seven o'clock, my secretary's been instructed to fax it to the Press Association in London.'

Ellis folded his arms.

Merrily looked at her watch. 'I make it you've got just under an hour.'

'To do what?' He leaned back, expressionless.

'Put on your white messiah gear,' Merrily said. 'Get out there and tell them it's all over. Tell them to go home. Or lead them all up to the village hall and keep them there.'

Ellis spread his hands. 'They'll be there, anyway. The police wanted them off the streets. I believe the Prossers have taken them to the hall.'

'Keep them there then. Tell them you don't want to risk their immortal souls by having them stepping onto the contaminated ground of St Michael's.'

He shrugged. 'OK, sure.' He leaned back, two fingers along the side of his head, curious. 'But I don't understand. Why do you care?'

She didn't follow him. She stayed on the edge of the school-yard, near the police vans, and saw lights eventually come on in what she reckoned was Ellis's house. Dr Coll came out of the surgery, but didn't so much as glance at her. Perhaps Judith hadn't told him. At the same time, two policemen went in, presumably to obtain statements from the injured man and his wife. Merrily resisted an impulse to yell at Dr Coll, 'Why did you kill Mrs Wilshire?' in the hope that some copper might hear.

The village was comparatively quiet again. The lights were still few and bleary. Or maybe it was her eyes. Was there more she could have done? If there was, she couldn't think what it might be. She was tired. She prayed that Ellis would see sense.

A few minutes later, she saw him coming down from the council estate, a Hollywood ghost in his white monk's habit. He walked past the school and didn't turned his head towards her. Leaving twenty or thirty yards between them, she followed him to the hall. A cameraman spotted him and ran ahead of him and crouched in the road, recording his weary, stately progress to his place of worship. A journalist, puffing out white steam, ran back to the pub to alert the others. Merrily prayed that they were all going to be very disappointed. Like the Christians.

'With respect, Father, what was the point of us coming at all?'

One man on his feet in the crowded hall. It was the biker with the black dragon.

Ellis brought his hands together. 'You came here because you were moved by the Holy Spirit. We must all obey those impulses which we recognize as a response to the will of God.'

'But,' the man persisted, 'what does God want us to *do*?'

Ellis let the question hang a while, then he said softly, 'You all saw what happened earlier to our brother. I can tell you that two men have been charged with assault causing actual bodily harm. That will be the least of *their* punishment. But, in allowing that to happen, God was telling us that a public demonstration is no longer the answer. The answer is prayer.'

'Praise God,' someone cried, but it was half-hearted. They wanted . . .

Blood? Merrily sat at the back, demoralized even in victory.

'There will be no more . . . violence.' Ellis emphasized it with open hands. There was desultory applause. 'But our task is still far from over.'

He told them they must pray for the intervention of St Michael to keep his church out of the hands of Satan, out of the red claws of the dragon. And if they prayed, if their faith in God was strong enough, the Devil would fail tonight. The Lord would yet intervene.

A frisson went through the hall; there were tentative moans.

'God' – Ellis's arms were suddenly extended, ramrod stiff – 'arises!'

A man arose from the floor, his own arms raised, a mirror image of the priest. Others followed, with a squeaking and scraping of chairs.

Hundreds of arms reaching for the ceiling.

A woman began to gabble, 'God, God, God, God, God!' orgasmically.

Soon, Merrily found she was the only one seated and was obliged to scramble to her feet. She looked up and saw that Ellis – who must surely know that this was as good as over, that there would be no more generating paranoia, no more wholesale exorcism, no more *internal ministry* – was aglow again, his eyes like foglamps, and they were focused, through the wintry forest of stiffened arms . . . focused on her.

'*God arises!*' Ellis snarled.

Merrily left the hall. He was showing her that even in defeat his power was undiminished. That the Holy Spirit was with *him*.

'A remarkable man, Mrs Watkins,' said Judith Prosser.

She was standing in the porch, in her long black quilted coat.

'Yes,' Merrily admitted.

Judith gently closed the doors on the assembly. She contemplated Merrily with a wryly tilted smile. 'I take it,' she said lightly, 'that you've made your decision.'

'I'm sorry?'

'Your "exorcism in reverse",' Judith said. 'The laying to rest of the poor moth in the jar.'

'Oh. Yes.'

'Jeffery will have left now, for his lodge. But perhaps this was not such a good idea.'

Inside the hall, a hymn was beginning. It would end in tongues. Ellis and his followers were, for the time being, contained. Jane, too, by Gomer and Sophie. Merrily had a couple of hours yet before she was due at St Michael's. She walked out into the cold and looked down on the meagre glimmer of the village. She shivered inside Jane's duffel coat.

'All right,' she said. 'Let's go and do it.'

FORTY-NINE

Cashmere and Tweed

Jane had never seen Gomer quite like this before, although she'd heard the tales. The legend.

Ciggy glowing malevolently in the centre of his teeth, like a ruby in the face of some Indian idol, he rode the mini-JCB into the middle of the field to where the earth was banked. The digger was the size of a heavy-duty ride-on mower. A big yellow Tonka toy. Nev's truck was parked a few yards back, engine running, headlights full beam. Next to it, at a slight angle, was Gomer's Land-Rover, with Sophie inside.

In any other situation, Jane would have found this deeply, shockingly thrilling, but tonight she only wanted to get it over with, and find Mum.

This was Prosser's ground, turned over to the archae- ologists who'd dug trenches all over the place, and then paid fat Nev to replace the tons of removed soil. Up here with Mum yesterday, Gomer had noticed a part that was not professionally finished. Not how he'd taught Nev to do it. Not seeded, but clumsily planted with turf. Not made good to Gomer Parry Plant Hire standards.

Gomer had taken it up with Nev. Nev had been offended. Nev said he'd left a bloody perfect job, banked up and seeded tidy.

Now, it could be that Gareth Prosser had buried some

sheep here, but no sheep grazed this area, and it was a long way to come for a dull, lazy bugger like Gareth.

'Eirion!' Gomer yelled. 'Do me a favour, boy, back the ole Land-Rover up a few feet, then we can see the top o' the mound.'

'OK.' Eirion ran through the mud.

'Jane!' Sophie called from the truck. 'Either you come in here, or I'm coming out for you.' Knowing Jane was quite keen to sneak away and snatch a look at the ruins of the church across the brook, to see if they were all lit up.

'Oh, Sophie, Gomer might need some help.'

'Very well.' The truck's passenger door creaked open. There was a squelch. 'Blast!'

Jane grinned. Sophie was not the kind to carry wellies in the boot.

The bucket of the little digger went into the soft bank like a spoon into chocolate fudge. Gomer had thought this mini-JCB might be more appropriate than a big one, in the circumstances, and also less conspicuous. It couldn't be an awful lot less conspicuous, with all the noise Gomer was making.

'This is quite ridiculous.' Sophie was now limping across the field, serious mud-splashes on her camel coat. 'I don't know how I ever agreed—'

'You didn't agree. We dragged you along. I'm sorry, Sophie. You've been, like, really brilliant today.'

'Shut up, Jane.'

'We could have told the police, I suppose, but they probably couldn't have done anything without going to a magistrate for a warrant or something, and that would have meant tomorrow.'

'Mind yourselves!' Gomer bawled. The arm of the digger swung, the bucket dipped with a slurping, sucking sound. Jane wondered if Minnie's exasperated spirit was watching him now.

The bucket clanged and shivered. '—*ucking Nora!*' Gomer snarled. The digger's hydraulic feet gripped at the slippery earth, the whole machine bucked and Gomer rose from the seat like a cowboy. He turned and spat out his cigarette end. 'Eirion! Can you get the ole torch to that, see what we got there?'

But it was a just a big rock, too big for the digger to shift. Gomer and Eirion had to manhandle it out of the way. It took ages; they both got filthy.

After about half an hour, there was a new bank of earth, three feet high, at right angles to the one they were excavating. It was like some First World War landscape. Jane wandered over to the digger.

'Gomer, look, suppose Sophie and I go back and see what's happened to Mum? Is that OK?'

'Sure t'be.' Gomer sat back in the headlight beams, his glasses brown-filmed. 'We en't gettin' nowhere fast yere. Bloody daft idea, most likely. Gotter put all this shit back, too, 'fore we leaves.'

'It was worth a *try*, Gomer. You aren't usually wrong. OK, look, we'll get back just as soon as we—'

'Mr Parry!' Eirion's face turned round from the gouged-out bank.

'Ar?'

'Oh bloody hell, Mr Parry.' Eirion slurped desperately out of the clay. He dropped the lamp and his muddy hands went to his mouth. Jane heard him vomiting, the sick slapping into the mud.

Gomer was out of his seat, grabbing the hand lamp from where it had rolled. 'Stay there, Jane. Bloody *stay* there!'

*

Jane froze where she was, in the clinging mud. All those crass remarks she'd made to Mum after Mumford had been, after the radio reports. It should have been her, not Eirion. She deserved to face this horror.

Sophie was hopping towards her. 'What is it?'

'They've found something.'

'Then let's call the police.'

'He needs to make sure, Sophie.'

Realizing, with a horrible, freezing feeling that Gomer wasn't in any position to make sure of this. Only *she* was.

She would *have* to face it.

'Sorry.' Eirion came back. His baseball cap had gone. His face gleamed with greasy clay and sweat. There were touchingly childish mud streaks around his mouth where he'd wiped it with his hand. 'That was inexcusable.'

'Irene . . .?'

'It was the smell, I suppose.' He shuddered. 'I just put my hand down this kind of fissure and this whole wall of stuff came down and like . . . Oh God.' He turned away, pushing slimy fingers through his hair.

Gomer came back for the spade.

'Is it?' Jane was shocked at the weakness of her own voice.

''Ang about,' Gomer said non-committally.

Sophie said, her voice dry and clipped, '*Is* it, Mr Parry?'

'Well . . . likely.'

'Oh, for heaven's sake, give me that torch!' Sophie snatched the rubber-covered lamp from a caterpillar of the mini-JCB and stalked off into the murk.

Gomer followed her with the spade, called back over his shoulder, 'Better stay there, girl. En't nothin' you can do.'

'I kind of think there is, actually,' Jane said sadly. She slithered after him towards the bank. Eirion plunged into the mud, grabbed her.

'No . . .'

'Irene, I'm the only one of us who's actually seen her.'

'Jane, believe me . . . that is not going to help you.'

'What?'

Even over the clatter of three engines, she heard Sophie's moan. Ahead of her, the newly unearthed soil and clay was shining almost white in the intersecting beams, and had that multihued, stretched look, like when you bent a Mars bar in half. Sophie came back, slapping dirt from her hands.

'Go back. Now!'

'Sophie . . .?'

'It's a woman.'

'Could it be Barb—?'

'Cashmere and tweed,' Sophie said. 'She's wearing cashmere and tweed.'

'What does she look like? I've seen her, you see. When she first came up to Mum at the funeral . . .'

'Come on, Jane.'

'I'm not a little kid, you know. Let me just—'

'Jane.' Eirion took her hand in his mud-encrusted paw. 'We don't know *what* she looks like.'

Sophie said coldly, 'Someone seems to have hacked her face to pieces before they buried her.'

Sophie's camel coat was ruined.

FIFTY

Scumbag

Alone in the yard, Robin looked back at the farmhouse, lit by the underfed porchlight, and it was like he was finally waking up.

Here were the once-white walls, stained and crumbling to reveal rubble underneath. There were the four front windows, small and sunken, like squinting eyes.

Then it just, like, hit him in the gut: *What a dump!* What was he doing here, stranded in this squalid hovel, with a coughing stove and a pile of wet wood, and his wife coming and going like some kind of elemental spirit, and his portfolios coming back marked 'Piece of shit', this whole god-forsaken place rejecting him?

All day he'd felt a madness around him, wild fluctuations of mood, chasms of disaster opening up at his feet, like the potholes in the yard . . . and then the sun suddenly breaking out again, the puddles streaked with rainbows.

'I still think Kirk could be persuaded to listen to reason.'

The elegant and cultured Ned Bain could change it all about, even though Bain was doing this not for Robin, whom he didn't really need, but for Betty, whom he apparently did. Whom everyone did.

Even witches talked in hushed tones about Betty. There were all kinds of people in Wicca, and the ones you needed to be most wary of tended to be the men – guys who'd read

483

about group sex and ritual flagellation, guys who'd heard you could learn to magic your dick into staying hard all night long. Every coven attracted a few of these, and they never stuck it long, and they were the trash end of the Craft. And at the other end were women like Betty, about whom even witches talked in hushed tones. *'I was very much looking forward to meeting her,'* Ned Bain had said. *'Word gets around.'*

And yet, since Betty had returned home, she and Bain seemed hardly to have spoken, as though neither wanted the other to read their private agenda. Because there sure as hell *were* private agendas here, even stupid and decidedly unpsychic Robin could sense that. Maybe – like high priest and high priestess – Bain and Betty were communicating without words. Robin's fists tightened. He couldn't bear the thought of that.

The night was as cold as you could get without inches of snow on the ground, but it was bright, with a last-quarter moon and a scattering of stars. So what, in the names of all the gods, were they waiting for?

The church itself was primed for its reversion to the Old Religion. A hundred fat candles were in place, plus garden torches and sconces and fireworks for when it was all over. There was a purposeful silence around the place, unbroken even by crazy Vivvie and fluty-voiced Max. Even the god-damned Christians had cooled their hymn-singing.

Robin had had to get out of the house; he couldn't stand the tension, had kept getting up and walking around, irritating the witches who were sitting in the parlour, hanging out, waiting, their robes – in view of the extreme cold, they were at least starting this one robed – stowed in bags at their feet, and the crown of lights ready in the centre of the room. But whose house was this anyway? He'd wanted Betty to come outside with him, confide in him. She was a great priestess but she was still his wife, for heaven's sake.

But Betty had avoided his eyes.

Was there something she didn't want him to know? Something secretly confided to her by Bain? He who would later join with her in the Great Rite – simulated. *Simulated, right?* Robin's nails dug into his palms. Bain was a handsome and, he guessed, very sexual guy.

Usually – invariably, in fact – the hours before any sabbat were lit with this gorgeous anticipation. Tonight was *the* sabbat. An event likely to be more resonant, in Robin's view, than the collapse of the Berlin Wall, than the return of Hong Kong to the Chinese. This should be the finest night of his life. So how come, as he walked back toward the house, all he felt was a sick apprehension?

The pub car park, the point where the village streets come together, is full of nothing much. Coppers and reporters, yes – but where were all the funny Christians, then?

Gomer leaves the truck on the double-yellows outside the school, and that boy Eirion brings the Land-Rover in behind him. Eirion's going along with Mrs Hill to tell the coppers what they've dug up. Better coming from somebody cultured, see, so the cops move faster. Besides which, Gomer and young Jane need to find the vicar in a hurry, on account of there's somebody out there has done for Barbara Thomas, then took what Gomer judges to be a log-splitter to her face, before her was planted in Prosser's ground.

One of the telly cameramen is pointing his lens at the mini-JCB. A bored-looking woman reporter asks, 'What have you been digging?'

'Sprouts,' Gomer tells her. He's spotted a light in the old school that's now become Dr Coll's surgery. 'Why don't we give this a try, girl?' he asks Jane. 'Vicar was in yere earlier, we knows that.'

They walk into the yard. Don't seem two minutes since this old place was a working school. Don't seem two minutes since Gomer had *friends* went to this school. That's life, too bloody short. Too short for bloody old wallop and bullshit.

So, who should they meet but Dr Coll himself in the doorway, coming out. Gomer stands his ground, and Dr Coll's got to take a step back into the building. Has to be a reason, going way back, that Gomer don't care for doctors, but he bloody don't, and that's the only mercy about the way Minnie went: no long years of being at the mercy of no bloody doctors.

'Look, I'm afraid surgery's long over.'

'It bloody en't, pal.' Gomer lets the youngster in, and then slams the door behind them all.

'I know you, don't I?' Dr Coll says, with a vague bit of a smile. Must be close on sixty now, but he never seems to change. Dapper, the word is. Beard a bit grey now, but never allowed to go ratty.

'Gomer Parry Plant Hire,' Gomer says.

'Ah, yes.'

'Never goes near no bloody doctors meself, but you might recall as how you used to peddle drugs to a friend o' mine, Danny Thomas.'

'I really don't think so.' The smile coming off like grease on a rag.

'And Terry Penney, remember? But that's all water up the ole brook, now, ennit?'

'If you're trying to tell me,' Dr Coll says severely, 'that you're hoping I'll supply you with proscribed drugs, I think you should decide to leave very quickly. In case you didn't notice, there's a police van parked directly outside.'

'Shows what kind of a bloody nerve you got then, ennit, Doc?'

'Mr Parry—'

'Them coppers knew what we knew, they'd be in yere, turnin' the place over.'

'Are you *drunk*, man?'

Young Jane picks up the thread now. '*We* know you killed that old lady in New Radnor. You've probably killed, like, *loads* of people. You're probably like that Dr Shipman.'

'All right!' Dr Coll turning nasty at last. 'I haven't got all night to listen to a lot of ludicrous nonsense. Out of here, the pair of you!'

Gomer shoves himself back against the door. Dr Coll's eight, maybe ten years younger than him. And taller, but then most blokes are. Don't make no odds when you're madder than what they are, and Gomer is sorely mad now.

'Guess who just got dug up, Doc.'

Dr Coll tries to grab the door handle, but Gomer knocks his wrist away with his own wrist, which hurts like buggery. Gomer grits his teeth.

'Remember Barbara Thomas? Come to see you the other week, 'bout her sister, Menna? Likely you're one o' the last people poor ole Barbara talked to 'fore some bugger ripped the face off her then planted her in Prosser's bottom field, down where the harchaeologists was.'

Colour drains out of the doc's face something beautiful. Gomer's well heartened by this.

'Course, the cops don't know Barbara seen *you* 'fore she got done. Cops don't know nothin' about you an' Weal, the bloody Hindwell Trust, all the doolally patients you recommended to Weal for sortin' their wills . . .'

'You're making no sense to me.' Dr Coll coming over with all the conviction of a bloke caught with a vanload of videos at two in the morning saying he's just been to a bloody car boot sale.

'Well, then.' Gomer folds his arms. 'I'll be straight with you, Dr Death. All we wants to know right now is where we finds the vicar. The lady vicar? We finds the vicar, we'll likely have that much to talk about, could be well into tomorrow 'fore we gets round to makin' police statements 'bout anythin' else – you gets my meanin'. Leavin' quite a bit o' time for a feller to pack his Range Rover with money and bugger off.'

'I've got a wife and family,' Dr Coll says. He blurts it out like he's just suddenly realized. Anybody else but a bloody doctor and Gomer could almost feel sorry for him.

'Where's my mum?' young Jane screams in his face.

A large chalice of red wine stood on the temple altar, with the scourge and the handbell, the wand for air, the sword for fire. Royally pissed off by now, sitting just inside the door, on the doormat for Chrissakes, Robin wanted to suggest they share it out or at least open another bottle.

Across the parlour, Betty sensed his impatience and sent him a small warning smile. The moment was close to intimate. Her face was warm and young and wonderful in the glow from the Tilley lamp which sat in the centre of the floor – what would have been the centre of the circle if they'd drawn one. But tonight's circle would be drawn outside.

If it ever happened, though they were robed and ready. Maybe this was no night for naked, and anyway Robin could appreciate the need for a sense of ceremony. He also loved to see Betty in the loose, green, medieval gown she'd made herself two, three years ago. Robin just wore this kind of grey woollen tunic; he didn't have anything more ceremonial. But then he would be peripheral tonight, an extra, a spear-carrier.

Ned Bain, in a long, black robe, sat on a bare flagstone

below the window, opposite the hearth, where the heatless twig-fire burned. He was obviously listening, but Robin suspected he was not listening to Max.

In preparation, Max had led a meditation on the nature of the border, and read to them, in translation, an old Welsh poem about the death of Pwyll, son of Llywarch the Old, who sang, 'When my son was killed, his hair was bloody and flowed on both banks of the brook.' Robin had been painting it in his head – that long, bloodied hair was a gift to an illustrator. Wicca worked in strange ways; he himself might not be able to see spirits or know the future, but his imagination could be sent into instant freeflow by any image you cared to pitch him. Hell, that was *something*.

'On this holy Celtic night,' Max intoned, 'let us close our eyes and picture – all around us – the ghostly monuments of our ancestors. We are in a wide, silent valley, the stones in a grey mist around us. But over it soars Burfa Hill, and we can dimly make out the notch marking the rising of the sun at the equinox. In the black of the night is born the bright day, the new spring. And we, too, shall be born again into a new day, a new era.'

That was it. There was silence. The stones had loomed out of the mist for Robin, his soul reached for the new day, but he dispatched it back to his subconscious. He'd had enough. He shifted uncomfortably on his mat and, across the room, closest to the altar, Betty saw him and knew he was about to say something.

Instead, *she* did. But first, she smiled sadly in the lamplight, and it was for him, and Robin thought his heart would burst with love.

And then Betty said, very quietly, 'Once, not so very long ago, there were two stepbrothers . . .'

*

Jane and Gomer hurried across the street, making for the hall. It was, Jane thought, crazy to let the doctor just *go*, but Gomer said that if they didn't want to spend the rest of the night in some police station, they didn't have a choice.

The doctor had told them Mum had gone off with Father Ellis, and he knew Father Ellis was up in the hall, conducting a service. The doctor had then put his dignity back together, walked out across the yard, his medical bag swinging from his wrist, as if he was off on a house call.

Scumbag.

You couldn't miss the village hall, with that cross lit up on the roof. As soon as you turned up the track to the steps, you could hear the singing. A song which had no tune but lots of tunes, and endless words but no sense.

Jane started racing up the steps, saw that the hall was blazing with light. But, at the same time, she became aware that Gomer, behind her, was panting quite painfully. It had been a gruelling night and you tended to forget how old he was and how many roll-ups he smoked. She stopped halfway up and waited for him to catch up.

She reckoned afterwards, after the glass in the porch burst and the flames came out in a great gouging *whooomp* of heat, that Gomer's lungs had probably saved their lives.

FIFTY-ONE

Laid to Unrest ·

The laurel alley.

Later, its leaves would be crisp with frost. Merrily could see only the alley's outline, rippling black walls under the worn pebble moon.

'We could use a torch.'

'Amply bright enough,' Judith said, 'if you know the way.'

Which she, of course, did. She took Merrily's arm, leading her down to the fork in the drive. 'Mind the step, now.' Merrily remembered Marianne's hand on her arm, as the police burst through. *Things you oughta know.*' Judith's grip was firmer. Judith was without trepidation. What did Judith believe in? Not ghosts, perhaps not even God – except maybe some strictly local deity, the guardian spirit of Old Hindwell.

At the corner of the rectory, where the drive split, Merrily looked for a car, but there was just an empty space. J.W. Weal had gone to don his Masonic apron. It must look like a postage stamp on him. Lodge night: a crude ritual structure to further stiffen his already rigid life.

The police had gone, too, now. There seemed to have been a winding-down of the action at the gates of St Michael's. Nothing to see or hear when Merrily and Judith had walked past the farm entrance.

They dropped down to the tarmac and then the crazy paving to the lawn. Sharp conifers were all around, pricking stars. Merrily glanced back once at the grey-stone rectory, at the angular bulge of the bay window: lightless, no magisterial shadows of furniture, no frenetic flickering, crackling . . .

Stop it!

'Something bothering you, Mrs Watkins?'

'Nothing at all, Mrs Prosser.'

At the end of the lawn, pale grey and shining slightly, was the squat conical building, the wine store . . . ice house . . . now tomb. Merrily stumbled on a lump in the lawn; Judith's arm easily found her waist, helped her up. Merrily tightened inside. It was about here that Weal had wrapped his arms around her, lifting her, whirling her around. *'Men-na.'*

Merrily shivered suddenly, and Judith knew.

'You're frightened.'

'I'm cold.' She clutched her blue airline bag to her side.

'As you wish.' Judith bit the end of one of her leather gloves to pull it off and produced from a pocket something that jingled: the keys to the mausoleum. 'But it will, I'm afraid, be even colder in here.'

When Betty had been talking for a while – calm, succinct, devastating – someone actually got up, went over and switched on all the lights. Hard reality time.

It was a starkly meaningful moment. Robin stared in cold dismay around the parlour, with its damp patches, its dull fire of smoky, sizzling green twigs, its sad assembly of robed witches and the crown of lights on the floor like some unfinished product of a kids' handicraft class left behind at the end of the semester.

It all looked like some half-assed fancy dress party that never quite took off. The air was sick with confusion, incomprehension, embarrassment – affecting everyone here, except for Ned Bain, who was still entirely relaxed in the lotus position, his butt on the stone-flag floor.

And Betty, in her green medieval robe, remained expressionless, having come out with stuff about Ned that Robin, with his famously huge imagination, couldn't begin to fathom how she'd gotten hold of. Was that where she'd been last night – obtaining Ned Bain's life story? And never saying a word to Robin because he was this big-mouthed asshole whom all subtlety deserted the second he put away his paints.

He felt royally betrayed, shafted up the ass, by everyone. Like, how many of them already knew this? How many knew that Nicholas Ellis was Bain's stepbrother, who covered up for his old lady after she stabbed Bain's father to death? Was this some British Wiccan conspiracy, to which only he was denied access?

But Robin only had to look at Vivvie's pinched and frozen face to be pretty damn sure that few, if any, of them had been aware of it all. They might've known about Ned's father and the lingering bitterness over his killing, but not about the real identity of the saintly Nick Ellis.

'Ned . . .' Max came to his feet, nervously massaging his massive beard. 'I do rather think we're due an explanation.'

All of them, except for Betty, were now looking over at black-robed Ned Bain, still relaxed, but moody now, kind of saturnine. Betty, having rolled a grenade into the room, just gazed down into her lap.

Ned brought his hands together, elbows tucked inside his knees, the sleeves of his robe falling back. He smiled ruefully, slowly shaking his head. Then, in the face of Max's evident disapproval, he brought out a packet of cigarettes and a small lighter, and they had to wait while he organized himself a smoke.

'First of all, what Betty says is broadly correct.' He sounded kind of detached, like it was dope he was smoking. 'My father married Frances Wesson, and our intelligent, free-thinking, liberal household changed almost overnight into a strict Christian, grace-at-mealtimes, church-twice-on-Sunday bloody purgatory. Icons on every wall, religious tracts on every flat surface . . . and the beatific face of my smug, pious little stepbrother. Well, of course I hated him. I hated him long before he lied to the police.'

There was another smoky silence.

'So Simon Wesson . . . changed his name?' Max prompted.

'I believe Ellis was Frances's maiden name. She'd already met the appalling Marshall McAllman during one of his early missions to the UK, but this only became evident later.'

'In other words,' said Max, too obviously anxious to help Ned clear up this little misunderstanding, 'with the promise of American nouveaux riches, your father had somewhat out-lived his usefulness.'

'Oh, I've conjured a number of scenarios, Max, in the years since – none of which allows for the possibility of my father's death being self-defence. Simon knows the truth. I realized part of my destiny was to make him bloody well confess it. It became a focus for me, led me into areas I might never have entered. Into Wicca.'

Robin saw Betty look up, her green eyes hard, but lit with intelligence and insight. There would be no get-outs, no short cuts. Ned Bain took another drag at his cigarette.

'I'd tried to be a simple iconoclast at first, telling myself I was an atheist. Then, for a while – I'd be about nineteen – I was into ceremonial magic. Until I realized that was as cramped and pompous as Frances's High Church Christianity. Only paganism appeared free of such crap, and there was a great sense of release. Naked, elemental, no hierarchy – it was what I needed.'

Betty said, without looking up, 'How long have you known about this place?'

'Oh, only since Simon arrived here. Since he took over the church hall. Since he became "Father Ellis". When he first came back to Britain, he was a curate in the North-East, but that was no use to me. He wasn't doing anything that left him . . . open. I'd had people watching him in America for years – there's an enormous pagan network over there now, happy to be accessed. And other links too.'

'Like Kali Three?' Betty said.

Robin saw Bain throw her a short, knife-like glance; she didn't even react. 'I used several agencies.' He turned away, like this was an irrelevance. 'And then, when "Father Ellis" began to make waves on the Welsh border, I came down to take a look for myself. Fell rather in love with the place.'

Bain then talked of how the archaeological excavation was under way at the time, just across the brook from the church; how the immense importance of the site as a place of ancient worship was becoming apparent. 'One of the archaeologists told me he'd dearly love to know what lay under that church. Circular churchyard, pre-Christian site. I took a walk over there myself, and met some eagle-eyed old boy who told me he'd just bought it.'

'Major Wilshire,' Robin said. He couldn't believe how this was shaping up.

'Something like that. I didn't pay too much attention to him, as I was being knocked sideways by the ambience. It was while I was talking to this guy that I had . . . the vision, I suppose. A moment beyond inspiration, when past and future collided in the present. *Boom.* I became aware how wonderful and apt it would be if the power of this place could be channelled. If this church was to become a temple again.'

'Under the very nose of your fundamentalist Christian brother,' Betty said quietly.

'In fact' – Bain raised his voice, irritated – 'it was rather the other way round. For the first time I was almost grateful to Simon, for bringing me here. Ironic, really. But the church had now been sold, and that was that. I went home to London. You can imagine my reaction when, just a few months later, I learned that St Michael's Farm and Old Hindwell Church were on the market again.'

'No,' Betty said coldly. 'What exactly *was* your reaction?'

'Betty,' said Max, 'I really don't think we should prejudge this.'

Ned said, 'Simply that I wanted it to be bought by someone sympathetic to the pagan cause.'

Bulbs finally started flashing big time inside Robin's head.

MENNA WEAL

The actual tomb was bigger than Merrily had expected: perhaps seven feet long, close to three feet wide, more than three feet deep. From outside, with the funeral party of Prossers, Dr Coll and Nick Ellis grouped around it, it had resembled a stone horse trough. Now, under the cream light from the wrought-iron electric lanterns hanging above the head and the foot of the tomb, she could see that it was far more ornate. A complex design of linked crosses had been carved out of the side panels. The lid was not stone, but perhaps as good as: an oak slab four inches thick. The great tomb had been concreted into its stone plinth.

'All *local* stone,' Judith said proudly. 'From the quarry.'

'Got that done quickly, didn't he?'

Judith closed the oak door, so their voices were sharpened by the walls of the mausoleum, which were solid concrete, inches thick. The chamber was about twenty feet square, nothing in it but the tomb, and the two of them, and dead Menna.

Judith said, 'Mal Walters, the monumental mason, is a long-established client of J.W. Mal worked through the night.'

'Right.'

Judith Prosser stood by the head of the tomb, disquietingly priest-like in her tubular black quilted coat – not quite cassock-length, but close. Her short, strong hair had been bleached, her pewter-coloured earrings were thin, metal pyramids. She was waiting, behind the shade of a sardonic smile.

'I thought . . .' Merrily put down the airline bag she'd brought from the car. The junior exorcist's starter kit. 'I thought I'd keep it simple.'

But should she even be doing it here, rather than in that big room behind the bay window, where the 'baptism' had taken place?

Yes, she should. She didn't want the complication of having to try to restore peace to a room where the atmosphere had apparently been ravaged by another priest. Also, she had been asked by Menna's next of kin to calm the spirit. No one had invited her to deal with that room, least of all Weal. She didn't want to go in there, didn't want to enter his actual house in his absence. She really needed guidance. If she'd predicted this situation might develop, she'd have rung her spiritual adviser, Huw Owen, in advance. But there'd been no time for that.

Judith moved to a double switch on the wall, and the lantern at the head of the tomb went out, leaving Menna's concrete cell softly lit, like a drawing room.

'Are you a Christian, Mrs Prosser?'

'That's a funny question.'

'I know you go to church. I know you support Father Ellis. I don't really know what you believe.'

'Nor will you ever,' Judith said tartly. 'What's your point? What are you getting at?'

'Do you *believe* in the unquiet dead?'

Judith Prosser regarded Merrily across the tomb, her eyes half closed. 'The dead are always quiet, Mrs Watkins. The dead are dead, and only the weak-minded are afraid of them. They cannot touch us. Nor, I assume . . .' She laid a forefinger gently on Menna's small inscription, '. . . can we touch them.'

'Meaning Mr Weal.'

'Mr Weal's a tragic figure, isn't it? He wanted what he *thought* Menna was. He liked it that she was quiet. He liked it that she was polite to her father and did not go with boys. A real, three-dimensional woman was far too complicated for J.W. He wanted, I suppose, a shadow of a woman.'

Oh my God.

Merrily said, 'You have to tell me this. If not you yourself, then has anyone else seen the . . . spirit of Menna Weal?'

Judith made a scornful *pfft* noise. She half turned and began to unbutton her coat. 'Anyway . . .' Sweeping the coat back to place her hands on her hips, turning to face Merrily. 'Time is getting on. What do you propose to do here, my girl?'

'Well . . . I'm going to say some prayers. What I really should be doing – I mean to be halfway sure of this – is holding a Requiem Eucharist. And for that there really ought to be a few of us. Like I said this morning, it would be better if we'd had Mr Weal with us. I mean *with* us.'

'And as *I* said, that would be imposs—'

'Or even Barbara. If Barbara were here, it—'

Merrily heard her own words rebound from the concrete walls. She lurched away from the tomb, as if it were mined.

Such a vast tomb for one small body.

Judith looked mildly curious. 'Someone walk over your grave, Mrs Watkins?'

Merrily knew she'd gone pale. 'Judith . . .?'

'Go ahead,' said Mrs Prosser. 'We're quite alone, almost.'

Merrily swallowed. The scarf felt tight around her throat.

'What do you think J.W. Weal would have done if he'd discovered that Barbara Buckingham had found out about Father Ellis's exorcism of Menna, performed at his behest?'

Judith's eyes were not laughing. 'What on *earth* am I supposed to say to that?' She stepped back.

Now they were both looking at the tomb.

'Oh, I *see*,' Judith said.

Merrily said nothing.

'You mean, after he dumped the *car* in the Claerwen Reservoir, what, precisely, did he do with the body?'

Merrily said nothing.

'Does Barbara perhaps lie below her poor sister? Were her remains, in those fine English clothes, already set in concrete when Menna's coffin was laid to . . . unrest?'

Merrily bit her lip.

'Come on, woman! Is that what you meant?'

'It looks very deep,' Merrily said. 'And . . . as you said, the monumental mason worked all night.'

'All right!' Judith's voice rang with challenge. 'Then let's find out, shall we?'

Merrily found she'd backed against the door.

'Oh, Mrs Watkins, did you think poor J.W. could bring himself to say such a *final* farewell to his beloved? What other reason would a man like him *have* for going to all this trouble?' She pointed.

From back here, Merrily didn't even have to bend down to see that the tomb's handsome oakwood lid was hinged.

'It's very heavy, all the same,' Judith said. 'You may have to help me.'

*

Merrily remembered, when she was a little kid, being towed along by her mother to make the arrangements for her gran's funeral, and how the undertaker's inner door had been left open. Merrily's mother thinking she was too young to understand. But not too young to absorb the smell of formaldehyde from the embalming room.

She'd been four years old, the formaldehyde alternating with the equally piercing tang of furniture polish, making her afraid to go to sleep that night, and she didn't know why. There was only this grim, opaque fear, the sense of a deep, unpleasant mystery.

Which returned when Judith threw back the solid oak lid of the tomb. Judith hadn't needed help with it after all. She looked down into the tomb and smiled.

'The dead are always quiet, Mrs Watkins. The dead are dead, and only the weak-minded are afraid of them.'

But Merrily who, since ordination, had seen any number of laid-out bodies *was* afraid. The same grim opaque fear, and she didn't know why.

What would be the point, anyway? Judith had only done this for effect, to put herself in control from the start. And if the body of Barbara Buckingham was in there too, it would be in the base, set in concrete, never to be discovered, certainly not in J.W. Weal's lifetime.

Menna, though – Menna was readily accessible. It was clear that Judith was not now looking down on merely a coffin lid.

'Close it, please,' Merrily said.

'How do you know it isn't Barbara? Come on, see for yourself.'

'This is intrusion,' Merrily said.

'It was always intrusion, Mrs Watkins.'

'Then close the lid and I'll say some prayers and we'll go.'

'If I close the lid,' Judith said, 'she won't be able to hear you, will she?'

The whole mausoleum stank of embalming fluid. Merrily needed air, a fortifying cigarette. She went back to the door.

'Don't open it, you silly girl. The light!' Judith let go of the lid and it hung for a moment and then fell against the stone side of the tomb with a shuddering crash, leaving the interior fully exposed. The single lantern, over the foot of the tomb, swung slightly, and Merrily saw a quiver of parchment-coloured lace from inside.

'Come over yere, Mrs Watkins,' Judith said.

'This is wrong.' Merrily's hand went to the centre of her breast where, under her coat, under her jumper, the pectoral cross lay. *Christ be with me, Christ within me, Christ behind me . . .*

'Come and see how peaceful she looks. It'll make you feel better. Then we'll say goodnight to her. Come yere.'

. . . Christ before me. Merrily walked into the centre of the mausoleum. If necessary, she'd close the lid herself.

'You *silly* girl.' Judith reached out suddenly and grabbed her by the arm, pulled her close. 'Don't be afraid. I'll look after you.'

I don't think so. As the formaldehyde seared the back of Merrily's throat, the lantern swung again at the sudden movement and shot spears of light and shadow from Menna's swaddled feet to Menna's exposed face.

'See how peaceful she looks.'

No.

That night in the hospital, with the freshly applied water on her brow, Menna had appeared simply and calmly dead. The body hadn't, from a distance, seemed much different during her funeral. Now, embalmed, only days later, her face was pinched and rigid, her mouth downturned, lips slightly parted to reveal the teeth . . . and that particularly, Merrily thought in revulsion, was surely not the work of the embalmer.

She recoiled slightly. Judith's arm was around her, gently squeezing.

'Thank you,' Merrily said. 'Now I know it isn't Barbara.'

'You're trembling.' Merrily felt Judith's breath on her face.

'Don't,' she said mildly.

'Things you oughta know,' Marianne had said. And earlier: *'That Judy. She took you outside, din't she? I was glad when she did that.'*

'It's been hard for you, Merrily, hasn't it?' Judith said, quite tenderly. 'All the pressures. All the things you didn't understand.'

'I'm getting there.' Marianne had been in shock. Marianne needed help. Marianne, who sometimes preyed on men, had herself become vulnerable, pitiable, accessible.

'Yes, I believe you are,' Judith said tonelessly.

FIFTY-TWO

Beast is Come

Jane watched, eaten up with dread, as the multitude assembled where two lanes in the village converged. The uniformed chief inspector in charge tried to organize some kind of roll-call, but it wasn't going to be easy. Only two people known to be missing, and one of them was Mum.

Once the fire brigade was in – four machines, two Welsh, two English – the police had sealed off Old Hindwell. Fire-fighters with breathing apparatus tried to get into the village hall but were eventually ordered out for their own safety. Jane was there when the order was given, and that was when she began to sob.

When – soon after the brigade got there – the porch's wooden roof had collapsed, lighting up the night and several Sitka spruce, many people fell down on their knees and prayed to the violent, orange sky. Jane was frantic and clung to Eirion, by the side of the police Transit in the filthy, choking air. She didn't remember when Eirion had appeared, or where he'd appeared from. Sophie was here too, now, and many local people had come out of their homes.

And Gomer . . . Gomer was a deeply reluctant hero. The media kept wanting to talk to him. They wanted to hear him describe how he'd spotted the flames and gone round to the rear entrance and opened it up and guided 350 Christians to safety. Gomer kept saying, 'Later, boys, all right?' But later he was muttering, '*Bugger off*,' as the firefighters went on blasting thousands of gallons into the roaring hall.

And still they hadn't found Mum.

Jane, by now hyperactive with fear, had dragged Eirion into the middle of the milling people, and she kept shouting through her tears, 'Small, dark woman in a tatty duffel coat, anybody? *Anybody!*'

But nobody had seen her. *Nobody*.

Though a number elected to pray for her.

Not nearly as many, however, as were praying for Father Ellis, last seen, apparently, stepping from the stage to sing with the crowd. Nobody, at that time, had been aware of the fire in the porch because of the fire doors, and nobody had heard it because of the glorious exultation of the Holy Spirit amplified through their hearts and lungs.

Nobody had known a thing, in fact, until a skinny little man with wild white hair and thick glasses had appeared at the bottom of the hall and had begun bawling at them to bloody well shut up and follow him. By then the fire doors were surrounded by flame and the air was turning brown and the tongues were torn with coughing.

Now Jane's arms were gripped firmly. Sophie said incisively into her ear, 'Jane, she is not *in* there, do you understand? She cannot *possibly* be in there.' Jane opened her mouth to protest and took in a wad of smoke, and was bent double with the coughing, and heard a man shouting in rage.

'They've found a petrol can!'

Obvious what this meant. Jane straightened up, eyes streaming.

A senior-looking policeman was saying, 'We don't know anything yet, so don't anybody go jumping to conclusions.' But he was wasting his breath, because everybody knew what the petrol can meant.

And then, suddenly, the white monk was there.

He was just suddenly *there*, about thirty yards away from the crowd, up against the schoolyard wall.

Jane's feeling was that he'd been sitting quietly in one of the cars or something, staying well out of it, and had come out casually when everyone's attention was diverted by the sound of the porch crashing down or something. Two women in their thirties noticed him first, and it was like Mary Magdalene and the other woman finding an empty tomb and then turning around and there He was. They ran towards him, shouting, 'Thank God, thank God, thank *God*.'

And it just kind of escalated like that. Jane saw all these people falling down on their knees at his feet and all shouting, 'Praise God,' and, 'Thank you, God,' and some of them even looked like local people. Jane heard a tut of disdain from Sophie, and, for the first time, felt something approaching genuine affection for the cool cathedral woman in the wreckage of her camel coat.

There wasn't a mark on the white monk.

'Please,' he was saying, 'don't you worry about me. I'm fine.' He bent to one of the women. 'Stand up, please.' He raised her up and hugged her and then he walked away from the wall. And his arms were raised, palms towards the crowd, fingers splayed. 'Stand up, everyone –

Stand up and smell the foetid stench of Satan!'

There was this shattering hush.

Feel the heat of the dragon's breath!'

A woman moaned.

And know that the beast is come!'

'It was *you*?' In the dingy parlour-turned-temple, Robin stared at Ned Bain; Bain didn't look at Robin. '*You* had the estate agents send us the stuff?'

'Not . . . directly.' For the first time, the guy was showing some discomfort. 'We put out feelers through the Pagan Federation to see if anyone might be interested.'

'We?' Betty said.

'I did.'

'But, like, how come you didn't just buy this place yourself?' Robin was still only half getting this.

'And reveal himself to Ellis?' Betty said. 'Before he could get his plans in hand?'

'Coulda bought it through a third party.'

'He has,' Betty said acidly.

'I don't think that's quite fair,' said Max. 'There was hardly time for *plans* – except, perhaps, in spheres beyond our own. I'm inclined to believe this came about as a spontaneous response to what one might call serendipitous circumstance.'

'Max.' Betty was laying on that heavy patience Robin knew too well. 'Do you think, for one minute, that we'd all be here today, trying to pull something together at the eleventh hour, if Vivvie hadn't crassly shot her mouth off on a piece of late-night trash television and alerted Ellis to what he immediately perceived as the Devil on his doorstep? No, Ned would have waited for Beltane, Lammas, Samhain . . . and got it all nicely set up for maximum impact.'

Max started to speak, then his beard knitted back together.

George was up now – squat, stubbly George, partner of Vivvie.

'Look, people, I think . . . that however this all came about, we've got to put it behind us for tonight. If we allow it to destroy this seminal sabbat, under the spotlight of the entire pagan world, we are going to regret it for the rest of our lives, man. I agree that maybe Ned's not been as upfront as he might've been. I know we could start to accuse him of only setting this thing up to have this Ellis man go down in history totally humiliated, as the priest who lost his church to the Old Religion, but . . .'

'It's more than that,' Betty said. 'For a start, he set *us* up. And in a place which none of us—'

'It doesn't *matter*, Betty. We cannot let personal issues fuck up a seminal event. We have to hold the sabbat, we have to reconsecrate this church in the names of Mannon and Brigid and . . .'

George stopped. Betty had stood up. In this damp, chilly room she was a heat source: the only one here who didn't look kind of tawdry. She looked like a goddess.

'Ask him what he's waiting for,' she demanded.

'Please . . .' George wilted back. 'Just leave it.'

Ned Bain didn't move.

'He's waiting for his stepbrother,' Betty said. 'He's waiting for the hymns to start up, only louder. He's waiting for his stepbrother to lead the enemy to the gate.'

'But, Betty, we *need* that tension,' George said. 'That's what this is about – the changeover. In the dawn of the year, the dawn of a millennium, a pretender is banished.'

'Christ, you mean?'

'If you like. I prefer to think in terms of the warlike Michael. I've got nothing against Christ, but he was, at best, an irrelevance. Yeah, Christ, if you like.'

'I *don't* like,' Betty said. 'We're an alternative. We're not the opposition. I mean, *he* might be – he and Ellis both. Whatever else they are, whatever they claim to represent, it's completely soured by what lies between them. I don't want that. I don't want to go into that old, fouled place on the back of twenty-five years of pent-up hatred. I suggest everybody gets changed and leaves now.'

Howls of protest and serious consternation at this, shared by Robin. In some ways, the recent revelations had made him feel better about the situation – the great Ned Bain brought down to human level.

'Bets, look,' he said hoarsely, 'you can't precisely say we

were set up. *We* decided to go for this place. All the omens said it was right at the time. Plus, we had the promise of the Blackmore deal and all that it could bring. We were on a roll.'

'Ah, yes,' Betty said, 'the Blackmore deal.'

Ned Bain shifted. Robin felt a pulse of alarm. *'I still think Kirk could be persuaded to listen to reason.'* This was all gonna crash now, the rainbows in the puddles turning black.

'Robin, love . . .' Betty's eyes had misted, or was it his own? 'Kirk Blackmore's been working you like a puppet, hasn't he? All your highs and all your lows.'

'He was important, sure.' Robin looked at Ned. Ned was staring at the stone flags in the floor, elbow on knee and arm outstretched, cigarette loose between his fingers.

And suddenly Robin knew.

'I guess *you're* Kirk Blackmore, huh?'

Bain didn't reply. The room was silent.

Robin turned to Betty. 'How did you find that out?' Inside his rough woollen tunic he was starting to sweat like a hog.

'Some . . . friends of mine got some information from the Internet. Blackmore's this notorious recluse supposedly living on a Welsh mountain and communicating only by fax. People speculate endlessly on the Net about the true identities of authors. Publishers often write novels under pseudonyms: usually lurid, mass-market novels they might not want to be associated with. I'm really sorry, Robin.'

Ned's brow was suddenly a little shiny.

'But he could've bought this place out of his small change,' Betty continued.

'It was your destiny, not mine,' Bain said calmly. 'At the time.'

'Bullshit,' Robin said quietly.

'Any time you wanted to get out, I'd have taken it off your hands.'

'You mean like after we ran out of money? After we'd taken all the shit from the local people? After Ellis got safely kicked out on his ass by the Church? After our marriage got smashed up on the fucking rocks?'

'There was always this growing atmosphere of turbulence,' Betty said. 'We were made to feel insecure from the first. He wanted us to feel beleaguered, maybe a little scared.' She looked down at Bain. 'You *needed* this, didn't you? Were you working on it with your coven, Ned, or was it some magical construction of your own – long and intricate, like one of your novels? Generating unrest – backed up by a campaign of mysterious letters and phone calls directed at Ellis. The dragon rising? Were you working towards some kind of cataclysm . . . only forestalled by stupid Vivvie giving it away – resulting in *this* farce.'

Vivvie snarled, 'What *are* you these days, Betty? Because you're not one of us any more.'

Bain said, 'If you really want to discuss this, I'm perfectly willing—'

'Did *you* buy the witch box from Major Wilshire? Did *you* have someone deliver it to us, place it on our doorstep?' Betty paused. 'And were you . . . were you *really* that surprised when Major Wilshire fell from his ladder?'

Ned Bain sprang up in a single movement. 'Don't you fucking *dare* . . '

His stiffened finger inches from Betty's soft cheek.

Which was enough.

Robin lurched across the room to the altar. George reached out to stop him, but Robin shook George savagely away. He felt the weight of his hair on his shoulders. He heard warbling sirens in the night. He saw through a deepening mist. He remembered the pit of desperation that swallowed him when Al Delaney, of Talisman, had called to say, *'He wants someone else to do it, Robin. He doesn't want you.'*

Robin wrenched from the altar the great ceremonial sword. No toy this, no lightweight replica, but three and a half feet of high-tensile steel.

Robin raised it in both hands, high above his head. He heard Vivvie screaming.

FIFTY-THREE

Snakeskin

Merrily said, 'You really did look after her, didn't you? You really took care of her.'

Judith Prosser adjusted a fold in the corpse's shroud. 'I was the only one *ever* took care of her.'

'Could we close the lid now?'

Judith didn't touch the lid. 'Why don't you conduct your ceremony, Merrily? Take off your coat, make yourself into a priest.'

Taking control again.

Merrily moved to the head of the coffin, looking down towards Menna's feet. Her airline bag, with the Bible, the prayer texts, the flask of holy water, stood by the door.

'Why don't you finally leave her alone? Why don't you just accept that maybe you've done enough harm?'

'Meaning *what* precisely, Mrs Watkins?' Judith said briskly. She went to stand at the foot of the coffin, from where she could observe the faces of both Merrily and Menna.

'You had her on the Pill from an early age. Dr Coll's good like that, isn't he? Ministering to the *real* needs of the local people? Dr Coll understands these things.'

'She'd have been pregnant by fourteen if we hadn't done something.'

'Mmm, her father really *was* abusing her, wasn't he? Maybe over quite a long period.'

Judith shrugged.

'And, of course, you knew that.'

'We didn't talk about such things then. Other people's domestic arrangements, that was their own affair.'

'Yeah, yeah, but also because . . . whenever it happened, she would come to you.'

'Oh, well, yes. Almost a mile.' Judith smiled. Incredibly, it looked like a smile of nostalgia. 'Almost a mile across the fields to our farm. To my parents' farm. In tears, usually – or you could see where the tears had dried in the wind.'

'And you would comfort her.'

Judith breathed in very slowly, her black coat flung back, breasts pushing out the rugby shirt. Merrily thought of her in the toilet at the village hall, tenderly ministering to Marianne. Always victims: always vulnerability, confusion, helplessness, terror, desperation. Like Menna, alone on that remote hill farm with her beast of a father.

'What a turn-on that must have been,' Merrily said.

Judith's face became granite. 'Don't overstep the mark, Mrs Watkins.'

'Why didn't you just take her to the police?'

'To give evidence against her own father? Apart from the fact that, as I say, such things were not *done* yere in those days, not talked about, how would she have managed on her own, with her father in prison? How would she have coped?'

'Probably have been taken into care. And that's probably the best thing that could have happened, in Menna's case.' Merrily paused. 'If not in yours.'

'You don't know *anything* about this area!' Judith snapped. 'Social services? *Pah!* We have always managed our own social services.'

'I'm sure. Especially after you got married and you were operating from the perfect, secure social platform.'

Marriage to Gareth Prosser. *'Councillor, magistrate, on this committee, that committee. Big man. Dull bugger, mind. Lucky he's got Judy to do his thinkin' for him.'*

A very satisfactory arrangement that, in almost all areas of life, Judith needed Gareth for the framework, the structure, the tradition: a facade, and a good one. What did sexual orientation have to do with it? Fancy, meaningless phrase from Off. Self-sacrifice was sometimes necessary – for a while.

'The foundations of rural life,' Merrily said. 'A husband, a farm and sons – preferably two of them, in case something happens to one of them, or the other grows up strange and wants to live in Cardiff and be an interior designer.'

Judith smiled thinly. 'Oh, you're such a clever little bitch. What about *your* life, Mrs Watkins? They say your husband died some years ago. Does the love of God meet *all* your needs?'

Merrily let it go. 'When you're married to a man like Gareth, nothing needs to change. You go to Menna, she comes to you. And then, when her father dies, you have the contingency plan for her: Jeffery Weal. Good old J.W., the solid, silent family solicitor. A local man, and discreet.'

'He was too old for her, yes. Too rigid in his ways, perhaps. But it was what she was used to, isn't it? She was a flimsy, delicate thing. She would always need protection.'

What could be more perfect? His clothes smelling of mothballs, and little or no experience of women. And living just a few hundred yards down the hill from the Prosser farm.

'*You* arranged that ideal marriage, Judith. You probably coached Menna in what would be expected of her. But she was used to all that, anyway, poor kid. She'd always been a kid – a sad, pale little girl. He must have frightened her a bit, at first, the size of him. He frightens *me*. But that would be no bad thing either, for you, if she needed a lot more comforting.'

Judith's hands were on her hips. 'Now you *have* overstepped the mark.'

'And of course she must continue to take her Pill because children would not be a good thing *at all*. Having a child can make someone grow up awfully quickly.'

'She was not strong enough for children,' Judith said sullenly.

'Was that how Weal eventually found out about you and Menna? Because *he* wanted children – with the family business to pass on to them. "Pills – what pills are these, Menna?" ' She put up a hand. 'No, all right. I reckon he did find out, though, didn't he?'

'You *reckon*,' Judith sneered, 'you *guess*, you *theorize*.'

'Is that why you wanted me to come here tonight? To find out what direction the speculation was taking? I'd guess the answer is that you don't really know for sure whether Weal knows about you and Menna, or not. But if he does, he wouldn't say a word to you. It's not the local way. Besides, I suppose you were useful to him. I expect there *were* aspects of Menna he couldn't deal with. Maybe she'd finally changed – becoming a woman.'

'You don't know what you're—'

'But that wouldn't be awfully good for you either, would it? To have Menna becoming a bit worldly-wise as she reached middle age? What actually *was* her mental state? I wouldn't know but, my God' – Merrily pointed into the tomb – 'look at her now. Look at her face. It's all coming out now, isn't it, in that face? God Almighty, Judith, it's almost turning into *your* face.'

Judith Prosser stood very still, seemed hardly to be breathing. Merrily moved away, back towards the door.

'You know what I think? What I'd bet big money on?' She was aware of her voice rising in pitch, more than a bit scared now of where this was inexorably leading. 'When Weal had Ellis exorcize his wife, that was nothing to do with her father at all. Ellis seemed to be able to demonize *anything* and then get rid of it. He stopped your boy from nicking cars, didn't he? So maybe Weal thought that Nicholas Ellis could purge Menna of the demon . . . the demon that was *you*.'

Merrily was shattered. She hadn't quite realized what she had been about to say. But the evident truth of it was explosive.

Judith took a swift step towards her, then stopped, and said brightly, too brightly, 'You are off your head, Mrs Watkins. You do *know* that?' She laughed, her eyes glittering with rage.

'That was only the half of it, though,' Merrily said, to defuse things a little. 'The next part would be the baptism of the two of them, in the same little bowl of holy water, I guess. Something medieval going on there: the fusion of two souls?'

Merrily stared down at the soured face in the tomb. In the medieval church, baptism *was* exorcism. Exorcism charms had been included in marriage services, or blessing of the sick. Pregnant women were exorcized too. In those days, demons were getting expelled from people like tapeworms.

A scenario: late afternoon, the sky like sheet metal. The bay-windowed room north-facing, so not much of the sunset visible. A cold room and a cold time of day. Menna standing there like some white slave, her skin waxy, her arms like straws. Perhaps a bruise forming blue where Ellis had gripped her roughly – in his mind gripping not her but *it*. Perhaps she was wrapping her arms around herself and shivering. Or was she entirely unmoved? Compliant? Accepting this ritual as just another of those things men liked to do to her.

'Do you embrace God?' Ellis's customizing of the rite.

J.W. Weal standing there, big as God.

Menna hesitating, perhaps a little worried by the word 'embrace' and thoughts of what else God might do to her after this.

'Do you embrace Him?'

'I . . . Yes . . . Yes.'

Around the high, white room, dark oak chairs with long pointed spines, standing like judge and jury.

'Do you renounce the evil which corrupts that which God has created? And the sick and sinful, perverted desires which draw you away from the love of God?'

Menna beginning to cry again.

'Say it!'

Her head going back. A sniff.

'Say, "I so renounce them"!'

'I s . . . so . . . renounce them.'

'I can't begin to know where Ellis derived that rite from,' Merrily said. 'Or if he made it up. But there's an awfully long tradition of bodged religion around the Forest, isn't there?'

'I don't know what you mean,' Judith Prosser said sulkily.

'Like, what's the good of religion if it isn't *practical?* Whatever he did, it was nasty and unhealthy and yet . . . and yet somehow it worked, Judith. In some horrible, insidious way, it bloody well *worked*. And he has her now.' Merrily felt she was drifting away on a formaldehyde fog, sailing so far from the land of normality that she was afraid of never getting back there. 'Got her to himself. At least part of her. Part of *something*. Something half realized, fluttering after him like a crippled bird. It's obscene.'

There was a slithering sound. Judith was shedding her long, black, quilted coat, like a snakeskin.

FIFTY-FOUR

No God's Land

Even Jane could see the police didn't quite know how to handle this any more. A routine peacekeeping assignment had turned into a confusion of arson and murder. They'd taken over the doctor's surgery as an incident room, for two separate investigations which might be totally unconnected.

Jane and Gomer were keeping well back from it all. They stood with Sophie and Eirion in the shadow of the rear entry to the pub yard. Gomer had a ciggy going, and looked more his old self. Jane, too, felt more in control since Sophie had taken her to the chief fire officer, and he'd confirmed that they'd now managed to get inside the hall and had found no bodies there.

But the police had a body: a body with no face, dug out of the mud. And now that the immediate fire crisis was over, this had become their priority again, and they wanted very much to talk to Gomer. Wanted to know why he'd been so sure that something was buried in the old archaeological site that he'd gone up there with a digger, at night. Sophie, her white hair in almost hag-like disarray, was trying to explain to him that all they wanted was a statement, to allay their suspicions.

Gomer didn't want to know, though. It was a plant hire thing that would take too long to explain; Jane understood this. 'It's stupid. Why would Gomer have sent you to tell the police if *he* had something to do with it?'

Eirion said to Gomer, 'I think what Mrs Hill's trying to say is it would be better if *you* approached *them*, rather than have them come find you.'

'Eirion, what can I tell 'em that's gonner be any help?' Gomer growled. 'I'll talk to the buggers tomorrow, ennit?'

And Jane realized that he was worrying about Mum.

She looked out of the entry to the street, where a sombre assembly had formed around two priests – or, at least, two men in dog collars. One of them was raising his hands as if holding up a huge rock he was about to smash down on something. Jane just knew that some crazy scenario was being manufactured around the village hall fire, involving not a furtive little green-haired plonker with a can of petrol and a grudge, but some great satanic panoply clanking through the night. They'd asked Father Ellis what he wanted them to do, but Ellis had said, cleverly, 'I'm not your leader. Listen to your hearts and let the Holy Spirit move within you.' And he had walked away, leaving bitter, apocalyptic stuff on the air amidst the hellfire fumes. He knew what they'd do. He just wasn't going to be seen to instigate it.

Watching this, Gomer had nodded knowingly. 'Truly a local man at last,' he'd said – which Jane didn't really understand.

Sophie appeared at her shoulder. 'There's one place we haven't tried,' Jane said.

'The church, I suppose,' Sophie said. 'She had a loose arrangement with that young pagan woman, didn't she? To do some sort of Deliverance work? You're probably right. If you and Gomer want to go down there, Eirion and I will stay here, in case she shows up.'

Gomer nodded. He never liked to stand still for very long. 'Thank you, Sophie,' Jane said. 'You've been—'

'Shut up, Jane,' Sophie said wearily. 'Just go. And perhaps you could warn them over at the church' – she nodded towards the assembly on the streets – 'about *that*.'

Robin and Betty were holding one another in some kind of sweet desperation. Everything seemed lost: Robin's work, the house, their friends, their religion, their future here. Everything smashed in an act of sacrilege so gross it was worthy of a Christian. The candle chopped in half, the scourge handle snapped, the pentacle sent skimming like a frisbee into the wall. The chalice of red wine draining into the rug.

Finally the one-time studio table hauled from its trestles, flung onto its side. Max's wife Bella screaming, Vivvie raging, calling down the vengeance of the gods, or some shit like that. This was before Ned Bain had come and stood, unflinching, in front of Robin, who still held the sword. Robin had felt like decapitating the bastard, but Ned Bain had remained impressively cool. That quiet power, even Robin felt it.

'Before I leave,' Bain said, 'I want to make it clear that no one else here was involved, no one conspired. No one else deserves to suffer.'

And then he turned and gathered his robe and walked out without another word.

There'd been a long period of quiet then, broken only by some weeping. Betty leaned against a wall, drained. Vivvie had her head in her hands. Even Max had nothing to say. His kids hovered in the doorway, the fiendish Hermes looking satisfyingly scared. The pregnant witch, whose name Robin couldn't recall, had left the room with her partner. Robin only hoped she was OK. He was starting to feel sick and cold. The twig-fire hissed. A thick piece of altar candle rolled into a corner.

Alexandra, who'd been sitting calmly, with the crown of lights on her knees to protect it, was the first to speak. 'I think we should all leave Betty and Robin alone for a while.'

And so Robin and Betty, covenless, had rediscovered one another. *I take thee to my hand, my heart and my spirit at the setting of the sun and rising of the stars.* Robin started to weep again and buried his face in her hair. Clinging together in their stupid robes, in the wreckage of the altar.

They went hand in hand to the door, and looked out at Winnebagos, the barn and puddles. Robin watched the moon in the puddles, icing over. You could almost get sentimental about those puddles. But not quite.

'We should get outa here tomorrow. Go check into a hotel someplace. Think things over. I love you.'

Betty had her red ski jacket around her shoulders. 'And I love you,' she said. 'But Robin, honey . . .'

Betty fell silent. He hated when Betty became silent.

'OK, what?' he said.

She held his hand to the centre of her breast, her emotional centre.

'We can't just leave it.'

'Watch me,' Robin said.

But his spirit took a dive. She'd already explained how she'd spent the night at a Christian priest's house. A woman priest, who was also the county exorcist or some such, and knew a lot of stuff. He had the idea it had all come about through Betty's meeting with Juliet Pottinger. A part of him still didn't want to know about any of this.

He thought he could hear distant voices, beyond the trees. Like from a barbecue. Or maybe he just thought barbecue on account of the red glow in the sky. Perhaps a glimmering of Imbolc.

'There's a fire somewhere,' Betty said. 'Can't you smell it? Didn't you hear the sirens?'

'I was maybe smashing things at the time. Coming on like the Reverend Penney.'

'Let me tell you the truth about Penney,' Betty said. 'He had a bad time in Old Hindwell Church. I think he was basically a very good man, probably determined to make a success of his ministry. But I think there were some aspects of what he found here that he couldn't handle. Began taking all kinds of drugs.'

'Didn't the Pottinger woman say, in her letter to the Major, she *didn't* think he was doing drugs?'

'She was wrong. He seems to have had a vision, or a hallucination . . . of a dragon . . . Satan . . . in the church. And he seems to have thought that by discontinuing active worship there, it would . . . make it go away.'

Nothing very new there. 'But?' Robin said.

'But I *don't* think what he experienced was anything to do with the Old Religion or the rise of the new paganism. I think he became aware of the dualistic nature of religion as it already existed in this area; that there *is* a paganism here, but it's all mixed in with Christianity. A kind of residual medieval Christianity – when magic was very much a part of the whole thing. When prayer was seen as a tool to get things done. It's practical. It suits the area. Marginal land. Hand to mouth.'

Robin thought of the witch box, the charm. Christian, but not entirely Christian. Those astrological symbols, and some of the words – using witchcraft against witchcraft.

'There are five St Michael churches,' Betty said. 'A pentagram of churches, apparently to confine the dragon. But it's an *inverted* pentagram, right?'

'That . . . doesn't sound good.'

'Perhaps,' Betty said, 'it was accepted that, at some time, they might need to *invoke* the dragon. It's border mentality. I met a bloke called Gomer Parry. Radnorshire born and bred. He'll tell you this place took a lot of hammering from both the English and the Welsh and survived, he reckons, by knowing when to sit on the fence and which side to come down on.'

Robin took some time to absorb this. He could smell those bonfire fumes on the air now. It was, in some ways, a sharp and exciting smell carrying the essence of paganism.

He said, 'You mean they're . . . I don't know this stuff, the Book of Revelation and all . . .'

'Sitting on the fence while the war in heaven rages,' Betty said. 'Five little old churches in a depopulated area with a rock-bottom economy. No-man's-land.'

'No-god's-land?' Robin said, awed. 'But, like . . . way back . . . way, *way* back . . . this place *was* something . . . the archaeology shows that.'

'Maybe that accounts for its inner strength. I don't know. We don't know what we're standing in front of. We don't know the full nature of what lies the other side of that barn.'

'Does Ellis?'

'I don't know.'

'Or Bain?'

'Partly. Maybe.'

'But Bain's big thing was personal. That's dark magic. *Low* magic.'

'There are people round here who would understand it. It's notorious for feuds lasting from generation to generation.'

Robin said, 'I wonder, how did Ned Bain get the box from the Major? He buy it? Or just push the old guy off of his ladder and steal it?'

'I don't think he'd push the Major off the ladder. But I don't think he'd have been averse to posting his name on the Kali Three web site.'

'What is that, anyway?'

'You don't want to know,' Betty said.

'Don't wanna dump on my idyll, huh? There's no idyll, babes. No more idyll. Where's that leave us?'

'Leaves us with eleven disappointed witches,' Betty said. 'And a contaminated church.'

Robin breathed in the distant smoke. 'What do we do?'

'I was expecting somebody. I thought she'd have come by now.'

'The woman priest? The Christian priest?'

'She's also an exorcist.'

'Excuse me,' Robin said, 'but didn't we pass this way before?'

'It would've been very wrong to let Ellis do it. You were right about that. From the start.'

'Don't try and get me on your side.'

'OK.'

They looked out over the freezing puddles to the barn on the other side of which the Church of St Michael overhung the restless Hindwell Brook, probably the very same brook into which that guy's son's blood flowed from his hair, in the old Welsh poem Max had read out.

'On account of you know you never need to,' Robin said eventually. 'You know that whatever shit comes down, I am on your side. Do what you think is best.'

He felt like crying. He wished for subsidence, an earthquake. He wished the freaking church would fall into that freaking brook.

Presently, Alexandra stood on the edge of one of the puddles, her long, grey hair loose, a thick woollen shawl wrapped around her.

The emissary. The negotiator. The one they were most likely to talk to.

'It has to be your decision,' Alexandra told them.

'I don't know what to say,' Betty said.

'Babes,' Robin said gently, 'it's getting late. And the priest isn't here. If she was ever gonna come at all.'

'We don't know what that place is really about.' Betty looked out into the night, in the direction of the church. 'We don't know what rituals they were performing, what kind of magic they were trying to arouse or for what purpose. All those millennia ago.'

'Bets,' Robin said, pained, 'the ancient powers locked into the land? The magic of the Old Ones? This is Blackmore shit.'

She looked at him, puzzled. She was probably thinking of him standing watching the water rushing below the church and ranting about the cool energy, him and George with their dowsing rods working out how many old, old bodies were under there, where the energy lines converged. She didn't understand – as Robin now did – that to do his paintings, to be what he was, a true creative artist, he just had to *live* the legend. That was all. That was as deep as it went.

Alexandra said hesitantly, 'May I make a suggestion?'

'Please,' said Robin.

'We abandon all reconsecration plans. That's been tainted now, anyway, because of Ned. And Ned's gone, and we talked about that and we were all relieved, even George, because Ned's . . . Ned's a little bit dark.'

'Fucker,' Robin said.

'So we forget all that. We forget the politics.'

'Even Vivvie?'

Alexandra glanced behind her. Robin saw the whole coven in the shadows.

Vivvie came forward, looking like some rescued urchin. She stood beside Alexandra. 'Whatever,' she said.

'My suggestion,' Alexandra said, 'is that we simply enact the Imbolc rite.'

'Who'd be the high priest?' Robin said.

'It should be you.'

Robin knew this was a major concession, with George and Max out there. Although he'd been through second-degree initiation, he'd never led a coven.

'And when we come to the Great Rite,' Alexandra said, 'we'll leave so that you can complete it.'

For Robin, the cold February night began to acquire luminosity.

Alexandra smiled. 'You've both had a bad time. We want this night to be yours.'

Robin tingled. He did not dare look at Betty.

FIFTY-FIVE

Grey, Lightless

Only a dead body.

Whatever else remained was not here; it was probably earthbound in that back room, where a medieval exorcism replayed itself again and again, until the spirit was flailing and crackling and beating at the glass. The grey and lightless thing that J.W. Weal brought home from Hereford County Hospital.

'Look at her . . .' said Merrily, in whom guilt constantly dwelt, like an old schoolmistress. 'That's what you all did. That's what you left behind. Take a proper look at her face. Go *on*.'

But Judith Prosser looked only at Merrily. And there was no guilt. Practical Judith in her tight blue jeans, the sleeves of her shirt pushed up to the elbows, her black coat in a heap on the floor. Practical Judith Prosser, ready to act, thinking what to do next, how to make her move. A smart woman, a hard woman, a survivor.

But Merrily, perhaps taking on the guilt that Judith would never feel, pushed harder.

'Maybe that's why J.W. invited you to the interment – you and Gareth and the good Dr Coll. Did Dr Coll, by the way, prescribe Valium to keep Menna afloat, keep her quiet when she threatened to be an embarrassment? Was there medication for Marianne, too? I thought Marianne seemed *awfully* compliant during her cleansing.'

'You have it all worked out, Mrs Watkins,' Judith said.

'Yeah,' Merrily said. 'I finally think I do. It stinks worse than this embalming stuff.'

'And what will you do with it all? Will you go to the police and make accusations against Dr Collard Banks-Morgan and Mr Weal, the solicitor, and Mrs Councillor Prosser?'

'It would help,' Merrily conceded, 'if Barbara Buckingham's body *was* in here.'

'So why don't you come back here with a pickaxe? Or with your good friend Gomer Parry and one of his road-breakers?'

It wasn't going to be there, was it? There was no one under Menna. Yet Merrily was sure now that Barbara Buckingham was dead.

'*Did* Barbara find out about the exorcism?'

Judith slowly shook her head, smiling her pasted-on smile, back on top of the situation, giving nothing away.

'Still,' Merrily said, '*Menna*'s here. For any time you want to look at her and remember the old days before she turned into a woman and became less malleable. And J.W.'s left you with a key. So you can come in any time and watch what you once had . . . see what you did. Watch it slowly decaying before your—'

Merrily sank to her knees.

She'd been expecting, if anything, a shriek of outrage and clawing hands. She hadn't seen this coming. Judith Prosser didn't seem to be close enough. Now Merrily was on her knees, with the flash memory of a fist out of nowhere, hard as a kitchen pestle. On a cheekbone.

She had never been hit like this before. It was shattering, like a car crash. She cried out in shock and agony.

Judith Prosser bent with a hand out as if to help her, and

then hit her again with the heel of it, full in the eye. Merrily even saw it, as if in slow motion, but still couldn't move. It drove her back into the wall, her head connecting with the concrete, her left eye closing.

'You can tell the police about that, too, Mrs Watkins.' Judith was panting with satisfaction. 'And see who they believe – a hysterical little pretend-priest from Off, or Mrs Councillor Prosser. Ah . . .'

One hand over her weeping eye, Merrily saw through the other one that the door had swung open. And the doorway was filled. Really filled.

'Good evening, Jeffery,' Judith said.

'You have me, Judith, as a witness that she hit you first.' Weal's voice was colourless and flat as card. 'But only if you make no further mess of her than that, or it would not be a reasonable defence.'

He was carrying what looked like a kind of garden implement. He came in and gently closed the door of the mausoleum behind him. He was wearing a charcoal grey three-piece suit and a white shirt, and a black tie to show he was still in mourning. His face was pouchy, red veins prominent in his grey cheeks.

He propped the garden implement against the door. Merrily saw that it was a double-barrelled twelve-bore shotgun.

'Thought it was the hippies, see.' He nodded at the twelve-bore. 'Some satanist hippies are parked up in the clearing by the Fedw Dingle. Father Ellis phoned to warn me. They break in anywhere.'

'Isn't loaded, is it, Jeffery?' Judith said.

'It's always loaded. There are foxes about. And feral cats. I hate cats, as you know.'

'Not going to the Masonic?'

'I *was* going, Judith, till I saw all those troublemakers in the village. Can't leave your house unguarded, all this going on, can you?'

Talking politely, like neighbours over the wall, people who knew each other but not that well.

They must have known one another for most of their lives.

Merrily didn't try to move. Judith looked down at her.

'Recognize this one, do you, Jeffery? Came to see me this morning. Asking all kinds of questions about Father Ellis. And about you, and Menna. When she left, I saw that the keys . . . You know where I keep your keys, on the hook beside the door? Stupid of me, I know, but I trust people, see, and we've never had anything stolen before. But when she left I seen the keys were gone.'

Weal stood over Merrily. 'Called the police?'

'Well, next thing, there she is coming down the lane tonight. I thought, I'll follow her, I will, and sure enough, up the drive she goes, lets herself in and when I came *in* here, she'd already done *that*.' They both looked at the open tomb. 'Disgusting little bitch. I shouldn't have touched her but, as you say, she went for me. Like a cat.'

'*I hate cats, as you know.*' How instinctive she was.

Merrily was able to open her swelling eye, just a little. She looked up at Weal. It was like standing under some weathered civic monument. She didn't think there was any point at all in telling him that Judith had lured her here, picking up, with psychopathic acumen, Merrily's guilt, her sense of responsibility for Barbara Buckingham.

'Why did you do this? Why do you keep coming here? Why do you keep wanting to see my wife?'

J.W. Weal gazing down at her sorrowfully, giving Merrily the first real indication that there was something wrong with him. His speech was slow, his voice was dry.

'The truth of it is,' Judith said, 'that she seems to have a vendetta against Father Ellis.'

'Father Ellis is . . . a good man,' Weal said calmly.

No, it wasn't calmness so much as depletion. Something missing – almost as if he was drugged, not fully here. As if part of him existed on some intermediate plane, at grey-and-lightless level. Lying there in a cocoon of pain, detached, Merrily felt her senses heightened, her objectivity sharpened.

'Supposed to be the exorcist for the Hereford Diocese, she is,' Judith told Weal. 'Doesn't like him working in her back yard – a priest whose feet she is not fit to wash. What good would a woman like *this* be at what he does?'

Merrily tried to stand. Judith immediately pushed her down again and she slid into the corner by the door. Judith was wearing her leather gloves again, perhaps to cover up any slight abrasions or bruising from the punches. Merrily's face felt numb and twisted. She wondered if her cheekbone was broken. She wondered where this would end. The way these two were talking to each other, it was like a bad play.

'Gave me some nonsense story,' Judith Prosser said. 'About Barbara Buckingham being murdered and buried in there.' Another nod to the open tomb.

Why, in God's name, didn't one of them close it?

'Buckingham?' Weal said vaguely. What was *wrong* with him?

'Barbara *Thomas*.'

'Murdered?'

'*She* thinks Barbara was murdered.' A gleeful, almost girlish lilt now. 'Thinks you did it, Jeffery.'

Merrily didn't look at him. She could almost hear his mind trying to make sense of it.

'Because . . . Barbara Thomas . . . came to see me, is it?' His voice thin and stretched, as though he was trying to remember something. 'Because she . . . accused me?'

'Did she?' Merrily said.

'Shut up!' Judith moved towards her. Merrily shrank back into the corner. If she could just get to her feet, she might . . . but then there was Weal.

'If you grievously injure her,' he told Judith earnestly, 'you know I may not be able to help you.'

Merrily shut her eyes. *Think!* Barbara believes Weal was responsible for Menna's death, so she goes to see Weal and accuses him of bringing about Menna's death by subjecting her to Ellis's perverse ritual. What does Weal do then? What does he do to Barbara?

Nothing.

The way he was talking now, viewing the situation, almost naively, from a pedantic legal perspective, made one thing clear: whatever else he was, this man was not a killer.

There's only one killer.

'J.W.,' Merrily said. 'When Barbara came to see you . . . when she went a little crazy and started accusing you of . . . things, did you . . .' She could hear the acceleration of Judith's breathing, but she didn't look at her; she was going to get this out if she was beaten into the ground for it. 'Did you send her to see Judith?'

Weal didn't answer. He glanced briefly at Judith, then down at Merrily. The question had thrown him. He looked at Judith again, his jaw moving uncertainly, as if he was trying to remember why it was that he hated her so much.

Merrily could suddenly see Weal and Barbara in the old rectory, Weal red-faced and anguished. *'Why are you plaguing me, you stupid, tiresome woman? Why don't you talk to the one person who, for twenty-five years, has been . . .?'*

Judith said, 'Jeffery, you're tired.'

'Yes,' he said. 'I'm always tired these days.'

'Why don't you go back to the house now?' Judith said kindly. 'I'll sort this out.'

He put his fingers vaguely to his forehead. 'You won't go doing anything stupid, will you, Judith? We are entitled to protect our property, but only . . .'

'Don't worry about me. I have never been a stupid woman. I was just carried away, see. Just carried away, Jeffery.'

He nodded.

'Here,' Judith picked up his shotgun. 'Take this with you and lock it away. No one will try to get in now.'

She held the gun upright and handed it to him. Weal accepted it, holding the barrel loosely.

'Right,' he said. 'Thank you, Judith.'

When Judith's gloved hand slid gracefully down the barrel, down the stock, the blast was like the end of the world. Merrily, shrinking into her corner, into herself, saw J.W. Weal's head burst like a melon in a rising red spray.

Felt it come down again, a warm hail.

FIFTY-SIX

Each of my Dyings

Judith still held the shotgun, her face creased in concern.

'Poor man,' she said. 'But, see, what did he have to live for now?'

Judith held the gun with both gloved hands, the stock under her arm.

'Not much,' she added. 'Not much at all.'

Weal's great body blocked the door. His blood and flesh and bone and brain blotched the walls, but most of the mess, still dripping, was on the ceiling. Merrily, sobbing, was still hearing the sound of Weal's head hitting the ceiling. Would hear it for ever.

'A terrible accident,' Judith said.

Two smells now: the embalming room and the slaughter-house. Merrily hung her head. She felt very cold. She heard something sliding stickily down the wall behind and above her.

'An accident, Mrs Watkins. A *terrible* accident.'

'Yes,' Merrily croaked.

'Or perhaps he meant to do it, do you think? You saw me handing it to him. Such a tall man, it was pointing directly under his chin.' She laughed shrilly. 'Such a big man. They calls him Big Weal in Kington and around. *Big Weal – The Big Wheel.*'

'That's very good,' Merrily said.

Judith said flatly, 'I'm making excuses, isn't it?'

Merrily felt something warm on her forehead, wiped it roughly away with her sleeve. She thought that maybe being squashed into a corner had protected her from most of the carnage. She remembered Judith jumping quickly back, snatching the gun away too. Not a speck on Judith.

She heard herself say, 'These things happen,' and felt a bubble of hysteria. She began to get up, levering herself, hands flat behind her pushing against the floor, her bottom against the wall. Now she could see J.W. Weal's huge shoes, shining in the lantern light, his legs . . .

'Oh no, you don't!' Judith swung round, the stock hard against her shoulder. 'You'll stay there while I think, or you'll have the other barrel.'

Merrily froze. Judith's eyes were pale – but not distant like J.W.'s had been. Her gaze was fixed hard on Merrily.

'*You* made me do that. It's *your* fault. You suggested to J.W. that he must've sent Barbara Thomas to me. He never did. He wouldn't do that.'

'Didn't she . . . tell you?' Merrily's gaze turned to the river of blood that had pumped from J.W. Weal's collar. She gagged.

'She was off her head, that woman,' Judith said. '*Off her head!* Screaming at me. Standing there, screaming at *me*, in her fancy clothes. How dare she run away, go *from* here, spend her life in cushy . . . where was it? Where *was* it?'

'Ham . . . Hampshire.'

'*Hampshire*. Soft, cushy place that is. How dare she come back from Hampshire, start screaming at me – *me* who's had it hard all my life. They comes here, the English, think they can say what they like.'

Half a mile over the border – just half a mile – and this myth of the English having it so good.

Judith's accent seemed to deepen as she remembered the

encounter. 'But a scrawny neck, she had, like an old bird. Trying to hide her scrawny neck with a fancy, silk scarf. But I found it, Mrs Watkins.'

Oh God. Merrily stiffened in her half-crouch against the wall. Sinewy hands around a scrawny neck. Maybe a silk scarf pulled tight.

'Going to tell everybody, she was, that bitch! *Everybody!* Going to shout it all over Radnorshire that Mrs Councillor Prosser was a lesbian! How *dare* the bitch call me a lesbian? "I'll sue you!" I said to her. "I'll hire *J.W.* to sue you. See how long your English money lasts you then!"'

Merrily retched again.

'Never seen blood before, Mrs Watkins? Used to kill all our own pigs, we did, when I was a girl. And whatever else we wanted to, until the regulations. Regulations about this and that . . . Regulations, it is, killing country life.' She calmed down, sighed. 'Poor Jeffery – it's just like putting down an old horse.'

'What was . . . the matter with him?'

'It was since she died.' A toss of her head towards the tomb. 'He was hardly awake since. Couldn't face being awake.'

'Was he . . . on medication? From Dr Coll?'

'Wouldn't have it. Said it was the mourning took his energy, eating him up inside.'

Took his energy?

Menna.

'Do you know what I think?' Judith said, brightening. 'I think he ought to have killed you, Mrs Watkins.'

Merrily felt the first spasm of a cramp in her right leg. She had to move.

'That's what I think. Meddling little bitch, you are, come to spy on Father Ellis.'

Merrily braced herself against the wall, straightened the

leg in front of her, looking up. Into the black, metal-smelling barrels of the twelve-bore hovering six inches from her face.

Judith said, 'Perhaps he *did* shoot you.' She raised a hand to her head for a moment, horribly childlike, as if putting something together in her mind. 'Likely he shot you before he killed himself. Blew your little head off with the one barrel, saved the other for himself. He was a solicitor. A logical man, see.'

She looked delighted – the woman was mad.

Merrily looked along the barrel of the great gun towards the stock. She saw two triggers, one slightly in front of the other, Judith's finger around the second one. The speed she'd managed it last time, there must be hardly any tension in those triggers.

Merrily jerked her head to one side, but the two holes followed her.

Judith was a practical woman.

'First used one of these when I was nine year old,' she said proudly, 'when I could hardly lift it. Saw my father shooting crows.' She smiled happily. 'Country girl, see, always the tomboy. Always a better shot than Councillor Prosser.'

The trigger finger relaxed. Merrily still held her breath. Could she summon the strength to throw herself from the wall, knock the barrel aside? As if she'd picked up the thought, Judith backed away smartly, smiling.

'Jeffery thought you were one of the hippies broken in. Thought you were a hippy, and you went for him and his gun went off. That's what they'll say, isn't it? Then, when he saw what he'd done, he turned the gun on himself. Suicide while the balance of mind was disturbed. Went to an inquest two year ago, we did, Councillor Prosser and I. One of our old neighbours hanged himself – verdict of suicide while the balance of mind was disturbed. Everyone here knew J.W.'s balance of mind was gone.'

Merrily shook her head helplessly.

Judith waggled her fingers to show she was still wearing gloves. 'Dropped the gun as he died. Two of you dead.' She glanced at the open tomb. 'Went to say goodbye to his wife, before he killed himself. Poor Jeffery, he's with her now – is that what you think, Mrs Watkins?'

'Yes.'

Judith's face turned red. 'Rubbish! Nonsense! How can a *woman* be so stupid. There is nothing after death! Menna waiting in the clouds with her arms open, waiting for her J.W. with no head? Is that what you would tell them in your church, Mrs Watkins?'

'Is that what you say to Father Ellis?'

The barrel moved down to Merrily's chest. At this range, the blast would cut her in half, and it could happen any time. If she moved too quickly, Judith would blow her apart. She wouldn't feel anything. She wouldn't even hear the shot. Her last moment would be a moment just like this.

'We could have been friends, you and I, Merrily Watkins.'

'I'm not sure that we could,' Merrily said honestly.

'I'm not a lesbian, you know. Are you calling me a lesbian?'

Merrily thought of Jane, glad that Gomer was with her. Would the kid later remember hearing a distant explosion from the village, hear it echoing down her life. Pray that these concrete walls were too thick. Pray: *Please, God, Oh God. Please, Jesus, hold me safe from the forces of evil. On each of my dyings shed your light and your love.* Would she die wearing Jane's coat? She saw not her own life flashing before her, but Jane's. Jane aged three on the beach in Pembrokeshire, following a ball, tripping over it, starting to cry because she thought she should, and then bursting into wild laughter, rolling over and over like a kitten.

Merrily tore herself wretchedly back into the present.

'Frankly, Judith, I couldn't care less where you stand sexually. It's insignificant.'

'Not to me, Mrs Watkins. Not to my reputation.'

'The real point is, you're a monster. A monster that feeds on the vulnerable. Anything that brings out pity in the rest of us, it just makes you more excited. Tears turn you on. You were probably everything to Menna – all she had sometimes. But she was nothing to you, no more than a slim, white, trembling body to play with.'

She stood up, looked at Judith and shrugged.

'You may close your eyes, if you wish,' Judith said coldly, but she'd squeezed the second trigger before Merrily even had time to decide.

Betty and the stately Alexandra drifted about the ruins like mother and daughter ghosts, moving things around while Robin watched and held the lamp.

The fat candles mostly stayed: on sills and ledges, and in glass lanterns on the top of the tower.

The altar got moved. This was an old workbench from the barn, with a wood vice still clamped on the side. Robin helped Alexandra carry it from the north wall to a place in the middle of the nave, opposite the tower but facing where Betty figured the chancel had been. East-facing, like a Christian altar, in case this Merrily Watkins turned up.

The ruins hung around them like old and tattered drapes, moonlight showing up all the moth-holes. The moon was real white now, like a slice of Philadelphia cheese over the tower. Robin thought he saw a movement up there. An owl, maybe.

Across the roofless nave, Betty was taking some crystals from a drawstring bag. She kept her eyes down.

When it was all ready, the coven was summoned in, and Alexandra said to Betty, 'Will it be?'

Robin looked at Betty, and he knew she had at last accepted that the Christian priest would not come.

Betty nodded.

Tapers and matches were handed out. The coven moved like shadows, dipping and bending, and when each one rose there was a new glimmering.

Max's wife Bella did the tower. 'Creepy,' she said when she came down. 'Felt I was being watched.'

In the end, there must have been seventy or eighty candles alight. Lined up in every jagged, glassless window. Along the walls of the roofless nave. In the arrow-cracks of the tower. On top of the cold battlements, in glass lanterns.

St Michael's, Old Hindwell, was ethereal, unearthly, shivering with lights, and the display reflected, crystallized, in the Hindwell Brook.

FIFTY-SEVEN

In Shock

Never had a gun, never wanted one, but Gomer knew about gunshots, how loud they could be at night, how the sound would carry miles, and he'd figured out roughly where this one had come from, and it wasn't likely to be poachers or lampers of hares – not tonight with all these coppers on the loose.

'The church?' young Jane said, scared.

'Further on, more like.'

He wasn't gonner say it was the ole rectory yet, but he was gonner check it out.

As they reached Prossers' farm, a police van shot past them – far too fast, in Gomer's view, to be heading for the entrance to the ole church. They wouldn't've heard the shot. Most likely they was heading for the camp the coppers would've now set up where they'd dug up Barbara Thomas.

Gomer had been worried they might get stopped. Under his bomber jacket, he had his sweatshirt on back to front, so it no longer said, 'Gomer Parry Plant Hire'.

Behind them, the fire was just fumes on the air, almost unnoticeable as they reached the St Michael's entrance. No protesters here yet. No coppers, neither. And no reporters. A woman's body and some bugger figuring to fry 300 people had to be more important than God and the Devil.

The five-bar gate was closed across the track, but the

padlock hung loose from the hasp on a chain. Gomer was about to open it when Jane let out a gasp.

Two women were approaching up the road.

Jane hesitates a moment, then starts to run. Gomer levels his torch.

It lights up Judy Prosser. Also the vicar.

The kiddie runs to her mam and they starts hugging, but Gomer knows straight off this en't normal. He walks over, slowly.

''Ow're you, Judy?''

But he's looking at the vicar in the torchlight, where her eye's black and swelled-up, her face lopsided.

Jane's now spotted it, too. 'Mum, what have you—'

But Judy cuts in. 'Gomer, we're looking for the police, we are. Something terrible's happened.'

'What's that, Judy?'

'I have to report a suicide.' She's holding herself up straight in this long, black quilted coat. 'Mr Weal – he's shot himself, I'm afraid to say.'

'Big Weal?'

'Blew his head off with a shotgun. In his wife's tomb, this was, poor man. Turned his mind, isn't it? The grief. Tried to stop him, didn't I, Mrs Watkins? Tried to talk him out of it.'

The vicar says, in this clear voice, like in the pulpit, 'No one could have done more, Mrs Prosser.'

'You all right, vicar?'

'Yeah, I'm . . . fine. Apart from a few bruises where . . . Mr Weal hit me.'

'I warned her not to approach him,' said Mrs Prosser. 'Silly girl.'

'Yes, I've been a very silly girl.'

Judy says, 'We all were terrified that he might do something stupid. So, as a close neighbour, I was keeping an eye on him. I go there every night, I do, to check he's all right, and sometimes I finds him beside the tomb, with the top open, just staring at Menna's remains. Mrs Watkins said she did not think this was healthy and she asked me to take her to see Mr Weal, and we finds the poor man in there, with his wife on show and his twelve-bore in his hands. Mrs Watkins panics, see—'

'Gomer . . .?' the vicar says.

'Ar?'

'Are there any police around? I thought there'd be some here.'

'Over the harchaeologist site, vicar,' Gomer says warily. 'Any number o' the buggers.'

'Could you take Mrs Prosser. Ask for a senior officer, and tell them Mrs Prosser has a lot of . . . information.'

'You can tell them my husband's on the police committee,' Judy says. 'That should expedite matters. But surely you're coming, too, Mrs Watkins?'

'I have to take my child back to the vicarage, Mrs Prosser. She's too young to hear about this kind of thing.'

The vicar hugs young Jane very close for a few seconds.

'Say goodnight to Gomer, Jane,' the vicar says.

The kiddie comes over, puts her arms round Gomer's neck and hugs him real tight, and in his ear in this shocked, trembling whisper, her says,

'Mum says to tell the police not to let her go. She's killed twice.'

They followed the path to the old archaeological site. Some thirty yards away, they could see two police cars lined up, a radio crackling from one of them. They could see the low, white tent, the orange tape. The second car was parked on the edge of a small wood full of dead trees, white branches shining like bone. Jane had told her what was probably still lying under the tent.

'Are you sure?' the kid kept saying. 'Are you *sure?*'

'I promised.'

'But with everything that's . . . And look at you . . . *Look* at you. You need a doctor.'

'Dr Coll?' Merrily started to laugh, and the laughter wouldn't stop.

'Stop it!' Jane screamed. 'What's that on your hands?'

Merrily looked down, still laughing.

'Oh.'

Thock, she heard. *Thock*.

Seeing the ridiculous dismay on Judith's face . . . watching her step back, angrily breaking open the gun, and coming out with that brilliantly dry observation.

'Wouldn't you know it, Mrs Watkins? A Radnor man to the core. Never load two cartridges when you may not even need the one.'

The funniest line Merrily had heard in a long time. Possibly, at that moment, the funniest line being spoken in the whole, insane world. When she started to laugh, she was half expecting Judith to come at her with both fists or take a swing at her with the shotgun. But smart Judith, canny Judith . . . this was not how Judith reacted at all. She simply laid down the empty gun, a few inches away from the half-curled hand out of which she'd snatched it before the fingers could spasm around its barrel.

'The stupid man.' Voice flat, eyes flat like aluminium. 'What did he want to do that for? You saw it, Mrs Watkins, you saw how I tried to stop him.'

As if the previous minutes had never happened – as if editing her life like a videotape. Instinctively compiling the alternative version, with an efficient jump-cut from the second the gun went off. So practical, this Judith.

And Merrily had reacted quickly for once, getting it exactly right.

'You'd better tell the police what happened then, Mrs Prosser.'

'It's my duty, Mrs Watkins. Give me a hand here, will you?'

Both of them then pulling the body away from the door, as though it was a huge dead sheep, so they could squeeze outside.

This was how Merrily had got the blood on her hands.

To the left, she could hear the sound of the Hindwell Brook.

Jane said, 'She killed Barbara Buckingham, that woman?'

'Yes.' *Strangled her with her own silk scarf. Beat her up first, probably.* 'Perhaps when Barbara went to see her and challenged her over . . . certain things. I think Gomer said her husband owned a digger. I suppose one of them would've driven her car over to the Elan Valley, with the other following.'

'Who *is* she?'

'She's Mrs Councillor Prosser, flower – fortified by the local community: the doctor, the lawyer, the councillor . . . even the priest. Solid as a rock, she was, until someone from Off blew it all open. Someone who hadn't always been from Off, and realized what she was seeing here.'

And Merrily couldn't help wondering to herself, then, if anything had ever gone on, way back, between Judith and Barbara – something Barbara had suppressed, erased from her memory as simply as Judith Prosser had erased from her mental tape the murder of Weal and the attempted murder of Merrily.

Over her shoulder was slung her airline bag, bought because it was blue and gold. She'd brought it out of the tomb with her, but there was no blood on it, a small miracle. It contained the Bibles, prayers, altar wine and holy water. So medieval?

They stopped at the bridge, and there was the church across the water, and also reflected in the water. Betty's birthday cake.

'It's beautiful,' Jane breathed. 'It's . . . *son et lumière*. Without the *son*.'

Merrily smiled wildly. Less than an hour ago, she was staring into eternity down the barrels of a twelve-bore. Now she was back in airy-fairyland.

'Are you *sure* about this?' Jane said. Merrily squeezed her arm.

'Jane . . . look . . . I don't want to have to worry about you, OK? So I'd like you to stay out of the way. I know you're sixteen and everything . . .'

'You're in shock, aren't you? I mean, you've just seen something totally horrific. You've been through a really horrifying—'

'Yeah, I probably am in shock.'

'You could do this tomorrow.'

'I said I'd do it tonight.'

'We could explain to Betty . . .'

They were halfway across the footbridge now. The ruins shimmered in a hollow of silence.

Then a woman's voice rose up.

'Dread lord of Death and Resurrection
Of life and the Giver of life
Lord within ourselves, whose name is Mystery of
    Mysteries encourage our hearts
Let thy light crystallize itself in our blood . . .'

Merrily slumped over the rail of the bridge.
Too late.

FIFTY-EIGHT

The Woman Clothed with the Sun

His coven around him, Robin lifted the wand high, in his right hand, until it divided the moon.

The wand was a slender, foot-long piece of hazel wood, cut from the tree with a single stroke on a Wednesday, as laid down in the Book of Shadows. In his left hand Robin held the scourge, a mild token thing like a riding crop with silken cords.

Behind him were the crone – Alexandra – and a woman called Ilana, who was twenty-four but looked a lot younger and represented the maiden tonight.

The flames rose straight up out of the tight nest of stones in the centre of the nave as he brought down the wand in a long diagonal, right to left, then left to right in a forty-five-degree angle and straight back horizontally and down . . . and up.

To a point. One point.

The positive, invoking pentagram of Earth . . . drawn before his high priestess, whose hair shone brighter than the fire, whose eyes were deeper than crystals.

'*Blessed be*,' Robin whispered.

And never had meant it more.

Merrily followed Jane around the church tower. The kid had a small torch, borrowed from Gomer, but they didn't need it; the church cast its own light. When she looked up to the top of the tower, she could no longer see the candle-lanterns, only the highlighted stones. She and Jane slipped – unseen, she assumed – from the tower, across a grassy, graveless churchyard, glittering with frost, to the side of what looked like a stone barn.

What to do? Watch and pray?

Christ be with us, Christ within us, Christ behind us.

They stood with their backs to the barn. From here, through an empty Gothic window in the nave, about twenty feet away, they could see the long candles on the altar, and they could see, by the fire and candlelight, Betty in her green robe. On one side of her was a girl of about eighteen, on the other a plump and placid woman, who looked like she ought to be running a day nursery. The girl was combing Betty's blond hair.

There was now music on the freezing air: vaguely Celtic, string and reed music from some boombox stereo concealed in the ruins. It all seemed gentle and poetic and harmless and not a lot, in Merrily's view, to do with religion.

The distance, the walls and the music allowed them to talk in low voices. Jane said, 'Doesn't look as if she's been, like, coerced, does it?'

Betty stood with her back to the altar, the other women on either side. The male witch, who looked like he should be playing bass with Primal Scream, appeared in the Gothic window.

'We saw him in the *Daily Mail*, right?' Merrily said.

'Yeah, I'm pretty sure that's Robin.'

'And is he the high priest? You know this stuff better than me.'

'Has to be.'

'Not Ned Bain, then.'

'Which is a mercy?' Jane said.

'Which has to be a mercy.'

A shadow moved beside her, as if off the barn. Any night but this, she might have cried out.

'A mercy, you think, then?' the shadow said.

'Hello, Ned,' said Merrily.

They'd customized the rite slightly, to allow for the place and the changed circumstances, but Robin thought it could still be OK. He tried to concentrate on the meaning of the ritual – the birth of spring. And the purpose – the bringing of fresh light to an old, dark place. He wondered if Terry Penney could see them in some way and feel what was happening. For in the absence of the woman priest, Betty said, this rite must also be a form of exorcism, to convey Terry's spirit into a place of peace.

But Robin couldn't dispel the awareness that they were doing this in a *church*. He would close his eyes for a moment and try to bring down the walls until there was only a circle of stones around them, but he was finding he couldn't hold that image, and this *wasn't* Robin Thorogood, visionary, seducer of souls, guardian of the softly lit doorways. He found himself wishing they were someplace else, in a frosted glade or on some open moorland . . . and *that* wasn't Robin Thorogood, custodian of an ancient site which tonight was entering its third incarnation, quietly and harmoniously, without tension, without friction.

He laid the wand and scourge upon the altar and helped the maiden to arrange the shawl around the shoulders of the crone.

From a jam jar on the altar, he took a small bunch of snowdrops – the flowers of Imbolc – which Alexandra had found growing behind the barn and had bound together with some early catkins.

He presented this humble bouquet to Ilana, the maiden.

He lifted the crown of lights from the altar and waited while the three women arranged themselves.

He raised the crown of lights and placed it on Betty's head, and the maiden and the crone tucked and curled her golden hair becomingly around it.

'Merely spectators,' Ned Bain whispered. 'Isn't it sad? Came for a baptism and they wouldn't even let us be godparents.'

Merrily said nothing, keeping her eyes on the Gothic window, full of moving lights.

'I've been barred,' he said. 'Might that be down to you?'

She flicked a glance at him. She hadn't seen him clearly, but he was not robed, like the others. He seemed to be wearing a jacket and jeans. She made sure she kept Jane on the other side of her.

'If you've been barred, why are you still here?'

'Because Simon will come,' Bain said. 'If he isn't here already.'

'Simon?'

'*You* know who I mean.'

'Maybe.'

'You really aren't on his side, are you, Merrily?'

'I'm not on anybody's side.' She was picking up a musky, sandy smell on him. It reminded her, for just a moment, of Sean. She made the sign of the cross and cloaked herself and Jane in the glow from the breastplate of St Patrick. The smell went away.

Bain said, 'Am I right in thinking Simon's offended you?'

'Am I supposed to think this is ESP, Ned? Your awesome powers at work?'

'Isn't Father Ellis performing exorcisms?'

'Is he?'

'Do they work?'

'Depends on what he intends them to do. That's where the problems arise.'

'Tell me.'

Jane touched her shoulder. 'Mum . . . I think they're coming.'

'If I tell you what he did,' Merrily said, 'will you bugger off?'

'OK.'

'He performed some kind of baptismal ritual which effectively bound together two people who never should have been brought together in the first place. And when the woman died, her . . . spirit would not leave the man. And instead of bringing him comfort, it oppressed him and sapped his energy, and turned him into . . . even less than he was before.'

'Mum . . .'

'Thank you,' Ned Bain said. 'What will you do about that?'

'I don't know that I can do anything.'

She moved behind Jane to the corner of the barn, looked out across a yard, past the farmhouse to where a track was marked out by a line of swinging torches and lamps.

She heard singing – inane, redneck gospel, with all the spirituality of a football chant.

We shall raise the sword of Christ and strike the Devil down.

'Sounds like your people, Merrily,' Ned Bain said. 'And my cue to disappear.'

In the night, with all the spearing torches, the hymn sounded dense and menacing. Merrily remembered the Christian biker with the dead dragon on his T-shirt.

'This is what you wanted, isn't it, Ned?'

'If I were you,' Ned Bain said, 'I'd stay well out of it. Call that a gentle warning. Call it a prophecy. Goodnight,

Merrily.' He turned and merged with the shadows. 'There's blood on your hands. Why's that, I wonder?'

She didn't see how, in this light, he could possibly have seen her hands. And she'd got it all off, hadn't she?

In the shimmering silence of the open ruins, with the tower rearing behind his priestess, Robin brought a taper from the fire and lit the candles around the crown of lights. The little flames sprang brightly. Robin said,

> 'Behold the Three-formed Goddess,
> She who is ever Three
> Yet is she ever One.
> For without Spring there can be no Summer,
> Without Summer, no Winter.
> Without Winter, no new Spring.'

Tears in his eyes as he gazed on his goddess. She was everything he'd ever imagined, the beautiful book cover he'd painted so often in his head for the book which was too profound, too poetic, too resonant for anyone yet to have written. He looked into Betty's eyes and then up at the blurred moon.

'Listen to the words of the Great Mother – She who, of old, was also called among men Artemis, Astarte, Athene, Dion, Melusine, Aphrodite, Ceridwen, Dana, Arianrhod, Isis, Brigid and by many other names.'

And so it went on, and when it was over, the maid took up a broomstick and walked clockwise around the fire, followed by the mother and the crone, sweeping away the old, and Robin prayed to the moon for the badness and torment in this place to be swept away for ever.

*

When the torch and lamp lights were enlarged, beams crossing in the air, and the hymn behind her began to sound like the baying of wolves, Merrily looked up and saw him.

Just a shadow against the stars, then faintly lit by the lanterns on the battlements. He was not in his white robes, which would have been too conspicuous; someone would have seen him getting into the tower.

'Oh Christ,' Merrily said. She turned to Jane. 'Stay there.'

'No chance,' Jane muttered, and followed her towards the church.

They kept close to the walls so they couldn't be seen from the tower itself, passed by the Gothic window full of lights, edged around the building to the opening, where the south porch had been. Merrily began to pray softly and realized, with horror, that she was praying to God for protection against His servants at the gate.

She was very anxious now.

Robin picked up, from outside the ring of stones surrounding the fire, two twigs of holly he'd cut a week ago and hung over the back door, so that they were now nicely brittle.

The coven gathered around him. He knelt before the fire and set light to each twig in turn and held it up for them all to see. Then he tossed each of the twigs into the flames. And the coven chanted with him, in what ought to have been joy and optimism but sounded scarily flat and formulaic,

> 'Thus we banish Winter,
> Thus we welcome Spring,
> Say farewell to what is dead
> And greet each living thing.
> Thus we banish Winter,
> Thus we welcome Spring.'

Then the coven melted away, into the shadows and out of the church, Max patting Robin on the shoulder as he passed. 'Well done, mate,' Max whispered.

All over.

All over, but for the Great Rite.

A double sleeping bag lay directly under the tower, protected from the wind, a candle-lantern quietly alight at either end.

Robin stood by the fire. Betty walked away toward the base of the tower and when she reached it, she turned around, all aglow in her nest of candles. But the glow came from more than the candles, and there was a strange moment of fusion, as if the whole church was a crown of lights around them both, and Betty's gown slipped down with a silken rustling, and Robin's heart leapt like a fawn and he moved toward her along the open nave.

And then he heard a voice, cold and strident on the night.

'Foul serpent!'

Robin looked up and saw the spectre on the battlements, its arms raised like the twin points of a pentagram upside down.

'O most glorious leader of the heavenly armies, defend us in our war against the dark spirits which rule this world and the spirits of wickedness in the high places. For the Holy Church venerates you as her guardian and the Lord has entrusted to You the souls of the redeemed, to be led into heaven.'

'St Michael,' Merrily explained. 'He's invoking St Michael. It's his exorcism.'

She stood in the entrance, with Jane.

'You've got to do something,' Jane said.

A bright light lanced over the kid's shoulder. A TV cameraman was moving up behind her. They were all piling in now, whether they'd come over the gate or across the bridge, forming a big circle around the ruins. But it had been a small church and she and Jane were blocking the narrow entrance. People began to push at her back.

'Make them go away!' A woman's voice she'd heard some-where before ... *I can show you a church with a tower and graves and everything* ... 'This is sacrilege!'

Merrily put an arm around Jane and didn't move.

Ellis boomed from the tower, his voice like a klaxon in the still, freezing air. *'In the name of Jesus Christ, our Lord, and of Michael, the Archangel, we confidently undertake to repulse the deceits of Satan!'*

Merrily was furious. He was not entitled. He was not *entitled* to wield the name of Christ like an axe ... or the cross of Christ like a dildo ...

Robin Thorogood couldn't seem to move. He stood in the nave, staring up, as if his blood had turned to ice. Impaled by TV lights, he looked like a prisoner caught in the search-lights escaping from some concentration camp. Merrily couldn't see Betty.

From the tower, in the haze of the lanterns, Ellis cried, *'God arises! His enemies are dissembled, and those who hate Him shall fall down before him. Just as the smoke of hellfire is driven away, so are they driven. Just as wax melts before the fire, so shall the wicked perish before the presence of God. Behold—'*

He stopped. Betty had walked out. She was robed again. She looked terrified, but she didn't look up, not once.

She was somehow still wearing the crown of lights.

And Merrily, in a vibrantly dark moment, was already hearing the verse from Revelation when he started to broad-cast the words.

'Now a great sign appeared in heaven ... a woman clothed with the sun, with the moon under her feet ... and on her head ... a garland of twelve stars ...!'

Robin Thorogood shouted, 'No . . . that's not . . .' Throwing out his arms in protest.

'*Serpent!*'

Merrily saw what she knew that Ellis was seeing. She saw the picture in his war room, the one by William Blake, and it turned Robin's arms into great webbed, leathery wings the colours of a freshly dug worm, and his wild hair into a ram's curling horns. She saw the Woman Clothed with the Sun, stars around her head, a twinkling lure for the Great Red Dragon.

Merrily at last gave way to the prods and thrusts at her back.

Robin saw the small, dark-haired woman running into the nave.

'*No . . .*' she was yelling. '*Please God, no.*'

And when he heard, from above, this sickening, crumbling, creaking, cracking sound, he realized he was screaming too as he hurled himself towards Betty, threw his arms around her and bore her to the ground, covering her with his body and closing his eyes as the first stone came out of the sky.

He didn't feel it. He couldn't feel anything. But he could hear other people's screams and, above them all, Ellis's bellow.

'*And there was war in heaven!*'

Robin just lay across his goddess on the sleeping bag, unmoving as the black sky tumbled.

He opened his eyes just once, to watch the crown of lights rolling away like a cheap Catherine wheel, the birthday candles going out one by one.

There were many other lights, too, but he closed his eyes on them; many other sounds, but he didn't listen to them. He heard only the heart of his goddess, and his own voice whispering the words which moved him beyond all others.

'In the fullness of time we shall be born again, at the same time and in the same place as each other, and we shall meet and know and remember . . . and love again . . .'

FIFTY-NINE

Damage

He was a tall, stooping man with a mournful, half-moon kind of face, a heavy grey moustache. He was the recently appointed head of Dyfed-Powys CID, a mere caretaker role, he said, before retirement. His name was Gwyn Arthur Jones, detective superintendent. Gomer Parry knew him from way back, which saved them some time.

But it was still close to 3 a.m. before they left the incident room – Dr Coll's waiting room – for the comparative privacy of Dr Coll's surgery. The door was closed, and a metal Anglepoise burned on a desk swept clean of all papers.

Formal statements had been taken and signed. Jane was asleep on Dr Coll's couch. Sophie had taken Eirion back to Hereford and his stepmother's car.

Detective Superintendent Gwyn Arthur Jones had brought out his pipe and discovered a bottle of single malt in Dr Coll's filing cabinet.

'Kept naggin' at me, see,' Gomer said, 'that piece o' ground. Amateur job, stood out a mile. Why would bloody Gareth dig it up again and put it back, 'less he was lookin' for treasure, and Gareth wouldn't know treasure 'less it come in a bloody brass-bound chest with "Treasure" wrote on it.'

'And Mrs Prosser?' The superintendent's accent was West Wales, quite soft, a first-language Welsh-speaker's voice. 'Did no one *ever* nurture uncharitable suspicions about her?'

'Judy?' Gomer shook his head as though he would go on shaking it for ever. 'Not me. Least nothin' I could get a ring-spanner to. But her kept croppin' up, ennit? I kept sayin' to the vicar, didn't I, vicar, you wanner talk to Judy . . . Judy's smart . . . Judy *knows*. Bloody hell, Gwyn, I never guessed Judy knowed it all.'

'And still holding out on us.' Gwyn Arthur sipped Dr Coll's whisky. Merrily had noticed that when he'd taken the bottle from the drawer he'd replaced it with a twenty-pound note. 'I don't somehow think she will ever do otherwise. "Mrs Councillor Prosser, wife of a former chairman of the police committee" – time and time again, like name, rank and number.'

'Local credentials,' Gomer said. 'Means everythin' here.'

'And Dr Collard Banks-Morgan, former acting police surgeon – the allegations about *him*, he tells us, are quite risible. As we would have been further assured by Mr Weal, had the poor man not taken his own life. I suspect people cleverer than me will have to spend many days among Mr Weal's files.'

Gwyn Arthur poured further measures of whisky into those little plastic measuring vessels you got with your medicine.

'All in all,' he said, 'never, in my experience, have so many eminently respectable, conspicuously guilty people lied so consistently through their teeth. I'm awfully afraid, Mrs Watkins, that you are destined for a considerable period in the witness box.'

'What will you do with Ellis?' Merrily asked.

'We'll hold him until the morning, then we shall have to think in terms of charges, and I'm very much afraid that my imagination, at present, will not stretch a great deal further than wilful damage – if that – regardless of the tragic conse-quences. He didn't even have to break into the tower. Just bolted himself in from the inside. What happened later was, he insists, an unfortunate accident. He hasn't even described it as the will of God. The tower parapet, as the late Major Wilshire discovered to his ultimate cost, was horribly unstable. He did not mean for all those stones to fall.'

'What about the TV pictures?'

'Almost gratuitously graphic when it comes to portraying the results. But the lights on the cameras were insufficiently powerful to reach the top of the tower – or to illuminate Ellis's movements in the moments before the stones were dislodged. I would give anything for it to be otherwise, but there we are.'

Merrily lit a cigarette with fingers which still would not stay steady. 'I'm not giving up on that bastard. Expect me at the station later today, with a Mrs Starkey, if I've got to drag her. But I don't think it'll come to that. Not now.'

'Yes, indecent assault is a better beginning.' Gwyn Arthur Jones drained his medicine measure and went to stand at the window. The only vehicles left on view in the village were the police cars and vans, Merrily's Volvo, Gomer's Land-Rover and Nev's truck with the digger on the back. Gwyn Arthur came back and sat down and contemplated Merrily. 'And what else? What else, in your wildest imaginings, Merrily, would you think Ellis might have done?'

She took a tiny sip of Scotch. 'Well . . . have you got anybody yet for the village hall?'

'Interesting,' Gwyn Arthur said, 'but no we haven't. The travellers we brought in were *most* indignant.'

'I mean, it was all getting a bit tame, wasn't it? A few hymns, a little placard-waving. He'd had his chance to convince 300 fundamentalist Christians that Satan was in residence in Old Hindwell, and he hadn't *really* pulled it off, had he?'

'You think he planned to inflame these people, as it were,

with the thought that the pagans wanted to burn them alive? Maybe to drive them to excesses?'

'Knowing full well he'd have been able to lead them to safety out of the rear entrance, even if Gomer hadn't turned up and received the credit? I think that's very much on the cards.'

'Hmm,' said the superintendent. 'Certainly, emotions among those decent, church-going Christians were running at a level possibly unparalleled since the days of the witch-hunts. There's no question in my mind that it *could* have become extremely nasty . . . if, ironically enough, those stones had not fallen when – and where – they did.'

'You could always check out his robe for petrol traces or something.'

'No one as yet, has been able to *find* his robe,' said Gwyn Arthur Jones regretfully. 'He doesn't remember where he left it. Unlike Mrs Prosser, he's being entirely cooperative. He tells us he chose to go alone to the church, one man against a horde of heathens, precisely because he did not want his legitimate Christian protest against the desecration of the house of God to become a bloodbath. Several witnesses confirm that he tried to stop them.'

Merrily closed her eyes. 'He doesn't *like* churches. Churches are disposable. Instead, he set up in this village hall because it was close to Old Hindwell Church . . . the battleground. He claimed he'd been getting anonymous letters, phone calls . . . signs on the Internet.' She sighed. 'Do you know the Book of Revelation at all? The paintings of William Blake?'

Betty stared down into the near-black water. She said slowly, 'O Lord, Jesus Christ, Saviour Salvator, I beseech the salvation of all who dwell within from witchcraft and from the power of all evil men or women or spirits or wizards or hardness of heart. Amen Amen Amen.'

An ambulance warbled across the city. Maybe the one which had brought her here several hours ago.

From the viewing platform above Victoria Bridge, the suspension footbridge over the Wye, bushes hid the sprawl of Hereford County Hospital.

It was dawn, that coldest time, with only a few lights across the river, shining through the bare, grey trees.

'Either the charm didn't work,' she said, 'or it worked all too well.'

'Get rid of it,' Merrily said.

Half an hour ago, she'd been waiting with Betty when the orthopaedic surgeon, who was called Frank, had explained that Robin's pelvis was smashed, and there was some spinal damage. 'Will he walk again?' Betty had asked. Frank couldn't answer that one, yet, but he said he was hopeful.

Merrily said bitterly, 'War in heaven, and all the casualties down here.'

'Don't you go losing your faith,' Betty said. 'It's only religion. Faith is faith, but religions are no better than the people who practise them.'

SIXTY

Lamplit

It was still only mid-morning when the bedside phone awoke her. She hadn't been in bed long enough for it to be a sleep of any depth – although the half-dreams were dark – and she was instantly focused and expecting the worst.

She didn't expect *him*.

'It all comes down to demonization, you see, Merrily,' he said, as if they'd been talking for hours. 'I was demonized from an early age – twelve, to be exact. He was the little Christ, and I was the Antichrist. He and his mother were always very efficient at the demonization of anything in their way. And he still is, of course.'

He sounded as if he'd been drinking. His voice was dark and smooth and intimate. Merrily sat up in bed, fumbling a cardigan around her shoulders.

'He wanted dragons, so I sent him dragons. I sent him serpents.'

'What do you mean?'

'It isn't *all* done by magic. The postal service can be equally effective, and now the Internet and email . . . almost as fast as one can transmit a thought. But then it's all electricity, isn't it? Everything's a form of electricity. Science is catching us up. Soon *everyone* will be doing magic. What a dispiriting thought.'

She heard the clink of a glass against his teeth.

'I've been a bad man, in my way. No worse, I would submit, than Simon, but bad enough. Sometimes I yearn for redemption. Is that possible, do you think, Merrily?'

'It's possible for everybody.'

The sunlight penetrated through the crack in the curtains and put a pale stripe down the bed. Celtic spring had come.

'I hoped you'd say that,' he said. 'So . . . will you help me? Will you help a poor sinner onto the . . . lamplit path?'

She froze. 'Who told you about that?'

He laughed. 'I know everything about you. You're in bed, aren't you?'

She felt his Sean-breath, the warm dusting, and she was afraid.

'I can just see you in bed,' he said, 'all rumpled, a little creased around the eyes. Rumpled and smelling of softness and sleep.'

She remembered the blood he could not have seen on her hands. She remembered the red and white lights on the motorway, false lights in a night of filth.

'Can we meet?' Ned Bain said. 'And discuss my redemption?'

'I don't think that's a good idea,' she said, and put down the phone and sat there in bed, shivering.

Notes and credits

Most of the stranger aspects of this novel are based (as closely as the law and the rules of fiction allow) on fact. The 'Abracadabra' charm can be seen at the charming Cascob Church; the Four Stones nestle behind their hedge off the Kinnerton road; and, although you may have difficulty finding Old Hindwell itself, the Hindwell Brook still meanders and sometimes rushes through the Radnor Valley. The area's huge importance in the Bronze Age was uncovered by the Clwyd-Powys Archaeological Trust and documented by Alex Gibson in *The Walton Basin Project*, published by the Council for British Archaeology.

My thanks to Glyn Morgan, who pointed me down the dark lane of border spirituality with a very timely photocopy of the witch charm, found in the wall of an old house in North Radnor.

The imperfect Radnor Pentagram also exists. It's true that only four churches are listed in the official tourism brochure, but the pentagram can be completed by adding St Michael's, Discoed, an ancient church with an even more ancient yew tree in front. Thanks to Carol for first suggesting what proved to be more than an idea, and to the distinguished medieval historian, Alun Lenny, of Carmarthen, for completing the picture, with the help of Francis Payne's classic work on Radnorshire.

Pam Baker told me a hospital ghost story and explained about oestrogen, etc. Quentin Cooper discussed a few of the problems involved in owning a church, and extra details were filled in by Brian Chave, Steve Empson and Steve Jenkins at the Church of England. Geoffrey Wansell and John Welch helped with the setting up of the *Livenight* programme.

Thanks also to Neil Bond, Sally Boyce, Jane Cook, Gina-Marie Douglas, Paul Gibbons, Gavin Hooson, Bob Jenkins, Dick Taylor and Ken Ratcliffe. And, for inspiration, to the white magic of XTC and 'Apple Venus'.

There was important help and fine-tuning from my editor at Macmillan, Peter Lavery, and my agents, Andrew Hewson and Elizabeth Fairbairn. And, of course, the thing would never have come together at all without my ingenious wife, Carol, who plot-doctored, character-trimmed and edited for weeks, with her usual inimitable flair, ruthlessness and lateral thinking. You *can* do it alone, but it's never as good.